Something Rad

playlist

Everybody Wants To Rule The World – Tears For Fears
You Give Love A Bad Name – Bon Jovi
These Dreams – Heart
Sledgehammer – Peter Gabriel
Hysteria – Def Leppard
Jessie's Girl – Rick Springfield
Heartbreaker – Pat Benatar
Rock You Like A Hurricane – Scorpions
Forever Young – Alphaville
What About Love? – Heart
Separate Ways (Worlds Apart) – Journey
Your Love – The Outfield
Time After Time – Cyndi Lauper
Love Is A Battlefield – Pat Benatar
Every Breath You Take – The Police
Alone – Heart
Run To You – Bryan Adams
Hungry Eyes – Eric Carmen
Tell It To My Heart – Taylor Dayne
Is This Love – Whitesnake
Should've Been Me – Tiffany

Stop Draggin' My Heart Around – Stevie Nicks & Tom Petty
Hold The Line – TOTO
Purple Rain – Prince
Crazy For You – Madonna
I Can't Hold Back – Survivor
Waiting For A Girl Like You – Foreigner
Head Over Heels – Tears For Fears
Sara – Starship
Little Lies – Fleetwood Mac
Harden My Heart – Quarterflash
Careless Whisper – George Michael
Don't Know What You Got (Till It's Gone) – Cinderella
Take Me Home Tonight – Eddie Money
With Or Without You – U2
Can't Fight This Feeling – REO Speedwagon
Take My Breath Away – Berlin
I Want To Know What Love Is – Foreigner
Lights – Journey
Burnin' for You – Blue Öyster Cult
The Flame – Cheap Trick
Sara Smile – Hall & Oates
Don't You (Forget About Me) – Simple Minds
Send Her My Love – Journey
The Promise – When In Rome
Nothing's Gonna Stop Us Now – Starship
Faithfully – Journey

To the people that escape into books, live inside of films, and exist within music. Your story is only just beginning.

Something Rad

NIKKI WITT

"Life moves pretty fast. If you don't stop and look around once in a while, you could miss it."

–John Hughes, *Ferris Bueller's Day Off*

1987
Bay View, California

one

SARA

"Can you feel it?"

Do you ever stop and think about how one moment in time can change everything?

A single word spoken? One choice made? One action taken?

Every minute of every day, every person on this planet is making decisions. Decisions that not only affect them and the route of the rest of their lives, but, often unknowingly, the lives of those around them as well.

Even though we all like to imagine we're the main character in our own movie, that's simply not the case. And it's in those moments– the ones where you lose control, the ones where things don't go your way, when you realize the spotlight of life actually isn't following you at all, but is just catching you in the periphery of someone else's main stage– that you realize it's all just a game. And it all just comes down to if you're willing to play. If you're willing to put yourself out there. If you're prepared to accept any possible consequence of your actions.

For some, that answer is yes. For others, they'd prefer to stay safe, to stay in the dark where solitude is comfort and ignorance is bliss.

And then there's others. The outliers. The ones that don't care who the star of the story is, as long as they get a say in writing it. As long as they have some control over this forever unpredictable world we live in. As long as they can contribute, can make it better, and can leave their mark behind, they'll be satisfied.

It's an incredible thing, to feel. But it's a purely magical thing to make *others* feel.

Or, at least, the thought of it is.

I wouldn't know.

But I'd like to, one day.

I just need to begin. I have to start somewhere. And I guess that somewhere will just have to be the halls of my small town high school.

One final year. I can do this. I *have* to do this.

"*Hello*, Earth to Sara?"

"Sorry–*What?*" I startle, breaking from my trance at the same moment our school bus rockets over the familiar entirely larger than necessary speed bump that I know means we are entering the school parking lot.

Welcome back, the speed bump seems to say.

Our blue Bay View High School marquee literally *does* say it though.

I turn fully to look at Alice, the sharer of my torn up back row bus seat and also my best friend since elementary school, seeing her dark brows raised at me.

I raise my own auburn ones in return. "What?" I repeat when she doesn't say anything.

Alice breathes out a laugh, rolling her eyes. "I asked if you can feel it," she says.

"Feel what?"

"The air!" Alice huffs, exasperated.

"You're asking if I can feel the air?"

"Not the actual air. But what's *in* the air."

"And what's in the air?" I question her as the bus pulls to a stop in front of the school.

"You know...*the feeling*," Alice pushes, bumping my shoulder with her own.

I tilt my head at her as I secure my backpack on my shoulders and shove the newspaper I was holding in my lap under my arm, standing up from the bus seat to let her out.

"That this year is going to be different!" Alice finally exclaims, making my look of confusion twitch into a smile.

"Alice, you say that literally every year."

She really does. And every year she catches me off guard with it.

Alice Quinn, forever the optimist.

And I love her for it.

"Okay, but this year I know it's true," Alice insists.

She also says that every year.

"How do you figure?" I ask her, as we start to follow the rest of the students off the bus.

"Well, for starters, I finally got my braces off over the summer. And I'm wearing this killer new dress. I mean, how cute is this?"

I glance back at her, taking in the puffy elbow length sleeves and soft colorful floral pattern.

"It is a lovely dress."

"*Right?* How could my day be bad when I own this dress? Much less my year?"

"I couldn't possibly imagine," I deadpan.

"And as for *you*," Alice starts, ignoring my sarcasm, "you're about to become *the* editor of Bay View High School's 1987-1988 yearbook!"

I stop in my tracks on the last step out of the bus, making Alice run into my back and causing both of us to nearly tumble face first into the parking lot. I clutch the door frame of the bus to brace us, but am not able to stop us from lurching forward before several small items fall from the haphazardly half-zipped pockets of my backpack and onto the concrete below.

"*Hey!*" Alice groans. "What gives?"

"That's not for sure yet," I tell her, spinning to face her. "Actually, it's not for sure at all."

"Oh, come on. It's totally for sure," Alice replies, rolling her eyes. "You've worked your butt off in journalism class, on the school newspaper, *and* on the yearbook for the last three years. Of course you're going to get it. And besides, Mr. Hughes loves you."

I begin to chew on my bottom lip. "I'm not so sure, Al."

"You've *got* this," Alice insists. "And I don't want to hear anything else about it. You're going to march into Mr. Hughes's classroom today and ask– no, *demand*– that he make you the editor."

"*Demand?*" I ask, raising my brows.

"Yes, *demand*. Come on," she says, motioning her hand in the air. "*Sara Cooper, Yearbook Editor*. Doesn't it just sound meant to be?"

I snort.

Nothing's just *meant* to be. You have to *make* it be.

That's something I've always known. But it'll just go in one ear and out the other for Alice. Like I said, *eternal optimist*.

"And besides, this year is going to be different! *Remember?*"

This year will never just *be* different. I have to *make it* different.

I know that also. But I don't say it. Instead, I let out a deep breath through my nose, closing my eyes.

"Hey, ladies. *Move it or lose it!*" the bus driver tells us.

"We're moving it. Sorry about that, Larry," Alice says.

"That's *Mr. Larry* to you, Alice Quinn," the old grumpy man we've had as our bus driver nearly our entire lives tells her.

"I know, I know. Sorry about that, Larry," Alice says, patting my shoulders and scooting us fully out of the bus and into the parking lot in front of the school.

I groan, looking down at the contents of my backpack scattered at our feet, including two of my most prized possessions: my journal and my red lipstick.

"Can you hold this for a second?" I ask Alice, handing her today's copy of the newspaper from under my arm and bending down to gather my things. School day or not, I've read the newspaper every day for as long as I can remember. Something I picked up from my dad, apparently.

"God, he's so hot," Alice whines.

I glance up at her, squinting from the sun. "Who?"

"Ronald."

"Ronald who?" I ask, scooping the last of my casualties into the front pocket of my backpack and zipping it closed.

Alice lets out a dreamy sigh. "Reagan."

I choke out a laugh. "On a first name basis with our president, are you?" I ask, snatching the newspaper from her hands, seeing the man himself plastered across the front cover.

"I could be," she says. "Once you make it big in Hollywood, you could introduce us. He was an actor, you know."

"I'm aware," I chuckle. "Pretty sure he'll be way out of his prime before I get anywhere near Hollywood, but I'll keep it in mind. What would Daniel say though?"

"Hey, Daniel knows he has my whole heart," Alice says. "He can share my eyes. Just a little bit."

I laugh, shaking my head.

Daniel is the boyfriend that Alice acquired approximately one week after getting her braces off over the summer. Though Alice was always confident, something about getting those braces off really unleashed her.

"Thank you for ditching him to be lame and ride the bus with me today by the way," I say, nudging her.

"Don't even mention it!" Alice nudges me back. "We've always ridden the bus together on the first day. No way was I going to let that tradition die in our senior year. Daniel can bring me to school any other day."

I open my mouth to thank her again but am quickly cut off by the sound of tires squealing and the growing volume of Bon Jovi's *You Give Love A Bad Name.*

Alice and I both turn at the same time to see a bright red 1985 Camaro tearing through the parking lot. The music only gets louder as the car comes to a stop in a space right in the front row, left open as if it was reserved for it.

For *him*.

I find myself rolling my eyes before I'm even consciously aware of my decision to do so.

"Speaking of hot guys..." Alice murmurs.

The driver's side door of the Camaro is pushed open and out he steps.

White Converse All-Stars come into view, then Levi's 501s. I already know it's him, but his signature gray Members Only jacket and Ray Ban sunglasses confirm it before his hand running through his sleek brown gravity-defying hair delivers the killing blow to half the girls in the parking lot.

Robbie Summers.

Most popular guy in school. Star of the basketball team. Boy of every girl's dreams and every somewhat average looking boy's nightmares. Son of Darren and Donna Summers, Bay View High School legends and current owners and operators of our only local eye doctor's office, Summers Optometry.

He's a walking cliché.

There's been a Robbie Summers in every movie of our decade, but, in this story, the arrogant popular jerk always wins in the end.

Alice whistles. "Somehow I manage to forget every summer that Robbie Summers sure knows how to wear a pair of jeans."

"Yeah, he sure knows how to be an ass, alright," I mutter, turning away just as I see Robbie slip his headphones over his ears.

"Yeah, totally– *Wait*. I don't think that's what I said," Alice calls after me, following in my path.

We make our way up the steps and through the front door of the school, immediately being greeted with a large blue and yellow hand painted banner hanging from the ceiling reading *Welcome Back Bears!*

Our bus is one of the later ones to arrive, so the hallways are already bustling with students. We hop in the short line in front of the office to pick up our class schedules and, by the time we have them, Alice spots Daniel walking through the front door.

"Go meet him," I tell Alice, nodding in Daniel's direction. "I'll catch you at lunch."

"Are you sure? Alice asks.

"Definitely," I insist. "I wanted to run to the library before first period to check in with Ms. Rose anyways."

"Aw, well okay. If you insist," Alice says sarcastically, leaning in to hug me. "I will definitely see you at lunch though. Let's meet on the steps?"

"You got it."

Alice pulls back from our hug, keeping her hands on my shoulders. "And I expect a full report on your conversation with Mr. Hughes."

Her eyes flick down to the class schedule in my hands and I quickly shove it behind my back, sighing. She obviously sneaked a look at it and saw that I have journalism third period.

"You've got this, Sara," Alice says.

"Yeah, okay."

"No, no," Alice shakes her head. "Say it with me. *You've got this.*"

I blow a breath out of my nose. "I've got this," I quickly mutter.

"*Louder!*" Alice nearly yells, causing several heads to turn in our direction.

"*I've got this!*" I whisper-shout back, chuckling as I remove her hands from my shoulders. "Now, go harass your boyfriend please."

"As you wish," Alice says, raising her hand to her forehead, saluting me. "And, even though you're trying to hide your schedule from me, I also noticed we have physics together sixth period. So you'll be blessed with even more harassment from me this afternoon."

She taps the end of my nose with her finger and starts to turn away, but then spins back suddenly. "Oh! I almost forgot," she says, pulling her backpack from off her shoulder and digging into the back pocket. "I brought you some liquid courage."

She pulls a bright red can out and tosses it to me, a smile

coming to my lips before the soda even reaches my hands. Once I have hold of it, I quickly spin it around, seeing the familiar logo containing a yellow lightning bolt.

"You brought me a Jolt Cola?" I ask, referring to the extra caffeinated soda in my hands that I consume entirely too many of in any given week.

Alice shrugs. "We all need a vice in life. I'm happy to support your singular one."

I glance back down at the can. *All the sugar and twice the caffeine.* I pop the tab, taking a large gulp. "Tastes like rebellion," I smile. "Thank you."

"Don't mention it," she replies, waving as she walks away. "Maybe we'll find you a few more vices this year while we're at it," she calls over her shoulder.

"Don't count on it," I call back.

I don't have time for vices. Not this year. There's too much on the line.

Daniel breaks out in a grin as Alice approaches him, slinging his arm around her shoulder and planting a kiss on her cheek. *"This year's going to be different,"* she mouths silently at me as he does so.

I chuckle, shaking my head. Daniel spots me and waves. I wave back, smiling at the both of them as I turn and walk away. I take another drink from my Jolt, lifting my schedule towards my face to double check what room my first period class is in as I head towards the library. Once I confirm it, I fold my schedule in half, moving to slip the paper in my back pocket as I take another sip of my soda. I don't manage to do so, however, before I slam into what feels like a brick wall.

My Jolt can goes flying, spilling all down my front. Brown liquid splatters me from my pale striped sweater, down my jeans, and to my white Keds. One hand lands on my shoulder as my body ricochets off of what is apparently another body rather than a brick wall like I originally thought. I register that even the entire left side of my hair and the white collar of my under shirt are completely drenched in soda.

"Hey, Denise, sweetheart, *wait up!*" a loud voice booms from directly in front of me.

I feel my blood run cold as I slowly raise my eyes to see Robbie Summers standing before me. He's waving at someone over my shoulder. Denise Davis, it sounds like. His girlfriend, last I heard. But that can change by the week. Clearly he's caught her attention, because I see his brown eyes light up, his lips pulling into a grin.

He slides his headphones off his ears, leaving them to rest around his neck. I can hear the loud rock music blaring out of the foam ear pads from here. It's a good thing he comes from a long line of eye doctors and not ear doctors, or I'm pretty sure he'd be committing a cardinal sin right now.

"*Yeah*, that's right," he nods towards her. "Where do you think you're going without me?"

I audibly scoff, throwing my hands in the air.

Robbie's eyes flick down to me and back up towards Denise so fast that I'm not sure they even really moved. "Hey, sorry about that," he says, bringing his other hand up so he can quickly pat both of my shoulders before sidestepping me and heading for Denise.

I spin, watching him with lasers in my eyes as he walks all the way over to her, smoothing his hand over her bouncy blonde hair before sliding his arm around her waist, both of them continuing down the hallway like nothing even happened.

I shake my head in disbelief, scooping up my now almost entirely empty soda can and completely ruined schedule before bolting to the nearest bathroom.

"*Son of a–*" I mutter, gritting my teeth, when I catch sight of myself in the mirror. I grab a wad of paper towels, trying in vain to salvage my ruined outfit, shaking my head the entire time.

Robbie Summers did this. And he didn't even have the decency to look me in the eye while he apologized.

Yep, sounds about right.

People like me don't exist to people like Robbie Summers.

I let out a sigh, shoving the paper towels into the trash and digging into my backpack for my journal. I furiously scribble down a few lines of notes until I am satisfied, then return the journal to my backpack. I push out of the bathroom door and back into the hallway, trying my best to pretend like I don't know my clothes look like they were dragged through a sewer this morning. I force a smile to my face.

Robbie Summers may have ruined my outfit, but he will *not* ruin my mood.

I just reach the door to the library when I'm forced to pause, hearing snickering coming from my side. I turn my head to see Jesse Lamonte and Paul Strothers pointing towards me, their faces alternating between looks of confusion and chuckles.

Great.

I roll my eyes, secretly flipping them the bird as I push by way into the library.

Sorry, Alice. If this is any indication of the start we're off to, I'm not sure this year will be so different after all.

two

ROBBIE

There's just something about it.

Every new day is a new opportunity for a kick ass time, but this day is like no other. I breathe deeply. It's as if I can smell it in the air.

Potential.

Or maybe it's just the culmination of the raging hormones from the upperclassmen and the anxious fear from the underclassmen.

Either way, it's like the nectar of the gods. And like music to my ears.

I sigh, stopping the tape on my Walkman and pulling my headphones down to my neck. "God, I love the first day of school," I say.

"Yeah, you've mentioned it," Paul says, rolling his eyes in my direction.

"Only every year," Jesse chimes in, slamming his locker closed next to me.

"Hey, well at least it's our last first day of school ever," Paul points out. "Well, high school, that is."

"Thank the sweet heavens above," Jesse nods in agreement, his dark shaggy hair falling in his face.

"Then," Paul starts, but then Jesse joins in, helping him finish his train of thought.

"*College.*"

"Oh yeah, baby," Jesse grins. He reaches out to slap hands with Paul, but I step between the two of them, blocking it.

"Oh, *c'mon,*" I groan, slinging my arms around their shoulders as we make our way down the hall. "You boys just have the wrong attitudes."

"Our attitudes are just fine, Summers," Paul says.

"See, this is where we have to disagree, my friend. Because why on earth would you be focusing on the future when there's so much potential for today? It's a beautiful freaking day, man. Just look at it," I insist, motioning my hand through the air around us.

"What's got you so high on life today, Summers?" Jesse asks, refusing to acknowledge how beautiful today, in fact, is. "And I mean, like, extra high on life than normal?"

"*Tsk tsk tsk,*" I click my tongue, shaking my head at him. "I'm gonna stop you right there. What is there *not* to be high on life about, boys?"

Jesse and Paul both raise their brows, clearly finding my question to be rhetorical.

"We're *seniors.* We rule this place. We got *one* last year," I say, holding up one finger on each hand for each of them to see. "One last basketball season with my teammates. There's games to be played. Dances to be attended. Parties to be crashed. Beers to be drunk. Bad things to get into with my boys. And good times to be had with my girl."

"Denise?" Jesse asks, clearing his throat.

"Of course, Denise," I say, swinging my head to look at him. "Who else?"

"I don't know, man," he replies, shrugging out from under my arm. "You tend to move on pretty fast is all."

"Not from Denise Davis. I'm not that much of a bonehead."

"Have you seen her today yet?" Jesse asks.

I unhook my Ray Bans from my collar and slide them on my face as we push through the doors to the back of the school where the portable buildings for overflow classes are located. The outdoor walk to our history class might be less than two minutes, but there's no need to mess with the protection of your eyes. You only get one pair of them in your lifetime.

Geez, I sound like my father.

I shake the thought from my head.

"Of course I've seen her today," I say, replying to Jesse.

"When?" he asks.

"I walked her to her first class," I reply, looking at him over my shoulder. "Are we playing twenty questions now?"

"Hey, excuse the hell out of me for giving a shit about my friend's life," Jesse says, raising his hands.

I spin around right before we reach our class building, hooking my arm around his neck. "Aw, buddy, I appreciate you caring about my life." I pull him closer, whispering in his ear. "But there is absolutely no need to be concerned with my love life. I got that one on lock." I yank him even closer, ruffling his hair.

"Okay, okay. Point taken, Summers," Jesse says, shoving me away.

Paul and I start laughing but are quickly cut off by the sound of Ms. Cage's voice. "Planning on joining us today, boys?" she asks, her pink lips pursed and one of her blonde eyebrows raised. She stands outside the doorway of the portable classroom with her arms crossed, tapping her foot impatiently.

"Why, yes ma'am, we are," I drawl, slipping my sunglasses off my face and back into the collar of my shirt. I dip my head to make better eye contact with our history teacher. "So sorry for the disturbance, Ms. Cage."

Though her lips press more firmly together in annoyance, I don't miss the way her cheeks flush. She takes a step back, motioning for us to come into the classroom. "Take your seat, Mr. Summers. Mr. Lamonte, Mr. Strothers," she adds, nodding at Jesse and Paul behind me.

"We'd love to," I say, adding a wink for extra effect as we file into the room.

I lead the way to my usual choice of seats in the back row, but Ms. Cage's voice halts our feet once again.

"Boys? Sit a little further up, please."

"Why?" Paul and Jesse ask at the same time.

"It wasn't a request, gentleman. Now, sit."

"You know, it was a valid question, Ms. Cage," I say, shrugging my shoulders as Jesse and Paul take two seats to the left of where we're standing, grumbling the whole way.

"I'm not required to answer your questions, Mr. Summers," Ms. Cage says, her back straightening. "But, considering you all managed to be late on the very first day of class..." she pauses, exhaling through her nose as she stares intently at me. "I just figured I should keep an extra close eye on you."

I slowly look her up and down, my tongue pushing into my bottom lip. I wonder how old she must be. Twenty-seven? Thirty-two, tops. I stare back at her until I feel the class starting to settle around me.

"Well, why didn't you just say so?" I finally say, smirking at her before stepping back to take the closest seat to the right of Jesse and Paul.

I maintain eye contact with Ms. Cage, who is caught somewhere between blushing and fuming, when my back brushes into someone behind me. I notice books and a notebook of some sort on the desk in front of me as I slide into the chair, but I refuse to forfeit the intense staring match I'm currently involved in with Ms. Cage, my grin only growing wider.

"Um, *excuse me?*" An unfamiliar voice sounds from behind me. "You just literally stole my seat out from under me. Do you mind?"

I flick my head in the direction of the female voice behind me.

"Hey, I'm sorry, baby. Just following orders. You heard Ms. Cage. She needs to keep an eye on me."

"She meant on *us*, jackass," Jesse whispers.

"Are you serious right now?" The voice huffs from behind me.

14

"Oh, I know exactly what she meant," I whisper back out of the corner of my mouth to Jesse, continuing to stare forward.

"Ms. Cooper, please take your seat so we can begin," I vaguely register Ms. Cage saying.

"You're both idiots," Paul whispers, leaning forward to shake his head at us.

"*Unbelievable,*" the voice behind me mutters. Books are swiped out from in front of me as I glance away from Paul and I hear the squeak of a chair against the ground somewhere in the background.

"Now, if we could *finally* get started," Ms. Cage begins, turning her back to us and strolling to the chalkboard at the front of the room.

She writes her name neatly on the board and starts to go over introductory items. I bring my elbow to the top of the table resting my fist just to the side of my mouth. As she turns back to us to speak, she seems to make an effort to look all around the room, but I notice her eyes flicking back to me far more often than the other students. She seems annoyed every time her gaze finds me, almost immediately forcing it away every time. It's like her eyes are magnets and my presence has created the perfect electromagnetic field, constantly drawing them back to me.

Jesse lets out a scoff. "You can't win 'em all, Summers. One of these days..."

"But not today, I guess," I say, grinning.

Jesse chuckles, shaking his head while Paul eyes me, his brows knitted.

"Did I mention I love the first day of school?"

three

SARA

My teeth clench down on the end of my pencil, leaving an indentation in the wood. My knee continues to bob anxiously as I glance back up at the clock, watching the second hand intently. I'm convinced this is the longest minute of my life.

I've got this. I can do this.

Tick, tick, tick.

You'll never know if you don't ask.

Tick, tick, tick.

The squeaky wheel gets the grease. That's what Mom always says.

Tick, tick, tick.

Well, I think it's actually what *Dad* used to always say. But still.

Tick, tick, tick.

What kind of grease does one even put on a wheel?

Bbrrrriiiiinnnnngggg!

I startle, biting down suddenly so hard on my pencil that I hear my jaw pop. "*Shit*," I mutter, rubbing the side of my face.

Once the pain somewhat subsides, and as the majority of the students start filing out of the classroom, I blow out a breath.

You've got this. Just go up there and ask–

No, *demand*, I hear Alice's voice correcting me in my head.

I straighten my stack of books unnecessarily for the third time, then force myself out of my seat and in the direction of Mr. Hughes's desk. The moment I do so, however, he spins around and starts rifling through some papers.

That makes me hesitate for some reason.

He seems busy. Now's probably not a good time.

I spin on my heel and make way for the door.

I'll just talk to him about it tomorrow. Or maybe next week. It's only the first day of school for crying out loud. And, besides, judging by the only two classes I've attended so far today, this clearly isn't my day. I'll just see myself out—

"What can I do for you, Sara?"

I freeze in place so fast that my journal slides forward off of the front of the stack of books in my hands. "What?" I sputter, bending down to grab it. "Oh, nothing I– *Crap*, ouch!"

I raise my hand, rubbing at the sore spot on my head from where I just banged it on a desk as I was standing up.

"Sara?"

I slowly spin back to face Mr. Hughes, attempting to smooth out my curled hair.

Yeah, that left a dent, alright.

I switch priorities, quickly fastening the middle button on my denim jacket. I wasn't seriously about to face my favorite teacher with a mess of a hair-do *and* a stained sweater on display. I force a smile on my face as one of Mr. Hughes's brows starts to raise.

"I–*Er...* Hi. I just wanted to say hi. Happy first day!" I wave my fist with enthusiasm like it's a cheerleading pom-pom wielded by Denise Davis, then start to turn away again.

"Sara, come on. What's on your mind?"

I hesitantly spin back around. "Nothing, I swear! No thoughts in my head."

Mr. Hughes lets out a sigh. "I'm pretty sure we both know that is never true, Sara. And I'm almost positive I know what it is this time, so why don't we just talk about it?"

When I don't respond for a moment, Mr. Hughes motions with his hand towards the open desk right in front of him.

My stare flicks between his hand and the desk several times before letting out a light sigh of defeat. Straightening my shoulders, I walk over to the desk and slide into its seat. I set my books down on the table in front of me, lacing my fingers together and training my eyes on them.

Just say it.

"I want to be the yearbook editor."

I gradually raise my gaze to meet Mr. Hughes's. He leans forward further in his seat, but his expression is unreadable. He doesn't say anything.

"I think I should be the yearbook editor."

I try to tell myself he didn't hear me the first time and that this is more in the range of a *demand* that would make Alice proud. But Mr. Hughes still doesn't respond. He just raises his hand to run it once over his mouth, then crosses his arms.

Okay, now I'm starting to feel silly.

"You should make me the yearbook editor."

Third time's the charm?

Mr. Hughes lets out a sigh, looking away and then back to me. "I heard you the first time, Sara."

I feel a crease form between my brows as I tilt my head. "Okay...?"

Then why didn't he answer me?

"And you know I agree with you," he says.

"I do? I mean– *Yes*, I do," I babble.

Mr. Hughes is silent for a few moments, and I hate the way I strongly sense a *but* coming with his next statement.

"But it isn't up to me."

I feel my face fall. I knew there was a *but* coming.

But, *how?*

"What do you mean it isn't up to you?" I ask, my face feeling very warm all of the sudden. "You're the journalism teacher. And the head of the yearbook club. You always choose the yearbook editor."

"You're right," Mr. Hughes says, running a hand through his hair as he turns to dig through the pile of papers behind him. "I usually do."

"Then what's different about this year?"

"Unfortunately, this," he says, turning back and handing a paper to me.

"What is this?" I ask, feeling incapable of reading with the way my mind is racing right now.

"A note from Principal Whileyman," Mr. Hughes says, frowning. "He let me know that he wants this year's yearbook editor to be the—"

"*What?*" I cut him off, suddenly regaining the ability to read the typed note in my hand. My grip tightens on the paper, creasing it, as my vision suddenly begins to blur. "He wants the yearbook editor to be the same person as...*the student body president?*"

Mr. Hughes nods. "It seems that way."

The temperature in the classroom suddenly feels like it has risen thirty degrees. I unbutton my jacket, fanning myself, not caring at this point if Mr. Hughes sees my pathetic stained wardrobe.

"But...*why?*" I finally ask, pushing the paper back onto Mr. Hughes's desk, decidedly done with reading for today. "I mean, how are the two even related?"

He takes the note back, shaking his head at it. "Principal Whileyman feels like the student body president is the best representative of the school. The true face of the student body. He feels it only makes sense that they be the person to oversee the creation of the class yearbook."

I keep shaking my head, not sure what else to do.

Well, there it goes. My one shot.

I shake my head some more.

No, it can't be. I'll think of something else. Some other way to prove myself.

My teeth sink into my bottom lip.

No. There is nothing else. This is it. This has always been it. And you were supposed to make it yours. There's gotta be a way around this. A way to convince Principal Whileyman–

"And I can't say I totally disagree with him."

My eyes snap back into focus.

"What?" I say, not sure I heard Mr. Hughes correctly.

"I can't say I totally disagree with Principal Whileyman," he repeats, confirming my fear.

My lips part, but no words make their way out.

"The student body president does tend to be the most involved person in school. They're the face of Bay View High in a lot of ways. I think it makes sense for them to have the final say on how their class year is documented and remembered by the students."

I stare at Mr. Hughes for a long time. "Okay," I finally say. I quickly push myself up and out of my seat and grab my things. "It was nice talking to you. See you tomorrow," I mutter over my shoulder as I start to walk away.

"Sara, wait," Mr. Hughes calls.

I turn back to him, trying to contain my composure as I raise my brows. "Yes?"

"Did you hear me?" he asks.

"Um, I believe so? And I just had my hearing checked over the summer, so," I say, with more attitude than I probably should towards a teacher. I can't help it though. I've worked so hard for this. Mr. Hughes *knows* how hard I've worked for this.

"What did I say?" Mr. Hughes questions me.

My brows pinch in both irritation and confusion. "You said you agree with Principal Whileyman. That the student body president should also be the yearbook editor. I heard you, Mr. Hughes. Now, I'd like to go to lunch." I start to turn away again, but don't even make it the full rotation before Mr. Hughes speaks again.

"I also said that I know you should be the editor."

I stare at him, shaking my head. "But...that couldn't happen."

"Why not?" he asks.

"Because...I'd have to be the student body president."

Mr. Hughes's graying brows raise, a smile pulling at his lips. "And?"

My shoulders drop. "*What?* You can't be serious, Mr. Hughes."

"I can't outright choose you as the yearbook editor, but Principal Whileyman didn't say anything about not encouraging my top choice of editor to run for the position."

I shake my head, trying to process. "Are you saying what I think you're saying?"

"You should run for student body president, Sara. And take the yearbook editor position you want and know you deserve."

I let out a groan, shaking my head as I approach Mr. Hughes's desk. "Mr. Hughes, that's insane."

"Why?"

"I would never win. You know that."

"I don't know anything," he says, mocking my same tone I used earlier when I said I had no thoughts in my head.

"It's just a popularity contest," I say. "That's how it is every year."

"Well," Mr. Hughes says, shrugging his shoulders. "Make this year different."

My mouth clamps shut as I stare back at Mr. Hughes, at a loss for words.

"Listen, Sara," he says, a sad smile on his face. "I checked with Principal Whileyman. Class elections will be happening the Friday before Homecoming. That's six weeks from now. You have plenty of time to campaign before then. If you're worried about it being a popularity contest, try putting yourself out there. There's a pep rally this Friday. Are you going?"

"Yes, I'm taking photos."

For the yearbook I won't be the editor of, I don't add.

"See, that's a great start! Mingle. Get to know some of your classmates."

"I've known them all since kindergarten."

"Okay, but do you ever actually speak to any of them?" Mr. Hughes questions me. "Other than that Quinn girl?"

My wince is answer enough for Mr. Hughes.

"That's what I thought," he says. "Maybe give it a try on Friday."

"Do I have to?" I ask.

"*Run for class president*," Mr. Hughes says, ignoring my questions. "You can do it, Sara. I have all my faith in you. Have a little faith in yourself."

I sigh, meeting his gaze. "I'm not sure how much faith can help me here, Mr. Hughes."

His lips purse. "Promise me you'll think about it at least?"

I look away for a moment before returning my gaze to him. I slowly force a soft smile to my face. "Sure," I say. "I'll think about it."

"Fantastic."

"Thanks, Mr. Hughes," I say, giving him a wave as I turn and make my way out of the classroom.

Yeah, that's an easy promise. I'll be thinking about it, alright.

Thinking about how I have no chance in hell of making this happen.

ROBBIE

I push my way out of the front door of the school, pausing at the top of the steps to slip my sunglasses on. I swivel my head from side to side for a few moments, scanning the parking lot. When I'm unsuccessful in finding my target, I slide my headphones off my head, as if the lack of music in my ears will suddenly make my eyesight better. Regardless, I tell myself it works.

Because there she is.

Bingo.

I jog down the steps, taking them two at a time, and across the parking lot, slowing my pace to a tiptoe as I approach her.

Well, look at that. She's walking right by my Camaro.

A grin pulls at my lips.

How convenient.

As soon as I'm at her back, I shoot my hands out, wrapping them around her face to cover her eyes.

Denise jolts against me, letting out a squeal of surprise.

"Oh my God!" she giggles. "You scared me!"

Ginger Matthews, her friend and fellow cheerleader that she was walking with, stops in her tracks, turning back to find the source of the commotion. I smile at her, greeting her with a nod. Her eyes dart between me and Denise, an odd expression that I don't understand passing over her face for a moment. But then she seems to snap out of it, giving me a small smile and a wave of her hand.

I pull Denise back so that she's flush with my chest, bending down to whisper in her ear, deepening my voice to disguise it. *"Guess who."*

She shakes her head and laughs before reaching up to pull my hands away. I let her, and she whips around to face me, a huge smile on her face. The moment Denise makes eye contact with me, however, her face flickers, her smile fading and shoulders seeming to stiffen.

"Oh. Robbie," she says. "Hey."

I bring my hand up to the back of her head, pulling her forward to kiss her forehead. "Hey, you." When I pull away, the smile is back on her face, but she seems uneasy, as if she was caught off guard. *I mean, I guess she was.* But when she doesn't seem to relax any further, I let out a chuckle. "What? Expecting someone else?" I ask, smirking.

Denise lets out a shaky laugh, shaking her head.

I reach out, pinching a piece of her blonde hair between my fingers and twirling it. "It's Thursday," I state.

"Yeah?" she says.

"Which means it's Friday eve," I grin.

Her brows pinch together. "Okay?"

"Which means it's basically the weekend."

"Does it really?" she chuckles, pushing the lock of hair I was twirling behind her ear.

"Close enough," I shrug. "What are we doing, sweetheart?"

"Doing?" she echoes me, raising her brows.

"This weekend."

Denise opens her mouth to answer, but I silence her with the press of a finger to her lips, leaning back against my car and pulling her with me.

"Actually, there's no need to answer. I've got a whole list of things I wanna do with you," I say.

"Oh?" Denise asks, her cheeks reddening.

"Yeah," I reply, pulling her closer. And it's true. It's been a long four days of school. As much as I've loved being back, I'm well overdue for some alone time with my girl. "How about we get an early start with this?"

I lean in, but Denise suddenly turns her head to the side, avoiding my kiss. "Um," she says, a weird giggle coming out of her as she pushes away from me. She stands up straight, smoothing out her blouse.

What was that about?

"What? Did the summer make you shy, sweetheart?" I mutter, reaching for Denise's hand. She lets me take it, holding my gaze from a moment before dropping her eyes to our intertwined fingers. After a few seconds, she wriggles her hand free, looking back at Ginger, who I honestly didn't realize was still there, and smiling tightly at her.

"Ginger, could you give us just a minute?" she asks her. "I'll meet you at your car."

"You're not going to ride home with me today?" I ask, my brows knitting together.

Denise looks from Ginger to me and back to Ginger. "Just...two minutes," she tells her.

Ginger nods at her, smiling briefly at me before turning and heading for her baby blue VW Bug across the parking lot.

Denise turns back to me, crossing her arms.

I stand up straight against my car, tilting my head. Denise's big blue eyes meet mine and, even though she has me puzzled as hell right now, I can't help but break into a grin.

God, she's something to look at.

She doesn't return my smile, however, her pouty lips pressing together. I reach out, forcing her to uncross her arms and taking her hands in mine. "What's going on, sweetheart?" I ask. "You and Ginger already have plans this weekend?"

I find it weird she wouldn't have mentioned plans with Ginger sooner, but it's not a big deal. I don't own her or her time. I guess I'll just hang with the guys. I wonder what the rest of the basketball team is up to this weekend. I'll see if I can track any of them down in the parking lot before they leave.

"I need to talk to you, Robbie," Denise says.

"We *are* talking," I smirk, reaching up to smooth a hand over her hair, but she pulls away suddenly from my touch. I drop my arm to my side, confusion swirling through me.

"No, Robbie," Denise says, shaking her head. "We need to *actually* talk."

I raise my brows, not sure what the difference is. "Okay, fine. What's going on?"

Denise's eyes land on the ground before slowly looking back up at me. "I don't think we should see each other anymore, Robbie."

A laugh works its way out of me. When Denise's expression doesn't change, I glance away, running a hand through my hair. "You're serious?" I ask.

She nods.

I look around, convinced this must be a prank or that I'm going crazy. "Sweetheart, how can you be serious?" I laugh again, but there's no humor in it.

She blows a breath out of her nose, crossing her arms again. "Because, you're *not*, Robbie. Ever"

"I'm not...what?" I question.

"*Serious!*" Denise responds, throwing her hands in the air before placing them on her hips.

I tilt my head, looking at her for a long time. "What does that even mean?"

Denise stares back at me for a few moments before her shoulders drop and her expression softens. She takes a step forward, grabbing my hand. "Look, Robbie," she says, "I like you. You know I do."

"Yeah, I know you do. So what's the problem?" I ask.

"Robbie, it's our senior year."

"Yeah, exactly, Denise," I say. "It's *our* senior year."

"And what are your plans for next year?" she asks.

"What?" I question, leaning back. "My plans for *next* year?"

"Yes, Robbie," she nods. "For college? For life?"

"For *life*?" I ask, shaking my head with a laugh. "Denise, come on–"

"I'm serious, Robbie."

"Denise, you said it yourself," I say. "It's our senior year! Why can't we just enjoy that? Enjoy the now?"

"Not everything's about the *now*, Robbie. I have a future to think about. You know I want to be a doctor."

She does?

"You do?"

Denise shakes her head looking down at the ground. "Look, Robbie. I just don't want to waste either of our time, okay? I just don't see us going long term, so it's better to just rip the bandage off now."

"Come on. Time with you could never be wasted." I take both of her hands in mine. "You know we're great together."

"I just think we'd be better as friends," she says.

I shake my head. "Sweetheart..."

"Thanks for understanding," Denise smiles, leaning forward to kiss my cheek.

"I don't remember saying that."

"I'll see ya later, Robbie," Denise says, turning away to prance in the direction of Ginger's car. "Take care of yourself, okay?" she calls over her shoulder before disappearing between the rows of cars.

"Um, what?" I ask myself outloud.

Did Denise Davis just...*break up* with me?

No one has *ever* broken up with me.

No. Denise clearly doesn't know what she's doing. Her head's not on straight. I mean, *come on*. We're perfect together. She has to know that. I mean, everyone else in the school does. No, she must just have a lot on her mind. I'm not sure what all it is exactly, but–

The pep rally.

That's it. Tomorrow is the first pep rally of the school year. That's got to be what's stressing her out and causing her to make irrational decisions. She's too focused on being on the top of the pyramid in front of everyone at school tomorrow to see what's right in front of her. To see *me*.

An idea works its way into my brain suddenly, and a smile comes to my face.

I'll just have to *make* her see.

I glance up, searching to see who's still left in the parking lot. An explosion of high pitched giggles sounds suddenly from right behind me, and it's like music to my ears. I spin around, seeing three other girls I recognize from the cheer team making their way down the steps of the school.

I turn to look at my reflection in the window of my car, quickly running my fingers through my hair and popping the collar of my jacket back up. I turn back just as the girls' feet hit the edge of the parking lot.

"*Sandy, Kate, and Lisa!*" I call to them.

All three of the cheerleaders stop dead in their tracks, looking like deer in headlights.

"Just the ladies I wanted to see," I smile, taking a step closer to them.

It's Kate that composes herself first, speaking up. "Um, hi, Robbie. What's up?"

I walk around the girls, throwing my long arms around all three of their shoulders, pulling them into my side. "I have a favor to ask you ladies."

All of them beam nervously at me in response.

"Think you can maybe help me out?"

SARA

"I just can't believe this."

Click.

Denise Davis twirls her blonde ponytail around her finger as she turns to say something to Lisa McDaniel.

Click.

A huge smile lights up Denise's face the second I take the picture, as if she sensed it. In a way, I'm sure she did. She's used to it. She's a girl with eyes on her at all times. A girl who is always thought of. Always noticed.

Though Denise might be completely unaware of what's going on around her, every person around her always knows exactly what's going on with Denise.

I wonder to myself if that's a blessing or a curse.

"I mean this just isn't right."

I shake my head, swiveling away from the cheer squad to focus on the band members in the bleachers.

Click. Click. Click.

I pause as students filing into the gym for the pep rally pass by in front of us, blocking my shot.

"I mean, here you are," Alice continues her rant as the last student passes in front of us, "slaving away for the sake of Bay View High journalism–"

Click.

"Slaving away is a bit dramatic, don't you think?" I ask, interrupting Alice.

"Absolutely not! Do *not* discredit yourself, Sara Cooper," Alice huffs, poking me in the shoulder. "You put your heart and soul into the newspaper and yearbook. You put in extra hours and show up to take pictures when it's not even asked of you. This is the first pep rally of the school year and while every other student is just here for the ride and to have a good time without a care in the world, only one is over here in the corner pouring out her blood, sweat, and tears!"

Click. Click.

"Pretty sure I'm not bleeding."

I can't say I haven't experienced the other two things today though.

Click.

Alice ignores me, continuing on. "Only *one* student is over here–"

"Well, technically, there's two of us over here."

I glance over at Alice, seeing her lips pressed into a thin line and her expression lacking amusement. "You're deflecting," she says.

I let out a sigh, returning my attention to the camera. "I sure am," I mutter.

Click.

"It's not fair, Sara. You know you deserve the editor position."

"Yeah, well, life isn't always fair, Al."

"Doesn't make it suck any less," Alice replies.

"You're definitely right about that," I say.

Click. Click. Click.

Alice is quiet for a few moments before she speaks again. "Have you...thought about it any more?" she finally asks. "If you'll run? For student body president?"

Click.

"I'm just not sure there's much to think about, Al. You know I'll never win."

"Do you know who else is running?" she asks. I notice how she doesn't try to pretend like I *will* win. Alice may always be my biggest hype woman and the most optimistic person I know, but she's not delusional.

"No, but Mr. Hughes said candidate sign ups and nominations aren't officially due until next Friday." *Seven days from now.* That's how long I have to decide whether or not I'd like to set myself up for disappointment. And most likely public humiliation.

"So you don't think you're going to do it?" Alice asks.

I immediately shake my head, but, when I open my mouth to speak, my voice gets caught in my throat. "I...don't know."

As much as I know there's no point, and as much as I keep telling myself I'm not going to run, I just can't make myself say it out loud.

"Sara..." Alice says. "You know how badly you want this. How badly you *need* this."

Click. Click.

"*Sara?*"

"Can we please talk about something else?" I ask Alice, dropping my shoulders. "Just for a little bit?"

I know she is only coming from a place of love, but I just need a breather from the love for a little bit. I need to process. And to come up with a plan B for my resume.

I suddenly register that my arrangement with Ms. Rose *was* my plan B, and I'm already doing that.

It also registers that it's not going to be enough.

"Okay," Alice mumbles. I'm busy looking through the camera viewfinder, but I can hear the frown in her voice.

As the flood of students coming into the gym begins to trickle to a stop, I let the camera's focus trail to the side. When my view reaches the far side of the gym, I spot Brad Marshall, Jesse Lamonte, Billy Montgomery, and a few other basketball players huddled to the side of the bleachers. I can't place my finger on what exactly it is, but something just seems off about the scene. My brows pinch together as I pull the camera away from my face. I find myself glancing around the gym and back to the group of boys.

I feel Alice step closer to me, peering over my shoulder. "Where's their fearless leader?" she asks.

"Great question," I reply, thinking to myself how odd it is that he's missing.

Robbie Summers would never miss a pep rally.

Wait.

Why do I care?

"Robbie Summers never misses a pep rally," Alice says, echoing my thoughts.

Ah, right. Of course we care.

Because Robbie is a boy with eyes on him at all times. A boy who is always thought of. Always noticed.

Though Robbie might be completely unaware of what's going on around him, every person around him *always* knows exactly what's going on with Robbie.

Lucky us.

"You're right," I say. "He'd never pass up on a chance to make himself the center of attention."

Alice scoffs out a laugh. "Well, to be fair, this pep rally is focused on the football team, not the basketball team."

"I'm sure he'd still find a way," I mutter.

Alice shakes her head, chuckling as Principal Whileyman walks to the middle of the gym floor, the long cord of his handheld microphone trailing behind him. I glance back towards the group of boys. They all have an air of suspicion to them, but Jesse looks especially guilty for some reason.

My gaze is forced away again as Principal Whileyman taps the top of the microphone a few times to get everyone's attention before he starts his usual welcome back spiel.

"How are we doing out there, Bears?!" he begins.

Back to work.

Click. Click. Click.

"Okay," Alice says, turning to me. "I'm going to find and sit with Daniel. Will you be okay over here in the corner?"

"Of course. I *own* this corner," I joke, smirking.

"Oh, right. I always forget," Alice says, rolling her eyes sarcastically. "Nobody puts Baby in a corner. Because it's already Sara's. She owns all the corners."

"Right," I deadpan. "That actually was the full line, but Patrick Swayze just got choked up on the last part."

"Right," Alice nods, playing along like a true best friend. "I suppose we forgive him?"

"Maybe someday," I shrug.

We both break off into laughter, shaking our heads.

"Okay, enough," Alice chuckles. "I'm going to find Daniel. We're going to the mall after school today. Do you want to come?"

"Can't. I'm with Ms. Rose after school. And then I'm working tonight."

"You're with Ms. Rose even on Fridays?" Alice asks, her brows raised.

I shrug. "Thank you for the offer though."

"Bay View doesn't deserve you, Sara," Alice says, squeezing my hand and turning to walk away.

"But you do," I call to her over Principal Whileyman's introduction of the cheer team.

Alice turns back to wink at me. "You got that right," she says. "Call you tomorrow?"

"You better," I reply, winking back at her as the band starts to play and the cheerleaders start flipping and cartwheeling their way into the center of the gym.

Alice nods, smiling, then weaves her way up into the bleachers in what I assume is Daniel's direction.

I return my attention to the gym floor as the cheer routine begins, Denise standing front and center of the pack as always. I carry on taking pictures, but people are hooting and hollering so loud that it totally drowns out the clicking of my camera.

I capture every twirl of a blue skirt and every pink lip gloss coated smile over the next minute until something draws my attention to the side.

The basketball boys have broken their tight huddle and are scurrying away from the bleachers, their heads tucked low as they bolt in the direction of the large double doors leading to the back parking lot of the school.

Huh?

I begin to pull the camera from my face but quickly snap back into gear as I hear a resounding *Ahh* from the bleachers, knowing that means the cheerleaders are assuming the formation of their signature pyramid.

I manage to snap a photo right as Denise spins into her place on top in the center of the group. Her stunt group tosses her high up into the air and her legs shoot out on either side, allowing her to perform a perfect toe touch before the girls below catch her again. The moment they do so, however, a loud slam rings out throughout the entire gym.

I jolt along with everyone else, and the band's music cuts off in an awkward sputter. Everyone in the gym glances around for the source of the disruption, looking confused.

I take note that all the cheerleaders, however, don't look that confused at all.

That is, except for the one that is front and center.

All of the girls are blushing and smiling at Denise as she stares back at them with wide eyes.

It all happens so fast.

Every cheerleader but Denise skips off of the floor, ducking behind the bleachers and out of view. I don't even have a moment to question what they are doing before the sound of a very particular and familiar set of horns and drums filters into the gym.

The volume of the music rises from a faint whisper to a blare of speakers in a matter of seconds, and I instantly register the tune as Peter Gabriel's *Sledgehammer*.

My eyes follow the sound like a magnet until I finally locate the mysterious missing basketball boys. They are split in two groups, each of them holding open the gym doors. I happen to realize Jesse Lamonte has suddenly disappeared from the group, but that thought is quickly lost to the void as my jaw all but hits the floor at the sight of a bright red car barrelling through the doors.

A red car driving into the gym.

A red car that is clearly the source of the music, its JVC speakers giving every ounce of their power and worth.

A red car–

No.

My jaw unhinges further.

Not just any red car.

The red car.

Robbie Summers honks his horn the moment his face comes into view, the sound reverberating throughout the entire gym. Right as I think he plans to drive straight into the bleachers, the Camaro skitters to a hard stop. Right in front of Denise.

Yeah, that's definitely going to leave a mark.

Robbie quickly hops out of the car and slams the door, Ray Bans still on his face along with a huge grin.

He walks right up to a very stunned Denise. The moment he gets directly in front of her, Robbie spins on his heel, breaking into dance and singing along to the song with so much swagger that you'd think he wrote the damn thing.

With absolutely impeccable timing, Kate Andrews appears out of nowhere with two *actual sledgehammers* in hand.

"*What in the–*" I mutter aloud, but break off, too stunned to speak even to myself.

Kate hands one hammer to Robbie right before he slides to his knees in front of Denise, using the handle of the hammer as an air guitar as he proclaims right along with Peter Gabriel that he wants to be her sledgehammer.

The gym goes berserk. Everyone jumps out of their seats, clapping loudly and whooping their praises and approvals of the performance. I manage to tear my eyes away from the absurd scene in front of me long enough to find Alice's gaze in the crowd. Her jaw is just as slack as mine. We both shake our heads with wide eyes, mouthing similar exclamations of shock to each other.

When I look back towards the middle of the gym, the rest of the cheer team has now joined in on the act, creating a circle around Denise and Robbie, swinging their own sledgehammers around in synchronized clearly pre-planned dance moves.

I shake my head in disbelief.

There is nothing this man can't do. This arrogant, entitled, infuriatingly perfect-haired man. This absolutely self absorbed jerk that steals seats and doesn't even apologize when ruining someone's outfit on the first day of school–

Okay, that might be personal, but *still*.

The man bent the *entire* cheer team to his will!

Well...

Not the entire *cheer team, it seems?*

Denise still looks shocked. Her mouth is open and her body language is rigid as Robbie continues to serenade her. He's slipping his jacket off now, letting it fall to the floor. That garners just a few hundred squeals from girls in the crowd.

I resist the involuntary urge to roll my eyes, but am unable to look away.

Robbie makes his way closer to Denise, closing the distance between them as the song continues, his head bobbing faster and his enthusiasm only continuing to grow. A light sheen of sweat covers his forehead and I hate that it makes him look even more attractive.

I feel a lump of nausea settle in my throat at that internal thought.

Just objectively *attractive. Of course that's all I meant.*

I shake my head.

The entire scene before me begins to turn my stomach sour, sending a million thoughts swirling through my mind. As much as I want to ignore the urge, I feel my fingers begin to twitch. I blow out a breath, feeling for the back pocket of my jeans.

I grind my teeth together when I realize my journal is in there just like I thought, and so easy to access. Before I can stop myself, I pull it out, flipping to the next free page and scribbling down the quickest thought I can manage before slamming it shut and shoving it back into my pocket. I hope I won't even be able to decipher its meaning later, but...I also secretly hope I *will*. This scene might be infuriating in a lot of ways, but, *God*, it'd make for great entertainment.

I raise my gaze again as Robbie abandons his sledgehammer, reaching out both of his hands instead for Denise's face. I feel my heart rate spike at the motion, a small gasp escaping me as Robbie starts to pull Denise to him. Right before he reaches her, however, the music abruptly stops all at once.

It's as if the lack of music jars me back to reality, the weight of my camera slung around my neck suddenly feeling very heavy. I realize at that moment that I didn't take a single picture of what just happened here in the midst of my shock.

Shit.

I'm sure this event wouldn't be school approved anyways, but still. It's a story. An unforgettable moment. Regardless of how sick it may make me to my stomach, it deserves to be documented.

Click. Click. Click. Click. Click.

I continue to snap photos as Principal Whileyman comes into view, holding up the keys to the Camaro. The entire gym goes dead silent.

"My office, Mr. Summers," he bellows. "*Now.*"

The smirk doesn't waver whatsoever from Robbie's face. He leans down slowly to pick up his jacket, like he has all the time in the world. After standing back up, jacket in hand, Robbie walks by Denise, leaning down to whisper something in her ear before continuing on. I can only see Denise's side profile, but I don't miss the way her teeth push into her bottom lip and her cheeks redden at whatever it was he had to say to her.

"*Mr. Summers.* Office!" Principal Whileyman repeats, more forcefully this time.

Robbie's gaze slowly shifts from Denise to the principal's, and I swear he chuckles before he starts walking forward. He has the audacity to clap Principal Whileyman on the shoulder as he passes by him on his way out of the gym.

"See ya there, bud," Robbie calls to him over his shoulder.

A few very long seconds of silence ensue before the entire gym erupts into cheers.

Principal Whileyman immediately begins shouting into his microphone repeatedly for everyone to settle down. But it doesn't do much.

I glance to the doorway, seeing Robbie's figure paused within it, slipping his sunglasses off and into his shirt collar. He hesitates there for a moment, his grin growing wider as he takes in the chaos he just caused. As he realizes the chaos he's *able* to cause. I roll my eyes one again, but feel my hands involuntarily move into action.

I raise my camera, zooming in on his face. I capture it right before he turns away. Right before the door closes.

Click.

I capture it.

The look of pure satisfaction, confidence, and power.

six

ROBBIE

My head falls back as the school bell rings.

Everybody around me scrambles to grab their things and get out the door as quickly as possible. But I just allow my eyes to close, take in the sound of the scene around me.

I have to chuckle to myself when I realize that it doesn't sound much different than a pack of mice scurrying after a piece of cheese, feet shuffling quickly against the ground and the squeaks of pent up excitement and chatter filling the air.

I don't blame them. They're teenagers. The very limited hours between 3:30 p.m. and bedtime *are* their cheese during the week. It's Monday afternoon and they're finally free. Free at this very moment to peruse an all-you-can-eat cheese buffet.

Free to *cheese* the day, if you will.

Can't say the same about myself, unfortunately.

No more cheese for me during the week.

Free afternoons, that is. At least not for a while. And though I'm not exactly thrilled about what my time after school will look like for the foreseeable future, I can't stop a grin from coming to my face.

That performance was absolutely bitchin'.

Was it worth it in the end?

Maybe not. Not yet at least. But still.

Bitchin'.

I push out of my desk once I'm the last student left in the classroom, nodding in Ms. Wenzel's direction before heading out into the hallway.

My interaction with Principal Whileyman after the pep rally last Friday replays in my head as I weave my way towards my destination, admittedly, a place I've visited less than a dozen times throughout my entire high school career, and definitely never by choice.

"Care to explain yourself, Mr. Summers?"

I lean back in my chair. "You want an explanation?"

"That's what I said, son."

I let out a sigh, my gaze falling to the floor. When I return my attention to the principal, I have on the best puppy dog face I can manage. "I did it for love, sir."

"Love," Principal Whileyman scoffs, echoing me. "I'm pretty sure you wouldn't know love if it bit you on your nose, kid."

"Denise is a very special girl, Principal Whileyman," I respond, deepening the frown on my face. "She makes me very happy."

"Yeah, well, happy isn't going to pay to remove the tire marks you just left on our gym floor. Or give those students back their first pep rally of the year."

I shake my head, fighting the grin pushing its way on to my face. "I gave them a memory they'll never forget instead, sir. And showed them the power of love all at the same time. I think it's by far a decent trade off."

Principal Whileyman blows out a long breath, staring down at his laced together fingers before returning his gaze to me. "Mr. Summers, I'm serious."

"So am I, sir," I say, holding up my hands. "Serious as cancer."

"No, actually, that's the thing," he says, an edge of grit to his voice. "You're never serious. About anything."

I drop my hands slowly, my brows pulling together.

"It's your senior year, kid. It's time to grow up."

A choked laugh escapes me. "Sir?"

"The stunts and wise cracks may have been cute your freshman and sophomore year, but they're not going to slide anymore. You're graduating this year. Why don't you act like it?"

"I don't know what you mean, sir."

"Clearly," Principal Whileyman says, shaking his head. "Look, kid. I've let you get away with far more than I'd let any other student. You know that. You know I respect your father. Your family."

I bite down on the inside of my cheek, looking away.

Right. He respects my father. My family.

But not me.

I look back at Principal Whileyman as he speaks again, pushing the thought away and forcing my usual indifferent smirk back on my face.

"I know you think you own this school, Robbie, but there's several hundred other students here that would say otherwise."

"I don't know anything, sir."

"Well, finally something we can agree on," he replies curtly, pulling a yellow notepad from his desk drawer. He clicks a pen open and scrawls across the paper for several seconds.

I lean forward, trying to catch a glimpse. "Whatcha got there, sir?"

"I know you weren't the only person involved in this little show," Principal Whileyman says. "And don't you worry, your basketball minions and the cheerleaders involved will all have detention for the next week."

I'm forced out of my seat. "Sir, no–"

"Don't bother," he says, holding up a hand and cutting me off. "They made their choice."

My mouth closes as quickly as it opened. I do feel a twinge of guilt... but he has a point. And besides, if we're all in detention together, how bad could it be?

"Well, if we did the crime together, I suppose we'll do the time together," I say.

"Oh, you won't be with them," Principal Whileyman says, tearing the yellow page from the notebook.

"Uh, sir?" I question, thinking I must have heard him wrong.

"You won't be in detention with them."

I blink hard. "You're not punishing me?" I ask.

Principal Whileyman laughs. "I didn't say that. How much of a punishment is time after school locked up with all your lackeys and sheep?"

"You mean...my friends?"

Principal Whileyman ignores my question, handing me the yellow slip. "You're on library aid duty after school, Mr. Summers. One month."

My jaw nearly hits the floor. "A month? Sir—"

"You said it yourself, Mr. Summers. You did the crime. Time to do the time."

"But, sir—"

"If it was any other student, they'd be getting suspended and a bill sent to their parents from the school district. Go home and thank your lucky stars for your privilege, kid."

I stare at Principal Whileyman for a long moment before dropping my gaze to the paper in my hands.

"You'll check in with the librarian Monday afternoon for your first shift."

I fold the paper, slipping it into my pocket. "Okay then. May I leave, sir?"

"Please," Principal Whileyman says, motioning for the door.

I move to exit his office but pause in the doorway when he speaks again.

"Was it worth it, kid?"

My lips pull up at the corners. I look back at the old man, removing my sunglasses from my shirt collar and slipping them on my face. "I guess we'll find out."

. . .

And so we will.

Denise had mentioned earlier last week that she'd be out of town all weekend and through Monday for her older sister's wedding in Hawaii, so I haven't been able to see or speak to her since the pep rally.

But it doesn't matter.

I know I won her over. I saw it in her eyes. Those big, blue, beautiful eyes. I know everybody loves blue eyes, but it's for a reason. Every time I see hers, I just wanna dive right in and swim the bottom of their depths until I drown. Those eyes are everything. And they were wide and shining just for me on Friday.

Yes, I already know I've won her back.

I don't think anyone could say no to a man who serenades them. Much less in front of the whole school.

No, Denise will know by now that she made a mistake. I'm sure she's come to her senses and that she spent the whole plane ride to Hawaii daydreaming about just how perfect we are together.

Yeah, she'll be over her obsession with the future and focus on the now.

The now *with me.*

And I'll do everything in my power to show her what a great time it can be.

After walking right past it on accident twice, I finally find the door to the library, pushing it open. I stick my head in, scanning the room. It's an absolute ghost town, just as I expected.

Well, this should be fun.

I take a few steps inside the room, glancing behind me at the clock over the door. It reads 3:46 p.m. One hour and fourteen minutes until freedom.

You got this, Summers.

I make my way over to the library counter and find it vacant. I place my hands on top of it, leaning forward to search for signs of movement in the librarian's office behind it. "Hello?" I call.

No answer.

I try walking over to the bookshelves next. I weave my way

through several of them, still not finding the librarian, or anyone else for that matter. "*Hello?* Anyone here?"

Only me and the ghosts apparently.

How hard is it for a guy to serve his detention in this school?

I continue to call out after any form of human life until I reach the very back of the library. "*Hello?*" I call even louder this time. "Ms. Rose? Are you in here–"

I cut off as the door to a supply closet flies open right in front of me and someone storms out of it with a pile of books so high that I can't even see their face.

I tilt my head as the floating books on legs continue forward in my direction. "Ms. Rose?"

The floating books skid to a stop, clearly startled, and begin to tumble out of the hands holding them.

"Oh, hey, sorry about that!" I say, bending down to pick up some of the fallen books. "I didn't mean to spook ya, Ms. Ro–"

My apology is cut off when a hand snatches a book I was about to grab right out from under my fingers. I raise my gaze slowly and find myself looking into a set of large gray eyes. Something about them seems somewhat familiar, but I can't place a finger on it before the eyes are quickly covered from my sight by a curtain of red hair and the somewhat familiar girl is darting around and away from me.

I rise to my feet, straightening my jacket before I turn to face the direction she stormed off in, following after her. She's standing behind the library counter now, flipping through books and stacking them in various piles at the speed of light. She doesn't acknowledge me as I approach. I look at her for several seconds, my eyes flicking between her face and the fast movements of her hands clearly organizing these books in a very meticulous fashion that my brain can't comprehend at the moment. Eventually, I break the silence.

"You're not Ms. Rose."

It takes her so long to respond that I start to think she's not going to. She starts slipping used due date cards out of the back pockets of the books and replacing them with fresh ones. She does it so fast that I wonder how she doesn't get a paper cut. I find myself getting so mesmerized by the action that I almost don't hear when she speaks.

"You're correct," she says.

Not sure what to say to that, I tilt my head at her. She glances up, making purposeful eye contact with me for this first time.

"Sorry, did you want a gold star or something?" she asks.

I scoff out a laugh. "Um, no thanks. But if you could tell me where Ms. Rose is, that would be great."

She suddenly scoops up a stack of books and whips around the counter, making a beeline for the bookshelves. I'm not sure why, but my feet automatically start to follow her.

"She's not here," she says over her shoulder without looking at me.

"Well, do you know when she'll be back?" I ask.

"Not until tomorrow," she says, weaving through the bookshelves and returning books to their rightful spots without so much as a second glance at where she's putting them. "She had to leave early today to pick up her grandson. He's sick."

"Oh," I say, stopping at the same time as she does to reorganize a particularly messy shelf. I put my hands on my hips. "Well, I sort of need to see her today."

In a matter of seconds, she's off again, heading back to the front counter. "Well, that's unfortunate," she says. "Guess you'll have to wait until tomorrow."

"Yeah, well, the thing is," I say, placing my hands on the counter as she gets back to work flipping through books, "I really can't."

"Yeah, well," she responds, not meeting my eyes as she does so, "as difficult as I'm sure patience and understanding are for you, you're just going to have to practice some for all of one day. I promise you'll survive."

My mouth falls open, but before I can say anything, she's slipping into Ms. Rose's office behind the counter with an armful of books.

"*What the...?*" I mutter to myself out loud.

I start to turn to leave but stop myself.

Yeah, no.

There's no way I can let that go without an explanation.

I turn my back fully to the counter, bracing my hands on it and pushing upwards. I swing my legs over the counter to the side, landing swiftly behind it and taking the few steps necessary to push my way into the office after the girl.

I find her standing behind Ms. Rose's desk, leaning over and writing in a record book of some sort. She glances up at me when she hears me enter, and I don't miss the way those gray eyes subtly roll before returning to the book.

"I'm sorry," I say, crossing my arms. "But do you have a problem with me?"

She rolls her eyes again, much more obviously this time, then pushes her auburn curls out of her face. "What do you want, Robbie?"

"I just want to start my one month of library aid duty so I can get it over with," I say, holding up my hands. Her brows raise in what looks to be genuine shock and concern, and then it registers that she just called me by my name. "*Wait*, you know me?" I ask.

Her brows immediately fall, her expression morphing into one that tells me I just said something extremely dumb. I suppose it's warranted. Of course she knows me.

But then it clicks.

I lean away, looking her up and down. I think I might just know her too.

"Cooper," I say.

Her eyebrows shoot up once again before she hides her face from me all together, skirting around me, out of the office, and back towards the bookshelves, picking up another stack of books on her way. I trail right after her.

"Sara Beth Cooper," I say.

She spins around on her heel, stopping me in my tracks. "It's just Sara," she says, spinning back around to place a book on the shelf. She quickly moves on, heading for another aisle.

"Just Sara?" I ask. "Are you sure?"

"Fairly."

"Huh," I mutter, running my hand through my hair. A wave of memory snippets and flashbacks flood through my brain. "Well damn, Cooper. Long time, no see, I guess. How long has it been? Since, like, the fourth grade?"

She makes her way over to one of the shorter waist-level shelves, and I stand opposite of her on the other side of it.

"Robbie, we've had a class together every year in high school," she says.

"*What?*" I question, taken aback. "No way, Sara Beth–"

"It's just Sara," she insists, pausing her movements to stare daggers up at me.

"Oh, right. Okay," I respond, starting to nod, but then shaking my head instead. "But I *swear* you went by Sara Beth."

"Well, I *did*," she confirms, exasperated. "Because Ms. Delgado mistakenly said my full name when she called attendance on the first day of kindergarten and I was too shy to correct her. But it's just Sara. My entire home life, and since the sixth grade of my school life, it's just been Sara."

"Okay, Sara Be–" I start, then stop myself. "You know what? This is confusing."

"It's really not. Just call me Sara–"

"I'm just going to call you Cooper."

"Well, I suppose I've been called worse," she replies, moving to the next shelf over.

I can tell she doesn't care to have this conversation. For what reason, I don't know, but I just can't wrap my head around what she's saying. And besides, I'm technically sentenced to the walls of this library for another hour. May as well make small talk to pass the time.

"Cooper, there's just no way we've had classes together all of high school."

She slips the last book from her stack onto the shelf in front of her then stands up straight to face me. She holds up her hand, counting off one finger at a time. "Geometry our freshman year, third period with Crocker. Chemistry our sophomore year, sixth period with Pavelski. Spanish last year with Jaramillo—"

"You're *loco*, Cooper," I interject.

"*Lo siento. Es la verdad*, Summers."

I raise a brow at her. Her face falls flat.

"I'm sorry. It's the truth," she translates.

Clearly I didn't retain much in that class. Including the fact that Sara Beth Cooper was a part of it, apparently.

Sara Cooper. Just Sara. My bad.

I shake my head. "Okay, fine. We had classes together the last few years maybe. But not this year—"

"History. Ms. Cage. Second period."

Her back is to me as she is putting another book away, but she turns around to look at me when I don't respond right away, seeing my pinched eyebrows.

She turns to face me fully, leaning against the book shelf and crossing her arms. "I sit directly behind you."

I let out a chuckle of disbelief, thinking she must be pulling my leg. When her eyes continue to narrow at me and a smile never comes to her face, I realize that must not be the case after all.

"Well shit, Cooper. My bad," I say, shaking my head.

Her red lips shift from a soft pout to a tight purse, and her gray eyes roll at me for what must be the tenth time in the last ten minutes.

She mumbles, nearly incoherently, but I think she says something along the lines of, "No worries. Checks out."

She starts to storm back to Ms. Rose's office but I stop her, reaching out and grabbing her by the arm.

"Hey," I say. Her eyes flick down to my hand on her arm with a look as if I've just touched her with a radioactive substance. I drop her from my grasp, taking a step back. "What's that about?"

She brushes off her shirt sleeve, keeping her eyes trained on it. "What's *what* about?"

"Why does that *check out?*" I ask, motioning my fingers into air quotes.

"You're Robbie Summers," she says, no hesitation whatsoever.

"You're correct," I say, echoing her from earlier. I leave out the part about the gold star though. "And what's that supposed to mean?"

She looks up at me through her lashes. I swear I've never seen eyes like hers in my life. I can't place what it is they remind me of, but I can't look away from them. Even if she is giving me a seriously hard time with them right now.

"Well it's just that, being Robbie Summers, I'm sure you're entirely too consumed with waxing your muscle car, and adding more product to your luscious hair, and winning basketball games, and taking your perfect girlfriend out, and just waiting in the wings to take over an legendary family business to concern yourself with the peasant likes of me."

Her cheeks are flushed by the time she finishes her monologue. We play the staring game for a solid five seconds before she shakes her head, turning away.

"Wait," I say.

She stops in her tracks, slowly turning back to me.

I take a step towards her, bracing one hand on the bookshelf to our side. "You think my hair is luscious?"

Cooper rolls her eyes once again, turning away again and making her way back to the front counter.

"Hey, hey, Cooper, wait," I say, jogging after her. She doesn't wait, but she does stay mostly in one place as she starts sorting through books behind the counter again. "Catch me up to speed here."

"How so?" she asks, not looking up at me.

"You don't like me."

"I didn't say that."

"You've heavily implied it. Physically and verbally."

She lets out a heavy sigh, closing her eyes for a few seconds before looking at me. "It's not that I don't like you, Robbie," she says, shaking her head. "Things are just different for people like you and...people like me."

I'm really not sure what she means by that, but I really don't like the way she says it with so much disdain in her voice. I clear my throat, attempting to lighten the suddenly heavy mood in the air.

"Well, we can't be that different," I say. "We both landed ourselves in detention. Speaking of, what the hell put you in here, Cooper?"

"Nothing *put* me here," she says, returning to her book stacking. When I tilt my head at her, she continues. "I'm here by choice. I volunteer for this. Library aiding. Shelving books," she clarifies, holding up a stack of paperbacks.

"Why in the world would you do that?" I ask her.

Cooper looks away, her lips pulling to the side. "Not everyone's world is the same as yours, Robbie. Maybe if you looked outside of your little bubble once in a while, you'd realize that."

And with that, she slips past me with her stack of books and out into the library, leaving me alone in Ms. Rose's office with raised eyebrows and a slack jaw. I slowly turn around, shaking my head. I lean against the office door frame, watching her from afar scurry from shelf to shelf without a glance in my direction.

"Well, Cooper, looks like we're in for an interesting month."

seven

SARA

The yellow locker door slams shut right in front of my face.

"I'm sorry, I don't think I heard you right," Alice says, her hand still resting on the door handle.

"I'm pretty sure you did, actually," I reply.

"Robbie Summers's punishment for the pep rally stunt is to hang out with you for the next month?"

"Okay, that's not exactly what I said—"

"You," Alice continues, ignoring my correction. "Him. Alone. The library after hours. For the next four weeks—"

"Well, Ms. Rose is usually there too—"

"*Sara*," Alice cries, grabbing me by the shoulders.

"What?" I groan.

"This is *nuts*."

I raise a brow at her. "I'm not sure *nuts* is the word I'd use."

More like unfortunate. Maybe devastating. *Definitely* infuriating.

Alice chuckles. "I can't believe this." She removes her hands from my shoulders and wraps them around herself. "You and Robbie Summers getting all *cozy* in the library." She draws out the word cozy, swaying her hips as she does so.

I grab her by the wrist, forcing her arms back down to her sides. "I'd rather get cozy with a cactus, Alice." I turn and continue walking down the hallway.

Alice trots after me. "Oh, c'mon Sara. You have to admit how wild this is." I pause in front of a water fountain, gathering my hair to one side. "Even if you're not the guy's biggest fan, there's worse people to have to look at. Robbie's face is way more exciting than the thousands of wrinkled pages of books you normally spend all your afternoons staring at."

"That's debatable," I say, shaking my head as I lean over the water fountain.

"I give it two weeks until you're drooling over him."

My throat constricts on the water I'm in the process of swallowing and I let out a sputter of coughs. "Alice, I think *you're* nuts," I say, wiping the back of my hand over my mouth.

"No, Sara, you're *in denial*."

"How so?" I question her.

"In thinking you're the one member of the female species completely immune to the glorious specimen that is Robbie Summers."

"Alice—"

"*And*," she cuts me off, "in thinking it'll take more than an hour alone together for him to see just how delicious *you* are."

Delicious?

"You're making me physically nauseous, Alice," I say, placing a hand on my stomach.

"Oh, come on. Can't you see it?" she asks.

"How much of a jerk he is?" I question her. "How he's being forced to work with Ms. Rose while I desperately *need* to be there? How my hour and a half of daily peace has now been crashed by an entitled, self-centered, slimy—"

"Okay, he is anything but slimy," Alice interjects. "And you are just further proving my point."

"And what point is that?"

"That this is the start to every movie ever."

My feet slow and I turn to look at Alice. "What kind of movies are you watching?"

"The kind where the super hot popular jock guy and the super cute but very quiet and reserved bookworm girl next door begrudgingly cross paths and are forced to spend time together and eventually the guy shows he has a sensitive side and the girl lets her hair down and they bond over the hardships of life until they make out, have an epic dance scene, and then live happily ever after."

My lips part, but no words come out. Alice stares back at me, a self satisfied smile on her face. "Tell me that I'm wrong," she says.

"I always wear my hair down," is the only sentence I manage to form in response to that.

"Well, start wearing it up," Alice says, and before I can stop her, she's circled around me and is pulling my hair up into a ponytail, sliding the red scrunchie off of her wrist and securing it around my hair. "*Voilà*," she smiles, stepping back to look at me. "Problem solved."

I can't stop myself from chuckling as I roll my eyes. "Okay, but it definitely doesn't solve the problem of Robbie Summers having approximately zero life hardships or sensitive sides to him. And that we most certainly will not be bonding. But I always appreciate your enthusiasm, Al."

Alice's gaze shifts to just behind me. "Speaking of enthusiasm," she says. "How are you feeling about that?"

I turn my head to see what she's pointing at, and my face instantly drops. There's a clipboard attached to the extra curricular activities bulletin board. The paper clipped into it reads *Class Election Sign-Ups and Nominations*. I purse my lips as I scan over the short list of names already scribbled on the paper. I stop after reading both *Ginger Matthews* and *Jesse Lamonte*.

That's enough.

Both of them would win over me without even trying.

I let out a sigh, pulling my bottom lip into my mouth with my teeth. I have no idea why, but I reach for the pen dangling from the clipboard. I can sense Alice taking a step closer behind me, but I ignore it. I keep my gaze on the pen, twirling it in between my fingers as I chew on my lip. Like something has taken over my body, I start to raise the pen to the paper. I'm just an inch away from it when something stops me. I feel a heat against the side of my face.

I glance to my side and freeze as I find Robbie standing right in front of me, just ten feet away. Time seems to slow down for a second as we stare at one another. I feel my pulse gradually begin to rise as my teeth push further into my lip. His expression is unreadable for a few moments as he just continues to look at me. He stares so hard at me that I begin to think he's going to stare a hole right through me. Then, suddenly, something in his eyes changes, his face breaking into a huge grin. My lip slips out from between my teeth instantly. He slides his Walkman headphones off of his head and down around his neck, running a hand through his hair once he's done so.

God, that stupid, absurdly voluminous, hair.

He nods in my direction in greeting.

What?

He does it again, taking a step forward this time. "Hey, you," he calls.

My mouth falls open, my brows pulling together.

"H–" I start to say but am cut off by a whip of wind and am quickly suffocated by a cloud of the unmistakable scent of Love's Baby Soft body spray.

An arm brushes against mine and suddenly I am looking at the back of Denise Davis's head as she walks right past me. And towards Robbie. I turn back, realizing she came up from right behind me. Right between me and Alice.

Oh.

The pen falls from my hand, clanking against the clipboard.

By the time I'm facing forward again, Robbie's arm is slung around Denise's shoulder and they are walking away down the hall.

I shake my head, feeling stupid. Then stop myself from shaking it, not even knowing why I'm feeling stupid. *Why would he have been looking at me?* Much less saying hi? We aren't even friends. He didn't even remember my existence until yesterday.

Part of me thinks I honestly liked it better when he didn't.

"Sara?" Alice speaks up.

I snap out of whatever weird trance I let myself slip into, turning to face her. "Hey, I just remembered. I have to run a quick errand before class." I straighten the stack of books in my hands, taking a few steps down the hall. "See you at lunch?"

"Okay," she says, eyeing me suspiciously. "See you at lunch, busy bee."

Before she can question me further, I spin on my heel and bolt down the hallway.

I shake my head, not even allowing myself to wonder what the hell any of that just was. I'm not sure which of the two things that just occurred makes me question my sanity more: me almost actually signing up for the student body president race or me thinking that Robbie Summers was actually paying me mind.

I was so sure he was looking right at me.

I shake my head, pushing the absurd thought away.

We spent one very heated hour and a half in the library together. That doesn't make us friends.

Not that I'd even want us to be.

I return to consciousness as I finish my unnecessary lap around the school to complete my imaginary errand, bringing me to the door that was around the corner from where I was just standing with Alice, leading outside and to my second period class. History with Ms. Cage.

And Robbie.

I roll my eyes at the realization as I move to push open the heavy metal door, it creaking the moment I do so.

"God, you're so tan, sweetheart. How did Hawaii make you even more beautiful?"

"Oh, stop it, Robbie."

I stop dead in tracks, my hand freezing on the door. I glance down, seeing the three inch crack of open space between the door and the frame allowing this conversation outside to float through and into my earshot.

I feel my heart pounding in my ears. Robbie and Denise are clearly right outside the door.

Right between me and the class I am definitely on the verge of being late for.

The only other option is to go out the front of the school and all the way around to the back, but the front office ladies will definitely question me, and there's no way I'd make it on time.

"*Denise, come on. I don't understand. You said you loved the show.*"

"*I did love it, but I'm sorry, Robbie. It doesn't change anything.*"

I can't do this. I'll just have to run to the front and sprint right past the front office ladies. I'll choose to ask for forgiveness rather than permission if they decide to chase after me. I start to let the door close but stop immediately, gritting my teeth together as it lets out a loud squeak.

"*How could it not change anything?*"

"*Because, Robbie. I'm still me. And...you're still you.*"

"*And what's wrong with that?*"

I blow a breath out of my nose. This definitely is not a conversation I should be overhearing. And not one I should even want to.

So why do I shift the books in my hands to one side of my body and lean flush against the door to hear it better?

"*Robbie, you just proved what I said before. You're fun and know how to have a good time, but you don't think beyond today.*"

"*But today is the best day. I mean, look at you, standing here. How could I think of anything beyond this?*"

"*You just don't get it, Robbie.*"

"*Then explain it to me, sweetheart. Tonight. Let me take you out. Mary Lou's. Your favorite.*"

Denise seems to hesitate, not responding right away. I push my ear further into the open crack of the door.

"*I don't think it's a good idea,*" she finally says.

"Come on," Robbie groans desperately. *"You love Mary Lou's. Burgers and strawberry sodas. On me."*

I have my ear so far into the opening that I hear Denise sigh.

"Okay, I will get a burger and strawberry soda with you–"

"Hallelujah–"

"As friends.*"*

I make out what sounds like Robbie clicking his tongue several times. I can't see him, but I just know he's shaking his head, not a strand of that annoyingly perfect hair falling out of place.

"I'll take what I can get," he eventually replies.

"I mean it, Robbie."

If it was somehow possible, I lean further into the door.

"I'll pick you up at 5:30."

The shrill sound of the bell ringing tears through the school, startling me and causing me to slam against the door. My journal goes flying off the stack of books in my hands and slips straight through the opening in the door before I can grab it. Out of panic, I reach for the door handle, yanking it back closed.

I stand inside the school, my jaw slack, holding the handle of the door in a death grip. I close my eyes, trying to catch my breath.

Shit. Very, smooth Sara.

I shake my head, telling myself to get it together. I'm late for class. I have to move.

Maybe they didn't even notice.

No, I'm sure the sound of the old rusty metal door being jolted into by the full weight of my body wasn't even that obvious.

Regardless, I'm out of time.

It's fine. He didn't notice.

I take a deep breath and open the door as casually as I can, taking a step outside.

And I find Robbie standing directly in front of me.

Holding out my journal to me.

The casual expression I had attempted to plaster on my face falls.

I quickly glance around and see that Denise is nowhere to be found. I wish that fact made my shoulders relax somewhat, but it doesn't.

I look back to Robbie, who hasn't moved. I open my mouth to speak, but no words come out. Robbie raises his brows at me. I close my mouth again and, ridiculously, snatch my journal from him and bolt in the direction of Ms. Cage's portable. In the direction of the first class I've ever been late for.

Robbie didn't say anything and still hasn't, but I can sense him hot on my heels now. I pick up my pace, really testing the soles of my Keds, and make it to the building right as Ms. Cage is closing the door.

She seems taken aback when she sees me. "*Ms. Cooper?*" Her shock and disappointment in my tardiness makes my face feel hot and my stomach twist in shame. I swallow down the bile rising in my throat as I make it through the doorway, holding the door open as Ms. Cage walks into the classroom in front of me.

"What a surprise–" she continues, but cuts off. "*Oh.* And Mr. Summers." I feel a heat against my back as I assume Robbie appears just behind me in the doorway as well. "Much less of a surprise," Ms. Cage says.

I don't look back as I let my arm fall away from the door. I can hear Robbie's hand immediately replace mine on the door but ignore it as I step into the classroom. Ms. Cage's eyes dart between the two of us, as I'm sure the rest of the classroom's do as well.

The silence in the room becomes deafening, my and Robbie's somewhat labored breathing being the only sound that breaks it.

Ms. Cage shakes her head, pulling a notepad out of her desk drawer. "Detention, both of you," she says, scrawling across the paper.

"Ms. Cage," I plead, stepping up to her desk. "I'm sorry, but I've never been late in my life–"

"Can we take it in the library?" Robbie's voice boldly interrupts me from behind.

"*What?*" I say, spinning towards him at the same time Ms. Cage says, "Excuse me?"

Robbie slides his Ray Bans off, rubbing them against his striped shirt to clean them. He takes time doing this, like he is having a casual conversation with a friend and not speaking to a teacher. "Our detention," he says, nodding towards the two slips of paper Ms. Cage has torn from the notepad as he slips his folded sunglasses into his shirt collar. "Can we take it in the library after school with Ms. Rose?"

Ms. Cage raises a brow, looking between both of us and the detention slips a few times. "Well, I suppose–"

"Great," Robbie grins, snatching the slips from Ms. Cage's desk. He hands me one of them without so much as a look in my direction. I don't even remember accepting it, but suddenly it's in my hand. And then he makes his way down the middle row of desks to take his usual seat.

Well, what would have been my *usual seat.*

But that's not important right now.

I spin back to Ms. Cage. "But Ms. Cage, still, this is my first offense. At, well, *anything*. I really don't think this deserves–"

"Take your seat, Ms. Cooper," she interjects. I start to argue further, but she's already turned away from me and is moving to write on the chalkboard.

I let out a sigh of defeat, looking down at my detention slip and gritting my teeth before following after Robbie.

He's already in his seat when I pass him, and he continues to stare forward, cool as a cucumber, without acknowledging me as I scoot past him and take my own seat with a huff.

"Thanks a lot," I mutter under my breath as I aggressively flip open my textbook.

I don't intend for Robbie to respond, and for a few seconds, he doesn't, but then I sense movement in front of me. I glance up to see him barely looking over his shoulder at me. "I don't appreciate the sarcasm, but, regardless, you're welcome," he says.

I bite down hard on the inside of my cheek.

Let it go, Sara.

I don't let it go.

"Sorry, for *what*, exactly?" I ask, lurching forward in my seat so that Robbie can hear my heated whispering.

He suddenly spins around fully to look at me, taking me by surprise and causing my spine to snap straight. "Seriously, Cooper? I know you're smarter than this."

"*Excuse me?*"

Robbie shakes his head, flexing his jaw. "You're already going to be in the library. *By choice*, apparently. I essentially got you out of detention."

"You didn't get me out of anything!" I whisper-shout. "This is still going to be on my record, Robbie."

His brows raise, and he lets out a whistle. "Your *record?* Oh no. Why didn't you say so in the first place? On second thought, better skip the library after school and run straight home. The Bay View Police Department could burst through the doors at any minute to haul you away."

My lips press into a firm line. "I don't appreciate sarcasm either," I say, echoing him. "And this isn't funny."

"Are you sure?" he asks. "I think it's getting funnier by the minute."

I shake my head, ignoring his comment. "You know, I was going to get out of it before you opened your big mouth."

Robbie straightens in his seat, towering over me. "Why did you need to get out of it at all?"

My brows pull together in confusion. "What do you mean? I already told you, this can't be on my record–"

"Why did you get detention in the first place?" he asks, cutting me off.

My mouth falls open, but before I can answer, Robbie leans forward, crowding my space, his eyes burning like pools of melted chocolate.

"Why were you late, Cooper?" he whispers, his voice low and daunting.

His eyes search my face and, when I don't respond, his lips pull into a smirk.

Yeah, I think he noticed.

"*Ms. Cooper?*" Ms. Cage's voice suddenly sounds out, making me jump in my seat. "Mr. Summers?" Robbie doesn't move a muscle, continuing to stare at me. "Care to actually join this class today? Or should we make it two days of detention?"

My back stiffens. *Two* days? "Yes, ma'am. No, ma'am. Sorry, ma'am," I answer for the both of us, dropping my gaze to my textbook.

Robbie clicks his tongue, and I can see the way he shakes his head at me in my peripheral vision before slowly turning back forwards.

I feel my face and the back of my neck warm. I start mindlessly scribbling in my notebook as Ms. Cage begins droning on about the American Revolution, but, after a few seconds, I can no longer ignore the heat of the gazes I swear I feel on me.

I glance to my left, seeing Jesse Lamonte and Paul Strothers eyeballing me with some sort of combination of suspicion, confusion, and...*interest?*

I slowly let my gaze drift away from them and then stiffen as I realize several people throughout the classroom have their eyes trained on me.

No, I shake my head, returning my gaze to my desk. They aren't looking at me.

I flex my fingers, pulling my journal out from underneath my notebook. I open it up to a new page and begin writing before the thought passes.

No, their eyes are clearly on Robbie.

Always on Robbie.

eight

ROBBIE

Despite the serious hostility from Cooper in Ms. Cage's class, library detention actually goes fairly smoothly this afternoon. Don't get me wrong, she's still being hostile towards me. But, rather than yelling at me with her mouth, she's yelling at me with her eyes.

Those huge gray eyes.

I still don't even understand what she has to be so angry about. I effectively got her out of detention. Her afternoon is as it would have been had she not been lurking in the hallway and eavesdropping on my and Denise's conversation until the tardy bell rang.

I don't know why she was listening to us, how long, or what all she heard. I also don't know why she tried to hide and scurry away from me like a little mouse once she had been caught, or how she suddenly turned from a mouse into a lion once her 'record' was on the line.

I don't know why she seems to so strongly dislike me, me not having said a word to her in years, or how she can verbally attack me in one breath while staring at me in the hallway as if I'm the ultimate answer to a question she's long been seeking in another.

I also don't know why she was gripping the pen attached to the class election sign-ups for dear life.

I also *don't know why I cared enough to go back and look at that clipboard later to confirm what it was.*

I just don't know what she has against me, or how her presence that was practically nonexistent to me just days ago is now somehow nagging at and invading everything around me.

And, most currently relevant, I don't know why she chooses to voluntarily spend her every afternoon working in the school library.

Come to think about it, there's a whole lot of things about Sara Beth Cooper that I just don't know.

But, what I do know right now, is that she must be on track for a world record in the number of library books returned to their rightful spot without actually looking at where they're being put. I know this because, over the last hour while Ms. Rose has been walking me through the introductory stuff that she missed showing me yesterday, every time I find myself glancing at Cooper, she's already looking at me.

Well, looking *is probably not the right word.* More like glaring. Or glowering. *Scowling, maybe?*

Regardless, she never lets me see it for long, always looking away the moment my eyes land on her.

After the first three times, it started to feel like a game. A very frustrating game. After the tenth time, however, the game started to turn kinda fun. Because every time I caught Cooper staring, she seemed to get more heated, her pace quickening and the aggressiveness with which she was shoving the books into the shelves intensifying.

Aside from my and Cooper's glaring match, the rest of library detention is a breeze. Ms. Rose, who is actually pretty cool by the way, gave me my short list of duties as library aid, explained the filing and shelving system, and set me up with a key to the library for days she might not be here or has to leave early. By the end, I think I have a basic concept of what it was that Cooper was flying around doing at light speed yesterday.

It's five minutes after 5 p.m. by the time Ms. Rose lets me go. Sara left right at five on the dot, smiling and waving at Ms. Rose and completely ignoring my existence as she grabbed her backpack and walked out the door.

I grab my own backpack, slipping on my Ray Bans and speed walking out to my Camaro. I have a little over twenty minutes before I need to pick Denise up for our date at Mary Lou's. That's just enough time for me to drop my things at home and freshen up real quick before I head her way.

I'm speeding out of the parking lot and halfway down the street when something catches my eye. I slow my speed and push my sunglasses down my nose just far enough to confirm that it's Cooper along the side of the street. I recognize her old backpack and the red scrunchie she decided to sport today. I also see that she's carrying some sort of clothing garment on a hanger for some reason.

I glance at the clock on my car radio, seeing that it's 5:11 p.m. I know I should keep on driving. I know that *she* would want me to. I know that she doesn't even want to speak to me. I know she'll just blow me off and most likely be rude to me in the process.

But I pull up right next to her anyway.

"Hey," I call.

Cooper shudders in surprise.

Jumpy little mouse, she is.

As soon as she realizes that it's me that's called out to her, her brows pull tightly together. She never stops walking, looking my car once over before turning her attention back to the road in front of her.

"Hey," I say again, driving along next to her. When she doesn't respond again, I call her by name. "Yo, *Cooper!*"

"I heard you the first time," she replies without looking my way.

"Well, maybe you should have answered the first time."

"Would have if I wanted to," she says, continuing forward.

I shake my head, my eyes rolling. "Hey, I was just trying to see if you were okay."

She finally slows to a stop, turning to face me. "If I was...*okay?*" she asks, her forehead scrunched in confusion.

"Well, yeah," I reply, stopping my Camaro next to her. "You know, if you needed a ride or anything."

Her auburn brows raise further, but she doesn't say anything.

"It's hot outside," I say, shrugging.

"It's really not," she responds. "And I always walk. But...thank you, I guess." Then she spins on her heel and continues her trek.

I glance back at the clock.

5:14.

I need to go. I shake my head, starting to accelerate but then letting off right away. I idle my car, waiting for Cooper to catch up.

"You really don't want me to just drop you at home?" I ask her once she does. "I'm pretty sure it's right on the way to mine."

She hesitates slightly, her shoulders stiffening uncomfortably.

"This is a small town. And I went to multiple of your birthday parties in elementary school. Don't make it weird, Cooper."

"Trust me, you don't need any of my help in that department," she mutters, continuing on.

"Well, weird *is* the new charming."

"According to who?" she questions, exasperated.

"Do you want a ride home or not?" I push, ignoring her question.

Cooper blows a breath out of her nose, seemingly resisting the urge to look in my direction. "I'm not going home. And I said no."

"I'm pretty sure you never actually said no, but fine. Have it your way." I shake my head, then find my eyes trailing down to the hanger she's carrying. Now that I see it up close, I recognize it as one of the burnt orange vests the employees of Groovy Movie wear. I guess she must work at the local video rental store

"Are you going to work?" I ask. "At Groovy Movie?"

"Are you stalking me or something?" she asks, throwing her hands in the air and finally turning sideways to glare at me as she walks.

"Hey, excuse me for trying to show a little Southern hospitality," I say.

"We live in California, doofus."

My foot accidentally slips and hits the brake for a second, causing my Camaro to stutter awkwardly.

Did she just call me a doofus?

"And not even *Southern* California," she continues.

I roll my lips into my mouth. "What even is *South?*" I ask, simply trying to egg her on at this point. "Isn't location really just a construct created by *The Man* when you think about it?"

Cooper's feet skid to a stop and she turns fully towards me. "What are you doing, Robbie?"

"Just trying to make polite conversation," I say, grinning. I see the simple action cause Cooper to tighten her balled fists, and I grin even wider.

"Don't you have a hot date to get to?" she asks.

"So you *were* eavesdropping."

Her face instantly goes pink.

Busted, Cooper.

"I wasn't eavesdropping," she insists, starting to walk again. "It's just impossible to ignore the grating sound of your voice. Now, please, go pretend to be somebody else's knight in shining armor"

I scoff out a laugh. "I don't have to pretend, Cooper." I could keep going all day with her, but my glance at the clock telling me it's 5:17 makes me cut my set short.

I really do have a hot date to get to, after all.

"Right, well, it's always a pleasure chatting with you, Cooper, but I really do have to get going. I've gotta pick up Denise and get to Mary Lou's– *Oh*, wait. You already knew that."

I see the color of her cheeks deepen even further, but she doesn't entertain me.

"And how silly of me," I continue. "I should've known you wouldn't find it hot outside. Hey, Cooper, say hi to your father, Satan, when you get home for me, will you?"

Cooper slowly turns to look at me, her lips parting and eyes narrowing.

I push my sunglasses back up my nose and flash her a huge grin in response. "Have a nice walk," I say, then hit the gas, speeding off.

I thought it would be worth my while to make a dramatic exit by flooring my car away from Cooper until I made my next turn, but it ends up biting me in the ass instead.

I am literally turning into my neighborhood when I hear the sound of police sirens behind me.

"*Goddammit,*" I curse, pulling off to the side of the road. I let out a huff as I put my car in park, glancing at the clock.

5:20.

I don't even need to turn my head to look at the man approaching my window.

"Evening, son."

"Can we please make this quick, Mr. Strothers?" I say. "I know the drill, and I have somewhere to be."

The cop leans down, furrowing his graying blonde brows before removing his sunglasses. His brown eyes narrow on me, full of disdain, his face twisting into a scowl.

He might be Paul's dad, and Paul and I have always been cool with each other for the most part, but, for whatever reason, Officer Strothers has never taken a liking to me. Actually, quite the opposite, I'd say. I'm not sure I want to know how many evenings of this man's life he's spent either glaring at me from the bleachers of our basketball games or pulling me over.

"Yeah, well, lots of people got places to be, kid," he grits. "And they're not going to ever be able to get there if you're plowing them down in the road. Just because your daddy bought you this showboat of a vehicle and lets you think you're the only person on the planet who matters doesn't make it true."

"I'm sure you matter to someone, Officer," I say sweetly, flashing him a smile.

His jaw flexes as he pulls out a pad of paper from his back pocket, scribbling something down on it.

"Now, are you taking me to jail? Or can I go?" I question him.

"Not today," he shakes his head, tearing off the warning slip and handing it to me to add to the pile already in my glove box. "But I'll get you one day, Summers. Mark my words."

"It's good to have dreams, Mr. Strothers."

"That's *Officer* Strothers–"

"Gotta go," I say, putting my car in drive and pulling away, leaving him standing on the side of the road.

It's 5:26 by the time I'm parking in front of my house and flying through the side door. Thankfully, Denise lives just down the street. I'll probably be a minute late to pick her up, but she can't hold that against me.

Can she?

When I enter my bedroom, I toss my backpack onto my bed and make a beeline for my closet. I quickly swap out my gray Members Only jacket for my black one, then head into my bathroom. Multitasking, I swish a cap full of mouthwash while refluffing my hair with my hands. Lastly, I spray on two spritzes of Calvin Klein Obsession and one an extra spritz of my secret weapon hairspray for good measure. I grab my keys, sunglasses, and wallet and am making my way back to my car with a good minute and a half to spare before I'll be late to get Denise.

I just touch the handle of the side door, however, when a voice barks out, making me freeze.

"*Robert?*"

I flex my jaw, my hand still on the door handle. "Yeah, Dad?"

"Come here, please."

"*Goddammit*," I mutter to myself.

So close yet so far.

My dad comes into view as I approach the dining room. "Dad," I say, nodding to him. I'm already not thrilled to be facing my father right now, but when I round the corner fully into the dining room, my muscles tense even further at the scene in front of me.

"Mom," I add, smiling tightly at my mother. "Janet, Will..." I continue, addressing my older sister and her husband.

Janet has always felt more like an acquaintance than a sibling. I usually feel like a stranger in my own home when she's around, and right now feels no different. She met Will when they were in optometry school together. The dude's nice enough, but I've never heard him utter any words that didn't have something to do with the anatomy of the eye or the stock market.

I have to let out a cough before acknowledging the last person seated at our dining table. "*Steven.*"

"Hiya, Bobbie," my older brother nods to me, a smug grin on his face.

Steven has always felt like less than an acquaintance. Or the *opposite* of a friend. Whichever of those is worse. He is the person in the world that I like the least, but he's the current working heir to Summers Optometry, meaning he's the person my father likes most in the world.

Yay for me.

I ignore him, turning to look at my dad. "What is going on here?"

"It's just family dinner, Robert," my mom says, an expression on her face like I've somehow managed to deeply offend her in the first thirty seconds I've been in her presence.

Wouldn't be the first time.

I tilt my head, trying to understand why this group of people would even care to have dinner together on a Tuesday night when they spend five days a week working together. This isn't a family dinner. It's an office happy hour. *Plus me*, for the moment.

"Yeah, c'mon, Bobbie," Steven chimes in. "Lighten up and join us, would you?"

"Can't unfortunately," I respond, not looking at my brother. "I wasn't informed of this shindig, and I actually have plans, so you guys have a blast. Meatloaf looks great, Mom," I say, patting the door frame as I turn to leave.

"Robert," my dad calls, making me stop in my tracks again.

I let out the lightest sigh I can manage, looking back at him. "Yes, sir?"

He wipes his napkin over his mouth, placing it neatly back in his lap. "Where were you this afternoon? Where did you just come from?"

"The library."

"The library?" my dad repeats, raising a brow.

"Yes, I was doing work there."

Well, it's not technically a lie.

"Work?"

"Yes, sir," I nod. I have to resist the urge to start tapping my foot. I have definitely burned up my minute and a half of time cushion at this point.

Dad leans back in his chair, narrowing his eyes at me. "How about we try that again, Robert. And you be honest this time." I swallow hard. "Why were you in the library this afternoon?"

Dammit.

I think he knows.

"And yesterday afternoon, for that matter?"

Yeah, he definitely knows.

Shit.

No point in lying now. "I had detention...sir."

"Yes, you did, didn't you?" my dad nods, his fingers flexing. "I heard all about your cute little performance."

Damn you, Whileyman.

"Yes, sir."

"And do you have anything to say for yourself?" he asks, his tone uncomfortably even. Steven and Janet exchange some sort of look that causes both of them to snicker under their breath. Dad doesn't acknowledge them, his eyes staying glued to me.

"Well, sir, I did it for a very special girl. And I'm doing the time for it. But that very special girl just so happens to be waiting on me, so I'll just get out of your hair." I turn to leave. "And let you get back to your Summers Optometry meeting here–"

"*Robert,*" my dad shouts, slamming his fist on the table.

The dining room grows deadly silent. I grind my teeth together, slowly turning back to my family. "*Yes, sir?*" I mutter.

"You know, it's called *Summers Optometry* for a reason."

Here we go again.

"Because it is a family business," my father continues. "A family *dynasty*."

I resist the urge to roll my eyes.

"And the intention is that the dynasty will continue."

"I know, Dad."

"*Do you?*" he asks, shoving away from the table to stand up. "Because you sure don't act like it."

I don't respond to him, slightly shaking my head as I glance away. We have this conversation at least once a month. My father's greatest fear has always seemed to be that his *dynasty* will one day fall apart. He has two children already who have followed the path he set out for them at birth step by step. Janet and Steven are there to carry on what he and my mother created. *Happily*, I might add. But it's still not good enough for my father. *I'm* not good enough for my father. Not that he's even given me a chance to prove it yet. I'm still in high school for crying out loud.

"You're too busy putting on stunts and acting like a child," he says, approaching me.

"Dad, it wasn't a big deal, I swear."

"Of course not. Because nothing is a big deal with you."

I take a step back. "Dad–"

"Where are your college applications?" he asks, cutting me off. "In the mail, I presume?"

"I...I'm, well, still working on them..." I stammer, rubbing the back of my neck.

"Unbelievable," my father scoffs, turning away from me.

"Dad, really. I'm almost done. And you said you had connections at the Dean's Office at the University of San Francisco. I figured you could–"

"Cover your ass? As always?" he asks, cutting me off.

"No," I shake my head. "I..." I trail off, shifting my gaze to the rest of my family. My mom and sister are staring straight down at their plates while Steven is staring at Dad, the greatest look of pride on his face. "I'm going to get them done," I insist, my voice firmer. "I'm serious, Dad."

He looks up slowly at me. "You're serious?"

"I am," I nod.

"You are," Dad agrees, nodding back. I start to feel the breath reenter my lungs, but it quickly dissolves at the next words he utters.

"A *serious* disappointment."

He shakes his head at me, returning his gaze to his plate and stabbing at his meatloaf loudly with his fork.

My mouth goes dry. I look away, flexing my jaw so hard that it aches. "I gotta go," I say, backing out of the room.

"Can't you stay for dinner?" my mother, suddenly finding her voice, calls.

"I have dinner plans–"

"Sit down, Robert," my dad says.

"Dad, I can't. I–"

"*Right now*, Robert."

My nails bite into my palms as I squeeze my hands into fists.

I walk slowly over to the table, not looking at anyone as I pull a chair out, not attempting at all to stop its wooden legs from scraping against the floor. I plop down as a plate appears in front of me at my mother's hands. No one says anything for a few minutes, just the sounds of utensils clanking against plates filling the air.

Finally, my dad breaks the silence.

"Steven, tell me about the laser peripheral iridotomy you performed today."

And so it continues.

nine

SARA

"I don't want to go."

Unfortunately the reflection of me in my vanity mirror doesn't respond to me.

Ugh, what a bitch.

I take a sip of the Jolt Cola I smuggled into the house last night after work. If my mother saw me drinking it before 8 a.m. like I currently am, she'd probably blow a gasket. But desperate times call for desperate measures.

I don't know why, but dragging myself to school today feels like climbing a mountain. I have a quiz this morning in physics, an essay due tomorrow in English that I need to get feedback on today, and pictures of the debate team I'm scheduled to take this afternoon. The morning of a day like this would typically have me jazzed and ready to rock, but all I want to do right now is crawl back under my covers and stare blankly at my ceiling until the sun goes down.

I reach for my Jolt again, hoping it'll be the magic elixir to turn my morning around. I'm pretty sure it's the opposite, however, because when I go to drink from it this time, I somehow manage to completely miss my mouth and spill it straight down the front of my white button-up shirt.

I let my eye contact shift between the reflection of the stain and my own eyes several times in the mirror before I find it in me to stand up and walk to my closet. By the time I get there though, I don't even have enough energy to fully change out of my stained shirt, instead just throwing a blue sweater over top of it and pulling my luckily unstained white collar through the top.

I make it back over to the vanity and plop down in the same spot.

Hey, look at that.

I still don't want to go.

I spy a scrunchie sitting on the table before me and raise a brow, reaching for it. I start to gather up my hair in the mirror, but never end up fastening it, letting out a sigh as I let it fall back down around my face.

"I don't want to go," I say out loud to myself again.

I turn my head to look at the clock on my nightstand. I still have ten minutes before I have to be outside to catch the bus. *Good.* I think I'm going to need every one of those ten minutes to convince myself to make it out there.

I let my gaze shift to the side of the clock, looking at the *Top Gun* movie poster on the back of my door. My eyes linger on it for a few seconds before I push out of my seat and walk over to stand in front of it.

"Do I have to go?" I ask Tom Cruise.

I take the furrow of his brow and hard set of his jaw as a *no.*

Of course. I should have known. Maverick always takes rules and orders as suggestions. I nod reassuringly to myself. Maverick would *not* go to school today.

"Great, glad we got that settled."

I kick off my Keds and jump back into my bed. I just get the covers up and over my face when I hear the door to my room open.

"Hey, Sara, remember, I'm working a double tonight. There's leftover spaghetti in the fridge for dinner– *Sara?*"

"Hi," I grumble in response to my mom, not removing the covers from my face.

"Um, are you not planning on going to school today?" she asks.

"Tom said I didn't have to."

The covers are suddenly pulled back, and I see my mom standing over me in her pink Dolly's Diner waitress uniform. I notice she's bedazzled herself a new name tag this week, the letters of *Sherri* standing out in hot pink crystals. "Who the heck is Tom?" she asks.

"Pete."

"*Huh?*"

"Maverick," I mumble, turning away.

My mom grabs my shoulder, spinning me back to her. "Hon, are you feeling okay?" she asks, her light brown curls tickling my face as she leans over and places her hand on my forehead, feeling for my temperature.

"Negative, ghost rider," I tell her.

The reference finally seems to click, and Mom glances back at the *Top Gun* poster, shaking her head and fighting a smile. "What hurts?" she asks.

"My will to live."

"Ah, right. I've heard that's serious," Mom nods, sarcastically. "Well, do you think it'll sort itself out in the next," she pauses, glancing at the clock, "four minutes?"

I let out a sigh, hesitating for just a moment before my head starts nodding involuntarily.

"That's my girl," Mom says, patting my cheek and hopping up off the bed.

I sit up and swing my legs over the side of the bed. Mom is already handing me my Keds before I even have a chance to ask her to. "*Gracias,*" I say, taking them from her.

"*De nada,*" she replies, ruffling my hair. I'm pretty sure it'll be an improvement at this point. "Alright, girlie, I gotta head out. Are you good?"

"I'm good," I nod at her as I lace up my first shoe.

I can sense her hesitating in the doorway. "But, really, are you good?" she pushes. "Are classes okay? Do you need any help with anything? Need any money?"

"I've got it covered, Mom," I reply, shaking my head. "Really, don't stress about me."

I can see the concern etched between my mom's brows. "You know that's not possible," she says.

"Well, try your best," I say, smiling at her.

Mom's quiet for a moment before she speaks again. "Any update on the scholarship front?" she asks, not quite meeting my eyes.

"I've got it handled. Don't worry," I say. I can tell she doesn't quite believe me, so I try again. "I'm...figuring some things out."

"Okay, hon," Mom says, smiling tightly. "I can swing by the community center tomorrow morning and see if there's any new smaller award applications out. We can fill them out together this weekend?"

I feel my throat constrict. I know anything helps, but the small awards will just never cut it. They're not what I need. Not the *one* that I need. I'd never say that out loud though. She's just trying to help. And I'll let her. "Sure, Mom. That sounds great. Thanks."

"Sure thing, baby girl," she winks. "I'll see ya tomorrow morning." I notice her eyes shift to the side and then widen. "Sara Beth Cooper, is that a Jolt Cola?" she asks, pointing to my vanity.

"See ya, Mom!" I shout, jumping off my bed, flashing her a grin as I start to push the door closed.

She rolls her eyes at me, accepting defeat for today and spinning on her heel to leave. "I'm proud of you!" she calls over her shoulder as she walks out the front door, just as she does every single day.

I let out a deep breath, still holding on to the door handle, and glance at the clock, seeing I need to be outside in two minutes.

"Alright, Maverick," I say, turning back to face the poster on the door, "let's give Mom something to be proud of."

I grab my backpack and head for the door.

———

I should have asked Ferris Bueller whether or not I should have gone to school.

Because it's just after first period and I'm already praying for Marty McFly to appear out of nowhere so he can take me back in time to slap Sara from earlier this morning for even considering leaving the house today.

First, I got stuck with the worst seat in the back of my bus, known for its painfully torn up vinyl seats and permanent odor that no one can seem to identify, much less remove. I made the mistake of not looking before throwing my backpack down on the seat and, once I grabbed it to leave, found that I had sat it in some sort of suspicious yellow-green sticky residue.

How did I notice, you ask?

Because when I went to take my backpack off and put it into my locker, it was stuck completely to me. I had to have Daniel physically detach it from my back, several threads of my sweater snagging in the process.

Why did Daniel help you and not Alice, you ask?

Well, Daniel was only at my locker to inform me that Alice was sick with a stomach bug and wouldn't be at school today, or probably the next few days for that matter.

One of the few times in a year that I am ready to welcome her eternal morning-person energy and unflinching optimism before 10 a.m. with open arms, and Alice Quinn is MIA.

Things continued on the downhill as I went to physics first period and definitely bombed the quiz I had spent hours studying for.

How could you have done so badly if you studied, you ask?

Well, I say *bombed*. By that I think I barely scraped by with a high *B-*, maybe a *B+* if I'm lucky. I swear I knew the information, but it was like my brain was in a fog. The answers were right there, but I just wasn't able to see them.

And that's not an acceptable excuse. Especially not for me.

I shook my head as I left the classroom, telling myself I would make up for it and thanking my lucky stars it was only a quiz. My focus was quickly drawn away from my subpar test grade, however, as my hand flew reflexively to cover my loudly rumbling stomach.

Why are you so hungry at barely 9:30 a.m., you ask?

Well, it seems I was too busy arguing with myself (and a poster) on whether or not I was going to go to school this morning to leave time for breakfast.

I sped up my walking pace so that I'd have time to hit the vending machine on the way to my second period, remembering there's one right by the door leading out to Ms. Cage's class.

I made it to the machine with plenty of time to spare, a tear nearly coming to my eye when I spotted the Carnation Breakfast Bars front and center on the top row. My stomach continued to growl painfully as I shoved my coins in the slot as fast as I could. I felt my mouth slowly start to water as the bar inched slowly forward.

And that has brought us here.

Where the bar has stopped moving forward.

I feel my face drop. "No, this isn't happening right now," I mutter to myself.

I smack my hand against the machine once, but the bar doesn't budge, the corner staying jammed firmly in the row slot.

I frantically dig in my jean pockets, looking for more coins. When I realize I am only one nickel short of being able to pay for another bar, I lose it.

"*Come on!*" I shout, slamming a shoulder into the machine. "What did I do to deserve this?"

I'm sure I'll be thankful later that this is a low traffic hallway, but right now, I don't have it in me to care about anything other than the peanut butter and chocolate of that Breakfast Bar that is rightfully mine making its way to my stomach in the next minute.

I continue to shove against the machine, adding in kicks when I remain unsuccessful. This goes on for a full thirty seconds until I am sweating like a pig and breathing like someone that just ran a marathon.

I rest my forehead against the machine. *"Please,"* I beg through strangled breaths.

"Sara?"

I startle, gripping the sides of the machine as I turn to find Mr. Hughes standing next to me. "Mr. Hughes," I say, not having the energy to peel myself away from the machine. "Hi."

He glances between me and the metal box from hell, a gray brow raising.

"Please, don't ask," I mumble, defeated.

"Okay," he says. "I'll ask about something else instead."

I let out a sigh.

Please, for the love of God, ask about anything other than—

"Have you decided to run for student body president?"

Dammit.

"The deadline to sign up is this Friday," Mr. Hughes adds.

This Friday.

The day after tomorrow.

I resist the urge to groan. "Right, Friday," I nod.

"So, is that a yes?" Mr. Hughes asks.

"I'm...still thinking about it."

A frown pulls at Mr. Hughes's face. He stares at me for a moment, sticking his hands into his pockets. "Well, I know you'll make the right decision."

I want to ask Mr. Hughes to define the word *right*. To ask him if *right* is a new way of saying *risky* or *most likely resulting in existential disappointment and pointless humiliation*, but I refrain, just nodding at him in response instead.

"Please let me know if there's anything I can do to help, Sara," he says.

I nod again.

"Right, well, I'll just, uh...let you get back to this." He motions in the general direction of where I'm laid up against the vending machine.

"Thanks, Mr. Hughes," I mutter, forcing the best smile I can manage at this moment on my face. I'm pretty sure it comes out as a mixed look of anxiety and pain, considering the speed with which he walks away from me.

The moment I see Mr. Hughes turn at the end of the hall, I continue my assault on the machine, slamming my knee against the glass. I only get three jabs in, however, before a very familiar voice distracts me.

"*Denise!*"

I whip my head to the side, seeing a heated and seemingly distressed Robbie Summers storming up the hallway in my direction after a tight faced Denise Davis. When Denise doesn't respond, Robbie breaks into a jog until he's right behind her.

"Denise, sweetheart, *wait*," he seems to plead, reaching out for her shoulder.

Denise spins around the second he makes contact, her blonde ponytail nearly whipping Robbie in the face. "*Save it*, Robbie. I knew I never should have thought about giving you a second chance, and you standing me up just confirmed it."

"Sweetheart, I'm trying to tell you," Robbie says, running a hand through his hair, which I note is far messier and a few millimeters less voluminous than normal, and wonder if this means that the world might just be ending. "This is all a misunderstanding–" Robbie continues, but then cuts off suddenly. "*Wait*...did you say...*a second chance?*"

Denise looks off to the side, not answering his question.

"You...you said it was just as friends," Robbie says, reaching out for her arm. She quickly shrugs him off, however, her gaze returning to his face.

"Yeah, well, I guess we'll never know now," Denise says, pursing her lips at him before taking off back the way her and Robbie came from, leaving him in the dust.

Robbie stares after her for a few seconds until she is out of sight and then doubles over, grabbing at his hair with both of his hands.

Things are eerily quiet for a stretch of time as he slowly stands back up straight and I find myself staring at the back of his head. Then, suddenly, Robbie breaks the silence.

"*Dammit!*" he grits, turning and kicking the blue and yellow set of lockers next to him. His hands go to rest on his hips, his chest rising and falling heavily. I haven't moved a muscle, but, evidently, I've somehow managed to catch his attention.

"*What*, Cooper?" Robbie demands suddenly. My heart stutters momentarily in my chest, but I don't let it show on the outside. "You got something to say?" He still hasn't looked at me yet, his gaze staying on the locker in front of him.

When I don't respond after a few seconds, he slowly turns to look at me. He raises his eyebrows at me, pushing me to answer him.

I tilt my head, my own brows raising. "No," I say simply, seeming to irritate him more.

Robbie, still breathing hard and now flexing his fingers at his sides, nods.

I don't know what's going on with him today, or what would have possibly have him so worked up, but I don't have the time or energy to care. Especially not this morning.

No, Robbie Summers and his shit are the absolute least of my concerns.

We both stare back at each other in some sort of annoying challenge for several seconds. We maintain eye contact for the most part, but, gradually, each of us starts glancing towards the door leading outside and to Ms. Cage's class, realizing the bell will be ringing soon.

We both suddenly storm for the door at the same time, Robbie moving away from the lockers and me finally pushing off of the vending machine. You can feel the irritation radiating off of both of us and culminating into one big ball of rage as we grow closer. Robbie makes it to the door half a second before me, getting a scoff out of me as he shoves it open. I am hot on his heels as he heads outside, but am quickly met with a sharp pain to my nose when Robbie suddenly stops in his tracks and I ram straight into the brick wall of his back.

"*What the—?*"

"*Hey, watch where you're going, would you, Cooper?*"

We both shout at each other at the same time.

When I step back, rubbing my already sore nose, I see the reason for our collision. Robbie apparently had to stop in place that very moment, after racing me to the door and insisting on walking out of it first, for the very important task of putting his sunglasses on.

I literally stomp my foot in irritation. "*Are you kidding me?*" I fume.

"*What?*" Robbie asks, looking back at me like I'm insane as he continues walking.

I storm right after him. "You seriously have to put your sunglasses on to walk fifty feet? Are your eyes going to burn up and melt out of your head in the time it takes us to get to the classroom? Your poor little pupils must be under so much stress–"

Robbie spins around, continuing to walk backwards as he addresses me. "*Actually*, the iris is what controls how much light is let into your eye–" he breaks off, seeming to cringe at something, then looks back at me, flexing his jaw. "Please, for the love of God, can we talk about anything other than eyes?"

I let out a laugh. "Well, that's rich coming from the optometry prince."

Robbie shakes his head, turning back forward. "Yeah, *you* would think so, wouldn't you?" he mutters under his breath.

I know I should ignore him, but I've simply hit my limit. "Excuse me, what is that supposed to mean?" I ask, speed walking right up next to him as we approach Ms. Cage's portable.

He stops, turning to me. "Well, you just got me all figured out, don't you, Cooper?"

My mouth falls open in surprise, but I don't shy away from him, steeling my spine. "Well, it's not like it's hard."

"Yeah?" Robbie asks, taking a step closer.

"*Yeah*," I confirm, taking my own step closer. "I don't have to figure you out, Robbie. I *know*. Because you just *make* everyone know about you. Even if they don't care, they just *have* to know." His brows pull together. "Gotta know all about the golden boy and his perfect family and the way he's just used to getting everything he wants without any effort on his part."

"You really think it's *that* easy?" Robbie asks, moving even closer. That you can just *know* me," he pauses, snapping his fingers between us, "just like that?"

I don't respond, blowing a deep breath out of my nose. I shake my head, moving to walk around him, but Robbie side steps, blocking me.

"Fine. Let me try," he says.

I start to question him, but he cuts me off.

"Sara Beth Cooper," Robbie starts, putting up one finger. "Comes from a perfectly content middle class nuclear working family." He puts up another finger. "School has always come naturally to her, but one of her parents, maybe even both, are always pushing her to do better, giving her resentment for both of them and a serious chip on her shoulder." He adds another finger, stepping closer. "She'll easily graduate first in her class and has had her college applications and decisions sorted since the first day of summer. She dreams of a stable yet excruciatingly boring career as a doctor or engineer where she can expect the same outcome out of each and every day for the rest of her life." He steps so close that I'm forced to retreat a step backwards as he raises another finger. "And, lastly, she never feels like she's good enough, no matter how much she succeeds or how hard she tries, so she voluntarily works a part-time job at the local movie rental shop and helps out at the library after school." He leans so close that I can smell his cologne, the warm woodsy amber scent invading my nose and fogging my brain. "Because she's *desperate* to feel something."

Robbie closes his fist, slowly lowering his hand. "How'd I do?" he asks, his chocolate brown eyes narrowing on me.

I ignore the painful lump in my throat and burning in my eyes, raising my chin as I close the remaining distance between us. "Couldn't be more wrong," I say. The smug expression on Robbie's face wavers slightly. "And you're a real *ass*."

"*Ms. Cooper!*"

I flick my gaze over Robbie's shoulder, seeing Ms. Cage standing in the doorway. I don't wait another second, stepping around Robbie and walking past Ms. Cage into the classroom and she calls after me. "*Language*, young lady!"

I don't look at anyone, keeping my eyes on the floor as I barrel to my seat. I start to open my textbook, but immediately swap it for my journal instead, frantically scrawling down all the things I'm already wishing I would have said.

I can sense a presence looming right in front of me, and look up to see Robbie standing to the side of his seat with an expression I can't read on his face. My instinct tells me to look away, but I refuse, holding his eye contact as I slam my journal closed. His gaze flicks down to it once before returning to my face, where it stays for several seconds. Eventually, he opens his mouth like he's going to say something, but then Ms. Cage's voice cuts through the classroom.

"Alright, everybody, who can tell me about the Boston Tea Party?"

Robbie's mouth closes again, and he slowly sinks into his seat, turning to face the front of the room as Jesse Lamonte tells Ms. Cage and the rest of the class all about the Boston Tea Party.

ten

ROBBIE

"*Shit!*" I curse, yanking my freshly paper-cut finger away from the book and shaking it out. After a few seconds, I raise my finger to my lips, sucking the blood away.

I register a snicker to my side and quickly turn my head, but I just see Cooper, turning away to add another stack of books to her shelving cart. I realize when she joins it with the other two that she has managed to check back in three stacks of books in the time I've barely managed to do half of one.

I shake my head, returning to my pile of books. I move to the next book, flipping it open and taking out the used check-out card to replace it with a fresh one. I try to pick up my pace, attempting to flip open the next book at the same time I'm adding the current one to the *done* pile, but immediately let out a hiss as my pointer finger is sliced open with another paper cut.

"*Goddammit!*" I grit, smacking my other hand down on the counter as I suck my pointer finger into my mouth again.

And, this time, I *know* I hear a laugh.

"Something funny, Cooper?" I ask.

Cooper's body freezes, and she slowly turns to look at me. Her face is completely void of emotion. "Nope," she replies. She keeps her eyes on me as she starts to push her cart– that now somehow has *five* stacks of books on it– out from behind the counter and towards the bookshelves.

I shake my head at her, and start to return to my pathetic stack of books when I hear the word *"amateur"* garbled within a cough.

I drop the book in my hands and hop over the top of the counter in one swift motion, ignoring the pain in my double paper-cut finger as I march up to Cooper. If she's surprised by my action, she doesn't show it, just glancing at me lazily over her shoulder as she continues to shelve books.

"Alright, enough of this, Cooper."

She says nothing, but returns to the shelving cart between us, picking up another book and examining it.

"Cooper, I'm serious."

She replaces the book on the cart, reaching for another one.

I let out a frustrated sigh, walking forward and bracing my hands on the cart directly across from her.

"Cooper, *please.*"

She slowly raises her gaze from the book in her hands to my face. She doesn't respond, but she does raise an eyebrow at me, which is more than I've managed to get out of her in the last hour that we've been here in the library together.

"Look," I say, "I'm clearly not having the best day. And– And I think I may have taken it out on you...somewhat. But, for the record, I'm pretty sure you didn't wake up on the right side of the bed today either."

Her other brow joins the one she currently has raised, her deep gray eyes narrowing on me. I still can't place what her eyes remind me of, and it's starting to drive me crazy. Along with just about everything else about this girl.

"Regardless, I didn't mean to...hurt your feelings...or whatever. I–I didn't mean to."

She just continues to stare at me, saying nothing.

"Cooper, can you just tell me what you need me to do? Because this silent treatment is gonna drive me insane real fast."

Cooper's hand holding the book falls to her side. My gaze flicks down to follow the movement and, when my eyes return to her face, I see a smile slowly spreading across her lips. I open my mouth to say something, but she surprises me, walking around the side of the cart to stand right next to me. I spin to face her as she comes closer, and the speed that she walks at makes her scent wash over me in a gust of wind.

She doesn't smell like anything I've ever smelled before.

It's like a mixture of flowers and rain. Floral and fresh. Sweet, but natural–

I'm suddenly pulled from my short trance as Cooper speaks to me for the first time since this morning.

"I'm not giving you the silent treatment, Robbie," she says.

"You– You're not?" I ask her.

"No," she laughs, her smile growing. She steps closer, looking up at me from under her lashes. "I'm just busy shelving books."

My shoulders fall. "Oh," I say, shaking my head, realizing how much I must have been overthinking this whole afternoon. "Really? You're not pissed at me?"

"No, Robbie," Cooper shakes her head, letting out another laugh. "I've really just been focused on the books." Her voice has this sweet note to it that she's never let me hear before, and it throws me off guard. She takes a step even closer, and I can feel the heat of her against me. I swallow painfully against the odd feeling building in my chest, and tilt my head at her. She reaches out, grabbing both sides of my open jacket in her hands.

"Cooper, what are you–"

She pulls me closer suddenly, and I have to grab onto the cart next us to keep from falling forward. Her lips are only a few inches from my ear when she speaks again.

"I've just been helping out in the library." She stands up on her tiptoes to get even closer. I find myself leaning into her, and I have no idea why. "Just in the library," she repeats. I feel my chest constrict even further the closer she gets, until she is right up against my ear, sending a shiver down my spine. *"That's all, Robbie."* Her voice is nearly at a whisper now. "I've just been here."

"Desperately trying to feel something," she grits out.

My body goes rigid and eyes go wide as she suddenly drops back down flat on her feet, pushing off of me and spinning away to shelve the book still in her hands.

I feel frozen for several long seconds as Cooper carries on putting books away like nothing just happened. I realize my mouth has been hanging open and I force it shut, shaking out the rest of my body to come back to reality.

"Okay, so I take it you *are* still pissed," I say.

She spins back to me, her hands on her hips. "Hmm...I don't know," she says. "Are you still an ass?" She doesn't wait for an answer, grabbing the cart and pushing it to a section further back in the library. I follow right after her.

"Apparently, according to you," I reply.

She lets out a laugh, turning back on me. "According to *me?* Oh, right, because nothing could ever just be on you."

"Excuse me?"

"Everything just *happens* to you, Robbie. Nothing's your fault. You're not an ass. I just *say* you're one. You didn't stand up Denise. She just rejected you for *no reason* whatsoever because she's clearly lost her marbles—"

"Hey." I stop Cooper from talking, storming right up to her and pointing at her with my paper-cut finger. "Don't talk about things you know nothing about."

She reaches up, grabbing my hand and forcing it down and out of her face. *"Ditto."*

I match her challenging gaze for several seconds before I take a step back, running a hand through my hair. "Alright, Cooper, fine."

"Fine?" she questions.

"You're right," I say.

She seems to glitch in place, doing a double take at me. "Sorry, what was that? Can you say that again?"

I halfway resist the urge to roll my eyes. "I said you were *right*. I don't—"

She holds up a hand. "Hold on, I'm just taking this in. Just a few more seconds." I fully roll my eyes this time. "Okay," she says, content. "About what, exactly?"

"I don't know anything about you."

"Well, obviously—"

"And you don't know anything about me," I finish, cutting her off.

Her posture straightens slightly, and she glances away.

"So why don't we fix that?" I say.

"Why?" Cooper asks. "Why do you even care?"

"I don't know that I do," I answer honestly, shrugging. "But I do know that we have to spend the next three and half weeks together, and I'd rather not spend all of those afternoons in heated silence."

"We could just spend them in regular silence," Cooper offers, returning her attention to the books.

"No," I shake my head, walking up to the bookshelf where she's shelving. "Tell me what I got wrong."

"What?" she asks, not looking at me. "When?"

"You know when," I say. "When I was...*reading you*. What did I get so wrong?"

Cooper just shakes her head, not responding to me. She grabs the cart, pushing it to the next row of shelves.

"What did I get wrong, Cooper?" I push.

"I believe I already told you," she says, turning to look at me. "*Everything*."

I let out a sigh. Sensing that just getting her to talk is going to be harder than pulling teeth, I decide to switch my method. "Okay, let's try something different," I say.

"Or we could not." Cooper says,.

I ignore her, pushing on. "I ask you a question, then you ask me a question. I'll go first. What are you doing here?"

"*Me?*" she asks, turning in my direction. "Well, you see, Robbie, I'm shelving books. Sorting them. Putting them back where they belong. Kinda like...what you're supposed to be doing. Ring any bells?"

"You know what I mean, Cooper. Why are you *here*?" I ask, stepping closer. "If it's not just to feel something." I see her throat bob, but she hides it by shaking her head. She turns back to the shelf, obviously not planning to answer. "I'm just going to keep asking, so you may as well tell me."

She slams a book down on the cart, putting her hands on her hips as she spins to face me. "*Why. Do. You. Care?*" She pauses so long between each word she grits out that they each sound like their own sentence.

"*Why. Are. You. Here?*" I ask her again, in the same low voice and manner she just used.

She stares at me, taking several deep breaths before standing up straight and crossing her arms. "Because I need to be."

"Why–"

"My turn," she says. "Why'd you stand Denise up?"

"*What?*" I shake my head, that being the last question I expected her to ask. "I didn't–"

"Then why did she say you did?"

"*My turn*," I cut in. "Why do you *need* to be here?"

She shakes her head in frustration, then gives in. "To build my resume."

"What does library aiding have to do with being a doctor?" I ask.

"I never said I wanted to be a doctor," she says. "That was all *you*."

"Well, then what do you want to–"

"*Nope*. My turn," she cuts me off.

"But I didn't even ask a question–"

"You did. And I answered–"

"Oh, come on, Cooper," I say. "That didn't count."

"I'm just playing your game by your rules, *Summers*."

"Fine, go," I grumble.

"Why were you so touchy about me bringing up your family business earlier?"

"*Pass*," I say, shaking my head.

"*Pass?*" Cooper asks, throwing her arms in the air. "You can't pass!"

"Ask a different question then," I tell her.

"*Fine*," she says, crossing her arms. She turns away from me, pacing back and forth a few times, seeming to think very hard about something. "Okay," she finally says, turning back to me. "What is your greatest dream?"

"What..." I trail off, tilting my head. "What kind of question is that?"

"What do you dream of?" Cooper repeats.

"When?" I ask.

"You know, in life," she says, waving a hand around her. "Where do you see yourself in ten years?"

My mouth falls open. "I have never once thought that far into the future, Cooper."

She raises a brow at me, looking me up and down several times. "Seriously? Even with your family's practice–"

"*Seriously*. And that's two questions–"

"That was *not* two!" she cries.

"It *was*–"

"The second one was a question of confirmation. Not an actual question–"

"Fine, whatever," I say, holding up my hands. "What are you always writing in that little red journal you carry around?"

Cooper's cheeks immediately turn a darker shade of pink, and she sinks back slightly into the bookshelf. "Pass," she says.

"I thought we couldn't pass?"

"Well, you did anyways," she says. "Ask a different question."

I roll my lips into my mouth. There's about a million things my brain is shouting at me to ask her, but I'm still stuck on the bizarre question she just asked me. "Fine, Cooper. What's *your* greatest dream?"

Her lips part, and then she closes them again. She glances away from me several times, then starts to shake her head. "Pass–"

"Okay, you definitely can't pass *twice*. And especially not on a question you asked me first–"

"I'm pretty sure you're just making the rules up as we go," she huffs.

"Well, it's my game," I say. "Spill it, Cooper."

She shakes her head again. "I– I'm not sure...I don't know how to put it into words."

I glance down, seeing her wringing her hands. My brows pull together, trying to understand why this question out of all of them makes her so nervous. And why it's so serious to begin with. "Try," I say.

She throws her hands up in front of her. "I– I don't know. I just... I want to...create something. *Things*."

I raise my brows, but don't say anything, pushing her to continue. The tactic works, and the minute she starts nervously babbling, she can't seem to stop.

"I want to...I guess...be able to... I want to make stories. *Write* them. I want to create moments that make *other people* feel something. I don't know how to explain it, because I don't even have *it* entirely nailed down. But I want to write. Anything I can. I want to tell stories. Write books. Make movies. I want to be able to reach people all across the world and leave them with something they've never experienced before. I want to evoke emotions in them that they didn't know existed. I– I want to leave something behind. I just want to create something that will be remembered..." she trails off, shaking her head. "I know that doesn't make any sense."

"No," I say, shaking my head. Cooper meets my eyes, and it looks like she just snapped back to reality. A look of embarrassment washes over her, and she looks away again. I swallow, my throat suddenly feeling dry. "I get it," I say.

"You...do?" she asks.

"Yeah, I do," I nod. "I get it. You want to do something rad."

Cooper's face relaxes, and a confused chuckle escapes out of her.

"Um, yeah," she says. "I guess that's a really simple way to put it." She pushes a lock of her red hair behind her ear, obviously still uncomfortable.

"And that's why you work in the library after school?" I ask. "Because...you want to write books?"

"It's...more complicated than that."

"Well, explain it, then."

Cooper blows out an exasperated breath. "I want to write," she echoes me. "At a screenwriting program...at NYU."

"NYU?" I repeat. "As in...*New York University?*"

"Yeah," she nods. She looks at me for a while, gathering her thoughts, and I can see her features re-hardening into the anger she had a few minutes ago by the second. She lets out a humorless laugh, shaking her head.

"What?" I question her.

"Well, it's just...my college plan? The one I had all figured out months ago with my *perfectly content and functioning two-parent family*?" she says, throwing my words at me from earlier today. "Well...turns out that's not quite the case."

"What do you mean? Why not?"

"For multiple reasons," she says, "but mainly...it's gonna cost a pretty penny. And we barely even have a *regular* penny. Not that that's something you'd be able to understand." She tries to walk away and continue sorting books, but I just follow right after her.

"Wait, so, that's why you work at Groovy Movie? You're saving up money for college?" She doesn't answer me. "And...and you work at the library for your resume... Meaning what? You're trying to get some scholarship money?"

Cooper scoffs out a laugh. "Yeah, *some* scholarship money isn't going to cut it."

"What does that mean?" Cooper seems to be on auto-pilot at this point, zooming between the bookshelves so fast that I'm having to nearly jog to keep up with her. "*Cooper?*"

She shakes her head, barely glancing at me. "It means that I need *the* scholarship. One of the three full-ride scholarships that

NYU offers to the top students admitted into the screen-writing program."

I skid to a stop next to her. "And you got that?"

"The scholarship?" she asks, not looking my way as she scans the shelf in front of her. "No, not yet. They don't announce the recipients until April of next year."

"But the program? The screenwriting one? You've already been accepted into it?"

Cooper pauses, blinking a few times. "Yeah. Yeah I was."

"Cooper...that's *awesome*," I say, shaking my head in true amazement.

She slowly turns to look at me. "Why am I telling you all of this?" she asks. She shakes her head in what looks like irritation with herself. She tries to turn around, but I walk around her side, stopping in front of her.

"Is that why you were in a bad mood today?" I ask. "Because you're stressed about the scholarship stuff?" I don't know why, but now that I've got Sara Beth Cooper talking, I can't seem to stop.

She rubs a hand down her face. "Robbie, *enough*."

"Is that *why*?" I push, stepping closer to her.

"*Oh my God*, yes. Sort of. Partially." She throws her hands in the air, turning the opposite way and moving around the corner to go down the next aisle of shelves.

I turn the opposite corner, meeting her halfway in the aisle.

"Partially, *how*?" I ask.

She startles at my presence in front of her, clutching at her heart. When she catches her breath, her eyes narrow on me. "Why do you care, Robbie?" she asks. "Is this fun for you? Is it entertaining? Hearing about my mess of a life?"

"Give yourself some credit, Cooper. It could be much messier."

"What do you–"

"Partially, *how*?" I ask again, not letting her derail the conversation.

She heaves a sigh, pinching the bridge of her nose. "Oh my God.

Okay, *fine*. I work for the school yearbook and newspaper. I'm sure you haven't noticed, right?"

I tilt my head at her, a blurry image forming in my mind.

A red head in the corner of the gym at our pep rallies...my basketball games...and sometimes even the school dances, a camera slung around her neck. She snaps away, taking photos while everyone else around her has fun. She sinks into the background... and I never look at her a second time. My brows pinch together, wondering now how I could have never looked a second time.

"I noticed," I say.

Cooper's shoulders stiffen at my answer. "Okay, well..." she stammers, clearly not having expected me to say yes. "I've worked on them every year of school and, this year, I was hoping...*expecting*...to be picked as the yearbook editor."

"The editor?" I question, not sure what that really means.

"It's basically the person in charge of the entire yearbook. Of what the final product will look like. The yearbook editor...they get to tell the story. The story of our senior year of high school. The story that our entire class will look back on for the rest of our lives," she shakes her head, and I can see the awe that the idea alone puts her in.

I'm pretty sure I've never felt as intensely about anything as she feels about this one tiny thought, and I'm not sure how I feel about that.

"And that means a lot to you." I don't phrase it as a question. I don't have to.

Cooper nods in response. "Yeah. And...I think– *I know*..." she trails off, shaking her head. "It's the final piece I really need on my scholarship resume to stand out. It's the closest leadership position of any sort that I can get at this small school to screenwriting."

"So, are you going to be the yearbook editor?"

She huffs out another sigh. "It's not that simple, unfortunately."

"And why not?" I demand. "Who's the yearbook teacher? That Hughes guy? Cooper, you need to walk into his office right now and–"

"You really think I haven't tried that, Robbie?" she asks, exasperated. "Things are different this year."

"How?"

Her head drops in defeat. "Principal Whileyman... He's insisting that the yearbook editor is also...the student body president."

Fucking Whileyman–

Wait.

I stand up straight, something suddenly clicking into place. "That's why you were looking at the sign-up sheet that day."

Cooper's eyes go wide. "Wh..*what?*"

"You're free to go, kids!"

Cooper and I both startle at Ms. Rose's voice, stepping back from each other and reaching out to grip the bookshelf for support at the same time.

"Oh, there you both are," she says, appearing around the corner. "It's 5:09. You guys get out of here."

It is? I look down at my watch in disbelief, but find she's right.

She starts to leave, then turns back. "Oh, I almost forgot. You guys are off the hook tomorrow."

"What do you mean?" Cooper asks, her voice straining.

"We're having the carpet cleaned in here tomorrow after school, so you guys get the day off."

"Really?" Cooper asks. "But–"

"Yes, Sara," Ms. Rose chuckles. "Enjoy your time off. Relax. Or, hey, go take the time to shop for a new outfit for the Back to School Dance next Friday!"

I blink a few times, realization hitting me.

Back to School Dance? Is that already next Friday?

An idea suddenly forms in my head, bringing a smile to my lips.

"Great, thanks, Ms. Rose," I say, my feet launching into gear. I pause briefly as I reach the end of the bookshelf. "Oh– Uh, see ya, Cooper," I call over my shoulder, throwing her a wave before grabbing my backpack and heading out the doors to freedom.

I've got a second chance to plan for.

eleven

SARA

I drain the last drop from my Jolt Cola, crushing the can in my fist before dropping it in the trash can.

Why?

It's basically the only thing that's been swirling through my mind since yesterday afternoon.

Just *Why? Why? Why?* With the occasional *Stupid* thrown in there.

I can't believe I let Robbie Summers of all people weasel his way into my brain like that. And so easily.

Why?

I've replayed our conversation from yesterday a hundred times in my head, and each time I find myself more irritated with Robbie and more embarrassed at myself. What business did he have asking me all of that? And what delusion did I have in telling him? It's not like we're friends. I find myself chuckling out loud. It's not even like we *like* each other.

Stupid.

He was just driving me insane making those completely absurd assumptions about me and then pestering me with all of his questions once I called him out on it. And then there was that little *game* of his, which I realized after the fact that he completely derailed at some point, only asking *me* a stream of questions until I just started word vomiting my whole life story to him.

Why?

Stupid.

I shake my head at myself.

Why would I tell him any of that? I barely open up to Alice and my mom about our financial struggles at home and my NYU situation. Much less do I babble on to them about my greatest hopes and dreams like some doe eyed child.

Stupid. Stupid. Stupid.

I suppose I *was* the one to start that whole topic of conversation, but...the question just came out.

Why?

I just can't understand why someone like Robbie, with such a clear and set future, would seem not to care at all about it. That he would...just be so willing to throw it away. Then again, I guess it's not much of a concern to rock the boat when you're riding in a yacht.

Still, I find it so hard to believe that there's a deeper side to Robbie Summers. I've always been so positive that what you see is what you get with him. But, then again, maybe that makes me a hypocrite. He clearly couldn't have had me more wrong.

And I still don't regret letting him know it. It was a split second decision, and I was afraid I might gag, forcing myself that close to him, but it turns out I'm a better actress than I thought. What I didn't expect, however, was the reaction my little skit seemed to get out of Robbie. I had pulled back from him and turned away so fast, but I swear I could sense him slightly leaning into me and hear a new harshness to his breathing just before I did.

I didn't think anything of it, and I still don't. *Boys will be boys*, I could hear my mom's voice saying in my head. But I won't say it didn't give me a renewed sense of power.

I turn down the main hallway of the school, my feet

automatically slowing as I approach a very specific bulletin board. I blow out a breath as I come to a stop in front of the class elections sign-up sheet, still pinned in the same spot and seemingly untouched since the last time I stood in this spot.

I blink hard, suddenly taken back to another part of our conversation from yesterday.

That's why you were looking at the sign-up sheet that day.

That day. He *was* looking at me. He was...*smiling* at me.

Why?

"Be careful there, you might short circuit."

I startle, my hand flying to rest on my pounding chest. I spin to face the voice at my back, my heartbeat now audible within my ears. I realize chugging an entire Jolt minutes before this encounter was poor timing on my part, but it doesn't help my pulse whatsoever when I find Robbie standing right behind me.

"*What?*" I question him.

He slips his headphones off his ears, sliding his hands into his jacket pockets. I register that it's a *blue* Members Only jacket today.

How many of those things does he have?

"You looked like you were about to blow a gasket," Robbie says, bringing my gaze back to his face.

"Do you talk to all the ladies like this?" I ask. "No wonder they're all falling at your feet."

Robbie rolls his eyes, ignoring my comment. "What were you thinking so hard about, Cooper?" When I don't respond, I see his eyes drift over my shoulder and narrow, I assume at the clipboard on the wall.

"Nothing. Great chat. See ya later," I say, bolting away in his distraction. I can sense his presence trailing after me just moments later.

"Cooper, would you wait–"

"I'm starting to think you really are stalking me," I say, turning around to face him.

He stops in his tracks, raising his brows and flicking his eyes down to where my hand rests on the door handle. I follow his gaze, registering that I am, in fact, opening the door on the way to Ms. Cage's class.

Where he is also going.

Stupid.

He slips on his Ray Bans, never breaking my eye contact. "Yeah, hate to break it to you, but you're not special this time, Cooper."

"Does that mean I was special before?" I ask, raising my voice an octave and batting my eyelashes in feigned flirtation.

Robbie rolls his eyes, motioning outside. "Would you just go?"

"Gladly," I say, pushing open the door and heading outside.

Robbie and I don't say anything else to each other all the way to Ms. Cage's classroom. Though I try my best to walk fast and put some distance between the two of us, his insanely long legs betray me, causing us to walk into the door one right after the other. It's not until every set of eyes in the room shoots to us like magnets that I realize this would be the third day in a row that Robbie and I have shown up to class together.

Only the first day we walked through the door not biting each other's heads off, though.

Time slows down for a moment as I become aware of everyone staring at us. I notice Ginger Matthews blowing an extra aggressive bubble from her chewing gum as she looks us up and down from the first row. Then my eyes shift to the back of the classroom, seeing Kate Andrews leaning over and covering her mouth as she whispers something to Lisa McDaniel, their eyes never leaving us, even as Kate pulls away and they both start giggling. Lastly, I find my gaze resting on Jesse Lamonte and Paul Strothers. Jesse is staring at the two of us with the oddest look on his face. It's like his brows are pinched in confusion but, at the same time, he's smirking at us with an air of...*awe?* Or relief? I can't place it, but am distracted anyways by Paul leaning forward in his seat and clapping his hands over both of Jesse's shoulders, shaking them in a friendly reassuring sort of way.

What in the hell is going on in this classroom?

"Cooper, do your feet work?" Robbie asks, startling me from my trance. I turn to shoot him the stink eye. "Seriously, move it or lose it," he says, waving his hands in a sweeping motion.

"My apologies, your highness," I grumble, leading us down the middle row to our seats. We both sink into our desks right as the tardy bell rings.

"Alright," Ms. Cage announces, clapping her hands to get our attention. "Let's get started, everyone. Today, we are going to be doing a partner activity."

There's an even split between those who groan and those who cheer in response to this news. Some people immediately start to shuffle their things and slide out of their desks, but Ms. Cage stops them.

"*Nuh-uh-uh*, not so fast. Stay put for a second." A few more groans result from this, and then the noise dies down. "Now," Ms. Cage continues, "like I said, this is going to be a partner activity. You all will pair up in groups of two, and you will interview each other." The classroom noise begins to start up again, but Ms. Cage silences everyone by putting her hands in the air. "But the catch is, you'll be interviewing each other about your views on the American Revolution." A few more groans sound. "*And*, there's another catch. One of you will pretend you are a Patriot while the other will pretend they are a Redcoat." Many more groans. "Now, won't this be fun?" Ms. Cage claps her hands, genuinely believing it *will*, in fact, be fun.

Honestly, I've had to do worse activities.

"Now," Ms. Cage continues, "so we don't have to move around and make this a big fuss, you'll just turn to partner with the person closest to you in your desk row."

My eyes widen, the lead of my pencil I was doodling with breaking off into my notebook.

Please say horizontally. For the love of God, Ms. Cage, please say horizontally–

"Across or long ways?" somebody calls out.

I start doing the mental math, counting the desks in the middle row and praying Robbie and I are not at an even split.

"Hmm..." Ms. Cage says, tapping her chin.

No such luck. We are desks five and six.

"Let's do vertically."

Goddammit.

"For example, Karen and Billy, Jesse and Paul, and Robbie and Sara–"

"*Got it, Ms. Cage*," I mutter under my breath, running a hand down my face.

Robbie takes his time spinning around in his seat. Once he's fully facing me, he raises his brows. "Come here often?" he asks.

"Unfortunately," I sigh. I lift up my notebook, tearing a sheet of paper from it to write on. "Alright, let's get this over with." When I glance back at Robbie, I notice his gaze focused on my journal. I quickly lay my notebook back down on top of it, and it seems to break whatever trance he was in, his eyes returning to my face. "Do you want to be the Patriot or the Redcoat?"

"Don't care," Robbie says immediately.

"Okay, then," I grit. "You can be the Redcoat–"

"Patriot," Robbie says at the same time.

My brows pinch together. "So, you *do* care?"

He doesn't respond with anything but a shrug. "Alright, fine. You're the Patriot," I say. I write down each of our roles at the top of the notebook paper.

How long is this class again?

"Do you want to go first?" I ask.

"Class election sign-ups are due tomorrow."

My mouth falls open, my eyebrows shooting up. "That's not a question," I say after a long few seconds.

"But it's true," Robbie says. "I saw it on the clipboard."

"What is your fascination with that clipboard?" I ask, my voice low.

Robbie scoffs out a laugh. "I should be asking you the same thing. I've caught you staring a hole in the thing multiple times now." I look away, feeling heat rush to my face. "And yet, you haven't signed up. Why?" he asks.

"Robbie, we have an assignment to do."

"No taxation without representation," Robbie says, catching me off guard.

"You know that?" I question him, surprised.

"Your name isn't on the list," he continues, ignoring my question.

"I'm glad to know you're not blind. Probably wouldn't be good for the family business."

Robbie's jaw flexes, but he doesn't address my comment. "Why haven't you signed up yet?"

I push my fingers into my temples, rubbing them in circles. "You're infuriating. Do you know that?"

"Just answer the question, Cooper."

"*You* just answer a single question for the assignment we're supposed to be doing!" I whisper-shout at him, exasperated.

"Fine."

"Fine?" I ask, surprised.

"That's what I said."

"Great," I smile. "What are your thoughts on the Boston Massacre?"

"No taxation without representation," Robbie recites.

Oh. So that's all *he knows.*

My face falls, and I start tapping the eraser of my pencil onto my desk in frustration.

"Now, tell me why," he says.

I let out a sigh. It has become clear to me that he's not going to give this up, so I may as well answer. "Because I don't know if I'm even going to sign up," I say, not meeting his eyes.

"What? *Why?*" Robbie asks.

"Why do you *think?*"

"But I don't understand," Robbie says. "You need to be president to be the yearbook editor. You need it for your scholarship–"

Before I know what I'm doing I'm covering Robbie's mouth with my hand. "*Jesus, Robbie.*" I see movement in my peripheral vision and glance to the side, seeing Jesse whipping back around like he had just been looking our way. I quickly remember that his name is on the sign-up sheet, and my face instantly turns three shades of pink darker.

I suddenly feel a wetness against my hand and gasp, yanking it away from Robbie's face. "Oh my God. Did you seriously just *lick* me?" I ask.

"Could've bitten you," Robbie says, wiping his mouth with his jacket sleeve.

"Are you actually five years old?"

"Turned six last week," Robbie replies, smirking.

"Hilarious," I deadpan. "Truly. And by the way, talk louder next time, won't you? I don't think the middle schoolers next door heard you."

"I don't get what the big deal is–"

"*Of course* you don't!" I cut Robbie off. "And that's exactly my point."

Robbie looks at me for a few seconds before slowly leaning closer, his voice at a whisper now. "Cooper, I'm just confused. You said yesterday that you wanted it. That you needed it."

"I do," I confirm. "But you and I both know I would never win student body president."

Robbie's brows pull together. "Why not?"

"Robbie," I say, shaking my head, "you didn't even know who I was until a few days ago."

"That's..." Robbie trails off. "That's not true."

"It *is*," I say. "And it's okay. It's reality. It's been *my* reality my whole life. And it's time I just accept it."

It's a few seconds before Robbie speaks again. "What does that mean? You're not even going to try? You're just going to give up the scholarship?"

A million responses race through my mind. I almost tell him that I'm not sure yet. That I can look into other options. That there might be a slight chance I could get the scholarship with my current resume. That maybe I'll just win the lottery in the next six months and not have to worry about the scholarship at all. I even think I might tell him that being the yearbook editor really wouldn't mean that much to me anyways, regardless of the scholarship, but I know it's a lie. I toggle back and forth between all of these answers to say in my mind, but instead, I ask a question. The same question I keep on asking him. Because continuing not knowing the answer just sends me further and further down a spiral.

"Why do you *care*?" I ask, with a lot more grit to my voice than I originally intended.

Robbie's back straightens. His eyes flick between mine several times. He opens his mouth and then closes it again, just staring at me. Then, all at once, his features seem to harden. "I guess I don't," he says.

"And *time!*" Ms. Cage's voice calls, drawing my attention to the side of the room where she stands. "How did we do, everyone?" I glance down at my paper that is completely blank aside from our names and roles and the words *no taxation without representation*.

I look back up to Robbie, but he's already turned back to face the front of the room, seemingly writing something in his own notebook and his headphones on his ears.

twelve

ROBBIE

My Converse All-Stars pad against the linoleum flooring perfectly on beat to Def Leppard's *Hysteria* as I make my way down the hallway, allowing me to completely zone out.

It isn't until I unsuccessfully attempt to pull open the library door for a second time and peer through the glass to find workers cleaning the carpet that I remember I don't have to go to detention today. A smile immediately comes to my face, but then an odd feeling pulls at my chest. I notice one of the carpet cleaners wheeling a shelving cart out of the way. And I can't help but picture it.

Cooper pushing around that cart like she's on a freaking mission. Like the entire town of Bay View will spontaneously implode if she doesn't reshelve every last book on that goddamn cart in the next five minutes.

I suddenly feel a prickling sensation in my right ear and reach up to readjust my headphones. Then I can't help but picture something else.

Cooper's lips at my ear, putting on the performance of a lifetime. A shiver reflexively works its way down my spine. The thought of having that girl so close had never crossed my mind. Especially not without it being a result of her attacking me. No, I had gathered by now that Sara Beth Cooper had some bark in her, but I definitely never thought I'd see her bite.

I can't say I haven't deserved it. I know I can be a prick. But she's got some venom in her too. It's definitely for the best that we spend an afternoon apart.

Why do you care?

Her voice involuntarily pops into my mind. I shake my head, pushing it away. I don't care. I know that I don't.

Why would I care?

Cooper said it herself. We come from two different worlds. It's best we keep it that way. I'm not sure one world is big enough for the both of us anyways.

I don't know why, but her voice comes into my head again.

"*Robbie.*"

Except she's not saying it normally. She's whispering it into my ear again.

I flick my headphones off my head in one fluid motion, needing the stimulation of the music gone. The second the headphones land around my neck, however, I'm startled by two hands clapping onto my shoulders and squeezing hard, pulling me backwards.

"*Hey, big boy.*"

I whip around, finding Paul standing right behind me with a goofy grin on his face.

"What the hell, man?" I ask, shoving at his chest. "You trying to give me a heart attack?"

"Well, just repaying the favor," Paul replies. "I think I just had an aneurysm when I saw Robbie Summers staring longingly into the doors of the closed library. You feeling okay? I didn't think you even knew we had a library."

I shake my head, starting down the hallway towards the front doors of the school, Paul trailing right behind me. "You're not going nerd on us are you?" Paul asks.

"No, dingus," I respond. "I have detention in the library this whole month."

"You do?" Paul asks.

"Yeah, I told you."

"Huh. I don't remember," Paul says. I slip on my sunglasses as we walk through the front door. "I just thought maybe Little Miss Valedictorian was rubbing off on you–"

"*What?*" I ask, spinning around to face him.

The smile on Paul's face flickers. "Well, you know. That Cooper girl. I figured you were getting at that–"

"Why?" I question him. "Why would you figure that?"

Paul's brows pinch together as he scoffs out a laugh. "I mean, I've just seen the way you two–"

I'm not listening to Paul anymore. Because the light catching a bright blond ponytail coming out of the door behind him already has my attention fully diverted.

"*Denise,*" I say, turning away from Paul to follow after her.

"I don't have anything to say to you, Robbie," she replies without turning back.

"Okay, well, I've got something to say to you," I say, jogging after her through the parking lot. We quickly reach her BMW parked in the front row, just a few spots over from my Camaro. "Actually, I've got something to ask you."

Denise freezes as she gets her car door unlocked, turning slowly to face me. "What is it?" she asks.

I lean up against the side of her car, leaning towards her. "Okay, I lied. I'm not asking anything."

"*Robbie,*" Denise groans. She starts to get into her car, but I stop her, gently grabbing her arm.

"I'm *telling* you..." I say, "that you're coming to the Back to School Dance with me next weekend." Denise's lips part and she glances away from me, her cheeks turning pink. I reach for her hands, holding them in mine. "So find something pretty to wear, sweetheart. And let's start over on starting this school year right."

Denise is still looking away from me, so I lean in close, tilting my head to try to regain her eye contact. "Sweetheart?"

She slowly starts shaking her head. "I can't," she says.

I click my tongue. "Denise, really. Can we stop this already? We had such a great summer. I know you can't say no to me—"

"I'm not saying no, Robbie," Denise says, her spine steeling. "I'm saying I can't."

"And why can't you?" I ask. "Are you doing something else that night?"

"No," she says, her eyes trailing on the parking lot at our feet.

"Then why can't you go to the dance with me?"

"*Because.*"

"Because why?"

"Because I'll already be there," Denise says, slowly meeting my eyes again, my brows pulling together. "With somebody else."

"Wh—what?" I stammer. "With *who*?"

Denise rolls her lips into her mouth, not answering right away. After a few long seconds, she finally fesses up. "Jesse Lamonte."

I let her hands fall from mine. "Jesse," I repeat.

"Yes," she replies, defensiveness in her tone.

"You're going to the dance...with *Jesse*?"

"Well, that's what I said!" Denise replies, exasperated.

"How?...*Why*?" I shake my head in disbelief.

"It's pretty simple, Robbie. He asked me at lunch today. And I said yes."

He asked her at lunch.

Today.

My head suddenly feels like it weighs ten pounds.

"Why would he do that?" I ask.

"Why *wouldn't* he?" Denise asks, taken aback.

"Because you're my—"

"I'm not your *anything*, Robbie. Not anymore. How many times do I have to make that clear?"

Until it starts making sense.

"Why Jesse, though? What does he have that I don't have?"

I truly wrack my brain to try to understand it. We're both seniors. We both run in the same social crowd, which honestly makes this entire situation that much more screwed up. We both come from well known families in town, and though an optometry clinic isn't necessarily the coolest business in town, it certainly beats being the town plumber. We both have sweet cars, mine being significantly sweeter, of course. We're both on the basketball team. Jesse might be the captain, but it's only because I turned down the role. I don't care for all the official leadership crap, but I'm definitely the star player at the end of the day, and everybody knows it, *including* Jesse. We definitely *don't* have many physical similarities, and I'm not saying that as a point towards Jesse.

What could it possibly be?

"Robbie..." Denise says, shaking her head. "Look, you're right. We did have a great summer, and I'll always remember it. Truly. But, come on..."

"What? What is it?" I push. "What is Jesse Lamonte that I'm not?"

Denise throws her hands in the air. "*Serious!*"

My face falls. "What?"

"Robbie...are you really gonna make me spell this out for you?" Denise asks.

"Yes. Spell it out. Please."

Denise crosses her arms, leaning back against her car. "Jesse's sweet. And funny–"

"I'm sweet and funny," I shake my head, interrupting her, not able to help myself.

"You *are*. But if you'd let me finish." She blows out a breath. "He's sweet, and funny, and kind. But most importantly...he has a future. A *plan* for a future."

My brows pull together.

"Jesse's going to college, Robbie. He's already accepted his offer, actually. UC Berkeley. Just like me. He's going for pre-med too."

"Jesse...wants to be a doctor?" I question.

"*Yes*," Denise says. "We both do." I shake my head, reminding myself that she also wants to be a doctor. "Jesse's smart. He tutors kids at the middle school after school sometimes."

A loud screeching sound breaks through the parking lot, pulling my gaze over the top of Denise's head. I quickly realize it was the sound of a school bus door opening. I start to look back to Denise, but then pause, a blur of something catching my eye.

A blur of something red.

"He volunteers at the community center on the weekends," Denise continues.

Cooper is standing in line a few people deep for the bus, her nose buried in a book she has lying open on top of the stack of other things she always has in her hands.

"He's president of the Italian club."

She moves forward, her eyes never leaving the book in her hands, her feet seeming to have a mind of their own. I look down at her scuffed white Keds and notice her frilly little bobby socks poking out of the top of them. I'm used to seeing her in jeans, but today she's wearing a skirt. I find myself tilting my head, taking in the baby blue plaid skirt and wondering how I didn't notice it earlier today.

"He's captain of the basketball team."

I shake my head back to reality, refocusing my attention on Denise.

What the hell?

"He takes honors math and science classes."

I grit my teeth, forcing myself to focus on the highlights of Jesse Lamonte's being, but am quickly distracted again by a loud voice in the distance.

"*Yo, go long!*" I glance back up, seeing a boy that looks like he's a freshman or sophomore throwing a football to another boy. The other boy is jogging backwards without looking where he's going. My eyes dart between where he is and where he's heading. I think I might intervene for a second, but it's a second too long.

"He's on the debate team."

The boy rams right into Cooper's shoulder, sending her

stumbling to the side. I find my body flinching automatically in her direction, but I don't move any further, seeing her quickly recover. I force my eyes back to Denise for a second, but my eyes automatically shift back to the scene. The boy seems to apologize to Cooper and she graciously accepts, even smiling in the process.

Freaking Cooper. I'll never figure you out.

"He's currently the class salutatorian."

All seems well again as Cooper turns back to the bus, stepping onto it as she's next in line. I let out a sigh through gritted teeth, starting to look back to Denise, but something catches my attention. Something on the ground. The bus doors shut as the last student gets on, and it pulls away from the front of the school. Once the area is empty of the bus and students, it's clear as day.

"He's even running for student body president!"

Cooper's journal.

Left on the ground.

"Are you even listening, Robbie?"

Denise's voice brings me back to reality, and my eyes back to her face. I take a deep breath. "Yeah, sweetheart. I hear you loud and clear."

And I do.

She'll never take me seriously.

Denise purses her lips, her blue eyes searching my face. "I'm really sorry, Robbie. I just...I have to think of the future. I have to be–"

"*Serious*," I say, finishing her sentence. "I get it."

And I do. But it still doesn't stop the pinch of defeat I feel in my chest. I shake my head, quickly forcing it away.

I reach up, pushing a lock of hair that escaped from Denise's ponytail behind her ear.

"I'll see ya?" I ask.

Denise nods, a sad smile pulling at her lips. "Yeah, I'll see you, Robbie."

I step back, letting Denise get into her car. I give her a wave as she puts it in reverse and drives away. I stand there for a moment, my hands in my pockets, staring after her until her car pulls out of the parking lot.

I'll think of something.

I'll get her back.

I start to walk the few steps over to my car, but then stop, my head turning. I see Cooper's little red journal, still lying face down and open on the bus porch where it must have fallen from off her stack of books. I blow a breath out of my nose, shaking my head. I spin on my heel, walking over to where it lays.

I'll think of something to get Denise back.

I crouch down, reaching for the journal.

But first...

thirteen

SARA

"Okay, I know it's the third time I've said it," my mom calls from the kitchen as she scrambles around to grab her things, "but what kind of sick joke is it that the one day you don't have to stay after school, I get the early shift?"

"I dunno, Mom," I call back, scrunching my nose at the same algebra homework problem I've been staring at for the last fifteen minutes. "I guess the universe just simply won't allow us to spend more than a few hours a week together."

"I *swear*," Mom says, her voice much closer now. I hear the familiar sound of her uncapping her blue Maybelline *Great Lash* mascara and know she's frantically applying it as usual in the mirror hanging on the wall right outside my door. "Ninety-five percent of *all* Thursdays for the last *fifteen years*, I go in to the diner at five, but just this *one* day when my girl is actually home—"

"*You get scheduled for four.*"

"*I get scheduled for four!*"

"Can you believe this?" Mom asks, recapping her mascara and shoving it into her purse.

"No, actually, I can't," I reply, erasing my math work once again,

114

nearing rubbing a hole straight through the paper. "In fact, I think you really aren't scheduled until five but just want an excuse to leave now. Because you hate me."

My back is to the cracked door of my room, but I can tell by the close sound of bracelets jangling together that my mom just stuck her head through my door. "Not funny," she says.

"Kidding," I say back.

I hear my mom let out a sigh, pulling away from the door. She starts moving about in the kitchen and living room again, the fridge and coat closet opening and closing several different times.

"Alright, well I gotta get going," she calls, opening the fridge again. "We have beef stroganoff leftovers, but I'm not sure if they're still good. Worst case scenario, we have things to make sandwiches–"

"I'm great with making a sandwich, Mom," I respond. I let out a huff, giving up and moving onto the next homework problem.

"Okay," Mom confirms. "Ah, *darn it*! I haven't checked the mail yet today, would you mind–"

"I can grab the mail, Mom. Don't worry."

"Okay, okay. Thanks, hon. *Oh*, and could you bring the trash cans in too?"

"Yes, Mom!" I reply, rereading the problem again, and wondering why we really care what x is in the first place.

"And don't forget, if you need anything while I'm gone, Mrs. Granger–"

"Is right next door!" *Just like she has been every day for the last seventeen and a half years.* "I'm good, Mom. You can go to work!"

"Alright, alright. I'm going!" she calls, her voice drifting farther away as she heads for the front door. "Love you!" I hear the lock click and the squeak of the door starting to open. "I'm proud of– *Oh*!"

Mom's voice breaks off, but I don't think much of it, too focused on my math problem and assuming she just remembered another thing she forgot. Several seconds go by as my eyes bounce back and forth between the numbers I've written down and my brain pretends to compute them.

"*Okay, Sara!*" Mom's voice comes again from afar. "I'm really leaving now! Your friend is here to see you!"

My pencil immediately drops from my hand, a smile coming to my face.

"I'll let you two lock the door behind me!"

"*Alice,*" I mutter to myself, my grin spreading.

I hear the front door close and suddenly become aware of the absurd amount of eraser shavings covering my homework paper and entire desk. I quickly gather them all into a pile and have just finished gently brushing them off of the side of my desk and into my trash can when I hear the creak of my bedroom door.

"About time you showed up, you little skank," I say to Alice.

Which would have been hilarious. Except, when I spin around to face the door, it's not Alice standing there.

"Well damn, Cooper. If you'd wanted me to come to your bedroom that badly, you could've just asked."

I feel all the blood drain from my face as I scramble to my feet. Then, once I take a second to really take in the fact that Robbie Summers is standing in the doorway of my bedroom right now, the blood rushes back to my head all at once.

I storm forward to him, my mouth agape but no words coming out. Once I reach the doorway, my head continues to swivel back and forth between him and the direction of the front door that my mother just left out of.

My mother.

Robbie Summers just interacted with my mother.

What alien planet did I wake up on today? Please, someone inform me.

I keep trying to speak, but only sputtering sounds manage to come out. "*Huh–Wha–Why–I–*"

"English might be helpful, Cooper."

"*Explain yourself!*" I demand, throwing my hands in the air. "How are you here right now?"

"Sherri let me in," Robbie replies nonchalantly, sliding past me and into my room. He does a full 360 degree turn, taking it all in before facing the doorway again. His head shifts slightly to the side, something catching his eye. "*Top Gun?*" he asks, a brow raising in my direction as he points to the back of my door.

I push my hair away from my face, pausing to rub my temples.

"Is that your favorite movie or something?" Robbie continues.

"*No,*" I say steadily.

"Then why do you have a huge poster–"

"No," I say, holding a hand out and cutting him off. "Not *no* as in *that's not my favorite movie*–"

"So it is?" Robbie asks.

I blow a breath out of my nose in frustration. "*Yes,* it's my favorite movie. *No,* as in: No, *you cannot just show up at my house and be standing in my bedroom and call my mother by her first name.*"

Robbie just lets out a chuckle, turning away from me as he continues to stare and snoop at the contents of my room.

"How did you get here? *Before* my mom–"

"Sherri," Robbie interjects.

"*Robbie,*" I grit. "Before my mom let you in, *how* did you get here?"

"Well, I drove, Cooper," he says. "I told you I was pretty sure I remembered where your house was." He glances over his shoulder at me. "Stop acting like Bay View is so big."

"It's getting smaller by the second. That's for sure," I say.

Robbie doesn't respond, moving to look through a stack of VHS tapes on my dresser.

"You know, you're really not helping your stalking case here," I say. Robbie picks up my VHS of *The Karate Kid,* and I cross the room, taking it from his hands. "Now, if you're done creeping through all my things, you're free to leave anytime."

Robbie scoffs out a laugh, then nods, his tongue in his cheek. He makes his way over to my doorway, spinning around and leaning against the door frame to face me. "You know, Cooper," he says.

"You just keep asking *how* I got here, but you haven't asked *why* I came in the first place."

"Because I don't care," I reply, crossing my arms.

Robbie tilts his head. "That so?"

"Yep," I respond, nodding my head in the direction of the front door. "You can leave the way you came."

Robbie shifts, his hand going behind his back, seeming to reach for his back jean pocket. Slowly, he raises his arm back up. "If you say so," he says. The moment his hand comes into view, my brows pinch in confusion, then my mouth falls open.

My gaze flies to my desk, seeing only my math textbook and a folder on its surface. I look back to Robbie, seeing something that looks exactly like my journal in his hand. Still not believing it, I dart over to where my backpack lays on my bed and start rifling through it frantically.

"I'll just see myself out, then," Robbie says, a tone of mischief to his voice.

I check every pocket of my backpack twice. My journal is nowhere to be found.

Because Robbie Summers is holding it in his hand.

"See you tomorrow, I guess," Robbie says, turning to leave.

"*Wait*," I demand, storming over to him and grabbing him by the shoulder. When I spin him back to face me, Robbie has a smug smile on his face. I snatch the journal straight from his hand, hugging it to my chest defensively. I slowly raise my gaze to Robbie's face. "*What did you do?*"

The smile on his face falters, then shifts into a look of irritation. "In my culture, we typically say *thank you*, but okay, Cooper."

"*Thank you?*" I laugh without humor. "Sorry, what am I thanking you for? Stealing my journal or breaking into my house? Or both?"

Robbie lets out a laugh of his own. "It's not breaking in if Sherri let me in the door–"

"*Oh my God*, if you call my mother Sherri one more time–"

"And I didn't steal your little diary, Cooper. I'm just returning it to you."

"It's not a *diary*," I insist. "And how did you end up with it if you didn't steal it?" Robbie just stares back at me for a second, not responding. "*Did you read through it?*" I ask, fuming.

Robbie runs a hand through his hair, frustrated. "*Jesus Christ,* Cooper. You really just have to think the worst of me all the time, don't you?"

I don't answer his question, stepping closer to him. "*Did. You. Read. It?*"

Robbie continues to shake his head at me. I can't be sure if he's answering my question or if he's just exasperated. I take another step closer, trying to keep my voice as even as possible.

"Where did you get it?" I ask again.

"You *dropped* it!"

I straighten my posture. "What?"

"Yeah, you can be a real klutz, Cooper," Robbie says, shaking his head.

"But, when–"

"After school. Bus porch. Freshman with a football. Ring any bells?" Robbie asks, an edge to his voice.

My brows pull together. I remember the freshman boys playing football and how one of them accidentally bumped into me. *Did I really drop my journal though? How wouldn't I have noticed?* A different thought quickly overshadows that one though. The thought that I almost lost it. That it could've been gone forever.

But it isn't lost.

Because Robbie apparently found it.

"I dropped it?" I ask. "And...you *picked it up?*"

"Genius, Cooper. Truly," Robbie replies, crossing his arms and leaning back into the doorframe. "Can't believe they're charging you to go to NYU at all."

All of the muscles in my face instantly tense, my eyes narrowing. "Yeah, well," I reply. "You're such a gentleman for returning it to me." I step forward, placing a hand on his arm and forcing a sweet smile onto my face. "Can't believe Denise Davis still wants nothing to do with you."

Robbie tongue slides over his top row of teeth. "Wow. You're ruthless, Cooper." He reaches up, removing my hand from my arm and taking it in his, making us handshake. "You'd be great in politics." He suddenly yanks me forward by my hand, bringing me within inches of him. "Too bad you're too chickenshit to even put your name in the running for student body president."

I swallow hard at the dryness in my throat. A wave of embarrassment tries to wash over me, but it's quickly put out by the fire of my quickly growing rage. "*Chickenshit?*" I repeat, shaking my head. "Oh, that's a good one."

"*Yeah?*" Robbie asks.

"*Yeah,*" I confirm, poking a finger into his chest. "Especially coming from you."

Robbie raises his brows in question.

"Coming from the boy that will put on a dance number in front of the whole school before he's willing to actually talk about the way he feels to a single girl."

I don't give Robbie a chance to respond, continuing.

"Coming from the boy that has everything he could possibly want or need in the world but is too lazy– *No*, too *scared* to take on the responsibility of it all. So, he hides behind an act. Hides behind his friends and this image he projects to the world. Hides behind humor and charm and attitude and his gorgeous hair and his *goddamn sunglasses*. Because it's *so* much easier. So much easier than having to try. So much easier than having to show anyone who he really is. Because how can anyone get disappointed by something that isn't real?"

I take a deep breath, looking directly into Robbie's blazing brown eyes. "Yeah, who's the real *chickenshit* now?"

We stare back at each other for several moments, both of us breathing deeply. Finally, Robbie breaks the silence.

"I don't know what to say."

I feel the crease between my eyebrows smooth out

momentarily, my shoulders falling. Guilt starts to seep in. Regret pricks at my chest. *You went too far, Sara–*

"I just can't decide if I want to focus on the fact that you just admitted you find me charming, or if we need to talk about how *deeply* obsessed you are with my hair."

My mouth falls open, and I turn away from him. "*Oh my God,*" I mutter to myself as I walk over to my desk, dropping my journal onto it. "Oh my God," I repeat, running my hands through my hair.

"God isn't here right now, Cooper," Robbie says from behind me. "Can I take a message?"

I spin back around, walking right up to him.

"I can't do this." I shake my head. "I'm going insane."

"Hate to break it to you, but I think you're already there, baby," Robbie states.

I continue to shake my head, dumbfounded. "Everything is a joke to you," I say to him. "*All* the time. Isn't it exhausting?"

"Is it exhausting *for me?*" Robbie asks, pointing to himself. "I mean, Cooper, come on. I think you should be more worried about yourself."

"Yeah? And why is that?"

Robbie takes a step closer, running a hand over the lower half of his face. "Everything with you, Cooper– *Everything* is just...*so*..."

"So *what?*"

"*Serious!*" Robbie cries. "You're so serious *all* the time, Cooper."

I let out an involuntary chuckle. "Yeah, well, I *have* to be serious, Robbie. Unfortunately, it's how you get taken *seriously.*"

Robbie's spine steels suddenly, his eyes flicking to the floor.

"I have to put in serious effort if I want serious results," I continue, on a rant now. "Serious time for a serious–"

Robbie holds up a hand, stopping me. "*That's it,*" he whispers.

A grin slowly creeps its way on to his face, and I find my eyebrows raising in response.

"*What's* it?"

fourteen

ROBBIE

"What's *it*, Robbie?" Cooper pushes when I don't respond.

My hand stays raised between us as I process the epiphany I just had. As I allow the thought that just popped into my mind to take form. As I work through the idea that just came to me.

The idea that's so ridiculous and insane...*that it might just freaking work.*

Cooper's gray eyes continue to widen and darken with every second I don't answer her.

"Robbie, I swear—"

I hold up a finger, quieting her. "Just hold on," I say, lowering my voice to a hushed tone. "Just...just hear me out."

"It's a little difficult to hear you out when you're not saying anything."

"Cooper, *please*."

She presses her lips together and crosses her arms, letting out a deep breath of resignation. "Fine," she says. "What is this about?"

"Serious," I say, letting out a breath of my own.

"Serious," she echoes. "Serious *what*?"

"*Being* serious," I say. "Being taken *seriously*."

"What about it?" she asks, raising one brow.

I shake my head, running a hand through my hair. I don't miss the way Cooper's eyes sharply follow the movement in the same way an animal's eyes stalk its prey. It makes me wonder if she's going to pounce.

Especially after what I'm about to suggest.

I think it through for a moment, wondering if I should forget it all together. But I can't. It's just too perfect. For both of us. Cooper will see that. She's too smart not to.

"Robbie?"

My gaze flicks up to meet Cooper's, and her expression seems to soften slightly.

"Just say it. Whatever it is," she insists.

Well, here goes nothing.

"Nobody takes me seriously," I say. Cooper opens her mouth to interject, but I carry on before she can. "Not my friends, not my teachers, not Principal Whileyman, not my family, and...especially not Denise."

Her brows pull together, her head tilting to the side.

"They all just see me as the *cool dude*," I continue. "The rich kid. The popular jock. The brainless womanizer. The life of the party. The fun guy that everyone wants to be friends with but...nobody really wants to *be* at the end of the day."

I swallow, shaking my head.

"But *you*," I say, pointing at Cooper. "Everyone takes you seriously. Nobody wants to be friends with you, but–"

"Excuse me?" she scoffs. "I have friends."

"You have *friend*," I correct her. "As in *one* friend."

"That is not true," Cooper retorts.

"Your mom doesn't count."

Cooper looks at me incredulously. "You know, I'm so glad I heard you out," she says. "Can you leave now?" She walks for her bedroom door, clearly trying to motion me out of it.

"Listen, Cooper, I'm not trying to offend you–"

She spins around in the doorway suddenly to face me, almost

making me run directly into her. "Yeah, well, you're doing a really crappy job of it," she says.

"Listen, please. I– I think we can use each other."

Cooper says nothing, her shoulders rising and falling with her irritated breathing. I find my eyes trailing down her figure, from those unexplainable eyes of hers, to her plaid skirt, and lastly to her old white Keds. When my gaze returns to her face, her cheeks appear much pinker and her lips are twisted into a frown of disgust.

"I'm not sleeping with you," she says.

I bark out a laugh. "I didn't say anything about that. And besides, *you* were the one dirty talking to me when I showed up here."

Cooper cheeks flush deeper. "Okay, *no*. I thought you were–"

"Really, Cooper, it's okay. I'm flattered. But I'd prefer for Hank to stay intact. So we don't need to talk about it any further." She tilts her head at me in confusion (and more disgust), and I motion downwards. "Something tells me you wouldn't be too kind to him."

Cooper's face falls flat. "Did you *seriously* name your junk *Hank?*"

I shrug.

"Well, you just tell Hank that there's not a fat chance in hell–"

"We're getting off track here, Cooper," I say.

"I wonder why," she huffs, throwing her hands in the air.

"As I was *trying* to say," I continue. "I think...that you and I..." I motion my finger between the two of us. "We have something to offer each other."

"I don't do drugs, Robbie."

"*Jesus Christ*, Cooper." I fist my hands in my hair. "*Socially*, we have something to offer each other." Her shoulders relax, the look of irritation on her face melting into something else. "For our mutual benefit."

Cooper glances away, crossing her arms. She shakes her head before looking back at me. "I don't know where you're going with this. But get there. Fast."

I roll my lips into my mouth, my pulse pounding in my ears. I'm halfway to just forgetting the idea all together.

God, she's infuriating.

My hands tighten into fists at my sides.

But you need her.

I force my hands to relax, my fingers uncurling.

Dammit.

I let Cooper's face come back into focus.

No turning back now.

"You need a way to stand out," I say. "And I need a way to... blend into the crowd."

Cooper blinks in a way that tells me this isn't at all the direction she thought this conversation was going to go in.

Guess that makes two of us, Cooper.

"I need a way to be taken seriously. To come off as somebody ambitious and determined and serious. And you, you need a way to be taken...*not* so seriously. To come off as somebody chill and easy going and interesting."

"Oh, so now you're saying I'm not interesting?" Cooper questions me, a humorless smile on her face.

"Not at all. You might be the most interesting person I've ever met." Cooper stays quiet, the smile fading from her face. "And for that reason," I say, "I'm willing to make a deal. But, only if you are."

"What does that mean?" she asks. "What kind of deal?"

I purse my lips, trying to find the best words. "One where we..." I trail off, tilting my head in thought. "Attach. Publicly."

Cooper's eyes widen, her mouth falling open. "I'm fairly certain that's illegal. And you're disgusting."

Okay, so I don't think I found the best words.

I pinch the bridge of my nose, my eyes closing. "Not like *that*."

"Then like how?" Cooper questions. "What are you saying?"

"I'm *saying*," I respond, throwing my hands out to the side. "I think we should appear to...you know..." I pause, waving a finger back and forth between the two of us.

"*What?*"

"*We should appear to be a thing.*" The words spill out of my mouth so fast that I'm not sure they even sound like English. "At school," I add, putting my hands on my hips.

Cooper's brows raise in slow motion. "You think we should appear to be a thing."

"Well, yeah," I nod.

"Are you saying that we should...*fake date?*"

Huh. What a simple way to put it.

"Yeah," I agree. "Something like that."

Cooper's face remains completely straight for so long, I start to think she's frozen. Just as I open my mouth to question her, she suddenly bursts into laughter.

"Did you run into a stop sign on the way over here? Or a tree, maybe?" she asks, shaking her head.

I roll my eyes at her. "Cooper, I'm being for real. This could work."

She starts to laugh some more, but then stops when she notices the look on my face. "You're serious," she says, steeling her spine.

"Trying to be," I mutter. She just continues to stare back at me, her eyes swirling with a mixture of confusion, disbelief, and irritation. "This could work," I say again when she doesn't speak for several seconds.

"Please explain in what world this could work, Robbie," Cooper says, shaking her head. "We couldn't be more different."

I take a step closer to her. "That's what *makes* it work."

"We can barely get along as *acquaintances*," she retorts, throwing her hands in the air. "Much less friends. How do you expect to make people believe we're...*into* each other?"

"I'm sure it can't be that hard."

"Oh, *right*. Because *everybody's* into you. I almost forgot." She rolls her eyes.

"Hey, I didn't say that."

"You imply it often enough," she quips, looking away. "It's easy to put two and two together."

"You're putting words in my mouth," I argue.

Cooper lets out a scoff of disagreement, shaking her head. After a few seconds she glances back at me. "Why?" she asks.

"Why *what*?"

"Why would you expect anyone to believe that?" she asks. "That we'd be together? That I'd be with you? That... That you'd be with *me*?" Her voice cracks on the last word, and she stops meeting my eyes.

I let out a sigh, bracing my arm on the door frame to my side. "Cooper, people believe what I want them to believe. Spend a little more time with me and you'll find out soon enough that with enough confidence you can make people think you're capable of anything."

"We don't run in the same crowd, Robbie."

"We would if you were my girlfriend."

Her lips part, a harsh puff of air escaping them. She blinks at me several times.

"You know I'm right," I say.

She shakes head, slowly at first, and then more aggressively the longer she thinks. "I know that you're crazy," she tells me.

"Cooper, please just allow yourself to think about it," I say. "It would only be a month."

"A *month*?" she chokes out.

"That's all it would take."

Her eyes squint, and I can see her internally shutting down.

"Hey," I say. Her gaze falls to the floor as her head continues to shake. I push off the door frame, circling behind her. "Cooper?" I place one hand on her shoulder, and she jolts in surprise. "Just try to picture it. Please?"

She says nothing, but I can feel her release a deep breath by the way her shoulder falls. I take it as an agreement.

I stretch my other arm out in front of both of us, motioning to a nonexistent picture with my hand.

"One month of us together," I begin. "People see you with Robbie Summers. *Who's that girl?*, they ask. *She must be something special. No, she* is *something special.* We put on a show, make our appearances. Everybody knows your name and, with my name attached to yours, you're a shoo-in for Homecoming Queen. You're a Bay View name. *The* Bay View name."

I see Cooper's throat bob in my peripheral vision, and it brings a grin to my face. I lean in closer to her side, continuing.

"Every guy *wants you* and every girl wants to *be you*. It's only natural you go on to win student body president. And, therefore, become..."

"*Yearbook editor*," Cooper whispers.

"Scholarship: *secured*," I state, snapping my fingers in front of us. "You attend the school of your dreams, graduate with honors, then go on to do something more rad than anyone at little old Bay View High could ever imagine."

Cooper's lips roll into her mouth, and I swear her eyes go glassy. I can see the gears turning in her mind. The puzzle pieces fitting together. She sees it. She can almost *taste* it.

Attagirl, Cooper.

"And in turn, people see me with this new mystery girl. *No*," I stop myself, fighting a smirk. "*Not* a mystery girl. A *smart* girl. A *serious* girl. The future valedictorian *and* student body president, in fact. Now, *what would a serious girl like that ever do with a goofball playboy like Robbie Summers?*, they'll ask. *He must have a deeper side. A bright future ahead of him. Look at him, in a committed relationship with Bay View High's 'Most Likely to Succeed'. You know what that means?* He'll *succeed. Yes, he has something to offer to the world other than his badass car and his luscious hair–*"

"Okay–" Cooper cuts me off, breaking from the trance I've seemed to put her in.

"Your words, not mine, Cooper," I say, continuing. "Yeah," I nod. "They'll all see. The teachers. My family." I click my tongue. "*Denise*."

Cooper pulls out from under my grasp, turning to face me. She looks at me with thoughtful gray eyes for several seconds.

"And...that's it?" she finally asks.

"That's it," I nod.

"One month?"

"One month," I confirm. "I get the girl of my dreams and every adult in this town off my back, and you get the presidency, yearbook editor, and the future you've always wanted."

Cooper's gaze focuses over my shoulder, and I can tell she's picturing it all over again. Her teeth push into her bottom lip, stifling what I know is a smile starting to come to her face. Suddenly, it's like she comes back to reality, and she refocuses on me standing in front of her. Her face slowly falls, a crease forming between her brows.

"Well?" I ask her.

"I... I don't know," she says. "I need to think about it."

"*C'mon, Cooper*," I groan, placing my hands on her shoulders. "Take the highway to the danger zone with me?" I nod towards the poster on the door next to us, a smile pulling at my lips.

Cooper eyes flick between Tom Cruise and me for a few seconds. "Negative, ghost rider."

My smile falls.

"I said I need to think about it," she says, attempting a firm tone.

I let my hands fall back to my sides. "What is there to think about?" I ask her.

"*Everything*," she says.

"Like what?"

She goes quiet, looking down and wringing her hands in front of her.

"Hey," I say softly, taking a step forward and gently lifting her chin with my thumb and forefinger so she'll look at me. "Talk to me, Goose."

The corners of her mouth pull up involuntarily, light flashing in her eyes. She quickly catches herself though, shaking her head and stepping back just out of my grasp. "I don't know," she says. "This just feels..."

"What?" I question.

She blows out a breath, looking up at me. "Icky."

"*Icky?*" I repeat. "Can't say I've ever had a girl describe me in *that* way."

"It's not *you*," Cooper assures me. "Well...not entirely—"

"I'm not *entirely* icky? Gee, thanks, Cooper."

She groans, running her hands over her face. "It's just...not honest. It doesn't feel right. And I don't know if anyone will buy it. I'm not sure I can be as good of an actress as you think I can." She crosses her arms. "And I'm not sure I even want to try."

"Cooper..."

"*Robbie*," Cooper cuts me off, holding up her hands. "Please. It's been a very long day, and now you've shown up here and made my brain hurt even more than it already did. And I need to start getting ready for work now. So, please, just go home."

I shake my head and start to argue with her, but stop myself.

"Fine," I nod, slipping out of her bedroom door and heading towards her front door. I hear her footsteps following after me as I slide my sunglasses on. I pull open the door and take a step out of it, but then stop in place.

I blow a breath out of my nose, turning my head to look behind me. Cooper is standing just inside the entryway, her arms crossed. "Cooper—"

"Goodbye, Robbie." She steps forward, moving to close the door.

I stick my arm out, stopping it from closing all the way.

Cooper's gaze snaps up, meeting mine through my sunglasses. "You'll think about it?"

She tilts her head, her eyes searching my face. What she's looking for, I have no idea. But she doesn't exactly seem satisfied with whatever it is she's finding.

"I said I would."

"Okay," I say.

"Okay," she says back.

When I don't move after a moment, Cooper glances at my arm still in the doorway. I pull it back.

"Bye," she says, closing the door in my face.

fifteen

SARA

Tap tap tap tap tap.

I continue to bounce the pen against the top of Groovy Movie's check-out counter as I take a sip of Jolt, doing anything I can to quiet the voices inside my head. Anything to disrupt the continuous swirl of thoughts and non-stop replay of the conversation that occurred in my bedroom just a few hours ago.

No, I'm not going to think about it. Not going to think about what was said. What was discussed. What was...*offered.*

Because it's ridiculous. And revolting.

But...it may just be the only chance you've got.

I shake my body out, brushing the invisible devil on my shoulder off.

No, it's not happening. I won't do it. I'll find another way. Or maybe I won't. Regardless, I'm not going to think about it right now.

About four seconds go by.

I mean, who does he think he is?

He shows up to my house—to my *bedroom*—completely unannounced and out of nowhere. He shows up with my *journal* of all things, is a complete ass as usual, insults me and throws my own problems that I never should have told him about in the first place back in my face. Then–*then*, he has the audacity to offer a simple solution to all those problems. The simple solution of *dating*–no, *fake dating* him?

I feel my face begin to heat and my stomach starts to bubble with nausea all over again.

Then I remember I'm not supposed to be thinking about this.

No, I'm not going to think about the absurd offer. Or the fact that tomorrow is the deadline to sign up for the student body president race. Or that I don't have any idea what I'm going to do when I don't sign up for it. When I don't become the yearbook editor or have anything more to put on my resume. I don't think about how slim my chances already are of getting one of the scholarships to the NYU screenwriting program.

I'm top of my class, I work a part-time job outside of school, I have lots of community service hours, and have participated in nearly a dozen extra curricular activities...but I know that every other person that was accepted into the program is most likely in the exact same boat.

A voice suddenly booms from behind me, making me jump. "Hey, good to see you again, Mrs. Roper!" I hear a door close as my boss and the owner of Groovy Movie, Mr. Ritter, walks into the store from the back office. It's then that I realize a customer is browsing a shelf of movies just a few feet away from the counter. I didn't even hear her come in.

God, I'm losing it. Get it together, Cooper–

I stand up straight, and resist the urge to slap myself in the face.

Sara. Get it together, Sara.

I run a hand through my hair and straighten out my burnt orange work vest, attempting to *actually* get myself together.

Think about anything else.

The older woman Mr. Ritter was talking to waves back to him. "Hi there, Jack," she says. "Always a pleasure. Just grabbing some movies to watch with the grandkids this weekend. They're coming into town."

"Oh, great! That's great," Mr. Ritter replies. "Well, as always, thank you for choosing us." Mrs. Roper waves Mr. Ritter off, telling him *"Of course"* before she continues on looking at movies. I sense Mr. Ritter turn in my direction and meet his gaze, smiling and waving. "Hey there, Sara. You doing okay?" he asks.

"I think so," I reply honestly. "I'm all caught up on checking rentals back in for now, and I think I switched around all the displays that we talked about yesterday."

"Awesome. Thanks, Sara."

"No problem," I say. "Just let me know if there's anything else."

"Will do," Mr. Ritter nods, smiling, before he disappears into the aisles of movies, most likely double checking my work and hoping for more inspiration to strike for ways to reorganize the same few hundred VHS tapes we have in stock to get our same handful of repeat customers excited. The thought brings a grin to my face. The man is passionate about his movies. And I don't blame him one bit.

Movies. Screenwriting. NYU.

And I'm thinking about it again. About *him* again.

Dammit.

I flip open a magazine laying on the counter, trying desperately to distract my mind.

Think about anything else.

I just barely flip through one page, however, before Mrs. Roper appears with a stack of movies in her hand.

"Find everything you were looking for?" I ask her, pushing the magazine aside.

"More than I was looking for, as always. I'm so indecisive. I'll just leave it up to the kids to choose. How many movies do you think we can watch in one weekend?"

"I think three is a good place to start," I reply with a smile.

I glance down at the stack of movies one more time before turning to the register. Then I do a double take.

National Lampoon's Vacation, Ferris Bueller's Day Off, and *Pretty in Pink.*

I swallow, blinking.

All John Hughes movies.

Hughes. Mr. Hughes. Yearbook. Yearbook editor.

I shake my head.

Nope. Not doing this.

"That'll be twelve dollars," I say.

Mrs. Roper fishes the money out of her purse and hands the bills over. I hit the few necessary buttons on the register and it opens. And now I'm staring at stacks of cash.

Cash. Money. Scholarship.

I throw the bills into the register and slam it shut. I hand Mrs. Roper her receipt. "Have a great weekend with your grandkids," I tell her, my voice slightly shaky.

"Oh, you have a great weekend as well, hon. Surely you've got a hot date."

My wrist slips, knocking over the plastic cup holding our pens and nearly my Jolt can with it.

Date. Dating. Fake Dating–

"No ma'am," I blurt, shoving the pens back into the cup and setting it upright. "No hot dates for me."

"Awe, I don't believe that. But, either way, have a nice weekend."

I nod at her. "Yes, ma'am."

Mrs. Roper walks towards the door to leave, and I immediately go back inside my head.

No more. No more thinking about this. About him. About even the idea of Robbie–

"Summers!"

"*Wha–what?*" I nearly choke.

Mr. Ritter's head pokes around the corner of a display at the front of the store. "Sara," he says, "the summer movies are still out in front. Remember we talked about switching the summers out for the fall themed movies?"

My unhinged jaw slowly reattaches itself.

Summers. As in the summer movies. Not as in...

Got it.

I run a hand through my hair. "Right, Mr. Ritter. I remember that now." I come around the side of the counter, heading in his direction. "I'll get those switched out right now."

I let out a happy sigh, thrilled to be distracted by anything else.

I just reach the display section Mr. Ritter is talking about when the song playing over the radio in the store fades out and the next one begins.

Sledgehammer by Peter Gabriel.

I groan, my forehead falling against the shelf.

———

When I get home, I flop straight down on my bed and stare at the ceiling. After a long time, I robotically get up to change out of my work clothes and get ready for bed. Then I flop back down on my bed and stare at the ceiling some more.

It's not until I hear the front door clicking open with my mom getting home from work that I realize my lamp is still on. I reach over and switch it off without looking at it just before my bedroom door creaks open. I shut my eyes just long enough for my mom to think I'm asleep, then I let them snap back open the moment the door closes.

Then I continue to stare at the ceiling some more.

I don't remember when I stopped staring at the ceiling and allowed myself to drift off to sleep, but when my alarm goes off, I'm suddenly staring at it again, not remembering a moment of dreams or feeling like I got a single hour of rest. I let out a sigh, reaching over and shutting off the alarm, then swing my legs over the side of the bed and sit up.

"I'm not doing it," I say out loud to nobody.

I push off of my bed and pad next door to the bathroom. I splash the coldest water I can on my face, then reach for a hairbrush, running it roughly through my extra tangled copper strands of hair that I neglected to brush last night. By the time I begin brushing my teeth, the backs of my eyes start to feel like they're burning. I cup water in my hands, bringing them up to my mouth to rinse. Once I finish, I meet my own gaze in the mirror, the grays of my eyes noticeably darker than usual.

"What are you so afraid of?" I ask the question to myself, not sure where it came from or why it was the one of many thoughts racing through my head that decided to make its way out of my mouth.

I think hard about the answer to my own question.

What am I so afraid of?

I shake my head, walking back into my room.

Discomfort. Laughter. Judgment. Embarrassment. Humiliation. The attention. Nobody believing it. Looking like a fool. Making a deal with the devil. Spending a month with my enemy. Doing something stupid.

Failure.

Regret.

I swipe through the clothes hangers in my closet, past all of my more decent but less comfortable clothes, and end up opting for an old sweater and my favorite worn jeans. I slip the clothes on then walk over to where I kicked off my Keds by my bed last night. I crouch down and reach out, but pause, my hand brushing against something under my bed. I immediately register what it is, the blood draining from my face. I blow out a deep breath before raising my bed skirt, finding the large envelope containing my acceptance letter to NYU and admissions information packet. Right where I left it.

I pull the envelope out slowly, running my fingers over where my mom wrote *Congrats!* on the outside of the envelope and drew several hearts in purple pen. I sigh, letting my eyes fall shut.

What are you so afraid of?

I stand up straight, bringing the envelope with me as I walk over to my vanity.

I'm afraid of all the things I thought of before. It's the truth. But, as scared as I am of those things, I have to ask myself, *What am I scared of even more?*

I set the packet down on top of the vanity, looking at myself in the mirror once again.

Complacency. Apathy. Indifference. Contentment. Withdrawal.
Never putting myself out there. Not believing in myself. Being a fool.
Being too scared to take a chance. Being my own worst enemy.
Never doing anything with my life.
Failure.
Regret.

My shoulders slowly relax, my jaw unclenching.

"Screw it."

I make a beeline for my closet, ripping my sweater and jeans off and flicking back through the hangers.

I come out two minutes later, a light sheen of sweat across my forehead from shimmying into the first pair of pantyhose I've worn in months and my nicest red skirt and blouse. I fasten a thick belt around my waist before crouching down to get back under my bed, feeling around for my black loafers I only wear strictly to special occasions.

If I'm playing a part, I'm going to play it all the way. I've never done anything halfway in life, and I'm not about to start now.

I gulp the moment the loafers are on my feet, still feeling uneasy but trying to ignore it. I glance at the clock, seeing I have a few more minutes before I have to walk to the bus stop. I decide to pop over to my bathroom one more time, teasing my hair a little extra and adding one or two more puffs of hairspray than is probably necessary.

Taking a page out of the Robbie Summers handbook, I tell myself, then instantly feel a wave of nausea bubbling in my stomach at the reminder of what's about to happen. What I'm about to agree to.

I put in a pair of hoop earrings and glide my favorite red lipstick on, then head back to my room, shoving my journal and work vest into my backpack before slinging it over my shoulder and walking into the kitchen to grab a granola bar from the pantry.

Am I really doing this? Am I really about to actually commit to this scheme? Am I really about to make this incredibly stupid decision?

A voice in the back of my head wonders if a decision can be stupid and good at the same time. Stupid and *right*.

I run a hand down my face, not knowing what I'm thinking, or feeling, and being so grateful that I can at least pretend this isn't happening for another hour or so. That I have until second period until I actually have to face this problem.

I unlock the front door, pulling the handle.

I start to think through exactly what it is that I'm going to say when that time comes, and tell myself that I'll spend the entire bus ride to school rehearsing it.

I have plenty of time–

The granola bar falls from my hands, bouncing off of my loafer and skittering onto the top step of my front porch.

The top step where Robbie is currently standing, his fist raised in the air like he was just about to knock on the door. He slowly lowers it, his brown eyes searching my face, then drifting down to the rest of me.

I open my mouth and close it several times.

What the hell?

No real words seem capable of coming out of my mouth right now, so I squat down to pick up my granola bar and buy myself a few more seconds to learn how to speak again.

When I stand back up to my full height, Robbie seems closer now. "Did you think about it?" he asks.

"What are you doing here?" I demand, my question overlapping with the end of his.

Neither one of us replies to the other, both of our brows pinching together. Something draws my attention away from his face and I realize for the first time that he has traded his usual Members Only jacket for a red down puffer vest and his usual t-shirt for a striped golf shirt. I tilt my head, taking in his unusually preppy look.

"*What are you wearing?*" We both ask each other at the same exact time.

My eyes shoot back to Robbie's face, and I realize his head is also tilted as he takes in my outfit. Our heads both snap straight in unison.

"*Don't worry about it,*" he says, at the same time I say, "*Nothing.*"

"Forget it," I say, holding up my hand. "Answer my first question."

"Well, I asked you my first question first," Robbie replies, putting his hands on his hips.

"...*What?*"

"I asked you a question before you asked me a question," he says. "Answer it."

I search my cloudy brain, replaying the last thirty seconds.

"*Did you think about it?*" Robbie repeats.

I blow out a breath. "I said that I would."

"And?"

I look at him for a long time, swallowing hard against the logical words threatening to come up my throat. I stand up straight, meeting his hard gaze.

So much for having time to rehearse this.

"I'm in," I say.

Robbie blinks once, rolling his lips into his mouth and nodding. "Okay," he says.

Okay?

"Okay," I nod back, crossing my arms. "Now, why are you here?"

Robbie slips his Ray Bans out from his collar and slides them on his face. "Because I knew you'd make the right decision."

I open my mouth to reply, but he turns away from me, walking down the porch steps and back to his Camaro parked in the street in front of my house. He opens the driver's side door and starts to get in but stops when he sees me still standing in the same place. "Well?" he says. "Are you waiting for a red carpet, Cooper?"

I shake my head in confusion. "What are you talking about?"

"Come on," Robbie says. "If we are—*were* dating, I'd be driving you to school."

"*What?*"

Robbie rests his hands on the roof of his Camaro, letting out a frustrated sigh. "Cooper, no girlfriend of mine is riding the bus to school." My cheeks flare with heat. "Now, come on," he says. "We're gonna be late." Then he settles down in the driver's seat, closing his door and starting the engine.

My feet feel like they're glued to the porch, but I force them forward and down the steps.

No turning back now.

I climb into the car, setting my backpack at my feet. I fasten my seatbelt then run my suddenly very sweaty palms down the front of my skirt, my gaze staying on the ground. It's like I'm telling myself that if I don't look at Robbie, this isn't real. That I'm not sitting in Robbie Summers's Camaro right now. That I'm not about to show up to school with him and have more sets of eyes on me than I've ever had in my life.

Robbie pulls away from my house, turning the radio on and immediately dialing the volume up to a level that vibrates the vehicle. Pat Benatar's *Heartbreaker* starts blaring through the speakers, and I can't help but chuckle at the irony.

"You good, Cooper?"

I turn my head, looking at Robbie for the first time since getting in his car. I can see his dark brows raise over the top of his Ray Bans. My eyes travel down to his singular hand resting on the steering wheel and back up to his face. I zone in on his features. The curve of his full lips. His straight white teeth. His perfectly imperfect skin, tanned and smooth in just the right areas, with the most precisely placed scattering of beauty marks that most of today's supermodels would kill for. The gravity defying swoop of chestnut brown hair curling just perfectly against his forehead. The eyes I know are hiding behind those sunglasses that can shift from the chocolate brown eyes of a little puppy dog to the amber eyes of a grown wolf on the hunt within seconds.

"You're the right kind of sinner to release my inner fantasy," blares through the otherwise silent car. *"The invincible winner. And you know that you were born to be a heartbreaker."*

I swallow.

Yeah, Pat. You got that right.

As much as he makes my blood boil, and as much as I would never admit this out loud, Robbie Summers has all the makings of a heartbreaker. The looks, the swagger, the attitude, the impulsivity, the...*undeniability.*

"*Dream maker, lover taker. Don't you mess around with me,*" Pat continues to sing.

I fist my skirt in my hands at my sides.

I won't let him. Not a chance in hell. This is strictly business.

"Cooper?"

I snap out of my trance, looking at Robbie.

He lowers his sunglasses just slightly. "You don't look so good."

My fists unclench.

Yep, trance successfully broken alright.

"Gee, thanks," I deadpan. "You tell all your girlfriends that?"

Robbie glances between me and the road a few times before he answers. "Only the ones I don't actually like."

My lips part.

Ouch.

"I mean–"

"I don't think it's a necessary requirement of our...*arrangement* that we talk when we're alone together," I interject, cutting Robbie off. "Is it?"

Robbie flexes his jaw. "I'm all for it not being a requirement."

"Good," I reply, an edge to my voice.

"*Good,*" Robbie says back immediately, matching my tone.

I cross my arms, turning to look out my passenger side window. I say nothing, but my mind is screaming a million thoughts. Most of which involve this being a horrible idea. We aren't even ten minutes into this, and we're already at each other's throats. How can we possibly go an entire school day without anybody noticing how *not* into each other we are? Without anyone noticing how we can barely occupy the same space without an explosion happening?

"Cooper, I can feel the heat radiating off of you."

My head snaps in Robbie's direction. "*What?*"

"You're fuming over there, and it's making it a little difficult to breathe," Robbie says. "So, why don't you just spill whatever it is that's burning a hole in your brain?"

"Has anyone ever told you how charming you are?" I ask.

"Lots of people, actually, yes."

"I think they all need to seek medical attention."

"*Cooper.* What is it?"

I blow a breath out of my nose. "The requirements."

Robbie raises his brows, clearly confused.

"Of our *arrangement*," I clarify.

"Why do you keep whispering the word *arrangement* like we're committing government espionage?"

I sit up straight, realizing I had, in fact, leaned in to whisper it. "*Espionage?*" I repeat. "Wow, big word, Robbie. Would you rather have a gold star or a cookie?"

"Why don't you shove your gold star up your—"

"*Wow,*" I exclaim, covering my ears before I can hear him finish that sentence.

Robbie grabs my left hand, pulling it away from my ear and rolling his eyes. "What *about* the requirements of our *arrangement*, Cooper?"

"Well," I say, clearing my throat, "I think we need to talk about them."

"Yeah, you're probably right," he agrees. "But not now."

"Why not?" I ask. But the sudden rocking of the Camaro as we cross over the familiar speed bump answers my question.

Because we're here.

I turn my head forward, seeing that we are actually pulling into the school parking lot. It occurs to me that it looks different today, and I don't know why that is. Then I realize, it's probably not the school that's different at all.

It's me. It's *this.* It's what's happening.

I gulp involuntarily, sliding down in my seat as far as I can go.

Robbie weaves his way through the parking lot, eventually

pulling to a stop in what I know is his typical front row parking spot. "Cooper?"

"Yep," I respond, not looking at him.

"Are you ready for this?"

"As ready as I'll ever be," I breathe.

"Good," Robbie nods, sliding his sunglasses down his nose and leaning closer to me. I slowly turn my head to meet his gaze. "Because I need you to be ready for this," he says. "Because once we step out of this car, once everyone sees us, there's no going back. Things will be different."

I stare at him for several seconds, not moving, then maintain eye contact with him as I push myself upwards, steeling my spine and flattening out my rumpled skirt. I lick my suddenly dry lips. His eyes flick down once before returning to mine.

"I'm counting on it," I say.

Robbie's throat bobs. "Me too."

Then, time seems to slow down. It slows down as Robbie pulls back, pushing his Ray Bans fully back onto his face. It gets even slower as he reaches over and cranks the stereo to full volume, Pat Benatar vibrating my very brain for the few moments it takes for Robbie to look away from me and to open his car door. He takes his time stepping out of the Camaro, occupying every bit of space and moment of time he's given, as per usual. When he's finally standing up straight outside of the car, he lets the engine run and the music continue to blast as he takes his time straightening out his vest and running a hand through his hair. I realize at that moment that my mouth is hanging open, and I snap it back shut, facing forward.

Robbie then makes his way to the trunk of his car, which I see in the rearview mirror. It's not until he has one strap of his backpack over his shoulder, his Walkman secured on his hip, and his headphones around his neck, that he closes his trunk and makes his way back to the front of the car. I swear he spends a full two seconds on each step he takes. When he leans back down into the car, reaching for the keys in the ignition, reality strikes me, and I move to grab my door handle, remembering I'm actually going to have to leave the car at some point today.

My hand pauses right as I grip the door handle, however, Robbie's wordless but firm shake of his head freezing me in place. I count to three while we stay in this position and before he finally shuts off the car, effectively silencing Pat Benatar.

It's not until I'm met with deafening silence that I realize every move Robbie just made was calculated. Calculated to draw as much attention to this car as possible. All it takes is one glance around to realize just how successful he was. Every head in the parking lot is turned in our direction. My heart rate instantly spikes, pounding in my ears and bringing a flush to my cheeks. I force my eyes to shut and breathe deeply, counting to three once again.

There's no going back. Everything will be different now.

I hear the door open to my side and let my eyes peel open. I square my shoulders, raising my chin as I turn my head to find Robbie standing in the doorway, his hand outstretched. I tilt my head back to meet his sunglasses-covered eyes. He drops his chin just slightly in a subtle nod that says nothing, but also everything.

Once I step out of this car, once everyone sees us, there's no going back. Things will be different.

I flick my head down in just as subtle of a nod. One that nobody but Robbie would even be able to register. I start to count to three again, but decide, *screw it.* I reach for his hand, wrapping my fingers around his and allowing him to pull me to my feet. I feel the heat of everyone's gazes all around us, but I don't allow myself to indulge them.

Robbie wouldn't.

I follow his lead, looking only at him. A few seconds go by as I try to keep my breathing under control. *No one else exists. Only him.* I feel myself start to wince at the thought, but force my expression to stay straight.

Suddenly, Robbie leans sharply forward, and a light gasp escapes me as I try to keep my posture firm. He ends up moving right past me, grazing my shoulder with his as he leans down to retrieve my backpack from under my seat.

"*Oh,*" I quietly mutter. "*I guess I probably need that, huh?*"

Robbie holds my backpack up by one strap so that I can easily slip it onto my shoulder. I move to reach for the other strap, but he's already there, grabbing my wrist and threading it through the opening. "*It might help,*" he replies quietly with a nod when he's in front of me again.

I automatically reach to grip my backpack straps at my shoulder as I always do out of an uncomfortable habit, but stop myself, forcing my arms to hang confidently at my sides. Robbie closes the car door, then lingers at my side for a moment, lowering his head just slightly to whisper in my ear. "*I'm going to do something. Try not to slap me when I do.*"

"*What are you—*" I start to question him through my teeth, but am immediately cut off by the shock of Robbie's hand encircling the side of my neck, the warmth of it sending a shiver down my spine. Before I have a moment to think about what is happening, Robbie is pulling me forward and pressing his lips to my forehead. He keeps us in the position for what feels like forever, but what I know is a few seconds at most, before he somewhat abruptly pulls us apart.

Our faces are only separated by a few inches when our gazes meet once again. I let out a breath I didn't realize I was holding, and a brick instantly feels like it settles in my stomach. Feeling like I'll crawl out of my skin if this silence doesn't get broken, I whisper, "*I didn't slap you.*"

"*Gold star or a cookie?*" Robbie whispers back, mocking me.

"*I still could though,*" I grit.

"*Good thing I'm in the perfect position to choke you.*"

Blood rushes my face, heat gathering at where I now realize Robbie's hand is still resting on my neck. He seems to glide his thumb down to the side just slightly, creating more of a gripping hold and proving his point.

"Hilarious, *honey,*" I mouth, a humorless grin coming to my face.

"Anything for you, *baby,*" Robbie replies.

We stare-off for another moment before Robbie lets out a chuckle that could even fool me. *"Don't make direct eye contact with anyone,"* he mutters before turning out, exposing me–*exposing us*– to the world. He slings an arm over my shoulder, pulling me closer to his side. *"Let the games begin,"* he whispers against my ear.

And we start walking.

sixteen

ROBBIE

I find the flash of blue I'm looking for floating around in my backpack and fish the cassette out.

Journey's *Frontiers*.

I open the plastic container, quickly slipping the tape into my Walkman as I make my way down the hallway. I snap the player shut and hit the play button, a grin immediately coming to my face as *Separate Ways* starts flowing through the speakers of my headphones.

Music on, *world* off.

I reach the lockers across the hall from the entrance to the library and lean up against them, my head falling back and my smile spreading. I just keep replaying it.

My and Cooper's performance today.

Though it may have felt like pulling teeth the whole way for the two of us, we had the entirety of Bay View High eating out of the palms of our hands. There wasn't a single person not looking at us. Not a single person not wondering what the hell was going on, whether the tides had reversed or Mercury was in retrograde. I could see it on every one of their faces.

What on earth is Robbie Summers doing with Sara Beth Cooper? And what on earth is she doing with him?

There was a short time on the ride to school this morning that I thought we both were nearly about to send each other running for the hills, but, in the end, I gotta give it up to Cooper. She played her part. And she played it well. I didn't miss the way she held her chin high as she let me help her out of my car, or the way she leaned into me as we walked through that parking lot. And she probably didn't miss the way I pulled her even closer when we passed Denise and half of the other girls on the cheer team. But it didn't matter. Cooper wasn't phased. Everybody was looking at her, but she was only looking straight forward.

Or at me.

I shake my head. *No,* she didn't give anyone any room to question us. To question *her.* We made our way through that entire parking lot and into the school foyer.

I could feel the buzz of anxiety coming off of Cooper, and I knew she wanted to pull away. I knew she wanted to bolt. But she didn't. She let me lead her through the doors and didn't slide out from under my arm until I brought us to a stop. She looked at me expectantly, her eyes swirling with shades of gray entirely new to me. She started to take a step back, but stopped herself, taking a small step towards me instead.

"What now?" she had asked.

"How about we start with this?" I said, pulling a pen out and holding it between us.

Her eyes flicked down to it, her brows raising.

I simply nodded to the side, to the bulletin board just feet away from us. To where the class election sign-up sheet was posted.

Cooper's shoulders fell, her mouth opening and closing several times. She immediately reached for her backpack straps like I've noticed she does when she's uneasy.

"Hey," I said, placing a hand on her shoulder. "Confidence looked good on you out there." I raised the pen in front of her face. "Don't stop now."

She swallowed hard, narrowing her eyes on me as if she was trying to read me. I didn't waver. The deed was done. Denise saw us. I'd make sure she continued to see us, along with every other person in the school that ever questioned me. Now it was time to keep up my end of the bargain. I wouldn't be in debt to anyone, much less Sara Beth Cooper.

I pushed the pen further in her direction. She glanced between me and the pen one more time, steeling herself, before she snatched it from my hand and stormed over to the bulletin board.

She wrote her name so frantically that I don't think she even realized that she took up multiple lines with it, pressing the pen so hard into the paper that it nearly tore. But when she stepped back, there it was: *Sara Cooper.* The last name on the list of student body president sign-ups and written three times larger and twice as dark as every other name there.

She didn't even take a second to admire it, simply spinning back around to face me. Her eyes found me first, but quickly shifted to the side, noticing basically every other person in the foyer noticing *her.* I could tell her automatic reaction was to slump her shoulders and retreat back into herself. She reached again for her backpack straps, but before she got to them, I saw the shift in her. She blew out a breath, instantly standing tall once again, and bypassed her backpack straps, instead running both of her hands through her hair to fluff it up.

Well I'll be damned, Cooper, I thought.

She'd forced a pouty smile on her face, instantly blocking everyone around us out once again and strutting forward to me. I held my hand out as she reached me and she dropped the pen back into it. "I did it," she said.

"*Attagirl,*" I nodded.

We stared back at each other for a few seconds, silence stretching between us. Eventually, we both started to say something at the same time, but the sound of the school bell drowned us both out, signaling that it was time to head to class.

After a quick and mostly amicable agreement with minimal eye rolling and gagging on how to handle Ms. Cage's class second period (*walk in together holding hands then just play it cool since we had a test to take today*), and a not as quick or amicable argument on our lunch plans (*Cooper insisting on needing to study in the library and me insisting that that's the opposite of what lunch is for and both of us eventually compromising that she'd study at a table in the courtyard with me sitting next to her mostly in silence*), we turned to go our separate ways.

I sensed Cooper hesitating and turned back to look at her. "Er... um...I..." she mumbled. I glanced down at her hands fidgeting. She took a step closer to me and I raised my brows at her.

"Yes, Cooper?" I asked.

She let out a huff. "Look, I've already been closer to you this morning than I care to ever be again, but I feel like we should probably look like we don't hate each other as we say goodbye."

"Can't say I disagree," I said, "but, yeah, that would probably be best."

"So..." Cooper said, taking another step closer and raising her hand awkwardly. She looked like she was going to place it on my cheek for a second then suddenly raised it further, starting to run it through my hair. "Well, bye—"

My shoulders tensed, and my hand shot up, wrapping around her wrist. Cooper froze in place as I grabbed her, her fingers still halfway into my hair.

"Cooper, I know we said we still need to fully discuss ground rules later, but I'd just like to go ahead and state my rule number one." Her brows pulled together in frustrated confusion. "*Hands off the hair.*"

She rolled her eyes at me, scoffing as she pulled her wrist from my grasp. "And you say *I'm* obsessed with it. Why don't you try getting over yourself, *Summers*?"

I leaned down closer to her, unable to help myself from matching her challenge. "How about you try getting under me instead?"

Her jaw dropped, and she started to angrily sputter out a

response, but both of our gazes snapped to the side, landing on Jesse and Paul walking by and looking straight in our direction. In automatic response, I reached for Cooper's shoulder and she grabbed a handful of my vest, each of us pulling the other to us.

I don't know why, but I found myself kissing her forehead again, just like I had in the parking lot, our chests slamming together awkwardly and causing both of us to let out a huff. We both played it off to the best of our ability, holding the forced hug for ten painfully long seconds– *literally*, with both of us counting out each number with gritted teeth– and then slowly pulled back from one another.

Jesse and Paul were much further down the hallway by then, neither of them looking in our direction any longer. I was still staring after them when Cooper suddenly spoke up.

"Okay, it's my turn now," she said.

"For what, exactly?" I asked.

"My first rule," Cooper replied, forcing a not so sweet smile on her face as she pulled me closer by my vest to whisper to me. "Put on a show. Put your arm around my shoulders. Press up against me if you have to." My brows raised, and she stood up on her tiptoes, getting close enough that I could smell whatever floral shampoo it was she used. "But touch your lips to any part of me again and I'll shave your head in your sleep."

And just like that, she dropped back down on her heels, giving my vest two gentle pats, before spinning around and walking off.

I guffawed. "See you later, baby," I called after her.

She turned around, walking backwards for a few steps, the most forced smile on her face.

I opened one side of my vest, hiding my hand and sticking out my thumb and pointer finger to mimic a gun. I flicked my hand up, motioning the finger gun like I was letting off a shot at her.

Cooper's hand went straight to her chest, a reaction to being fake shot to my eyes but a sweet gesture to all the other eyes still left lurking in the hallways. "I'll miss you so much, honey," she called back, raising her other hand to brush her hair away from her face. I scoffed out a laugh when I noticed her pushing her hair aside with only her middle finger, tilting her head at me with a tight grin as she did so.

Jesus, Cooper, I'd thought.

But it worked.

It worked so damn well.

People aren't nearly as subtle as they think they are. The cocked heads, the points, the questioning glances between friend groups, the hands half covering mouths, the whispers. They were all giving us exactly what we wanted. It was almost too easy. Too good to be true.

Something catches my attention in front of me and I glance up, seeing Denise passing right in front of me. She turns her head back forward at first, acting like she's going to keep on walking by, but then her feet start to slow. I push my headphones off as she comes to a complete stop before me.

"Hey," she says.

"Hey yourself," I say back.

We stand there for a moment, neither of us saying anything more. And as the seconds go on, I start to feel it.

Denise clears her throat, pulling the textbook in her hands closer to her chest.

I swear I'm not just imagining it.

"So, you moved on pretty easily, didn't you?"

I can barely stop the smile from spreading across my face.

There it is.

I push off of the lockers, taking a step closer to her. "Noticed, did you?"

Denise purses her lips. "Was pretty hard not to with the two of you strutting all over school all day plastered to each other."

"Be careful, Denise," I tsk. "You're on the verge of making me think you care." She narrows her eyes at me, and I take another step closer. "Or maybe even that you're jealous."

"I'm not jealous," she laughs dryly.

"Right, of course not," I nod. "Just a little hypocritical." Denise raises a brow in confusion. "How's Jesse?" I ask.

"He's one of your best friends. Why don't you ask him?"

I test her, taking another step closer. She takes a half step back. "Because I'd rather talk to you," I say.

Denise tosses her blonde hair over her shoulder and the strong scent of her wafts over me. My nose scrunches involuntarily. She smells so clean, but not in a natural way. There's something harsh about it. Something forced. I know she's always worn this same perfume, but I don't know why it seems to be hitting me differently today. I shake my head, playing it off and refocusing.

"So, can I assume I'll see you at the dance tomorrow?" Denise asks. "With your next innocent choice of prey on your arm?"

I lean back, tilting my head at her. "Yes to the first. No to the last."

Denise's brows raise. "You're going by yourself?"

I chuckle. "Is that really a question?" Denise gives me a confused look. "I'm spoken for," I say.

"But...who...?" Denise shakes her head as I tilt my own at her, and I can see it in her eyes the moment it clicks. She rears back. "You're bringing *Sara Cooper* to the Back to School Dance?"

"Of course I am," I reply, crossing my arms over my chest. "She's my girlfriend."

Denise breathes out a laugh. "You can't be serious."

"Apparently, I can be." I take a step forward. Denise doesn't take a step backwards this time. "Sara Cooper sure thinks so."

Denise stares at me, her blue eyes blinking.

I stare back until something catches my attention in my peripheral vision. I ignore it at first, but then realize it's a blur of red. I glance to the side, finding Cooper standing at the door to the library, backpack straps in an iron grip.

A weird feeling pricks at my chest when I meet her eyes. Something like guilt, and I don't know why, but it's quickly replaced with a flood of warmth that I don't quite understand either. I ignore both, a smile spreading across my face. "Baby," I say, my back straightening, "there you are."

Cooper tilts her head, an odd expression flashing briefly over her face as she looks back and forth between me and Denise. Suddenly, she snaps out of whatever trance she's in, plastering her own smile on her face and letting her hands fall. "Here I am," she says. She leans against the library door frame, jutting out one hip while placing a hand on the other, drawing my eyes to her waistline. My gaze trails further down as she crosses one ankle over the other. And suddenly, that red skirt is a lot shorter than I remembered.

"Wanna come and get me?" she asks.

My eyes snap straight back up to Cooper's face. She reaches up with one hand pushing her coppery curls behind her ear, her red lips pulling into a smirk. And right about the time I start wondering if my ears just played a trick on me, she speaks up again. "*Honey?*" she adds, cocking her head at me.

I let out a low whistle. "Absolutely, I do." I stroll straight over to Cooper, not giving a glance in Denise's direction as I do so. I notice that Cooper's eyes, however, stay glued specifically to Denise. Right as I reach her, she flashes Denise the sweetest smile.

God, she's good.

Then she turns that smile on me as I sling my arm over her shoulder, pushing open the door to the library and leading the both of us through it.

One, two, three steps across the threshold. The door closes behind us and, the moment that it does, Cooper's smile falls and my arm slips off her shoulder. We put a few feet between us, me straightening my vest and Cooper shaking out her hands like she was just touching a dead animal rather than me.

"Sheesh, Cooper, you can at least be subtle about it."

"What?" she asks, her eyes shooting up to meet mine, her hands still twitching at her sides and her shoulders nearly touching her ears. She seems to realize, glancing down at her body and relaxing. "Oh, whatever– I mean...Sorry. I guess," she sputters.

I stare at her as she starts to pace back and forth within the five foot radius around her. Something is clearly bothering her.

"You good, Cooper?"

"You talked to Denise?" she asks, not answering my question.

I tilt my head. There's that weird feeling in my chest again. *What is that?* "Yeah," I nod. "You saw me talking to her."

"And?"

"*And*, what?"

Cooper stops in her tracks, turning to face me. "Did she believe it? Is it working?"

I don't respond right away, making her take a step closer to me.

"*Well?*" she pushes.

I can see the anxiety bouncing around like crazy in those big eyes of hers. The hard set of her shoulders. The way she's clenching her fists so hard that she's leaving nail marks in her palms. She's really so worried about this. So worried about what people think of us. Of *her*. I don't understand the feeling. Maybe I've started to somewhat recently, but never to this extent. I've been stressed out by so few things in my life. What other people are doing in *their* lives, much less what they're *thinking* about, hasn't even been in the realm of my concerns. *Why does she do this to herself? Doesn't she know it's all in her head?*

"Robbie, if you don't answer me, I'm going to have to scream. And considering we're in a library that feels extremely sacrilegious."

"Cooper, of course she believed it."

Her posture straightens. "What? *Really?*"

"Yes."

"*Seriously?*"

"If I say yes, are you just going to ask me to confirm it again?"

Cooper's lips part. "Probably," she mumbles. There's a moment of silence between us, then she says, "But, really. She did? You're serious?" I just stare back at her in response. "But, why?"

I let out a breath, shaking my head. "Cooper, I told you. People will believe what you want them to believe. Just don't ever give them the opportunity to question you."

I think back to Denise's split second of doubt, her mere moment of disbelief back in the hallway.

That would be the only moment I let her have.

"We all get to write our own stories, Cooper. Write a gripping enough story for yourself and everyone will be forced to read it." Her gaze flicks up to meet mine, her brows pulling together. "And, besides, a story doesn't have to be real for you to believe it. People believe with their emotions as much as they believe with their minds. Learn how to master people's emotions and you can have anyone in the palm of your hand."

Cooper blinks at me. I swear her eyes are a different shade of gray every time she opens them. *How does she do that?*

Her mouth slowly opens. "Oh..." she finally says. "Okay then."

"Yeah," I respond, not sure what else to say. A few seconds go by, and Cooper's gaze goes out of focus, like she's clearly thinking very hard about something.

What now?

"But, anyways," I continue, holding my fist out, attempting to lighten the mood, "great first day performance, Cooper."

She glances between my face and my fist a few times before returning the gesture, bumping her fist against mine. "Thanks," she mutters. "I guess we may have actually convinced a few people that we don't wanna rip each other's heads off."

"I'd venture to say they don't even think we want to scratch each other's eyes out," I counter. "Good work."

Cooper rolls her eyes, the smallest smile flashing across her face before she moves around me to head for Ms. Rose's office, shrugging her backpack off as she does so. "Good thing we have the entire weekend apart to recover," she says right as she makes her way through the door.

I follow after her, leaning against the doorframe. Her back is to me, and her head is down, doing something in her backpack.

"Yeah," I reach up, rubbing the back of my neck. "About that..."

Cooper's body shifts a quarter-turn in my direction, and I see her scribbling furiously in her little journal. She glances up at me. "What about it?"

seventeen

SARA

"Do we seriously have to go to this?" I groan.

"Yes, Cooper," Robbie insists. "We absolutely do."

"The whole school is going to be there though."

"Exactly," he says.

"There will be so many people there. They won't even notice we're missing."

Robbie turns his eyes away from the road, giving me a pointed look.

I let out a sigh. He doesn't even have to say it. That look communicates it just fine.

Everyone will notice he's *missing.*

"I feel like we could come up with a story," I say, fiddling with the powder blue fabric of the dress I borrowed from my mother's closet. I've never been to a single dance in my high school career that I wasn't taking photos at, and, considering that I had zero intentions of breaking that streak in my senior year, I had nothing even remotely appropriate to wear to a dance. The one semi-dressy outfit I own, I already wore on Friday.

"Like what?" Robbie questions.

I pause, taking a moment to think.

"You want me to tell everyone that we never got out of your driveway because you couldn't keep your hands off of me and that we were too deep in the throes of passion to make it to the dance?" he offers.

I mimic a gagging sound. "Fine, let's go to the stupid dance," I mutter, crossing my arms.

"We're already going, Cooper. We've *been* going."

I slam my head dramatically into the headrest.

"Even if you give yourself brain damage before we get there, I'm still dragging you into the school gym behind me," Robbie says.

"Is that a genuine offer?" I ask. "Because I might be willing to compromise on that." Robbie gives me a side-eye right as we roll over the speed bump I've been dreading.

Shit.

I bump my head several more times against the headrest.

"Mind telling everyone giving us funny looks as you drag me behind you to vote for me for president?" I ask.

"Now you're just getting greedy, Cooper," Robbie says, pulling into a parking spot. He turns to face me. "You've got to put some work in here too, you know."

I close my eyes tightly, turning my head in his direction. "I know," I say. "I'm sorry. This just..."

"Isn't your thing?"

I open my eyes again, seeing him staring at me with a crease between his brows. I glance down, taking in his outfit for the first time, considering I didn't get much of a look at it as he was fighting me into his Camaro.

Darker jeans than normal, a button up shirt, and a black leather jacket. I lean forward just enough to get a glimpse of his shoes and see that he's traded his Converse for Nikes. I suppose this is Robbie Summers, *elevated.*

I must admit, it's nice. *He* looks nice.

And that makes me want to walk in there on his arm even less.

I know every girl in there is going to be looking at him. Which means they'll all be looking at me too.

Great.

"Yeah...you could say that," I nod.

"You'll survive. I promise," Robbie assures me, killing the engine. He pulls the key from the ignition, the Heart album he had been playing immediately cutting off as he does so, making it entirely too quiet all of the sudden. It seems obvious that Robbie finds the silence uncomfortable too by the way he clears his throat and quickly reaches for his door handle.

"*Wait,*" I say, wrapping a hand around his upper arm and pulling him back.

"What, Cooper?" he grunts.

My mouth hangs open as I stare at him, not actually knowing *what* it was I intended to say, but just knowing I'm not ready to go inside yet.

"Shouldn't we make a fashionably late entrance?" I suggest.

Robbie's lips press together. "Cooper, I *planned* for us to make a fashionably late entrance. And then it took over twenty minutes to convince you to get in my car. Now we are just *late*."

I blow out a deep breath, letting Robbie's arm go.

"Can we go in now?" he asks, grabbing the door handle again.

"No."

"Cooper–"

"*Ground rules!*" I blurt.

Robbie blinks at me. "What?"

"Ground rules," I repeat. "We still haven't talked about our ground rules yet. For us. For *this*." I motion my finger between us. "We need to."

"Right now?"

"If I'm about to walk into that lion's den, then yes," I confirm.

"Lion's den?" Robbie repeats, raising his brows. "Cooper, it's our Back to School Dance. You know, it's safe in there. Some might even call it *fun*."

I stare blankly at him, not willing to budge. When he realizes

I'm not going to let it go, he takes his hand off the door handle, running it down his face instead.

"We might have gotten away with one day at school together," I say, "but this is a whole different ball game. That was a practice run. A fun little show. But this...us going in there together...that makes it real."

"It was already real."

My shoulders tense.

"Cooper," Robbie adds, shaking his head. "We were all anyone was talking about at school yesterday. *You* were all they were talking about."

"Gee, good to know. That really makes me want to run into that dance now," I deadpan.

"I'm just saying, we seem to have this down. I don't see the need to complicate it."

"Ground rules *prevent* us from complicating this," I counter. "We might have gotten through one day, but we need to be on the same page to make this believable for a full month. We need to set expectations and limitations."

Robbie's eyes search my face, only a hint of irritation within them. "Alright, Cooper. Why don't you start us off then."

"Oh...I..." I look away, my teeth going into my bottom lip as I realize I haven't really thought this through. "Well, it's probably best to start with our goals, right?"

"We know those already," he reminds me.

"Right, okay."

Robbie breathes an exasperated laugh, taking over. "Okay. We're doing this for the next month. Until class elections when you win student body president."

My stomach flips at the easy confidence in his statement, but then something occurs to me. "What about you?" I ask.

"What *about* me?" Robbie asks.

"Well, we're setting my goal as the deadline on this whole thing. What about you? What if you don't achieve what you're going for by that date?"

I don't know why I don't elaborate. I know what he's going for, but I keep it vague. I don't say it. I don't say *her* name.

Robbie's mouth pulls into a smirk, and he lets out a chuckle. "Don't worry about me, Cooper."

"But–"

"I'll get exactly what I want," Robbie cuts me off.

"I suppose you always do," I automatically mutter.

That seems to catch Robbie off guard. We're quiet for a few moments before he clears his throat. "Rules?" he asks.

"Rules, right," I nod.

"I already know your first one," he says. "I can touch you with anything but my lips."

"I don't think that's exactly what I said–"

"And you know mine," Robbie continues.

"Right. I'm not to lay a finger on the glorious locks." I roll my eyes.

"Yep. That's exactly what I said." Robbie looks straight forward out the windshield. "What's next?" he asks.

There are several possible rules bouncing around in my head, but somehow they all decide to congeal into this one statement. "Robbie?" I breathe. He turns his head to look at me. "Just...don't make me look stupid, okay?"

Robbie's brows pull together. At the angle he's looking at me, one of the lamp posts in the parking lot is shining directly in one of his eyes. The comparison between that eye and his other right now reminds me of milk chocolate and dark chocolate. I don't like dark chocolate. It's bitter and always seems to taste the same. It never surprises me, just always disappoints me. But milk chocolate, on the other hand... I love milk chocolate. It's sweet. And bright. I never know what exactly to expect from it. I could try a different bar of milk chocolate every day and none of them would taste exactly the same. They'd always surprise me. But it would always be a good thing. Milk chocolate always finds a way to make me happy. I can *trust* milk chocolate, even if it's unpredictable. But dark chocolate is always just predictably, consistently bad.

I try not to think about how other things in my life can relate to chocolate. Or people.

Robbie still hasn't said anything, so I continue. "Just... If you don't want to do this anymore, just tell me."

"Cooper, I—"

I hold up a hand. "Just be honest with me. If you're suddenly happy with the way you're perceived by people next week or if Denise Davis comes up to you tomorrow and begs for you back, please just tell me you're done with this. Let us have a clean and simple fake break up to our fake relationship." I shift my eyes from Robbie's face to my lap. "Me agreeing to this was in an effort to better my reputation. I just ask that you don't do anything purposely to make it any worse. Okay?"

Robbie is quiet. I count to ten in my head before I risk a look at him. His facial expression is unreadable when I do. He's just staring at me. Slowly, he starts to nod. "Yeah. Okay, Cooper. I promise."

I look at him, noticing the light is now shining in both of his eyes.

Double milk chocolate.

I look away. "Okay. Well, I think that's all I have. You?"

I hear Robbie sigh, and am forced to look back at him. He has a tinge of a smile pulling at his lips. "I think this is the part where I'm supposed to drop the cheesy line of saying you're not allowed to fall in love with me."

The air freezes painfully in my lungs, my brows shooting up to my forehead. *What?*

"But I think we both know there's no point in adding that rule," Robbie finishes.

My lungs and eyebrows return to their usual forms, everything normal in the world once again. "Yeah, glad we're on the same page about that—"

"Because we both know you're already too far gone for me anyways."

I punch his arm.

I don't know why, but my automatic response was to punch

Robbie Summers right in his bicep. I also involuntarily accompanied the punch with a groan of disgust.

"Did you just *punch* me?" Robbie questions, gripping his upper arm.

"Are you gonna cry about it?" I ask.

We've clearly resorted to playground bully level as our form of defense.

Okay, Sara.

"Do we need to add no physical violence as a rule?" Robbie asks.

"Why?" I tilt my head at him. "Think you might be tempted to hit on me?"

Robbie's tongue pushes into the side of his cheek. He leans forward, matching my challenge. "I'm more concerned with your inevitable desire to bang me."

"You're vile."

"You too, baby," Robbie replies. "Can we go to the dance now?"

———

The gym doors seemed so far away as we first stepped into the long hallway of the school, and now, suddenly, they are right there. And Robbie isn't slowing down. The muffled music coming out from under the doors gets louder and louder as we approach, my pulse pounding in my ears matching it step for step.

"Robbie?" I call, two steps behind him.

"We're going in, Cooper. You can't stop me."

"I–We– Would you *wait?*"

"Nope. Nothing's stopping me from walking through those doors, Cooper."

"We should probably touch each other, don't you think?" I demand, throwing my hands in the air.

Robbie's feet skid against the floor with a squeak. He continues walking, but more slowly now, looking over his shoulder at me. "Would you like that?"

"Not particularly, but I think it has to be done."

Robbie lets out a whistle, staring back at me with a smug grin on his face. It clicks in my head what he's thinking, and I roll my eyes. "Not like that, you freak. Can you act mature for five seconds?"

"Sorry, someone didn't make that a part of the rules," Robbie says, turning to the side and holding out his arm.

I jog the few steps it takes to be at his side. The moment I reach him, Robbie relaxes his arm, his hand landing on my lower back. Then it goes lower. *Too low.*

I smack at his hand.

"*Ouch*, Cooper. *Shit*," Robbie curses, shaking out his hand.

I give him a look, telling him he deserved it. "Not like that.".

"Fine," he quips, hooking his arm around my neck and pulling me to his side. But it's not in a *friendly couple* kind of way. More like a *little brother you're about to give a noogie* kind of way. Or like *someone you're trying to strangle* kind of way.

"*Robbie*," I grit as I grab at his forearm currently wrapped around the front of my neck. I finally manage to untangle myself by spinning outwards from him, my hand still gripping one of his wrists. I drop his wrist, then realize we are walking through the doors. Panicking, I grab his wrist right back up, sliding my hand down it until my fingers interlace with his. We both dig our nails into each other's skin right as the gym doors are thrown open, the colorful lights blinding and the music of Madonna blaring.

I glance over at Robbie, seeing a smile spread across his face, a deep sigh leaving him.

He's in his element. He *loves* this.

We take a few steps further inside, both of us looking around and getting a lay of the land. The dance floor is packed. So are the tables and chairs sprinkled around it. And so are the snack and punch tables.

Great.

I see a swish of bright blonde hair just across the room from us and look up, spotting Denise standing on the edge of the dance floor. There are several cheerleaders standing around her and a few guys from the basketball team. She leans forward to whisper something to Ginger Matthews, and that's when I realize she has her arm hooked with Jesse Lamonte's.

My shoulders tense, and I swivel my head to look at Robbie. He's seeing exactly what I'm seeing.

"Are Denise and Jesse..."

"Yeah," Robbie responds, not taking his eyes off of them.

One of my eyebrows shoots up. "Isn't he, like...one of your best friends?"

"Yeah," Robbie nods. "I guess he is."

Damn. I shake my head, feeling an extremely unexpected but true pang of sympathy for Robbie Summers. His girlfriend and his best friend? That's awful. He must hate them.

"Let's go talk to them," he says.

"*What?*" I question him, blinking, but Robbie is already dragging me in the direction of the group.

It's Paul Strothers that spots us approaching first, a huge grin spreading across his face. "Hey, man," he says, clapping Robbie's shoulder.

"Hey, doing good, man?" Robbie replies, pulling me to his side to join in the circle. I'm certain I look like a deer in headlights as I take in everyone's heads turning in our direction. Denise and Jesse are the last to follow suit, and, like clockwork, Robbie's arm slings around my shoulder the minute their eyes land on us. I watch Denise's smile waver as she takes us in, and it somehow makes me relax some. I force a smile on my face, reaching up and taking Robbie's hand in mine, pulling him a little closer.

"I'm better now," Paul says, bringing my attention back to him. I meet his gaze and he smiles. "Hi, Sara."

My stomach twists in response. Of course Paul knows my name. We've gone to school together all of our lives and, as Robbie loves to remind me, Bay View isn't that big. But it's just now occurring to me that we haven't directly spoken to each other since elementary school, if even then. I take a quick glance around the circle and realize I can say that about basically everyone in it. *Great.*

"Hi, Paul," I say, returning his smile and trying my best to sound nonchalant.

He looks between Robbie and I, his head tilting and brows pinching. "So, this is a thing then? You two?"

"Sure looks that way doesn't it?" Robbie responds, and I resist the urge to shoot daggers at him.

Why can't he ever just answer a question straight? Why wouldn't he just say yes?

Paul nods. "It does. You guys look great together."

"Thanks, man," Robbie replies.

I feel a blush creep to my cheeks. I suddenly hear his voice inside my head, clear as day, as if he's responding directly to my thoughts.

I don't have to answer anyone's questions. Make them answer their questions themselves. Don't tell them. Show *them.*

I shake my head. *What the hell?* I let out a laugh, trying to cover the whole thing by leaning my head against Robbie's shoulder.

"I gotta say though," Paul speaks up again, pointing between Robbie and me. "Who would've thought?"

I feel Robbie tense slightly.

"Never in a million years would I have–"

Robbie chuckles dryly, cutting Paul off. "Well, we don't want you thinking too hard, Strothers. Wouldn't want you to hurt yourself." He taps a knuckle against the side of Paul's head.

"Right," Paul murmurs, his eyes narrowing on us as he takes a sip of his punch.

I laugh again, pulling Robbie down just far enough that I can whisper in his ear. "What was that about?"

"Nothing," he replies. "Don't worry about him."

"Hi, Robbie," another voice calls, this one much higher pitched than Paul's.

Denise.

We both turn to look at her. She has Jesse's arm in an iron grip at her side as she smiles sweetly at us. She's wearing bright pink eyeshadow and has her hair done in a style that would give Farrah

Fawcett a run for her money. She looks stunning. And I can't even hate her for it.

"Hey, Denise," Robbie says, his voice perfectly even. Not too interested, not too disinterested.

He's an evil genius.

"Good to see you, man," Jesse speaks up.

I watch the way Robbie's eyes sharply shift to Jesse.

"Jesse," he nods. His fingers flex while intertwined with my own, our hands laying flat now against my chest. He starts guiding them in stroking circular motions. I assume he's doing it as a way to distract himself, but it doesn't stop the goosebumps from spreading across my body. I clear my throat, trying to signal to him to stop. He just pulls me closer, continuing.

Denise's gaze flicks between the two of us. She looks calm, *happy* even. But I swear there's something in her eyes that's betraying her content facade. "You look really pretty, Sara," she says suddenly, completely throwing me off guard.

"Oh," I say, glancing down at myself. "Thanks...Denise. You do too."

"I'm pretty sure my mom has that same dress," she says.

I swallow against the sudden dryness in my throat, refusing to let the embarrassment show on my face.

"She got it on clearance at a Nordstrom in San Francisco a few years back."

Yeah, this dress definitely isn't from a Nordstrom. And Denise definitely knows that.

"Total steal. Super cute," she adds, tilting her head at me and smiling like a school teacher would smile at a kindergartener.

"Thanks," I mutter, not knowing what else to say. I keep scanning her from top to bottom, searching for something I can backhanded compliment, but there's nothing to be found. Physically, at least.

"So," Jesse says, cutting in. "I heard you're running for student body president, Sara?"

He's asking me, but his eyes keep flicking over to Robbie. I open my mouth to answer him, but Robbie speaks up first.

"I don't know why you're looking at me. She can answer you."

Jesse's eyes immediately snap to me, his throat bobbing and back straightening.

Something flutters low in my belly at that. Jesse has the upper hand here. Well, technically at least. He's managed to steal Robbie's girlfriend right out from under him. *And yet...he's still scared of Robbie.* Still affected by him. I take a quick look around, seeing everyone in the circle's eyes glued to us. They're all *so* affected by him.

I was always aware of the power that Robbie Summers held. But seeing it first hand, being a part of it...it's something else entirely. I feel like there's electricity under my skin. Like everything around us moves with us. Like I'm in total control. I don't know the last time I felt that way. It's scary. But it's also...*empowering.*

"Yes, I'm running," I reply to Jesse, standing tall.

Jesse lips press together tightly, like that wasn't the answer he was hoping for. "I am too," he says.

"Oh, you are?" I ask, tilting my head like I had no idea.

"So is Ginger," Denise adds. Ginger smiles tightly at me, holding up her punch glass.

I think they're trying to intimidate me.

I also think it's working.

With enough confidence you can make people think you're capable of anything, Robbie's irritating voice sounds in my head. I mentally swat him away, but listen to it anyway.

I raise my brows, holding my free arm out to the side and opening my mouth in feigned happy surprise. "Well, this should be fun, shouldn't it?" I ask rhetorically, not appearing to have a care in the world.

They're all quiet, simply staring back at me for a few seconds, then Denise breaks the silence with a laugh. The rest join in, the tension significantly easing.

"Well, let the best man win," Jesse says, holding out his hand for me to shake.

I take his hand in mine. "Or woman," I add, throwing Ginger a wink. She leans back, giving me a small smile in return.

"Right," Jesse nods, releasing my hand. "Good luck."

"She won't be needing it," Robbie says with a grin that could bring half this dance to their knees, dropping his hand to my waist and pulling me in tighter.

Jesse's eyes follow Robbie's action, his throat bobbing. "Fair enough," he says, then turns to Denise, who is also staring a hole in me at the moment. "You want some more punch, sweetheart?"

Robbie's hand tightens on my waist.

Sweetheart.

That's what he'd always call Denise.

Jesus.

"Sounds perfect," Denise says, leaning in to kiss Jesse's cheek, the two of them turning away to head to the punch table only a few feet away.

Air feels like it reenters my lungs for the first time in five minutes the moment they step away, my shoulders relaxing.

It doesn't last long, my body immediately tensing as Robbie leans down to whisper in my ear. "Do you want to stay here?" he asks, pointing to the floor where we're standing.

"I would like to do absolutely anything other than stand in this circle for another second," I reply through my teeth, smiling at him for the sake of any onlookers.

Robbie smiles back. "Great," he says. "Let's dance."

I start to shake my head. "I don't want to–"

"You said *absolutely anything*," he insists, cutting me off.

My mouth snaps shut, knowing he's right. *Dammit.*

"Three songs, and we can leave," Robbie says, making me immediately perk up.

"Like, the whole dance?" I ask.

He nods. "I think we'll have made a significant enough impression to sneak out by then."

I eye him suspiciously. "One song," I counter.

"*Three.*"

"*Two,*" I shoot back.

"Fine, two songs," Robbie agrees. Our compromise in place, he starts leading us to the dance floor. I register the intro guitar and drums of *Rock You Like a Hurricane* by Scorpions playing as Robbie strategically places us perfectly between the group we just left and the middle of the dance floor. Optimal exposure. The most eyes possible.

Great.

Robbie spins me once, then he begins to dance on the spot. I stand awkwardly in front of him, stepping side to side and not really sure what to do. Robbie eyes me as he makes the motion of a guitar, his head bobbing to the music. He leans in slightly, trying to talk to me over the song. "Cooper, if we're only doing two songs, you're gonna have to do better than that."

"What do you mean?" I ask, holding out my arms.

"I led you to the water," he says, motioning around us. "Now it's time for you to drink."

I just stare back at him, my mouth opening and closing.

"C'mon, Miss Valedictorian," Robbie says, rolling his eyes. "It's an analogy."

"It's actually a *metaphor*," I correct him, earning me another eye roll. "And I know it."

You can lead a horse to water, but you can't make it drink.

"Then giddy up, horsey," Robbie says, nodding in my direction.

I burst out in laughter, shaking my head. "I can't stand you."

"Good to know," he says, shimmying closer to me. "Let's make everyone in here think the opposite so we can go home."

My laughter fades as I stare up at him, knowing he's right. Robbie got me to the dance. I'm here, a place I would never be. Robbie's here, with a girl he'd never be with. We've got the school on the edge of their seats when it comes to this charade. Might as well knock them all the way off.

"Fine," I say, nudging closer to Robbie and grabbing two fistfuls of his leather jacket.

He glances down between us, his brows raising. He opens his mouth, seemingly about to ask me something, but I don't give him the chance, pushing off of him and spinning around. The chorus kicks in, and I think to myself, *Screw it.*

I throw my head forward, bending at the waist then immediately snapping straight again, sending my hair flying as I move my head in a circular motion. I sway my hips back and forth, running my fingers back through my hair, stealing a glance up at Robbie from under my eyelashes. His jaw is slack, and he seems to be frozen in place for a full second before his body resets, his fist pumping into the air and a huge smile landing on his face. I move closer to him, and he matches me step for step. I throw my hands in the air, headbanging to the beat of the music. Robbie's teeth sink into his bottom lip as he starts his air guitar solo once again. I laugh at the absurdity of what's happening right now, turning my back to Robbie and bringing a hand to my waist as I sway my hips back and forth. I circle my other hand in the air in a tornado sort of motion that I like to think resembles a hurricane, closing my eyes and allowing myself to act like I'm dancing alone in my bedroom. *Nobody else is here.* I let my head fall back. And it thumps lightly against something. *Wait.* Not something...

Someone.

It's Robbie's chest.

My eyes snap open.

I can feel the heat of him behind me. If I were to straighten and take half a step back, my body would be fully flush with his. I tilt my head back slightly further, the side of Robbie's face coming into view. His eyes are closed. He seems focused, his brow furrowed as he mouths the words to the song. It brings an unexpected grin to my face. Suddenly, as if he could feel me looking at him, Robbie's eyes open.

Double dark chocolate in this light.

I'm not sure what to think of that.

He doesn't give me a chance to think much of anything, his lips pulling into a smirk. He reaches up grabbing my hand that's currently in the air, giving it one gentle squeeze before releasing it, letting his hand slide down. His grip glides slowly over my wrist, then continues further, dragging down the entire length of my arm. He reaches the sensitive skin at the side of my torso, sending a shiver through me as he reaches my waist, digging his fingers in there and guiding my hips from side to side.

I don't know what's happening, but I know it has to be a damn convincing performance. I keep my eyes mostly closed, not allowing myself to break the illusion. If I open my eyes, this moment becomes everybody's, and I'm not ready for that.

I know my acting won't be nearly as believable if I allow myself to think there's actually an audience to this show. *No*, I keep my eyes closed. I focus on the music, on keeping our movements in sync. I focus on Robbie's hands on me and the odd sensation it's sending throughout my body. I lean my head back further, focusing on deciphering the spicy, woodsy, scent with the slightest hint of sweetness rolling off of him and positively invading my senses.

We stay this way through most of a verse, both of our bodies beginning to glisten with sweat and our breathing becoming labored, until Robbie reaches for my hand again and spins me away from him. We each continue to sway and step in front of each other, freestyling to the rhythm with shameless grins on our faces. Robbie reaches out to spin me again, and I realize how lost in the music I've gotten when the song changes the moment I crash into his chest.

Forever Young by Alphaville begins flowing through the speakers, making time slow drastically down. I open my eyes, becoming aware of my two hands laying flat against Robbie's chest and just how rapidly I'm breathing all at once. I force myself to tear my eyes away from the leather jacket in front of me, glancing around the dance floor.

People are equally filtering on and off. Couples take their places, hands finding hips and encircling necks as the slow dance begins. I swallow against the newly present dryness in my throat as I realize just about every person that just got off the dance floor is looking directly at Robbie and me.

"We can skip this song," I mutter. I move to leave the dance floor, but a hand shoots out, landing on my hip and stopping me in place.

"Cooper."

I blink hard, slowly turning my head up to look at Robbie. His lips roll into his mouth, his eyes dark. "Yes?" I ask.

"Let's finish strong," he says.

My lips part, and I start to shake my head. "But, what–"

Robbie silences me, taking each of my hands in his and guiding them up and around his neck. Once they're securely in place, Robbie brings his hands down, resting them on my hips.

"*I don't know how–* I've never slow danced," I confess.

Robbie's eyes stay on our feet as he starts stepping side to side, guiding me to follow his lead.

"If you're capable of whatever it was you just did, I promise you can do this," he says.

I nod, staring down at our feet as well and forcing past the lump in my throat.

After a few seconds, we find an easy pace and rhythm. Our heads both raise at the same time, our eyes meeting. My first reaction is to look away, *but to where?* It's either looking at Robbie or being forced to meet the hundreds of eyes currently burning into us. I'm reminded of the feeling of us all being magnets again, except, this time, I'm drawn to all of them instead. Robbie's unreadable eyes still glued to my face, I risk a casual glance around us, swiveling my head from side to side.

My stomach instantly drops to my feet. It's like we're the star exhibit at the zoo, everyone caging us in around the perimeter of the dance floor, eyes trained on us like they're waiting for us to do our next trick. I catch most of the people dancing around us even stealing glances over their dance partner's shoulder. I try not to let my reaction show on my face, but I can feel the pink working its way into my cheeks. *How can it not?*

I know this was the point of our entire arrangement, but I never expected *this*. I wonder if this is what Robbie feels like all the time. What he deals with all the time. No wonder he has a chip on his shoulder the size of Texas.

"Hey," Robbie whispers, making me look back up to him. "Talk to me, Goose. Where'd you go?"

I shake my head, hoping my face isn't as red as it feels. "Nowhere, unfortunately."

Robbie chuckles. His laughter fades out, several moments of silence stretching between us. The temperature of the room and pressure around us seems to increase by the moment, regardless of how much I try to ignore it. I blow out a deep breath, forcing myself to push it all away and focus on Robbie. I look up and find him already watching me. I tilt my head at him, sensing a thought behind his eyes. He gives it up instantly.

"You've got everyone looking, Cooper," he says. "What're you gonna do with it?"

"*Me?*" I question. "I'm pretty sure *I* just gave myself whiplash."

Robbie smirks, shaking his head. His gaze shifts to the side and the smirk wavers slightly.

"What happened to both of us pulling our weight?" I finish.

Robbie is still looking to our side, so I follow the line of his eyes. My shoulders fall slightly, seeing Denise and Jesse dancing just a few feet away from us. Denise is smiling at Jesse, but I catch her stealing glances our way every few seconds. I don't know why, but it sends a wave of irritation through me.

"You're right," Robbie's voice sounds from in front of me, bringing me back to him.

"About what?" I say, still distracted by Denise and everyone else staring at us.

Robbie pulls me closer suddenly, tilting his head down to whisper in my ear. "Do you trust me?"

I pull back just enough to meet his eyes. "Not really."

Robbie blows a breath out of his nose. "*Will* you trust me?" he asks, his eyes softening. "Right now?"

My brows pull together, uneasiness pinching my throat. "No breaking the rules?"

"No rules broken," Robbie confirms.

I nod, slowly, and then on the verge of frantically, afraid I'll back out from whatever Robbie's about to do if I give myself a moment to think about it.

He doesn't give me a moment.

The second I agree, he pulls one of my hands down from around his neck, spinning me out from him dramatically. Time seems to slow down as this happens, and I swear I manage to make brief eye contact with every person in the gym over the course of the 360 degree turn.

Suddenly, however, it's over, and Robbie's bringing me back to him. My hands land on his shoulders, his going back to my hips. I'm frozen in place for what feels like forever, but what I know is only a moment, staring straight ahead at his chest, my hair hanging in thick curtains around my face. My arms feel shaky and my lips quiver with the buzz of energy happening around us and nerves over what's happening between us all at once.

Robbie's thumb and forefinger brush against the underside of my chin, tilting my head up just enough so that I meet his gaze. "*Trust me*," he mouths, inaudible.

I give him the slightest nod, one he would never have been able to notice if he wasn't holding my chin in his hand right now. His gaze flicks from my eyes downward several times, and I register the sound of my pulse pounding in my ears. He leans closer, so painfully slow, and my heart is pounding so hard against my chest that it hurts.

He's millimeters away, and I can feel the back of my eyes burning, confusion, nausea, and something else I can't identify swimming low in my belly. It becomes evident he's not about to stop. "*Robbie*," I breathe.

The chorus of *Forever Young* breaks out, and, at the last possible moment before his mouth connects with mine, Robbie's thumb slides up from my chin, pressing directly into the middle of my lips, creating a barrier between us. There's a hair's width of space between us, but his lips aren't touching me.

Just like the rules state.

My eyes are half open as I process what's happening. Robbie pulls me tighter to him, bringing his other hand up and threading his fingers through the hair on the right side of my head, pulling it inwards and cupping my cheek, successfully blocking our non-connected lips from anyone's view.

For two long seconds, I'm rigid, unmoving, *panicked*. Then, Robbie's warmth seems to make its way across our thin barrier, and his touch seems to soften. My eyes fall completely shut, and I feel myself melt against him. My fingers curl around the lapel of his leather jacket, pulling him further down to me. At the same moment, Robbie's fingers tug at my hair just enough to sting.

It's the oddest sensation. We're flush with one another everywhere that doesn't matter and not even touching in the place that matters most, yet I've never felt something so intense in my life. It's *everything*.

And then it's nothing.

Both of us suddenly pull back, without any sort of communication prompting us to do so, at exactly the same time.

Robbie's eyes are on fire when he opens them, a deep crease set between his brows. I feel how flushed my cheeks are as I blink back at him, trying to rationalize if it's anger or something much more heated passing between us right now.

Robbie steps back abruptly as the song ends, looking me up and down. He seems to realize his action and quickly tries to recover by running a hand over the top of my hair in what I think was supposed to be a show of affection. I reach for his hand, trying my best to feign my own display. Robbie's fingers are rigid against my own, both of us squeezing each other's hands too tightly.

We both glance around the room at the same moment and are met with a whole lot of raised eyebrows, every person snapping back to reality and turning away to mind their own business the second we catch them watching us.

"Can we go now?" I mutter, not meeting Robbie's eyes, still feeling confused and, for some reason, slightly embarrassed.

"Yeah," Robbie nods. "I think that's enough torture for tonight."

eighteen

ROBBIE

Cooper and I don't say a word to each other over the short ride back to her house. The tension is so thick that you could cut it with a knife. I swear it raises the temperature inside my damn Camaro.

We haven't even looked at each other since we walked out of the gym. Since...whatever just happened. I can only deal with the stiff quiet for a minute or so before I have to turn the radio on, *Waiting For a Girl Like You* by Foreigner now the only thing slicing through the silence.

I love this song. I love the entire album it comes from actually. But something about it is just rubbing me the wrong way right now. It's sort of making me itch, like I want to crawl out of my skin, the words feeling like a needle poking at my already scrambled brain. I reach for the dial to change the radio station.

"No."

I halt, hearing Cooper's voice for the first time in the last fifteen minutes. I glance over at her and see her looking out her passenger side window, her hands folded in her lap.

"Leave it," she says, not turning to look at me.

I swallow, leaning back in my chair.

178

"You like this song?" I ask her after a few moments.

She shrugs, still not looking at me. "It's better than anything else you'd probably play instead."

I scoff out a dry laugh.

As if this girl hasn't tested me enough tonight, she's really going to sit in my own car and question my music taste. I shake my head, running a hand through my hair.

The song comes to an end just as I pull up in front of Cooper's house. I shut the radio off altogether, blowing a breath out of my nose. I dip my head down, looking at her driveway and finding it empty. I guess Sherri is still at work. I consider asking the question out loud, knowing it would piss Cooper off to hear me call her mom by her first name again, but I hold off. Instead I let my mind wander, questioning if Cooper's usually home alone this late. I wonder for a moment what her Dad does. I've only been to her house twice and have managed to miss him both times. He must travel for work or something.

I don't realize I've zoned out until I hear a car door open and see Cooper start to slide out of her seat. She pauses for just a moment once she gets her feet on the ground, her back to me. "Goodnight," she says.

I clear my throat, nodding even though she can't see me through the back of her head. "Night, Cooper."

I see her shoulders rise and fall with a light sigh and the slightest shake of her head. I don't get a chance to question her on it though before she hops out of my car, slamming the door just a little harder than necessary and making a beeline for her front door. I watch to make sure she gets in okay, and she doesn't look back once as she unlocks her front door, steps inside the house, and turns on her front porch light, letting the door fall closed behind her.

"*Jesus Christ, Cooper,*" I mutter under my breath.

I pull away from her house, turning the radio back on. There's nothing but commercials playing on the handful of stations I scan through, but I somehow prefer that to the alternative right now. I stop on a random station, letting an ad for New Coke play for a few seconds before I give up, shutting the radio off again.

I glance at the clock on my dashboard, seeing it's barely 9:30. I haven't been home this early on a Friday night in, *well*, ever. I know everyone will be leaving the dance soon and heading to Dusty's, the old drive-in movie spot in town that we pay to get into most Fridays and Saturdays and basically never watch the movies. It's just become the meeting spot to grab snacks and hang around until we decide where to go next.

I should go. It would be weird for me *not* to go. *Unheard of,* honestly. But where would I say Cooper is? I know it's the first thing everyone will ask. And I don't have the energy to act for anyone any further tonight. With how Cooper and I left the dance, further plans for the night hadn't even crossed my mind. I didn't even think about taking her to Dusty's. Not that she would have agreed anyways. It was nearly impossible enough to just get her to the dance.

But once she was there...

I never thought I'd see something like that out of her. The way she handled my friends, the way she *owned* that entire gym... You never would have known I had to practically wrestle her into my car an hour before. Or that the entire thing was just a show.

I'd even say that I might have forgotten for a minute there.

But, God, it was fantastic. *We* were fantastic. It was all going *so* perfectly.

Until it wasn't.

I keep trying to pinpoint where we went wrong. When did it shift from us doing what we were supposed to be doing, putting on a good show, both of us in agreement and on the same page, to something that crossed a line?

Was it when I pulled her closer than necessary while Jesse was talking out of his ass to her? Or maybe when she grabbed me by my jacket and looked up at me with those gray doe eyes like nothing I've ever seen before? It could have been when I dug my fingers into her hips. But that was only after her head fell against my chest, her flowery scent hitting me like a ton of bricks. And what was I supposed to do with that? The girl drives me insane, but she smells like a goddamn spring meadow sprinkled with morning dew. Like a fresh shower in the middle of a forest. Like what I imagine a waterfall in a fairyland would smell like. Not that I'd ever given any thought to what that scent might be until Sara Beth freaking Cooper walked–*no, trampled*– her way into my life.

I don't know what to think when it comes to her. And never once have I had to think about *what to think*. That's what she does to my brain. I need to make it stop though. I'm letting this become complicated, and it doesn't need to be complicated. We both agreed to this. We both had to know it wouldn't be easy, that there would be an adjustment period. She was putting on an act tonight. That's what we were *both* there to do. The point was to be convincing. For her to get the school's attention. She did her job. And so did I. That's all.

My non-kiss-kiss stunt at the end might have thrown her for a loop, but it had to be done. Everyone's eyes were on us. We had to take advantage. We had to make them believe. I...just *wanted* them to believe. That's it.

I knew in the split second that I decided to go through with it that it might catch Cooper off guard. I figured she'd go rigid in my arms and that the entire thing would last for approximately one and a half seconds before she pulled back. I expected that I would have to hear her pretend to gag the whole car ride home and be prepared to respond when she reminded me how much she couldn't stand me, reminding *her* that the feeling was mutual. I expected her to maybe even yell at me, even though I didn't break her rules. My lips never touched her.

But what I never expected in a million years was for *none* of that to happen. For her to trust me, if only for a few seconds. For her to *soften* against me. For her to go up on her tiptoes and pull me closer and tilt her head as if asking for more, like we were doing the real thing. I didn't expect the little noises that would come out of her, or the way her breathing would quicken, or the reaction my body would have to all of it. The way it felt almost natural for a moment. Like we don't get under each other's skin and test each other's nerves every second we spend in each other's presence. Like we weren't doing a damn thing for the sake of everyone around us and *everything* for just the two of us.

I was questioning my sanity in the seconds all of this was going through my brain, in those mere moments where time seemed to slow down. Then, just like that, it was like a switch flipped. Reality set back in. We both seemed to remember who we were. And who we *weren't*. Where we were. What this was.

So I guess everything was right in the world again.

I'm just not sure why it suddenly feels so fucked.

I shake my head. It's nothing. I'm overthinking it. Monday will come and we'll be fine. Or not fine. Because Cooper and I are never really *fine* together. But it'll be normal. And that's okay with me. We've got less than four weeks to go. We'll get through it, then put this all behind us. That's what I want. I'm sure that's what I want.

I shake my head, forcing my mind elsewhere, trying to focus on the positives.

I think about Denise.

Boy, did she look incredible tonight. That dress. That fluffy cloud of gorgeous blonde hair. Her pink painted lips.

I zone out further, tightening my hands on the steering wheel.

Fair skin, flushed cheeks, that sparkle in her eyes. I can't deny it. I wanted her. And can you blame me? Cooper is a complete knockout–

My spine steels in my seat. I blink several times, shaking my head out. *Denise.* Denise is a complete knockout.

What the hell?

I'm only a minute or two from my house, but silence is no longer working for me. I click the radio back on.

I grin, happily distracted when one of my favorite songs by Journey comes on. I realize quickly though that it's at the very end of the song. The music fades out and another song begins. My smile falls.

It's *Rock You Like a Hurricane.*

I turn the radio off again.

I count the remaining seconds it takes me to get home, keeping my mind busy. I hit seventy-four just as I pull into my driveway.

I make my way into the house, locking the door behind me like always, and start towards the stairs to head up to my room.

"Hello, Robert."

My hand grips the banister, my head slowly turning to see my dad sitting in his armchair in the living room. He closes the book in his lap, taking off his glasses and setting them on the side table next to him.

"You're home earlier than expected," he says.

"When did you expect me?" I ask.

He tilts his head at me, looking me up and down with not a hint of pride in his expression. "I never do, I suppose."

Of course. "Well, surprise," I say, nodding at him and starting up the stairs again.

"Would you come here for a moment?" my dad asks. I hesitate, not moving. "Oh, how hard is it to talk to your old man for a few minutes?"

You have no idea.

I step down the couple of stairs I managed to climb already and walk over to where my dad sits, giving us a comfortable ten feet of space apart.

"Where were you tonight?" he asks.

"The Back to School Dance," I reply stiffly.

My dad blinks. I swear only this man can say so much with a singular blink of his eyes.

"And I assume you were with your typical basketball motley crew?"

I fight the urge to roll my eyes, knowing it won't get me anywhere. "They were there, yes–"

"Of course," my dad grunts, rolling his eyes for the both of us.

"But I wasn't *with* them."

"Right," he says, reaching for his book again. "Which party

bimbo or cheerleader floozy had the honor of your presence this week?"

I grit my teeth. "None of them, actually."

My dad is fully looking at his book now.

Why did he ask me to come down here again?

"They were all busy? How unfortunate. I hope it didn't ruin your evening," he says, sarcastic.

"No," I shake my head, forcing myself closer to him. "Actually, I was there with my girlfriend."

My dad's eyes flick up at me from over top of his book. "Girlfriend?" he questions.

I nod, my fists clenching at my side.

"And who is this girl?"

"Sara Beth Cooper," I say, practically before he even has the question out.

"And where did we find her?" my dad asks, his brows raising. "The street corner?"

I feel heat rush to the back of my neck.

"Is she maybe president of the lip gloss and glitter club at school?" he continues. "The underage and underachieving drinking society perhaps?"

"*Gee, so clever,*" I mutter under my breath.

"What's that?" my dad asks, leaning forward.

"I said she's neither," I say, more forcefully this time. "Actually, she's the valedictorian of our class."

My dad sits up slightly in his chair, surprise flashing briefly across his face. "Is that so?"

"Yes. And she's about to be elected as our student body president."

His eyebrows raise, and I can tell that he is genuinely impressed.

"She's on the yearbook and newspaper committee and volunteers in the library after school."

My dad tilts his head at me, his eyes narrowing. "Ah," he nods. "So that's how you must have met her. Serving your detention duty in the library."

Shit. I swallow. *How does he always find something?*

"She must have very high standards," he deadpans.

C'mon, Robbie. Recover.

"She does," I say. "She's actually going to NYU in the fall. She got accepted to a prestigious screenwriting program there."

My dad leans back in his chair. "NYU, huh?" he asks.

"Yep," I nod, a grin of pride on my face. *Try to find something about that to pick apart.*

"And how are your college application efforts coming along?"

My face falls. "Well– Um, I–" I stutter.

A smile spreads across my dad's face. "Sounds about right," he nods. "Couldn't expect too much out of you."

"But I–"

"My mistake," he says, closing his book and rising from his seat, coming over to stand in front of me. I don't meet his eyes. "But don't worry, it won't happen again," he says, reaching up and ruffling my hair. Too roughly.

Just like always.

"Dad–"

"Goodnight, Robert," he says, not even looking at me as he continues walking past me.

I push my tongue into the side of my cheek, my fists nearly shaking at my side. I wait until the moment I hear the door to my parents' room click shut and storm up the stairs. My head hits my pillow less than a second after my own door slams closed.

I cross my arms behind my head, staring at the ceiling.

"What a fucking night."

nineteen

SARA

I tap my fingers anxiously against the phonebook as the dial tone continues. I blink hard, shaking my head in an attempt to fight off an incoming yawn and wake myself up.

I didn't sleep well last night. Well, the last *two* nights actually. Every time I closed my eyes, I was back in the Bay View High gym. I tossed and turned, unable to get comfortable, continuing to feel the sensation of fingers in my hair and warmth against my lips. No matter how many pillows I buried my head under, I couldn't keep myself from hearing the same songs from the dance on a loop. Over time, *Forever Young* started popping up more frequently in the line up, until it was the only song playing on repeat. I was so desperate to sleep that I even resorted to counting sheep, but all of the sheep eventually turned into chocolate sheep. That's when I knew I was losing it.

My heart suddenly drops into my stomach at the sound of someone picking up the phone on the other end of the line, making me realize how truly out of it I must be for not having expected that to happen.

"Summers residence. This is Donna speaking."

I let out a breath I didn't realize I was holding in. "Hi, Mrs. Summers. This is Sara Cooper. Robbie's...um...girlfriend."

I lightly smack my palm against my forehead. I didn't *want* Robbie to be the one to pick up the phone. Mostly because the whole purpose of me calling is because I don't want to talk to him. I'm realizing now how I didn't really think this through. But I hadn't thought of the possibility of one of his parents picking up instead. I don't know what Robbie's told them. And if we're keeping this thing going, I suppose it's best we cover all our tracks.

"Oh," Robbie's mom says. I can't totally decipher if she knows of my existence by that *oh* or not, but I'm weirdly leaning towards yes. "Right. One moment, I'll just get Robert for you–"

"*No*," I say, entirely too fast and entirely too aggressively. "That's okay," I say, sweetening my tone. "Could you just pass on a message to him for me, please?"

There is a short pause on the line, and I worry for a moment that she may have gone to get Robbie anyways. "I suppose," her voice comes back, making me sigh with relief.

"Great," I say. "Could you please just let him know that he doesn't have to pick me up this morning on his way to school? I have a...*uh*– dentist appointment. So my mom will be dropping me off instead."

Another pause. "I'll let him know."

"Thanks so much, Mrs. Summers–"

The line goes dead, her hanging up.

Oh well. I don't even care that Robbie's mother seems to be just as pleasant as he is. I'm off the hook. At least for another hour. And I'll honestly take anything I can get. I'm not ready to see him yet. I'm still processing the mess that was Saturday night and all of the emotions (expected and...*not so expected*) that came out of it.

I hang the phone up just as my mom appears from her bedroom. This is one of the rare mornings she doesn't have a double shift at the diner and is actually here. "Good morning, hon," she says. "Who was that?"

"Nobody," I say, closing the phonebook and sneaking it back into the kitchen drawer. "Telemarketer."

"Gross," Mom says, pulling the orange juice out of the fridge.

I spin around to face her. "Agreed," I nod.

She pours herself a glass of juice, taking a sip.

"Hey, Mom?"

"Yeah, hon?" she replies.

"Would you mind taking me to school this morning?"

Mom smiles, her eyes lighting up. "I thought you'd never ask." She sets down her glass. "Let me just get some shoes on."

———

Mom and I pull up to the school in her old station wagon fifteen minutes later. It's quite a bit before Robbie usually gets to school, but I do a quick scan of the parking lot anyways. My shoulders instantly relax when I see his car isn't here yet.

"Your chariot has arrived," Mom says, motioning dramatically with her hand as she stops the car.

I chuckle, taking my compact mirror and red lipstick out of the front pocket of my backpack. "Thanks for bringing me," I say.

"Anytime, honey. Well, anytime I can, at least."

I finish applying my lipstick, pressing my lips together a few times before returning the tube and compact to my bag. "I appreciate it," I say, smiling at my mom.

"I swear we never get to spend any time together anymore," she says. "I'm sorry about that."

"It's okay, Mom," I insist. "You're working a lot. I have school and work. Things are busy. I don't blame you for it."

"But still," she says, brushing my hair out of my eyes. "I feel so disconnected from you lately. What's new?"

I open my mouth to answer, but my eyes instantly shift over my mom's shoulder at the unmistakable sound of *Bon Jovi* tearing its way into the parking lot.

"*Absolutely nothing,*" I reply, frantically reaching for the door handle. "Sorry, Mom, but I have to go. I have some, um, homework to get done before class starts."

Mom's brows pull together. "Oh, okay, hon. Well, have a nice day. I'm thinking of making lasagna for dinner–"

"Sounds fantastic. I love you so much. Thanks again. Bye, Mom," I sputter, stumbling out of the car and slamming the door shut just as Robbie pulls into his parking place. I instantly spin on my heel, walking as quickly as I can towards the front door of the school.

I glance over my shoulder, seeing Robbie stepping out of his Camaro and securing his Walkman on his hip. I swivel my head back forward, increasing my speed, trying my best to be subtle.

I reach the steps and nearly jog up them. *Were there always this many?* I reach the top and find a bit of a traffic jam as several people are trying to walk in and out of the doors at the same time.

Don't look, Sara. Don't look, I think to myself.

I look.

And instantly make eye contact with Robbie as he's putting his headphones on his head.

"*Shit,*" I mutter, spinning back around. I force myself through the very slowly moving crowd as quickly as possible, nearly out of breath as I make my way into the foyer of the school.

I rest my hands on my knees for a moment, shaking my head and getting my breathing under control for a few seconds before standing back up straight. I push my hair out of my face, raising my head and planning to bolt for the library.

But my gaze instantly hits twenty feet in front of me. Right where Alice is standing with a giant smile on her face, throwing her arms out to the side.

"Alice!" I squeal.

"I'm *baaack!*" she sings.

I take a step in her direction. "It feels like forever–"

But I'm quickly cut off by a hand on my shoulder, spinning me around.

"Cooper, what gives?" Robbie asks, shoving his headphones off his head.

"Wha–*what*?" I stutter.

"Why didn't you let me take you to school?" he demands.

"I...Well, I–"

"You clearly didn't have a dentist appointment. So, what gives?"

I don't say anything for a few seconds, my brain firing at a million miles an hour.

Robbie shakes his head. "Well, while you're learning to speak again, come here at least." He pulls me in, wrapping me in a tight hug, threading his fingers through the back of my hair and pressing his cheek against the top of my head. "Can't let the kids see us fighting," he whispers. He pulls back, looking down at me. "I've missed you so much since Saturday, baby," he says far louder than necessary to make sure the people around us here.

The people around us.

I go pale as I slowly turn my head, seeing Alice frozen in place, a look of pure shock on her face.

I shake my head, opening and closing my mouth several times as Alice's eyes flick between me and Robbie. I suddenly register that his hand is still resting on my hip, and it feels like a hot iron.

"Hello, Earth to Cooper?" Robbie says. When I don't respond for a few more seconds, Robbie grabs both of my shoulders, spinning me towards him. "Cooper, what's going on?"

I continue to shake my head, but start flicking it backwards in Alice's direction.

"What?" Robbie questions, still not getting it.

"*Alice*," I finally manage to spit out.

Robbie's eyes narrow, shifting over my shoulder. When I assume he spots Alice, he stands up straight. I hold my breath, not sure what he's about to do. He *smiles*, nodding in her direction.

"*Stop it!*" I whisper-shout at him.

He blinks, looking back down at me. "Stop *what*?"

"Don't *smile* at her!"

"Okay, Cooper," he snorts. "I didn't peg you for the jealous type–"

"I'm not *jealous!*" I say, swatting at his chest. "But I can't have her thinking that we like each other."

"Um, isn't that exactly what we're *trying* to do, Cooper?"

I run my hands down my face. "Yes," I groan. "But not with her. It can't be with her." I start to turn away, but Robbie pulls me back.

"It *has* to be with her, Cooper. It has to be with everyone. If your best friend won't believe it, who will?"

"Are you crazy? I can't keep this from her. I won't. I'm going to tell her right now that this isn't what it looks like–"

I don't even get to fully spin around before Robbie grabs my hand and yanks me in the opposite direction, dragging me behind him.

"*What the hell are you–*"

I don't get to finish my question before Robbie shoves us both through the door of the nearest janitor closet. The door shuts behind me and we're instantly plunged into darkness. I throw my hands in the air, feeling around for a string to turn on the light. I do after a few seconds and yank it, the singular light bulb barely illuminating the dingy space. But it's enough to see Robbie standing right in front of me.

"What is the *matter* with you?" I ask.

"The matter with *me?*" Robbie retorts, pointing a finger at his chest. "You were about to blow our entire operation!"

"Alice is my *best friend.*"

"Exactly!"

"I can't lie to her," I say.

"Well, you can't tell her the truth."

I lean back, raising my brows. "And why not?"

"*Because,*" Robbie says, throwing his hands in the air. "This is all or nothing, Cooper. It's never going to work if we pick and choose who thinks we're dating. *You* were the one who was so concerned with people finding us out and looking like a fool."

My shoulders fall. "But this is just Alice... She wouldn't tell anyone."

"You can't know that," Robbie says, shaking his head. "And even if she doesn't tell anyone else, what if someone overhears you talking about it? It's too risky, Cooper. We've come this far. We have to see it through."

I can feel how red my cheeks are. "I strongly dislike you," I say, crossing my arms like a child. I strongly dislike even more that I know he's right.

Robbie laughs. "You're not my favorite tool in the shed either, Cooper."

"What does that even mean?"

He puts his arm up on the shelf to our side, pinching the bridge of his nose. "Just...don't tell her, Cooper. You can't."

I shake my head, staring back at him for several seconds. He raises his head, staring right back at me, not breaking my eye contact. A single strand of hair falls onto his forehead, perfectly curling right above his right eye. The ridiculous movie star-ness of it all makes me desperately want to reach up and shove the hair away, but I resist, following the rules.

I blow a breath out of my nose. "Fine," I say. "I won't tell her."

Robbie stands up straighter, his brows raising.

"But I do need to talk to her right now."

His brows instantly fall.

"She's been sick at home the last several days. She doesn't know about any of this. The last time we spoke, I was telling her how much you nauseate me."

"So you've talked about me before?" Robbie asks, a self-satisfied smile creeping its way onto his face.

"Not positively."

"You're so sweet to me," he says, rubbing a knuckle against my cheek. I reach up to swat at his hand, but I'm a second too late, waving at the air.

"*Baby*," Robbie fake frowns, fighting a grin.

I roll my eyes, done with this game. "I'm going to talk to her," I say.

He stiffens, his face becoming serious again. "You won't tell her?"

"I won't tell her we're not dating," I confirm.

Robbie tilts his head, his eyes searching me.

I let out a sigh, turning to leave.

"Well, just in case you change your mind," Robbie's voice sounds from behind me.

"What?" I say, turning back around. I let out a gasp as I see Robbie charging for me. I don't even get a chance to question him before he reaches up with his thumb, dragging it across my lips, smearing my lipstick.

My jaw falls open, time going in slow motion as I look up, seeing Robbie drag his same thumb across his own lips, transferring the red of my lipstick onto his mouth.

"Now she won't believe you," he grins.

I continue to stare at him, fire burning in my eyes as I clench my fists at my side. "You *didn't*."

Robbie puckers his lips, blowing a kiss in my direction.

"You're free to go," he says. And before I have time to process, he pushes the closet door open, shoving me out. I stumble, spinning around and coming face to face with Alice standing right outside the closet, her eyes wide.

"I–"

Her eyes flick upwards, and I turn to see Robbie stepping nonchalantly out of the closet, straightening his gray jacket. He slowly looks up at me and Alice, wiping at the corner of his lips with his thumb. "Sorry about that," he says, flashing a grin and nodding at Alice. "She just gets me so worked up."

I swallow hard, narrowing my eyes at him.

"See you later, baby," he says, winking at me as he slips his headphones on and turns to walk down the hall, completely leaving me out to dry.

I turn slowly back to Alice, a rock in my throat. "Alice, I–"

"I can't believe you." Alice cuts me off.

I freeze in place, my heartbeat in my ears. "Alice, please, let me explain–"

"I freaking *called it*," she squeals, grabbing me by the shoulders.

"...*What?*" I question, leaning back.

"All it takes is five days of me being out of commission and you totally fall for Robbie Summers!" she says.

I shake my head. "I wouldn't say that's what happened–"

"No, Sara, I totally get it. All those evenings in the library. Those close quarters. All that angst. All the banter. It was inevitable. I *told* you. The movies get it right every time. You should know that better than anyone."

I blink slowly at her. "Yeah...Yeah, I guess you were right."

Alice jumps up and down, clapping. "Aren't I always?"

She loops her arm through mine, walking us down the hall. "So, what else did I miss?"

I roll my lips into my mouth, trying to kill time as I process how that conversation was just so short and easy, then remember that my lipstick is smeared all over my face. As if reading my mind, Alice leads us into the restroom. I grab a few paper towels, wiping away the red stain and salvaging my lipstick the best I can.

I glance up at Alice in the mirror. "I'm running for student body president."

Alice's mouth falls open, a huge smile coming to her face. "Look at you go, Sara!" she says, hugging my shoulders from behind. "You're transforming right before our eyes! I'm so proud."

I chuckle, shaking my head.

Alice puts her hands on her hips. "*See*, I told you this year was going to be different."

twenty

ROBBIE

I finally find the shelf I'm looking for, feeling a tinge of accomplishment as I slip the book in its rightful place. I glance back to the cart behind me, seeing about fifty more to go and groan, no longer feeling so accomplished.

I run a hand through my hair and steal a look at my watch, smiling when I realize that it's 4:59 p.m. I look back at the cart and shrug. "Guess there's always tomorrow," I tell the books.

Yes, I've been working in a library for two whole weeks, and I'm talking to books now.

What can I say? It gets lonely in here when Cooper is giving me the cold shoulder half the time.

Speak of the devil...

I see a flash of red across the library and look up to see Cooper making her way into Ms. Rose's office, book cart entirely empty, of course. I shake my head, abandoning my own pathetic cart and following after her.

Though we've certainly had our moments, Cooper and I managed to settle into somewhat of a steady routine this week. We'd still argue during most of our car rides to school and barely spoke to one another during our library shifts, but during the day, we were golden. Cooper would bat her eyes at me during lunch and I would hold her hand in the hallways. We always made a point to interact with each of our friend groups— well, really just *my friend group* and *Alice*, and sometimes her boyfriend, Daniel, I guess— at least once a day to save face. We've packed on enough subtle PDA to make it believable, but I haven't fake-kissed her again.

She tore me a new one after the incident in the janitor's closet on Monday, and I can't say I blame her. I also can't say I regret it either. That shit was genius. And just seeing the fire crackling behind her eyes and the heated blush in her cheeks was enough to entertain me for the whole day.

Regardless, we made it through the week. But now it's Friday. And there's no way we can afford to be off the hook the entire weekend.

I lean against the door frame, watching Cooper grab her journal and books from Ms. Rose's desk and drop them into her backpack. I tap my knuckle against the metal frame twice, making her look up at me. "Hey," I say.

"Hola, Roberto," she replies, returning to gathering her things.

My brows pull together, and after a few seconds of silence, she glances back up at me. "Hello, Robbie?" she translates, a look of exasperation on her face.

"I know what you said," I tell her. "You're just weird."

"Gee, thanks, honey" she deadpans. "Well, have a great weekend." She comes around the desk, heading for the door.

"Wait," I say, holding a hand up, stopping her. "What are you doing tonight?"

She holds up her hand, showing me her orange Groovy Movie vest I didn't realize she was holding. "Going to a soirée," she says, straightfaced. "Do you think my outfit will impress?"

I give her a pointed look, annoyed, though admittedly impressed, by her sarcasm.

"I'm working," she says, dropping the act. "Why?" she asks after a few seconds, suspicion in her tone.

"Lisa McDaniel is having a party tonight," I tell her.

"Okay?" she says. "And?"

"We need to go."

Cooper lets out a groan. "You're joking, right?"

"I don't know," I say. "Is it funny?"

"Not at all."

"Then, no, obviously."

She rolls her eyes. "I don't want to go."

"Well that's too bad, Cooper," I retort. "Because I want to go."

"And what does that have to do with me?" she asks, raising her brows.

"Don't you think it would be a bit of a bad look to show up without my current girlfriend to a house party where my ex-girlfriend will certainly be?"

Cooper stiffens, her eyes shifting to the side. "Denise will be there?" she asks.

"Definitely," I say. "She's on the cheer team with Lisa."

"*Right*," Cooper mutters, nodding slowly, chewing on her bottom lip.

"And besides, there's only two weeks left until class elections. You need to get your name out there."

"I put up posters," Cooper mumbles.

"Cooper," I say, leaning forward, "your little construction paper and magic marker monstrosities were adorable, but you and I both know that isn't gonna cut it."

She lets out a deep sigh, and I know she knows I'm right.

"I have to work," she says.

"And when do you get off work?" I ask.

She rolls her eyes again before looking back at me.

So stubborn, Cooper.

"Nine."

"Perfect," I clap. "The party starts at nine. I'll pick you up from Groovy Movie and we'll go straight there."

"Fine," Cooper says, moving past me in the door. "Don't be late or I'm walking home."

"You got it, Cooper." I turn around, watching her leave. "Hey, do you want a ride to work now?"

She spins around with a look on her face like I just asked her if she enjoys kicking puppies for fun. "Absolutely not." She shakes her head. "I think we will have been in enclosed spaces together for more than enough time by the end of today."

"Whatever you say, Cooper," I reply, holding my hands up. "As always."

"Whatever *I* say?" she asks, raising her eyebrows. "Are you actually ser–" She stops herself, inhaling and releasing a deep breath. "I don't have time for this right now," she says. "I'm going to be late." She spins on her heel and makes her way out the library door.

"Wouldn't be late if you weren't so damn hard-headed and let me drive you," I call after her.

She pokes her head back inside. "Maybe when hell freezes over," she says, grinning. "But thanks anyways."

———

I was at Groovy Movie by 8:55.

Just because I wanted to see the look on Cooper's face when she thought I wasn't there and that she was going to get out of going to the party, I parked at the far corner of the parking lot. It was absolutely worth it when she practically tiptoed her way out of the door at nine sharp, work vest in one hand and a can of Jolt Cola in the other, glancing hesitantly from side to side like a little kitten. She didn't see me at first, and I swear she nearly broke out in a happy dance. It was short lived though as she spotted my car a few seconds later, her shoulders instantly slumping. I shook my head at her in my rear-view mirror, chuckling.

I pushed open my car door, stepping out into the parking lot and walking around to open the passenger side door for her. "Nice try, Cooper," I said.

Ten minutes and one just slightly hostile car ride later, we're pulling up to Lisa McDaniel's house. I weave through the twenty or so cars already parked up and down the street in front of her house, eventually finding a spot.

"Jesus, it looks like the whole town is here," Cooper says, her face pressed up against the window like a kid looking at an aquarium for the first time.

"Well, they basically are." Cooper whips her head around to look at me. "All the cool kids anyways," I correct, flashing her a grin.

She flops back against the headrest, groaning. "I hate it."

"Well, I hate to break it to you, baby," I say, putting my car in park, "but you're one of us now."

"Only for two more weeks," she mutters.

I pause on my way to grab the door handle. "Right," I say, then clear my throat. "Hallelujah."

I push open my door, hopping out and walking up to the sidewalk. After a few seconds, I realize Cooper isn't following me. I turn around, leaning down to glance through my car window to see what the hold up is.

I find her staring into a little compact mirror, applying her red lipstick. My brows pull together as I watch her swipe the color onto her already naturally red lips, her eyes hooded and mouth pouted as she does so. She raises her hand to her face, swiping at the corners of her mouth with her pointer finger and pressing her lips together. Then she puts the lipstick down, flipping her head over once in front and back up, fluffing up her hair. She finally opens the door, signaling me to stand up straight again.

She steps out of the car, her full lips freshly painted and her auburn waves falling over her shoulders, and I guess I'm staring at her, because she looks up at me with a weird expression. "What?" she asks.

"Nothing," I say, shaking my head. I just don't know why my throat feels tight all of the sudden. "Ready?"

"As I'll ever be."

We make our way up to the front door, Cooper automatically putting her arm around my waist and me slinging mine over her shoulder the second we cross the threshold like the well-oiled machine we are.

I wasn't kidding when I said every cool kid in Bay View is here. The foyer alone is packed with people, and the crowd only gets more dense as we push our way into the living room. I knew we couldn't miss this tonight. When Lisa McDaniel's parents say they're going out of town for the weekend, there's only one place to be on Friday night.

The lights are dim and AC/DC's *Back in Black* album is blaring from a record player in the corner as people mingle around in groups, cans of cheap beer and wine coolers in hand.

I glance down at Cooper and find her stiff at my side, looking something like a deer in headlights. "You good?" I ask her.

She nods slowly. "We're here," she says.

"Good observation, Cooper."

She doesn't even have a snarky comeback, just looking up at me. "What now?"

I open my mouth, but don't even get a chance to form an answer as a loud voice appears at our side.

"Well, look who it is!"

I glance up, realizing it's coming from Brad Marshall, one of my basketball teammates, right as he throws his arms around me.

No, not just me.

Me *and* Cooper. "Hey, man," I say. "How's it going?"

"Fantastic, man," he grins, his crazy blue eyes having a more suspicious gleam in them than usual as he looks between me and Cooper. "Especially now."

I laugh. "What do you mean by th–"

I don't get to finish my question before Brad raises his thumb and forefinger to his mouth, letting out a whistle. "Look who I found!"

An eruption of cheers sounds from behind us, and Cooper and I both spin around to find it coming from a group of people on the living room couches. I just have to squint my eyes slightly in the dark to immediately make out Jesse, Denise, Paul, Ginger, and Lisa within the bunch.

"Well looky here!" Paul whistles, standing and grinning at us.

"The happy couple!" Denise says, far too enthusiastically. "Come join us!"

Cooper and I exchange a subtle glance, me just as unsure as her as to why they're acting so weird. Eventually, I shrug, and we make our way over to the couches, Brad's hands practically guiding us from behind. Paul and Ginger scoot over, leaving a spot open. I motion for Cooper to sit in it but she gives me a look telling me that's the last thing she wants to do, so I plop down in it instead. She's still standing, and I try to motion with my head for her to at least sit on the arm rest of the couch. She glances between it and me several times, and I eventually give up, turning my head back forward.

Stubborn, stubborn, Cooper–

She completely catches me off guard by sitting right down on my lap. I go stick straight, but she doesn't seem to notice, looping her right arm around the back of my neck. I try to look at her, but her eyes are scanning the rest of the party, her body relaxing into me as if this situation is entirely normal.

She never fails to surprise me. I'll give her that.

"I'm so glad you're here, Sara," Denise says suddenly, bringing me back to reality.

What?

I feel the slightest dig of Cooper's nails into the back of my neck, making goosebumps prickle down my spine. I swallow nervously as I glance up at her, but am surprised to find that she appears completely unphased. "Thanks, Denise," she says. "I'm glad to be here."

"You don't usually come to things like this," Denise states.

It's not a question, but Cooper answers it anyway. "I haven't in the past, no," she says.

Denise tilts her head, smiling in a patronizing kind of way, and makes a show of leaning against Jesse on the couch next to her.

Something twists in my stomach as she does it, but I'm not sure what to call the feeling. I grind my teeth together, ready to speak up, but Cooper beats me to it.

"But what can I say? It's just been a whole new world since I've been with Robbie. He makes anything seem possible. He always has me pushing my limits and living just off the edge of my comfort zone. I guess you could say he's making me a better me."

I blink several times, then turn my head to look up at Cooper. I find her already looking at me and meet her eye contact, my lips involuntarily pulling up at one side. She gives me a soft, closed-mouth smile in return. "But I'm sure you understand that," she suddenly adds, turning back to Denise.

I stiffen, forcing my brows not to shoot to my forehead.

Holy shit, Cooper.

When I look at Denise, her smile is gone, her brows pulled together and lips parted. Cooper just leans further into me, resting her head on top of mine and smiling even more sweetly right at Denise, shameless.

It takes everything in me not to jump up off this couch and high-five Cooper right now. Maybe even pick her up in a hug and spin around.

Jesse clears his throat. "You guys didn't get anything to drink yet?" he asks. Denise seems to snap back to life, sitting up in her seat.

"We hadn't had the chance," I reply, "but I guess we'll head that way now."

"Don't bother," Paul speaks up.

"Yeah," Jesse adds, "we just grabbed a couple of extra beers when we were in the kitchen a minute ago." He makes a show of looking around, moving the cushions on the couch and peering behind them.

I start to sit up, Cooper shifting to the side on my lap. "Thanks, really. But, it's okay. We can go grab some ourselves."

"Wait," Denise says, looking directly at me but grabbing Lisa's arm to her side. "Didn't you have them, Lisa?"

A huge smile spreads across Lisa's face. "Oh, right. Duh," she says, moving aside the pillows next to her. I spot a gleam of something familiar and my jaw clenches.

Shit. You've got to be kidding me.

"Here it is!" Lisa squeals, whipping out the big gold hand bell and shaking it for all it's worth, the sounds ringing out throughout the whole living room. I start to run a hand down my face but stop myself, realizing this isn't something I should be looking upset about. I force out a dry chuckle instead, throwing my hands in the air.

"You know what that means!" Jesse claps.

Cooper's head is swiveling around frantically. *"What does that mean?"* she whispers out of the corner of her mouth the me, her voice shaky.

Paul is suddenly off the couch, and his and Brad's hands are on my and Cooper's shoulders.

"Seven Minutes in Heaven!" half of the living room yells practically in unison, followed by an explosion of claps and cheers.

Within seconds, Cooper and I are pulled up off the couch and being shoved into the living room game closet. I spin us around as we stumble inside, taking the impact as we slam into the back shelf, throw blankets and nearly an entire box of Scrabble raining down on our heads.

"You kids have fun in there!" Paul says, before slamming the door shut and plunging us into darkness again.

"Robbie, *what the hell?"* Cooper grunts, shoving herself off of me. *"What* is going on?"

I shake my head, even though she probably can't even make it out in the darkness. I put my arms out to the sides, feeling around for a light switch, and end up tangled within Cooper's arms that are doing the same thing. Neither of us have any luck, and I swing my arms around in the air looking for a pull cord of some sort, but it's no help. I end up snagging my foot on something (probably a rogue throw blanket) and stumbling forward, accidentally taking Cooper with me. Her back thuds flat against the closet door and my arms shoot out, one hand landing somewhere near her head and the other probably somewhere near her waist. We both let out some sort of startled grunts in response, and they're almost immediately drowned out by the sound of giggles coming from the other side of the door. I reach blindly for the door handle with one hand, giving it a hard twist.

Locked. Definitely locked.

"*Robbie–*" Cooper hisses, but she's immediately cut off by another voice.

Denise's voice.

"Seven minutes, *starting now!*" she calls, knocking twice on the door. I feel my brows pull together, a wave of confusion and irritation washing over me.

What the hell is her game here?

"Seven minutes of *what*?" Cooper demands.

"You know what, Cooper," I breathe.

Lisa's voice sounds from the other side of the door. "Try to keep your clothes on, will you? I don't want to have to disinfect the whole closet."

"Wow, I'm so honored to be one of the cool kids," Cooper deadpans. "Are all your parties this fun?"

"Actually..." I press my tongue against my top lip. "Yeah, usually."

I can't see her, but I just know she's rolling those gray eyes straight into the back of her head.

A knock bangs against the door. "It's a little quiet in there, kids," Paul's voice comes through. "Robbie, have you killed the poor girl? Or maybe you just made her pass out from boredom?" I shake my head.

Prick.

There's a few seconds of silence before Paul adds, "Do I need to come in there and show her how it's done?"

My spine steels, my jaw clenching. A wave of heat rushes down my neck, and I don't like the way it feels. *Not one bit.*

I lean forward, dropping my voice to barely a whisper. "Cooper, I need you to moan for me."

I sense her stiffen in front of me, her voice getting caught in her throat. "Wha–*Excuse me?*"

I blow out a breath. "We just need to make some noises. Those idiots will get bored after thirty seconds and then we're free to stand on opposite sides of the closet until seven minutes is up."

"Those *idiots*? The ones you call your friends?"

"*Cooper*, focus."

She scoffs, incredulous. "You're asking me to...*make noises*?" My head falls back in frustration. "...*For you?*" she adds.

I blink, then bring my head back forward slowly, swallowing hard. "Yes."

There's no sound but her shallow breathing for several seconds. And then, finally...

"Robbie, I'm not going to–"

"*Jesus Christ, Cooper,*" I groan, going straight for her side, digging my fingers hard into her waist, circling them against her skin.

She lets out the craziest mixture of a moan and squeal, the sound ringing out for a solid three seconds.

Ticklish, are we, Cooper?

I hear an obvious full range of reactions from the side of the door from cheering to gagging. I grin to myself, satisfied.

Cooper swats at my chest. "*Robbie, what the hell are you doing?*" she whisper-shouts.

"*Yeah, you like that, baby?*" I ask, an edge of mischief to my entirely louder than necessary voice.

She doesn't even get a chance to reply before I grab onto her other side, just a bit higher this time, causing her to immediately yelp in response.

We play this game for thirty or so more seconds, me tickling Cooper, her moaning and groaning, and me adding in my own sound effects where I see fit, until we're both on the verge of breathless and, much like I predicted, the party outside clearly seems to have gotten bored, the normal hum of scattered mingling and music returning.

Cooper shoves me away once and for all, and I let her, holding my hands up in defeat.

"*Satisfied?*" she demands.

"Not at all," I reply. "But I'd say they are."

"Well, I guess that's all that matters then," she quips.

"Isn't it?" I ask.

She blows out a frustrated breath. "*What* did I say about enclosed spaces?"

"You say a lot of things, Cooper. Especially complaints and demands. It's hard to keep up at times."

I can sense her pacing in front of me. "One closet per week with you is more than enough for me."

"Oh, so you want to make this a regular thing?" I ask. "What time in your little red diary do you want to pencil me in for next week?"

She stops pacing. I don't know how I know. I guess I can just feel it. "It's not a diary," she says. "Or an *agenda* for that matter."

"What is it then?"

"What it *is* is none of your business," she snaps.

"What's the big deal—"

"*Let it go.*"

I let out a scoff. "Fine."

"*Fine,*" Cooper echoes me.

We each step backwards, getting as far apart as two people in one small closet can get from each other. A few seconds go by, and I hear what sounds like Cooper sliding down the wall to sit on the floor. I wait a few seconds, and then do the same, not wanting her to think I did it just because she did because I'm in an immature mood apparently. She huffs out a breath anyways.

We stay quiet for a little bit, and let me tell you, silence in pure darkness seems significantly longer and is much more painful. I try to look at my watch to check how much time we have left, then shake my head at myself, remembering that it's dark and I can't.

I'm about to break. I don't think I've ever gone this long without speaking in my life. But surprisingly, I don't have to. Cooper breaks first.

"Can I ask you a question?" she says, an odd tone to her voice that I can't place.

"Knock yourself out, Cooper."

"Why do you even like Denise?"

My mouth falls open, and I'm suddenly thankful we're sitting in the dark. "What do you mean?" I ask her.

"She's kinda awful."

I snort, caught off guard by her bluntness. "Yeah, and you're a total walk in the park, Cooper."

She's quiet for a few seconds, and I find myself swallowing, my throat tight all of the sudden. "Just forget it," she finally says.

"No, no," I say, shaking my head. "Look, I...I don't know. I just do."

"You just...*do*?"

"Yeah," I nod to myself. "I mean, I know she's not always the most pleasant person to be around. She has basically no filter and is a little full of herself–"

"A *little*?"

"Okay, Cooper, okay," I chuckle. "She might not be perfect...on the inside, at least."

"On the inside," Cooper says, her voice dry. "Right."

Because her outside is obviously perfect, I know she wants to add, but doesn't.

I can't even say I'd disagree with her. Denise is stunning. She's completely perfect on paper. Shiny blonde hair, bright blue eyes, perfectly symmetrical face, smooth skin, full lips, fit body. There's not a thing you could physically point to that needs changing. She really is *perfect*. But...the more I think about it, the more I start to question what that really means. I look at Denise's eyes, I've looked at them a million times, and I know they're beautiful. But, if I really think about it, I don't know that I've ever really looked *into* them. You know? Don't know that I've just sat there thinking about them.

Don't know if they've popped into my head when I'm trying to sleep, questioning exactly what shade they are or what they resemble and why it's making me want to crawl out of my skin not knowing.

Denise's hair is always polished and smooth and, *God*, so pretty. But, it's almost too pretty to touch. I have always just grazed my hand over top of it, not wanting to force a single strand out of place. That would be wrong. *No*, I've never just looked at her hair and had the desire to thread my fingers through it and just pull. Never wanted to test it just to see what would happen. It never reminded me of anything like fire. Something eye catching and inviting, but also wild and dangerous. Something that feels electric to the touch. Like a good kind of sizzling pain that you don't necessarily want but just can't seem to pull away from.

No...nothing like that.

But, *yeah*. Denise, she's beautiful. *Yeah*. Perfect.

I hear Cooper clear her throat, snapping me back to reality. "*But?*" she prompts me.

"But..." I trail off, my head falling back. "She's mine, you know? Or...she *was*. And...I don't know. I just want her back."

Cooper seems to think for a few moments before speaking again. "What exactly is it that you want from her?"

"What do you mean?" I question her.

"What does she do for you?"

"Well," I say, letting out a whistle. "There was this one Saturday night back in July in the back of her dad's Cadillac where she did this thing with her tongue–"

"*Ew*, stop," Cooper cuts me off. "Not what I meant." She sighs. "I mean...what do you love about her?"

My brows pull together. "What?"

"How does she make you feel?" Cooper asks. "What do you like about being around her? How do you think she makes you better?"

My lips part.

It's just been a whole new world since I've been with Robbie. I guess you could say he's making me a better me.

I shake my head, Cooper's words from out in the living room a few minutes ago bouncing around in my brain.

So, that wasn't just some bullshit she made up on the fly? She actually believes in something like that?

"*I...*" I chuckle, breaking off. "Shit, is this an interrogation or something, Cooper?"

"Just making conversation," she says.

"Well most people when making conversation ask about a person's favorite color or their zodiac sign or shit like that."

She actually laughs. And it occurs to me that I'm not sure I've heard her really laugh before. It makes my chest feel kinda weird. I rub at it with my hand, and the tightness settles as quickly as it came. "Well, now you may as well tell me," she says.

"Red. And Leo."

"Right," she says.

Right? "What about you?" I ask.

"Don't have one. And I don't know."

"Of course you'd be the person to not have a favorite color," I say.

"What is that supposed to mean?"

"Nothing, Cooper," I chuckle. "Forget it."

"There's so many options."

"God forbid."

"I feel like my answer changes weekly, so I just choose not to give one," she says. "There's no point. It all depends on how I'm feeling. Or what's currently...tickling my brain, I guess?"

"Tickling your brain," I snort. "Right. Have I told you you're weird today, Cooper?"

"Yes."

"Good, just making sure," I say, grinning into the dark. "So, what color's on your mind this week, Cooper?"

It takes her a few moments to answer. "Brown."

"Huh," I mutter.

Brown, really?

I get a few more seconds of silence as a response, and then, "Favorite food?"

"Pizza," I say instantly. "Yours?"

"Chocolate cake."

"I... Does that count as a food?" I ask.

"Pretty sure you can eat it."

"Shit, you got me there, Cooper," I say. "Sorry, I just expected you to say, like...chicken casserole. Or meatloaf. Or something like that."

"I don't even want to begin to understand what you mean by that," Cooper says. "*Meatloaf?* Why?"

I shrug. "Just seems like something you'd say."

"Because you know me so well," she retorts.

"What, like you know me?"

"Favorite sport?" she asks, a challenging tone to her voice.

"*Basketball,*" we say at the same time.

"Gee, gold star, Cooper. Should we guess what my first name is next?"

"Fine," she says. "That was an easy one. What's your favorite type of music?"

"*Rock,*" we both say, together again.

"Okay," I shake my head. "It's not like that's not a well-known fact. And, besides, you've been riding in the car listening to music with me for weeks now."

"Fine," Cooper says. "What's your favorite season?"

"*Summer,*" we say.

"Okay, but whose isn't?" I ask.

"Mine," she says. "I like spring."

"Of course you do."

She smells like spring, I think to myself and don't know why.

"And what's your favorite movie?" Cooper asks. I open my mouth to answer, but she cuts me off. "Wait, no. Let me guess. *Star Wars? Back to the Future?*"

"What's wrong with those movies?" I question her.

"I never said there was anything wrong with them," she says. "They're fantastic movies. Just...obvious, I suppose."

"Huh. Well, that's interesting, considering you're wrong."

"Really?" she questions me. "What, is it *Terminator*? *Raiders of the Lost Ark*?"

"I guess you have me pegged as an action boy, Miss Groovy Movie?"

"Well, Mister *Month of Detention*," she retorts, "I think you've made it clear you don't shy away from a thrill. And that you don't mind living in a fantasy world."

That statement hits me right between the eyebrows and somewhere deep in my stomach, a pain settling there. "Right," I mutter.

I think Cooper senses the shift in mood. She throws a Scrabble piece at me in what I think is her attempt at easing it.

Weirdo.

"So, what is it then?" she asks.

I toss the Scrabble piece right back at her. I'm pretty sure it bounces off her head based on the *oof* noise she lets out. "*The Outsiders*," I tell her.

"Oh..." she says, sounding completely shocked and trailing off.

"Not what you expected?" I ask.

"Yeah...not at all."

"In a good way?"

"Yeah," she confirms. "In a good way. Interesting choice."

If I've learned anything about Cooper thus far, her saying something is *interesting* could mean about a million different things. "Yeah, well," I say, clearing my throat. "I guess Tom Cruise was a lot dreamier by the time *Top Gun* came out." She doesn't say anything in response to that. "Or is it Goose you're sweet on?" I ask.

"Yeah, because that's the only possible explanation for why that's my favorite movie," she says, her voice low.

"Well, humor me then, Cooper."

"No."

The grin on my face falls slightly. I don't know why, but she seems genuinely annoyed. Even upset. "Hey, Cooper," I say, softening my tone. "I'm just yanking your chain."

She stays silent. I squint in the darkness, but I can't make out a damn thing other than the vague outline of her form across from me. I push off the wall behind me, scooting a little closer to her. "C'mon," I insist. "Tell me. Why's it your favorite movie?"

"It's just good," she says quickly. Way too quickly.

"No." I shake my head. "It's more than that. Good isn't good enough for you."

She clicks her tongue. "I…"

I find myself reaching for her. My fingers just graze the top of her hand, but then I pull back, feeling her stiffen. "What?" I ask, too invested now to let this go. "What is it, Cooper?"

"My Dad was a Navy pilot."

My brows raise, a million thoughts running through my mind. One stands out from them all though.

Was a Navy pilot.

Shit.

"*Was?*" I question, hoping it's not what I think it is.

"Yeah," she breathes. "I know. It's stupid—"

"It's not."

She lets out a sigh. "He died when I was four."

Dammit.

"He was doing a training exercise. It was a freak accident."

"I'm…" I say, shaking my head. "I'm really sorry, Cooper."

"I have some memories of him," she continues, "but not many. I was just barely a kid when I knew him. But…I don't know. I know you probably think I'm a dork."

I don't tell her that I think she is. Now's not the time.

"But movies have always just made me feel things. *So* deeply. A lot more deeply than I think they make other people feel things. And the first time I saw *Top Gun*…" She goes quiet for a moment, seeming lost in thought. "My dad wasn't in the Navy long. He'd just barely gotten his wings by the time he died. But I guess I just like to imagine, if he wouldn't have gotten in the accident, that he would have gone on to be someone like Maverick. That he would've done amazing things. Been a hero. That he would have just done something...been something..."

"Rad?"

I see her shift in the darkness, and I think she turns her head to look at me. "Yeah," she mutters. "Yeah, I suppose. And I guess thinking that is better than the reality. The reality that it was all for nothing and now he's just...gone. That he'll never get the chance to do something rad. Or just...be my dad." We're quiet for a few seconds, and then Cooper lets out a dry chuckle. "I guess maybe I'm the one that likes to live in a fantasy world after all."

I just sit there, lips parted, not having a damn clue of what I'm supposed to say to her, but knowing that I should definitely say something. "Cooper, I–"

We both startle, the door handle suddenly starting to jiggle behind us. I feel Cooper start to sit up in front of me. "Hey, Cooper–"

"Yeah," she says. "I know the drill." I shake my head, brows pulled together, just as the door barely cracks open, a line of light streaming in. I find Cooper right in front of me, just inches away. I open my mouth to say something, but a heavy lump has settled its way into my throat, preventing me. She leans in further, and I feel my stomach drop. When we're just a breath apart, she reaches up, swipes her fingers over her lips, then brushes her fingers across my mouth, transferring her lipstick onto me. Like I did back in the janitor's closet on Monday.

A million years ago.

Cooper's gaze flashes once from my now red stained lips to my eyes, then she slowly raises to her feet. "I'm going to find a bathroom," she says. Then she walks out of the closet, leaving me sitting here on the floor with my heart in my stomach.

I hear a scoffing sound and turn my head to find Jesse holding open the door, making me immediately push myself to my feet. I don't even realize Denise is at his side at first, her hand on his shoulder and her head peering around the side of him. "Geez, man," Jesse says, looking me up and down. "I was thinking of giving you an apology, but now I'm thinking you owe me a thank you instead."

I straighten out my jacket, walking right up to Jesse until I'm looking down on him. He tries not to look intimidated, but he's not very good at it, his dark eyes going wide and his tan cheeks going pink as he has to tilt his head back to meet my gaze. "I don't need you to give me an opportunity to be with my girl," I tell him, taking a step closer. "She wants me all on her own. First and foremost," I say, smirking in a way that I know will keep Denise up tonight. Even though I'm not really thinking about her right now. "Now, if you'll excuse me."

I walk right past them, feeling Denise's eyes burning into me the entire way. I don't give her the satisfaction of looking back.

twenty-one

SARA

I open my locker door, reaching for my camera and stuffing a few extra rolls of film into the front pocket of my jeans.

Even though I got to leave class a few minutes early, the halls are already buzzing with students anxious for our midday pep rally. Our girls volleyball team is taking on our archrival, Golden Gate High, in their game tonight, and it's an annual tradition that we have a mini pep rally before lunch on the Tuesday of the game to get everyone in the fighting spirit.

I usually love this pep rally. It's a nice change to see the whole school hyping up the girls once in a while. Our boy athletes get drooled over enough on a daily basis as it is. I can think of a few right off the top of my head...

Well, maybe just one right now.

For some reason that's all my brain's been able to think about lately. The thing is, I can't even decipher the thoughts. It's not like there's something in particular. He's just...*there*. Which is unfortunate because there are about a million other things that should be there in his place right now. Like the photos I'm about to take of this pep rally for the spread in the school newspaper I need to create tomorrow. Or my algebra test on Thursday. Or my physics project that's due on Monday. Or the scholarship essay I need to get started on for NYU. Or the speech I have to give next Friday so that I'm elected student body president so that I have even a fraction of a chance of getting said NYU scholarship.

I blow out a breath, securing my camera strap around my neck. I turn to look into the little magnetic mirror I have on the inside of my locker door, pulling my hair out from under the strap and attempting to fluff it into a reasonable state. I find my eyes trailing up, landing on the stickers stuck to the door above my mirror. First to the Bay View Bears one, then over to the one in the shape of an F-14 Tomcat. My lips automatically pull up into a smile when I see it. I reach my hand up, grazing my fingers over the little fighter jet sticker, remembering how Mr. Ritter gave it to me in a Christmas card last year as an ode to my favorite movie. He had no idea how much it really meant to me. But that's okay. Nobody really does.

My smile falls.

Well, I guess *somebody* does now.

I refrain from slamming my head against my locker door.

I've never talked to anybody about my obsession with *Top Gun* and my delusional fixation on how it connects to my life before. Not even Alice. I'm sure my mom can connect the dots, but she's never brought it up. We figured out a long time ago that it was just easier to not talk about things that make us sad and that we didn't have the control over to fix. So I decided to just keep it to myself. Nobody needed to know.

So why on earth did I tell Robbie Summers?

I don't have the slightest clue. He just pulled it out of me. He has a way of doing that, and it's becoming downright infuriating. Every once in a while, when he actually decides to stop talking, suddenly I *can't stop* talking. One minute he's arrogant and annoying, never shutting up, pushing my buttons and making me want to pull my hair out. And then the next...he's quiet, curious, attentive, almost on the verge of comforting, and possibly even, dare I say...*sweet?*

I don't know, but I don't have time for it. I just have to get through this next week and a half. I'll give my speech next Friday (that I still have to write) and then I'll be elected president the following Monday.

Or I won't. And this will have all been for nothing.

And then we'll go our separate ways. I'll never have to speak to Robbie again. My stomach dips at the thought, but I know it has to just be the stress of what's coming. That has to be all it is. My and Robbie's little arrangement is going to expire, just like it was meant to. Just like we both planned for. Just like we both want.

My stomach sinks further.

I just have to get through my speech next Friday. Then we're done.

But why am I feeling like I'm forgetting something?

"Hey you!" Alice's head appears around the side of my locker door, making me jump. I grip the door, my heart stuttering it my chest.

"Hey, you menace," I say. "You nearly gave me a heart attack."

Alice tilts her head at me. "What were you so deep in thought over?" she asks. "Or should I say *who*?" Her eyes narrow playfully at me.

I play off her question with a chuckle, closing my locker door. "Did you come to walk with me to the gym?" I ask, starting to walk down the hallway.

"No, actually," she says, following after me, "I'm meeting Daniel in a minute. But I did want to ask you if you have next Monday off of work?"

"Oh." Monday is the only day a week I technically have off from Groovy Movie, but I often end up picking up an extra shift that day anyways. "Yeah, as of right now."

"Great!" Alice claps. "We're going dress shopping. I'll pick you up from school after your library shift."

I spin to look at Alice. "*Dress shopping*? For what?"

"Well, Homecoming, of course."

My feet slow. *Shit. I knew I was forgetting something.*

"Robbie asked you, right?" Alice asks, one brow raised.

"Oh, well, yeah. Of course he has," I mumble.

He hasn't. I'm hoping he won't. Maybe he'll just forget about it.

He won't forget about it. I know there's no way I'm that lucky. He talked about it when he came up with the idea of...well, *us*. But he hasn't said anything since. I can't believe I've been so hung up on the election that I completely forgot that Homecoming was the next day.

"So you'll go then?" Alice asks. "Dress shopping?"

"Umm..." I think about the probability that Robbie won't make me go to the dance and decide it is approximately a zero percent chance. "Yeah, sure. Let's go." Worst case scenario, I'll return the dress.

"*Yay!*" Alice sings, jumping up and down. "How fun is this? Both of us going to our senior year Homecoming with boyfriends?"

"*So* fun," I nod, entertaining her.

Alice pulls me into a hug right outside the gym door. "I can't wait. This is already the best year ever. I'm so happy. Especially for you."

I swallow down the urge to scream that it's a lie. "Me too, Al."

"Oh, there's Daniel," she says, spotting him over my shoulder and pulling back. "See you later?"

"Sure. See ya."

Alice scurries off, hooking her arm with Daniel's and heading towards the far main entrance to the gym where the rest of the students are filing in. I duck inside the door to my side where the athletes and staff are meant to enter.

I find my usual spot in the corner of the room and begin fiddling with my camera, making sure it's all set to begin taking pictures. Once it's good to go, I inch around the edge of the bleachers, taking in the scene as the band starts to play. The students in the bleachers instantly get excited by the sound, many jumping out of their seats.

Suddenly, a gust of wind passes behind me, startling me, as the cheer team comes jogging around the corner and spreads out in front of the bleachers, some doing cartwheels and flips to get to their places. The crowd goes wild, and I take it as a perfect opportunity to grab some pictures, already mentally writing the newspaper article in my head. When I pull the camera back a few moments later, I see all of the cheerleaders gathered around a handful of plastic bins in front of the bleachers. They start pulling the contents out and tossing whatever the small items are into the bleachers. People have their hands in the air and are jumping up and down trying to get the attention of whatever cheerleader is closest to them so they'll send one in their direction. It isn't until Kate Andrews sets one off, quickly followed by every other cheerleader and a good portion of the students in the bleachers, that I realize they're confetti poppers.

A smile instantly comes to my face and I raise my camera again, snapping as many pictures as I can. This will be awful for cleaning up, but absolutely incredible as yearbook photos.

I run out of film, and start fishing another roll out of my pocket. It's then that I spot Robbie walking into the gym with Brad Marshall and Paul Strothers. His head shifts in my direction and we make eye contact for a fraction of a second before I look away, pulling the film from my jeans. The volume of music coming from the band starts rising, the roar from the crowd becoming crazy between all of the people talking, cheering, and setting off confetti poppers. It all becomes suddenly twice as intense as Principal Whileyman's voice comes over the speakers, introducing the volleyball team.

"*Crap*," I mutter, working to swap out the film rolls as quickly as possible. I just barely get the used film roll out of the camera when a shadow appears in front of me.

"Oh my gosh! Hi, Sara!"

My brows immediately pull together at the voice I swear I recognize. I look up slowly, finding Denise standing in front of me with her hands on her hips, a huge smile on her face. "Uh– Hi, Denise?" I say, trying to mask the confusion in my voice as I work to get the new roll of film into the camera and ready to go.

"You're here!" she says, that too big smile growing even wider.

"Um, well, the whole school is here," I say.

She lets out a laugh that somehow sounds like angels singing in heaven. "Well, yeah," she says. "But I guess I just meant *here*. Like, right here."

"Right," I say, narrowing my eyes at her. "Well, I always take photos over here during pep rallies."

"You do?" Denise asks, tilting her head. "I've never noticed."

Of course you haven't.

The volleyball team starts running into the gym and I raise my camera, trying to get a picture. Denise immediately steps in front of me. "Sorry, excuse me," I say, trying to get around her. She just keeps stepping to the side, staying in my path and blocking my shot.

"Why don't you come and join the fun?" Denise asks. "Take the day off. Come hang out in the bleachers."

"I can't." I shake my head. "I have to get photos for the newspaper and yearbook."

I move to the left this time, trying to trip her up, but Denise doesn't miss a beat, continuing to block me. "Oh, come on," she says. "Live a little. We have party poppers and everything." She holds up her hands to show me the handful of poppers she's holding.

"I noticed," I say, trying not to sound as frustrated as I feel. "It looks like fun, but I can't." I manage to get one half decent shot over Denise's shoulder of the volleyball team waving to the crowd of students, but half decent won't cut it.

Suddenly, Ginger Matthews appears, jogging up from behind Denise. "Hi, Den," she says. "What's going on?"

"Oh, I was just trying to get Sara involved in the fun, but she says she's not interested," Denise says, flashing Ginger a puppy dog face.

"What?" Ginger questions, an exaggerated look of surprise crossing her face. "Oh, c'mon, Sara, you totally should!"

"See, I told you!" Denise says. "Come on, just for a few minutes."

"I told you I can't." I stand on my tiptoes, snapping whatever photos I can without Denise's blonde ponytail in the frame.

Denise grabs me by the elbow. "Surely you have enough. Let's go to the bleachers."

"Let go of me, please," I demand, pulling out of her grasp.

"You know you want to," Ginger chimes in.

"No, I can't."

"Can't or won't?" one of them asks. I can't even tell the difference right now with my camera up to my face.

"Does it really matter?" I ask.

"Here, just take one of these and come on," Denise says, trying to shove a popper into my hand that is currently holding the camera.

"Okay, *seriously*," I grit, yanking the camera down from my face. "Do you mind–"

I don't get the full question out before a confetti popper goes on in my face, shooting directly into my left eye. I'm thankful my camera is strapped around my neck, because I immediately drop it, doubling over in pain as both of my hands go to my eye. I try to open it, but it feels like there's a mixture of sand and razor blades floating around on its surface. I try to catch my breath, knowing it's just pieces of paper and glittery sequins, but it doesn't make it hurt any less. All the sound in the room goes muffled for several moments, until one stands out clear as day from the rest.

"*What the hell, Denise?*"

I feel hands on my shoulders, but I can't move, my teeth digging into my lower lip in an attempt to distract from the throbbing pain in my eye.

"*Oopsies*," I hear Denise say. "So sorry. Total accident."

Accident, my ass, I think to myself, not sure I'm able to speak yet.

I'm not sure by what force, but I'm being led out of the gym, walking with my head down and being guided by the hands on my shoulders. Once we get outside, we take a handful more steps until we walk through another door. I am able to tell by the change of the flooring that I see through my squinted good eye that we're in a bathroom now. I hear the sink turn on and it's not a moment later that my head is being forced under the stream of water, letting it run over my injured eye. I let out a hiss of discomfort as the pain only gets worse. It takes me a few moments to realize one of the hands on my shoulder is now rubbing circles across my back.

After the water runs over my eye for twenty seconds or so, the pain goes from sharp to dull, but the ache is definitely still there. I try to force my eye to open further but can't, immediately wincing. The water shuts off and I feel fingers under my chin, forcing my head up. I squeeze both of my eyes closed as I stand up straight, trying to gauge the difference of feeling between the two.

Yeah, the right one definitely feels normal and the left one feels like it's on fire.

"Let me see ya, Cooper," a voice whispers in front of me.

My good eye snaps open, finding Robbie standing right in front of me, his fingers still resting under my chin, his head tilted, and his eyes full of concern.

I reflexively jump back, my mouth falling open. "I–You–*What*–"

"Are you okay?" he asks, ignoring my stammering.

I shake my head. "You can't be in here!" I say, not sure why him being in the girls' bathroom is the first coherent thought I'm able to get out.

Robbie raises his brows. "That's your main concern right now, Cooper? Seriously?"

"It's the girls' bathroom!" I say, throwing my arms out.

Robbie rolls his eyes, stepping closer to me. "Would you let me see your eye?"

I flinch as his thumb brushes across my left eyebrow. "I can't open it."

"You can," Robbie insists. "You're just scared."

"Yeah, well, blame it on your girlfriend," I mutter.

Robbie's gaze flicks down, meeting my single good eye. He flexes his jaw, his head shaking slightly. "You're my girlfriend, remember?"

I swallow, pressing my lips together.

"Here, let me help you," Robbie says, pressing his thumb down and pulling up on my eyebrow just a little, forcing my eye open. I suck in a sharp breath as Robbie's other thumb presses just below my eye, pulling down. "*Shhh*, I got you," he says, ducking his head to get a better look.

He goes quiet as he examines my eye. Several seconds go by before I ask, "What's it look like?"

Robbie doesn't answer at first, distracted.

"Robbie?" I say.

"*Hmmm?*"

"What's it look like?" I ask. "My eye?"

"I don't have a damn clue," he breathes.

My brows try to pull together, but don't have much luck with the way Robbie is currently manhandling the left one. "*What?*"

Robbie seems to suddenly snap out of whatever trance he went into, letting my face go and stepping back. He rubs the back of his neck. "Yeah, gonna be honest, Cooper. It doesn't look great."

"Well, great," I murmur.

Robbie puts his hands on his hips, staring at the floor. He lets out a deep sigh, then reaches for my wrist. "Okay, let's go," he says.

My feet stay glued to the ground as he tries to pull me along with him. "Go *where?*"

Robbie shakes his head. "I can't do anything else for you," he mutters. "We need to get you to a doctor."

My spine steels. "I don't want to go to the doctor. I'm fine."

Robbie tilts his head at me, giving me a pointed look. "Cooper, can you even open your left eye without crying right now?"

"Yes, totally," I insist. "*See?*" I go all in, trying to force my eye open. I don't even get halfway before I automatically wince in pain, a fat tear rolling out of the corner of my eye as if on command. "Shit, ow," I cry, reaching up to wipe it away.

"We're going," Robbie says, turning to leave again.

"I don't want to," I grunt, yanking him back.

His tongue goes into the side of his cheek. "Would you rather stay here in the boys' bathroom instead?"

"I–*What?*"

The boys' *bathroom?*

I turn my head, needing my right eye to see the wall of urinals to my side. "Oh my God, *Robbie!*" I say, whacking at his shoulder with my other hand. "Why would you drag me in here?"

"Well, I couldn't go into the girls' bathroom," Robbie says, a smirk on his face.

"You're the worst," I groan.

"You're welcome," Robbie nods. "Can we go to the doctor now?"

———

I'm resting my head against my passenger side window, swearing the pulse pounding in my eye is perfectly matching up with the beat of whatever song is playing on the radio. At *full volume*, I must add. It may be playing at full volume because I wouldn't stop protesting about going to the doctor and Robbie decided to crank the radio up instead of continuing to argue with me, but I don't think that's an important detail.

I'm brought out of the daze of my pain when Robbie suddenly turns off the main road and I glance up to see that we're pulling into the parking lot of Summers Optometry. I sit up straight in my seat, it for some reason not clicking in my brain until right now that he was bringing me here. I mean, *of course* he's bringing me here. It's the only eye doctor's office in town. But still.

I'm about to meet Robbie's family.

Like, all of them.

I sink back down into my seat as Robbie parks, taking the keys out of the ignition. "Uh, Robbie. I really think I'm okay–"

"Shut up, Cooper." Robbie is out of the car and around to open my door before I have a chance to argue any further.

I accept his hand with a groan, letting him pull me from the car, then drop it once I'm standing upright. He immediately moves to rest his hand on my shoulder, guiding me towards the front door. I turn to look at him with my one open eye. "You don't have to do that," I say, motioning to his hand. "I'm not entirely blind, you know?"

Robbie takes back his hand, holding it up with his other hand defensively. "Suit yourself, Cooper." He moves in front of me, stepping up on the curb and heading for the front door.

"Thank you," I say, following after him.

I take two steps before I walk directly into a parking sign, smacking the left side of my head on it. "*Agh!*" I step back, rubbing at the quickly forming bump on my temple. I glance up at the culprit, seeing the sign reads *Reserved for Dr. Darren Summers.*

I hear a sigh and turn my head to see Robbie walking back to me. He puts his hand back on my shoulder. "Wanna try that again, Cooper?"

I clear my throat. "Yes, please."

Robbie leads me through the front door and into the lobby, telling me to sit down in a chair while he goes to talk to the receptionist. I'm nearly across the room, but can still just make out his voice as he reaches the desk.

"Hey, Doris," he says.

The older woman looks up at him, her head pulling back. "*Robbie?* What are you doing here?" she asks. "Shouldn't you be at school?"

"Yeah, well, it's my...girlfriend," Robbie says, motioning his head in my direction. I quickly glance the other way, keeping my hand covering my bad eye and pretending to be very interested in the wall. "She had a little accident. Messed up her eye. Figured she should have it looked at. And, besides, it's lunchtime right now."

I steal a glance back at the desk, seeing Doris looking right at me. I give her a little smile and wave. Her eyebrows raise, and then she waves back before sitting back down. "Well, isn't she just darling?" I hear her ask Robbie. I look away, my cheeks feeling warm all of the sudden.

Robbie clears his throat. "Can you get her squeezed in real quick?"

"Oh, I'm sure that'll be fine. Let me go get your father—"

"*No*," Robbie says forcefully, making me look back in his direction. I see him holding out his hand to stop Doris from getting up.

My brows pull together at his odd reaction.

What's up with that?

Robbie smiles tightly at Doris. "Can you see if Will's available? Or Janet? Or my mom, if neither of them are? Please?"

There's an awkward pause before Doris responds. "Sure, hon. Let me take a look." She appears to flip through a binder, I assume looking at today's appointments. "It looks like Dr. Richards is free right now."

"Awesome," Robbie says, visibly relaxing.

"Let's get her in an exam room and I'll go get him," Doris says. Then she stands up suddenly, looking in my direction. I snap my head in the other direction, pretending I wasn't eavesdropping on the whole encounter.

"Honey, you can come on back," she calls to me, motioning with her hand for me to walk through the door to the side of the reception desk.

"Great," I squeak. "Thank you." I hop up and scramble for the door, but Robbie beats me there, holding it open for me. After I walk through, he follows behind me, letting the door fall shut. I glance back at him with my one good eye, seeing his unusually guarded expression, his posture slumped. The way he keeps his head ducked almost looks like he's...*hiding?*

"Here we go. Just in here," Doris says, making me return my attention forward to where she's leading me (*us*, apparently) into an exam room. I try to take one of the small chairs in the corner of the room, but Robbie grunts out a sound telling me no, and I look up to see him pointing towards the very big and dramatic exam chair in the center of the room. I cock my head at him, attempting to challenge him, but he just shakes his head, pointing at the exam chair again as he plops down in the seat I was about to take. I roll my one good eye at him, begrudgingly making my way over to the ridiculous chair. "Dr. Richards should be in here in just a minute, hon," Doris announces, closing the door and leaving Robbie and me alone.

It's quiet for a few moments before I look over at him. It takes me a beat to realize what looks so off about him. He's glancing around the room with his arms crossed like it's just as new to him as it is to me. He looks *uncomfortable*. That's definitely a new look on Robbie Summers. I question why it would be in action at his family's business of all places. Then something occurs to me.

"Dr. *Richards*?" I ask him. Robbie's head shifts in my direction. "You guys let someone infiltrate the legendary family business?"

"He's my sister Janet's husband," he says. "Will."

"Your sister's married to an optometrist too?"

"They met in school," he confirms.

"Wow. You guys really...love eyes."

Robbie's gaze snaps to meet mine, his eyes narrowing the only response I get to my silly statement. Luckily, there's no time for the silence to get awkward. The exam room door opens, Doris's voice sounding. "Here you go, Doctor."

My eyes are still on Robbie as his shift to the door, and he instantly stiffens in a way I've never seen before. I scrunch my brows together, looking from him to the door and seeing a much older salt and pepper haired version of Robbie making his way past Doris and into the room. In the blink of an eye, Robbie is on his feet next to me.

"*Dad*," he says.

I gulp, looking between the two of them.

Dad?

The man doesn't spare a glance in either of our directions, walking over to the small sink in the room and beginning to wash his hands. "Robert," he grunts.

Robert?

I'm starting to quickly understand why Robbie looked so

unhappy coming in here. And that makes me question all the more why he insisted that we do.

"Dad, I–"

"And who do we have here?" Dr. Summers asks, cutting Robbie off and looking directly at me, acting as if Robbie isn't even standing there.

It takes the man raising his eyebrows at me for me to realize I actually need to respond. "Um, Sara?" I say dumbly.

Dr. Summers' jaw flexes. "Sara Beth Cooper, is it?" he asks, his gaze finally trailing over to Robbie at a snail's pace. I glance at Robbie, seeing his throat bob, his eyes squinting.

"Just Sara," I correct him, an odd feeling settling in my stomach at the realization that I've definitely been talked about in the Summers household.

"I thought Doris said Will was free," Robbie interjects suddenly.

"Something came up," his father responds, not looking at him.

"I didn't want to bother you," Robbie mutters.

Dr. Summers lets out a scoff. "Concerned about that suddenly, are you?"

My mouth falls silently open. *What did I just walk into?*

"Anyways, Sara Beth–"

"Just *Sara*," I insist, interrupting Robbie's dad. *What is it with these Summers men?*

"Well, *just* Sara," he smiles, gritting his teeth, "I see my son has made fast work of getting you into trouble."

"*Dad*–"

"What?"

Robbie and I both speak at the same time.

"What seems to be the issue?" Dr. Summers cuts us both off, snapping on a pair of rubber gloves.

"It was just an accident," I say, irritation in my voice as a response to the disdain in his.

"We were at a pep rally with the rest of the school," Robbie speaks up. "People were setting off confetti poppers. She was busy taking photos for the school newspaper and didn't notice one going off right in front of her. It hit her in her left eye."

I take note of Robbie's summarized version of the events, finding it interesting the details he chose to include and the ones he left out, but I don't comment on either.

"I helped her flush her eye out as best I could," he continues, "but it still seems to be really irritated. Maybe even scratched."

Dr. Summers sits down on a rolling chair, wheeling his way over to me. I feel goosebumps prickle at the back of my neck as he draws closer. "That your professional opinion, son?" He laughs and winks at Robbie when he says it, but I don't miss the condescending tone in his question. For a moment, I find myself questioning how I ever thought *Robbie* was a prick. And now I wonder if I could even blame him for being one.

"No," Robbie replies, his voice low. "That's why I brought her here."

Dr. Summers ignores Robbie's comment, scooting even closer to me and raising an eye exam tool with a light up to his face. "Let's take a look, shall we?" I try my best not to flinch away from his touch as he reaches for my hurt eye, gently pulling up on the lid. It feels like sandpaper, and I immediately try to close it again, but Dr. Summers keeps a firm hold on me. "There, there. Just a second."

He spends a few more seconds examining my eye before he lets my eyelid go, standing up from his chair and walking over the trash can to remove his gloves.

"It's just a minor corneal abrasion," he says, grabbing a notepad from the counter next to him and scribbling something down.

"A...*what?*" I ask.

"A scratched eye," he replies without looking up.

"So, I was right?" Robbie asks.

His dad ignores him. "It should heal on its own in one to three days. I'll send you home with some saline solution to rinse it out with during that time." He walks over to my side, tearing the top paper from the notepad and handing it to me. "Show this to Doris on your way out. She'll get you what you need."

"Um, thank you," I say, taking the paper from him, "Dr. Summers."

"It's what I do," he nods. "Now, Robert, how about you get this young woman back to school?" Robbie reaches out a hand to help me out of the chair. I fumble for it, accepting his help, standing up next to him. We start to turn away, but Robbie's dad speaks up again. "And, son?"

Robbie slowly spins back to face him. "Yes?"

"Next time, maybe just save yourself some time and come straight here." He smiles tightly at Robbie, reaching up and roughly ruffling his hair. I see Robbie's jaw flex at the same moment mine comes unhinged. "So good to see you, son."

Robbie's hair is a complete mess, but he doesn't make any move to fix it. "Right," he grits. "Thanks, Dad."

Robbie scoots us both out the door before Dr. Summers has a chance to say anything further, but we don't make it far, running directly into another variation of Robbie on our first step into the hallway.

"*Whoa,*" the man stops in his tracks, eyeing me and Robbie, and then my hand in Robbie's. He's about an inch shorter than Robbie and his hair has a bit sandier of a hue to it. His eyes are also a darker shade of brown. "What do we have here?" he questions. "Hi, Dr. Summers," he says, holding a hand out and winking at me. He gives me a smirk, and as confident as he seems to be in it, it just doesn't have the same effect as his little brother. I shake his hand limply.

"Um, hi," I mutter. "Sara."

The moment the *second* Dr. Summers drops my hand, he immediately moves to muss Robbie's hair further. My eyes narrow in response. "Hi, Bobbie," he grins. "I didn't know you were here, little brother."

"Well, Steven, it doesn't really matter," Robbie grits. "Because we're leaving right now."

And without another word, Robbie drags me into the lobby, snatching the paper silently from my hand and handing it to Doris. She gives us a tight smile as she hands Robbie the saline solution and he mutters his thanks before hauling me out to his car, almost physically putting me into the passenger seat and buckling me in before I snap him out of his robotic trance, telling him I can do it.

He doesn't say anything to me the entire ride back to school or the rest of the day, and I don't ask anything of him, both of us wordlessly agreeing to temporarily lay down our weapons.

I think we've both had more than enough for today.

twenty-two

ROBBIE

I watch as Cooper turns over a book to read its library label, and my stomach sinks when I see her squint her left eye to read it.

It's been three days since *the incident,* as Cooper and I have settled on calling it, since she doesn't want to talk about what happened at the pep rally and I don't care to talk about what followed it. I know she's embarrassed about what happened to her, which is completely ridiculous, since it wasn't her fault whatsoever. I know because I watched the whole thing unfold.

As much as I tried to avoid looking her way at the pep rally, Cooper's fiery head of hair was the only thing I could manage to keep my eyes on from the moment I walked in the gym.

She had no idea, I'm sure, hard at work, taking all of her newspaper pictures like it was the most important task in the world. Since she was too busy to notice me, I know she was also too busy to notice Denise conspiring with Ginger from the second she stepped through the doors.

Denise had that look in her eye, a look I know all too well. She was out for blood. I just have no idea why. What I do know though, was that nothing was going to end well the moment she started sauntering over to Cooper, her blonde ponytail bouncing behind her. I tried to stay out of it. I tried to just focus on the conversation with Paul and Brad and my other friends sitting around me that I felt like I hadn't talked to in ages, but I couldn't look away. And let me tell you, I'm glad I didn't.

The moment that confetti popper went off right in Cooper's eye, I thought I was gonna lose my shit. I'm not sure my feet have ever moved so fast. The basketball team is certainly going to be expecting a whole lot more from me this season after seeing the way I sprinted over to her.

I saw red. I was so angry with Denise for being so childish and petty. I wish I would've given her more of a mouthful, but I was too distracted by Cooper bent over in pain.

I knew. I definitely knew right in that moment where I was going to have to take her. It still didn't make it any easier. I'm not sure my father and brother could've made me feel any smaller while we were at the optometry office. I'm used to that at home, but Cooper having to see me in that state, truly having to experience my family dynamic, was not something I was ever anticipating. No one sees that side of my life, and that's definitely on purpose.

Regardless, I guess I have to say it was worth it. Cooper's eye is totally back to normal today, or so she says. I swear she keeps squinting it.

I shake my head, sliding my headphones off my ears and telling myself to let it go. I don't even know why I'm so worked up over the whole thing.

"You kids go ahead and get out of here," Ms. Rose's voice sounds behind me, making me turn away from the shelf I've been organizing to look at her.

I glance over at the clock, seeing that it's only 4:30 p.m.

"Are you sure, Ms. Rose?" Cooper asks. "We still have a half hour."

I chuckle under my breath, rolling my eyes. Cooper doesn't *have* any hours. She has zero obligation to be here, yet she feels bad leaving early. I don't know why anything from her surprises me anymore.

"Absolutely, Sara," Ms. Rose says. "It's Friday. Go soak up some sunshine and enjoy your weekend. I'm certainly going to."

"Okay then," Cooper smiles at her. "If you insist."

"I do," Ms. Rose nods, slinging her bag over her shoulder. "Have a great evening. I'll see you kids on Monday." She takes a few steps towards the door before she pauses, spinning back around. "Oh, well, actually," she says, "I suppose I'll just see you *kid* on Monday." She looks pointedly at Cooper, making her brows raise. "Today's Robbie's last day of detention."

My and Cooper's lips both part at the same time.

Shit, is it really?, I think, but instead, I nod and say, "That's right."

"Oh," Cooper says, looking over at me with an unreadable expression on her face.

"Well, thank you for all you've done, Robbie. It's been great getting to know you," Ms. Rose says. "I'm not one to listen to rumors anyways, but it turns out you're actually a very decent young man. It's been a pleasure having you in my library this last month."

A genuine smile pulls at my lips. "Thanks, Ms. Rose. It's actually been a lot of fun."

Ms. Rose flashes us a final grin and waves as she walks out. When I turn back around, I find Cooper back hard at work, flipping through a stack of books with her head down. I scoff out a laugh, walking over to her. "Cooper, would you give it a rest? She said we can go."

"I just want to get to a stopping place," she says, not looking at me as she spins around to slide a book onto the shelf behind her. When she turns back to her stack of books, I lean up against the bookshelf. As she spins back around with another book, I stick my hand in the open spot on the shelf she's moving to place it in, stopping the book in its tracks.

"Would you look at that?" I say. "A stopping place. You're welcome."

She rolls her eyes at me, dropping the book back onto the stack. "Gee, thanks so much," she deadpans. "What will I ever do without you now?" She gets behind the cart, rolling it back behind the library counter.

"Oh, come on, Cooper, admit it," I say, following after her.

She parks the cart and heads into Ms. Rose's office. "And what am I admitting?" she asks.

I walk in behind her, plopping down on top of Ms. Rose's desk as Cooper starts to gather her things. "That you're gonna miss me so much."

She pauses as she's unzipping her backpack, looking up at me. She stares at me for a moment before she chuckles. "Yeah, I don't think so. Do you have any idea how much money I'm going to save on Tylenol and Jolt Cola now?"

"You and I both know you'd drink the Jolt regardless," I tell her. "And besides, Cooper, I think you secretly enjoy me wearing you out."

It's not until she raises her brows at me that I really think about what I just said. I don't address it though, my tongue pushing into the side of my cheek as I hold back a smirk.

Cooper narrows her eyes at me. "I get plenty worn out without needing any extra help from you," she says, then starts shuffling around the contents of her backpack, looking for something.

My mind is clearly in the absolute gutter at the moment, because a vague image flashes through my head of Cooper...*wearing herself out.*

I blink hard, pushing it away.

Get a grip, Summers.

"Maybe so," I say. "But, you know, it's okay to want things you don't need. Some would say it's even good for you once in awhile."

She continues looking through her bag, barely glancing in my direction as she questions me. "What are you even saying?"

Then, at the same moment, her and I both spot what she's

obviously been searching for. Her little red journal is sitting right behind me on Ms. Rose's desk.

Open.

The scribblings of her curly handwriting in every color and form of writing utensil jump out at me. I swallow, forcing my eyes out of focus as I reach down and pick up the notebook, standing up from the desk and handing it to her. Her cheeks are several shades of pink darker as she takes it from me.

"I was just saying," I continue, "it's okay to loosen up once in a while, Cooper. It's alright to let go."

"I don't have time to let go," she says, not meeting my eyes.

I tilt my head at her as she stuffs her journal into her backpack and pulls out her Groovy Movie vest. The words just slip out of me in a near whisper.

"I wish you'd take the time anyways."

Her face softens as she looks up at me, and, even though it was really a thought meant to stay in my head, I don't regret saying it out loud. I just have a feeling.

Letting go would look good on her.

I definitely keep *that* thought to myself though.

Silence stretches between us for a long few seconds, Cooper not having replied. I clear my throat, deciding to soothe the awkward tension. "You know, you'd have plenty more time if you didn't spend your free afternoons in the library." I step over to her, bumping her shoulder with mine. "*Nerd.*"

Cooper's eyebrows pinch together before she lets out a laugh, shaking her head. "Yeah, you're right. I'm totally going to miss you *so* much," she says, her voice full of sarcasm.

I grab my backpack and follow her as she walks out of the office and heads for the library exit door. "Well, at least you're not entirely rid of me yet. We've still got the Homecoming dance next Saturday."

Cooper stops in her tracks in the doorway. She blows out a breath, slowly turning to look at me. "I was wondering if you were going to bring that up."

"Well, I did," I nod. "And *yes*, we have to go."

She throws her head back dramatically, groaning. "I swear we *just* had a dance."

"Yeah. And now it's time for another one. It's high school. We have dances. It's *fun*, remember?"

She grumbles a bunch of words I can't make out, pushing through the door far more aggressively than necessarily.

"You know, I guess you don't *have* to go," I say, following her out into the empty hallway.

"*Really?*" Cooper asks, perking up.

"Yeah," I shrug, slipping on my sunglasses. "And then everyone will just question why you aren't there at the dance with me. That'll just look a *little* odd. Especially considering you will have just given your winning student body president speech the day before."

Her spine steels, the smile fading from her face.

"Yeah," I nod. "People will probably think that's just a *tiny* bit weird that we'd break up the day you win president and the day before Homecoming, but it's fine. I'm sure no one will think the whole thing was a sham–"

"*Fine*," she groans. "I get it. I'll go."

"That's what I thought."

She presses her lips together. "But if I bomb my speech and know I'm losing the election, I'm not going."

I tilt my head at her. *Yeah, right.*

"Fair enough," I agree. "I'll pick you up for the football game at 4:45 next Saturday."

"*Game?*" she questions. "Why do we have to go to the game?"

"Because, Cooper, *everybody* goes to the game. It's *Homecoming*. You go to the game at five o'clock and then to the dance at eight." I start to look at her like she's crazy, but then it occurs to me.

Of course she doesn't know this information. She's never participated in any of this stuff before. This stuff that just seems like second nature to me now. That fact sends a weird feeling through my chest.

"Well, I can't go," she shakes her head, starting to walk down the hall again. "I have work until nine on Saturdays."

"Work?" I question her. "Can't you request off?"

"No, actually, I can't," she snaps back. "I need to work, Robbie."

I open my mouth, but no words come out, realization hitting me again of just how different my and Cooper's high school lives have been. Of course I'd just assume she can take work off. None of my friends really have jobs, and the few that do just have them for fun, to kill time or earn some pocket money to buy cigarettes or beer without having to use their parents' money. And for the second time in the last minute, I feel like a total prick.

"We are usually pretty slow on Saturday nights," Cooper says, "so I'll see if I can get off by 8:30. I can bring a change of clothes for the dance with me to Groovy Movie and you can just pick me up from there. We can be *fashionably late* for the dance." She drawls the words, mimicking me. "But, I'm sorry, I can't make the game. I'm already going to have to take off some time around finals to study, so I just can't swing that."

She's already factoring in and planning for the time she's going to have to take off nearly three months from now? That pain in my chest intensifies, forcing me to rub my hand over my heart. "Alright, that's fine, Cooper," I say. "Don't worry about it. We'll get it worked out."

Her eyes stay on the floor as she nods at me.

I reach the front door of the school first and pull it open, standing to the side for Cooper to walk through it. We both end up pausing in the doorway, however, when a loud crack of thunder goes off and we catch sight of the heavy rain pouring from the sky.

"*Oh*," Cooper gasps.

"Well, so much for the sunshine Ms. Rose was talking about," I say.

We step outside under the protection of the overhang, but before the door closes, Cooper stops it with her hand. "I'm gonna go grab my umbrella from my locker."

I can see the gears working behind her eyes as she fidgets with her Groovy Movie vest in her other hand. There's no way she can walk to work in this weather, but something tells me that if I offer to drive her again, she'll bite my head off.

The *something* is having spent nearly every day of the last three weeks with this girl. I know how she operates now, and there's not a chance in hell she'd ever let me or anyone else think she needs our help.

"Okay," I nod.

"I'll see you Monday I guess," she says, her eyes shifting between me and the dark sky behind me.

"Yeah, alright." It's on the tip of my tongue to ask her if she's like a ride even though I know the answer, but I don't. Instead, I secretly hope she'll swallow her pride and ask me herself.

"Okay, bye," she says, inching back inside the school.

No such luck.

"See ya, Cooper." I turn away from her and grab my headphones from around my neck. I slide them back onto my head, but I don't hit the play button on my tape just yet. I take the few stairs down at a ridiculously slow pace, keeping my ears open as I pretend to fiddle with my Walkman. Just as I reach the bottom of the stairs and have accepted that Cooper is determined to rent movies out fully soaked this evening, I hear her voice.

"Um...Robbie?"

Bingo.

I push my headphones off, hiding the smirk that's come to my face as I look back at her. "Yeah, Cooper?"

"Could you... I mean, do you think... Would you maybe mind—"

"C'mon, Cooper." I nod in the direction of the parking lot. "I'll give you a ride to work."

She doesn't meet my eyes as she mumbles a red-faced *"Thank you."*

We both jog to the short distance to my Camaro, ducking inside and closing the doors to the quickly worsening downpour. We don't say anything as I pull out of the parking lot, me focusing on the road and Cooper too busy putting on her work vest and sorting out her damp hair. As we approach the first red light, the weather and traffic report playing on the radio comes to an end, and I instantly smile when the following song starts playing, the piano intro all too familiar to me. I start nodding along to the melody, getting ready for the lyrics to begin.

"*Highway run—*"

My head snaps to the right when the song cuts off suddenly, replaced by the garbled staticky sound of the radio scanning for another station. My response is so reflexive, I don't even know what's happening before I'm snapping my middle finger and thumb against Cooper's hand, making her jolt and pull her hand away from the dial.

"*Ow!*" she yelps, holding her hand to her chest. She looks between her hand and me with wide eyes several times before asking, "Did you just *flick* me?"

The light turns green and I take off. I reach for the dial, tuning the radio back to the original station, glancing over at Cooper over top of my sunglasses as the song resumes once again. "I did. And you deserved the flick."

"*Why?*"

I hold my finger up, shaking it at her. "You don't turn Journey off in Linda."

"*Linda?*" she repeats.

I simply double tap my knuckle on the dashboard.

Cooper's brows raise. "You named your junk Hank...and named your car...*Linda?*"

"Beautiful, ain't she?" I ask, glossing over the first part of her question.

"If I say she's gorgeous, will you let me change the station?"

I shake my head, grabbing my chest like I've been fatally wounded. In fact, I think I have. "Cooper, you're hurting me. They're from our very own Bay Area."

"Who is?"

"Journey!" I snap.

She rears back. "Okay...? That's great. Go, Bay Area. Their song is still making me fall asleep."

I scoff, incredulous as I shoot her a look.

"What's the big deal?" she asks. "The song's just slow."

I bark out a laugh. "*You're* slow."

She just blinks at me.

Wow, good one, Robbie.

Hey, *cut me some slack. I'm under duress here.*

"So is that a yes to changing it...or...?"

I shoot daggers at Cooper, and she pauses her reach towards the radio again. "Cooper, I think we need to add to our ground rules."

"Don't you think it's a little late in the game for that?"

I ignore her question, holding up three fingers. "In this car, we worship the Father, the Son, and *the* Steve Perry." Cooper opens her mouth to argue, but I cut her off. "And I won't hear any more disrespect from you on the matter, young lady."

She lets out a scoff. "But–"

"Hey, look at that!" I grin, pulling into the Groovy Movie parking lot. "We're here anyways. So it doesn't even matter."

Cooper's still staring at me open-mouthed as I come to a stop right in front of the building. She shakes her head at me, an exasperated half-smile coming to her face. "You're ridiculous. You know that, right?"

"Oh, I know it. But I love it when you remind me, baby." I wink at her and she makes a show of pretending to gag as she opens the door.

I sneak a chuckle out before she can turn back around to face me. "Thank you for the ride," she says.

I tilt my head at her. "Well, we couldn't have you coming down with pneumonia before the big election."

"Yeah, I suppose that would have been pretty tragic." She laughs, somewhat uncomfortably. "Well...I really appreciate it. Thanks again."

"Don't mention it."

She nods, giving me a small wave as she moves to close the door.

"*Hey, Cooper?*" I call after her.

She turns back, ducking down to look at me. "Yeah?"

I turn around grabbing my backpack from the back seat. I open the front pocket, digging through it for a few seconds before I find the flash of dark blue that I'm looking for. "Here," I say, tossing her my Journey *Frontiers* cassette tape. She barely catches it, bouncing it in her hands a few times before getting a firm grip on it. Once she does, she stares down at it, her brows pulling together. I wait until she looks back up at me again.

"Educate yourself over the weekend, will you?" I tell her.

"Um, I–"

"Bye, Cooper," I say, giving her a tight grin and motioning for her to shut the door.

She does, and I take off the minute she steps back, wondering as I pull out of the parking lot of Groovy Movie if I'll ever see the cassette of my favorite album again.

twenty-three

SARA

It's quiet. *Too quiet.*

I always found so much comfort in the silence of the empty library in the afternoons. It was honestly my favorite time of day, the only time I could really hear myself think. But now, my thoughts just feel entirely too loud.

As much as it felt like Robbie had crashed my serenity space when he started his detention sentence here—and as much as I hate to admit this—I really grew accustomed to him over the last month.

I got used to the silence being replaced with the sound of his foot tapping and him humming along to his music. I adapted to the once empty space around me being taken up by him, the movements of him pushing around book carts or bobbing his head to whatever song he was listening to becoming a fixture in my peripheral vision. Even though my library volunteer shifts used to be an hour where I would fully zone out of the rest of life and focus in on my task at hand, and even though he may have driven me crazy the first week, I learned to appreciate the interruption and brain break of Robbie asking me questions every few minutes, whether they be related to the library or entirely random.

I always knew his time here had an expiration date on it, and I was completely fine with that. I had zero attachment to Robbie Summers. If anything, I'd call it the opposite of that. Or, at least...*I would have*. But now, it's Monday, and it's the first afternoon in a month that he hasn't been here with me.

I should be thrilled. I should be frolicking through the bookshelves and thanking my lucky stars that my afternoons are my own again. But instead, in the barely five minutes I've been in the library, I've already lost track of the amount of times I've glanced up or over my shoulder, just expecting to see Robbie there.

But he isn't, and then I feel silly. Without him here, and with Ms. Rose running errands around the school, I keep finding myself clearing my throat just to break the silence.

It doesn't help.

Just a minute ago, I turned a corner and found a wadded up piece of notebook paper on the ground, and instead of picking it up with the intention of tossing it in the trash, my first reaction was to scoop it up and throw it at Robbie.

Only, Robbie isn't here.

I let out a breath as I walk through the door to Ms. Rose's office, setting a stack of books down on her desk. I stand there for a moment, just listening to the quiet nothingness. You could hear a pin drop, only the sound of my steady breathing filling the space. I run my hands through my hair, then glance up at the office door. I immediately look away, irritated with myself for picturing Robbie leaning up against the door frame. I imagine what snide remark he'd make. Or what goofy unwarranted comment he'd offer. Or what ridiculous question he'd ask me. It would all depend on his mood. I start to feel like I may be going insane when I swear I hear "*Cooper?*" echoing in my ears.

I shake my head, digging through my backpack for the candy bar I put in there earlier, looking for a distraction. I still have nearly forty minutes to kill. Forty minutes until I can leave and not be constantly reminded of Robbie. It's not until I find the Charleston Chew bar at the bottom of my backpack that I remember I'm going dress shopping with Alice after school today. Dress shopping for the Homecoming dance...with *Robbie*. I groan, tearing open the end of the candy bar wrapper and taking a bite. I let out a hum of satisfaction at the chewy nougat chocolate bar, telepathically thanking my mom for leaving it for me on the kitchen counter this morning.

As I take another bite, a flash of silver in my backpack catches my eye. I pull open my backpack and spot the Walkman staring back at me. I purse my lips, thinking back on my weekend.

I slept restlessly on Friday night, then found myself wide awake and staring at my ceiling by six in the morning. After multiple failed attempts at falling back asleep, I gave up, kicking my covers off.

By the time my mom was up and making breakfast at nine o'clock, I had already finished all of my homework and studying I had planned to do over the weekend, and even gotten ahead.

I cleaned the kitchen after breakfast, then found myself wandering back into my room, not sure what to do with myself for the next several hours until I had to leave for work. I tried to start working on my scholarship essay, but found myself too anxious to focus on it, my mind continually wandering to the class election this coming Friday and the speech I have to give for it. I switched to attempting to write my speech, but then I just felt like I was going to throw up, so I gave up on that too.

I pushed harshly away from my desk, and when I did so, my backpack that had been hanging by a strap on the back of my chair slipped off. I spun around as I heard some of the contents skittering across the floor. I let out a heavy breath as I bent down to pick up the small items that had slid out, and I found my head tilting when my gaze locked in on the little blue cassette tape. The one Robbie had tossed at me the day before, for reasons I still don't understand.

I had completely forgotten about it, shoving the thing inside my bag as I walked into Groovy Movie after Robbie peeled away from me in his Camaro. I picked it up then, examining it for the first time. The cassette was colored dark blue, with artwork of some sort of alien figure pictured along with the band and album name.

I knew a few Journey songs. They were good, I guess. But I didn't understand why Robbie was so hellbent on me listening to this album. Or why he had felt the need to inflict pain on me for changing the station during one of their songs.

"*Lunatic*," I muttered to myself as I stood back up.

I started to shove the cassette back into my backpack, but I hesitated, flipping the tape over to look at the back side.

"You have work today, right, hon?"

I startled at my mom's voice, looking up to see her applying her mascara in the mirror next to my doorway, dressed in her work uniform.

"Yep, like always," I nodded.

"Alright. Well, be safe. There's leftover meatloaf in the fridge."

My brows pulled together, a memory instantly popping into my head of Robbie saying he'd expect my favorite food to be meatloaf. I still didn't know what I thought of that.

"Okay. Thanks, Mom," I replied.

"Sure, hon. Well, I'm off now," Mom said, dropping her mascara into her purse. "Have a good evening. I won't be back until late. Love you." She moved away from the doorway, heading for the front door.

"Alright, love you too," I said. Then, something pushed my feet forward. "*Hey*, Mom?"

"Yeah, hon?" she questioned, spinning to face me with her hand on the door handle.

"Do you mind if I borrow your Walkman?" I asked her.

"Oh," she said, her brows pulling together. "Sure, hon. Of course. It's in my nightstand in my bedroom."

"Cool, thanks," I smiled at her. "Have a good shift."

She tossed me a wink before walking out of the door.

I quickly found the Walkman right where she said it'd be, and attached it to my hip before sliding the Journey tape inside and placing the headphones over my ears. I needed to clear my head, and cleaning always helped me to do that. I decided to start in my bedroom, pressing play on the tape.

The first track caught me off guard as it began, the fast-paced addictive melody instantly putting me in the zone. As much as I mentally tried to fight it, the *Separate Ways* song sucked me in, and, before I knew it, I had cleaned every room in the house from top to bottom and listened to the entire album two and a half times through. I ended up continuing to listen as I got ready for work and even ended up taking the Walkman with me for my walk to Groovy Movie.

By Sunday evening, I knew the album front and back, and by this morning, as I was snagging the Walkman from my desk after failing to convince myself to leave it at home, I was cursing Robbie Summers for being right about something.

I loved it. I loved the entire thing. I couldn't get the songs out of my head. Even the one from his car that I had tried to change, *Faithfully*. I might have truly deserved that flick after all. That song is a religious experience. I have chills all over my body just thinking about it now

It took everything in me not to use the Walkman in the halls during the passing periods today where I cross paths with Robbie, or at lunch while I was studying at one of the tables out in the courtyard while he was tossing a football around with some of his basketball teammates. I knew he'd ask questions, and I was not prepared to admit defeat. *But now...*

Well, he's not here now, is he?

A mischievous smile comes to my lips as I pull the Walkman out of my backpack. I hook it onto the front pocket of my jeans, sliding the headphones onto my head as I make my way back into the library. I weave my way through the rows of bookshelves, finding the full book cart I previously abandoned back here when my mind was too all over the place to focus and I put four books in a row in completely the wrong spot.

I weave the fingers of each of my hands together, stretch my arms over my head.

Well, we're not gonna have that issue now.

Book cart, prepare to meet your maker.

I hit the play button, and the intro the *Separate Ways* starts flowing through my headphones.

Game on.

I start putting away books like it's nobody's business, my head bobbing along to the music. As the song builds, so does my pace. I feel like I'm stuck in a trance, totally alone in my own world as I put away book after book, barely needing to glance at the covers before I'm already drifting exactly towards where they need to go. The further into the song I get, the fancier I get with my movements, doing a little shimmy as I slide the book on to the shelf or adding in a little spin as I'm turning corners of aisles.

By the second chorus, I'm fully using the library as my dance floor, my eyes half closed as I sway my head from side to side, mouthing along to the lyrics that are basically imprinted on my brain at this point. I start to question if I'm going crazy when the lights of the library suddenly seem like spotlights between the bookshelves, and I *know* I'm crazy when the blurry image of Robbie leaning up against a bookshelf and grinning at me flashes through my mind mid-spin. The moment I'm back forward, facing the bookshelf, the chorus hits again, and I throw my head back, bobbing it back and forth, whisper-shouting the lyrics into the silent space.

"*Someday, love will find you! Break those chains that bind you!*"

My eyes flutter open slightly, and I catch a flash of movement behind me.

Then I register that I am, in fact, *not* crazy.

Because Robbie *is* leaning up against a bookshelf, with his arms crossed, grinning at me.

I throw my headphones off of my head so fast that it nearly rips a wad of hair out of my scalp. I don't know what to do with my hands, alternating between trying to casually hang them at my sides and grappling for the book cart and attempting to nonchalantly grab onto the bookshelf behind me. I eventually settle for one hand on the book cart and one on my hip.

"Hi," I say, blowing a strand of hair out of my face.

Robbie's brows raise, his smile spreading. "Hi."

"You're here," I state, not knowing what else to say. Then I become aware of the faint sounds of music still playing and glance down, stabbing the stop button on my Walkman far more aggressively than necessary.

Robbie's eyes flick down to follow my movement, then settle back on my face, his smile never wavering. "I am," he nods.

"But you don't have to be," I say.

He tilts his head, his tongue pressing into his bottom lip. "Whatcha listening to, Cooper?"

"Music," I blurt. I have to refrain from smacking my palm against my forehead, instead deciding to look very enthralled with one of the books on the cart.

"Oh, okay," Robbie nods. "Because I totally thought it was the Gettysburg Address."

My head snaps up, my brows raising. "'No taxation without representation' *and* the Gettysburg Address? Are you sure you don't come from a family of historians? Truly, I'm impressed."

Robbie winces, but quickly plays it off. If I didn't realize after our visit to Summers Optometry, I definitely know now that Robbie's family is a sore subject for him. I open my mouth to try to apologize, but Robbie cuts me off, glazing over the subject completely.

"Excuse me for asking," he says, pushing off the bookshelf and taking a few steps closer to me. "It's just that you seemed really into whatever *music* you were listening to."

I feel heat rush to my cheeks and look away from him. "It was alright, I guess," I mutter.

"So *alright* that it made you," Robbie holds up a finger, spinning it around in a circle, "do a little twirl?"

I drop the book in my hands back onto the cart. "I did not *twirl*."

"Oh, don't worry, Cooper," Robbie says, holding up his hands and leaning in closer. "It was the cutest little twirl I've ever seen."

I turn to fully face him, putting my hand on my hip. "Sorry, why did you say you were here? You just couldn't stay away from me?"

Robbie shakes his head, suppressing a grin. And after all the time I've spent with him, I know, for now, that he'll let this go. I let out a subtle sigh of relief as Robbie says, "Coach Parsons called a meeting with the senior basketball players after school today to plan for try-outs."

"Oh," I say. "I guess the season is coming up."

"Try-outs are in two weeks," he nods.

A silence settles between us for a few moments as I'm pretty sure we're both thinking the same thing. There won't be any more *us* by that time. Suddenly, two weeks seems like both one second and an entire lifetime away.

"It's too bad. I guess you're gonna miss out on being my Bleacher Babe, huh?" Robbie says, breaking the trance we've found ourselves in.

"Your *what?*" I ask, rearing back.

Robbie lets out a chuckle. "You know, my *Bleacher Babe*. One of the girlfriends that sits on the sideline wearing a t-shirt with their boyfriend's name and number on the back and does little cheers." He holds up his hands, making a cheerleading type motion.

"That's a real thing?"

"Afraid it is," Robbie confirms. "You know, some even consider it an *honor*, Cooper."

"Well I guess that's a good thing. You'll have a whole line of girls ready to take my place."

Robbie's brows pinch for a second before he nods. "Yeah, I guess so."

A weird feeling twists through my stomach. Even though I brought up the *whole line of girls*, the image of them in my head right now leaves a bad taste in my mouth. "I'm sure Denise would love to do it," I say, trying to mask the tightness in my throat.

"Yeah," Robbie agrees, his voice low. "She would."

"I guess I wouldn't mind having a t-shirt," I blurt out before my brain even has time to process the words.

I slowly look up at Robbie to find his forehead creased. "Yeah?"

"I mean, I believe I'll have earned it after being your fake girlfriend for a whole month. I think it's only fair for all my trouble."

Robbie snorts, a smirk pulling at his lips. He takes a step closer, resting his hand on the book cart next to my hip. "*You're* trouble, Cooper."

I roll my lips into my mouth, trying not to smile, and Robbie's eyes flick down to watch me do it before meeting my eyes again.

My mind starts racing at a million miles an hour as Robbie and I stare at each other. I start to remember all of the things I have to do and worry about over the coming week. Hell, the coming *months*. A stupid t-shirt should be the last thing on my mind. Much less a t-shirt for the sake of Robbie Summers. I'm sure I won't hear another word from him the minute Homecoming is over. The minute he has Denise back on his arm and I win student body president...or *don't*. I feel my smile fade from my face. I guess it won't really matter to him at that point. I swallow hard, suddenly feeling very foolish. I force my eyes away from Robbie's, my gaze trailing down to his chest. I start to turn back towards the book cart, but Robbie nudges my shoulder with his.

"Hey."

I glance up at him hesitantly, and he tilts his at me.

"I'll get you a shirt, Cooper."

My lips press together as I search for the hint of sarcasm or teasing in his tone or on his face, but I can't find it. "Okay," I breathe.

Robbie's throat bobs, something conflicting flashing through his eyes before he steels himself, taking a step back from me. "How are you feeling about this Friday? The election? Your speech?" he asks.

I blow a breath out of my nose, irritated with the way he can seem to read my mind. "I'm trying not to feel anything at all about any of it." I pick up a stack of books from the cart, turning around to put them away on the bookshelf behind us.

"I overheard Jesse and Paul talking at our basketball meeting,"

Robbie says, coming around to lean against the bookshelf at my side. "Ginger dropped out of the race."

"What?" I question, nearly dropping the book in my hand. "*Why?*"

"This is a *good* thing, Cooper."

"But why did she drop out?"

Robbie crosses his arms, a mischievous grin spreading across his face.

"What is it?" I ask, raising an eyebrow at him. "Tell me."

Robbie's tongue pushes into the side of his cheek. "She didn't think she had a chance against you."

My lips part, and I shake my head, not believing it for a second. "That's really funny, Robbie," I deadpan.

"It's not a joke," he insists.

I look at him and can see in his face that he's serious. "You heard someone say that?"

He nods. "Paul."

Paul and Ginger are close. I'm pretty sure they've dated on and off all of junior high and high school. Something in me knows that if Paul said that, it's the truth. I just have no idea of *how* it's the truth.

"But...why?" I mutter. "How? Why would she feel that way?"

"Because everything is going exactly according to plan, Cooper. Don't you see it?"

"See what?"

Robbie scoffs a laugh. "You really haven't noticed it? The way everybody looks at you when you walk into a room? You haven't heard them all whispering?"

My brows knit together. "I mean, sure. I've seen some people looking at us—"

"Not us," Robbie says. "*You*, Cooper. They're all fascinated with you."

"Because I'm with *you*," I retort.

Robbie shakes his head. "Maybe for the first week. But now you've got everyone's attention all on your own."

My mouth falls open, my brain clouding with this absurd

information. I know this was what I hoped for when I agreed to Robbie's deal, but...I guess I just never thought in a million years that it would actually *work*. That there would be a world where *Ginger Matthews* would be intimidated by *me*.

"I also heard something else," Robbie says, pulling me from my thoughts.

"What's that?" I ask.

"The other couple of other people that signed up to run either didn't meet the qualifications or never followed through on turning in their paperwork," Robbie states. My back straightens, realization hitting me. "So it's just–"

"*Me and Jesse.*"

"You and Jesse," Robbie confirms.

A boulder settles its weight on top of my chest. "Wow," I mumble.

"Cooper."

"Yeah?" I croak. My gaze raises, and I find Robbie's eyes darting between mine.

"I meant what I said. I don't know if it makes me an evil genius, but this plan...our arrangement...it's going exactly like I told you it would. You really *do* have all the attention on you." He takes a step closer to me. "Now, the question is, what are you gonna do with it?"

I swallow against the gravel in my throat. "I guess I'm gonna try to win this damn election."

"Damn right you are," Robbie nods, smirking. "Do you want all this time we've spent together to be for nothing?"

"Oh, God," I shake my head. "Well, when you put it that way..."

"There we go."

"Yeah, I don't know about what weird crap you're into," I say, "but I'm no masochist."

"Cooper, I may be into plenty of weird crap, but masochism surely isn't one of those things," Robbie insists. "We can go over the rest of the things on the list though if you're free later–"

"No, really," I hold up a hand, "that won't be necessary."

Robbie chuckles, which makes me chuckle. I let out a sigh, rolling my eyes at him.

"You know, you've got this, Cooper." I look up at Robbie, waiting for another punchline to hit. But it doesn't. He ducks his head, holding my eyes. "I mean it. I believe in you."

I blink back at him, not believing myself.

Because I think I might actually believe that he believes in me.

twenty-four

ROBBIE

I shake my head, taking a bite of my sandwich as I hit the play button on my Walkman, Van Halen's *1984* album beginning to flow through my headphones. I glance over at Cooper, watching her from five tables across the courtyard.

Why is Cooper five tables across the courtyard?, you ask?

Because apparently my mere presence was distracting her. My existence alone was going to drive her to her breaking point. I was *so* bothersome, that she had to put twenty-five feet of space between us.

I roll my eyes behind my sunglasses.

First, we had an argument over how I was crunching my Doritos (*How does one* not *crunch Doritos?*). Then, she forbade me from *looking* at her (*Where was I supposed to look? We were sitting alone together at a table*). Next, we had a minor (*major*) disagreement following my asking Cooper if she could stop clicking her pen (*like, non-stop clicking—I thought I was going to go insane*). Then, finally, when my *breathing*, of all things, wasn't to her liking (*Seriously?*), Cooper declared she was sitting on her own for the rest of lunch today to work on her speech.

I get that she's stressed. I know there's a lot riding on this for her. *Everything*, really. But she has it in the bag. I don't know how I know, but I just know.

She's played her part perfectly throughout this whole month. There's not a guy in this school that doesn't look Cooper's way when she walks past them—on *my* arm, of course. But that just makes them look even more. Same for the girls. I couldn't tell you if they love her or hate her, but they *envy* her. And that's all that matters. The guys will vote for her because they *want* her, and the girls will vote for her because they want to *be* her.

Either way, in the end, she comes out on top.

Right where she belongs.

I look up at her again, but she doesn't look at me. Cooper's totally in her own bubble over there. Her gray eyes are glued to the notebook in front of her, her brows pulled together in concentration. She keeps alternating between writing, chewing on the top of her pen, and scratching out what she's written. Usually in that order. On repeat.

I watch as a strand of hair falls from her scrunchie ponytail and into her line of sight. She blows the lock of hair away from her face as she reaches for her can of Jolt, taking a long sip. Now that I think about it, I'm pretty sure that's the third one she's had today. There's no way that's helping her nerves or her already testy temper. I consider saying something to her, but decide against it. She'll just fight me on it, so there's no point. Her speech is the day after tomorrow. I'll let her focus on that.

Although, she might have some difficulty giving her speech if she doesn't sleep for the next two nights due to all the caffeine she's inhaling.

Whatever. She's fine, I tell myself.

I stand up with a huff, crumpling my sandwich wrapper and Doritos bag into a ball before tossing it into the trash can on my way inside, not allowing myself to look back at Cooper as I do it.

After going to the bathroom, I stop at the vending machine in the hall on my way back outside. I dig a couple of coins out of my pocket, feeding them into the machine and hitting the button for Pepsi. I bend over to retrieve my soda from the little flap door at the bottom of the machine, and when I stand back up, I find myself face to face with Jesse Lamonte.

"Hey, Robbie," he says.

My spine steels, and I try my best not to show how caught off guard I am on my face as I slide my headphones off my head. "Hey, man. What's up?"

Jesse glances around before looking back at me. "Where's your girl?"

I tilt my head at him, squeezing my can of Pepsi tightly in my hand. I don't know why, but I didn't like the look in his eyes when he asked me that. My first urge is to ask him, *What's it to you?* But, after a deep breath, I relax slightly. "She's outside." I nod towards the door just behind him.

Jesse takes a step back, peering through the glass window on the door. I can see the moment his eyes lock on Cooper, and something about it makes my skin crawl. "What's she doing out there?"

"Waiting for me to get back to her."

It was the opposite of the truth, but he didn't need to know that.

"Oh," Jesse says, his lips pressing together. He throws one more look in her direction, and I feel my patience wearing dangerously thin.

"Why do you ask, Jesse? Don't you have your own girl to worry about?"

"No reason," he replies, completely ignoring my second question. "She just seems to be working really hard on something out there."

"She's always working really hard." I flash him a fake grin. "Now, if you'll excuse me–"

Before I can get around him, Jesse's hand shoots out to grip my arm. "Is it her speech?"

I turn my head slowly, my gaze cutting into him. I flick my eyes down to his hand on my arm, and he instantly drops it.

Smart man.

"And what if it is?" I ask him, my voice low.

Jesse shakes his head slowly. "C'mon, man."

"What?" I question him.

He exhales, his jaw tight. "Don't you think it's time to give it a rest?"

I scoff. "I'm sure I don't have a damn clue what you're talking about, man."

"This is getting ridiculous. Why don't you just tell little Sara Beth she can call off the charade?"

My shoulders stiffen, anger flowing through my blood like boiling water. "Two things, Lamonte." I hold up two fingers. "*One*, I don't know who the hell you think you are, talking to me like *this* and calling my girlfriend *that*." Jesse's throat bobs roughly as I take a step closer. "And *two*," I drop my second finger, "*what* charade?"

Jesse looks away, flexing his jaw. "Look, man, I get it."

"And what exactly do you get?"

"You're pissed," he says, flicking his eyes back to mine with fire in his gaze. "You're pissed about Denise. Pissed that, for *once* in your life, you lost."

My mouth falls open, my brows knitting together.

"You've made your point," he continues. "I hear you, loud and clear. Now tell Sara to drop out of the student body president race already."

A choked laugh comes out of me. "*Excuse me?*"

"I get that you're butthurt that I stole your girl, *alright?*" Jesse says, throwing his hands in the air. "Yeah, it was a dick move of me. But, if you haven't noticed, you're kind of a dick *all the time*. And I've still been your friend all these years."

"*Some friend*," I mutter under my breath, incredulous.

"But this is my future we're talking about here," Jesses continues. "I *need* this."

"And you think she *doesn't?*" I practically growl, getting in his face. "You think she's just running for student body president because *I* want her to? To get back at *you?*"

I shake my head in disbelief, my rage blurring the edges of my vision. I don't even know what's going through my head right now. I'm caught between staggering relief that the *charade* Jesse was referring to was this ridiculous concept and not my and Cooper's relationship and dumbfounding anger that he thinks of Cooper as someone who could be so easily manipulated. As someone without their own hopes and dreams. Someone he can just *take* this away from.

"What about *her* future?" I demand.

"Dude," Jesse shakes his head, a humorless smile pulling at his lips. "Who even *is* she?"

My eyes narrow at him. I stay calm, slowly standing up to my full height. I slip my sunglasses back on, rolling my lips into my mouth. "She's the girl that's gonna kick your ass in this election." I step back, pulling open the door to outside.

I take a step, then pause in the doorway, looking back. "And Jesse?"

His dark eyes snap up to meet mine, his nostrils flaring. I immediately smile in response, cracking open my Pepsi and taking a sip.

"I didn't lose a damn thing. I never do. Don't forget that."

twenty-five

SARA

Click.

I feel like I'm gonna be sick.

Click. Click.

My head feels so foggy. Between the lack of sleep and non-stop nerves I've been experiencing over the last week, my mind is in overdrive. I can't even think clearly.

Click.

Every time I try to, it feels like my brain is a swamp and I'm having to wade knee-deep through the deepest, murkiest, swirling pools of thoughts to find just one that makes any logical sense.

Huh. That's pretty good.

I drop the camera from my face, leaving it to hang around my neck as I reach into my back pocket for my journal. I turn away, grabbing the pencil from behind my ear and scribbling down the thought onto a page. Once I'm done, I close the journal, and the moment I look up, I spot Robbie walking into the gym. He's with Brad and a couple of junior basketball players named Michael and Billy, but he doesn't look too engaged in their conversation, his head swiveling around like he's looking for something.

Or someone.

It's Denise, obviously.

I turn my head, looking around the gym, but find the cheerleaders all gathered in the far corner. Nowhere near where Robbie keeps looking. My gaze flicks between him and his line of sight, and I realize he keeps looking around the little stage riser set up in the middle of the gym.

The one that Jesse is standing off to the side of, chatting with Principal Whileyman.

The one I probably should've been standing by about ten minutes ago. I swallow hard.

Just a few more minutes. It'll be fine.

I raise my camera once again.

Click. Click.

A few minutes later, Principal Whileyman steps up on stage to open up the Homecoming pep rally, welcoming the cheerleaders to the floor.

Click. Click. Click.

I try to take pictures of every cheerleader *but* Denise, but my camera just keeps finding her.

Click. Cli–

My camera is suddenly ripped away from my face.

"Hey, what the–"

"What the hell do you think you're doing?"

I look up with wide eyes at the voice that cut me off, finding Alice standing in front of me.

"Oh, hi, Al," I say, forcing a tight smile to my face.

"Sara, why are you taking photos right now?" she demands, her dark brows furrowed.

"Well, it's kind of my job."

"Not today, it isn't. Your only job today is to get your ass on that stage and deliver your kickass speech."

"I... I will," I stammer. "I'm going to. But I need to take photos first. The newspaper. The yearbook–"

"Mr. Hughes will understand," Alice interrupts me. "He's

rooting for you more than anyone. You know it's more important to him that you're the editor of the yearbook than it is to have a hundred photos of this pep rally to choose from to include in it."

My lips press together, because I fully know that she's right. But if I stop taking pictures, then that makes this real. Then I really have to walk over to that stage. I'll have nothing else to occupy my mind other than the speech I'm about to give in front of the whole school. The speech I have to give to try to convince them to vote for *me* over Jesse Lamonte for student body president. The speech that will be my ticket to the yearbook editor position I've always wanted and very possibly to the future beyond high school that I've always dreamed of.

"But..." I mutter, my voice weak.

"Here," Alice says, gently pulling the camera strap from around my neck and placing it around her own. "I'll take pictures for you."

"What–*Really?* But I–"

"I got it, Sara," Alice insists. "Now get over to that stage and be ready to knock 'em dead."

I slowly nod. "Okay."

"You've got this, girl," Alice smiles, rubbing her hand softly over the side of my arm. "You deserve it."

I try my best to return her smile as I turn away from her, forcing my feet across the perimeter of the gym.

I try to make my way to the stage as quietly as possible behind where the cheerleaders are currently doing their routine. Though I am attempting to be as discreet as possible, I can feel the warmth of gazes on me. I don't allow myself to look towards the bleachers, keeping my eyes glued to the floor. When I'm halfway to the stage, I feel a particularly searing heat against the side of my face, and somehow I just know that Robbie's spotted me. I drop my head even further, him being the absolute last person I need to look at right now. I've had at least three nightmares in the last week that I froze on stage and ended up blurting out to the entire school that my and Robbie's relationship was a complete sham. I have no plans of doing that, but I don't need Robbie's face as a reminder of the possibility.

By the time I reach the stage, the cheerleaders are just finishing their routine.

"There you are, Ms. Cooper," Principal Whileyman says.

Jesse's head snaps in my direction as he says it, and I can visibly see him stiffen, a look of irritation washing over his face. I wonder what that's about. I try to replay the last few times I was around Jesse and what I could have done to make him angry with me, but I come up empty. If anything, *I* should be angry at *him* for that whole *Seven Minutes in Heaven* stunt. That's the least of my worries right now though. I give a gentle shake of my head, deciding to let it go.

"Sorry, Principal Whileyman," I say. "I had to take pictures for the yearbook."

"Oh, right. Of course," he nods, realization hitting him. "Mr. Hughes told me all about your yearbook work. Not a problem, dear. That's great actually. I'm just glad you made it." He gives me a genuine smile, and I return it, the stress in my shoulders settling some. "Get any good ones?"

"*Er*...Pictures?" I ask.

He nods.

"Yes, sir," I confirm. "Lots."

"Fantastic," Principal Whileyman says, clapping his hands. "Now, are you kids ready?"

"Uh–"

"Yes," Jesse says immediately, talking over me.

"Great. I'll just go up and get everything started. Would either one of you prefer to go first?"

"Me, sir," Jesse says before I even have a chance to take a breath.

I turn my head to look at him.

"Only if that's okay with you, Sara, of course," he says, not even meeting my eyes.

I find myself gritting my teeth. "Sure, Jesse. Whatever you need to make you most comfortable."

My patronizing tone finally forces him to look at me, and the look in his eyes is not a kind one. I don't let the grin on my face waver.

You are not going to bully me today, Jesse Lamonte.

If I lose, it's because I deserved to lose. Not because I let some spoiled rich kid taunt me out of even trying.

Maybe Sara from a month ago, but not Sara from today.

Not a chance.

"Alright, great," Principal Whileyman says, completely oblivious to the tension between me and Jesse, effectively ending our stare-off. "I'll introduce you first, Mr. Lamonte. Best of luck to both of you."

I feel my heart slowly drop into my stomach as Principal Whileyman ascends the stage. He taps the microphone on the podium to get everyone's attention, and when the gym grows silent, the ringing of my own thoughts in my head becomes deafening.

"Alright, everybody," Principal Whileyman begins, "I know we're all very excited to kick off Homecoming weekend here at Bay View." Cheers erupt from the crowd, and he waves his hands in the air, prompting everyone to settle down. "That's exactly what we plan to do at this pep rally, but we also have something else equally exciting happening this afternoon. In just a few minutes, you're going to be hearing from your student body president candidates, and then, you all, as a school, will get to vote on who will represent you this year."

More cheers sound, and I specifically pull out the handful of people shouting some form of "*Go Jesse!*" from the crowd. I blow out a steady breath, trying with everything I have to not let it phase me.

"You can pick up ballots at the gym door exits on your way out and drop them off at the front office once you've made your choice. The winner will be announced during the morning announcements this coming Monday." I start to tap my foot nervously, trying not to think about how I'll have to go all weekend without knowing whether or not I won. "Make your choice wisely. The person you select will not only be your student body president, but also the editor for this year's school yearbook.

You want to choose the person you feel best represents Bay View High as a whole. And, for you, seniors, the person you want responsible for maintaining the memory of your class for years to come. So, without further ado, let's hear first from Mr. Jesse Lamonte."

Applause, shouts, and whistles sound from all throughout the bleachers as Jesse steps up onto the stage, replacing Principal Whileyman at the podium. I cross my arms, steeling my spine as I get ready for Jesse to begin. I don't know how I feel about him going first. Part of me wishes that I could've gone first just to get it over with. But also, I guess there's some advantage to seeing what I'm up against. I shake my head, knowing, truly, that it wouldn't matter. Either way, I know I wouldn't be feeling great right now. There's nothing I can do to change it now. I just have to give it my all.

Principal Whileyman pats my shoulder as he steps off the stage, giving me a wink. Something about that comforts me. I try to tell myself he's secretly rooting for me. Not that it really matters. It's all in the hands of the students now.

Jesse lets out a sort of chuckle into the microphone as the cheers die down. "Well, well, well, here we are!" he says, and I resist the expression of annoyance that my face is trying to twist into. "You know, it feels natural to start this sort of thing out with the whole 'For those of you who don't know me' thing, but let's be real here. This is Bay View High, and I know you all know exactly who I am."

More claps and cheers erupt, and my stomach twists further with every single one.

"I'm Jesse. But, more importantly than who I am, is *what* I am. And that's a proven leader." Hoots and hollers burst from the room, making Jesse's smug smile only grow wider. "Throughout my three years here at Bay View, I've become a top honor student, an active community servant, a star debate team member, president of the Italian club, and the captain of the varsity basketball team."

A roar of deep cheers sounds from one area of the bleachers, and I just know it's the basketball team. I refuse to even glance that way, clenching my hands into fists to stop myself, because something tells me that if I see Robbie included in the mix, I may not make it on that stage.

"I've had my path set for as long as I can remember," Jesse continues. "I'm going off to UC Berkeley in the fall, and then I'll head to medical school to become a doctor. Being in this position is the perfect way to spend my senior year and the best way to cap off my high school experience. You all have known and trusted me to lead you these last three years. Let's finish off strong. Vote me for your student body president."

Jesse steps away from the podium, nodding and grinning towards the crowd as they burst into applause. I feel frozen in place as Principal Whileyman steps past me to get back on the stage. I barely register Jesse stepping down, other than the dirty look I know he threw in my direction. I don't have the energy to spare for him anymore.

This is it.

"Thank you for that, Mr. Lamonte," Principal Whileyman says into the microphone, clapping his hands. "And now, we have Ms. Sara Cooper."

My teeth sink hard into my lower lip the minute my name is said.

Walk, Sara. Walk, I tell myself.

Keeping my eyes on the floor, I make my way onto the stage, and am surprised when I hear a decently loud applause as I do. I mean, it doesn't have near the passion that Jesse's welcome had, but considering that I was met with pure silence every time this scene played out in my nightmares this week, this is certainly an upgrade.

I make it to the podium, gripping onto it with shaky hands. I'm still keeping my gaze out of focus, not ready to face the crowd yet. Once the clapping fizzles out, however, I realize I'm out of time. I do my best to appear completely at ease, letting out a relaxed laugh. "Wow, great job, Jesse," I say into the microphone as I pull my journal out of my back pocket. "I feel bad for whoever has to follow that up."

A couple (and I mean *a couple*) of chuckles rattle off at my lame joke, before full silence settles in the room. I roll my lips into my mouth as I open my journal on top of the podium, pulling out the folded up piece of notebook paper I shoved inside it containing my speech. I nearly rip it as I try to open it with my jittery fingers. After two failed attempts, I finally get the paper unfolded, but when I stare down at it, my vision blurs, all the letters and words jumbling together.

Panicking, feeling like I've been quiet for too long, I try to get some words out. "S–so, thank you all f–for being here. I–uh..."

I blink hard, trying to focus on the words of my written speech, but I can't. It's not working. My chest starts to become painfully tight, and I find myself clenching onto the side of the podium with my hand.

Breathe, Sara. Just breathe.

I listen to myself, closing my eyes and forcing myself to take a deep breath, letting it out slowly through my nose. Then I face my biggest fear of all. I open my eyes, looking out into the crowd.

And there he is.

I find Robbie instantly, our gazes snapping together like two magnets finding each other. He's smack in the middle of the crowd, sitting at the front of the cluster of basketball boys, his entire attention fully focused on me. Even from here, I can see his eyes are sporting milk chocolate this afternoon, and something about that sends a wave of warm comfort through me.

I find myself snapping to attention, however, when I realize Robbie is trying to say something to me. I zero in on his lips, watching him mouth to me, *You got this, Cooper.*

My spine straightens, and when he realizes I've understood him, Robbie nods at me. I nod back.

I've got this.

"So, I must admit," I say, leaning into the microphone with newfound confidence, "Jesse really beat me to it with the '*For those who don't know me*' schtick, but I'm going to do it anyway. Because, even though this *is* Bay View High, I know with certainty that there's plenty of you who *don't* know me. I mean, we are a small town and a small school, so of course you know me. But I know you don't really *know* me. You know?"

I expect a handful of laughs from the audience at the absurd amount of *know*s I just uttered, but it stays completely silent. I swallow my remaining hesitation, carrying on.

"So, I'm Sara Cooper. Some of you might remember me as Sara Beth Cooper back in elementary school. There's a story behind that, but I won't burden you with it right now." I let out a nervous chuckle, shaking my head. "You see, the truth is, I haven't actually spoken to the majority of you here. Sure, we've had classes together over the years, but most of you have probably never given me a second thought. Until maybe these last few weeks at least."

My eyes reflexively flick to Robbie, and I see his tongue pushing into the side of his cheek as he stifles a smirk. He nods at me again, and I know he's urging me to continue.

"You see, I've always been on the outskirts of things. I've attended every pep rally these last three years, and countless other school events. But I've never truly been *in* them. I've always been off to the side, too focused on capturing the moment all of you were having rather than living in it myself. And, honestly, I've loved it that way. Before this year, I hadn't been to a single school dance or sports game that I wasn't taking photos at. Genuinely, I'm not sure I've spent a single lunch hour without working on homework or planning out a newspaper or yearbook spread. I've really been a silent bystander at this school..." I take a breath, my lips rolling into my mouth.

"But, when you really think about it...aren't those the people that actually take the most in? Not the people that live in the scene, but those that observe it? I know every in and out of this school. I know who is who, what they're involved in, where they're going. I know what gets people excited, what bothers them, even what scares them."

I decide to steal a glance at the crowd. I'm not sure if it was a mistake, because every person staring back at me is still, dead silent, and wearing an absolutely unreadable expression, including Robbie.

Well, there's no turning back now.

"The fact is, most of you have probably never noticed me in the corner taking pictures. But I've noticed all of you. I know what Bay View's student body is and what it can be." I feel my cheeks flush as a smile spreads across my face. "I wanna tell our story. And I want to play a part in writing it during my final year here." I shake my head, feeling my throat threatening to close up. "The thing is, I've *never* had a path set. And because of that, I've had to make my own. That's what I'm trying to do now. I hope you'll give me the opportunity." I pause for a moment, pushing my tongue out to wet my dry lips. "Thank you."

I step back from the podium.

Nothing.

I count to three in my mind.

Still nothing.

My head suddenly starts to feel very heavy, and I force myself to turn away, embarrassment flooding me.

I immediately make eye contact with Jesse off the side of the stage, and find him with a look of what I can only call disgust on his face. Just as I think I'm about to melt onto the floor right there, the entire gym explodes.

My back straightens in surprise at the sudden sound. I slowly spin back forwards and find nearly everyone in the bleachers on their feet, clapping and cheering with everything in them. My eyes scan the crowd, finding support from every range of group in the student body, and my lips involuntarily part.

My gaze finds Robbie, and I see he's on his feet with everyone else, his head shaking at me in something like awe. I mouth to him, *Holy shit.*

The biggest grin spreads across his face as he continues to shake his head. Then, he mouths back, *Holy shit, Cooper.*

twenty-six

ROBBIE

I make my way up into the stands after I spot Billy Montgomery in the crowd, cheers sounding all around me as our football team makes their way back onto the field. As I get closer to him, I see some more of my teammates sitting behind and around him, including Paul and Brad. I try not to make too much of a show of looking, but I know I definitely don't see Jesse.

"Summers, how's it goin' man?" Billy says as I plop down next to him, holding out his box of popcorn to me.

I gladly grab a small handful, tossing it into my mouth. "Good, man, thanks. How about you?" I glance at the scoreboard, seeing we're currently ahead by seven. I'm not totally sure why, but I took my time getting here. The first quarter is nearly over already.

"I'm all gravy, man," Billy replies to me, grinning. "Hey, where's your girl at?"

"Ah, she has to work tonight."

"On *Homecoming*?" Billy questions.

"Unfortunately," I reply. "She'll be out in time for the dance though."

"Damn," Billy says, shaking his head. "Well that's good at least. You couldn't pay me enough to work tonight."

I turn to look at him. I know he didn't mean anything by that, but I can't help but think about the fact that he would never *need* to be paid to work. His dad is the mayor of Bay View and his mom's a lawyer. Cooper doesn't have that luxury. Billy's really a nice guy though, so I decide to let it go.

I suddenly feel two sets of hands clap me on the shoulders and startle, turning to find Brad and Michael.

"*Jesus*, hey guys," I say.

"Hey, man," Michael says, shaking my hand. "Where's your lady?"

I had a feeling this was going to be a recurring question tonight.

"Working. But I'm picking her up for the dance."

"Work? Tonight? Are you kidding?" Brad asks, his brows pulled together.

"Nope," I say, not offering any other explanation.

"Well, I just have to say," Michael pauses, whistling, "Sara murdered that speech yesterday."

I find a smirk coming to my face. "Yeah, she did. Didn't she?"

And that's the truth.

I couldn't believe what she did up there on that stage. I mean, I had faith in the girl, but she came *alive* up there. Became a whole new version of herself. The confidence was radiating off of her, and she had that entire gym eating out of the palm of her hand. I know we aren't finding out the results until Monday, but I don't have a doubt in my mind. Cooper stole that election fair and square. I did what I could to help get her to where she was yesterday when it came to the social status and popularity aspect, but I didn't make that speech for her. I couldn't. That was all her. We made the cake together, but she put the cherry on top. She *earned* it.

"Yeah, man. I mean, don't tell him I said this," Brad mutters, leaning in and blocking the side view of his mouth with his hand, "but she kind of left Jesse with egg on his face."

I push my tongue in the side of my cheek, forcing myself to not respond to that statement. "Hey, where is Jesse?"

"Not sure," Brad shrugs. "Paul was saying he was running late or something."

"Interesting," I state. I'm dying to ask more questions, but I refrain.

Is Jesse seriously avoiding showing his face after yesterday?

Cooper did totally wipe the floor with him, but come on. I feel like it's way more embarrassing to hide like this. At the end of the day, it's not that deep. Jesse's life will go on. And a hell of a lot easier that Cooper's would have if the roles were reversed. I guess whether or not he shows up to the dance will be the real test.

A voice suddenly comes over the loudspeaker, announcing the end of the first quarter and that Bay View is currently up 10-7 over Golden Gate High. Claps and cheers sound off throughout the stands as I sense movement to my side. I glance up, seeing Paul making his way down the stand. When we make eye contact, his steps slow.

"Hey there, Robbie," he says. It feels like he's eyeing me, but I try not to think too far into it.

"Hey, man," I nod. "How goes it?"

"Alright," he says, glancing over my shoulder. "Where's Sara at?"

My teeth reflexively grind together. "Work. She'll be at the dance."

Paul's eyebrows raise, a deep chuckle coming out of him. "*Work?*"

"That's what I said."

"And what's little Cooper do for work?"

Suddenly this conversation isn't one that I want to have looking up at Paul. I rise to my feet, facing him.

"She works at Groovy Movie. The rental shop on Cali Avenue."

Paul snorts. "Well, shucks. Isn't that cute?"

I find my fists flexing at my sides. "Yeah. It's pretty adorable, actually. She likes movies. That a problem for you or something?" I grit.

Paul's still chuckling, not even registering what I'm saying by the looks of it. "I mean, who works on Saturday nights? Much less on Homecoming?"

I take a step closer to him, and I'm pretty positive the eyes of every one of our teammates are on us now, but I couldn't care less. "I'm not sure what's so funny," I say, my voice low. "Believe it or not, Paul, some people actually actually have to work for what they have."

Paul stops laughing, but the grin stays on his face. "Oh, like you, Summers?"

Angry heat rushes my face, and I decide to bite the inside of my cheek to keep myself from saying something I'll regret later. I slowly spin back to face Billy, Brad, and Michael behind me, finding them with wide eyes, their hands all frozen in place between Billy's popcorn bucket and their faces, like they're watching a damn movie. I can't help but scoff out a laugh.

"I'm gonna go grab a Pepsi," I tell them.

They all nod back at me in unison like sheep, but I'm already turning away from them, not sparing Paul another glance as I head down the bleachers. I'm still gritting my teeth together as I reach the bottom, trying with everything in me to block out the last few minutes.

Let it go, Robbie.

I shake my head at myself. I'm not sure what makes me feel like more of an idiot: the fact that Paul just threw my own privilege right back in my face after I confronted him for laughing at Cooper or the fact that I know I would've been laughing right along with him if it were just over a month ago.

Hell, I would have been leading the charge.

I make it out of the bleachers and turn right, heading for the concession stand. At the exact moment I round the corner, somebody steps out of the girls' restroom. I just catch a flash of a blonde ponytail before I nearly run smack into them.

"*Sheesh,*" I mutter, grabbing the girl's shoulder to stop myself before I take her out.

The blonde ponytail flicks in my face as the girl's head turns, and I find my lips parting as I come face to face with Denise.

"Oh, Robbie. Hi," she says, a little smile lighting up her face as she turns to fully face me. I glance down, taking in her blue and yellow cheerleading uniform. I swallow, forcing myself to look back at her face as the fantasies I've had about that uniform start flashing through my mind like a highlight reel. "What're you doing?" she asks, tilting her head at me with a knowing look in her eye.

I take a step back, clearing my throat. "I was just grabbing a drink from the concession stand." I turn and start walking that way, and Denise follows right after me. "Don't you need to get back on the field?" I ask her when I reach the stand, stopping behind the two people currently in line.

"They won't miss me for just a few minutes," she says, sidling up next to me.

I let out a chuckle, shaking my head at her. "You think you can just get away with anything, don't you?"

"No, silly," Denise grins, batting her eyelashes as she takes a step closer to me. "I *know* I can."

I open my mouth to respond, but the person running the concession stand stops me, calling out "*Next!*"

"Go on," Denise says, nodding towards the counter. "Can't have you thirsty."

I blink at her, pressing my lips together before I step up to the counter. "Just a Pepsi, please," I say. I take out my wallet to pay, then look back at Denise. "Ah– Did you want anything?"

She looks at me for a few seconds before slowly shaking her head, a smile on her lips.

The person behind the counter hands me a can of Pepsi in exchange for my money, and I step off to the side to open it.

"Where's Sara?" Denise decides to ask the moment I take a sip.

I nearly choke on the soda, but recover, wiping my mouth with the back of my hand. "She has to work until 8:30. I'm picking her up from work to take her to the dance."

I wait for Denise to make a snide comment about Cooper having to work, but surprisingly, she doesn't, just nodding and continuing to stare up at me in response.

"Where's Jesse?" I ask.

That question seems to break whatever trance she's in. She blinks a few times, crossing her arms. "You know, I'm not too sure."

My brows pull together. "What do you mean?"

"We aren't really seeing each other anymore."

My spine steels, and I think I leave a dent in my Pepsi can with how hard I squeeze it. "Since when?"

Denise shrugs, not looking at all bothered by the revelation she just spoke, and something in me tells me this is very fresh news.

Damn. Why do I almost *feel sorry for Jesse?*

Almost.

"Robbie, can I say something?"

I glance up, meeting Denise's ocean blue eyes. "I'm not sure I could stop you if I tried."

She laughs, looking down and shaking her head before meeting my eyes again, her expression softening and a smile coming to her face. "I... I'm really proud of you."

I tilt my head at her, a weird feeling settling in my stomach. I think that may have been the absolute last thing I expected her to say.

"I feel like..." Denise continues. "No, I *know* that you've changed this last month. I'm not quite sure what it is...but you're just...different."

"Good different?"

Denise smiles, stepping closer to me. "*Really* good different."

I roll my lips into my mouth, and I don't miss the way her eyes flick down to my mouth as I do it.

"Can I say something else?" she asks.

I nod.

She reaches up, fiddling with the zipper of my jacket like she has so many times before. I always loved it when she did that. Which makes me wonder why my first instinct was to pull away when she started doing it now.

"I miss you," she says, looking up at me from under her eyelashes. "Have you missed me?"

My throat bobs, my lips pulling into a smirk. "Sure I have."

Haven't I?

Denise bites her bottom lip, and it's written all over her face that that was exactly the answer she was expecting.

"C'mon though," I say. "You're Denise Davis. You don't need me to validate you, sweethea–"

I freeze, cutting off my own words. The *word* that was so natural to roll off my tongue.

Denise's eyes widen, her smile spreading.

Yeah, she definitely caught that.

And she loved it.

"So..." Denise muses. "Do you like Sara?"

"She's my girlfriend," I say, my tongue pressing into my bottom lip. "Of course I like her."

Denise refuses to pull her gaze away from mine, and it only makes my brain and stomach swim further with uneasiness.

"Hmmm..." she hums, her lips twisting to the side. "Do you like me?"

My mouth slowly falls open. "I–"

"*Denise!*"

Denise and I both turn to see Coach McKinley, the cheer coach, with her hands in the air. "What are you doing? Get back out there."

"Yes, Coach!" Denise sings, smoothing out her skirt and snapping to attention. She tightens her bow on her head before gently touching my arm. "See you at the dance, Robbie."

And then she leaves me standing there, with a half empty Pepsi and an overloaded mind.

twenty-seven

SARA

Another honk sounds as I barrel through the back door of Groovy Movie, my backpack in one hand and my school clothes (*that I didn't get a chance to shove inside of my backpack because* someone *starting honking their car horn when I was not ready approximately thirty seconds after 8:30*) in the other.

I spot Robbie's Camaro right outside of the door and take the only step necessary before flinging the passenger door open. "Is the honking entirely necessary?"

"Places to go, people to see, Cooper," Robbie states, not looking my way as he combs his hair in his rear view mirror.

"I don't think *the people*, all of which you *just* came from seeing at the football game, will mind if we arrive two minutes later than planned."

Robbie lets out a huff, slicking the side of his hair back. "Cooper, we have already discussed the difference between fashionably late and just *late*. One of them is the social standard and the other is just plain frowned upon."

"I still don't think that justifies obnoxiously honking your horn at me two feet from the door to my job. Are you trying to get me fired?"

Robbie lets out a scoff. "As if they'd fire the queen of cinema herself from Groovy Movie."

"The queen...of...cinema?" My brows pull together. "Are you high?"

Robbie rakes one last hand through his hair as he reaches over and opens his glove box, tossing his comb inside of it. "Wish I was about now if I'm being honest." He starts to close the glove box then stops. "Actually, hang on a second." He lets the door fall back open, digging his hand inside and shuffling some contents around before he pulls something small and white out. "*Ah*, here we go." I think at first that he's holding a little rolled up wad of paper, but as I squint at it in the light of the barely lit parking lot, I let out a gasp, realizing what it actually is.

"*Robbie!* Oh my God!" I squeal, smacking the joint out of his hand.

"Cooper, *what the hell?*"

"*A joint?*" I whisper-shout. "*Pot?* Are you *insane?* We are literally at my place of work!"

Robbie ducks back and starts fishing around the floor of his back seat, looking frantically for his lost treasure. "We are in the *parking lot* of your place of work," he retorts. And we'd already be out of it by now if you'd stop lollygagging and get in the damn car." He sits upright again, and I see the joint between his fingers. I immediately dart out to grab it from him, but he fights me for it.

"*Robbie!*"

I finally drop all of the contents I'd been carrying on the floor by my passenger seat so I can wrangle with him with two hands.

"Cooper, *would you just stop–*" Robbie looks up at me for the first time and suddenly cuts off. I take whatever caused his momentary distraction to pluck the joint from between his fingers, shoving it back in the glovebox under a pile of papers and slamming the door shut.

"*Wow,*" I hear Robbie mutter.

"Oh, don't cry about it. You can go smoke pot as much as you want, wherever you want, the minute you drop me off at home."

I let out a huff, finally looking up at Robbie, and when I do, something on his face tells me he's not thinking at all about the pot anymore. I glance down at myself, checking my baby blue ruffled tulle dress. The way Robbie continues to stare at it makes me wonder if I should've fought Alice when she insisted I buy it. It was more money that I should have spent anyway. I was excited though at the thought of borrowing some of my mom's shimmery blue eyeshadow she always wears to work since it matched perfectly. Now I'm wondering if I regret that decision too. I find my cheeks heating as Robbie's gaze continues to burn into me.

That's it, I'm returning the dress Monday afternoon.

I finally muster up the courage to ask him, "What?"

Robbie suddenly snaps out of whatever trance he's in, his eyes meeting mine. "Nothing," he says, clearing his throat.

"Nothing?" I question him. "Is something wrong?"

"Not a thing," he says, shaking his head.

I tilt my head at him, not convinced.

"Just..." Robbie trails off, gripping his steering wheel. "You clean up pretty okay, Cooper."

"Oh," I breathe, my brows knitting together as I look down at myself once more. "Thank you?"

"Anytime," Robbie says. "Now, please, for the love of God, get in the car."

———

We arrive at the dance fifteen minutes later to find it already packed. Luckily, *Your Love* by The Outfield is playing when we walk in, so everyone is too busy singing it at the top of their lungs shoulder-to-shoulder on the dancefloor to notice us walking in.

After the Back to School Dance, I feel a lot more comfortable in this environment.

Well, as comfortable as I could ever be.

Robbie and I grab a few glasses of punch, make some small talk, and even stop to take a photo together at the type of booth I've manned so many times in the past. We have a bit of a debacle over Robbie's hand placement in the photo, and my timid freshman friend from yearbook, Eugene, who was working the camera may have uncomfortably laughed as he gently reminded me and Robbie to *look like we liked each other* as he took the photo, but I think it's going to turn out okay. Hopefully.

I wonder for a minute what will even happen to the photo. If it's something I'll even want to keep. I imagine myself forty years from now, pulling the photo out of an old shoebox to show my grandkids. *Look kids! It's Grandma at her senior Homecoming Dance with her fake boyfriend!* Or maybe it'll make it into the yearbook. I ponder that for a moment, realizing I might actually have a chance in deciding that.

I suppose we'll find out on Monday.

We make some more rounds after the photo, stopping to chat with some of Robbie's teammates and their dates, several of which surprisingly praise me on my speech and let me know they voted for me. I hope my cheeks didn't flush as intensely as I felt they did when they made those declarations. I end up spotting Denise hanging out in a corner with some of the cheerleaders. I realize that I may have been subconsciously scanning for her since the moment we walked in, and, even though I knew she would be here, I can't say I'm thrilled to have found her. She's wearing a cream colored dress with soft off-the-shoulder puffy sleeves and matching satin gloves up to her elbows. Her hair is perfectly styled and her makeup is shimmery and pink and I just frankly want to dump the punch bowl over her head because it's just not fair that someone can look that much like a literal angel on Earth.

Luckily, I'm able to force my eyes away from Denise as we find Alice and Daniel over by the food table. We spend a few minutes catching up with them before Alice drags me onto the dance floor when her favorite Whitney Houston song comes on.

As the song starts to fade out, we begin making our way back to the guys. I don't ever make it off the dance floor, however, because

Separate Ways by Journey starts playing, and Robbie doesn't hesitate for a single second, practically throwing me over his shoulder to force me back onto the dance floor. He refuses to wipe the smug smile off his face as my stream of complaints eventually gets lots in giggles and I finally have to give in and dance along with him to the song that's been stuck in my head for a full week now.

"Ready to admit defeat yet, Cooper?" Robbie asks me over the music as we bounce around on the dance floor.

"To you? Never," I shake my head. "But what exactly are we talking about?"

"That you were wrong and Journey totally rocks."

My mouth falls open. "I never said they *didn't* rock."

"Maybe not exactly," Robbie says, narrowing his eyes at me, "but you did try to change the station when they came on in my car."

"I did," I agree.

"Which is deeply offensive on so many levels."

I follow Robbie's lead, taking his hand as he spins me around. "I understand that now."

"Good," Robbie nods. "Just glad that we can keep the status quo."

"The status quo?" I question him, my brows pulling together.

"That I'm always right," Robbie grins, stating it like it's a fact.

I bark out a laugh. "That's comical."

"When have I ever been wrong, Cooper?"

"Hold on, do you have a pen and paper?" I ask. "I need to make a list."

"Hilarious," he sneers. "Just admit it. I'm always right."

I look up at him, my lips pulling up at the corners. "Fine, I'll admit it." Robbie starts to slowly raise his fist in the air in success, but I cut him off, placing a hand on his chest. "On one condition."

"What's that, Cooper?" he asks.

"I get to keep the cassette."

Robbie's tongue pushes into the side of his cheek. "Not a chance in hell."

"Then I guess you're not always right." I give him a self-satisfied grin.

Robbie tilts his head at me, studying me. "You know what, Cooper–"

"*Can I have everyone's attention please?*"

The music cuts off abruptly, and Robbie and I both jolt away from one another, not realizing how close we had gotten until the lights in the gym suddenly turned back up. Our eyes stay on each other for one more long second before we both spin forward to face the stage where Principal Whileyman is currently standing.

"Now, I see you all are having a great time tonight," he says into the microphone in his hand. "Is that right?" Cheers sound from all over the gym in response. "Great, great, we love to see that," Principal Whileyman continues. "I don't want to hold you too long, but we're getting late into the evening, so it's about time we announce our Homecoming King and Queen!"

Everyone erupts into more claps and whistles as the blood drains from my face. *Why had I completely forgotten about this part of Homecoming?* I glance shakily behind me, realizing I walked right past the table set up for people to cast their votes when we walked in.

"Now, I know the anticipation is killing all of you, so let's just get to it!" Principal Whileyman says.

More applause sounds. I swallow hard, my mouth suddenly feeling bone dry.

"Your Homecoming King and Queen for 1987 are…"

I reach out for Robbie, not able to look at him. "I– I need to go to the bathroom," I say, turning away. "I'll be right back–"

"*Robbie Summers!*"

The gym goes nuts, and a few people nearby clap Robbie on the shoulder, shoving me closer into him. I feel like the air has been stolen from my lungs. I manage to pull back just slightly, spinning away as I mutter under my breath, "I'm just gonna go–"

"*And Sara Cooper!*"

I freeze in place, feeling like a deer caught in headlights.

Wha–what?

I don't move on my own, but suddenly I'm twirling around. It's not until I'm facing forward that I realize Robbie's hand is on my waist, controlling my body. "That's our cue, Cooper."

"I–Um–*What?*" I stutter.

Robbie ducks down so his mouth is next to my ear. "To the stage, baby," he says, then plasters a grin on his face, nodding at the hoard of people around us cheering for and congratulating us. He gives my waist a little pinch, pushing me to move forward.

Everything is a blur as we make our way onto the stage and somebody places a plastic sparkly crown on my head. Principal Whileyman places a larger king's crown on Robbie's head, and I vaguely register him patting Robbie's shoulder, a look of something like pride on his face as he nods at him. I don't get much time to process it, however, my attention turning out toward the gym, the lights completely blinding me as I stare into the crowd. The crowd of people that apparently voted for us. Not just for Robbie, but for *me*. I shake my head in pure disbelief. I try to force myself to smile, but I feel like the look on my face probably just makes me appear like I'm nauseous. I suppose that makes sense though, since I am.

I spot Alice barrelling her way through the crowd to stand at the front. She jumps up and down cheering for me as if I'm Whitney Houston herself and she has a front row seat to her concert. I let out a laugh, a true smile coming to my face for the first time as I look down at her. She throws her hands in the air, mouthing *Oh my God* at me. I shrug my shoulders, laughing, since I don't know how else to respond. I'm completely dumbfounded. But it makes me so happy to see my best friend so happy. So happy for *me*.

I feel my smile waver for a second as the realization hits me. The realization that this isn't real. I mean, not really. I didn't *earn* this. If Homecoming Queen is even something that you can earn. It's not like I didn't already know this, but it really hits me at this moment that people only voted for me because I'm dating Robbie. Or because *they think* I'm dating him. I wonder if I should feel guilty. If I shouldn't be standing up here in awe right now. But the deeper I dig into what I'm feeling in my gut right now, the more I find myself just wanting to enjoy the moment. This absolutely crazy, once-in-a-lifetime moment. I don't know how I ended up here, but I decide, for now, to just go with it.

"Now, if everybody could please spread out and leave some space," Principal Whileyman says, motioning with his hand, "I'd like to open the dance floor for our Homecoming King and Queen's first dance."

My spine steels as *Ooos* and *Ahhs* sound from around the gym, everyone immediately falling in line to leave a circle open in the middle of the dance floor. My mouth falls open as I stare at the scene with wide eyes.

"I'm sorry," I whisper, my voice cracking. "Our...*what?*"

Cyndi Lauper's *Time After Time* starts playing through the speakers as I hear Robbie chuckle at my side. "C'mon, Cooper," he says, reaching for my hand. "I've got you."

Robbie gently pulls me behind him as we make our way down the couple of steps off the stage. The gym lights lower further, showing the disco ball off in all its glory. A spotlight comes on, shining right in the spot we are headed for, instantly sending a shiver of nerves down my spine. Robbie spins me as we reach the middle of the open circle, and, somehow, I don't fall down. I swallow hard, glancing around at all the eyes on us as I place my hands on Robbie's shoulder.

"Hey," Robbie whispers, his finger pushing my chin up lightly to force me to look at him. "They're not even here, Cooper."

I swallow again, with more force this time, as Robbie's hands move to my hips and we start swaying side to side. "Just you and me?" I ask.

"Unfortunately." He frowns in disgust for just a second before he breaks, the frown turning into a grin.

I scoff out a laugh, shaking my head at him. "What a lucky girl I am."

Robbie chuckles, eventually fading into a sigh. "I do just have to point something out," he says.

"What's that?" I ask.

"The fact that this is yet another thing I was right about."

I tilt my head at him.

Robbie smirks. "I told you that you'd be a shoo-in for Homecoming Queen."

My lips part, the memory coming back to me, the conversation that feels like it was a million years ago. "You did, didn't you?"

"Can't say this has turned out to be too bad of a deal for you, has it, Cooper?"

"No, I guess I can't," I answer honestly. "So far, you've managed to give me everything you promised. Well, except the election. We don't know about that yet–"

"We *do* know about it," Robbie cuts me off. "You won it, no doubt. But, regardless, I didn't give you that, Cooper. That was all you."

My throat bobs, a small smile coming to my lips. "You know what I mean," I say. I clear my throat, trying to lighten the mood. "And, you know, aside from all that, I guess it's been nice to have a chauffeur."

Robbie's brows raise. "Oh yeah? Is that all I am to you, Cooper?"

I shrug my shoulders playfully. "I mean, as much as I love walking, I suppose it hasn't been entirely painful having a ride to places. Even if it has to be with you."

Robbie cocks his head to the side, leaning in closer to me. "Is that so?"

I duck my head, letting out a chuckle. "Yep. I'll admit it. I don't *hate* riding with you." Robbie digs his fingers into my side, tickling me. I throw my head back in laughter, the spotlight shining right in my eyes. "Even if Journey is playing the entire time and there aren't even storms going on outside to force me into it."

Robbie's feet slow, and, aside from my still swaying hips, we've almost stopped dancing entirely. His gaze is heavy on my face as he mutters something inaudible.

"What?" I ask.

"*Storms,*" he mutters. "I'll be damned."

I press my lips together, glancing down at Robbie's still unmoving feet, and that seems to somewhat snap him out of whatever trance he's in as he starts to dance with me again. "What are you talking about?" I question him.

"Storms," Robbie says again, his lips pulling up at one side as he shakes his head. "That's what your eyes look like. Two little storms."

I tilt my head back to look at him. My lips part, but I'm at a loss for words. Apparently Robbie is as well, as he just continues to smirk at me, his eyes darting between mine. Goosebumps prickle the back of my neck and a heavy feeling settles low in my belly as he refuses to break my eye contact. I lick my dry lips, my mind racing.

"Do you think you should kiss me?" I blurt.

Robbie's brows shoot up.

"Like you did before, I mean?" I clarify. "Since everybody's watching?"

It's Robbie's turn to lick his lips now. He nods. "Sure, Cooper. Good idea."

I drop my chin, shaking my hair forward to try to block people's view as much as possible as Robbie cups my face with one hand, leaning down. Just like before, he doesn't hesitate, not allowing anyone to question what's happening. He waits until he's a hair's width away from my mouth before his thumb glides up, pressing into the center of my lips just before his own lips come down over top. Once again, we're not touching. But we're *so* very close. I can feel the warmth of him, his scent invading my every sense.

I know if I pressed forward just the slightest bit, just applied the tiniest bit of pressure, my lips would brush his for real, and something about that knowledge sends heat flowing through me. I wrap my arms just a little tighter around Robbie's neck, and I swear he groans against his thumb when I do it. The entire act makes my knees suddenly very weak and sends a fluttering pulse between my thighs.

Then, just like before, it ends as quickly as it begins. Robbie's hand falls from my face and he stands back up to his full height, leaving me feeling satisfied in our mission but otherwise unexplainably empty.

I force myself to smile as a round of squeals sound from all of the girls around the dance circle, but I don't look at them, keeping my eyes on Robbie's and trying to decipher his unreadable expression. Still not successful after several seconds, I decide to break the silence.

"What about you?" I ask.

Robbie's throat bobs, a tight smile coming to his face. "What *about* me?"

"Do you feel like you've gotten some of your end of the bargain at least? With our...arrangement?"

"I do," Robbie nods. "I really do, Cooper."

"Well, as long as you're satisfied." I clear my throat, not meeting his eyes as I say what I'm about to say. "Denise looks really pretty tonight."

Robbie's dancing slows for just a moment. I'm still not looking at him, so I don't know what his face looks like. "Yeah," he agrees, his voice hoarse. "Yeah, I guess she does."

I blow a slow breath out of my nose, my face feeling hot all of the sudden. "I didn't see Jesse with her earlier. I wonder where he is."

Robbie's fingers flex against my hip, but I don't react to it. "They–eh... They broke up."

My heart feels like it drops to the floor as I snap my head up to look at him. "They *what?*"

Robbie shrugs his shoulders, his jaw tight.

"When did this happen?" I ask, blinking.

"I'm not sure," he says quietly.

I blink back at him for several seconds, and it's not until I register a swirl of movement around us that I realize the song has come to an end. People rejoin the dance floor, swaying all around us as *Every Breath You Take* by The Police begins to play through the speakers.

My feet are still rooted to the floor, my throat tight as I try to speak. "Robbie, are you–"

"Hey there," a sweet voice cuts me off, and I dart my gaze to the side to find Denise. My eyes flick down as I take notice of her hand resting on Robbie's bicep. My lips flatten into a line, those little white satin gloves of hers suddenly not looking so angelic anymore.

"Denise, hey," Robbie says.

"I'm sorry," Denise smiles, "but would you mind if I stole the Homecoming King for just one little dance?" It takes a full three seconds for me to realize that she's talking to me. That's she asking me for *permission*. "Just for old times' sake?" she adds on, as if that makes her request better. As if that will somehow soothe the burning ball of hate currently sitting in my chest for her. Robbie and I aren't actually together, but she thinks we are. Yet she doesn't care. Clearly.

Bitch.

I keep the thought to myself though. Knowing that I'm not allowed to care. Not actually. I also have to remind myself of what Robbie and I just discussed. *Our agreement.* Us each getting what we wanted out of it. Robbie said he was satisfied, that he'd gotten his end of the bargain. *Denise* was a part of that bargain. She's what he always wanted. She's a huge reason why we are even here together in the first place. Of course I have to let her dance with him. Because that's exactly what he wants, exactly what he deserves after helping me go after everything I've wanted.

I swallow against the lump in my throat, forcing a bright smile on my face. "Of course," I say. "If that's what Robbie wants."

Robbie's head snaps in my direction, his gaze flicking back and forth between me and Denise.

"Great!" Denise grins. "Robbie?" She grabs his hand, and he only hesitates for a second, looking back at me, his brows pulling together.

"See you in a minute?" he says.

I nod, keeping my happy face intact. "Have fun."

I let out a heavy sigh the moment they both turn away from me to weave their way deeper into the crowd of dancers.

I don't know where I'm planning on going, but I know I can't stand here in the middle of the dance floor watching them dance together, so I spin on my heel in the general direction of the food and drink tables. I don't make it far, however, immediately finding myself bumping into a hard chest.

"Oh my God– Sorry– Excuse me," I stammer, pulling back from my victim. I immediately tilt my head to the side when I find myself staring up into the hazel eyes of Paul Strothers.

"Hey, you're fine. It's a small dance floor," he grins.

I choke out a laugh. "Right. Doesn't help when I'm already clumsy. Sorry, Paul, you'll have to excuse me"

"Don't even mention it." He rakes a hand through his sandy dark blonde hair, and, though it certainly doesn't have the same effect as when Robbie does it, I have to admit I don't mind watching it.

"Well," I clear my throat. "I'll just carry on before I cause any more damage."

I go to move around Paul, but his hand catches my wrist. "Hey, Sara, wait."

"Yeah?" I question, looking back at him.

"Do you, maybe..." he pauses, rolling his lips into his mouth as motions over his shoulder with his thumb. "Do you wanna dance?"

"Oh," I breathe, my back straightening. "I..."

I find my eyes trailing to the dance floor, and, like a magnet, my gaze immediately locks on Robbie and Denise. On him smiling down at her and his hands on her hips, *just like* they just were on mine. I zero in on her bouncy blonde hair swishing side to side as they sway together and the way her eyes light up as she looks up into those eyes I *know* are milk chocolate in the disco ball lights.

My shoulders drop, my fists uncurling at my sides. "I would love to dance, Paul."

Paul wastes no time guiding me on to the dance floor as the second chorus starts up. My hands land on his shoulders and his land on my hips, and I make myself focus my full attention on him, reminding myself for the second time tonight to just enjoy the moment I'm in.

Which would be so easy to do if I didn't feel a gaze I know all too well burning into my face. I try to stop myself, but I can't keep my eyes from flicking up over Paul's shoulder. I find Robbie immediately, his eyes locked on me over the top of Denise's head as he dances with her just ten feet away. When he realizes I've caught him, his gaze falls back down to Denise. He says something to her, smiling tightly. I know I should look away, but I don't. Not until he looks back up at me again. Then, suddenly, Paul's face is the most interesting thing I've ever seen. I smile at him and he smiles back. I try to distract my mind from Robbie by trying to figure out what Paul's eyes look like, but, aside from swamp water, I come up blank. I steal one more glance at Robbie, and find he's already looking at me. The only difference is, this time, he doesn't look away.

And neither do I.

twenty-eight

ROBBIE

I'm on edge.

I've tried cycling through four different tapes in my Walkman to distract myself, hoping that music would drown out my thoughts like it has for me so many times before, but it's done nothing for me this morning.

Cooper and I didn't say much of anything to each other on the ride to school this morning, pretty much mirroring our ride home from the dance on Saturday. There's a tension between us that's different than what's been there before. Something shifted when I danced with Denise. Or maybe it really happened when she danced with Paul.

Fucking Paul.

I've never really had an issue with Paul. Not until recently. He was always kind of a bonehead, but he was my buddy. We had a comfortable friendship. We played basketball, we partied, end of story. Things were simple between us.

I guess leave it up to Cooper to find another way to un-simplify my life.

I know I chose to dance with Denise. I know that that was

maybe a crappy thing to do five minutes after me and Cooper won Homecoming King and Queen. But Cooper said it was fine. I'd even venture to say she encouraged it.

I'm not saying that I mind, I'm just saying that... I think that matters.

It also matters that Denise was always a part of the deal. She was a factor Cooper could expect in the screwed up equation of our fake relationship.

Paul, on the other hand...

That prick came out of nowhere. I'm not sure what he's playing at. But him making a joke out of Cooper in front of our friends at the Homecoming game and then having the *audacity* to ask her to dance just a few hours later...

It made me want to do things that would probably undo every ounce of progress I've made with Principal Whileyman over the last month.

Or would probably land me a spot in the back of Paul's dad's cop car.

I don't care what his motives are. I don't care what he wants. I don't care if he secretly really likes Cooper. *Hell, I can't even say I would blame him—*

Wait, what?

I clear my throat, shaking the odd thought away.

Regardless, he can't have her. Not on my watch. We have rules. If Cooper decides she wants him, I can't stop her. That's her call to make. But until she utters those words, there's not a chance in hell I'm even going to give Paul the pleasure of *daydreaming* that she'll ever be his.

Because she deserves so much better.

I slide into my regular desk in my homeroom class. I might not be listening to any music, but my headphones are still on. I needed the barrier from the outside world this morning. But since I'm not listening to anything, that means I can hear every word of Brad and Billy's heated debate behind me about which Star Wars movie Princess Leia was the hottest in.

I rub my hand over my face as I shake my head, honestly

welcoming the distraction but not wanting them to know I can hear them.

"Dude, how is this even a discussion right now?" Brad questions Billy.

"I think it's a very valid discussion, thank you very much," Billy shoots back.

"Bro, you *know* it's Return of the Jedi," Brad insists. "I mean, the gold bikini. Come on!"

"I dunno man, I can see a bikini any day of the week," Billy retorts. "But those little hair buns really did something for me in the first movie."

The ridiculous conversation behind me suddenly gets drowned out by the staticky sound of the intercom coming over the classroom speakers.

"Good morning, Bay View Bears! Happy Monday," Principal Whileyman's voice begins.

"I can't believe you right now," Brad says to Billy.

My back straightens as I slide one side of my headphones off my ear.

"We have a few regular announcements to get to this morning, but I believe it's best we get our most exciting announcement out of the way first."

"I can't believe *you*, man!" Billy exclaims. "Is a beautiful woman nothing but a body to you?"

"So, without further ado," Principal Whileyman continues, making me slide my headphones fully off my head, "I'd like to announce the winner of our student body president race."

"I'm just saying, dude," Brad scoffs. "I think you're priorities are seriously messed up when it comes to what *buns* you're concerned with–"

"Holy Christ, would you two *shut up?*" I huff, spinning around. I only intended for Billy and Brad to hear me, but, judging by every set of eyes in the classroom being turned on me, I think I may have been a little more aggressive than I thought in my request.

"Shit, sorry, man," Brad mumbles, giving Billy a look that says I've gone insane, but I'm too preoccupied to care right now.

"I'd like to thank our two candidates for their dedication to our student body and willingness to serve it. I also appreciate everyone that took the time to vote after the pep rally on Friday. Your voice really does matter at Bay View."

"*Yeah, yeah, blah, blah. Get to it, bud,*" I mutter under my breath.

"So, here we go. Drumroll, please."

A handful of people around the classroom drum their hands against the top of their desk, probably to poke fun at me about how invested I seem to be in this announcement.

Screw them.

"Your student body president for the 1987-88 school year is..."

My teeth grind together as my fist clenches at my side. My foot starts tapping on its own. I pull my shirt collar away from my neck, trying to get some air. I think I'm sweating.

Why am I sweating?

Principal Whileyman clears his throat.

My head is going to explode.

"Sara Cooper!"

I slump against my chair, letting out a breath I didn't know I was holding.

"Congratulations to Ms. Cooper! Again, thank you to all who entered. If you see your new president and yearbook editor in the halls today, make sure to give her your congrats. Sara, when you have a few minutes, come see me in my office."

Oh. My. God.

Principal Whileyman continues droning on with the rest of the regular announcements, but I tune them all out. I slide my headphones back on my head, not even trying to hide my smirk. I hit the play button to start the Bon Jovi *Slippery When Wet* tape in my Walkman, my brain suddenly completely clear.

You freaking did it, Cooper.

———

I practically break down the door the minute the bell dismisses us to head to second period, making a beeline for Ms. Cage's class. My head is on a swivel looking for her. A few people try to say hi to me on the way, but I pretend I don't notice them. Hopefully they'll think I couldn't hear them through my headphones. Realistically though, I don't really care what they think. Not right now.

Within a minute, I'm turning the corner at the end of the hall, still no sight of her.

But then, there she is, rounding her corner at the exact same time.

We both skid to a stop, and Cooper looks like she's seen a ghost. Her eyes are wide, her shoulders stiff, her lips slowly parting. We continue to stare at each other from ten feet away, neither of us speaking. The tension from before is still there, but I can feel it thinning, slowly whittling away.

Looking at Cooper right now, it's as if she's frozen, and the heat of my gaze is slowly melting her from the outside in. I watch as her shoulders slowly relax, as the rise and fall of her chest gradually deepens, and as her look of shock gently fades into a smile.

"Cooper." I break the silence, shaking my head..

"I...I don't..." she stammers, blinking rapidly. "...I can't...I..."

"Yeah?" I smirk.

Her teeth sink into her lower lip. "We did it," she breathes.

I shake my head firmly. "*You* did it."

Her mouth opens, but she doesn't say anything. She starts rocking on her heels, fidgeting with her hands.

Then we both start moving, closing the distance between each other. I open my arms and Cooper jumps right into them. I lean back from the force of her impact, her feet coming off the ground and my left arm settling at her lower back to hold her to me. Cooper's head settles against the crook of my shoulder as her arms wrap around my neck.

"I can't believe it," she whispers just below my ear, shaking her head.

The scent of her flowery shampoo washes over me, and I just

have to run my hand over her copper hair. I may even press my nose against it and breathe deep. I couldn't tell you. Everything feels like a blur right now with Cooper closer to me than ever before.

"Well, believe it, baby," I say, my voice low.

Cooper pulls back just enough to meet my eyes, gently sliding down to stand on her feet again. Her arms stay around my neck, and it occurs to me just how much her skin smells like early morning rain.

Wildflowers for hair, rain for skin, and storms for eyes.

God, is she something.

"Thank you," she says, making me tilt my head at her. "For your help. I know I almost didn't agree to your deal. I really didn't want to do this. I was...*scared* to do this, to even try. But thank you for pushing me. I don't think I would have gone for it if it weren't for you. If it weren't...*with* you."

I shake my head at her. "Cooper, you may be a total pain in my ass...but I'm really proud of you."

She rolls her eyes with a grin, finally taking a step back and putting some distance between us. "Thanks," she mumbles.

"We gotta celebrate," I say.

She lets out a shy laugh, waving her hand at me.

"I mean it, Cooper. You have Monday nights off, right?"

She goes still, looking up at me when she realizes I'm serious. "Um, yeah. I do."

"I'm sure people will be hanging out at Dusty's tonight."

"The drive-in movie theater?" Cooper questions. "On a Monday?"

"Mondays are free admission for students. We always go on Mondays."

"Oh." It's obvious by the way she says it that she had no idea. I guess I can't blame her. I said *we* always go on Mondays, but the fact is, I haven't been in a month now.

I see Cooper roll her lips into her mouth like I have realized she always does when she's nervous about something. "We should go,"

I tell her, giving her shoulder a gentle shove. "You deserve to let loose a little."

"I don't know..."

"Cooper, you won freaking student body president. Who would've ever thought in a million years you would have done that?"

"Well, clearly not you," she huffs, crossing her arms and looking away.

I give her a knowing look, waiting for her to look back at me.

"I guess not me either," she admits when she finally does.

"Exactly," I nod. "So take it in. Come out tonight."

Her lips twist to the side before she lets out a resigned sigh. "I guess it could be fun."

I reach out and poke her nose, and she swats my hand away.

"I'll pick you up at seven."

———

I can feel the gentle bounce of Cooper's knee as she leans against the side of my car next to me. I glance to the side, looking her up and down.

"*What?*" she demands, raising her brows at me.

"What's the matter, Cooper?" I ask.

She hugs her arms tighter around herself as she shrugs. "Nothing."

"Really? Nothing at all?"

"T–that's what I said," she insists, and I don't miss the way her teeth chatter as she does.

I had shown up at Cooper's house at seven o'clock sharp, and the moment she stepped outside in her little denim skirt and short sleeve blouse, I knew she was going to be freezing tonight.

"Are you going like that?" I had questioned her.

"Like *what?*" she asked, her brows furrowing.

"Well, *that*," I said, motioning to her outfit.

She scoffed. "You know, Robbie, now that you mentioned it, I don't have to go at all." She spun on her heel to go back inside, but I grabbed her by the arm before she could slam the door in my face.

"Cooper, relax. I'm just saying, I don't think you're going to be comfortable."

"Really? That's weird. Because I'm always *so* comfortable around you."

I rolled my eyes at her sarcasm. "I just mean that I think you're gonna freeze. The drive-in is out in the middle of a field, and it's supposed to really cool down tonight."

"I'll be fine," she insisted, yanking her arm from my grasp.

"Are you sure? You don't want to put anything else on?"

"Robbie," she huffed, "if I go back inside that house, you're gonna have to drag me out by my hair to get me to leave it again."

"Well, don't tempt me with a good time, Cooper–"

"Shut up," she cut me off, walking past me out the door. "Let's go."

Now, we're at the drive-in, the sun has gone down, and I'm watching Cooper shake like a leaf with her arms crossed so tightly that she has to partially be cutting off her own air supply. It doesn't bring me any satisfaction to see her shivering and uncomfortable like this.

But also, it kind of does.

"Just making sure," I say. "You're not...I don't know...*cold?* Or anything?"

"N–no," she stutters.

"C'mon." I nudge her shoulder. "Talk to me, Goose."

Cooper's head snaps in my direction as she stares daggers at me.

"You know, Cooper, fun fact: geese fly south for the winter."

She raises her brows at me.

"Because they get cold."

I turn away before I can see the look I know she's giving me (*one that could kill*), opening the trunk to my Camaro. I duck down, quickly spotting my blue and yellow letterman jacket, and pluck it out. I close the trunk, tossing the jacket in Cooper's direction. "Here."

She flinches as it flies towards her, just barely catching it before it falls to the ground. She holds the jacket up with both of her hands, inspecting it, her eyes flicking between it and me. "What is this?" she asks.

"A jacket."

"But I don't need a jacket," she says, insisting on being stubborn.

"Then let's call it a peace offering."

"B–but–"

"Cooper, put on the damn jacket."

Her lips press together, her eyes boring into me for several seconds before she finally resigns, letting out a sigh and turning away from me to shrug on the jacket. She threads her hands under the curtain of her hair, pulling it free from the collar. I watch as it falls naturally down her back, splaying out like flames licking the top of the letters of my last name that are sewn across the back of the jacket.

Something about that sends a strange rush of heat through me. I swallow at the sudden tightness in my throat, my eyes still glued to the mural of red hair and *Summers* when Cooper calls my name.

"Robbie?"

My gaze snaps up, seeing her looking over her shoulder at me with her brows pulled together. "Are you okay?" she asks.

"Yep," I mutter. "Why wouldn't I be?"

She opens her mouth to respond, but I don't give her a chance when I see Michael and Brad's cars pulling into the lot, along with several others I recognize. "There everyone is," I say. "Come on, let's go."

"Go where?" Cooper questions.

"To socialize, Cooper."

"But why–"

"Unless you'd rather be alone with me all night," I cut her off, raising my brows.

I watch her throat bob as she glances between the hoard of Bay View students exiting their cars and me. "Let's go," she says, practically taking off jogging.

I huff a laugh, following behind her as she makes her way over to my friends. I find my eyes trailing down and realize that my letterman jacket is big enough on her that her skirt is barely visible from the back. I force my gaze away, shaking my head to push away the unwarranted unholy thoughts that come from that realization. My eyes land on the large screen at the same moment the feature presentation begins, and Cooper skids to a stop before three seconds of the opening to the movie even play out.

"*OhMyGosh!*" she squeals out, running her words together from how excited she is. "You didn't tell me *Dirty Dancing* was playing! It's been out for almost two months! I figured they had stopped showing it by now! Oh my gosh– I'm *so* excited!"

She's practically jumping up and down as we approach the small mob of Bay View students, half of which are wearing lettermans just like the one Cooper is currently wearing. "You haven't seen it yet?" I question her, surprised.

"Oh, no, I've seen it!" Cooper says, her head swiveling between the screen and me. "Twice!" I let out a chuckle at how excited she is to see a movie (*for the* third *time*). "I just love it. So much."

"More than *Top Gun?*"

She turns her head in my direction, continuing to bounce on her heels as she gives me a look like I'm crazy. "Now, don't be ridiculous." She looks back at the screen, tilting her head and grinning. "But it's up there."

She continues to watch the movie while I watch her, my tongue pushing into the side of my cheek as I wonder if I'll ever be as passionate about anything as Sara Cooper is about everything she loves.

"Well look what the cat drug in."

I turn to see Brad with his arm slung around Lisa McDaniel, smirking at me.

I chuckle, returning the fist bump he's extending my way. "If I'm what the cat drug in, what the hell kinda creature hauled you here?"

"That would be me," Lisa says, flashing me a grin before turning in Cooper's direction. "Hey Sara. Congrats on winning president. You totally killed that speech."

"Oh," Cooper smiles, a blush spreads across her cheeks. "Thanks, Lisa."

"Yeah, I gotta say, you really warmed my cold, dead heart with that one, Madam President," Brad muses, patting his chest.

The sound of a handful of car doors closing draws my attention across the lot, where I see Jesse and Paul getting out of one car and Denise, Ginger Matthews, and Kate Andrews getting out of another. In a matter of seconds, Jesse and Denise spot each other, each of them visibly shifting with discomfort, then, at exactly the same time, both of their gazes land on me.

"Thank you, Brad," Cooper chuckles. "Really, I take that as the highest form of compliment–"

"Hey, Cooper, you wanna grab some snacks?" I interject, grabbing her arm.

Denise's gaze shifts from my face to where I'm grabbing Cooper, her eyes narrowing when she sees her wearing my jacket. Then, for whatever reason, she smiles.

I don't like the look of it. Not when it's coming from Denise. A conflicting feeling settles in my chest, and I know I can't deal with this right now.

One girl at a time.

"I'm not really hungry–" Cooper starts, but I cut her off.

"You're thirsty. Got it. Let's go." Before she has a chance to argue, I take off, hauling her behind me.

"See you guys, later, I guess," Brad calls after us.

I throw him a thumbs up over my shoulder as I continue towards the concession stand.

"Robbie, what's wrong?" Cooper asks.

"Nothing. Just can't have my girlfriend thirsty. That's not a good look."

"*Robbie*," she pushes right as we reach the concession stand window.

"Hi there," I tell the girl behind the counter. "One Pepsi and one Jolt Cola, please."

"We don't have Jolt," the girl responds, blowing a bubble with her gum.

"Another Pepsi, then?" I question, looking at Cooper.

Her brows knit together. "Coke."

"Okay, Coke then." The girl starts to turn away to grab our drinks, but I stop her. "Oh, and a bag of Skittles please." I glance at Cooper. "And a Charleston Chew."

"Coming right up."

"How did you know I like Charleston Chews?" Cooper questions me.

"I've seen the wrappers in your backpack."

She tilts her head, studying me. The girl comes back, handing me our sodas and candy in exchange for a couple of bills. I hand Cooper her candy bar as we step away from the window, and she sighs, shoving it into the pocket of my jacket. "Robbie, we need to talk."

I practically shove her Coke into her hands, and she gives me an exasperated look. "*Robbie.*"

"About what?" I ask her, keeping my voice casual.

"A couple of things," she says. "First of all, you just freaked out because Denise looked at us." *Shit, she saw that?* "And second, you just called me your girlfriend." *What?*

I spin to face her. "Okay, first of all, I don't know what you're talking about. And second, what's wrong with that? You *are* my girlfriend." I give her a look that lets her know I'm tacking the word *fake* on before *girlfriend* in my mind.

"But I'm not." She shakes her head. "I mean, not anymore...right?"

My brows pull together, and, after a few long seconds, realization hits me. "Oh," I say.

"We hit our expiration date," Cooper breathes, looking off to the side. "I mean, I understood you wanting to celebrate tonight, but I figured—"

"No, you're right," I nod. "We're done."

I mean...we are.

This was what we always planned for. We were going to run with this little scheme until Homecoming. Until the people at this school took me more seriously. Until Cooper won president. Now that all of those things are done, we have no reason to continue. I just...*forgot*. Just had a momentary mental lapse. But she's right.

Cooper clears her throat, bringing my focus back to her face. She pushes a loose strand of hair behind her ear, not meeting my eyes. "So, I guess we're broken up then."

"I guess we are." I rub the back of my neck, a veil of awkward tension settling between us.

"You know," Cooper speaks up, "a month felt like it would be so long. But, in the end, it kind of feels like it flew by."

"It does, doesn't it?" I agree with her.

"And, surprisingly, I don't even think it was the worst month of my life," she adds.

"Awe, c'mon, baby, you're too kind to me."

Cooper chuckles, shaking her head. "You don't need to call me that anymore."

"*Cooper?* I think it's a little late for that—"

"No," she says. "I mean...*baby*."

"Oh," I mutter. I hadn't even realized I'd said it. "Sorry. Habit."

"I get it," she breathes, meeting my eyes. We look at each other for a few seconds, neither of us saying anything out loud, but a million things passing between our locked gazes.

"Well," I break the silence, holding my soda up to her, "here's to a successful campaign, Cooper." She clinks her soda can against mine with a small smile. "The student body president one and... well...*you know*." I shoot her a wink.

She purses her lips, taking a sip of her Coke. "I still can't believe I won. I can't believe I'm really the yearbook editor. This...this really means so much to me."

"I know, Cooper," I say, wrapping my arm around her to squeeze her to my side. The action is automatic, and she doesn't even fight me on it, leaning into my shoulder and letting out a sigh. I rest my chin on top of her head, but the moment I catch a whiff of her fresh floral scent and my eyes start to flutter shut, I pull back, putting some distance between us. I dust off my sleeves, trying to look natural as I gather myself, putting the same distance between us mentally as I have physically. "So, are you going to go home and write about this in your diary?"

Cooper scoffs, rolling her eyes. "I've told you a million times, it's not a diary."

"Yeah, well, you may have told me a trillion times what it *isn't*, but you've never told me what *is*. So what's a guy supposed to think? You know we have dirty minds."

She crosses her arms, giving me an annoyed look before turning back towards where the movie screen is playing in the distance. I move to stand beside her, crossing my arms as well.

I try to watch the movie for a few seconds, watching as Jennifer Grey's character lays eyes on Patrick Swayze's for the first time. The quiet innocent little girl with big dreams of making a difference and seeing the world, completely enamored with the smooth-talking bad boy that her family would never approve of and can't do a damn thing for her.

My throat bobs as I glance over at Cooper. She appears on the surface to be completely enthralled in the movie, but I can tell that she's holding something back, that she's trying really hard not to look over at me as well. I bump my shoulder against hers, but she pretends not to notice. "Tell me, Cooper," I say. "What's in the journal?"

Her eyes slowly drop from the movie screen before she turns her head to look at me. Her lips press into a flat line as she seems to be fighting some sort of internal battle. I don't break her eye contact as she works through whatever she needs to in her head. After what feels like forever, her shoulders relax. "Ideas," she says.

"Ideas?"

She nods slowly, her voice low when she speaks again. "Inspiration. Writing snippets. Story concepts. Anything that provokes thought or stokes my passion. Anything small that I think could help me to create something so much bigger. Anything I come across in my daily simple life that makes it feel extraordinary. Anything that makes me feel something that I might like to use some day to make other people feel something as well."

My lips part as I stare back at her. "So only your deepest hopes, dreams, and desires?"

Cooper's brows pull together, her face looking so serious for a full three seconds before she breaks, barking out a laugh and shaking her head. "Yeah. Yeah, I guess you could say that."

"I ever make it into your rolodex of future smash hit movie ideas?" I ask her.

Cooper swipes her tongue against her bottom lip as she looks up at me. She takes a breath, looking like she's about to say something, then suddenly turns her head away, taking a long sip of her soda.

I'll take that as a yes. I let out a chuckle. "Well, where are you gonna get all your inspiration now without me, Cooper?"

"I'll have plenty going on, don't you worry," she says. "Now that I actually have a strong chance, I need to focus on filling out my scholarship application. Plus I'll be more involved in the yearbook than ever. Also whatever my new student body president duties entail. And, of course, work. And–"

"Everything else you do," I finish for her.

"Right," she nods. A couple of seconds of silence stretch by before she asks, "Are you excited for basketball to start next week?"

"Oh," I breathe. "Yeah, of course, I'm excited. Jesus, that's already next week, isn't it?" I ask, running a hand through my hair.

"This semester really is flying by. It'll be Thanksgiving before we know it."

"Fuck, I hope not."

The words come tumbling out of my mouth before I can stop them, accompanied by my reflexive wince.

Cooper eyes me, her brows raised. "Uh...What's wrong with Thanksgiving?"

"Nothing," I shake my head, looking away. I try my best to look casual, but just the word alone is making my skin crawl.

"Robbie?" Cooper puts her hand on my shoulder. I try to shrug it off, but that just makes her grip my arm with both hands, forcibly spinning me to face her. "*Hey*, what is it?"

I flex my jaw, not meeting her eyes. "I said it was nothing, Cooper. Just drop it, please."

"Not a chance." My head snaps up as I'm completely caught off guard by her response. "*Now*," she says, now that she has my full attention, "talk to me, Goose."

I blow a heavy breath out of my nose. "I just... I hate Thanksgiving. Gonna be honest, Cooper. It may just be my least favorite day of the whole year."

She tilts her head at me thoughtfully. "Why?"

"Because it's my parents' favorite," I admit. "I think because they like to torture me."

"What do you mean?" she asks.

I grind my teeth together. I don't want to talk about this. I never talk about this–or about anything having to do with my family– to *anyone*.

So why is my gut telling me to word vomit every thought that's been swirling in my mind for most of my life to Cooper right now?

"They hardly even acknowledge every other holiday," I begin. "Most of them, they are both on-call for emergency cases at the optometry office, and on Christmas we basically always take an extravagant vacation where they can dump me on a beach and ignore me for the week while they go off on their own itinerary of things to do. But, for whatever reason, Thanksgiving is the one day a year where my parents like to pretend like we are one big happy family. My dad makes us get dressed up like we're going to the freaking Oscars and sit around our stiff uncomfortable dining room table in our stuffy loveless home and pretend that we're thankful for all of it. I don't know what it is. It's like my dad feeds off of it.

Like it makes him feel like he's meeting his yearly quota of parenting. Like he can actually pretend we are the shining golden family he wants the rest of the town to think we are."

"Aren't you?" Cooper asks, her voice barely audible.

I scoff out a laugh. "I guess it depends on how you define it. Sure, my family's successful. We've made a name for ourselves, like my father likes to remind me every five minutes. But, at the end of the day, once we're all just together with each other under one roof...none of us are happy. Because my dad's never happy. Not really. I mean, my mom, older brother, and sister at least make him content. Because they try. They *want* to please him. But I figured out a long time ago that there just wasn't any point. I was never going to be who he wanted me to be."

I swallow, stealing a glance at Cooper. She's watching me intently, her lips pressed together and expression unreadable.

"So I just stopped trying," I continue. "And I'm usually able to hide from him for the most part every other day of the year. I'm just at home as little as possible. If he can't see me, he can't give me shit for not being half of the son he always wanted. *Hell*, not even half of the son he already has."

"Steven?" Cooper asks.

I nod. "Yeah, Steven." His name feels like acid on my tongue.

"The rest of the year, I'm usually able to remain under the radar. I never show up to family occasions, and ninety-nine percent of the time, I'm not questioned on it. But on Thanksgiving...there's no exceptions. And...I don't know. It just sucks."

The air goes silent as I finish off my rant, and, as time goes on, a deep feeling of remorse starts to twist in my stomach. I rake a hand through my hair, trying to play off the embarrassment tinging the tips of my ears pink over just spilling all of my shit to Cooper. I start to fidget with my jacket. I *never* fidget. I don't know what's gotten into me tonight. Enough time eventually passes that I'm convinced Cooper isn't going to say anything, but then she surprises me, suddenly speaking up.

"Does anyone else ever go to your Thanksgiving?" she asks.

I turn to look at her, caught off guard by her question. "Uh...no. Not usually. My grandparents are all dead, and my only aunt and uncle don't get along with my parents." *Of course they don't*, I frown to myself. "So, yeah, I guess nobody usually comes. Well, nobody except my sister's husband. And a couple of my brother's girlfriends in the past."

Cooper's gray eyes are glossy as she stares up at me. Her throat bobs once before she says, "My mom always works on Thanksgiving." My brows raise at her statement. "It pays overtime, and people at the diner are always really generous with tips on holidays. Since it's just the two of us, it just makes sense for her to take the shift. I usually spend the day watching movies and baking a chocolate cake until she gets home a little before midnight with leftovers from the diner. It's kind of a sad little tradition we've developed. But I love it."

"Oh," I say, not really sure how else to respond.

Cooper threads her fingers together, glancing away. "That being said...I'm free for Thanksgiving dinner. You know, if you'd like some emotional support. Or back-up. Or whatever..." She slowly raises her eyes to meet mine again.

"*Oh*," I say again, with much more certainty this time. "I–Uh–Cooper...You don't have to do that... Not for me..."

"I don't mind," she responds softly. "Really, I mean it. It might actually be nice to not spend the day alone for a change."

I swallow hard. It's on the tip of my tongue to tell her no. To insist that it's not necessary. To tell her I don't need her to be there and that I take it all back. *But the truth is...*

"That would be really great, Cooper."

She smiles tightly up at me. "Okay then. I'll be there."

"Okay," I breathe, nodding slowly.

I watch as Cooper's smile falters, her brows pinching. "The only thing is...well..."

"What?" I ask.

"They think I'm your girlfriend."

"Oh... right," I mutter.

But she's not anymore.

Cooper chews on her bottom lip, her eyes squinting. "I guess... we could..."

"What?" I question her.

"I mean...should we maybe just...continue? To pretend?"

My back straightens, a fluttery feeling pounding against my ribcage. "I suppose we could."

"Yeah?"

"Yeah," I nod. Cooper looks apprehensive, and I fully understand the feeling. "You know, it probably makes the most sense anyways."

"You think?" she asks.

"Yeah," I insist. "Everyone thinks we're the power couple of the school right now. We just won Homecoming King and Queen."

Cooper nods, processing what I'm saying. "Yeah, you're right. And I did just win student body president. It would probably look a little weird for us to so abruptly break up."

"Exactly," I agree. "It only makes sense to stretch it out a little longer."

"Right. We don't want anyone asking any questions," Cooper says.

"Now *that* would be a catastrophe."

Cooper pulls my jacket closed tighter around herself, blowing out a steady breath. "Okay. So we continue for a little longer. Until... winter break?"

"Winter break," I confirm. "Yes, that works."

She clears her throat, shifting on her feet. "What about Denise?"

"I've got Denise handled. Don't worry about it, Cooper."

"What does that mean?"

I open my mouth and then close it again. Because I don't really know what it means. Not yet. *But I suppose I can figure it out as I go?* "Can I just ask you to trust me?"

Cooper studies me hesitantly, her eyes darting between mine. "If we do this..." she says, not addressing my question, "the same rules apply?"

"Same rules," I agree.

"If either of us wants out at any time, we're honest, and we end it," Cooper says.

"Deal."

"And?" she questions me.

"I won't kiss you."

She flattens her lips, her gaze flicking away. "And?"

"And I won't make you look stupid."

"Great," Cooper nods, satisfied for now. "We've come to an agreement. Now, can we please go watch the rest of *Dirty Dancing*?"

My lips pull slowly into a smirk.

"Sure thing, baby."

twenty-nine

SARA

"Are you sure you want to do this?" Robbie asks.

I slide out of the passenger seat of his Camaro, straightening my dress. "I'm sure, Robbie."

He closes my door behind me, coming to walk by my side. He seems stiff, not like his normal self. I'm not sure if it's the suit jacket he's traded his usual Members Only jacket in for, or the way his usually tousled front strands of hair are slicked back with no chance of slipping into his line of sight, but he seems uncomfortable in his own skin. It's as if he's actually putting thought into how he looks and acts, and something tells me that's not a daily activity for Robbie Summers.

"Really, Cooper, I mean, there's still time to back out."

"As we are actively walking to your front door? Only feet away?" I question him.

"If we're not past the threshold that means we haven't reached the point of no return," he insists.

"Robbie," I say gently, waiting for him to look at me. "We've made it this far. We are going to Thanksgiving with your family."

The last six weeks have gone by in a blur. It felt so far away when I committed to helping Robbie through Thanksgiving, but, between him starting basketball and me being busier than ever with everything else going on in my life, we settled into an easy routine that made the weeks fly by.

Aside from a few basketball games that I was coerced into attending as a *Bleacher Babe* (*I don't want to talk about it*), and a Halloween party at the school that began with an argument over both Robbie and me unknowingly dressing as Tom Cruise's character in *Risky Business* (*don't ask*) and ended with a dance battle to Michael Jackson's *Thriller* that left me with a knot on my head and Robbie with a sprained ankle that kept him out of basketball practice for three days (*you don't want to know*), we've managed to get by fairly civilly.

Well, as civilly as you could expect from us.

We've held hands in the hall and eaten lunch at the same table. I've maintained my work, extra curricular, and volunteer schedule as best I can while Robbie's kept up with his basketball one, both of us compromising on one at least semi-public outing per week. I haven't asked Robbie what's going on with Denise, and he hasn't told me. It's worked. It's been fine.

Completely and totally *fine.*

"Really, it's going to be fine," I tell Robbie.

"You don't know that–"

"*I do,*" I insist. "Because I'm saying it's going to be fine. I've *decided* it's going to be. So it will be."

Robbie's throat bobs and he turns his head away from me. "When the hell did you become the voice of reason out of the two of us, Cooper?"

That makes my feet stop moving.

I'm pretty sure I always had reason. Just no voice, I think to myself.

"Not sure," I say, shaking my head, "but get used to it, Summers." I grab Robbie by the elbow, practically dragging him the rest of the way to the front door. "Should we ring the doorbell?"

"I live here, Cooper," Robbie grumbles, reaching for the door handle.

"Well, I was just trying to be polite."

Robbie shoves the door open and we come face to face with who I assume must be Robbie's mother. Her hair is bleach blonde and her eyes are more green than brown, but she has Robbie's same golden skin tone and exactly the same formation of beauty marks across her face as him.

"My goodness!" she squeaks, clutching her chest.

"Oh, hi, Mom," Robbie says.

"Robert, you could have rang the doorbell. I wasn't prepared."

Robbie glances back at me and I press my lips together to suppress the smug grin attempting to make its way onto my face. "Sorry, Mom," he replies to her, standing up straight and stepping aside to make room for me to enter.

"Have I taught you no manners, my boy?" she asks him.

I let out a chuckle, assuming she's taking a lighthearted jab at Robbie, but when her hazel eyes narrow on me, I realize she's being entirely serious. I clear my throat, forcing my grin to fall.

Yikes. Is it hot in here all of a sudden?

"Sorry, Mom," Robbie says. "I'll try to remember next time." I can sense she wants to push him further, probably insisting that *trying* isn't good enough if I had to guess, but she doesn't. "Anyways," he continues. "Mom, this is my girlfriend." It's been months of him saying that, but, for some reason, it still sends a shot of electricity down my spine. "Sara Beth Cooper." I want to correct him, telling her to just call me Sara, but something makes me refrain. "This is my mom, Donna."

"Robert, there you are."

I glance up at the new voice, seeing Robbie's dad stepping into the foyer.

"Well, Sara Beth," Donna Summers says, "I have been very... intrigued to meet you." She extends her hand to me, but not before she looks me up and down with a look on her face like someone

313

would have as they examine the bottom of their shoe after stepping in something.

I take her slender hand in mine, shaking it, putting the sweetest smile on my face as Mr. Summers comes to stand behind his wife. "I've been very intrigued to meet you as well, Mrs. Summers. You know, you and Mr. Summers are a bit of Bay View legends."

"Honored to know it," Mr. Summers says, patting his wife's shoulder. "Proud to keep it that way." He smiles tightly, his gaze shifting over my shoulder. "Right, Robert?"

It's a few seconds before Robbie answers, his voice low when he does. "Yes, sir."

I can feel a thick air of tension forming between Robbie and his parents and, remembering the reason I'm here, try my best to diffuse it. "Well, you have a beautiful home. Thank you so much for letting me join you all today."

Mrs. Summers blinks a few times before focusing on me again. "Yes, well, shall we head into the kitchen?" she asks. "The food should be just about ready to bring into the dining room."

I look in Robbie's direction, but his eyes are on the ceiling, his jaw tight.

"Sounds great, Mrs. Summers," I say.

Robbie and I follow after his parents, weaving through their house that could fit probably six of mine inside of it, until we reach the kitchen. As we walk in, I immediately spot Robbie's brother, Steven, recognizing him from the optometry office on the day of *the incident*.

He's leaning against the kitchen counter with a glass of red wine in his hand, the collar of his white dress shirt popped straight up and the pink sweater tied around his neck perfectly ironed. It takes every ounce of me to not snort at how comically pretentious he looks. His head swivels in our direction, and the gleam he gets in his eyes when he sees me forces my gaze to shoot away.

My eyes end up landing on who I have to assume is Robbie's older sister, Janet, and her husband. I think Robbie said his name was Will, but, considering the way neither one of them seems to plan on acting like I exist, I'm not sure that it's that important I remember.

"Robert, aren't you going to introduce Sara Beth to the rest of the family?" his father asks.

"Well, you kind of just did," Robbie says. "And Steven's already met her."

Mr. Summers simply raises his eyebrows at Robbie, and the way it makes Robbie fold sends a wave of nausea through me.

"Right, I apologize, sir," Robbie grumbles. He attempts to run a hand through his hair, but it doesn't have the same effect with the way he has it sealed in place today. "This is my girlfriend."

"Such a treat to see you again, Sara Beth," Steven says, raising his wine glass in my direction. The smile he flashes me makes my skin crawl, but I force my own to my face, crossing my arms over my chest.

"Nice to see you as well," I say. "Thankfully, this time, it's not because I was lucky enough to have any exploding objects near my eyeball today."

Nobody laughs at my attempt at a joke. The only response I get is a steady exhale and a shake of the head from Robbie.

Great.

Fortunately, the kitchen timer chooses now to go off and save me from my spotlight of embarrassment.

"Ah, that'll be the turkey," Mrs. Summers says. "Robbie, if you could just grab that out of the oven?"

"Sure, Mom," he agrees.

"Everything else is already on the table in the dining room," she continues. "Let's go ahead and take our seats. I'll grab another bottle of wine."

I try my best to hang back and wait for Robbie to handle the turkey, but his mother shoos me into the dining room as soon as she has another bottle of red in hand. I make my way to the seat she points at when I look confused, pulling the chair out as slowly as possible, not wanting to sit down until Robbie does for some reason. I'm simply not slow enough, however, settling into my seat right as Robbie makes his way through the doorway carrying a platter with a massive turkey on it.

"So, Sara Beth," Steven begins, instantly making my spine steel, "not that we're not thrilled to have you here, but, can I ask, how does one find themselves without plans on Thanksgiving?"

My mouth falls open at the bluntness of his unexpected question. "Oh– Well, I wouldn't say I don't have plans. They're just not until later." Steven and Janet raise a singular brow practically in sync with one another. "It's just– My Mom. She always works on Thanksgiving."

Robbie finally makes it to the table, balancing the heavy platter in his hands.

"Oh, well isn't that commendable?" Mrs. Summers speaks up. "Is she a doctor?"

"Eh...no," I mutter. "She's a waitress."

I think Robbie's mom nearly chokes on her wine.

"A waitress, you say?" Robbie's father asks.

"Your mom's a *waitress?*" Steven adds.

Suddenly, the turkey platter is slammed down onto the table, rattling every dish and wine glass sitting on it. Six heads turn in Robbie's direction. "That's what she said, isn't it?" he snaps.

"Hey, I was just making sure I heard her correctly," Steven retorts.

"Yeah?" Robbie questions. "Are you due for a hearing check? Do you need me to bring you to the doctor?"

"*Enough*, Robert," Mr. Summers states. "Sit down."

Robbie's fists clench at his side as he throws one more heated look in his brother's direction before taking his seat next to me.

"Sara Beth, what's your mother's name?" Mrs. Summers asks.

"Sherri Cooper," I tell her.

"Ah," she sighs, exchanging a look with Robbie's father. "Formerly Sherri Rogers?"

"Yes...that's her," I reply hesitantly.

"Hmmm," Robbie's mother hums.

"Do you two know her?" I ask.

"Oh, we certainly remember Sherri from high school, don't we, Donna?" Mr. Summers asks his wife.

"Of course," she confirms. "I mean, who could forget *Airy Sherri?*"

"Excuse me?" My brows raise.

Robbie's parents pass a look between each other.

"Did you say...*Airy...Sherri?*"

"Oh, it's nothing, dear," Mrs. Summers assures me. "Just a silly little high school nickname."

"And where would that nickname come from?" I question her.

Her lips purse. "Oh, you know," she waves her hand. "Your mother was always such a cute, sweet girl. But people just like to make jokes."

When I still appear confused, Mr. Summers chimes in. "Just that she didn't have too much...going on up here." He taps on his temple.

Heat instantly blooms across my cheeks.

"Again, it was just a joke," he insists, holding his hands up defensively. Mrs. Summers chuckles, taking a sip of her wine. "But we need people like her around. To keep the mood light and fun."

"*And to wipe down tables*," I hear Steven mutter into his wine glass, and my head instantly snaps in his direction.

Robbie pushes back from the table, standing up.

"Oh, great, Robert," Mrs. Summers says, "since you're up, I just remembered I left the gravy sitting on the counter. Could you grab it?"

"I—"

"Do as your mother says, Robert," Mr. Summers says, cutting off whatever Robbie was about to stay.

My gaze is fixed on the table when I see a bowl of mashed potatoes being thrust into my peripheral vision. I glance to the side to see Will holding them out to me. I hadn't even realized we had started passing around food. I robotically grab the bowl from him, adding a single scoop to my plate as Robbie storms back into the kitchen for the gravy.

"I remember her going with that ginger-headed boy back in school," Mrs. Summers muses. "What was his name? Charles?"

"Chris," I breathe.

"Oh, *Chris*!" she claps. "Chris Cooper, that's right."

"And what ever happened to your father?" Mr. Summers asks.

"He died."

Robbie freezes in the doorway, gravy boat in hand. His gaze slowly shifts between his parents and me, his tongue pushing into the side of his cheek.

"Oh?" Mr. Summers says, straight-faced. "I'm sorry to hear that."

Somehow, I'm not convinced.

"Right over here is fine, Robert." Mrs. Summers motions to a spot on the table for Robbie to set the gravy.

"So, Sara Beth," Mr. Summers says, drawing my attention back to him, "Robert has told me all about this bright future you have."

"Oh. I– *Really?*" I stammer, glancing at Robbie. He meets my eyes, but doesn't say anything. "Well, I'm planning to attend NYU for screenwriting–"

"Any chance you could maybe rub some of that ambition off on our son?" Mr. Summers cuts me off.

I rear back, caught off guard. "What?"

I can see Robbie stiffen in my peripheral vision, his gaze raising slowly to his father.

"Oh, you know," Mr. Summers says, "it would just be nice if you could teach him to put a little effort in. To something other than his hair, of course."

My mouth falls open, but my voice is caught in my throat.

"I mean, as someone who has no example to follow in life, you've managed to make something of yourself. Robert has absolutely no excuse to have no desire to be worth something."

I feel the last ounce of blood drain from my face the moment the last drop of wine is emptied from Robbie's father's glass.

Robbie's. Father.

Does he even deserve to be called that?

Mr. Summers's head swivels around, looking for something else to fill his glass with. His eyes land on the wine bottle just to the side of Robbie. I assume he's about to ask him to pass it to him, but instead, he pushes back from the table, walking over to stand by Robbie as he pours himself another glass of wine. The dining room is silent, but, as I look around the table, I realize the rest of Robbie's family aren't quiet because of shock or mortification in the way I am. In fact, most of them look barely half-interested to be here. Janet's examining her fingernail polish while her husband picks absentmindedly at his mashed potatoes. Mrs. Summers is staring off into space, like her mind is in a totally different place. Steven is the only one showing any ounce of emotion, yet he's the one infuriating me the most, unable to wipe the shit-eating grin off his face.

Finally finding my voice, I look up at Mr. Summers. "I...I can't believe you'd say that. *Any* of that."

He looks completely unfazed by my statement, setting the wine bottle down and taking a sip from his glass. "Just being truthful, Sara Beth. I think Robert has a lot to learn from you. That's more than I could say about any of his previous trysts."

"I–" I begin, but am immediately cut off by Robbie.

"She's not just a *tryst*, Dad," he grits. "And she just goes by Sara."

Robbie's father narrows his eyes at him, but I don't give him a chance to say anything in response.

"I don't think you're giving your son enough credit, Mr. Summers."

He breathes a laugh. "I think maybe you're the one giving him too much credit, dear. The boy hasn't even filled out a single college application. He's an embarrassment. But it's nothing he doesn't know. Right, son?"

I can already feel the rage flowing hot through my body, but it makes me feel like I'm about to burst into flames when Mr. Summers reaches down and roughly messes up Robbie's hair until it's entirely disheveled, the chestnut brown strands jutting off his head in every which way.

I'm out of my chair before I even realize it, my hand slamming down on the table. "Why do you do that to him? He's not a child, you know."

"*Cooper, it's fine,*" Robbie mutters, subtly pushing his hair out of his eyes.

"No, Robbie, actually, it's not."

Mr. Summers laughs, looking taken aback. "If he's not a child, maybe he shouldn't insist on acting like one. And I think I'm perfectly aware of who my son is."

"*Really?* Because I'm not so sure."

"Young lady—"

"*No,*" I hold up a hand, cutting him off. "I don't know who you think your son is at home. *Worthless?* An *embarrassment?*" I shake my head, my cheeks burning with heat. "I don't know about any of that. But what I *do* know is, at school, he's a *god.* Everybody knows who he is. Everybody looks up to him. People make a path for him when he walks into a room because they look up to him as a leader. In fact, up until a few months ago, many people would consider *me* the embarrassment. I wasn't anybody until Robbie came into my life. He's opened my eyes to so many things and possibilities I never thought existed. He might not be applying to Ivy League schools, but he's one of the smartest people I know. There are some things you simply can't be taught in school, and he's the master of every single one of them. Because of that, people at Bay View value him. They *respect* him. Maybe if you opened your eyes for two seconds—something I'd think a family of *optometrists* would be at least somewhat decent at— you might just see what everyone else sees. And you might respect him too. He doesn't have to be a carbon copy of you to be worth something. And, you know what? As far as I'm aware, every person I've ever met that *wipes down tables* deserves a whole lot more respect from me than any of you do."

I place my hands on my hips, taking a moment to catch my breath before I scan the room to find six sets of wide eyes glued to me. "Well, with that being said. Thank you for allowing me into your home. It's truly been as unpleasant as I could've imagined. I'd say I'm sorry for causing a scene, but I have a feeling it was well overdue." I turn, glancing down at the chair to my side. "Robbie, would you care to take me home now?"

I swear I watch Robbie's eyes shift from dark to milk chocolate in real time, his lips pulling up ever so slightly at one corner.

"Yeah," he nods. "Yeah, I would."

thirty

ROBBIE

Neither Cooper or I have said a word to each other by the time I pull to a stop in front of her house. I swear she still hasn't caught her breath since her epic speech she laid on my father.

The same one that still has my heartbeat pounding in my ears.

I glance over at her in my passenger seat, still seeing the shallow rise and fall of her chest. She's chewing on her bottom lip and tapping her foot as she stares out the window at the evening sky. With our early exit from my house, it's barely half past six. She has several hours before her mom is supposed to come home, and I feel an odd sensation of guilt pinching in my chest at the thought of leaving her here for all that time.

I also feel an equally strong sense of dread at having to go back home to face my family. God only knows how they'll react. Either my dad will yell, or he won't speak to me for the next two weeks. I'm crossing every finger I have that it's the latter.

Hell, if I'm lucky, maybe he'll extend his usual silent treatment sentence to a month.

Whatever he does though, I know it'll be worth it. Every ounce of punishment will be worth getting to see that flabbergasted look across my dad's face. The look of someone that hasn't been challenged in eighteen years. I wasn't aware he was even capable of having that look.

Looks like Cooper's short temper and sharp tongue are good for something after all.

I'm suddenly brought back to reality at the sound of a car door opening, and, when my eyes refocus, I find Cooper out of her seat. Her gaze keeps flicking between the ground and my face, her mouth opening and closing. After a few seconds, she blurts, "See you at school, I guess. Bye."

She slams the door shut before I even have a chance to respond, practically jogging to her front door.

See you at school, I guess?

What the hell?

I shake my head in confusion, throwing my door open and barrelling after her. I catch her by the arm just as she is pushing her front door open.

"What do you want?" she asks.

"Cooper, what I want is for you to explain to me what the hell that just was."

Her lips press together tightly as she glances away from me. "I was just trying to do the right thing."

"*The right thing?*" I question her.

"Yes," she insists. "I'm sorry, but I just snapped. Someone can only be in an enclosed place with such a raging asshole for so long."

My brows pull together, my mouth falling open, ready to fight her as always, but then, after a few seconds, I realize.

"You're talking about my father."

"Yes?" she confirms, tilting her head at me. "Who else would I be talking about?"

Me.

"No one. I don't know." I shake my head.

It's quiet for a few moments as I stare down at the stained concrete of Cooper's front porch steps beneath my feet, until she breaks the silence, practically whispering, "Are you mad at me?"

My head snaps up. "What?"

"I know your relationship with your family is strained, and that you're not your father's biggest fan– and honestly, vice versa– but I probably shouldn't have gone off as hard as I did. It wasn't my place." I cock my head, my eyes traveling between the lines of concern etched in Cooper's forehead and her wringing hands. "You're totally mad. I *was* too much, wasn't I?"

I take a moment to take in what she's saying, how she's *apologizing* for defending me. It takes everything in me not to reach out and shake her by her shoulders. Instead, I blow out a puff of air, keeping my face neutral. "I mean, you give *one* successful speech, Cooper, and now you just have to bust them out everywhere you go." Her spine steels when she catches my sarcasm. "You think you can dial it back a bit? Really, you've got us all walking on eggshells around here–"

Cooper whacks my chest with the back of her hand, making me chuckle.

"Goodnight, Robbie." She rolls her eyes, moving to close the door, but I catch it with my hand.

"Hey, wait a second," I say, pushing the door back open and leaning against the frame.

"What?" she huffs, crossing her arms.

"Thank you."

Her brows raise, but she doesn't respond.

"For coming tonight," I elaborate, "even if it was only for, like, twenty minutes."

Cooper's cheeks flush, and she starts to turn her head away, but I reach out, catching her chin between my thumb and forefinger, forcing her to look at me.

"And for what you said. And how you said it." I swallow. "Really. It was..."

"Insane?" she asks.

"I was thinking *badass*."

She blows a breath out of her nose, a smile tugging at the corners of her mouth. It suddenly occurs to me how close we are, and I drop my hand away from her face, taking a slight step back. An odd look passes over Cooper's face as I do so, but she hides it well, clearing her throat.

"Well, I just..." she stammers. "I couldn't listen to your dad talk about you like that. I might have said some things to you in the past...I mean we've both said things...but I would never really...I don't mean..."

"I get it, Cooper."

"Yeah?" she questions hesitantly.

"Yeah," I nod. "Only we're allowed to give each other shit."

Her mouth falls open, and she shakes her head, chuckling. "Close enough."

I have to laugh as well.

"Really though," Cooper says, "you may get on my absolute last nerve, and you may act like an entitled jerk sometimes, and you may be a lot better at the whole playing thing than the working thing...but I'd never call you worthless."

My lips roll into my mouth as I try to meet Cooper's eyes, but fail. As much as I'd rather not let her–or anyone– know, the whole *worthless* thing really strikes a chord with me.

Maybe because you've heard it your whole life.

"I know I've judged you before," she continues. "I've made a lot of assumptions about who you are and the family you come from–"

"I've done the same for you, Cooper."

"Yeah, and you were wrong," she nods. "But so was I. And just because your life looks a whole lot shinier on the surface than mine does, doesn't mean that you can't have a whole lot worse happening on the inside than I do." I blink at her, unsure of how to respond. "I'm just trying to say that I'm sorry, okay?"

My throat bobs as I slowly dip my head in agreement. "Yeah. I'm sorry too, Cooper."

"For what?" she asks.

About a hundred things fly through my mind to apologize to her over, which is surprising to me. Before a few months ago, I could probably count on one hand the times in my life that I was genuinely sorry for something. I try to pinpoint one specific thing to say, or try to think of a way to summarize all of it, but, because I'm me, I decide to go with the route I know best.

"I'm sorry my dad referred to you as a *tryst*."

Cooper practically snorts, her head falling back. "Oh my God," she chuckles. "If only he knew."

"Yeah," I agree. "If only he knew you were the least exciting tryst to ever exist."

"*Hey!*" Cooper scoffs, feigning offense as she swats at me.

"I'm sorry, baby. But there isn't much *tryst*-ing going on here. Especially not enough to warrant everything else that comes along with you that I have to endure." She tries to swat me again, but I dodge her. "Hey, at least you can say you're definitely not a cheap date."

"I hate you," Cooper says, shaking her head.

"See what I mean?" I raise my brows.

We both laugh, but eventually, as the sound fades away, we're both left in silence.

"Well..." Cooper sighs, glancing over her shoulder inside her house.

"I guess I should get going," I say.

"Okay," she nods.

My feet don't move. Cooper crosses her arms, looking me up and down.

"Uh...you're not going," she says after several seconds.

"Yeah, I know," I respond. "I guess...I don't really want to." I glance up at her, seeing her brows raise. "Go home, that is."

"Oh," she breathes, her shoulders falling. "That makes sense."

I run a hand through my hair, and, when I find it still messy, that just makes me want to go home even less. I huff out a breath. "But you gotta do what you gotta do. So, see ya, Cooper." I start to spin around, but Cooper's voice makes me pause.

"You know...I'm just going to watch movies until my mom gets home later. I already baked my chocolate cake this morning. So, I mean, if you wanted to..."

"Yeah?" I question her, my spine steeling.

"You can join me," she offers. "But you have to promise not to talk during the movies. Or to try to make me into a *tryst*, because there's not a chance in hell."

My lips pull into a smirk. "I can't guarantee the first, but we should be safe on the second."

Cooper rolls her eyes before pushing the door open further, stepping aside. "Deal."

I step inside her house, letting her close the door behind me.

"I'm just going to get out of my dress," Cooper says.

"Excuse me?"

She shakes her head, covering her face. "I mean, I'm going to put on something more comfortable."

"No, I get it. You're using reverse psychology on me, Cooper. You invite me into your home, telling me I have to keep my hands to myself, just to lock me in and pounce the first chance you get."

"Robbie, I didn't–"

"You know, Cooper, I'd like to fight you on this. To say it's a double standard and wrong for you to objectify me in this way, but, if I'm being honest, I kinda think being objectified turns me on."

"*Oh my God.*" Cooper throws her hands in the air in defeat, heading towards her bedroom door. "I'm going to change now. The most recent movies I brought home from Groovy Movie are sitting on the TV stand. Pick one out and please figure out how to stop talking by the time I'm back."

I open my mouth, but Cooper slams her bedroom door closed before I can say anything else. I let out a chuckle, shrugging off my suit jacket and tossing it onto the couch. I untuck my dress shirt and undo another button at the top of it, feeling like I can breathe a little better as I walk over to the TV stand and crouch down to look at the small stack of VHS tapes sitting on top of it. The first three are *Footloose*, *Grease*, and *Flashdance*.

In a musical mood this week, are we, Cooper?

I almost decide to just go with *Grease* before the last movie on the bottom of the stack that I didn't see before catches my eye.

"*No freaking way,*" I whisper to myself, grinning.

I pick up the tape, standing up to my full height right as the door to Cooper's room opens and she reappears in the living room. "Did you pick something?"

I glance up, finding her in a pair of gray sweatpants and a blue Bay View Bears sweatshirt. "Uh, yeah. I think I did." I flash her a teasing smile, making her tilt her head at me.

"What?" she asks.

I take a few steps closer to her, holding up *The Outsiders* for her to see.

"Oh…" she mutters, her shoulders dropping. "I– Uh…forgot I got that."

"I'm sure you did," I nod.

She narrows her eyes at me, plucking the tape from my hand and moving to TV to get the movie started.

Once she does, she settles on the couch, raising her brows at me in a way of asking me if I'm going to sit down. I shake my head, plopping down next to her, leaving a few feet of space between us.

"Are you going to fast forward through the previews?" I ask.

Cooper shakes her head. "It's all a part of the experience."

"Oh, of course it is," I deadpan.

"And besides," she shrugs. "I figured I'd give you the time to get all your talking out."

"How considerate of you."

"Well, it *is* the season of giving."

I breathe out a laugh.

"I'm going to grab a drink before the movie starts," Cooper says, pushing off the couch. "You want a Coke?"

"I'd prefer a Pepsi."

"And I'd prefer to be watching this movie with Rob Lowe, but we get what we get."

I hear the fridge close, and, a few seconds later, Cooper is holding out a Coke to me. I let out a scoff. "Fair enough, Cooper," I say, taking it from her.

I don't think it's intentional, but when she sits back down on the couch, her knees pulled up to her chest, Cooper's a lot closer to me now. We crack open our cans of Coke in unison, each of us taking a sip.

"So, speaking of the season of giving, do you have any plans for the holidays?" I ask.

Cooper shakes her head. "It'll just be the same old, same old for me. I'll go hang out with Alice's family on Christmas Eve until my mom is off work, and then it'll just be me and Mom on Christmas day. Nothing extravagant. But I don't even feel like I can think about the holidays right now. The next two weeks are going to be crazy."

"The next two weeks?" I question her.

She takes another sip of her Coke, her brows pulling together. "Finals, Robbie."

"Oh, right. Those."

Cooper lets out a sigh. "I *have* to be valedictorian. I've worked so hard for it now. I can't let it slip my last year. And especially now with me applying for the NYU scholarship."

"Right," I nod. "I get it."

I don't. At all. But I know it's important to her.

"You've got it in the bag, Cooper."

"We can only hope," she mutters.

"So, other than finals," I say, "there is something coming up in the next couple of weeks that I wanted to talk to you about."

"Oh? What's that?"

I blow out a breath, meeting her eyes. "Denise's annual holiday party."

"Oh..." Cooper says, her face scrunching.

"She has it every year on the last Friday night before winter break. It's huge."

"Is it?" she asks, suddenly very enthralled with the tab on her soda can.

I nod. "Her parents go out of town to give her the house for it and everything."

"*Seriously?*" Cooper questions, looking up at me.

"Yep. Everybody goes. It always gets pretty crazy."

Cooper lets out a heavy sigh, her mouth twisting to the side. "So, we should probably go."

"Yeah, I want to go."

Cooper stiffens in her seat. She shifts slightly away from me, looking down and fidgeting with her sweatshirt. "Then you should go," she says.

"And what about you?" I ask.

"Oh, well, if you think it'll look best if I go with you...to keep selling *us*. It's up to you. Or if you just want to call it off a couple weeks earlier. It doesn't matter–"

"Cooper," I cut her off, grabbing her knee to stop her turning away from me any further. "Let me rephrase. I want to go to Denise's party," I pause, waiting until she meets my eyes, "with you."

Cooper's eyes flick between my own, reflecting the gray and blue of her outfit and looking like the most complex set of stormy skies I've ever seen. "Okay," she says softly. "If that's what you want."

I tilt my head at her. "What do *you* want?"

Her lips part, and I find myself glancing down at them. When my eyes return to hers, I find her looking down at mine. I notice a faint flush of color appearing across her cheeks, and it hits me right then how much she reminds me of Cherry Valance from *The Outsiders*. In fact, physically, you could believe they're sisters. Same copper red hair and big doe eyes. Same fair skin and full, heart-shaped lips. *Yeah*, the physical features are all there. But I know, more than anything...she's got the same fire as Cherry. She's no cheerleader, and she definitely isn't the most popular girl in school, but she doesn't need any of that. She has the same strong-willed attitude. The same short fuse and refusal to back down. Seeing as this is my favorite movie, I'm confused how it took me this long to make the connection.

I'm not sure when I reached for it, but it suddenly occurs to me that I'm twirling a strand of Cooper's hair in between my fingers. I look up from my hand to meet her eyes again. She takes an unsteady breath like she's about to say something, but she doesn't get a chance to, both of our heads turning towards the TV at the familiar sound of *Stay Gold* by Stevie Wonder and the opening credits of *The Outsiders* begin.

We both snap apart, Cooper's hair falling from my fingers and both of our backs hitting the couch like it's a fridge and we're heavy duty magnets.

"*Movie's on,*" Cooper mumbles unnecessarily.

"*Right,*" I mutter back.

And we watch it.

And I don't fail at either of Cooper's conditions.

I don't say another word. Not during my favorite parts. Not when Cooper scoffs or giggles or gasps throughout the movie. Not even when Cherry Valance mouths off to Dallas Winston at the drive-in movie and I'm itching to tell Cooper that's her.

I don't lay a finger on her either. Not when her hair falls in her face. Not when she hugs her legs closer to her as she shivers, and everything in my body is urging me to move closer to her. Not even when I see a single tear falling from her eye at the end of the movie and my hand twitches at my side as I fight the urge to reach up and swipe it away for her.

No. I watch the movie. And then I leave.

Because reality has hit me. And because I know this little social experiment is coming to an end. And even though neither of us planned to enjoy any aspect of it, you simply can't plan for life, as much as Cooper or Denise or Jesse or anyone else I know might disagree.

Unfortunately, it's occurring to me, at the least convenient time possible, that I might just not dislike Cooper as much as I think I do. In fact, I'm realizing, I might actually *enjoy* her presence. It's suddenly apparent, just as I feel her starting to drift away, that in the absolute shitshow that is my life, she's been an anchor. Like a lighthouse in a storm. Like a flame in the darkness. But it doesn't matter. Because we weren't ever made to last. So that's why I leave her house tonight with a curt nod and not so much as a goodbye.

Because, after Denise's holiday party, I know we'll be done. I know she'll be done. Because that's how it was always supposed to be. Because we are who we are. Because, as frustrating as it may be, it really is true.

Nothing gold can stay.

thirty-one

SARA

After a painfully quiet viewing of *The Outsiders*, two weeks of time apart filled with me studying and test-taking like my life depends on it and Robbie doing...*I'm not sure what*, and one semi-awkward car ride where we didn't discuss any of it, Robbie and I are walking through the front door of Denise Davis's house.

This will be fine, I tell myself as the two of us quickly become engulfed in the low lights, blaring music, and mass of underage drinking students from our high school. At first, the crowd seems intimidating, but the further we make our way into the house, the more I feel like I just disappear, and the more comfortable I get.

Just as I start to think this may be a fairly uneventful evening spent under the radar, a voice I've come to know all too well comes ringing through my ears.

"Oh, look! You two are just in time!" Denise calls the moment Robbie and I step into the living room. She claps her hands, hopping up from where she's sitting cross-legged on the floor and flitting over to us.

Jesus Christ.

I try to look to Robbie for any possible out from whatever this situation is about to be, but Denise is clasping both of our wrists in her hands before I even get a chance to turn my head.

"Just in time for what?" I ask her, shifting uncomfortably.

"*Spin the Bottle*, of course," she says, a devilish grin pulling at her baby pink lips.

I instantly feel my heart sink, my throat drying. I successfully glance up at Robbie, but he doesn't offer any help, his expression stoic as he stares back at Denise. Something about that frustrates me, and I find myself letting out a harsh breath. "Do any of your party games *not* involve swapping spit?" I ask.

"None of the fun ones," Denise replies with a wink, tightening her hold on our wrists and dragging us over to the circle of people sitting on the floor. She ends up plopping each of us down a few people apart from each other, then reclaims her own seat, creating a perfect triangle between the three of us. I glance between Denise and Robbie, and then down at my wringing hands and try not to think of the ridiculous irony of this situation.

My eyes eventually settle on Robbie, and I desperately try to send a telepathic message to him, telling him I want out of this, but he's not looking at me. He's too busy running his hand through his hair and talking with Brad to his left. I blow out a breath, setting my hands flat on the floor to force myself to my feet, but pause when I feel a tap on my shoulder.

I turn to see Paul behind me. He bends down, his hazel eyes becoming level with mine. "Hey, Cooper," he says. My brows pull together, a weird feeling settling in my stomach at him calling me that.

"Um, hi, Paul," I say. "What's up?"

"You just looked like you could use one of these," he says, holding up a green bottle. He hands it to me and I realize it's a Bartles and Jaymes wine cooler.

"Oh, I don't–" I'm about to say that I don't drink, but the sandpaper feeling in my throat and the anxiety of the current situation stops me. "Thank you," I say instead, taking a long drink from the bottle. I don't know what to expect from it, but it definitely isn't the sweet citrusy flavor that bursts on my tongue and tastes absolutely nothing like alcohol. My cheeks instantly warms as I down nearly half the bottle in a few gulps. "*Mmm,*" I hum, pulling the bottle away and licking the few drops that escape off my lips.

Paul lets out a chuckle. "You like that?" he asks.

I nod. "It's really good."

"Well, here," he says, holding up a second bottle. "I was bringing this to Ginger, but how about I just tell her we ran out?" He sets the bottle down to the side of my left thigh as I take another drink. "You'll be done with that one in no time."

I swallow, smiling at him. "Thanks."

Paul suddenly reaches up, swiping at the corner of my mouth with his thumb. I stiffen in surprise as he wipes away the drop of wine cooler. "Anytime, Sara," he says, smirking at me before standing up straight again.

I immediately take another drink from the bottle, finishing it. *Geez, these go down easy.* I reach for the second bottle, twisting off the cap. I take a sip, my eyes closing as the flavor and warmth rushes through me once again. When I open my eyes again, however, the warmth turns to a blistering heat when I find Robbie shooting daggers at me from across the circle, his jaw working.

Double dark chocolate, I instantly think.

I tilt my head at him as a way of questioning him, but he doesn't acknowledge it, his fists clenching at his side. Paul takes a seat to his right, and I watch as Robbie's head flicks in his direction for a fraction of a second before he turns his glare back on me. My lips part, a question starting to form, but it doesn't get the chance to as Denise calls my name.

"*Saraaa!*"

My head turns away from Robbie, finding Denise across the circle. "Yeah?"

She pushes forward onto her knees, crawling towards the middle of the circle. "C'mon, Madam President," she says, pushing the empty wine bottle on the floor in my direction. "Your turn."

My head shakes automatically. "Uh– Yeah, no. I'm okay."

"Really?" Denise frowns. "You don't want to spin?"

"No, thanks." I can feel Robbie's stare, but I refuse to look at him, taking another drink of my wine cooler.

"Suit yourself," Denise says, shrugging. "Guess I'll go then." She gives the bottle a sharp twist with a flick of her pink painted nails then sits back on her heels. The bottle is a blur, making several rotations before it eventually starts to slow. I feel goosebumps rise on the back of my neck. *What a stupid, ridiculous game.* I shake my head, raising my bottle to take another sip. But then the game bottle comes to a stop.

And so do I.

I follow the line of the bottle with my eyes, raising them at a snail's pace to see it pointing directly at Robbie's chest.

My mouth opens and closes several times.

I find Robbie looking at Denise. So I look at Denise.

She's looking at Robbie.

I look at Robbie.

Now he's looking at me.

He looks between Denise and me, settling finally on me.

The expression on his face is unreadable. His brows are pinched, his lips rolling into his mouth.

The circle lets out a chorus of *Ooos,* and heat rushes to my face, my hand gripping the neck of the bottle in my hands.

"Oh my goodness!" Denise squeals. "Well, isn't this just hilarious?"

Robbie's eyes are still on me. I notice the tiniest flick of his head, as if he's about to start shaking it, but Denise distracts me, bringing my eyes back to her face. "Well, I suppose this is just how the game is played," she says. "You don't mind, do you, Sara?" She's asking, but she's already inching towards Robbie, crawling towards him like an evil lioness.

Maybe that's why I suddenly have the urge to claw her eyes out.

No. I stop my thoughts in their tracks, gritting my teeth together.

This is perfect, actually.

Isn't this the whole point of what we're doing? Isn't this what Robbie wants? I swallow against the lump in my throat.

Yeah, this is exactly what he wants.

I got what I wanted. I'm the student body president. I'm the yearbook editor. My scholarship application is as strong as it can be. I got my end of the bargain.

It's time Robbie gets his.

I glance up at him, seeing his tongue dart out to wet his bottom lip.

Have at it, Summers.

"No," I say. Robbie's spine steels. Denise pauses her stalking, looking in my direction. "Of course I don't mind," I finish. "It's only fair."

A huge grin spreads across Denise's face. I take another long drink, watching Robbie's eyes narrow on me. His lips pull up at one side, and I hear him scoff out the quietest of laughs.

This is fine.

I can watch this happen. I may have realized sometime in the near past that I may not hate Robbie as much as I thought I did, but that should mean that I should want him to be happy. That I should want him to have fun. This is good. This is fine.

Denise closes in, grabbing Robbie by the front of his shirt and pulling him forward to her. Their lips crash together. Robbie's eyes fall shut.

And my heart drops straight into my stomach.

I can see Denise smiling against Robbie's mouth, loving every second of this. Though Robbie seems stiffer than usual, he eventually shifts his head to the side, allowing her slightly better access to him.

It feels like somebody has dumped boiling water straight over the top of my head, every inch of my skin sizzling and itching with an emotion I can only compare to rage.

This isn't good.

This isn't fine.

Why isn't it fine?

I see the fingers of Robbie's left hand flexing, reaching up and grappling for something to hold. But when they graze Denise's waist, his eyes open just enough to meet mine over Denise's shoulder, and his hand drops back to his side. I look away, biting into the side of my cheek and trying my absolute best to seem completely unfazed. Luckily, all eyes are on Denise and Robbie.

Of course they are. This is how it's always been. How it's always going to be.

I guess Denise pulls away, because everybody is clapping now and Denise is scooting back into her spot in the circle. I stare at her, because I am willing to look anywhere other than at Robbie right now.

"Sorry, Sara. I think I got a little carried away there. Old habits die hard, I guess." She shoots a wink in Robbie's direction, and I resist every urge to hurl my wine cooler straight at her head. "Thanks for letting me borrow your boyfriend."

"Don't even mention it," I grit, flashing her the most pathetic excuse for a smile that I can manage.

She smiles right back at me, unbothered.

Bitch.

"Okay, Paul," Denise sings. "Your turn."

I shift my attention to the shag carpet at my feet, twiddling a few of the fibers between my fingers, trying to get my heart rate under control and praying that my face doesn't look as red as it feels. The sounds of the party around me start blurring together until they're just a whirring in my ear. Eventually, a gasp and the sound of clapping break through the fog.

"My, how the tables have turned!" Denise's voice says.

"Shit," I hear Brad chuckle. "Revenge is best served piping hot, I guess."

A few seconds go by, then everything goes eerily quiet, making me finally glance up.

First, I see Robbie, jaw dropped and shoulders stiff.

Second, my gaze shifts to the left, seeing Denise clapping and smiling harder than she ever has at any pep rally.

Third, my eyes graze back to the right, past Robbie, and towards the middle of the circle, where I find Paul, a smirk playing on his face and his tongue pushing in the side of his cheek.

Fourth, I'm drawn back to Robbie, as I suppose I often infuriatingly am as of late, and find his gaze on the floor, his brows drawn together.

Lastly, my eyes find the target of that double dark chocolate glare. And, suddenly, the whole scene before me makes a whole lot more sense.

The bottle.

Pointed directly at me.

Paul.

I meet his hazel eyes across the circle, and they light up the second I do. I make myself count to three in my head, then I take a long drink from my wine cooler, finishing it off.

"*Welll?*" Denise questions, a devious tone of joy in her voice.

I haven't taken my eyes off Paul, and he hasn't made a move.

Robbie speaks up suddenly. "She said she didn't want to play."

And that's why Paul hasn't made a move.

What a gentleman.

"Well, Robbie," Denise says. "Maybe she's changed her mind. Your girlfriend's a big girl, you know. She's allowed to do that."

"Cooper?" Robbie says.

I don't break Paul's eye contact, my heartbeat in my ears.

"Cooper, you don't have to," Robbie insists. "Let's just move on. Who's next?"

I watch the rise and fall of Paul's chest and measure the indecision and conflicting emotions in his eyes. He watches me do so, then his face cracks into a smile, a single chuckle escaping him. My lips part, the smallest smile coming to my face as well.

"*Sara.*"

My head snaps in Robbie's direction at his call, my brows shooting up.

...Sara?

He's up on his knees, his jaw clenched and the veins in his neck straining. A strand of his perfect hair has gone rogue, falling out of place and curling down in front of his left eye. I can see the slightest tinge of pink topping his cheekbones and ears, a color I'm not sure I've ever truly seen on him before. But then he tilts his head forward, and I catch another shade of pink in the light.

Baby pink lip gloss still painting his lips where Denise just attached herself to him.

Heat creeps up my chest at the image.

Her skin on his. His lips on hers. Her knees and chest brushing up against body. His hand on her waist. Her laughter tickling his mouth. His brown eyes fluttering shut.

Because. Of. Her.

I set my empty bottle down, sitting up on my knees.

"Okay," Robbie says, nodding, his body relaxing. I turn my head back in Paul's direction. He's sat back down, but his eyes are still glued to me, his brows pinched.

I see Robbie sit up taller on his knees in my peripheral vision. "I think we're done with this game–"

But I don't hear anything else.

Because I'm too busy crawling across the circle and launching myself into Paul's arms.

thirty-two

ROBBIE

Sara sets down her bottle, sitting up, and the sweetest sense of relief washes over me.

Sara.

Yeah. I guess I let that slip. Not sure what came over me.

I clear my throat. "I think we're done with this game–"

I don't even get my full sentence out before the relief is immediately replaced with an entirely different feeling that I can't even explain. It feels like a white hot fire poker is being shoved directly into my chest as I watch Cooper fall to her hands and knees and crawl straight forward across the game circle...

And just to the right of me.

Straight onto Paul Strothers's lap.

Within the blink of an eye, she's basically straddling him, her green skirt riding up and falling to the sides, exposing and pooling around her creamy white thighs.

"C–Coop–" My sputtered attempt at questioning her dies on my tongue when she grabs two fistfuls of Paul's shirt collar and yanks him forward. He happily obliges, eyeing her with heavy lids like she's a four course meal and flashing her a lazy grin just before she sinks her mouth into his.

The fire poker gives a harsh twist in my chest before it yanks itself free. I snap my jaw shut, gritting my teeth and trying to swallow against the gravel in my throat. I watch Cooper's ruby red lips work against Paul's, slow and deep and all-consuming, and my blood suddenly feels like it turns to ice in my veins, freezing me to the spot. I don't know what's happening. I feel like I'm going to combust. I don't think my heart and mind have ever raced so fast. And especially never at the same time.

But *why?*

This is *Cooper.*

Why do I care what she does?

She can kiss whoever she wants. Good for her, honestly. It would do her good to live a little. Loosen up some. If it was up to me, I'd go with just about anyone other than Paul fucking Strothers, but I guess that doesn't matter.

You're right. It doesn't. Because it's not up to you.

I blink hard. *This is crazy. Why am I worked up over this?* This was the point of all of this at the end of the day, right? Cooper and I aren't from each other's worlds. We don't run in the same circles. We stay in our lanes. *This* is my lane. The point of our arrangement was to push her outside of her comfort zone.

I just didn't know that would mean pushing her into Paul Strothers's lap...

Stop. Breathe. This is nothing. *She's nothing to you.*

You're nothing to her.

My eyes snap into focus as I see Paul's slimy little hands reach up to grip Cooper's thighs, giving them each a light squeeze, his fingers digging in.

The blood in my veins definitely isn't frozen anymore. It's rushing hotter than ever. I think I'm going to lunge forward and break each one of his fingers individually, but I hold myself back, knowing Cooper can fight her own battles and that she is surely going to brush him off in the next millisecond.

I watch his fingers graze one inch higher and dig in once more. She pauses.

And she does the opposite of brushing him off.

Still attached to his mouth, she pulls back just a fraction of an inch and lets out the lightest little moan, her cheeks flushing with color.

The prick *smiles* against her mouth.

And that's when I'm done.

It's a good thing Cooper chooses that moment to pull back for air, because I'm already on my feet, hooking an arm under each of her armpits and hauling her up off his lap. Paul smiles a shit-eating grin up at me as I do, and it takes every ounce of willpower not to kick him twice straight in the teeth and once in his surely half-hard dick for good measure.

"*Robbie, what the–*" Cooper stammers, kicking her feet in confusion as I drag her to her feet and take off, pulling her behind me.

Hoots and hollers sound off from the circle and I hear Brad shout "*Ooo, lovers quarrel!*" But I don't even care. They're already in the background. Out of sight and out of mind.

Speaking of *mind*, I'm not sure at this moment if I'll ever think straight again. Right now, all I can focus on is moving my feet forward and bringing Sara Beth Cooper– the infuriating, intoxicating, mind-bending, psychosis-inducing, and, most currently, very strongly protesting and violent, girl of my nightmares– with me if it's the last thing I ever do. My plan was to take us to my car and to get the hell out of here, but there's no way I'm going to make it that far. I feel like I'm going to explode if I don't speak to her right now. I let out a huff and skid my feet to a stop, throwing open the nearest door and shoving Cooper inside. I realize after I follow her inside and slam the door behind us that it's a closet.

"*What the fuck, Robbie?*" she rages, throwing her hands in the air.

"Wow, *fuck*? Big dirty word, Cooper. Just learn it today?" I put my hands on my hips, narrowing my eyes at her. I need to get myself under control. My chest feels so heavy it's hard to breathe right now.

She scoffs. "Yeah, maybe I did. Here, let me use it in a different way to prove it. What's your *fucking* problem?"

I let out a humorless laugh. "You know, that's not very ladylike, Cooper. You should watch your tongue. Oh, *wait*. I think you left it back there in Paul's mouth."

Cooper's spine steels, a brand new storm raging in her eyes. "You're...*mad*? About what just happened?" she asks, pointing over her shoulder in the direction of the living room.

I say nothing, blowing a breath out of my nose. I let my eyes trace her face, and when I take in the light sheen across his skin, her flushed cheeks, and her swollen, redder than usual lips, I think I'm gonna lose it. I'd be a damn liar if I tried to tell myself I'd never pictured her this way. But in whatever fucked up fantasy world that was, she never looked this way because of...someone else.

Someone other than me.

I tear my gaze away from her, biting down on my knuckle.

I need to get my head straight.

"You're mad," Cooper repeats, stepping up behind me. "You're *mad* about *Paul?*"

I spin around to face her. "I'm not mad." I shake my head.

"Well, good," she says, crossing her arms. "Because you have *zero* right to be."

"Right." *Because we're only pretending. This isn't real.*

"Because you kissed Denise first."

"Right," I reply automatically.

Wait.

"Wait," I say, shaking my head. "What?"

She lets out a frustrated sigh. "You being mad about me kissing Paul is entirely hypocritical when you just kissed Denise."

"*That's* why I have zero right to be mad?" I ask.

"Well, yeah?" she says, exasperated.

Interesting.

"So let me see if I have this straight, Cooper. It's hypocritical for me to get mad about seeing you kiss Paul?"

"*Yes*. Are we speaking the same language?"

"Okay," I nod. "So that means it made you mad to watch me kiss Denise."

Her spine straightens, and she blinks at me several times. "Not sure what logic you used to deduce that, but no, that's not what that means." She tries to move around me for the door, but I block her path.

"What's it mean then, Cooper?"

"What is your obsession with keeping me captive in closets?" she asks, diverting. "It's becoming concerning." She tries to take another step towards the door, but I hold my ground. She lets out a huff, looking up at me with irritation in her gaze.

"What does it mean, Cooper?" I repeat, more slowly this time.

She stares back at me for a dozen long seconds, her eyes darting between mine, before she answers. "It means that I didn't care." My head pulls back. "So you shouldn't have cared about Paul," she finishes, crossing her arms.

Now it's my turn to stare at her for an extended amount of time. I swallow, standing up to my full height. "Good."

"Good?" she questions.

"Yeah," I nod. "*Good*. Because I didn't." Cooper raises a questioning brow at me. "*Care*."

It's subtle, but I see her face fall, her facade faltering for just a moment before she corrects herself. "Good," she repeats, her voice even.

We stare off in silence for a few more moments before Cooper side-steps me for the door again. I let her this time. I tell myself I'm going to let her go, but the second I start to hear the door handle twist, I turn around, and the filter between my thoughts and my voice cracks wide open.

"But if we're playing everything equal here," I say, making her pause in place, "my allowing Denise to kiss me– well, technically, *you* allowing her to kiss me– "

"*I* allowed her?" Cooper questions, spinning back around to face me.

"Uh, *yeah*?" I laugh. "If anything, I'd say you encouraged her."

Cooper lips part, her eyes narrowing on me. "What was I supposed to say?"

I tilt my head at her.

"Did you not *want* to kiss her?" she asks me.

My mouth falls open, but no answer comes out.

I don't know why. If she would have asked me a month ago if I wanted to kiss Denise, my answer would've been immediate. Absolutely, without a doubt, any minute of any day– *yes*. But, tonight, I...*I don't know*. I'm not sure when exactly it happened, but nothing seems so black and white anymore. I'm not sure when the color red stormed into the picture and took the whole thing over. *How could I have let that happen?* I never *wanted* that to happen.

Cooper is staring at me expectantly, waiting for an answer I don't have to give to her. So I respond to her question with a question of my own.

"Did you want me to kiss her?"

She shakes her head, a humorless smile on her face. "I don't really care what you do or who you do it with, Robbie."

I can see it in the slight twitch of her lips and the way she refuses to let those gray eyes meet mine for more than a second before she looks away again.

She's lying.

"That's not true," I say.

"Excuse me?"

"You were mad," I insist, taking a small step forward.

She lets out a scoff, taking a step forward to match me. "I'm starting to think *you're* mad," she states. "Actually, I'm *convinced*. Why are you mad, Robbie?" She tilts her head at me, her tone mocking

"I'm not *mad*, Cooper," I chuckle dryly. "But, as I was *trying* to say before, Denise being allowed to kiss me doesn't exactly equate to you climbing Paul Strothers like a tree and wrapping yourself around him like a damn spider monkey."

She barks out a laugh, raking her fingers through her fiery hair. "Oh, you're *unbelievable!*"

"*Me?*" I question her, pointing toward myself. "I think my eyes are still trying to process that little show you put on out there," I say, turning my finger in the direction of the living room.

She laughs, clapping her hands together. "Well, my apologies, Robbie. I'm *so* sorry. *Truly.* I apologize if I shattered your little image of me tonight."

"And what image is that?" I ask.

"Oh, you know," Cooper says, waving her hands, "the one of the quiet little girl who stands in the corner all night with her mouth shut, observing everything around her and never participating. The one of the prudish, fun-allergic, untouchable little school nerd."

A wave of heat rushes over me, and I automatically move forward, closing the distance between us. "*Cooper...*" I say, shaking my head, my voice low. "I can assure you, if I've ever had an image of you in my head at any point, it certainly wasn't *that.*"

She slowly raises her gaze to meet mine as she inches backwards away from me. Her lips part like she's thinking about saying something, but then her back hits the door.

"Now, Cooper," I say, ducking my head, "tell me why you were mad."

"I wasn't mad," she replies instantly.

"Then why were you *upset?*" I ask.

Silence.

"You told Denise it was okay, Cooper," I push.

She turns her head, not meeting my eyes. "Well, she shouldn't have asked in the first place," she grits.

Bingo.

"And why's that?"

"Because..." she trails off.

"*Because?*"

She throws her hands in the air. "Because we're supposed to be *dating!*" she fumes.

Her outburst dies out, and I don't respond right away, only returning her burning stare. The air between us is silent, save for the sound of Cooper's labored breathing. I let my eyes rake her figure once, doubling back when I graze over her thighs. I think about Paul's hands on them and reflexively tighten my fists. When I force my gaze back to Cooper's face, her expression is dead serious, an unmistakable depth within her gray eyes. I roll my lips into my mouth.

"I thought it was just supposed to be a game?" I say.

Cooper's back straightens, and she pushes off the door, lessening the already small distance between us. "What, *Spin the Bottle?*" she questions, an edge to her voice as she tilts her head at me. "Or *us?*"

My brows shoot up. *Jesus, Cooper.* I suddenly take in how close she is and my throat bobs. Her pouty red lips are only inches away. An image flashes through my head of dragging the lower one through my teeth, but I instantly shake my head, forcing it away.

"I don't know, Cooper," I breathe. "Which are you willing to play at?"

"I don't think I even know the rules anymore," she mutters.

I force myself even closer to her, bending down to whisper in her ear. "*Fuck* rules."

I can feel the pace of her breathing quicken by the rise and fall of her shoulders. I don't move as she slowly raises her hands, grabbing two fistfuls of my jacket. A shiver runs down my spine and a smile comes to my face as I try to anticipate what this crazy, unpredictable, undeniably, *painfully* beautiful girl is going to do next. Somehow, she manages to completely surprise me, suddenly shoving me away so hard that I stumble, reaching up and grabbing a shelf to steady myself.

"Fuck *you,*" she growls.

I regain my footing, charging back up to her. "*What's your problem?*"

"The same as always! *You.*" I rear back, and Cooper shakes her head, fire blooming in her cheeks. "I mean, what are we even doing anymore, Robbie?"

"What do you mean–" I start to question her, but she cuts me off.

"I got my end of the deal," she says, pointing to her chest. "I'm student body president, yearbook editor, and not a total loser to the school anymore. And *you*," she turns her finger on me, poking it into my chest. "You stood up to your friends and your family. You showed them you could get a serious old boring girl like me to give you a chance. Denise is clearly dying to jump your bones again. So, *again*, I ask, *what the* hell *are we still doing*?"

Cooper's finger stays pressed into my chest and my eyes stay locked on hers. I clench my jaw, slowly raising my hand to wrap around hers. Her eyes squint as they flick down to our joined hands. My voice nearly at a whisper, I ask her, "Why wasn't I allowed to get mad about Paul?"

Her eyes dart back up to mine and her face twists in irritation. "I'm sorry," she laughs, "did we just hit rewind? Or teleport to an alternate dimension? We've been over this." She tries to pry her hand free from mine but fails as I just squeeze it tighter.

"Tell me again, Cooper."

She continues her attempt to pull her hand free. "*Because you kissed Denise first*," she grits, glaring up at me from under her eyelashes.

I catch her off guard, yanking her closer to me by our joined hands. "And not because none of this is supposed to be real?"

Cooper's shoulders drop. I loosen my grip on her hand and it falls from mine, landing at her side. Her mouth opens, but no words come out. Not for a very long and heated moment.

"Well...*yeah*," she finally mutters, her voice barely audible. "That too. Obviously." She rolls her eyes and turns her head away from me.

I push my tongue into the side of my cheek, hiding my incredulous smile in response to the absolute bullshit coming out of Cooper's mouth right now. "Well then, if that's the case," I murmur, taking a step forward, "I gotta know, what were you thinking about?"

"What?" she questions me, still not meeting my gaze. "When?"

I place my left hand flat against the door to the side of her head, caging her in as I lean forward. "What were you thinking about, Cooper," I repeat, reaching up with my right hand and cupping the outer edge of her jaw, forcing her to look at me, "when you were on top of Paul..." I pause, letting go of her face to brush the backs of my fingers over her right cheek, right in the spot where that deep pinkish red color rushes to her face "...cheeks flushed...eyes shut *so* tight...and you let out that little sound." Her eyes widen to the size of the night sky, darkening to nearly its same color. "That...*soft little moan*, Cooper–"

Something like a growl comes out of her as she slaps my hand away from her face. "*I hate you*," she grits.

"Yeah," I nod. "*I hate you too.*"

At least that's the only thing I know to call this emotion that makes my heart feel like it's on fire and like my brain is about to explode and like electricity is dancing across every inch of my skin.

She twists her body to the side, reaching for the door knob again, but I stop her, beating her to it, holding it in an impenetrable iron fist. She freezes in place, staring at my hand on the door knob as she realizes defeat.

"*What were you thinking about, Cooper?*"

She remains stone-still for ten harsh beats of my heart before she stands up tall. When she turns to face me, the absolutely devious look in her eyes makes my stomach do a somersault. Cooper pushes up onto her tiptoes, forcing me to stand up straight. She puts her hands on my shoulders, pulling me closer.

"You know..." she whispers, letting out a breathy little laugh that sends goosebumps straight down my spine, "your eyes were shut too. Your body went all stiff and rigid." She releases me with one hand to trace her finger across her shoulder and down my chest. I swallow hard, trying to focus on getting my heart rate under control so she can't feel it right through my two layers of clothing.

"Breathing...*so* shallow," she continues, her lips forming into a playful smile. "Your face was so twisted up in focus. Right...*here*." She removes her hand from my chest, reaching up and pressing her thumb hard right between my eyebrows, smoothing out where they pull together.

Something in me snaps, and I reach up, snatching her wrist away from my face and pulling her in as I push us both back against the closet door, her back hitting it with a light thud.

"*Yeah, Cooper?*" I breathe, our faces a mere inch apart. "Ask me what *I* was thinking about."

Her eyes bore into mine. A few seconds go by, and her tightly pulled together brows slowly begin to relax at the same time she starts to shake her head. Her lips part. "Robbie–"

Cooper doesn't get to finish that thought as the door is suddenly ripped open behind her and she goes falling full force from my arms.

And straight into Paul's.

"*Whoa there,*" he chuckles, steadying her. My eyes dart down to where his hands are on her body, and I once again have the sudden desire to rip them straight off his arms. I don't get to fantasize about it any further, however, as Denise's voice distracts me,

"There you two are!" she squeaks. Denise grabs my hand in hers at the same moment Paul grabs Cooper's and, before I even realize what's happening, the two of us are being dragged back to the living room and straight into the game circle from hell. "We just have one final round to play," Denise says, pulling me through the crowd against my will.

"I don't want–" Cooper's voice sounds from just behind me.

"Denise, we're done playing for tonight," I say, finishing her thought for her.

"Oh c'mon, I promise you'll like it," Denise insists. "It'll give us all the closure we need."

"What is that supposed to mean–"

I don't get my full sentence out before Cooper and I are shoved into the middle of the circle together. We both push off of each other as our bodies get tangled, irritation still spilling over from our closet interaction.

"Ready, kids?" Denise calls.

I blow out a breath, taking a step closer to Cooper and keeping my voice low. "Cooper, you don't have to–"

"I want this over," she interrupts me, her voice at a volume only I can hear.

"*Hellooo?*" Denise's voice sounds again, a clear smile in it.

"Let her finish her fun already so we can leave," Cooper says. "You know she's not gonna let it go."

We stare at each other for a long moment, frustration clear in both of our stances. As much as I hate to admit it, I know she's right. "Fine."

Cooper turns away from me, looking at Denise, who is standing just inside the circle with Paul, her arms crossed and a huge smile on her face. "Where's the bottle?" Cooper asks her.

Denise lets out a pixie-like laugh. "Oh, no bottle for this round," she says.

I run a hand through my hair, exasperated. "So what are we supposed to–"

"Kiss and make up."

Cooper and I both stutter in place before saying in unison, "*What?*"

Denise waves a hand in our direction, coming closer, Paul for some reason hot on her trail. "You've been through the ringer," she says. "It was just supposed to be a fun game. The last thing we would want is to drive a wedge between you two. So kiss *each other*. You've earned it. Then we'll call the game done and all go get another round of drinks." Denise claps her hands and grins like this is totally the most obvious and reasonable resolution to this whole event.

My feet feel frozen to the ground, my jaw tight and fists clenched at my sides. I steal a glance in Cooper's direction and find her the exact same way, her eyes widening like a deer in headlights when I meet them.

352

Shit.

We can't stay like this. We have to do something. Say something.

Dammit, say something, Robbie.

"I—"

"What's the matter?" Denise cuts me off, tilting her head in a patronizing sort of way. "It's just a kiss. I mean, just what you guys do all the time."

Neither Cooper or me make any sort of move. My throat goes tight as I become aware of all of the eyes on us right now. The eyes of the circle were enough, but now there's an entire crowd forming *around* the circle anxious to observe the scene. *Our* scene.

I've never been intimidated by the spotlight. In fact, typically there's nothing that could get me going like a room full of people's attention on nothing but me. A room full of people expecting a show out of me.

But this is different. This isn't just me. This doesn't affect *just* me. They aren't expecting something from *just* me.

It's *us.*

Her.

Cooper.

Her voice comes into my head suddenly, the conversation of our rules replaying. The only two rules she really had. *Don't kiss her. And don't make her look stupid.*

Never in a million years would I have thought those two simple rules wouldn't be possible to follow. Much less that a situation would occur where breaking one of the rules would be necessary to maintain the other.

I squeeze my fists tighter as I spin to fully face Cooper. I force myself to focus in on the crackling music coming from the record player in the corner, and all of the sounds of people around us slowly start to blur together, turning to a low pitched hum in the background, until all I can hear is TOTO's *Hold the Line*, the beat of it pounding in the deepest parts of my eardrums.

Then Ginger's voice breaks through like nails on a chalkboard.

"You know, it's kind of weird how willing you guys were to kiss other people, but you're so hesitant to kiss each other. I mean, that's weird, right?"

The hum of people's voices rise as several others audibly agree with Ginger.

Can't say I blame them.

I see Denise take a step closer in my peripheral vision as she moves in front of me. "Kiss your girlfriend, Robbie."

I narrow my eyes at her and she raises her blonde brows in challenge. I refuse to give in, looking back at Cooper. She stares back at me, her expression unreadable, landing somewhere on the scale between exasperation, fear, and anger.

"C'mon, man," Brad speaks up. "We don't have all night."

I don't respond to him, staying focused on Cooper before me, that being my safest bet.

Until Paul's steps into the picture, sidling up just behind her.

"Denise," he says, making Cooper flinch slightly, "are you thinking what I'm thinking?" He takes a step closer to her and my jaw instantly tightens.

I barely register Denise as she also takes a step closer to me. "What are you thinking, Paul?"

Yeah, what are you thinking, Paul? I fume in my head but can't manage to say out loud.

"Maybe they're each looking for a round two." My brows knit together as Paul reaches for Cooper's wrist. She pulls her gaze away from me to look down at where his hand wraps around her. *"Whatcha say, Cooper?"*

Three words.

All it takes is those three words and I'm seeing red.

Who the fuck does he think he is?

I start to take a step forward but stop when I feel a hand on my chest.

"Robbie, baby?" I tear my gaze away from Paul and Cooper to find Denise standing just to my side. Her hand drops from my chest, trailing down to grab my wrist.

Even though I used to wish I could dive in and take a swim inside of the bright blue depths of Denise's eyes, they do absolutely nothing to hold my attention now. In fact, they suddenly seem entirely too shallow to even dream of it. I break her eye contact, looking down to where her hand is encircling my wrist. It doesn't last long, however, as I quickly feel the heat of Cooper's gaze and look up to find her eyes locked on where Denise is touching me.

Seeming to sense me watching her watch me, Cooper's eyes snap up to meet mine with fire. I stare right back at her, my gaze only shifting when I see Paul's hand landing on her shoulder. I grind my teeth together so hard they feel like they could crack.

I don't know if I'm crazy, but the music suddenly seems so much louder. Like TOTO's performing a live concert right outside the damn living room. I feel it in my chest. I feel it down to my toes.

I see Paul's fingers flex against Cooper's skin, and my gaze shoots instantly back to her face, immediately finding her stormy eyes.

Time seems to slow down. The air. The music. The people around us. The dot of sweat running down my back. The pressing together of Cooper's ruby red lips. Seconds go by like hours.

One...

...Two...

...Three...

Then it's like a switch flips. We both shake out of Denise and Paul's holds, darting forward.

Fuck rules.

Cooper goes up on her tiptoes, my hands grab her face, her arms sling around my neck, and, all at once, our lips crash together.

When it happens, it's not like anything I could have imagined. It's like fire and electricity burst from where our mouths connect, shooting straight down my spine and settling in my core.

We're kissing.

Cooper and I...*are kissing.*

If you can even call it that. I've certainly never experienced a kiss anything like this before.

It's angry. Rushed. Furious. Rough. Frantic.

Necessary.

It had to be done. There was no way out. We broke the rules. Everyone was watching us, waiting. *Expecting.* We're doing this for show. *Only* for show. We broke the rules. But only because we had to. We didn't choose to do this. We never *wanted* to do this...

So why does it feel so goddamn incredible?

Cooper's mouth on mine feels like a tall glass of lemonade after a long hot day. Crisp, refreshing, electric, and sweet. *God, she tastes so sweet.* Like citrus and honey. Sugar and wine. Candy and the slightest hint of mint. I flex my fingers, antsy and eager for more but forcing myself to hold back. Without thinking, my right hand slides up the side of Cooper's neck and tangles into her hair. I stiffen for a fraction of a second.

I probably shouldn't do that. It feels hypocritical. I told her not to touch my hair. I...I don't like it–

A sound escapes Cooper that's barely audible, but with the way it feels against my mouth combined with the way she suddenly seems to melt against me, softening in my arms as she lets it out, it puts the amateur little moan she gave to Paul to shame. I can't help but smile into her kiss.

I think it's safe to say Cooper likes it.

Not able to help myself, I grab a bigger fistful of her fiery hair, giving it the slightest tug to the side so Cooper will angle her head, giving me better access to her. I can taste the wine coolers she was drinking still lingering on her lips and it's all I can do not to brush my tongue against the seam of her mouth in hopes of diving deeper for a stronger hit.

Approximately one second later, right as I think I'm about to lose my restraint, Cooper beats me to it, opening for me. She's hesitant at first, slow to explore. I don't want to push her, not wanting to cross a line or go past her comfort zone. I'll let her come to me.

And God, does she ever.

Cooper's tongue just barely grazes against mine, the candy

sweetness nearly forcing me to let out a groan of my own, before she tightens her hold on my neck and pulls me down further, completely entangling with me in just about every way possible.

Heat rushes through my chest, prickling, setting my every sense on fire. It continues its path, traveling downward.

And settling right in my groin.

Shit.

Cooper and I must become aware of the hard weight growing between us at the exact same time, because both of our eyes shoot open. Our gazes are both heavy lidded and cloudy as we stare back at each other until, suddenly, another switch is flipped, realization hitting us and reality crashing down.

The reality that we're in a room packed with half of our class. That all of them are looking right at us. That they're looking at us as we have our tongues halfway down each other's throats. That Cooper and I are standing in the middle of a circle. That we're entirely wrapped around each other. That we're *kissing*. That we're kissing *each other*. And, most presently concerning, that her red lipstick has smeared and stained across both of our faces, Cooper's cheeks are flushed the color of a fire truck, and my dick is *painfully* straining against the seam of my Levi's.

Both of our eyes snap fully open, wide with panic. Cooper is the first to pull away, pushing off of my chest so hard that I nearly lose my balance and she goes stumbling a few steps backwards. We're both breathing hard, varying looks of shock and bewilderment flashing across our faces. I reach up slowly, wiping the back of my hand over my damp mouth. As I do so, Cooper's brows pull together, her expression melting into one like anger. I tilt my head at her, looking between the smear of red on the back of my hand and her twisted up face.

"Well, holy shit." Ginger's voice breaks through the bubble that is me and Cooper.

"*Damn*," Brad mutters.

A chuckle sounds, and I think it's Kate Andrews, but I can't peel my eyes away from Cooper. "Geez, is it hot in here or what?"

I hear a throat clear to my side. It's Denise. "Well, that was...interesting."

"To say the least," Paul says.

Cooper's spine slowly steels, her face relaxing. She reaches up, swiping at the corner of her mouth as she turns to face Paul, walking right up to him. "I'm glad you enjoyed the show," she says. She attempts a half-hearted flash of a sexy grin and spins on her heel, not meeting my eyes as she storms past me. "You're taking me home now," she mutters as she brushes harshly against my shoulder.

"Well, shit," Paul raises his voice, calling after her. "Who knew you were hiding all of that, Cooper? If I'd have known a few years ago, I would've been all up in–"

I storm forward, grabbing two fistfuls of Paul's shirt and dragging him forward and up until he's practically nose to nose with me. "Finish that sentence about my girlfriend and you'll have no more fucking teeth in your useless mouth to talk with."

Paul's lips slowly spread into a smile. "Your girlfriend didn't find my mouth that useless just a few minutes ago, pal."

I let out a growl, yanking him up harder, stretching out the material of his shirt. I think about hitting him. I think about making him look as stupid as I fucking feel right now. But then I remember the girl that's out in my car waiting for me. And none of the other stuff seems to matter right now. "*Enough*," I grit, releasing Paul and shoving him away from me.

I turn around, straightening my jacket out and making a beeline for the door, the crowd parting like the Red Sea as I do so.

Denise attempts to step in my path, her fingers grazing the side of my forearm as I pass her. "*Robbie–*"

I snatch my hand away, not looking at her. "*No.*"

I don't stop until I'm out the door and the cool night air hits my face.

thirty-three

SARA

I'm already sitting in the Camaro when I hear the driver's side door open and Robbie settles into his seat. I'm not watching him, but I can sense his movements behind me as I stare intently out of the passenger side window and chew on my bottom lip with everything in me. It's starting to hurt, but I'm afraid of what will happen if I stop. I've had equal urges to scream, cry, and puke since I got in the car and finished cleaning up the murder scene that was my red lipstick smeared all over my face. Since the moment reality really hit.

I knew I had to leave. I knew I couldn't stay a single more second at that party, but I'm not sure why I didn't take a moment to comprehend the alternative. At least at the party, I could have run to the bathroom for a breather and then sunk in amongst the crowd once I was ready. I could've hunted down another sweet drink to warm my skin and settle my nerves. *Heck*, I could have even snuck out the back door and made a run for it if I really wanted to. *But, no.* I didn't choose to do any of that. I didn't take a moment to weigh my options. And now I'm sincerely regretting it as I'm finding

359

myself enclosed in a metal box with just the person I'd like to be around the least right now.

Robbie's door slams closed harshly, and the way it makes me flinch seems to perfectly represent the jarring shove I am given back into reality. The one where I'm reminded of the last hour of my life. Of how I spent it and who I spent it with. Of what I did. Of what I allowed to happen. As I feel my cheeks bloom with heat, I force my already strained neck to rotate even further away from Robbie, making my head almost completely parallel with the passenger side window.

Between the dark night and the lights lining the street, I unfortunately have a pretty clear reflection of Robbie to look at in the glass. I pray he doesn't have an equally clear reflection of me, but that fear fades quickly when I don't see any indication on his face that he does. He's too preoccupied looking between the back of my head and at his lap, his jaw working. My eyes are drawn to his lips, still the faintest stain of red across them. Goosebumps prickle across my skin at the reminder that I put that there. Then they quickly fade away, the prickling sensation transferring to my stomach in the form of nausea at the image of him wiping his mouth just after.

Wiping away what we just did. What just happened between us. Like the remnants of my kiss on his lips was the same as a bug on his shoe. I'm not sure I've ever been more mortified. I'm still trying to process how we even got to that point. What could have possibly led us there.

I sense movement and allow my eyes to refocus on Robbie's reflection. His body is turned in my direction, his brows pulled together. Time seems to slow down for a moment as I watch his lips part and see him raise his hand as if he's about to touch my shoulder and say something. But something stops him. He freezes in place for a long few seconds, his eyes boring into the back of my head. I swear I can feel the heat of them. But then, all at once, he pulls away, dropping and shaking his head as he turns the key in the ignition with a heavy sigh. I use the cover of the engine roaring to life to let out a shaky breath I didn't even realize I was holding. I shake my own head now, forcing myself to focus on the now moving view outside of my window.

I knew coming to the party was a bad idea. I knew continuing our entire charade longer than necessary was an ever worse idea. But, for some reason, I ignored that little voice in the back of my head telling me that. Now that I think of it, I'm pretty sure I've been ignoring it since the moment Robbie first spoke to me back during his first detention shift in the library.

How could I be so stupid?

I know I'm a lot of things, but I take pride in *stupid* never being one of them.

I try to pinpoint when exactly it was this evening that my common sense went out the window. I try to pretend for a second that it could be a number of things. The stress of my upcoming scholarship application due date. The pressure of all the eyes on me. The two wine coolers I drank that made my brain just a fraction fuzzier than usual. But, *no*. I can't lie to myself. I know exactly when it was. The moment Denise kissed Robbie, it was gone. My common sense was simply nowhere to be found. It was *so* misplaced that I threw myself at Paul Strothers. So far gone that...I *also* threw myself at Robbie Summers.

I kissed Robbie Summers.

It feels like my brain and guts have simultaneously been put into a blender as I try to mentally unpack that.

I was so *angry* at him.

As much as I would never admit it out loud, and especially not to him, it infuriated me to see Denise touching him. To see him touching *her*.

I had no right to be infuriated. He was more hers than he would ever be mine.

Right?

I don't know.

But what I do know is that the moment an opportunity

presented itself to prove I couldn't care less (and maybe...*just maybe*...to see if I could get an equal rise out of him), I took it.

Was it worth it? I ask myself, knowing I don't have an answer.

I run my fingers over my lips.

I kissed Robbie Summers.

I repeat the statement to myself in my head, but it just doesn't seem right. I keep replaying the events in my head. I keep seeing Denise standing between us, making her ridiculous attention-seeking demands. And then I see her fading into nothing, the only thing between Robbie and me being a thick cloud of tension and the blaring music of TOTO. I see it all, and I just know. I know that's not the full true story.

Because Robbie Summers *kissed* me.

Just as much, if not more than, *I kissed him.*

A sharp tingle shoots its way down my spine at the realization.

I kissed Paul, and that infuriated *him*.

I resist the urge to slide down in my seat and melt into a puddle of hot embarrassment on the car floor at the next thought that makes itself known in my mind.

Apparently I made a sound while I did it too.

I try to remember it. Try to recall when that little noise might have escaped me. I try to replay the scene of me and Paul. Of me allegedly *climbing him like a tree...*

But I can't. It's been totally replaced. Recorded over. Wiped out. *Demolished* and entirely rebuilt with the wrecking ball of the memory that is *Robbie*. His mouth on mine. His skin on my skin. Every soft part of him pressed against me.

And every...not so soft part–

"Cooper?"

I jolt slightly, blinking hard and swallowing down the gravel in my throat. "Yeah?" I breathe.

He doesn't respond right away. Long enough goes by for the voices in my head to quiet and for me to register the beginning of Prince's *Purple Rain* coming out of the car speakers. The air becomes thick as the seconds go by, and with each flick of Robbie's head in my direction. I keep my eyes on his reflection, not ready to truly look at him yet.

"Can we talk?" Robbie finally asks, an unusual huskiness to his voice

"I'd prefer it if we didn't," I say.

"Why not?"

I don't answer him.

"Why?" he asks again.

Again, I don't respond. I can see the irritation forming between his brows as he continues to shift his stare between me and the road. And then it finally happens. His gaze shifts and he makes eye contact with my reflection in the window. He shakes his head.

"Cooper–" His arm reaches out to grip my shoulder, but I whip my body around, ducking out of his reach and going for the dial on the radio, giving the volume control knob a hard twist to the right.

Purple Rain turns to full blast and, with the help of Robbie's upgraded JVC speaker system, full blast is very *very* loud. So loud it makes Robbie jerk the wheel slightly in surprise, sending me slamming against my door and drowning out the rest of whatever Robbie was trying to say.

Robbie reaches out, turning the volume back down to its previous level, shooting me a look like I'm insane. "*Jesus, Cooper.* What the hell was that?"

I stare forward, pretending I don't hear him. We're not that far from my house. If I just ignore him, he'll have to stop. *Right?*

"Listen, Cooper."

Not right, apparently.

"Things got a little out of hand back there," Robbie continues. "I never meant for–"

Nope.

I thrust my arm out, turning up the volume once again before he can finish that thought.

Robbie blows out a breath, turning it back down. "Big Prince fan, Cooper?" he asks, deadpan.

"The biggest," I say, not meeting his eyes as I turn the music back up.

Robbie immediately turns it back down. "Cooper, I just don't want you to think I would ever–"

Volume up.

Volume down.

"Cooper, I'm not interested–"

Up.

Down.

"*Cooper–*"

I reach for the volume control before he can stop me, firmly meeting Robbie's eyes for the first time since we left the party. "*No,*" I say.

Volume back up.

Volume back down.

"*Why not?*" Robbie demands.

"*Because,*" I insist.

Up.

Down.

"Because *why?*" Robbie questions me.

I turn the volume up so loud my ears hurt.

"*Dammit, Sara!*" Robbie fumes, peeling off to the side of the road and yanking his keys out of the ignition, effectively silencing the radio. It all happens so fast, and now my jaw is unhinged and I'm staring at Robbie in silence.

I reach out and jam my finger down on the radio's power button in desperation.

"Yeah, that's not gonna work," Robbie says matter-of-factly.

I shoot him a glare, then lunge, trying to grab his keys from his hands.

He immediately catches on though, dropping them. I grapple for the keys in the air, but I'm too late. The keys land right between his legs, hitting the leather seat with a light thump and sliding down, settling perfectly in the apex of his thighs.

I shoot daggers at the keys, blowing out a frustrated breath. And then realize I'm staring right at Robbie's crotch. Leaned over actually, getting a real good look.

My head snaps up, my eyes meeting his. He raises his eyebrows at me, and it takes me about two seconds to weigh my available options before I am turning around, whipping the car door open, and darting outside and into the roadside foliage.

I hear Robbie's door fling open. "Are you *insane?*" he calls after me. "*Where are you going, Cooper?*"

I don't turn back, much less respond to him, scurrying down the short decline and weaving my way through the trees. I get just far enough into the brush that I'm convinced Robbie won't be able to make out my figure in the dark, then duck behind the first shrub I see. I refuse to look down to see the damage to my white Keds as I hear the pounding of Robbie's hurried footsteps following after me.

"*Cooper?!*" he calls out, just feet from me. I crouch down further, concealing myself. He curses under his breath and it sounds like he kicks at the ground in frustration. "You know, if I get attacked by a grizzly bear, you're going to be riding the bus to school the rest of the year!"

I have to bite my tongue in an effort to not shout back at him that I've survived perfectly fine riding the bus to school for my entire life and that I don't need him for car rides or anything else.

I *also* have to resist the urge to inform him that if he *were* to be attacked by a bear, it would be a black bear and not a grizzly bear as those haven't existed in California, much less the Bay Area, in over half a century. But that's much less important at the moment.

I hear the crunch of Robbie's Converses against the ground and swear he sounds farther away now.

"*Cooper, c'mon!*" he bellows.

My shoulder relax. *Yep.* The sound of his voice is definitely further in the distance now. Not by much, but it's something. Without giving myself another second to think about it, I push to my feet and dart out from behind the bush and back in the direction of the Camaro.

Within ten seconds, it comes into view, both front doors

hanging wide open. It occurs to me that I didn't really plan this escape well and that I have no idea what I plan to do next. I do know, however, that if I stop my feet from moving, I'll probably just collapse onto the ground, so I jog around to the driver's side of the car. A glint of something in the seat catches my eyes when I reach the open door and my heart starts racing immediately in response.

I don't know what I'm doing as I reach for the keys. They jingle as I pick them up and start sorting through them, my hands shaking from nerves as I pinpoint the key to the Camaro. The second I locate it, I'm bending over, inserting it into the ignition and giving it a forward twist.

Have I mentioned I have no idea what I'm doing?

The engine just barely roars to life when the radio comes back on full blast, *Purple Rain* resuming.

"*Shit!*" I croak out, releasing my hold on the keys and jolting backwards a step in surprise.

After taking half a second to gather myself, I move to duck back inside the car but am quickly halted in my movement by two arms wrapping around my midsection from behind and pulling me back.

Hands land on my waist, spinning me around, and I find myself face to face with an enraged Robbie.

thirty-four

ROBBIE

"*Seriously, Cooper?*" I fume over the ridiculously loud music. "*Grand theft auto? That's what you've resorted to just to avoid talking to me?*"

"*Well, you didn't give me much of a choice!*" she shouts back, throwing her hands in the air.

"*Oh,* right!" I bark out a humorless laugh. "*Because* this *was clearly the* only *possible alternative!*"

Cooper scoffs, shoving at my shoulders. "*Anything beats spending another minute with you!*"

"*Oh, yeah. And you're such a ray of fucking sunshine yourself, Cooper!*"

Her eyes narrow at me. "*You know what?*"

"*What?*" I demand for her to tell me, since I'm not sure I know anything right now. Since this blaring music and blinding rage towards Cooper are the only things occupying my brain at the moment.

"*I* am *a ray of sunshine!*" she shouts, stomping her foot. "*Especially compared to* you!"

"*And what's that supposed to mean?*" I question her.

"*That you–you're–*ugh!" she sputters.

"*C'mon!*" I push, waving my hands in her direction. "*Spit it out, Cooper!*"

"*You are a fucking* hurricane!*"

My eyes squint at her, my brows drawing together.

A hurricane?

Cooper lets out a shaky breath, indecision flickering across her face, before she clearly decides to shove her filter away.

"*You just come and go as you please!*" she shouts, waving a hand in front of my face. "*You just come out of nowhere, make yourself known, wreck everything in your path without a care in the world, and then move on with your life! No concern for the damage in your wake.* And then, *guess what!*"

My jaw flexes as I meet Cooper's burning gaze with everything I have. "What, *Cooper? Tell me.*"

"*Then you just do it all over again! Because you can! Because no one can stop you!*" She shakes her head, and something tells me we both know we aren't talking about weather anymore.

We stare at each other for a long time, top volume Prince and our unsteady breathing the only sound breaking through the silent night.

"*You think that's* me?" I finally ask, raising my voice over the music.

"*I* know *it's you.*"

I take a step closer to her, forcing her backwards. It's obvious that she thought she had a lot more buffer space to work with when her back hits my car and she lets out a silent gasp, realizing she has nowhere else to run.

"*You're so full of shit, Cooper,*" I grit, my eyes darting all over her face.

She blinks back at me. We're close enough now that we don't have to scream at one another to be heard. "What?" she breathes.

"Either that or you clearly have no idea the effect you have." The statement flies heatedly out of my mouth before I instantly snap my jaw shut, looking away from her.

Goddammit.

Cooper's spine steels. "The *effect* I have?" she questions me. "On *what*?"

I shake my head, still not meeting her eyes. I can sense her getting angrier the longer I avoid her gaze, and something about that satisfies me.

Time for a taste of your own medicine, Cooper.

"What effect could I have, Robbie? *Please* tell me. Because, if I remember correctly, the entire reason that we're in this mess together is because you agreed with me that I have *no* effect, *right*? That I'm *invisible*?" I don't answer her right away, and she doesn't give me a spare moment to, pushing on. "That I'm just an unextraordinary antisocial poindexter that nobody wants to be friends with. That nobody wants to know–"

"I wish you'd stop talking that way about yourself," I cut her off, my eyes slowly shifting to meet hers, a heaviness settling between us as I tilt my head at her. And when I speak again, there's a deep strain to my voice that I don't expect. "Really, Cooper, it's killing me."

She swallows hard, trying her best to stand her ground, but I don't miss the way a shiver seems to go down her spine. She raises her chin, and the next words out of her mouth are like a knife to my chest. "It's not anything you haven't said yourself."

"*Cooper...*" I shake my head. "We need to get one thing clear. I have never once said...or even remotely thought...that you were anything less than extraordinary."

Her lips part, and the flush that makes its way to her cheeks has my heartbeat pounding in my eardrums.

"And, for the record," I continue, my tongue pushing into the center of my lower lip, my gaze settling on her mouth, "I think anyone that doesn't care to know you is a damn fool."

I can see the gears turning in Cooper's brain. I can see the way she's leaning on the car more for support. I can see the speed of her breathing increase with each passing moment. I'm just not sure what any of it means. I'm not sure of what I'm doing right now. All I know is that I'm frozen to the spot where I stand, and I can't manage to peel my eyes away from the girl I spent the last two weeks of my life convincing myself I'd be fine to never see again.

"Why is this song so long?" she suddenly mutters.

"You're Prince's biggest fan," I reply, not missing a beat, finally tearing my gaze from her lips to find her eyes instead. "You tell me."

For a girl so in love with stories, she's entirely too good at straying from the plot. But if that's how she wants to play this. I'll roll with it.

"Yeah," she says, swallowing hard. "Right."

"Aren't you?" I question her. "I mean, that's what you said."

Cooper appears to force herself to nod.

"Which is the only reason why you're insisting on playing this nearly nine minute masterpiece at top volume in the middle of the night," I say, my voice even.

She presses her lips together, blowing a breath out of her nose.

"That's the only reason," I repeat. "Right, Cooper?"

Her eyes slice into mine so fast, I have to stop myself from flinching.

"*No*," she mutters.

"What was that?" I ask, raising an eyebrow and ducking down, testing her.

Cooper stands up to her full height, which brings us even closer together, and I ignore the flower field's worth of heavenly scent that crashes over me as she does it. "It's not the only reason," she says firmly.

"*Then what's the other reason?*" I ask, pronouncing every individual word.

I can tell she's wavering on the inside, that she wants to back down from me, but she refuses.

"So that I didn't have to talk to you," she tells me.

I nod slowly, rolling my lips into my mouth. "And why didn't you want to talk to me?"

She doesn't answer me. It looks like she wants to say the words, but she just doesn't have them yet.

"Why, Cooper?" I question her, my voice intensifying.

And that's the moment she breaks. Her shoulders fall, her eyes dropping to my chest. A few moments of silence go by, and my lungs seem to struggle to process air the longer she leaves me without a response.

I inch just the slightest bit closer, dropping my head so that my lips nearly brush the top of Cooper's head as I ask her my next question. "Were you scared?"

She rears back, her gaze snapping back up to meet mine, and it's clear she's absolutely thrown by my question.

"Were you scared, Cooper?" I repeat.

A mixture of panic and anger swirls across her facial features. She moves to turn away from me, but I stop her, grabbing her face in my hands. At first, it's urgent, the way I force her to look at me, but then I feel the way she softens into my touch, and it makes me soften too, just a little bit. I look down at her, the pads of my thumbs brushing lightly across her cheekbones.

When I speak again, my voice is low and slow, making sure she doesn't miss a word. *"Tell me what you're scared of, Cooper."*

Her eyes dart between mine, and I can see the way they start to gloss over as she looks back at me. A tightness settles in my throat, an uneasy feeling rushing through me. One I'm not sure I've ever been met with before. I don't know why, but I'm still stroking her cheeks with my thumbs. It just feels natural at the moment, and I'm trying my best to follow that impulse.

"What I'm *scared of?*" Cooper croaks out, as if I didn't just ask her the same question three different times.

I stare back at her for a moment, my jaw flexing. Then I slowly nod.

"I'm..." she trails off, her tongue darting out to wet her lips.

"*Cooper,*" I nearly growl.

The confession bursts out of her, her voice rising three octaves. "I'm scared to *be here*, okay?! I'm scared to be around *you!*"

Her back slumps harshly against the car behind her, as if she's just realized what she just said. I immediately remove one of my hands from her face. I think for a second that I'm about to step away from her entirely, but when I ask myself what feels natural, I do the exact opposite. While my other hand remains on Cooper's face, I lean forward, resting my now free hand on the roof of my car to her side, caging her in.

"Go on," I say, probably too calmly.

Cooper's teeth sink into her bottom lip, and it's as if I can see the events of this evening—*hell, this entire* semester— replaying in her eyes. And I'm fucking tired. Emotionally and physically, I'm exhausted. So, as the indecision plays across Cooper's face, I just pray she decides to give in. Whether it's to scream at me or slap me or do anything else she desires,

I just need this all out in the open. Just need to know that it's not just me that feels like they're out of their damn mind right now. I just want her to talk.

Please, Cooper, say anything.

As if she can read my mind, she suddenly releases her lip from her teeth, raising her chin to look at me. "I'm scared of the way you make me feel," she admits.

She doesn't look at my face for a reaction, nor does she give me a chance to respond, barrelling on.

"I'm scared of how you make me feel like my skin is on fire and like my heart's going to beat out of my chest and like every neuron in my brain is firing at once. I guess I'm scared to feel this...*alive*. I don't know what to do with it. And I *never* don't know what to do. And that scares me too. I'm scared of letting go of control, of the way you make me feel like I'm losing it, and the way that I'm almost *okay* with losing it. I'm scared of the things you make me believe are possible. Of all the things I never thought I needed before but... now..." She pauses, swallowing hard. "I'm scared of...the things you make me want."

A few seconds go by before I realize just how rigid my body has become. How my hand is still glued to Cooper's cheek and I'm still crowding her space, but that I've somehow stopped breathing, her confession knocking all of the wind out of me. I allow my vision to refocus, looking deeply into Cooper's eyes to see if I find any hint of regret in them, but there is none. I tilt my head at her.

"You want to know what I'm scared of?" I ask her.

She takes a moment before she nods.

I let out a breathy laugh. Cooper just got as honest as it gets. I guess it's my turn now.

"I'm scared...of *getting* what I want."

Her brows pull together. "Why?"

"Because," I shake my head, "I *always* get what I want. But, this time, it's different."

Her eyes search my face. "And what do you want?" she asks, her voice hoarse.

"What I *want*...Cooper..." I drawl, leaning impossibly closer to her, "is the willpower to walk away from you. Because...I'm scared of what will happen to me if I succeed in resisting every painstaking urge, desire, and impulse I have to touch you right now. To shove you up against this car and show you just how extraordinary I think you are. Then, just so you really get the picture, lay you down across my backseat and do it all over again." I pause, licking my lips. "But what I think I'm even more scared of, Cooper...what I'm goddamn *terrified* of...is giving in...and you never letting me do it again."

The heat between us is blazing. Within the mere inches of space between our faces, I can feel the sharp crackle of tension drawing us together. I feel frozen in place. A million thoughts running through my mind at what Cooper could possibly be thinking, about what I could possibly expect her to respond to what I just said. But, as per usual, she completely surprises me.

"*You kissed me*," she whispers.

"Yeah," I nod, my eyes flicking down to her lips. *To the scene of the crime.* "I did."

"But it was only because you had to." She doesn't say it as a question, but more as a statement.

I reach up, pushing a loose strand of her hair behind her ear. "Was it?"

"Yes," she confirms, breathless.

"How are you so sure?"

"Because it would be crazy if not," she says.

"Crazy," I repeat, nodding. "Yeah. I guess that would be crazy."

"Right," she agrees, giving her own nod.

I tilt my head in the opposite direction, a playful smirk pulling at my lips. "You know what would be crazier?"

She raises her brows, questioning me.

"If I did it again."

Cooper's spine straightens, her throat bobbing. "You shouldn't."

I lean closer, grazing her nose with mine. "What if I want to anyway?"

"You can't," she insists, her voice trembling.

I lean back just slightly to look at her. "Why not?"

"Because we don't do that."

"Hate to break it to you, Cooper, but we *did* do that," I retort. "You kissed me too."

Cooper shakes her head, slowly at first, and then almost frantically. When her words come out, they're barely a whisper, her voice cracking as she tries desperately to convince herself more than anyone else. "I hate you."

"Yeah, I don't really think you do," I tell her.

She slowly raises her gaze to meet mine, and I can feel her exterior cracking as she does, the wall we've built between us slowly crumbling down.

"Do you feel it? Right now?" I ask, brushing the back of my hand across the warm skin of her cheek, causing her to suck in a sharp breath.

"Feel what?" she asks.

My eyes follow the stroking path of my knuckles against the side of Cooper's face. "The fire?" I breathe.

Her eyelids become heavy all of the sudden.

I can see her thoughts all over her face. I know that that's something she was scared to tell me. I know she's probably questioned it every second since it came out of her mouth. But it doesn't look like she's questioning it now. I think she's glad for me to know how she really feels. That I'm aware of this heat between us. In fact, with the way she's looking at me right now, I'm convinced she'd let me burn her alive if I wanted to. She reaches up slowly, wrapping her fingers around mine, holding them in place against her cheek.

I let out the lightest groan when she squeezes my fingers in hers, my resolve stripping away. I drop my head, leaning into her as I do. "*Sara*," I mutter against her neck. I see the goosebumps that instantly prickle across her fair skin and feel the way her body responds to me. Something tells me it's not far from how my body's responding to her as well.

"That's three times tonight," she whispers against my ear.

"What?" I question her.

"That you've called me Sara."

I pull back enough to look at her. "Isn't that your name?"

"Not to you."

My lips press together. "And what do you think you are to me?"

"I'd like you to tell me," she says.

My throat bobs once before I reach up to push another escaped strand of hair out of her face, but this time, instead of just pushing it behind her ear, I follow through, threading my fingers all the way into the hair on the side of her head, giving it the lightest tug. Just light enough to pull her closer to me and just hard enough that a wanting whimper escapes her lips, sending a jolt of electricity straight down my spine and into the straining place behind my jeans where I'm already aching for her .

"How about I show you instead?" I ask.

Cooper doesn't respond, her gaze swaying between my eyes and my mouth that is so dangerously close to hers. Desperately trying to hold back, *needing* for her to be the one to start this, I give the faintest brush of my lips against hers. Her back arches and her mouth instantly reaches for more of mine in response. I pull just a hair's width away, my tongue poking out to trace her top lip with the lightest of touches.

"That okay, Cooper?"

She says nothing, looking completely lost in a daze, her body somehow both soft and rigid in my hands at the same time.

"Hey," I whisper against her mouth. "Talk to me, Goose."

Her hand is shaky as she pulls it away from mine, her grip sliding past my wrist and all the way down my arm until she reaches my chest, her hand splaying out flat across it.

"I...I like the way you feel," she admits.

I rest my forehead against hers, a sigh of relief escaping me.

Holy shit, Cooper.

"I like...the way you *make me* feel," I say. "The things you make me *do*. Even if you drive me absolutely crazy because of it."

Cooper breathes out a laugh. "You're Robbie Summers. Nobody could ever *make you* do anything."

I scoff a chuckle of my own. "Yeah, well, a few months ago, I definitely would have agreed with you. But now..." I trail off.

"But now?"

I pull my forehead away from Cooper's, looking down at her, wondering what the hell has come over me, but also not convinced that I really care.

Here we are. All bets are off.

"I'm pretty sure there's not a thing in the world I wouldn't do if you asked me to, Sara Cooper. I'd burn the whole thing down to the ground if that's what you wanted."

Her cheeks flush, a smile coming to her face that she doesn't even bother to fight. "Well, if you're planning on burning the world to the ground anyways...you may as well...."

I draw closer to her as she trails off.

"May as well what, Cooper?"

Her mouth opens, but no words come out.

I shake my head. *Finish the damn sentence, Cooper.*

"Say it," I breathe. "Say it and it's yours." I suddenly feel like a caged animal, desperate to break free, and Cooper's the only one with the key to the lock. I can tell the words are right there on the tip of her tongue, but something's holding her back. Before I know what I'm doing, my cheek is against hers and I'm whispering into her ear, my voice barely audible. *"Ask me, and I'm yours."*

Cooper pulls back slowly, leaving just enough distance between us for her to tilt her head up to look up at me. When her eyes meet mine, I can see it. I watch as she lets every last fear and apprehension she has slowly melt away. I witness the moment, the one where she finally allows herself to give in to what she wants. What she really wants.

"Kiss me, Robbie."

thirty-five

SARA

Robbie doesn't take a spare second. The moment the words leave my lips, his fingers are winding tighter into my hair and his mouth is sinking down onto mine.

My body responds immediately, my back arching and my chest pressing up against him. A surge of warmth rushes from everywhere we touch, enveloping the two of us in a dreamy haze consisting of only us, the brisk night breeze, and *Purple Rain*. It's like something out of only the most ridiculous, cheesy, and *absolute best* movies.

I don't know what I expected to happen when I asked Robbie to kiss me. I don't know if I simply anticipated an encore of the show we put on back at Denise's party. But, if that was the case, I'd be shocked to learn that Robbie had an entirely new performance up his sleeve. One meant for an audience of exactly two and not recommended for the faint of heart or weak in the knees.

No, this is so completely, unbelievably, overwhelmingly *different*.

Before, it was rushed, haphazard, *frenzied*. Like we had an impossibly short time limit to complete a never ending task. Like there was a ticking time bomb strapped to both of our chests and the only instructions to defuse it were hidden deep within each other. Like we were a swarm of bees and a bear fighting for the rights to a beehive, the result being a messy explosion of sweet honey between us that we each were too blinded by the battle to enjoy. It was a necessary release of frustration and a finally bursting dam of months' worth of tension. What happened between us at the party... It was sudden and fast and catastrophic, burning hot, full of fury, and completely taking the both of us over. It was like a raging fire.

But *this*...what's happening between us now, it's not fire at all. Not in the traditional way. Sure, it's hot. *Searing*, even. It's an all-consuming, transformative feeling, scorching us from the inside out and setting the air around us ablaze. But, still, it's not fire. No, a better way to describe it—the only comparison I can even think to make— would be...*lava*. What's happening between Robbie and me now...it's languid, taking its time, fully absorbing the moment. Instead of trying to destroy each other, we are melting together and becoming one.

Robbie's kissing me like we're the last two people on earth and like he has all the time in the world savor every last inch of me. And I have to say...*it may just be the greatest feeling in the world.*

I push up onto my tiptoes, desperately wanting to be closer to him. It never occurred to me just how much taller than me he was until now. As much as I secretly enjoy the thought, it's frustrating at this moment when all I want to do is be at eye level with him. But the screaming of my straining calf muscles and the grinding of the toes of my Keds into the asphalt is completely worth it with every heated slide of Robbie's lips against mine.

Seeming to read my mind, Robbie's hands slowly untwist from my hair, sliding down to rest on my hips. "Let me help you out," he mutters against my mouth. Then, before I can blink, his hands are on the backs of my thighs and he's hiking me up against the car. I let out a yelp of surprise, but my body is ahead of my brain, my legs automatically wrapping around Robbie's waist as he settles me at eye-level with him.

"This okay, Cooper?" he asks, looking at me from under heavy lids.

"Just what I needed," I nod.

Robbie's teeth sink into his lower lip as he watches me, his head shaking. Then he leans down and latches his lips onto my neck. I let out a breathy sigh, tilting my head to the side to give him better access. Goosebumps prickle across my skin and shivers are sent down my spine with every hot press of his mouth, settling low in my belly and forming a ball of what feels like crackling electricity.

"I must admit," I murmur between heavy breaths, "I like this tree much better."

Robbie pauses his movements, and my eyes peel open just slightly. Just as regret begins to swarm my mind over the genius idea to bring up Paul right now, and I start to fear that I've entirely ruined the moment, Robbie surprises me with a sharp bite of his teeth into my shoulder. I let out some type of mixture of a gasp and a moan at the pleasantly painful sensation and the odd rush of warmth it sends through me.

"*Damn right you do,*" Robbie mutters into my shoulder before tracing over the sensitive spot he just bit into with his tongue, pressing a kiss to it after and continuing his trail up the side of my neck.

"You said you like the way I feel?" he asks between kisses.

"*Yes,*" I barely whisper.

Robbie's right at my ear as he asks, "Want to feel some more?"

I'm nodding before he even has the question out.

"I need to hear you say the words, Cooper."

"*Yes,*" I croak out. "*Please.*"

Robbie pulls back, his heated gaze meeting mine for a brief moment before he stands to his full height, hitching me up higher with him. Before my next breath is out, Robbie's pushing me harder up against the car and gently forcing my thighs apart just enough for him to fully settle between them. When it feels like he can't get any closer, he catches me by surprise and presses into me. A sound I've never heard myself make before escapes my lips when I feel the hard press of him against my center. My head automatically falls back as another pathetic whimper comes out of me. I can't help it. Between the way my hands are frantically grappling at Robbie's chest for purchase and the wet heat quickly soaking the spot between my thighs, I feel completely out of control of my body.

It only gets worse–yet *so much better*–as Robbie grinds himself against me. I send out a silent *thank you* to the universe that we live in a small town where ninety-nine percent of the population is off the roads by eight o'clock at night, because I know the scene that we're creating on the side of the street right now is unholy. I know my hair is a tangled mess and that my fair skin is coated with red patches and a sheen of sweat. My skirt is pushed so far up my thighs that it's basically useless. Only my cotton underwear are there to protect me from the rough rub of the full length of Robbie in his Levi's.

He lays into me so hard now that I see stars entirely different from those currently present in the night sky. I shudder, letting out a moan.

"*These sounds*," Robbie groans. "You're killing me, Cooper."

My head falls forward again and I look at Robbie. I'm not even aware of what sounds I'm making. I just know I need more of him. My hands move up his chest and around to the back of his neck. Everything in me wants to wrap my fingers in his ridiculously perfect hair. *God, I love his stupid hair.* But I stop myself, knowing he doesn't like that. Knowing now *why* he doesn't like that, I settle on the nape of his neck.

Robbie's brows pull together just slightly. "Cooper, are you okay–"

He doesn't get to finish his question before I'm yanking him to me, crashing his lips into mine. He lets out a hum of satisfaction against my mouth, and, I must confess, it brings me an immense amount of pride to know I'm making him feel as good as he's making me feel.

I don't know what's come over me. I try not to think about it too hard. I also try not to simply think about the reality of the situation I'm currently in. About the fact that I–*Sara Cooper*– am making out with *Robbie Summers*. That I'm letting him practically dry hump me on the side of the road up against his Camaro.

I also try with everything in me not to think about how much I like it. How I want even more.

If I could go back in time and tell the girl he dumped Jolt Cola all over on the first day of school what she'd be in for this year...

A smile involuntarily comes to my lips against Robbie's, and he takes it as a cue to deepen the kiss. His head tilts, and the moment his tongue brushes mine, I feel his fingers dig into my hips. He slowly slides one hand up, grabbing another handful of my hair and tugging my head to the side to keep me right where he wants me. My body doesn't know where to focus its attention, feeling overstimulated everywhere. From the pull of my hair in my scalp, to my bruised and busy lips, to my suddenly tight and heavy breasts, to the blissfully aching place down below – it's all too much, but also...*not nearly enough.*

I pull away suddenly. "Robbie, put me down," I pant.

Though his eyes are hazy and full of confusion when he opens them, Robbie responds immediately, gently setting me down.

"Please step back," I whisper, placing a hand on his chest and giving him a gentle shove.

Concern etches between his brows as he takes a large step back.

"Cooper," Robbie shakes his head, "I'm so sorry." I don't break his eye contact as I reach behind me. "It was too much–"

"I need more," I say, cutting him off. Then, without ever looking away from Robbie, I open the back door of his Camaro and settle down onto the backseat, pushing backwards until I'm fully stretched across it on my back, propped up on my elbows. "You said something about a backseat?"

Robbie's jaw unhinges itself as he stares back at me, his worried facial expression slowly melting into a grin.

"What are you still doing out there?" I ask him.

Robbie shakes his head at me, his tongue pushing into his cheek. "Don't have to tell me twice," he drawls before crawling in after me, closing the door behind him.

With the doors closed, the music is suddenly deafeningly loud. Both Robbie and I make a show of covering our ears and end up chuckling at the ridiculousness of it before he sits back on his knees and leans over the front seat to turn the radio down to a reasonable volume. The final seconds of *Purple Rain* fade out just as he settles over top of me. I can feel my heart thudding against my chest when he reaches up, pushing my hair out of my face. The next song begins, and I immediately recognize it as *Waiting for a Girl Like You* by Foreigner. It appears Robbie does too, his hand freezing in its movement. I catch the way his face twists up in the moonlight streaming through the car windows and tilt my head at him.

"Do you want to change the station?" I ask him, remember how he didn't seem to like this song before when it came on in his car after the Back to School Dance.

Robbie's eyes appear to refocus, staring directly into mine. "No," he says, shaking his head, a soft grin spreading across his face. "Absolutely not."

He swipes his tongue once over his bottom lip before leaning down and kissing me. It's so gentle, like he's trying to whisper a secret to me with the featherlight touch of his lips against mine and the brush of his hand across my cheek.

By the time Robbie pulls back, I feel like putty in his hands, warm, soft, and pliable. "You know," I say, "your eyes look like something too."

"Yeah?" Robbie questions, brushing his lips against the hollow behind my ear. "What's that?"

I let out a hum of satisfaction. "Chocolate," I breathe. "Sometimes milk, sometimes dark."

Robbie pulls back to look at me, amusement flickering across his face. "Well, aren't you cute, Cooper?"

"Shut up," I chuckle.

"Been daydreaming about my chocolate eyes?" Robbie teases.

I shake my head. "Never."

Robbie twirls a strand of my hair between his fingers. "Wanna dive inside them like that kid dove into the chocolate river in Willy Wonka?"

"*Augustus Gloop*?" I rear back, feigning offense. "Do I remind you of him?"

"Absolutely not," Robbie deadpans. "You're much more of a Veruca Salt."

My mouth falls open, and I almost have to stifle a laugh. "How dare you!"

"*Hey*, I like Veruca," Robbie says, holding a hand up in defense. "She's got a fire in her. She wants what she wants and she doesn't take no for an answer. Not many girls have the guts to be a Veruca. We need more of them in the world. They'd keep us honest and make life a hell of a lot more interesting."

My face slowly relaxes as I take in Robbie's statement. "Oh..." I mutter, not sure how else to respond to the most odd and roundabout, yet maybe the best, compliment I've ever received.

Robbie lets out a sigh, leaning down and grazing my nose with his from top to bottom. "It's okay, Cooper," he whispers against my lips. "I'll let you fantasize about how my eyes look like chocolate."

"Oh, will you now?"

Robbie nods, then catches me off guard, kissing me deeply enough that I nearly need to gasp for air when he pulls away. He rolls his lips into his mouth, looking down at me. "It's only fair since I'm going to be dreaming about how you taste like candy." He runs his thumb across my bottom lip. "How am I supposed to think about anything else every time I look at you now?"

My heart feels painfully heavy in my chest all of the sudden. I swallow against the lump in my throat, trying to buy time to form a coherent response. When nothing comes to me, I impulsively bite down on Robbie's thumb. "Sounds like a personal problem to me," I say.

Robbie's eyes narrow at me at the same time a smirk spreads across his face. "You're a little shit, Cooper. You know that?"

He pulls his hand away from my face, reaching down and digging his fingers into the side of my waist, tickling me. I let out a strangled giggle, trying to twist away from him, but it's useless. He's fully got the upper hand in this situation.

Several seconds go by before Robbie finally relents, collapsing on top of me with a chuckle at my expense. When his weight shifts on top of me, a wave of his scent crashes over me so hard that it makes my mouth water and causes me to let out an involuntary groan that Robbie crushes with his lips against mine.

"You smell so good," I mutter between kisses.

"Me?" Robbie asks coyly.

"*Mhmm,*" I hum in response. I'm realizing that every press of Robbie against me just clouds my brain more and shreds away further at my filter, but I'm too intoxicated by it all to care. "Spicy and sweet and woodsy and warm," I continue. He kisses me again. "Like Christmas morning." His hand traces lazy circles across the sensitive skin of my neck. "Or a walk on the beach." His teeth tug at my bottom lip. "Like sitting by a campfire and toasting marshmallows."

Robbie lets out a rough chuckle against my cheek. "Sounds like you've put a lot of thought into this."

"I think about you a lot," I confess. I don't think my brain even processed the words before they were out of my mouth.

Robbie stiffens, and when he pulls back to look at me, all traces of humor are gone from his face as his eyes flick between mine. He brushes a rogue strand out hair away from my face and lets out a gentle sigh. "I think about you too, Cooper. More than I care to admit."

Silence stretches between us as I take in Robbie's words. Though I haven't responded, I know the effect they're having on me is showing all over my face, in my flushed cheeks and glossy eyes. Just when I think I may be down for the count, Robbie absolutely knocks me out with his next words.

"You're so beautiful like this," he breathes, shaking his head and tracing his fingers across my features. "You know that, right, Cooper? That you're beautiful? So damn pretty that it hurts?"

I bite down on my lower lip, stifling the smile that comes to my face. "I mean, I knew I wasn't entirely repulsive."

Robbie breathes out a laugh. "Yeah, try the exact opposite." He tilts his head, surveying me. "You're so fucking beautiful all the time. And I'm sick of it." He tries to feign a look of irritation, but breaks, grinning at me and making me laugh in response. Robbie leans down, nipping at my neck and making me giggle more. His lips drag up the side of my neck, leaving my skin pebbling in his wake before he goes for my earlobe, tugging on it with his teeth.

And with that one action, things suddenly don't seem so funny anymore as heat rushes to my skin and a heavy feeling settles low in my belly.

My hands reach up to cup the back of Robbie's neck as he continues his assault on my neck, moving slowly down and across my upper chest. I find myself arching into him, my toes curling in my Keds at the sensation his mouth on my skin creates. "You know," I manage to mutter, "you're not too bad yourself." Robbie plants featherlight kisses across the neckline of my blouse, resting his nose in the exposed place between my breasts.

"Yeah?" he breathes. "I think that's gotta be a glowing review coming from you, Cooper. You really mean that?" A shiver runs down my spine and causes a groan to escape me as Robbie's teeth graze my collarbone. He sits forward, returning to eye-level with me, and I find my hands fisting in the fabric of his shirt.

"Every word," I confirm. "Has anyone ever told you that you have pretty nice hair?"

Robbie shakes his head with a mischievous grin, and I can't take it anymore.

I need him closer.

I have a feeling Robbie feels the same by the way that he responds immediately when I trail my fingers up his chest to push his jacket off of his shoulders.

Now free from the extra restriction, it's like Robbie becomes an entirely different person. He practically lunges for me, adjusting his position so that his knee is settled between my legs, not touching me, but just close enough that I can feel the heat of him. He moves up slightly, forcing my thighs to spread just a fraction and my body to soften with awareness.

The moment Robbie's lips are back on mine, my skin comes to life, a pressure settling low within me that nearly bursts at the seams as Robbie moves closer, his knee pressing into the spot between my legs. I utter a deep cry against Robbie's mouth at the foreign euphoric feeling, not knowing exactly what I'm experiencing but knowing that I want more of it. Robbie seems to understand the signal, rubbing harder against me at the same moment his tongue intertwines with mine. I squeeze my eyes tight, unlatching my mouth from Robbie's to gasp for the air I so desperately need.

Oh. My. God.

"You like that, Cooper?" Robbie asks, his voice low.

"I–*Er*–Uh–*Ahh*–" I stutter, my squirming body beneath Robbie acting as a better response than any words I'm capable of saying right now. My skirt has ridden so far up on my hips, but I don't have it in me to pull it back down. In fact, I don't think that I'd even want to if I could.

Robbie bites his lower lip as he watches me, a predatory look flashing through his eyes that should probably terrify me, but just excites me more. Slowly, he slides his knee down to join his other one, and I find myself frustrated at the loss of pressure. Then he raises up just slightly on his elbows, and it feels like fire laces through me when his gaze snaps to meet mine. Several seconds go by as he looks down on me, never once breaking my eye contact, before, without any warning, he pushes forward, grinding the hard length of himself against my center. I automatically throw my head back, letting out a strangled moan. Robbie lets out a groan of his own, pulling away before thrusting back into me, only the rough denim of his Levi's and my thin cotton underwear separating our most intimate parts from one another.

"What about *that*, Cooper?" Robbie rasps. "You like that?"

"*Yes*," I choke.

He presses into me again, harder this time, and the place between my thighs throbs so hard that my vision blurs.

"Wow, I never thought I'd see the day," Robbie grins, continuing his languid movements. "Sara Cooper admitted it. She likes me."

"Hey, I said I like *this*," I clarify, my fingers digging into Robbie's biceps as I motion my head towards the space between us. "Not that I like *you*."

Robbie's motions come to a stop, and I have to refrain with everything in me from whining at the loss of sensation. "That so?" Robbie asks.

"*Mhmm*," I nod.

Robbie raises one brow, leaning down close so that his lips brush against mine as he asks his next question. "So then I guess that means," he whispers, then reaches down between us with one hand, and, starting at my knee, slowly trails his fingers up my inner thigh, "that if I keep going, I wouldn't find your little white panties soaking wet right now?"

My throat constricts, my cheeks heating at the realization that Robbie has already caught a glimpse of my underwear tonight and my heart pounding in anticipation of what's still to come. "I don't know," I say, trying my best to keep my voice neutral. "I guess there's only one way to find out for sure."

Robbie's tongue darts out to wet his lips. "May I?" he asks, grazing an inch higher on my inner thigh.

I nod, my chest heavy with my next breath.

"I need the words, Cooper," Robbie grunts, the tips of his fingers tracing a line on my skin just to the side of my underwear.

"*Touch me*, Robbie," I practically beg. "*Please*."

It feels like we take one large inhale of breath together, our eyes frantically darting between each other's, before Robbie's hand shifts painfully slowly to the side. I can feel his hand hovering just millimeters away from where I need it, heat pulsing between us. Then, after an excruciating beat of silence, two of his long fingers press against me, running so very slowly from the bottom to the top of my slit. The rub of my underwear against my most sensitive flesh feels like fire and ice colliding, an answering gush a wetness rushing out of me as a result.

"*Oh my God*," I moan at the exact same moment Robbie groans, "*Jesus Christ.*"

Robbie's fingers slide back down, then repeat the same journey upwards, adding in a circular motion around a particular bundle of nerves when he reaches the top this time, making me cry out and automatically throw my thighs open further.

Robbie blows out a deep breath, and it looks like he's on the verge of coming undone. He slides down some and sits up so that his knees are now supporting him rather than his elbow, then reaches for the bottom hem of my skirt. "Can I see?" he asks. The note of pleading in his voice washes away any last shred of embarrassment or apprehension I might have had.

"Yes," I breathe.

Robbie shakes his head and licks his lips before slowly leaning down and using one hand to gently push my thigh open while using the other to peel my skirt back the mere inches it requires for my panty covered sex to be fully on display.

"*Holy fuck*," Robbie mutters, dropping his head. I feel his breath fan across my exposed inner thighs, making me shudder. Before I have time to recover, Robbie's reaching up and brushing his thumb over the damp fabric, increasing the pressure as he swipes it back and forth and making me feel like I could go into cardiac arrest at any moment. When he suddenly presses hard and twists upwards against my mound, it feels like an explosion of fireworks goes off in my lower belly.

"You're absolutely *drenched*, Cooper," Robbie chokes out over the sounds of my moans. "Is this all for me?"

"Maybe I like you a little bit after all," I pant, unable to keep up the charade any longer.

"Yeah," Robbie nods, eyes glued to the triangle of my panties. "I think the feeling is mutual." He pauses, pulling back one hand to adjust himself in his jeans.

As he returns his full attention to me, he asks, "Is this okay?"

"Yes," I reassure him. "Don't stop."

Without stopping the languid strokes of his hand against me, Robbie leans forward so he's over top of me again. "Cooper?"

"Yeah?" I ask. He chooses that exact moment to grind the heel of his palm against my swollen bud, making me choke out a sob of pleasure.

Robbie takes the opportunity to press a few heated kisses against my neck. "*So good*," he mutters. "*You're doing so good*."

I'm running my tongue against my drying lips when Robbie sits back up and crushes his mouth against mine. He pulls away just enough to meet my eyes. "Do you trust me?" he asks.

My lips part as I take a moment to look at him, *really* look at him. My head tilts as I stare back into the darkest chocolate eyes I have yet to see. Whether it makes me an idiot or not, I know I have my answer. "Yes," I whisper.

Robbie's throat bobs as he stares back at me, then his hand pulls away from me, shifting it to the side. "Can I touch you?" he asks. He dips one finger just under the seam of my panties, pulling the sticky fabric back from me just enough that the cold air hits my sensitive flesh and sends a shudder through me. Robbie slides the tip of his finger up and down the fabric, toying with it, his finger so close to me that it makes me pulse with need. "*Really* touch you?"

My back arches, trying to meet his touch, but Robbie stays firm, pulling back from me until I verbally agree. "Yes. *Take it*," I insist. "Whatever you want, Robbie."

His nose grazes mine. "What is it *you* want, Cooper?"

"You. Just you," I swallow thickly. "All of you."

Something shifts in Robbie's eyes. *Milk chocolate*. He leans down, kissing my lips and then the tip of my nose. "Then I'm yours, baby." He reaches up, slowly pushing two fingers into his mouth, brushing them across his tongue.

I feel my brows pull together in confusion, but I don't get a chance to ask any questions, cool air suddenly hitting my sex as Robbie fully pulls my panties to the side, exposing me and making me unleash a guttural cry. Before my next breath, Robbie's other hand is dropping down between us and his two fingers, wet from his tongue, are sliding easily through my drenched folds.

My eyes roll to the back of my head as he strokes me up and down, sinking deeper into me and slowly making me come apart with every heated touch. There are fireworks in my vision, a pressure quickly building in the deepest part of me. Reflexively, I try to snap my thighs closed, but Robbie anticipates my action, rooting his knee firmly down into the car seat against my thigh, preventing me. *"Relax, baby,"* he mutters above me, pressing his lips to my temple. *"You're okay. I've got you."*

Baby.

He's called me that name so many times before, but it's never sounded like this. It's never *meant* this. Somehow the nickname that once made my skin crawl is now the same one that is setting my skin ablaze.

Robbie rakes his fingers upwards, stopping this time to circle that sensitive sweet spot. I squeeze my eyes shut even tighter, digging my teeth into my lower lip.

"Eyes on me, Cooper." My eyes immediately snap open at Robbie's demand, meeting his heavy lidded gaze. "There we go," he breathes, leaning down to kiss my swollen lips. "I wanna see those storms when you come apart for me."

He swirls his two fingers in my wetness, sliding downwards as his thumb pushes against me where I'm throbbing with the most raw, unexplainable mixture of sensations. I feel something building, like I'm climbing higher. I feel like I want it to stop, but also that if it *does* stop, I may die on the spot. Just as I think this feeling couldn't possibly be any more intensified, Robbie shifts the angle of his hand, positioning his two fingers at my entrance. At the most deliberate, leisurely pace possible, Robbie's fingers slowly sink into me.

"Robbie," I whine, squirming beneath him. *It's too much.*

"*Breathe*, baby," Robbie whispers. "You can take it."

I try to listen to him, letting out a sharp breath. I'm not sure he's right. I'm not sure I can handle it, handle what he's doing to me. But, gradually, and then all at once, my body adjusts to the stretch. There's no longer a sting, every minor pinch of pain now replaced with pure pleasure. I blow out a heavy breath and find myself pushing against Robbie's fingers.

"*Yeah*," Robbie rasps, nodding, "*that's right, baby. So good. Let it go.*"

He curls his fingers inside me and my head falls back, turning to the side as I exhale what feels like my final breath. The air has just barely left my lips before Robbie's hand is raking through my hair, gripping the back of my neck and twisting my head back around to face him. He plants his elbow onto the car seat, supporting my head in his hand as he drops his forehead to mine. "I said, *eyes on me.*"

"Yes, your highness," I mutter against his mouth.

Robbie shakes his head, something like a growl sounding from inside his throat as his lips pull into a devilish smirk.

I start to ask him what that look is for, but I don't get a chance before he suddenly pulls his fingers out of me, immediately twisting his hand around, sliding up, and roughly pinching my swollen bud between his middle and forefinger knuckles.

And just like that, I explode, the view before me shattering as I let out a strangled gasp, my body spasming out of control under Robbie's touch. My movements are completely unconscious until Robbie's fingernails dig into my scalp. He doesn't say anything, but I know he's reminding me to keep my eyes on his. I obey, fastening my gaze to his wild one.

"*God, Sara,*" he mutters. "*So fucking good for me.*" He dips his head, trailing wet kisses from the base of my neck up to my mouth and back again as I slowly come back down to earth.

Eventually, I can see clearly again, the scene around me slowly starting to come back into focus. I can hear the music again. I'm able to recognize the lyrics of REO Speedwagon's *Can't Fight This*

Feeling, and my first reaction is to smile at the ridiculous irony of this song playing right now. *But then...*

I can feel the car seat below me. I can feel Robbie above me.

Robbie. Above. Me.

Right as the thought occurs to me, he raises his head, meeting my eyes.

And suddenly, with the heat of the moment now gone, everything comes crashing down on me so hard. The blissful light feeling in my stomach quickly twists and tightens into nausea. I become painfully aware of my mangled panties, still half exposed sex, and my skirt that's pushed completely up around my waist. I feel the slick heat between my thighs begin to cool and the tightened points of my breasts begin to relax.

But what I feel, more than anything, is the press of Robbie's length against my thigh, just as hard as ever.

My lips part, and I feel my throat slowly start to constrict as Robbie's eyes dart between mine, a line settling between his brows.

I think I'm starting to panic

Actually, no– I'm absolutely losing my shit.

The realization is hitting me of everything I just did with Robbie. Every part of me I allowed him to see. More of me than any other person has seen before. I've never been so vulnerable. I know I shouldn't, but I feel embarrassed. My heart feels like it's going to beat out of my chest. I feel like I need to get out of here. But I am also very aware of something else.

Robbie just...did so much. He did so much *for me.* Surely he's expecting the same in return. I can't just *not* give it to him. *That wouldn't be fair, right?* Even though it may be my first rodeo, I know it certainly isn't his.

"Cooper?"

My eyes refocus, finding Robbie.

"Hi," I say weakly.

He tilts his head at me. "Are you okay?" he asks.

I nod, too much, too fast. The back of my eyes start to burn as I reach for Robbie. I just barely grip him through his jeans when he lets out a low grunt. He shakes his head, pushing my head away. "You don't need to do that."

"Oh," I squeak, barely audible. "Sorry." I push up onto my elbow, shuffling back and away from Robbie, trying to battle with the conflicting emotions of relief at his letting me off the hook and also the sting of his rejection. I can't look at him. I shift to the side, swinging my legs off the seat to face forward, pulling my skirt down to where it should be.

"Cooper, what's wrong?" Robbie asks.

"Nothing," I say, fidgeting with my wrinkled blouse. "All good. You ready to take me home?"

I see Robbie also turn his body to a normal sitting position in my peripheral vision. He slides closer to me, and I turn my head away, unwanted tears clouding my eyes.

"Hey," Robbie says, gripping my forearm and turning me to face him. When I keep my head low, Robbie reaches up, holding my face in his hands. He pushes my hair away from my forehead, revealing my glossy eyes. His brows pull together in concern as he brushes his thumbs across my cheeks. "Talk to me, Goose."

My lips press into a flat line. I'm not sure what to say. I'm not even totally sure what all I'm thinking. It feels like a hurricane inside my brain right now.

"Cooper, please talk to me," Robbie says softly. "Are you okay?"

"Yes," I murmur. "I'm okay. I just—I'm just..."

"Freaking out?" Robbie questions.

I roll my lips into my mouth, nodding slowly. I feel so dumb right now. And I don't even totally know why.

Robbie lets out a pained sigh. "That was a lot. We went way too fast. I got caught up in the moment, Cooper. I should've taken it slower with you. I'm so sorry."

"Don't be," I shake my head. "I wanted it." Robbie's shoulders relax just slightly, but his expression remains tight. "Really, I did. It's just..."

"What?" Robbie asks gently.

I meet his eyes, swallowing hard. "I think I'm scared."

I didn't realize Robbie's thumbs were still sweeping across my cheeks until they come to a stop. "Of what?" he whispers.

I take a deep breath, reaching up and pulling one of Robbie's hands away from my face, bringing it down to settle on my chest. His eyes follow the path before they meet mine once again. "I meant what I said before," I breathe. "I'm scared...of the way you make me feel. I'm scared to allow myself to *let you* make me feel this way. I know I said I trusted you before..." I trail off, shaking my head. "But I need to know if you meant it. You said it twice, but...I need to know how serious you were."

"What did I say?" Robbie asks.

I push against the lump in my throat, forcing myself to hold his eye contact. "*I'm yours,*" I whisper. Robbie's face falls, and I'm not sure how to read his expression. "Are you? Are you...really *mine?*"

He doesn't reply right away, and that only makes the rock in my stomach sink further. He lifts his hand from my chest, and I pull my own hand away to let him. He brings it to the back of my neck, encircling it with his fingers. "*Cooper...*"

I shake my head, attempting to shrug him off. "It's fine," I say, turning from him. "Things got heated. I'm sure we both said things we didn't mean. It happens—"

"Wait, Cooper—" Robbie says.

"Forget it."

"*Hey,*" he demands, tugging just hard enough against the back of my neck so that I have to look at him. "I don't want to forget it."

I feel the redness rushing to my cheeks as I press my lips together.

"Did you really say things you didn't mean?" Robbie asks.

I blink at him. "No."

His jaw flexes, and he nods. "Good. Because neither did I."

My spine steels. "Really?"

"I meant every word, Cooper," Robbie says, his lips pulling up at one side. "I'm yours." His hand rubs affectionate circles across the back of my neck. "If you'll have me, of course."

I can't stop the smile that spreads across my face. Then,

completely in sync, we both lean in. This time, when we kiss, it's saying something different. It's sweet and gentle. It feels like a long time coming.

"Holy shit," I say against Robbie's mouth.

His shoulders shake with laughter. "Yeah, Cooper? You good?"

I nod. "I'm good. Just...having a hard time believing this is real life right now."

"Can't say I disagree," Robbie says, running a hand through my hair. "Who would have thought, right?"

"Not me," I say, shaking my head.

Robbie presses a kiss to my forehead, and I know he can sense the subtle way that I tense up. "What is it, baby?" he asks, his lips in my hair.

I blow a breath out of my nose. "Look," I say, reaching for Robbie's hand, "I'm happy about this. I really *really* am. It's just..."

"Really fast?" Robbie says, reading my mind once again.

"Extremely fast," I confirm. "I mean, I know it's been a few months, but...it feels like we've crammed a few more months all into a few hours tonight. I just...think I need to take a breath. I trust you, and I believe what you're saying, but I just really want to make sure. I think we should take a little time to make sure this isn't just the result of built up tension and teenage angst." I take a deep breath and look up to find Robbie staring at me. "Is that...okay?" I ask.

He shakes his head, and I feel my stomach dip. "Of course it's okay, Cooper. Let's take a minute. Whatever you need. I'll be here."

When he smiles at me, the knot of tension in my chest completely melts away. "So we wait," I say. "Until...after holiday break?"

Robbie lets out a dramatic groan, dropping his head to my shoulder. "That long?"

I chuckle. "It's only two weeks, Summers. You'll survive."

"You're a cruel woman, Sara Beth Cooper," Robbie says, pressing a kiss to the hollow of my throat. "But you're worth it. And I'll prove it to you."

My heart squeezes in my chest at his words as he lets out a sigh, raising his head. "Okay, let me take you home." He pushes a strand of hair behind my ear and leans in to kiss me once softly. He's a perfect gentleman, pulling away after only a second, but it's useless, because I pull him right back for another taste. After a much deeper kiss this time, Robbie starts to turn away, but then looks back at me, his eyes flicking between my eyes and my lips. "Maybe I could take you home in a few minutes instead?"

I smile at him, shrugging sheepishly. "A few more minutes couldn't hurt."

thirty-six

ROBBIE

I'm practically tweaking as I push my way through the front door of the school. I can't even pinpoint a particular emotion running through me right now. I'm all over the place. All I know is that I'm dying to see her. This isn't something that I ever thought I'd say, but, *God*, it's been a long two weeks without Cooper.

I was happy to give her the time she needed. I didn't even disagree with her that it was a smart thing for us to do, to take some time apart to cool down. But that didn't make it any less difficult. Even though Cooper and I agreed that we wouldn't make any contact with each other for the rest of the holiday break, I couldn't help myself. I'd like to say that I tried, but the truth is, I knew exactly what I was doing when I pulled out the phonebook and wrote down her home number on a piece of notebook paper. I also knew what I was doing when I slipped it into the suitcase I was taking on my family's vacation to Cabo. I knew it would be just like every year. That I'd spend my days alone on the beach and my evenings alone in our penthouse hotel suite while my parents and siblings were off doing...whatever it is they do. The only difference this year was that they didn't even have to pretend they cared about leaving me alone. We haven't exactly been on speaking terms since Thanksgiving, and that's honestly fine by me. But that just made it all the easier to rack up my father's hotel bill with a long distance phone call to Bay View, California on New Year's Eve after I'd helped myself to our room's mini bar.

"Hello?" Her voice came over the line, and I felt myself smile for the first time in two weeks.

"Hey, Cooper," I said.

"*Robbie?*" she questioned. "Are you calling me from *Mexico?*"

"*Sí.*"

"Are you serious?"

"*Sí,*" I said again.

"I can see your Spanish has drastically improved," Cooper deadpanned. "Ms. Jaramillo would be so proud."

I chuckled into the phone. "Cooper, I have to tell you something."

"Well, that's a problem," she said. "Because you're not supposed to be telling me anything. Not for three more days."

"Cooper, please. It's *reallyyy* important," I drawled.

"Are you drunk?" she asked.

I glanced back, seeing somewhere between four and six empty and half-empty mini bottles of tequila strewn across the kitchenette counter. *Huh, how did that happen?* "Not relevant," I mumbled. "But maybe a little. Now, would you shut up so I can tell you what I need to tell you?"

"Fine. I'm listening."

I walked over to the window, pushing aside the curtain to watch the fireworks erupting over the beach resort skyline. "Happy New Year," I announced. "Welcome to 1988, baby."

A chuckle sounded over the phone, making my brows pull together. "What?" I asked.

"You're an hour ahead of me, you ding-dong," Cooper laughed. "But I suppose it's the thought that counts. Happy New Year to you too, Robbie."

"Did you just call me a *ding-dong?*" I questioned her.

"Nope. I think you must be hearing things," Cooper quipped. "You should probably drink some water and go to bed. And don't talk to me again until you see me at school on Monday."

I sat up straight at the last little comment she tried to casually throw in there. "Am I not picking you up for school?"

"No," she said. "My mom's gonna drive me for the first day back."

"Oh..." I trailed off, trying not to let the unexpected wave of disappointment that sent through me show. "Well, speaking of..." I leaned against the window, putting on the smoothest tone of voice. "How is Miss Sherri doing?"

"I'm hanging up now."

"*Wait*," I blurted.

"*What?*" Cooper laughed, exasperated.

"Did you get your NYU scholarship application submitted?" I asked her, knowing she'd planned to spend the majority of her holiday break focusing on that.

"I did," she confirmed. "Had it postmarked the day before the due date."

"Well, look at you go, Cooper. How do you feel about it?"

I obviously couldn't actually see her, but I knew she was shrugging at that moment. "As good as I can. I think it's the best essay I've ever written. And my resume is as strong as it really can be. It's out of my hands now though."

"You'll get it," I told her. "I know you will."

"I hope so. I really do..." she trailed off, and the line went silent for a few long seconds.

"Cooper?"

"Yeah?"

"Just making sure you're still there," I said. "Do you have any New Year's resolutions?"

Cooper laughed, clearly caught off guard by my question. Honestly, I think I was as well. I don't even remember choosing to ask her that question. I think, secretly, I just didn't want her to hang up yet.

"I don't really believe in those," Cooper said.

Of course she doesn't.

"Fine. Then tell me a wish instead."

"A *wish?*" she echoed me. "Like, a New Year's wish? Is that even a thing?"

"It is now," I declared.

"*Hmmm...*"

"C'mon, you can wish for anything," I pushed. "What about a new car?"

"Why would I need that when I have the school bus and you to drive me around anywhere I need to go?"

I chuckled. "Fair enough, Cooper. What else then?"

"I'm not sure..."

"A *Top Gun* sequel?" I suggested.

Cooper barked out a laugh. "They would never do that."

"Yeah, you're probably right," I agreed. "Then what's it going to be?"

"I..." Her voice faded out, and I waited several seconds for her to continue. "Robbie, I just wish–" She was cut off suddenly, a voice sounding in the background that I assumed was her mom. "Hey, I'm sorry, but I have to go. My mom needs my help with something."

"Okay," I agreed. "Yeah."

"Happy New Year, Robbie," she said. Then, before I could say anything else, she hung up the phone.

I never got to hear her wish, and it's been eating me up inside ever since. I want to hear what she was holding back from me, what was causing her hesitation and the strain in her voice. For some reason I can't explain, something in me tells me that whatever it is that she wants, it's up to me to make sure she gets it.

I know Cooper still doesn't trust me, not fully at least. And I can't even say I blame her. Half the time, I don't trust myself. I've never committed to anything in my life, never put every ounce of myself into something. I've always held back, keeping myself at an arm's length. I think part of me knows the truth about why that is. That I always figured if I didn't allow myself to care, if I didn't let myself put my all into anything, I couldn't truly disappoint anyone.

I mean, you can't fail at something you don't really attempt, right?

But, as much as it might secretly scare the daylights out of me...I know I can't fight it any longer. I wanna *attempt* Cooper...in whatever capacity she'll let me.

I still don't have a damn clue what I'm doing with my life, or what my future looks like. But all I know is, right now, I just wanna do whatever gets me more time with Sara Cooper. I still don't think I'm good enough for her. I still don't think I can give her what she wants in life. But that doesn't mean I can't try. Whatever *trying* looks like for me.

In all honesty, I'm not sure that I've ever really had to do it before.

But I'll just handle it the way I handle everything in life. One step at a time.

I turn the corner, and am startled when a hand immediately claps my shoulder. I shove my headphones off my head, returning to the real world as I find several of the basketball guys in front of me, Billy being the one that grabbed me.

"Summers, holy shit, man. Aren't you a sight for sore eyes?"

I let out a chuckle. "Awe, did Santa forget to put me under your tree again this year?"

"That old fat son of a bitch did it again," Billy plays along, shaking his head.

"Okay," Brad says, stepping up next to Billy, "this is just bullshit. How did the golden boy get even more golden over the holiday break? You're all tan and shit. You look like a damn model, Summers."

"Gee, thanks, honey," I say, reaching out and pinching Brad's cheek for just a second before he swats me away with his hand. "I was on the beach in Mexico for a week, so unfortunately, that'll happen. Well...unfortunately for you suckers, I guess." I shoot him a grin that he promptly rolls his eyes at.

"Maybe save some ladies for the rest of us, would you, killer?" he retorts.

"Speaking of ladies," Michael pipes up, sliding in next to Billy. "What the hell went down at Denise's party, Summers?"

"And in what cruel world did both of us miss it?" Billy adds, motioning between himself and Michael.

I blow out a breath, not really sure how to respond. "It's a long story, man."

"Not really that long," Brad jumps in. "I was there, unlike you losers. It started with an innocent little game of *Spin the Bottle*–"

"Brad, we really don't need to talk about it–"

"*Yes, we do*," Billy and Michael say at the same time, cutting me off.

"On Denise's turn, she landed on Robbie," Brad begins, motioning dramatically with his hands. "So, obviously, they had to kiss. She had this little pink dress on and she shimmied over to Robbie all seductively while Sara watched–"

"Okay, Jesus Christ, Brad, maybe a briefer recap–"

Billy and Michael are already waving their hands in my face to shush me.

Brad sighs, rolling his eyes. "Long story short: Robbie tongued Denise–"

"I did not *tongue* her–"

"Then Sara tongued Paul."

"*Paul?*" Billy and Michael ask together in the exact same shocked tone.

I grind my teeth together, knowing I can't even argue that she didn't, in fact, tongue Paul.

"And then Robbie went all *Karate Kid* on Paul–"

"*Holy shit*," Billy and Michael both say at the same time I say, "I did *what?*"

"He drug Sara away to...I don't know," Brad shrugs, "I guess hate-tongue her in the closet–"

"*Hate-tongue?* Seriously?" I raise my brows.

Honestly, now that I think about it, that sounds like something Cooper and I would do.

"And then Paul and Denise drug Robbie and Sara both out of the closet and they did..." Brad pauses, scrunching his brows, "whatever the next step above tonguing is, right in the middle of the *Spin the Bottle* circle for the whole party to see!"

"You *did?*" Billy questions me, shocked.

"Summers, *holy shit!*" Michael grins, shoving at my shoulder.

I find myself starting to get frustrated. "That's not exactly what happened–"

"Uh, it's actually *exactly* what happened," Brad insists.

I shake my head. "It's not–"

"Hey ladies."

My spine steels when I hear the last possible voice I'd like to hear right now, and, when the second to last possible voice I'd like to hear right now joins in, I feel a vein in my neck bulge.

"How's it going, guys?"

I turn my head slowly, finding Paul and Jesse standing just to the side of us. I also realize that my other teammates that were lingering when I walked up have slowly worked their way closer, obviously eavesdropping on the shitshow of a conversation that just went down.

"Hey," I mutter, my voice low.

Paul grins at me, and I'd like nothing more than to knock the teeth out of his mouth like I promised.

"What are we talking about?" he asks, his tone irritatingly cheerful.

"Oh, we were just getting filled in on the events of Denise's holiday party here," Michael speaks up, chuckling. "And Jesus, man, you're ruthless."

I resist the urge to shoot daggers at Michael, knowing he doesn't mean any harm and that he wasn't at the party to witness what went down. But still, it's difficult.

"Oh, yeah, I heard about that," Jesse says. "Seemed like it was a fun night."

"Yeah," I nod. "Where were you during it again?" Everything in me wants to add: *crying in your bedroom?* But I refrain.

"Something came up," Jesse responds, playing it cool, "but it's

all good. Sounds like Paul here had fun enough for the both of us."
He pats Paul's back like he's a proud father or some shit.

"Awe, it was nothing, really," Paul shrugs.

I narrow my eyes at him, irritation starting to pulse through me.
"Yeah? *Nothing?*"

"Nah," Paul waves me off. "Just confirmed what we already
knew."

"And what's that?" Brad chuckles.

Paul's face spreads into a wide grin. "That Robbie's got himself
a wild one." And then the asshole shoves his fingers against my
chest. Like we're friends. Like this is all one big joke.

The guys let off a range of responses, all of which play into Paul
and only make me more angry.

"C'mon, man," I murmur, shaking my head, telling him to
stop now.

"What?" Paul questions me. "We're happy for you, man! I mean,
I knew redheads were known to be crazy, but it looks like you hit the
jackpot." My fists clench at my sides, my teeth grinding. "Come on,
man, please, share with the class," Paul continues, moving closer to
me. "Tell us what it's like."

"What *what* is like?" I grit, on the verge of exploding.

"Getting to use Little Miss Valedictorian any way you like,"
Paul says. "*Wherever* you like. Closets. Your shiny Camaro, I'm
sure. *Hell*, I bet you probably even got her to spread her pretty little
legs for you all those afternoons in the library, huh? While you
were there serving detention for trying to get Denise back?
Remember, that was the reason you were even there in the first
place? It's why you two even started talking. I'm sure you got to
have your cake and eat it too, huh? Tell us, Robbie, what was it
like? What did Cooper *taste* like? In the ways I don't already know,
of course."

I see red. A red so intense that it clouds my vision and makes my
head ache.

"What does Cooper do for you?" Paul pushes, raising his chin
at me.

I'm so caught off guard and flooded with fury that my reactions don't even make sense, and I burst out laughing.

"It's not like that with Cooper," I chuckle darkly, taking a step towards Paul. "You've got it so twisted, alright? She doesn't mean what you think she means to me. She's not that kinda girl. She doesn't *do* anything for me. I don't need her for that. I don't even want her for that. If I wanted sex, I could get that from any girl in this school *right now*."

"Then why don't you do it, Robbie?" Paul questions me.

I bark out a laugh. "Maybe I will if it'll get you to never say another word about Cooper to me again. The shit coming out of your mouth is making my skin crawl."

Everyone around us gradually falls silent, Paul included, his face unreadable. "Now, does anyone have a fucking cigarette?" I ask.

I don't smoke. Not regularly, anyways. I haven't picked up a cigarette in at least a month. But I'm afraid if I don't do something to distract myself right now, to calm myself down, I'll lose my shit completely. And I figure it's not a good look to get detention or a suspension on the first day back at school.

Billy digs into his back pocket, wordlessly pulling out and holding open his pack of cigarettes to me. "Thank you," I say, plucking one out and putting it between my teeth. "Now, if you all will excuse me," I mutter behind the cigarette, spinning on my heel to head outside to smoke before homeroom starts. But my feet stop in place, the cigarette falling from my lips and into my hand when I come directly face to face with Alice.

And I can just tell, between the absolutely heartbroken look on her face and the quick mental replay of the things I just said, that she definitely must have come in right at the tail end of our conversation. Right at the point that the things I said without context pretty much made me look like the biggest prick in the world.

Certainly not a prick that any girl would want her best friend to be dating.

Shit.

"Alice, I–"

"*Good morning, Bay View Bears!*" Principal Whileyman's crackly voice comes over the speaker.

Goddammit.

"As a reminder," he continues, "we are beginning our new semester with an assembly in the gymnasium during your homeroom period this morning. So, go ahead and start making your way there! We've got some exciting things to discuss about what's to come the rest of the semester, and, if you remember those votes you all placed for senior class superlatives during the last week before the holidays, we will be announcing the winners shortly into the assembly! So, if you want to see who won the '*Best, Biggest,* and *Most'* in Bay View's senior class for every category, don't be late!"

The second the intercom harshly cuts off, I dart forward.

"Alice, listen–"

But she turns away, practically *running* from me.

I try to follow after her, calling her name, but the hallways quickly fill with loud bustling students all making their way towards the gym.

"*Dammit!*" I groan.

"Hey, you good, man?" Brad's voice sounds from behind me as he clamps onto both of my shoulders with his hands.

"No."

I shake my head, running a hand through my hair.

"I need to find my girlfriend."

thirty-seven

SARA

I smile.

"Everything good to go?"

I don't know why I'm smiling.

I'm staring off at a dingy faded gymnasium wall with chipped blue and yellow paint running across it that's older than dirt and desperately in need of a retouch. I shouldn't be smiling. But, for some reason, I can't stop. I haven't been able to stop for two weeks.

"Yes, sir. I think we're ready."

I haven't seen Robbie yet. I want to see him. But also, I don't. I'm nervous. I don't know why I'm nervous. But at all the same times I've caught myself smiling over the last two weeks, I've also found my stomach in knots. Everything in me is battling over this, the current state of my life. The absolutely bizarre situation that I've found myself in. The one where I might have just accidentally let myself fall for Robbie freaking Summers. The one where I opened myself up to him.

In more ways than one...

I feel my cheeks heat at the reminder. At the *memory*. It keeps playing through my head on a loop.

Robbie and I crossed a line. A line I know we can't come back from. And even though I know that should terrify me...I'm not sure that it does. I think that, maybe, for once in my life, I'd like to tell my brain to shut up.

I have no concept of what a future would look like with Robbie. My life has existed solely on a timeline of *start* to *NYU scholarship application acceptance/rejection*. From there, it's really not been possible for me to plan further. Not when either answer would send me in dramatically different directions. I know that the last thing I need is to throw a wild card like Robbie into the crazy mix that is my life right now, but I think...if he's really been honest about what he wants...if this isn't all just a phase for us...for him...

Well, now that I think of it, I'm not sure I've really thought through what I'll do if he's decided it's just a phase for him. I mean, it's what I always assumed. It's the reason I've been so hesitant with him. But if it turns out I was right...

"And Sara? What about you?"

Actually, there's nothing to think through. As we said, if one of us decides we're done, we tell the other, and we move on. I've lived my life alone for eighteen years. I don't need *Robbie in it.*

"Ms. Cooper?"

But...I might like *him in it. It might be...just a little bit better...if he was* in it. Is it so bad to feel that way? *God, what has happened to me?*

"*Hello, Earth to Sara?*"

The hand waving in front of my face makes me snap to attention, Eugene and Principal Whileyman coming into view.

"*Oh*, yes– *Sorry*. I'm all good to go!" I smile sheepishly, fumbling for my camera around my neck and holding it up.

"Great," Principal Whileyman says. "As students come in, I'll just have a few announcements to make, and then we can get into announcing the superlatives. We'll keep it fairly short and sweet. You all are welcome to wait behind the stage until we get into announcing students for awards, then you can come up to take their pictures in front of these lovely backdrops you two set up."

"*Us two*," Eugene cough-chuckles under his breath.

Okay, maybe it was mostly him. I might have been a little distracted while I attempted to help him set up the blue fabric photo booths on the makeshift stage this morning before school.

"Sounds good to me," I respond to Principal Whileyman, ignoring Eugene's jab.

"Perfect," he says, adjusting his tie. "And thank you both again for helping out with this on the first day back."

"Of course. No problem at all. Just doing our jobs," I nod.

And, with that, Eugene and I park it behind the stage as students start to file into the gym. I find myself staring at the floor and back at my dingy wall of choice, getting a nervous fluttery feeling in my stomach at the thought of seeing Robbie again. I know it's going to happen this morning, if not at this assembly then during Ms. Cage's class, but, for some reason, I'd just rather not see him from afar. Not when I can't talk to him. Not when I can't see his facial expressions up close. I know myself, and I know I'll need approximately ten seconds face to face with Robbie to know where we stand. To know if he suddenly woke up this morning completely over what happened between us, completely over the thought of an *us* at all. I just...*I just need ten seconds.*

The assembly starts and, as promised, Principal Whileyman keeps the introductory pieces short. He welcomes everyone back to school, hypes up the continuation of the basketball team's current fantastic record, rattles off some upcoming events, and reminds everyone to keep their focus for the next four and a half months.

As he begins his opening spiel for announcing the winners of our senior class superlatives, Eugene and I make our way out from behind the stage to take our places off to the side of the stage by our respective photo backdrops. We decided we'd alternate which booth people are sent to so Principal Whileyman can get through every category as quickly as possible. It occurred to me, as I wasn't doing a very great job of helping Eugene to set up these backdrops on the stage this morning, that I never even voted for superlatives. I'm not even positive what all categories there will be. I was way too stressed out during finals week to pay any attention.

I guess I'll be surprised with whatever's to come.

Principal Whileyman jumps right into it, starting with the award for *Most Athletic*. The captain of our football team is called for the boy and the captain of our volleyball team is called for the girl, a round of cheers and applause going off, before they make their way to my booth for me to take their photo together.

And so it begins.

I get in the zone, snapping photos left and right as I trade off with Eugene. It only takes a few categories before Robbie is called, which is honestly a few more than I thought it would take. He wins the boy's award for *Biggest Class Clown*, and thankfully it's Eugene's turn to take photos at that point. I feel my gaze drawn to him, but I refuse to look, focusing on the people in my booth. I even feel like I see him trying to catch my attention out of the corner of my eye as he swaps places at Eugene's booth with Brad, who has just won for *Biggest Flirt*, but I shake off the feeling, grinning to myself.

You can wait, Robbie.

A couple more categories are called out until Principal Whileyman announces that *Best Hair* will be next, and I immediately let out a snort. Lisa McDaniel is called out as the girl winner and Robbie is *shockingly* called out for the boy winner. Again, I'm thanking the probability gods that Eugene is up again to take their photo. I don't think I could take the smug grin on Robbie's face or the ridiculous commentary he'd have to make to me about winning that particular award.

I click the button on my camera, taking a picture of Bay View's *Most Musical* boy and girl, when I feel a hand grip my arm and turn to find a wide-eyed Alice standing beside me.

"Oh, Alice, hey. What's up? How'd you get down here–"

"Sara, I need to talk to you," Alice cuts me off, her voice low.

"Oh," I say, my brows scrunching. "I mean, *now*?"

"Yes, now."

"I'm...uh...a little bit busy here." I hold up my camera. "Can we just talk about whatever it is at lunch?" I start to turn back towards the stage, and, in the process, my eyes snag on Robbie, who seems to be frozen at his photo booth, his eyes darting frantically between me and Alice as Lisa poses next to him for the camera. I start to tilt my head at him, wondering what that look is for, before Alice gives my arm a gentle yank, forcing my attention back on her.

"Sara, it really can't wait until then. I mean it," Alice insists.

"Okay," I breathe. "Al, honestly, you're scaring me. What is it?"

"I..." she trails off, swallowing hard. "I need you to prepare yourself, okay?"

"*Prepare myself?*" I question her. "Alice, please, just spit it out."

"Hey, are you gonna take our picture?" a girl's voice calls out.

My attention snaps forward, as I see the winners I just heard Principal Whileyman call out for *Best Eyes*. "Yes!" I blurt. "So sorry." I turn to Alice. "It's gonna have to wait, Al, I'm sorry."

"But, Sara–"

I'm already moving away from her, stepping forward to take Mark Davies and Nancy Fuller's photo.

Once I've gotten what I need, I spin around to find Alice still standing there.

"Alice–"

"Sara–"

We both speak at the same time, but are both cut off by the voice of Principal Whileyman.

"We're winding down with our last few awards here. Next up we have *Most Likely to Succeed*. For the boys, we have Jesse Lamonte!"

Cheers erupt from the crowd as I step closer to Alice.

"Alice, I don't understand what you could possibly have to tell me."

She rolls her lips into her mouth before she speaks again, her voice barely at a whisper. "It's Robbie," she says.

"*Robbie?*" My brows raise. My first reaction is to ask if he's okay, but I know he's okay. I just laid eyes on him mere seconds ago. "What about him?"

"It's something...something I heard him say. Sara, I'm so sorry, but–"

"*Sara Cooper!* Come on up here, hard worker."

My spine steels as I spin in the direction of Principal Whileyman's voice.

What?

He motions towards the stage. "Yep, that's you Ms. Cooper. You won. Get up here."

I...won? Most Likely to Succeed?

"Oh, shit," Alice mutters from behind me. "Well, go on," she says when I don't move for several seconds, nudging me towards the stage.

I force my feet forward, heading for the steps that lead up to where Eugene's photo booth is on the stage. Jesse gives me a tight smile as I join him, and I give him an equally stiff nod back. We scoot as close together as we can without touching at all, ready for the picture. I find a genuine smile coming to my face as Eugene takes it, realizing this is yet another thing I never expected to happen this year.

Jesse exits the stage first, and my smile is still lingering as I follow shortly after her. I just reach the bottom of the steps, ready to spin on my heel and head back to my photo station, when someone catches my wrist.

"Oh," I breathe, feeling myself blushing against my will. "Hi, Robbie." Whatever smile is left on my face falters when I realize how frantic Robbie looks.

"*I need to talk to you,*" he blurts out, his tone urgent.

"Um..." I chuckle awkwardly. I try desperately not to jump to any rash conclusions, but my brain is failing me.

What the hell is going on?

"Cooper, really–"

"What is with everyone dying to talk to me today?" I ask.

Robbie stiffens, his shoulders falling. "What are you talking about?"

I tilt my head at him, trying to understand. I'm not sure what. But *anything* would be nice about now. When I don't say anything, Robbie speaks up again.

"Alice? You're talking about Alice?" he asks, his voice low.

My brows knit together as I stare up at him. "Yeah... How did you know that?"

He doesn't answer my question, instead asking another one of his own. "Did she say anything to you yet?"

"Um, well...no. She hadn't gotten the chance to."

Robbie visibly relaxes just a fraction, and, somehow, that doesn't make me feel any better.

"Why do you ask?" I question him. "What would she be telling me?"

Principal Whileyman's voice comes over the microphone again as Robbie just looks at me, his mouth open, but no answers coming out. He announces that the final category of *Best All–Around* is up.

Robbie's hand is still wrapped around my wrist, and I hate that I can still register the electricity it sends up my arm. Even right now, as I know I should pull away, that feeling makes me not want to. Fortunately, my mind is able to win the battle against my heart, and I slip myself from his grasp.

Or at least I try. Robbie doesn't let me, holding on even tighter to me. I glance up at him and find a look in his eyes I can't decipher. It's some kind of mixture of panic and sheer desperation.

"I have to go take this photo, Robbie."

He doesn't move a muscle.

"Let me go, please," I say.

Robbie's throat bobs once before he finally releases me, unwrapping one finger at a time from my wrist. As he gets down to his last finger, I prepare myself to bolt, but he pauses his movement.

"*Cooper*," he mutters.

I look up at him, exasperated and so confused.

"I'm begging you," he says.

"Begging me to *what*?" I ask him, irritation clear in my tone.

He presses his lips together tightly, shaking his head before speaking again.

"Don't listen to Alice."

My heart instantly drops to my stomach. I yank my hand out of Robbie's grasp. "*What?*"

"Cooper, she–"

"*Robbie Summers!* Please make your way back to the stage."

thirty-eight

ROBBIE

I just need her to listen.

I fucked up, but it's not too late. It can't be too late. I don't want to be a fuck up. I don't *have* to be a fuck up. She's the only person that's ever made me feel that way.

I can't let her get away just because Paul Strothers succeeded at getting under my skin and made me break. I meant what I said to him, at least in the first part of my heated response. But now that I've had the time to replay it a hundred times over, I understand how bad it could sound. How I didn't choose my words very carefully. It's hard to choose your words when they're flying out of your mouth faster than your brain can process them.

It's not like that with Cooper.

I don't want her like that.

She doesn't mean what you think she means to me.

She doesn't do anything for me.

I don't even want her for that.

All things I said. All things I mean. But I just know Alice doesn't understand the *way* that I mean them. And I understand why. I know the reputation I've had. I know what's been expected of me.

416

And it's exactly what I'm sure Alice is thinking. That I'm the player of the Bay View High. That I'm the spoiled rich jock with the best hair in the school and zero need to stick to one woman. Because they all want me. I'm not the guy that dates the girl who is *Most Likely to Succeed*. I'm the jerk that says shit like...

If I wanted sex, I could get that from any girl in this school right now.

That one, I have no explanation for. No excuse.

Because it's true. And it just came out. And if Cooper heard me say that after what went down with us after Denise's holiday party...well, I'd probably have a really hard time talking my way out of that. Because there's no way to. All I can do is tell her that, regardless if that's the truth or not, it doesn't matter. Because even if every girl in this school really does want me...there's only one I care to give myself to.

I just need to get her to listen to me.

I don't know what to say though. Where to begin. What will get her to hear me out.

"Don't listen to Alice," I beg her.

The look Cooper's face molds into tells me that was definitely not the right thing to say.

"*What?*" she asks, tearing her hand away from my grasp.

Shit.

Please, just listen.

"Cooper, she–"

"*Robbie Summers!* Please make your way back to the stage."

My words get caught in my throat.

"*Mr. Summers?*" Principal Whileyman calls again. He must spot me on the side of the stage, because he adds, "*Ah,* there you are. Get up here, son!"

I shake my head. "Cooper–"

"You're needed on stage," she says, her tone clipped. "And I have to take your picture."

She turns on her heel and walks away.

"*Dammit!*" I grunt under my breath, biting down hard on my knuckles as I watch Cooper walk straight over to where Alice is still standing. Where she's clearly waiting to finish their conversation from earlier. The conversation I just thought I was able to successfully intercept before it ever happened. Cooper takes her spot in front of the photo booth, and, even though she's trying to be subtle about it, lowering her head and talking out of the side of her mouth, I can see her speaking to Alice. I just know she's asking her about what just went down. I also know I'm screwed.

I force myself up the steps and onto the stage just as Principal Whileyman is calling my name for a third time. I walk up to the podium and shake my head. He's saying things to me, but I'm not listening to a word. My eyes are glued to Cooper and Alice. I'm watching as every word that comes out of Alice's mouth makes Cooper's eyebrows bunch further together and her face turn redder. It feels like a punch to my gut.

Principal Whileyman places a sash over my head and motions for me to go stand by the backdrop in front of Cooper. It feels like the world moves in slow motion as I make my way over there, as I watch her avoid my eye contact as I approach, as I get to see the slump of her shoulders and the hard set of her jaw as I take my place.

I'm treading water. I'm on the verge of drowning. I don't have any idea how I'm going to dig myself out of this situation with her. This was certainly not the way I envisioned our first day back at school together, the first day of us making it through Cooper's mandated two week rest period. The one that she put in place so she could determine if what we had was real, if she could actually trust me. She never said those words exactly, but I knew it. I saw it in her eyes. As much as she wanted to trust me, she had to keep herself safe. I can't say I blame her. Especially not now. But *fuck*. This is so messed up. *How did it get so messed up?* I'm not sure that this could possibly get worse.

"And for the ladies, your *Best All-Around* for the class of 1988 is...*Denise Davis!*"

My spine steels. My and Cooper's gazes instantly snap to one another, and I see it, on full display, how absolutely done she is.

Fuck. Me.

Ooos and *ahhs* sound off from around the gym. Some of them are cheerleaders cheering on Denise. Some of them definitely sound like they are people reveling in the scandal of the exes being paired together for this award. Half of them are probably my friends.

I can see the swish of Denise's blonde hair as she hops up on stage and gets her sash from Principal Whileyman. When she joins me at my side for the photo, I feel numb. My eyes are on the floor, because I can't even look at Cooper anymore. My mind is racing through the quickly dwindling possibilities for how I can convincingly talk myself out of this and talk her down from completely shutting me out when Denise's hand touches my arm.

"Robbie?"

I raise my head slowly to look at her. "What?"

"Well, this is fun, isn't it?" she asks, beaming at me.

A laugh bursts out of my lips. But it's not a humorous one, it's an incredulous one, an *exasperated* one. I promise Denise doesn't notice the difference though. Or, if she does, she just doesn't care. I *have* to laugh. Because this situation is just so ridiculous. Because Denise is standing in front of me right now, and she used to be the girl of my dreams. I used to think I cared about her. I thought she made me happy. I never once thought about whether or not she made me a better version of myself. Or if she made my brain work in ways I didn't know it could. Or if the entire universe around me could be chaos, but she could be the one to bring me back down to Earth. I never thought about those things because I didn't even *think* to think about them. I didn't know they were possible. Or that they mattered. Not until I found someone that made them matter.

Someone I'm probably about to lose.

Denise giggles, squeezing my arm. "Well, let's take this picture, shall we?"

"If we must." I say it completely emotionless, but Denise still laughs.

I begrudgingly turn forward to face Cooper, but I don't actually get to. She already has her camera up to her face, ready to take the picture. "On three," she says, her voice all-business. I don't even pretend to put a smile on my face as she begins the countdown. "One...two...*three*."

"*Well isn't that just a picture perfect couple?*" A voice calls from the crowd the moment the flash goes on.

Paul.

I reflexively take a step forward, looking for him.

"One more," Cooper says, standing up straighter with her camera.

"Robbie?" Denise whispers.

I turn to look at her again. "Yes?"

"Sorry, I feel like my lipstick may be smeared," she says, shyly. "Could you help me?"

I'm ready to tell her it looks fine so we can just get off this stage, but when she tilts her head to the side, I can clearly see her pink lipstick smudged out at the corner of her mouth. "Oh," I mutter, not sure what to do.

"Do you see it?" she asks. "Could you just...?"

Without thinking about it any further, I reach up, swiping the lipstick away with my thumb. She freezes in place after I do so, staring up at me for a second before her smile spreads wide across her face.

"*Three*," Cooper says, an edge to her voice. I turn back to face the camera in a daze, feeling physically and emotionally whiplashed from the events of the last hour.

"Two."

What the hell am I gonna do?

"One."

"Robbie," Denise says.

I barely turn my head to look at her when she grabs me by the collar of my jacket and yanks me down, crashing my lips to hers the moment the camera's flash goes off.

thirty-nine

SARA

I press the button.

The flash goes off.

Denise kisses Robbie.

And everything goes black.

Luckily I'm wearing my camera strapped around my neck, because it nearly slips right from my fingers. I don't think I'd even care if I wasn't though. If it fell to the ground and smashed to a million pieces, that might actually make me feel better. Because it would mean that my heart isn't the only thing in this room that's absolutely shattered and destroyed.

I don't know why she did it.

But after what Alice told me Robbie had to say–*very loudly, in the middle of the hallway, where the entire school could hear him*–something tells me that I don't know much of anything anymore.

Robbie looks surprised by Denise kissing him, but that doesn't really mean anything. Not really. It just means that he's not completely heartless. Not enough to smear the fact that he doesn't really need me right in front of my face. *No,* he'd wait to do it behind my back. But Denise doesn't need to do that.

Because she felt confident enough to do it. Right here on this stage. In front of everyone. In front of *me*.

Because she's that kinda girl.

No wonder she does things for Robbie.

It feels like there's gravel in my throat as I swallow.

"Okay, kids, whoa there," Principal Whileyman chuckles uncomfortably. I can see his gaze swinging between me and Robbie, and I don't have the heart to look at him and address the confusion he's clearly feeling.

Denise pulls away from Robbie, flashing him a grin before she spins and walks off the stage. I don't stick around any longer to see what Robbie does. Alice tries to call my name, but I ignore her, heading straight for the door.

"Alright, settle down everyone," Principal Whileyman says over the roaring crowd of students. "You're about to be dismissed to go to your second period classes—"

I don't hear anymore as the gym door swings closed behind me, muffling the sound.

I force myself to keep moving, because the ache in my knees tells me that, if I stop, I'll collapse. I breathe deeply, forcing air into my lungs, but it's useless. I can't get enough. I'm feeling so many emotions that I don't even know which one to focus on. There's so many voices in my head shouting over one another to make their thoughts known that they're all blurring together. My chest and head feel like a jumbled mess, but the one thing I feel above it all is stupidity.

Absolute utter *stupidity*.

I reach my locker, robotically spinning the dial as fast as I can and entering the code to unlock it. I throw the door open, setting my camera inside and grabbing my things for my next few classes. I start to close the door, but have to pause, gripping the side of it as I take a deep, shuddering breath.

I can't believe I let myself fall for it. Fall for him.

I always knew. I knew what he was, *who* he was. And I also knew who *I* was. And that the two of us just don't *work*. We'll never work.

I always knew. But I guess, if I was going to find out for sure, it's nice that I know now.

God, it feels like there is a gaping hole in my chest.

"*Cooper!*"

My spine snaps straight, my head shaking.

No.

Robbie's hand lands on my shoulder, spinning me around.

"Cooper—"

I slap his hand away, taking a step back.

His brows pull together, his mouth opening to speak again.

"*No,*" I practically growl.

"Cooper, please just let me—"

"Robbie, I can't even look at you right now, much less let you do anything."

The school bell rings, and the gym doors burst open down the hall moments later, students immediately filling the halls.

"Cooper—" Robbie starts, but I cut him off.

"In fact, I think I've let you do more than enough to me. I'm done."

He reaches out for me. "But—"

I unzip my backpack where it hangs from my locker door, digging inside and pulling out his Journey *Frontiers* tape. I toss it at his chest, and his hands reach up, fumbling for it.

"That's the only thing of yours that I have to return to you," I tell him. "Unfortunately, you can't give me back anything of mine that you took. Nothing that matters."

His throat bobs. "Cooper—"

"No." I shake my head. "I'm done," I repeat, turning away from him.

And because that bell meant it's time to go to second period, and because that means it's time for history with Ms. Cage, for the first time in my life, I skip a class.

I head straight for the library. Ms. Rose is talking to a student at the front desk when I walk in, but she sees my face, and because of that, she doesn't question me as I walk behind the counter and into her back office, closing the door behind me.

I lock the door, figuring Ms. Rose will knock when she needs inside or insists on talking to me. I lean my back against the hard wood and sink slowly to the ground. I assumed I'd cry once I got here, but I don't. I just stare off into space, the anger, embarrassment, disappointment, and betrayal simmering within me.

Ms. Rose never knocks.

I suppose she owes me one.

ROBBIE

I skipped Ms. Cage's class.

I wasn't going to. I figured it would be a good opportunity to trap Cooper and force her to listen to me. But she didn't show.

Sara Cooper skipped class.

Because of me.

The moment I realized she wasn't coming, I got up and walked out.

Now I'm sitting in my Camaro in the school parking lot, smoking the cigarette I desperately needed an hour ago. But now, it does nothing for me. It's just a distraction. A distraction that's not really working.

How do I fix this?

I'm so pissed. Pissed at Cooper for not hearing me out. Pissed at myself for saying the shit I did. Pissed at Paul for bringing it out of me. Pissed at Denise for pulling that stunt.

God, I still can't believe it.

Before I even knew what was happening, my lips were on hers. And it was all wrong.

When you've become accustomed to red, pink just doesn't do it for you anymore.

I felt nothing. The kiss did *nothing* for me. The only thing I could even register was the simultaneous burst of panic and anger running through me once I realized what Denise had done.

Then, like it was nothing, she just walked away. She pulled the pin out of the grenade and threw it. She even smiled while she did it. I wanted so badly to demand she explain herself, but with her walking one way and Cooper walking the other, I had to make a choice. It was a choice that had my feet walking in the correct direction before my brain could even process that there was a choice at all.

Too bad that it was too little too late.

I'm done, Cooper said. *Twice.*

Could she really be done?

Because I'm sure as hell not.

I need to do something. I need to show her I'm serious about this. Serious about *her*. I just need to get her attention long enough that she'll let me speak. If I can do anything, I can talk. I just need her to let me talk.

But how?

I let my head fall back against the headrest of my seat as I stick my arm out the car window, flicking off the ash at the end of my cigarette. I let my eyes fall shut, blowing out a deep breath as I wrack my brain for something–*anything* that might work. The car becomes quiet as I zone out against the seat, only the steady ambience of the radio playing filling the space.

And then I hear it.

"Storms are brewing in your eyes."

My eyes snap open.

"Sara, Sara..."

I sit up, turning the Starship song I've heard a million times up to full blast.

"No time is a good time for goodbyes."

My mouth falls open as I stare at the radio as if it's about to grow a face and speak to me.

Sara by Starship.

How in the hell had I never thought of it before? Never put two and two together?

I spin around, feeling around the floor of my back seat until my hand touches the handle of my briefcase. I pull it up and onto my lap, quickly opening it and running my fingers over the organized cassette tapes until I find the one I'm looking for. When I land on it, my fist pumps in celebration. I slide the cassette out of its spot in the case, flipping it back and forth between my fingers as I examine it.

Starship's *Knee Deep in the Hoopla.*

"That's it," I mutter to myself. "That has to be it."

I shut off the car, stepping out and dropping my cigarette onto the asphalt, crushing it beneath my Converse All-Star.

I check my watch, seeing that second period is just about over. "T-minus an hour to showtime, Summers."

———

I tap my foot as I wait, listening to the song for the third time in a row. Just when I start to get antsy, Lisa McDaniel reappears from the door to the cheer locker room. I slide my headphones off my head, holding out my hands as a question to her. She gives me an apologetic look as she steps out of the door, which nearly makes me curse under my breath, but then I relax when she fully steps out and I see her carrying the boombox in her right hand.

"Sorry," Lisa says as she approaches me, "I ran into Coach McKinley. I had to come up with an excuse for why I was stealing the boombox. I told her some of the girls wanted to practice our new routine over lunch. I'm not quite sure she bought it, but she didn't stop me." She holds the boombox out to me. "Please just return it in one piece."

427

"I'll try my best," I assure her, grabbing the handle. "Thanks, Lisa."

I start to turn away but feel resistance and realize Lisa still has a hand on the boombox handle as well. "Also," she murmurs, if we could just...*not* mention to Denise that I helped you with this..."

"She certainly won't hear it from me," I say.

"Thanks, Robbie," she smiles. "I'm rooting for you."

I give her a tight smile and a nod before turning away, speed-walking down the hall.

And then, when I turn the corner...

Speak of the devil.

My feet skid to a stop as I come face to face with Denise.

"Oh, hey, Robbie," she grins.

I push my tongue into the side of my cheek, my fist tightening at my side.

"Whatcha got there?" Denise asks, glancing down towards the boombox, specifically at the tape on the back reading *Cheer Team*.

"Nothing that concerns you," I grit.

She lets out a musical laugh. "I think it concerns me if you're using the cheer team's property. How did you even–"

"*In fact*," I cut her off, "*nothing* that happens in my life concerns you anymore. Because, Denise, if you remember, *you* made sure of that."

She tilts her head at me, the corner of her mouth twitching. "What?" she questions me.

"*You* broke up with me. Remember that?"

She chuckles, shaking her head. "Robbie–"

"You decided I wasn't good enough for you. That I didn't have enough to offer. That I wasn't *serious*." She opens her mouth to try to argue, but I hold up a hand, not letting her. "And I fought you on it, because I wanted you. I wanted *you* to *want me*. But you didn't, no matter what I said. No matter what I tried. *No*, you didn't want me until you saw *someone else* have me. Until you saw someone that was a whole lot more serious than you claim to be wanting me. Even though you had already moved on, with one of my *closest friends*, I might add. You still just...couldn't stand that, could you? The thought of me being happy with someone else? Someone that wasn't anything like you? Someone that actually cares about me and listens to me and fights for me? "

Denise shakes her head. "I just...I didn't know you and Sara were ever that serious..."

"So you decided to test that theory by embarrassing her in front of the entire school? After already making a show of her in front of everyone at your holiday party?"

"I..." Denise stammers. "I just didn't think–"

"Yeah, clearly," I start to move past her, but she stops me with a hand on my arm.

"Is it such a crime that I missed you?" she asks. "That I realized I made a mistake?"

"No," I shake my head. "We all make mistakes, Denise. And one of mine is letting you pull me away from the girl that actually makes me feel like I'm worth something on the inside for another second."

"Robbie–" Denise whines.

"Denise, I truly wish you the best," I say, pulling my arm from her grasp. "But we have no reason to speak anymore. And I have another mistake I need to go fix."

And, with that, I make a beeline for the courtyard.

I know that's where she'll be, and I know that if I let my feet stop moving, if I let myself question what I'm about to do, I might miss my chance.

Just do it.

It'll work.

The lunch bell already rang over fifteen minutes ago. With the time it took to track down Lisa, convince her to help me, and wait for her to get the boombox, I'm sure there will be a pretty healthy crowd of students already settled in the courtyard eating lunch. I can't decide if that's better or worse. It's not like I've ever shied away from a crowd before, but I can't explain it. This feels different.

It's not different. It's going to be fine.

It'll work.

I push open the door, sliding on my sunglasses with one hand the moment I'm outside. I don't stop walking until I reach the most central table in the courtyard, which, surprisingly, is open.

It's like it was waiting for me, I think.

This is gonna work.

I set the boombox on one of the seats and make quick work of transferring the tape from my Walkman into it, getting it to the place in the album where I need it and ready to play. I blow out one deep breath before I hop up on the table. I stand tall, telling myself I'm searching for her, but the truth is, I already know she's here.

I was aware of her presence the moment I stepped into the courtyard, like a spark in the air or the smell of flowers in the breeze; you can't see it, but you just know it's there, invading your every sense. I stand tall, scanning the area around me, and it takes approximately three seconds before I spot the fiery head of hair I'm looking for.

There she is.

Cooper's sitting at a table with Alice and Daniel, a textbook open in front of her next to her brown lunch bag and can of Jolt. She hasn't spotted me yet. I see her talking to Alice, taking a sip from her soda, and then, as if she can sense me calling out to her, she stands up from the table. She has the Jolt can in one hand and grabs the brown bag with the other as she finishes her thought to Alice. And then she steps out of her seat, headed for the trash can.

The trash can that is right in the middle of the courtyard.

Go time.

I bend down, hitting the play button on the boombox and turning the volume up to the max before I can give it another thought.

Sara by Starship starts blasting at full volume.

Every head in the courtyard immediately snaps in my direction, but the one I care about seems to take her time, apparently not phased by the initial piano intro. When she finally glances up, it's right on cue for me to spin around to the electronic whistle sound that really begins the song. Applause and cheers sound out from the surrounding tables as I begin dancing and singing along to the music, completely letting go and giving it my all.

I watch as the levels of realization dawn on Cooper's face.

When she realizes the music is coming from inside the courtyard.

When she meets my eyes and discovers that I'm the person responsible.

When it registers in her head what song this is.

When her lunch bag and soda can fall from her hands.

When I really play it up to the line, *"I'll never find another girl like you,"* and she's forced to understand what I'm trying to do here.

When I stare right at her with a massive smirk on my face every time the song says, *"Storms are brewing in your eyes,"* pointing right at her so that she *knows* that's her. That *she's* Sara. *Literally.*

When she notices every single person around once again has their eyes on us. And that they *love* us. That they're cheering for us.

And when the song dwindles down to the end, and she realizes I'm hopping down from the table and heading straight for her with every intention of making her forget that kiss with Denise ever happened.

I approach Cooper halfway through the chorus, her shoulders relaxed and eyes wider and grayer than ever as they look up at me. Her expression is soft and not totally readable, her brows pulled slightly together and her lips half parted. I grin at her, mouthing *Sara* along to the song.

I slowly reach for her face. She doesn't stop me, frozen in place. The approving cheers around us only grow louder as I lean in towards her, letting my eyes fall shut.

I'm just inches away from her, anticipating the feel of her soft lips on mine and the coming hours together where everything will just be back to whatever crazy version of normal Cooper and I have created together.

And then the entire image shatters as a loud sound cracks out.

And it takes a moment before I realize, slowly registering the ache in my jaw, the fogginess in my brain, and the loud simultaneous gasps of the crowd around us, that the sound was from Cooper slapping me across the face.

I rear back, reaching for my hot and sore cheek, my eyes snapping open. When I see Cooper this time, her expression has totally changed, her skin flushed and facial features sharp as she stares back at me with a searing gaze.

"*What the hell?*" I murmur.

"Is this some kind of sick joke?" Cooper questions me.

I shake my head immediately, so confused how this went so wrong. I try to respond to her, but no words come out when I open my mouth.

"Let me save you the time," Cooper says, her voice husky, taking a step towards me. She's so close now that I can see the glossy sheen in her eyes, making my brows knit together. "I'm not Denise. And this does nothing for me."

I stare back at her, my eyes narrowing.

When did words become so hard?

I guess it doesn't matter. Because Cooper never gives me a chance to try any, storming off and around the side of the school building.

She gets ten paces away before my brain starts functioning again, my eyes blinking fast and my heartbeat sounding in my ears. My back straightens slowly as I replay everything that just happened, everything that was said, and it only takes Cooper walking five more steps for my reaction to all of it to form.

"*What the fuck?*" I mutter to myself.

I'm not Denise.

I know that. That's kind of the whole point.

And this does nothing for me.

Well, I'd like to know what exactly *does* do something for Cooper. Because, last time I checked, getting publicly serenaded was pretty fucking rad by every standard.

I don't even remember making the decision to run after her until I'm right behind her again.

"Cooper!" I call to her.

"*Leave me alone, Robbie,*" she grits, not looking back at me.

"Not a chance."

I catch her by the elbow, spinning her to face me. The moment she's turned around, Cooper's free arm is flying back to slap me once again. I catch her wrist in my hand right before she makes contact, gripping it tightly. I force her to step backwards until she's pressed against the brick wall of the school behind her, completely caged in by me. Anger flows through me as I watch her grit her teeth, looking up at me with such hatred and breathing heavily through her nose. It only makes my fingers dig harder into her wrist.

She tries to resist me, pushing her hand closer to my face, but she doesn't have a chance. I have all the control, slowly pulling her wrist down until it's resting against her hip. I lean in closer to her, using the hand I have on her other arm to draw her closer to me. She looks furious, but she doesn't back down, meeting my challenge.

"*Do* not *do that again,*" I grit, my voice low and face only inches from hers.

"No problem," Cooper breathes. "Because I don't plan to give you the privilege of touching me ever again. In fact, don't even speak to me." She's trying to stay strong, and my first reaction is to fume at her, but I didn't miss the crack in her voice at the end of her proclamation. Or the moisture currently pooling at the corners of her eyes.

I pull back just slightly, releasing my grip on her by a small fraction. It's still enough for her to break free, and she doesn't hesitate, pulling out of my grasp and escaping her cage against the wall.

"Cooper, come on—"

"*No.*"

"*Why not?*" I demand, throwing my hands in the air.

She spins around fully, locking eyes with me. "Robbie, what did I ask of you?"

"What?" I rear back. "When?"

"I asked you not to make me look stupid," Cooper says, her voice strained.

My posture straightens as I look at her.

"I asked this one thing of you, and you agreed," she continues. "And then, after everything we've been through–after everything *you* made me believe–you announce to Paul and a whole audience that I don't mean anything to you. That you don't even want me."

I shake my head so fast it feels like my brain rattles. "Cooper, you got it all wrong–"

"Do I?" she asks, raising a brow. "So that means that you *didn't* say you could sleep with any girl in the school if you wanted? You didn't say that you *would*, in fact, do just that?"

My throat closes up. "I..."

"Did you say that, or didn't you?"

I press my lips together, not sure what to say, knowing she already knows the answer, that she clearly talked to Alice.

"I asked you a question, Robbie."

I blow out a breath. "Look, I did, but–"

"Right. And then, mere minutes later, after you had just humiliated me and illegitimized everything between us in front of the entire basketball team and a full hallway of our classmates, you let Denise kiss you in front of the whole school–"

"I didn't *let* her kiss me, Cooper–" I grit.

"Right, I'll give you that. But you also weren't the one to pull away."

My head pulls back.

Okay...she's not wrong.

"And you certainly didn't try too hard to get her off of you."

"My God, Cooper." I run a hand down my face. "She caught me off guard, okay? She totally shocked me. What was I supposed to do? Throw her off of me?"

"That would have been better than what you *did* do," she laughs humorlessly. "Which was nothing."

I'm getting frustrated. I don't see a way out of this. It's like Cooper has already made up her mind about how this conversation is going to go, already planned for all of her responses without even knowing what I'm going to say. It feels useless to even try. I may as well ask her to fill in the gaps for me.

The words tumble out of my mouth. "What do you want me to say?"

"What?" she asks, her shoulders dropping.

"You heard me," I tell her. "I asked what you want me to say. Because clearly you aren't going to be satisfied with anything I come up with. You won't even hear me out. I just..." I trail off, my tongue pushing into the side of my cheek. "How did this get so messed up so fast?"

Cooper rolls her lips into her mouth, shaking her head. "The fact that you don't even know tells me that you may as well not say anything else. You're just wasting both our time."

I tilt my head at her, and she breaks my eye contact, dropping her head and looking away.

I'm so mad at her. I don't know what she wants. She's frustrating the hell out of me.

So why do I just wanna wrap her in my arms and kiss her?

"Cooper..." I reach for her wrist, and surprisingly, she doesn't stop me. "Please, I'm trying, okay? You know I'm not good at this. You know I've never even really had to *try* to be good at this. But that's because...this is different. You're different. My usual shit doesn't work on you. And, as frustrating as it is, I live for that. You make me put in the work. You make me work for it."

She bites down on her bottom lip, still not looking at me. "Robbie, I never expected that much of you. But do you really have to work that hard to just...*not* break my heart?"

"I guess I do," I whisper, completely honest.

"Please let me go," Cooper breathes. I let her pull out of my grasp, but I don't let her walk away, sticking my arm out and blocking her way.

"Look, I get the stuff in the hallway. I know what you're thinking. I know it sounded awful–that it *was* awful, but I'm trying to tell you, Alice walked up late and missed a lot of context. Paul said some vile shit. I know that doesn't excuse what I said, but he made me snap. I wish I could take back what I said about the other girls. I didn't mean it. But I know that doesn't matter now. Regardless, I understand why you're mad about that."

Cooper raises her head just slightly, and it makes me think for the first time that I may be getting somewhere.

"When it comes to the courtyard though," I continue, "I don't understand why you're mad about that. I did that for you. I had to get your attention. And that song... Cooper, it's *you*. I heard it earlier today and it was just too perfect. I wasn't recycling some previous performance and I wasn't thinking about anyone else when I did it. If you thought I was, I guess I can get why you'd be mad." She looks up at me now, her brows pulling together.

"But the Denise thing... C'mon, Cooper. You were there. It wasn't my fault we both won *Best All Around*. I haven't spoken to Denise by choice in months. You saw she grabbed me. That she initiated the kiss. And yeah, I didn't immediately shove her off. But it all happened so fast. My brain was running on such overdrive that it took a few seconds for me to even realize what was happening, and, by then, it was too late." I pause, swallowing as I maintain Cooper's unwavering gaze. "Cooper, I was so focused on *you*. I was just trying to get to you. To *talk* to you."

"So that you could cover your ass over what you said in the hallway before Alice could get to me first?" she jumps in.

My shoulders relax as it seems she's finally putting the pieces together. "Yes," I nod, "exactly."

"But then you got called up for the award."

"Yes," I agree, urging her on.

"And then, probably because she saw me taking the photo, Denise kissed you."

"*Yes*," I say again, feeling like a broken record but just happy to finally be heard.

Cooper's lips press together. "And I'm not supposed to be mad at you because..." she trails off. At first, I think she's going to continue speaking, but she doesn't, instead quirking her head at me like she'd like me to finish for her.

"Well..." I say. "Because it wasn't my fault. I didn't want her to kiss me. I didn't expect it."

Cooper looks at me for a moment, nodding slowly. "Right," she says. But I can tell that something's off about the way she says it.

"You know what *I* didn't expect, Robbie?" she asks, her voice even.

I search her face, not finding any indication of where this is going. "What?" I question her.

She takes a deep and steady breath, blowing it out of her nose before she begins.

"I didn't expect to come back to school today feeling like it was the very first day of the year all over again. I didn't expect to learn that I was right about you all along. I didn't expect to realize that, somewhere along the way, I had managed to fall into the trap that is Robbie Summers. The one I used to be proud to say I so clearly saw through. I didn't expect to watch you utterly destroy me with both your words and your actions. I didn't expect you to give what I thought was now only mine–because *you* said it was– to the one girl in the world that has ever truly made me feel like I'm nothing. And I didn't expect to watch it happen, much less along with the entire school." Cooper shakes her head, pausing only long enough to quickly swipe away the first tear that spills from her eye. "And I *especially* didn't expect you to have the audacity to use your same absurd apology tactic you used on her–*also* in front of the whole school–on me."

I stare at Cooper for several long seconds. "Absurd apology tactic?" I question her.

"Oh my God," she mutters, barely audible. "That's what you're taking away from what I just said. Okay, wow." She runs both of her hands through her hair, beyond frustrated. "Yes, Robbie. *Absurd.* Ridiculous. Wildly unreasonable. Illogical. Inappropriate–"

"I don't need the definition of the word *absurd*, Cooper. Jesus Christ," I huff.

"Then what *do* you need, Robbie?"

I start to respond, but Cooper cuts me off, throwing her hand out.

"Actually, don't tell me. I don't care what you need, because clearly you couldn't even dream of caring about what I need, much less what I want."

"Fine," I snap, throwing my hands in the air. "Have it your way. I'm an asshole and I don't know anything. I'm absolutely fucking clueless. So enlighten me. What is it that *you* want, Cooper?"

She takes a step forward, looking like she's ready to fight me with everything she has, but then I see it. The moment she truly breaks. Her shoulders fall, her eyes filling with tears, her voice cracking when she speaks. "I just wanted you to be honest with me. I wanted you to mean what you said. I wanted this to be a world where we could work. Where you and I made any sort of sense. I wanted to believe that you saw me for who I really was. I wanted to be able to trust you. I wanted to be okay with the fact that I showed more of myself to you than I ever have to anyone else. I wanted to feel comfortable knowing that I gave you things I can never take back and to trust that you would keep them safe."

She averts her gaze, flushed embarrassment coating her cheeks. When she speaks again, her voice is strained.

"I wanted you to be the guy I thought you'd shown me you were capable of being. I wanted you to, for once, not give me a goddamn performance, but instead, *you*. I just...wanted you. The you that is deep, and caring, and isn't afraid to drop the front and let me know that he's scared. I wanted the real you. Or what I thought was the real you. *That*, Robbie, is what I wanted. But I guess, if I've learned anything in this life, we don't usually get what we want."

I feel my heart slowly sink in my chest, until it feels like it drops right into my stomach. I'm at a loss for words. I don't know where to begin. She's telling me what she wants from me–or what she *wanted*–but...I don't know. I don't know how to give it to her. Where to begin. What problem to address first. I'm feeling so many emotions, but the one that manages to make it to the forefront is anger.

"Cooper, just admit it. It doesn't matter what I say to you. You've already made up your mind that you're never gonna trust me. Don't put this on me. I know I fucked up, I know I'm not perfect, but who the hell is?" I demand.

We stare back at each other for several seconds, our chest rising and falling but neither of us speaking. As time ticks by, I feel the fire of frustration within me slowly fizzling out until it's just a dull ache at the base of my throat.

"Cooper, don't do this," I say leaning towards her. "Don't push me away because you're scared. Because that's bullshit. Don't be so quick to just let this go."

"You broke the rules," she rasps, shaking her head as she blinks away the tears in her eyes. "You made me look *so* stupid."

"Yeah, well, I also kissed you. But you got over that."

Cooper's spine steels, her chin tipping up. When I catch sight of her eyes, they're as stormy as ever, and it brings me right back to the time I did a lot more than just kiss her.

"Don't let this go," I repeat.

The corners of Cooper's mouth pull down, and she scoffs out a dry chuckle. "How can I let go of something that was never even real?"

My mouth falls open.

And then the school bell rings, signaling the end of lunch. I look up towards the sky, turning my head towards where the sound is coming, trying to pretend that if I glare at the air long enough, the bell will stop. That time will reverse, and that I'll have just a few more minutes to sort this shit out. But then, I start to wonder.

Is there really anything to sort out?

It sounds to me like Cooper's made up her mind.

And apparently, in her mind, we never even existed.

The realization sends a wave of confusion and irritation crashing over me. I just don't understand. But maybe I don't need to. Maybe there's no point in even trying. Maybe, after all of this, Cooper's made some valid points.

She's gone on and on about what she wants and about the person she *thought* I was. And she's right. I'm not that guy. I've never been *that* guy. What would make me think that I suddenly could be? That a couple months with a girl like her could make a guy like me someone worth believing in? I never cared about being believed in before. Frankly, I fought against it. I've never answered to anyone. Not at this school

How could I be expected to start now?

Maybe Cooper's right. Maybe her and I just aren't meant to work. Maybe we are both just too set in our ways, too damn stubborn to let the other in. Maybe I've known this all along. Maybe we were always doomed.

But maybe...I want to try anyway...

But I guess it doesn't matter. Because I'm not the only person in this equation. And when I lower my head, planning to find the gaze of the other, she's already gone.

SARA

I slam the front door of my house and am face down on my bed within seconds. My head feels so heavy, my entire body aching like I just ran a marathon. I couldn't even tell you how the rest of the school day went after lunch.

After...

I don't even want to say his name. Even if it's just in my head. It feels like acid on my tongue and a stab to my chest to even think it.

When it was time to head to the library after school, I practically sprinted there. I couldn't wait. I needed my refuge, my safe haven. The one place in the world where I don't think about anything else.

Or, at least, that's what it used to be.

I forced every thought and memory of him away, keeping my head down and flying through book returns and stacks of inventory to reshelve like my life depended on it. I needed my hands working, or my mind would start working, and nothing good would come out of that. If I gave myself access to my mind, my heart was just a hop and a skip south, and something tells me the two of them would have a hard time getting along today. I didn't want to give my heart the opportunity to be the persuasive, nonsensical little wildflower that she is. She doesn't know what she's doing. She only cares about what she wants and not what she needs, not what's best for her. That's why she needs my mind. My mind protects her. My mind knows she's been through a lot.

"*Sara, was that you?*" I hear my mom's voice call.

I groan into the pillow, barely audible.

"Sara?" she calls out again when I don't answer.

I love my mother, but she loves to talk. And I simply do not want to talk right now.

Maybe if I just stay quiet, she'll forget she heard me. Maybe she'll just think she's crazy and that she just imagined the front door slamming. That's a solution that works for me. I just need to stay quiet until she goes to work. And then I don't have to talk.

I let my eyes fall shut.

Then I hear the sound of our front door banging open and closed. I register the creak of a door hinge near me and feel a whoosh of air at my side. My brows pull together as I slowly peel my face away from my pillow, opening one eye to peek at the source of the commotion.

Alice is standing at my bedside, her hands on her hips. "We need to talk," she says.

"I don't want to talk," I tell her, flopping back down on the pillow.

"Alice? Is that your voice I hear?" my mom says, poking her head in the door. "Oh, Sara. You *are* here. I was calling for you."

"Sorry, I was busy," I mumble into my pillow.

"Hi, Miss Sherri," Alice says, a grin in her voice.

"Hi, hon," she tells Alice. "Sara, I wanted to see if you had an extra pair of pantyhose I could borrow? My last pair has an awful run–" My mom's voice suddenly cuts off as our house phone starts ringing. "Oh, dangit. I'll be right back, girls," she tells us, the door hinge creaking once again as she leaves my room.

I hear Alice gently close the door behind my mom, then, a few seconds later, the bed dips at my side as she sits down next to me. "Sara..."

"I don't want to talk about it, Al, really."

"Yeah, well, I don't really care," she snaps.

I crane my neck up, my tired eyes blinking at her. "Well, that's not very nice."

"Who ever said I was nice?" Alice questions me. "Have you never heard of tough love? That's what friendship's all about. And I can tell you need a whole lot of that right about now."

"Alice, I know you mean well," I say. "And I *will* talk to you. But can't I just have twenty-four hours to simmer in my emotions?"

"Sara." Alice shakes her head, placing her hand on top of mine. "We have been friends a long time. I know how you operate. You are a busy girl. I knew damn well that if I did not catch you this afternoon on your day off from work that we would absolutely never discuss this. You'd just bottle this up with everything else you feel and shove it aside while you distract yourself with even more responsibilities you already don't have time for. So, no, you may not have twenty-four hours."

I stare up at her, open-mouthed, for several seconds. When I realize there's no way she's going to let this go, I flop over onto my back and let out a groan. I think I may even kick my feet a little in frustration.

"Great," Alice nods. "That's a great first step. Now, talk."

I blink at my ceiling, blowing a deep breath out of my nose. "I honestly don't even know where to start."

"How about the beginning?" Alice suggests. "How do you feel? What are you thinking? I know I've been a little out of the loop since you and Ro–"

"Please don't say his name," I cut her off, my voice tight.

Alice is quiet for a few seconds. "Okay," she says. "Well, I guess I just want to know what happened. Since you and...*him*...started dating. You guys really seemed so happy. I was so sure..." she trails off, twisting her lips to the side. "It just really seemed like he had gotten you out of your shell and like you had helped him turn a new leaf. I was convinced you guys were the real deal."

I let out a puff of air, something between a laugh and a scoff, because Alice's choice of wording couldn't be more spot-on ridiculous.

I was convinced you guys were the real deal.

I cover my face with my hands, shaking my head.

"Sara? What is it?" Alice asks, wrapping a hand around my wrist.

I run my hands down my face just enough so that I can peek up at her. "Alice...I..."

"What?" she urges me on.

"I have to tell you something."

I may as well. There's no need to keep it a secret anymore. There's nothing to keep under wraps. We've had a very public break-up to our...(*Very? Almost entirely? Somewhat?*) fake relationship.

"*Sara.*" Alice pushes, yanking both of my hands away from my face.

In a flash, my back jolts off the bed, and I'm sitting up straight at Alice's eye-level. "It wasn't real, *okay?*"

"What?" Alice questions me. "What wasn't real?"

I swallow against the lump in my throat, fighting the urge to look away from my best friend out of embarrassment. "*Us,*" I breathe. "Me and him. None of it was real. We both had things we needed and the other could help us get them. If people thought we were dating, it benefitted both of us."

Alice appears to have frozen in place, staring back at me with wide eyes.

"We were...just faking it," I continue. "Acting like we were a couple. Pretending to like each other. It was all a lie."

Several painfully long seconds go by, and Alice still hasn't moved. I'm not even sure she's breathing. Just as I'm starting to genuinely get concerned, she breaks form out of nowhere, completely startling me. I rear back, clutching my chest, and it takes me a long moment to realize that she's...laughing.

No, actually, she's not laughing. She's *hysterical.* She's chuckling so hard that her face is pink and she's squeezing a hand over her stomach.

"Wh–Why...*What?*" I stutter.

Alice continues to laugh deeply, swiping at the tears quickly forming at the corners of her eyes. "*Oh my God, that's a good one,*" she manages to hiccup out.

"What are you talking about?" I question her.

"Sara..." Alice shakes her head, finally managing to calm down. "I mean, you've got to be kidding me."

I raise my brows at her, still so completely confused.

"*Sara,*" she says, more firmly this time, "come on. The only lie here is the one you just told me through your teeth."

I rear back. "What do you mean?"

"I mean, Sara," Alice scoffs, "I said you two looked happy but... what I really meant was...you have been *glowing* these last few weeks."

I start to disagree with her, but I feel heat slowly creeping into my cheeks and turn my face away.

"It's like you've been on top of the world," Alice continues. "All of high school, I've never seen you so vibrant and outgoing. So *confident.* And even Rob–*him.*" She catches herself like the good friend she is, obeying my wishes. "It's like he's been a totally different person. He's been smiling–and I don't mean in that cocky, make-you-drop-your-panties kind of way–"

"*Ugh, God,*" I complain, trying to hide my face again, but Alice grabs my hand before I can.

"What I mean to say is," she corrects herself, "he's been smiling like he's...genuinely happy. It's like he went from arrogant to self-assured. Like he wasn't constantly trying to one-up himself. Like... he didn't think he needed to. He just seemed more...I don't even know how to explain it..."

"Serious?" I offer under my breath.

"Yeah," Alice instantly agrees. "Exactly."

"Well, that's exactly what he was going for," I mumble. "So I guess we put on a pretty good show."

"Sara...no," Alice insists, and I can see her head swiveling back and forth out of the corner of my eye. "This was different."

My eyes land on my floral duvet cover and stay there, tracing the petals and vines of the flowers woven into the fabric. "It wasn't," I assure her.

I can sense Alice trying to gain my eye contact in my peripheral vision. "Hey," she says, and I tear my eyes away from the red flower I'm currently staring a hole into to give her what she wants. "Look, believe me, I am not Rob–*Ugh*. Can I please just say his name now?"

"No."

"Fine," Alice huffs. "You know I'm not his biggest fan right now. What he said in the hallway was messed up. I mean, it broke my heart in half hearing it for you."

I wince, feeling my own heart breaking once again just at the reminder.

"And, even though I know that bitch initiated it–"

"*Alice!*" I cut in, a shocked laugh coming out of me. "My God."

She just continues on, completely ignoring my interruption. "It was crappy that he kissed Denise. It was even crappier that the whole school had to see it happen."

"Yeah," I croak out.

"And I know we're probably going to have different opinions about him serenading you..."

I snap my gaze up to meet hers, and Alice holds up her hands defensively.

"And that's fine," she insists. "These are all very real issues. Very real things you both need to work through–"

"Alice, there's nothing to work through," I interject. "We made a deal, we hit our expiration date, we both got what we wanted...for the most part...and now, we're done."

Alice tilts her head at me, her eyes thoughtful. "You know...you don't have to be."

"What?"

"You two," Alice clarifies. "You don't *have* to be done."

"But we–"

446

"It doesn't matter." Alice shakes her head, seeming to read my thoughts. "Sure, you two may have started out as one thing, but that doesn't mean it has to stay that way. That it has to *end* that way."

"I think it does," I insist.

"Why?"

"*Because*, Alice," I say, raking a hand through my hair. "It's just the way it's meant to be."

"Says who?" she asks.

"I...I don't know," I stammer. "But, come on. You know I'm right. Me and him...we were never meant to be together. Hell, we weren't even meant to be *friends*. Much less something more. We're two very different people from very different worlds...with very different paths."

It occurs to me now, for the first time, that I had never really taken the time to picture a future for me and...*you know who*. It was like I had a mental block that prevented me from even going there, from even imagining the possibility. But now that I let myself, the whole picture becomes even more clear.

I'm leaving. I'm going to NYU...*hopefully*. And, even if I don't get in, I'd spend every waking moment this next year getting the best possible grades I could at our local community college and working at Groovy Movie to reapply for the scholarship the following year. This is my dream. It's what I've always wanted. It's not something I could imagine letting go for anything... Much less a boy.

And when it comes to him...I have no idea what his future holds. What his next steps after high school will be. And I know he doesn't either. That's a huge reason why we even found ourselves in this situation in the first place. And, honestly, that's fine. Lots of people don't have a clear picture of what they want to do after they graduate. A lot of people don't have any idea what they want in life. A lot of people are fine to just go with the flow and figure it out.

But I'm not one of those people.

And the last thing I need is the distraction of one of those people holding me back. And I'm sure the last thing he needs is the pressure of someone like me pushing him to be someone he just simply...isn't. Someone he doesn't want to be. That's not fair. Everyone deserves a choice. We've both made plenty of our own. I can't say I'm one hundred percent happy with every single choice I've made...but at least they were my own. They've always been my own. I've always been in control. I've always *felt* in control.

Except for when I've been with him.

And I'm not sure how I feel about that. I think I don't like it. I think it feels dangerous. I think it serves to threaten every single thing that I've worked for and I think that...there's just no way that it can be worth it.

"It's just the way things are," I say, finally finishing my thought. "The way they've always been. And I think that's for a good reason. No matter what I may feel...I need to do what's right, what's smart."

Alice's eyes shift between each of mine, a sigh slowly escaping her. "Okay," she says. "If it's what you think is best."

I bob my head in a sort of nod.

"I just want you to be happy, Sara. Even if that doesn't mean always doing what's smart. Just...sleep on it, okay? Don't be so quick to let a good thing go just because it might not be the easiest thing."

"When have I ever been one to take the easy route?" I question her, oddly defensive over that particular comment.

"*Exactly,*" she smiles.

I purse my lips at her, annoyed to have fallen in her trap.

"Look, I meant what I said," Alice tells me. "I support you. But I'm also going to be watching you. If I see your sparkly new glow rapidly declining, we're going to have another talk." She points a finger at me and I roll my eyes.

"Deal," I say.

Alice opens her mouth to say something else, but that is the exact moment my mom decides to burst back through the door, her work uniform dress swishing around her thighs. "So, sorry about that. Telemarketers," she grumbles. She starts to shake her head, but then she catches sight of me and Alice and the position we're sitting in. "Oh, no." Her spine straightens. "What's the matter? What's with the serious faces?"

"Sorry, Miss Sherri," Alice responds immediately for the both of us. "Nothing too major. Just boy trouble."

My head snaps in Alice's direction, but she doesn't catch my heated gaze before my mom is already replying to her.

"What's going on with Daniel?" she questions her.

"Oh, nothing." Alice shakes her head. "It's Sara—"

My mom lets out a gasp. "Sara, you have a *boy?*"

I could launch myself at Alice right now, and I think she knows that, realizing now that she's definitely said too much.

"No, Mom," I insist. "Really, I don't."

My mom doesn't look like she believes me for a second, her eyes shifting over to Alice. She keeps her gaze on her, raising her brows when I don't say anything more.

"Well...not anymore," Alice mutters, completely cracking under pressure.

"*Alice,*" I groan, smacking a palm to my forehead.

"*Not anymore?*" my mom asks.

Everyone goes quiet. I don't say a word. Alice thankfully doesn't either. I see it as realization slowly dawns on my mom, her shoulders dropping and her mouth falling open. "Oh my God, *Sara Beth Cooper!* Was it that Summers boy?"

I let out a strangled sigh. "I—"

"Oh, for the love of God," my mom grits, resting a hand on top of her head. "You know, his parents are two of the worst people I know?"

"I can certainly imagine," I mumble, half to myself.

"But, I must say," my mom continues, shaking her head, "that boy was a charming little shit when I met him."

A sound like choking comes out of Alice at the same time I take the opportunity to flop back down on my bed. "Yeah, well, it was all a lie," I mutter, resting my forearm over my eyes.

"Oh, I'm sorry, hon," my mom says. "I don't know what happened between you two."

I don't say anything, and, as a result, it grows silent in my bedroom. I can feel the awkward tension thickening, but I let it continue to build, keeping my eyes shielded from the outside world. I start to think that maybe my mom left, but she quickly corrects my thoughts when she speaks up again, her voice in a hushed whisper.

"I have to say...he also has really great hair."

My forearm pulls away from my face, my eyelids heavy.

"He does, doesn't he?" Alice whispers back to my mom. "It's annoying, honestly."

"Oh my God. I love you both, but can you please leave." I sit up on my elbows and find both Alice and my mom with wide eyes, looking like they were just caught red-handed. "I'm sorry. I don't mean to be rude, but I've had a really long and crappy day and I'd just like to be alone now."

The two of them exchange one more look before Alice rises from my bed and my mom takes a step back. "Sure, of course, hon," my mom says. "I just really do need a pair of pantyhose–"

"Right," I say, remembering her saying that when she originally walked in. "In my closet, either in the bin on the top shelf or thrown somewhere on the floor."

My mom gives me a nod, slipping into my closet to begin her search.

"*Are you okay?*" Alice mouths to me when she's out of earshot.

"*Not yet*," I whisper back, being completely honest. "*But I will be.*"

I hear a grumble from the closet. "I'm not sure I'm having any luck here, Sara. We may need to make a trip to the store this weekend– *Oh*, wait. Here we are!" I see my mom's back as she starts to back out of the closet, pantyhose in one hand, but then she pauses. "Hey," she says, reaching up and plucking something off the shelf, "where did this come from?" When she turns around, I see she's holding something sparkly, and my stomach instantly drops.

She's staring down at the plastic thing in her hand. "What is this?"

"*Nothing,*" I mumble at the same time Alice says, "Oh, that's her Homecoming Queen crown."

My hands cover my face once again.

Dammit, Alice.

"You won *Homecoming Queen?*" my mom asks, shocked.

"*Oh my God,*" I say into my hands.

"Oh...I was...*just kidding?*" Alice offers.

"Sara?" my mom questions me, not taking the bait.

"It's a long story," I tell her.

I feel the bed dip right beside me. "I have to leave for work in seven minutes," my mom says. "Get started."

ROBBIE

I pull to a stop in front of the gas station, because it's just become a habit at this point.

I'm on my way home from basketball practice, which means she will have just left the library and will be heading for her shift at Groovy Movie. But she almost never goes straight there. No, she almost always stops at this gas station on the way to grab a Jolt Cola. Sometimes, she also gets a Charleston Chew. And, some days, even a bag of potato chips, if she's feeling crazy. I'm pretty sure they're salt and vinegar flavored. I don't know why, but that just makes sense to me. It seems to fit her. Somewhat polarizing, a little rough around the edges, can make you ache if you have too much but also constantly leaves you wanting more.

Yeah, that makes almost too much sense to be her flavor of choice.

Or maybe I'm just completely off my rocker.

She certainly makes me feel that way.

It's been three weeks since Cooper and I have spoken. Three weeks since everything fell apart. Since I managed to screw up and she refused to give me a second chance. Three weeks since we went our separate ways in the courtyard, so much left to be said but none of it that really mattered.

It's over. We're over. Things are back to the way they should be. Or at least we're both pretending that they are.

It took a full week for me to get out of the habit of picking Cooper up before school. For three days in a row, it's like I was in a daze, driving straight there on autopilot. Then, on day four, I was so mad at myself over the previous three days that I spent the whole drive repeating to myself that I would go straight to school, only to find myself still making the wrong turn when I got to the stop sign that separated my routes and still ending up at her house anyways. On day five, I just gave into it, telling myself I was just going to drive by, convincing myself that if I stopped fighting it, maybe I'd just get over it. But then she was walking out of her front door at the exact moment I turned on her street. Our eyes caught immediately, and I didn't know what to do. I slowed the car, waiting to see how she'd react. She didn't. She never moved.

I still ask myself what I would have done if she *had* moved. What would have happened. If I would have given her a ride. If we would have just slid back into our easy rhythm, forgetting everything that had happened the week before. But then I made myself stop thinking about it. Because she didn't move. And I brought my car back up to speed again, pretending I wasn't watching her the whole way behind the shield of my sunglasses as I passed by her. I thought for a moment that maybe that was a mistake. I thought she might bring it up in Ms. Cage's class that morning. But she didn't. She didn't say a word to me. And she still hasn't.

But she hasn't been perfect either.

I've caught her a few times with her head in a book, her body operating on autopilot, taking her to the places we used to meet one another. I've found her lingering by my locker as I approach it, only to catch herself before I get there, her body jolting when she realizes where she is and her feet carrying her away before I can ever confront her on it. I've caught her taking pictures of me at the basketball games. Far more pictures than she's taking of anyone else on the team. Part of me wonders if she has some nefarious purpose for that, if she's taking those pictures so she can bring them home and draw little impolite doodles on them or set them on fire. But another part of me hopes, for whatever sick reason, that she is simply using her photographer duties as an excuse to shamelessly watch me the way I've been watching her, her camera her shield in the way that my sunglasses and headphones are mine, making me looking totally oblivious to the outside world when, in reality, my entire world, my entire *focus*, has been one particular thing for the better part of the last few months.

Watching Cooper is like watching a car crash to me; I don't want to look, but I also can't seem to look away. It's like she's a flame and I'm a particularly stupid moth. Like I'm a recovering addict and she's the last hit of drugs around. She's like a guilty pleasure. Like a beautiful disaster. Like a bag of salt and vinegar chips.

I don't want to want her.

I don't know what to do, with or without her.

I can't let her go.

So that's why I'm here again, on a Tuesday night, coming home from basketball practice, and stopping to watch the red-haired, stormy eyed girl of my nightmares buy a soda.

My eyes catch movement behind the windows of the gas station's convenience store, and I see Cooper placing her can on the counter to check out.

Along with a bag of salt and vinegar chips.

I sink down in the seat of my car, letting my head fall back against the headrest as I shake my head.

"*What the hell am I doing?*" I ask myself.

I turn my head back towards the window just in time to see Cooper handing over cash to the boy behind the counter, giving him a huge smile. A smile that makes my heart thud painfully against my rib cage, because I'm not sure the last time I've seen her smile like that. It registers then that I know him. The boy she's giving that smile to. It's Doug Wells.

He's on the football team; a starter, but not a star. He's on the honor roll; one of the smarter kids in school and in one of the top spots in our class, but obviously not as high up as Cooper. He's on student council; not a major officer position, but at least he's involved. He's a clean cut guy; tall frame, narrow waist, eyes that are always kind and not a hair out of place. He comes from a wholesome, well-rounded, All-American family; middle class, still-married parents, mom's a teacher at our high school, dad owns our town's auto shop, family dinners and church on Sundays. I'm pretty sure I overheard that he's going to San Francisco State University in the fall; got some sort of scholarship that made his parents and teachers really proud.

That's about the sum of what I personally know about Doug Wells, but it's all I need to know to know that he's the type of guy that could make Sara Cooper smile like that. The type of guy that could *keep* her smiling like that. The type of guy that I could never be for her. The type of guy that she wants, and is willing to take a chance on, because she knows she won't be disappointed in the end. Doug wouldn't drag her down. Doug wouldn't have ever tried to change her.

That's why girls like Cooper pick guys like Doug.

That's why persistent and hardworking people like Cooper and Doug go on to live long, fulfilling lives taking the world by storm while the people like me who peaked in high school are left in their dust with the aftermath of us never having put the effort in to be anything more.

That's the way it's always been.

It's about time I accept that.

I pull away from the gas station, heading in the opposite direction of my home and towards Billy Montgomery's house. Towards the kickback with the guys he invited me to during practice with the promise of bottomless beers to get me out of whatever 'slump' I've been in and back in 'the game'.

A voice in my head had told me to turn him down when he asked, and I listened to it then. But now, I'm realizing that it was the voice of a ghost. The voice of a girl that's no longer in my life and won't be coming back. A voice I've been holding on to as much as I've been pushing it away.

I'm not sure when exactly I let her go, but she's quiet now. And I take that as my sign.

Time to let the past be the past and to come back to the present. To the place I've always been the most comfortable. To the place where I thrive.

To the only place I've ever really belonged.

forty-three

SARA

I just finish hanging the last sparkly green four-leaf clover garland when I hear the front door bell chime.

"Welcome to Groovy Movie," I say, spinning around. "Can I help you find anything– *Oh.* Hey, Alice."

Alice marches right up to the check-out counter, putting her hands on her hips. "Sara, what are you doing?"

"Uh..." I mutter, glancing at the garlands behind me. "Decorating for Saint Patrick's Day?"

"No," Alice shakes her head. "I mean, what are you *doing?*"

I cross my arms, tilting my head at her. "What do you mean? I'm working."

"It's Saturday night."

"I always work on Saturday night."

"Yes, I know," Alice says, shaking her head. "But, Sara, for nearly the last two months, you've been working *every* night."

"And what's wrong with that?" I question her.

"You doing absolutely nothing else besides it."

I scrunch my eyebrows at her. "I do lots of other things."

"Really?" Alice questions me. "Like what?"

"Well, I–"

"Something that doesn't involve volunteering at the library, student government duties, the yearbook, the school newspaper, or school at all for that matter," Alice says, giving me a knowing look.

My mouth snaps shut.

"That's what I thought," Alice sighs. "Sara, we gotta get you out."

I turn away from her, fiddling with some papers on the counter. "What is this 'out' you speak of? And why do I need to go there?"

Alice moves around the side of the counter to stand in front of me. "It was something you were finally learning about and experiencing. But then Rob–"

"*Don't.*" I cut her off, my gaze snapping up to her.

She holds her hands up defensively, rolling her eyes. "I'm just saying, Sara, it's our senior year. We have just about two months left. You can't just spend your every free moment throwing yourself into work or waiting at home by the mailbox for your scholarship application response to come in."

"Ouch," I scoff under my breath.

"Hey," Alice says, her voice gentler. "I'm only saying what you've said before. It's out of your hands now. You either got it or you didn't. You spending the remainder of your final year of high school as a hermit won't increase your chances of going to NYU at this point."

"I know that," I mutter, not meeting her eyes.

"*Good,*" Alice grins, grabbing my hand. "So we need to do something tonight." I start to groan, but she cuts me off, waving her finger in my face. "Nope, none of that. You've been dodging all my calls and blowing off any plans I've tried to make for weeks. Daniel is out of town this weekend and I miss my best friend so much. We are doing something fun."

"You act like we're some type of regular socialites," I chuckle, pulling my hand out of Alice's and reaching for my can of soda behind the register. "What would we even do?"

Alice tilts her head, seemingly trying to think of an answer. "Well, maybe–"

She's cut off by the front door opening, a loud commotion of music and voices instantly seeping in from the outside.

"*Hurry up, man, will ya?*" a voice calls from the car outside.

I can't tell who is standing in the doorway between the darkness outside and their head turned back towards whoever is yelling at them. "I told you, it'll just be a minute. I just need to drop these off for my mom. If we get a late fee because I put it off another day, it's coming out of my pocket."

"*Whatever! Just get to it,*" the voice calls back over the sound of music.

"I'm trying!" the guy in the doorway calls back.

"*Okay, okay– Hey! Wait, man!*"

"*What?*" the guy asks, exasperated, rebalancing the stack of VHS tapes in his hands.

"*If they have Red Vines, can you grab me a pack?*"

"Dude, no. If you want some freaking candy, come get it yourself. I'm not your mom."

A few seconds later, a car door slams and somebody is pushing through the front door with the original guy. When they both step into the light of the store, I realize it's Jesse and Paul.

"Oh, for the love of God," I mutter to Alice, running a hand through my hair.

Paul doesn't even take notice of me, turning and making a beeline for the snack wall, but Jesse spots me right away. I don't know what I expected his reaction to be, but it certainly wasn't a small smile and a gentle nod of his head.

I push myself into my robotic customer service mode, forcing a smile on my face. "Hey, Jesse," I say. "What can I help you with?"

"Hey, Sara," he replies, approaching the counter. "Just have a few returns."

"Oh, great," I say. "I can take those from you."

As Jesse is handing me the stack of movies over the counter, Alice speaks up.

"Hey, Jesse," she grins.

It takes everything in me not to shoot her a look like she's crazy.

"Oh, hey, Alice," Jesse says, his voice hesitant. Probably because these two have most certainly not spoken a word to each other since elementary school. "How's it going?"

"Just great, really. I was just dropping in on Sara here at work so we could decide what to do tonight after she gets off."

"Oh, sweet," Jesse nods.

"Yeah," Alice says, smiling wider. "Are you up to anything fun tonight?"

If my hands weren't full of VHS tapes right now, I'd probably be chucking my soda can at her head. I try to make eye contact with her to ask her through my gaze what exactly it is that she's doing, but she won't look at me for more than half a second.

"Well, actually–" Jesse starts to respond, but is interrupted by Paul reappearing around the corner with two family size bags of Red Vines in his hands, letting out a *whoop*.

"*Bingooo*," Paul drawls, plopping the two bags on the counter. "Found 'em." He looks at Jesse then swings his gaze in my direction, and, when he finds me, his spine straightens. "Oh, shit. Long time, no see," he smiles. "Hey, Cooper."

Every muscle in my body automatically stiffens at the name I haven't been called in months. Not since the only person that called me it finally stopped calling me at all.

Because you asked him to.

I clear my throat, pushing the thought away. "Hey, Paul," I nod, giving him a smile. "That'll be two dollars."

"Sure thing," he says, not taking his eyes off me or letting the grin leave his face as he reaches for his wallet in his back pocket.

"Do you think that's enough to get you through the car ride?" Jesse asks Paul, motioning towards the giant bags of candy. "Jesus, man."

"If not, I guess we know where to find more," Paul replies, still looking at me.

I let out a fake chuckle as I take the cash from his hands, turning towards the register to make change.

"So," Jesse begins, "I was just telling the girls—"

"Cooper, Jesse's throwing a party tonight," Paul interjects. "You should totally come."

My finger slips and I accidentally hit the button to open the register, making the drawer fly out into my stomach and knock the wind out of me.

"What?" I manage to choke out.

"People have missed you around lately," Paul says. "It's been awhile. You should come to the party. Both of you, if you want."

My brain is still processing what just happened when Alice speaks up.

"Well, that sounds so fun," she sings. "Doesn't it, Sara?"

I narrow my eyes at her out of view of the boys, but it doesn't faze her. "I don't know, I wouldn't wanna impose on Jesse..." I say.

"It's not a problem at all," Jesse insists. "You guys should come."

My head snaps in his direction, and I find both him and Paul looking completely casual about this entire thing, looking at me expectantly.

I swallow against the sudden lump in my throat, looking between them and Alice. Alice tilts her head towards me, raising her dark brows as a way to tell me to answer them.

"We'll think about it," I blurt. "Thanks for the invite."

"No problem, sounds good," Jesse says, tapping a knuckle on the counter before turning to head back to their car with a backseat full of girls whose faces I can't make out from here.

"See you later," Paul grins, taking a few extra seconds to look me up and down before he follows after Jesse.

As soon as the door closes, I let out a massive breath I didn't realize I was holding, immediately turning on Alice. "Do you care to explain yourself?" I ask her.

"What?" she questions me, an innocent look on her face. "We needed something fun to do tonight."

"No *we* didn't," I correct her. "And how is that your definition of fun? You want to go to a party with Jesse Lamonte and Paul Strothers?"

"You act like they're the only two people that'll be there," she rolls her eyes. "Sara, the whole school will be there, and you know it."

"Just knowing they're there at all is enough for me to not care to engage," I tell her. "If you've somehow forgotten, Jesse is sort of my arch-nemesis–"

"Is he? Really?"

"Well, yeah, kinda," I stammer. "I mean, he *was*, at least."

"He wasn't really acting like it now. He seemed plenty nice. And besides, you won. You beat him. If he seems cool with being in the same room with you, why do you care?"

"Well–I mean–I..." I trail off, pushing my hair out of my face. *Could she please* not *make logical sense right now?*

"And, come on, arch-nemesis seems a little dramatic. I'd think if that was anybody it'd be–"

"Don't even think about saying it," I cut her off.

"Well, regardless," Alice continues, "no matter who your arch-nemesis is, I would think the best thing you could possibly do is show them how unbothered you are by them. Show them how much fun you're having and how little you're thinking about them."

I blow out a steady breath, letting my eyes fall shut. I refuse to think into what she's saying, much less respond to it. Mostly because I know she's right.

"What's your next excuse not to go?" Alice asks.

I open my eyes again, looking at her. "Well, Paul..." I groan.

"What about him?" she asks.

"Well, if you're forgetting, we kind of made out once."

"Right," she nods, waiting for me to elaborate. When I don't, she suggests, "You could...do that again?"

"*Alice!*" I bark out a laugh.

"What?" she questions me, feigning innocence.

"Absolutely not. No thank you."

"It was just a suggestion," she shrugs. "He's hot, and you only have a couple more months to make dumb decisions before graduation."

"I think I'm good with passing on *that* particular dumb decision," I assure her.

"Fine," she says. "But what about the dumb decision of going to the party at all?" She wiggles her brows at me, an impish grin on her face.

I let out a heavy sigh. "If I say we can go, will you not make me go out the rest of the school year?"

Alice thinks about my offer for a moment, then holds out her hand to shake. "You're coming to Prom, but otherwise, deal."

"*Prom?*"

"Yes. And it's not up for discussion," she states. "But, if you go to Jesse's party with me tonight, I won't otherwise force you to socialize in public for the rest of the school year."

I chew on my bottom lip, my gaze flashing between Alice's hand and her face. "This is a horrible idea," I say.

"Which is why it's a great idea," she insists. When I don't respond for a few moments, she adds, "Sara, you need this. Come on."

I blow out a breath, shaking her hand before I can think about it any further. "Fine."

"Great. Now give me your keys." Alice holds out her hand.

"For what?"

"This place closes in half an hour," Alice grins. "I'm running to your house to grab you a change of clothes and leave a note for your mom that you'll be home late and then will be back here to pick you up."

I glance down at my jeans and striped sweater. "What's wrong with the clothes I'm wearing?"

"Sara, remember that talk we had."

"Which one?"

"About your glow."

My face falls.

"You haven't glowed in a while. And you're certainly not going to in those old things."

I open my mouth to protest, but Alice cuts me off, shoving her hand closer to my face. "Your keys, please."

I press my lips together, blowing out a breath before pulling my keys from my pocket and dropping them in her hand.

forty-four

ROBBIE

I tap my hands on the steering wheel along to the AC/DC song playing on the radio. I'm aware of Groovy Movie in my peripheral vision as I pass by it, but I don't turn my head.

I haven't turned my head towards it in two months, and I'm not gonna start now.

Just as I pass the building, I'm hit with a red light at the upcoming intersection. I blow out a puff of air as I bring my car to a stop, the neon lights of the forbidden movie rental store feeling like they're burning the back of my neck. I ignore them, reaching over and turning up the volume on the radio. When my hand pulls back from the dial, I catch sight of my fuel gauge and see I'm nearly empty.

"*Shit*," I grumble, taking off as the light turns green again. I'm already late getting to Brad's place, but I'm sure the guys won't even notice. Billy and Michael wouldn't have been a minute late since Brad told us his parents were out of town and that they left their liquor cabinet unlocked. I'll take advantage of them occupying his attention for a few more minutes. I'm barely a hundred yards down the road before I'm pulling off into the nearest gas station, parking my car at the first gas pump.

I keep my music turned up as I roll my car window down and open the door, jogging the handful of steps it takes to get inside and pay the station attendant. Then, I'm back at my car, just beginning to pump my gas when loud music drowns out my own as a new car tears into the parking lot. I shake out my hands as I release the pump and zip my jacket up, the unusually cold night breeze sending a shiver through me.

The loud car stops on the other side of the pump, parallel from me, and it only takes me barely craning my head before I recognize the brown Chevy Nova.

I take a deep breath, leaning against my Camaro and crossing my arms. The music coming from the other car gets even louder as the driver-side door opens, then it becomes muffled again once it slams shut.

Jesse and I immediately make eye contact as he steps around the pump to head to pay. His spine snaps straight and he blinks hard when the recognition sinks in, but then he quickly relaxes, bobbing his head at me. "Hey, man," he says.

I give him a nod. "Hey, Jess."

It's been two months.

Jesse and I never had a problem before this year. We're on the same team. There's no girls between us anymore. We both got the short end of the stick in some way or another from our situations. There's no need for bad blood. We've handled our shit like men and have moved on. We may not be throwing slumber parties or frolicking through fields together, but we're cool, which is all we need to be. I haven't given him much thought or overanalyzed the way he's treated me quite awhile now. I haven't felt the need.

So I'm wondering why now, as Jesse is watching me his entire way inside the gas station, his lips slowly pulling into a smirk as he does so, alarm bells are going off in my head.

I force myself to shake off the feeling, turning back to the pump to check on my gas. When I see it's only half full, I take the opportunity to wipe down my windshield and clear out trash from inside my car, needing to distract myself all of the sudden.

I grab a couple of Pepsi cans and food wrappers from the driver's side floor, then make my way around to the passenger side to get anything that may have made its way over there. I open the door, bending down to reach under the seat. When I don't find anything, I start to stand back up, but then pause, something catching my eye in the light.

I lean forward, squinting at the seat headrest and hoping that my mind was just playing tricks on me. But unfortunately, I'm just not that lucky, and it was not. I reach forward, plucking the distinctly long and red strand of hair from the headrest. I stand up straight, twirling the hair between my thumb and forefinger, watching as the gas station canopy lights above me make the single strand shift from orange to red to auburn, like the burning flame of a tiny match between my fingers.

I lean against my car to steady myself and shake my head, gritting my teeth together, my breath fogging in front of me from the cold air.

Even when she's not here, even when I've finally gotten to a place where I'm fine to not be thinking about her every minute of every day, even now when I'm able to turn the other way with the energy of her *so* close, just across the road, she still finds a way to make herself known. To make herself present. No matter how much I try to pretend like Cooper never happened, that she never happened *to* me, there's no use. She's everywhere. She's left her mark on everything. In the same way this hair of hers has lived in my car for months now, not consciously known but still there, she's left pieces of herself within me as well. And I'm tired of it. I'm tired of not being able to escape her. How did a girl that used to keep herself so invisible somehow become the only thing I can manage to see?

"*Robbie?*"

My head snaps up at the harsh voice, breaking me out of my trance, the strand of hair slipping from my fingers. I let it fall, swallowing against the dryness in my throat as my eyes find Jesse again. He's standing right in front of me with a case of beer in each of his hands.

It's funny. Bay View is small. Everyone knows everyone, which means the people who work at this gas station and every other place that sells alcohol in town know we are in high school. Yet they let guys like Jesse and me buy whatever we want, no questions asked. I remember now, a few years back, the first time he and I went to go try to buy beer together. We attempted to put together these ridiculous fake IDs. They looked awful, and we spent a full Saturday making them, but we never even got carded. Every adult just shrugged and let us buy the booze. I've never really thought about it until now why that is, or how other kids haven't been as lucky. Sucks for them, I guess.

"Are you good, man?" Jesse asks.

"Yeah," I say, too quickly. "Yeah, fine. Why?"

"Well, I had to call your name three times before you answered."

Oh.

"My bad," I say. "Just zoned out."

Jesse raises a brow at me. "Okay then," he replies, his voice skeptical. "Well, I was just going to ask if you're up to anything tonight."

"Why?" I ask, the question blurting out of me.

"Just wondering," Jesse says with a grin, glancing over to his car that I realize now is full of people. I try to see if I can recognize anyone, but I can't see who's inside through the dark windows.

"I'm throwing a little party tonight at my place."

Now it's coming back to me. I thought I overheard him saying something about a party in the locker room earlier this week. "It should be pretty cool. My parents are gone this weekend."

Of course they are.

"You can come, if you'd like," Jesse says, making me return my attention to his face.

"Oh," I mutter, rubbing a hand over the back of my neck. "Thanks, man, but I can't."

"You sure?" Jesse asks. "Lots of people will be coming out. It's just about to start up. We just stopped here to fill up and get some rations." He holds up the beer cases in his hand, which I assume is what he's referring to as rations. "I really don't think you're gonna want to miss this."

"I'm sure it'd be fun, but I've got plans."

"Okay," Jesse nods. I think for a minute that he's going to turn away, but then he says, "With who?"

"Oh...um...Brad. And some of the guys," I stammer, caught off guard by the question. *Why does it matter?*

"Huh. Alright," Jesse says, tilting his head at me. "Well, if you change your mind, you know where my place is."

"Yep," I agree. "I'll keep it in mind. Thanks, man."

And with that, we both get in our cars and drive in opposite directions.

———

When I walk in the front door of Brad's place about ten minutes later, Van Halen is blasting from the crackling speakers of a record player and Brad, Billy, and Michael are well on their way to tipsy.

"Well, well, well, if it isn't *Robbie the Heartthrob-ie!*" Brad slurs, throwing his hand in the air and hopping off his couch as soon as I make it into the living room.

I bark out a laugh. "Excuse me? What the hell did you just say?"

"Only what everyone else is already thinking," Brad replies, giving me a lazy wink and patting a hand against the side of my cheek.

"That's a good one," Billy calls from his spot on the couch.

"We should do something with that," Michael agrees.

"I clearly have some catching up to do here," I say, nodding towards the cup in Brad's hand.

"You sure do," Brad agrees enthusiastically. "That's what happens when you're late. You miss out."

So I guess they did notice. Oops.

"Here, I'll go get you something to get started with," Brad says, pushing me towards the couch. "Just make yourself at home, *Heartthrob-ie*."

"You know, we don't have to make that a thing," I insist.

"Too late," Billy drawls, yanking me down to the couch.

Brad makes his way into the kitchen, and I can hear him in the background tinkering around with some cups and liquor bottles as Michael starts off on some story about a girl he met at Dusty's Drive-In last night and how he and that same girl proceeded to nearly get banned for life. The shrill sound of a phone ringing breaks through the air, and it must startle Brad in the kitchen, because I hear something that sounds like a cup full of liquid hitting the floor and him letting out a curse. He must pick up the phone, because the ringing cuts off a few seconds later. Michael's just getting to a part in his story where I'm equally invested but also desperately in need of a drink now to continue, when Brad reappears in the doorway.

"Uh, did you forget something, Brad?" I ask him, motioning to his empty hands.

"Change of plans, losers," Brad says, walking forward and swinging over the back of the armchair in front of him.

"What do you mean?" Billy asks.

And, somehow, before Brad even says it, I already know the answer.

"Party at Jesse Lamonte's."

"*Really?*" all three of us ask at the same time. But, the difference is, Billy and Michael's '*Really?*' is out of excitement. It's an '*Are you serious? Woohoo!*' kind of '*Really?*', while mine is a hesitant '*Are you sure you really want to do that?*' kind of '*Really?*'.

"Yes, really," Brad confirms, not seeming to distinguish between our different forms of the question. "Robbie, can you drive?"

I blow out a breath, looking between the three guys around me.

It's Saturday night. Are we really gonna sit here on Brad's couch when we could be at a party with half of our senior class? This wouldn't even be a question that the old me would have asked. I wouldn't even have given it a second thought. Whatever weird feeling is in my gut that's trying to caution me about this party is just gonna have to take a hike. Because my brain's telling me I belong at this party tonight. In fact, now that I've allowed the idea to simmer, I *need* to be at this party.

I pull my car keys from my pocket, holding them up and twirling them by the ring.

"Why the hell not?"

forty-five

SARA

"Alice, what in the hell?"

"You're going to look amazing," she says back to me from the other side of the bathroom door.

"I thought you were going to my house?"

"I did," she confirms.

"But...where did you get this?" I ask her, looking at the red dress with black lace overlay in my hands. "This isn't mine."

"Oh, your mom's closet," she says casually.

"*My mom–*" I choke out, holding up the red dress to examine again. I *thought* it looked somewhat familiar.. "Alice, you went into my mom's closet?"

"Nothing in yours was doing it for me."

I bark out a laugh. "Was this really even necessary? I mean, it's just a house party. And besides, don't you think I'm going to freeze in this? That cold front came through this evening–"

"Oh, trust me," Alice cuts me off. "You'll be plenty *hot* in that."

"Okay, but you're wearing multiple layers and a jacket, and you still look hot–"

"Oh, Sara, would you just shut up and put it on already?" Alice whines. "The party's waiting, and I can't wait to see all the heads you turn in that little number."

I let out a groan, but comply, shimmying the red dress over my head and securing the spaghetti straps on my shoulders. I swap out my Keds for black loafers, then step out of the bathroom. I shoot Alice a look, doing a half-hearted twirl and throwing my arms in the air in a way of saying, *Are you happy now?*

"That's more like it," she nods, her lips pulling into a grin.

I lock the front door of Groovy Movie, then toss my other set of clothes into the back seat of the car Alice is borrowing from her mom, climbing into the passenger seat.

Within ten minutes, and before I have any time to change my mind about going, Alice is parked around the corner from Jesse Lamonte's house and is pulling me in tow behind her as she storms for the front door.

As we make our way, my arms crossed over my already shivering body, I begin to realize how many cars we are passing and just how far down the street they are parked, and it occurs to me that I was probably a fool for thinking this was some little house party. Nobody in Jesse's circle does anything *little*.

I gulp hard as Alice finally brings our feet to a halt on the front porch, her fist rapping against the door. Nobody answers, but, judging by the blaring music coming from the backyard and the muffled sound of tons of people on the other side of the door, Alice takes that as a sign that we can just let ourselves in.

There's lots of people mingling around in the house, but it's clear the majority of the party is happening in the backyard, so Alice grabs my hand, taking off, the handful of people that are in the foyer parting like the Red Sea for us. We don't stop until we pass over the threshold of the back door, Eddie Money's *Take Me Home Tonight* hitting us at full blast as we join the scene out back.

My jaw nearly comes unhinged as I take in the amount of people here. It's easily the same amount of people that were at Denise's holiday party, if not more. And the roster of people is practically identical, which doesn't do anything to settle my nerves.

Speaking of Denise, my eyes catch on a blonde ponytail, and I spot her with Ginger Matthews and Kate Andrews sitting cross legged on the edge of the pool, laughing with one another without a care in the world. As if she can sense me looking at her, Denise's head slowly shifts in my direction. My spine straightens as her eyes meet mine, and, for a moment, her expression is unreadable, her head tilting. I swallow against the sudden dryness in my throat, my hand that's not in Alice's clenching into a fist at my side. And then...

She smiles at me.

Or, at least, I think she does. It's so subtle. The slightest lift of the corner of her mouth. The tiniest indent of her cheek dimple showing through. The gentlest nod of her head.

And then it's over.

She turns back toward her friends, reinserting herself into their conversation like she never even left it.

Oh.

My shoulders relax, my brows pulling together.

Well, what am I supposed to do with that?

"Should we get a drink?" Alice's voice sounds, bringing me back to reality.

"That's a fantastic idea," I reply immediately, my teeth practically chattering as I finally tear my eyes away from Denise. I'm not usually the first in line for alcohol, but I'm willing to take anything that will warm me up right about now. I follow Alice off to the side of the pool where everyone seems to be grabbing drinks from.

I scan over the choices, looking from the keg of beer to the random assortment of coolers filled with all sorts of cans and bottles. A gasp of pleasant surprise escapes me and my mouth instantly begins to water when I spot a familiar green bottle. I snatch the wine cooler from the cooler, opening it and taking a long sip from it before Alice even has a plastic cup in her hand and is getting in line for the beer keg. By the time she waits her turns behind three other girls attempting to use the keg, I've nearly polished off my bottle.

"*God, these go down easy,*" I mutter to myself, finishing off the last of the sweet wine.

"And that's why they'll get you in trouble," a smooth voice comes from behind me.

I spin around, finding Paul standing right behind me. "Oh, Paul, hi," I mumble. I push my hair away from my face, noticing how my cheeks already feel a tad warmer and my anxiety has somewhat calmed.

I have to admit, alcohol can be a beautiful thing.

I suppose, until it gets ugly, that is.

Paul grins, his eyes tracing my face. "Looks like you need another one of those."

"Oh, um, I–" I start, and then, I don't know why, but I start laughing.

"What is it?" Paul questions me.

"Sorry, nothing," I chuckle. "Just...having déjà vu."

I shouldn't be laughing. Because if this moment is anything like the original moment that's causing my déjà vu right now, we are in for a mess of a night. Last time I checked, nothing good has come out of Paul offering me a second wine cooler.

Paul just stares back at me for a moment, and I start to feel ridiculous, but then he lets out a soft chuckle of his own. "Yeah, I guess you're right."

I smile at him, holding up the bottle in my hands and letting out a breath of laughter. I assume our moment is over, and that, with the awkward ice successfully broken between the two of us, that Paul and I will now go our separate ways. But, clearly, Paul doesn't see it the same way as he takes a step closer to me, his voice lowering an octave.

"We just keep finding our way back to each other, don't we?"

My mouth falls open, my eyes immediately shifting over Paul's shoulder, trying to find Alice. Unfortunately, she isn't able to come to my rescue, her focus fully on getting the keg to work, one of the girls that was in front of her in line helping her along with a boy I recognize as Daniel's cousin.

How many high schoolers does it take to make a beer keg operate?

"So, what do you say?" Paul asks.

My gaze returns to Paul in front of me. "What?"

His tongue pushes into the side of his cheek. "There's no more of those wine coolers in this cooler." He motions his thumb over his shoulder toward the cooler I just took this bottle from. "But I have some in my cooler on the other side of the pool. Want to go grab one together?"

"I..." I trail off, desperately looking in Alice's direction again, still not finding any luck.

"You know, I'd love to. But I shouldn't leave Alice here. Could you maybe just go get it and bring it back to me while I wait for her?" I attempt, fully intending for neither Alice or me to still be in this spot when Paul returns.

"Really?" Paul laughs.

I'm not looking at him, still focused on Alice.

"C'mon, Cooper."

My eyes snap back to Paul. "*Sara*," I tell him. "Please just call me Sara."

Paul's eyes squint at me, and he lets out a sigh. "You really sure don't want to come with me to get you another one?"

"Yes, I'm sure. I really need to stay here with Alice—"

I cut off, my words getting caught in my throat as my eyes snag on a dark blur just behind Alice.

It's him.

Walking into the backyard with Brad and Billy, arms around their shoulders, a huge smile on his face, and every hair just perfectly out of place.

Robbie.

"Okay, well, I guess I'll be right back—"

"*No*," I blurt, reaching out and grabbing Paul by the arm and stopping him in place. His brows raise, his gaze lowering to where my hand rests on the crook of his elbow. I clear my throat, my eyes flicking between Paul's face and where Robbie is. He hasn't seen me yet, and I'd love to keep it that way. I don't know if it's possible to keep it up all night, but it's definitely impossible if I stay here right now. He'll walk directly into me at the rate he's going. I try my best to seem casual, slowly sliding my hand forward enough so that I can hook arms with Paul. "Actually, I'd love to go with you. I'm sure Alice won't even miss me."

Paul gives me a confused look. "But I thought you just said–"

"*Please*, Paul. Can I go with you? I really want to." I give my best attempt at batting my eyelashes, my teeth grinding together as I smile at him, just needing him to buy my act and for his feet to move.

Paul lets out a whistle. "Shit, I'd take you anywhere you'd let me, Cooper."

My jaw aches as I grit my teeth together harder at the name I just told him not to call me. The one that only ever sounded right coming from the one person who I'm currently trying to get as far away as possible from.

Luckily, Paul starts walking. We make our way off the back deck and begin weaving through the people crowded around the pool. I can't help it. Once I feel like I am sufficiently camouflaged by the crowd, I have to glance over my shoulder. Robbie is still completely unaware of me and now has a can of beer in his hands, taking a sip and laughing at something Jesse is telling him.

Wait.

I do a double take, confirming that I'm not crazy.

Jesse?

I shake my head, confused. I guess the two of them are cool again. I guess it's also not any of my business. They're teammates. *Why wouldn't they be cool?*

I blink a few times, taking one more look. Jesse is clapping Robbie's shoulder, acting like the two of them are the best of friends again. I force my eyes back forward, staring at the back of Paul's head as he comes to a stop in front of a cooler hiding behind a pool chair. I wonder for a moment if Jesse knew that Robbie would be here when he invited me tonight. I wonder if Paul knew too.

Maybe I'm overthinking this.

I didn't notice Paul initially bending over until now as he stands back up, wine cooler in one hand and a bottle of beer in his other hand. He opens my drink for me then hands it to me, holding his bottle out for me to cheers with. I clink my bottle with his, running through excuses in my head that I can give to get away from Paul in the next thirty seconds.

Sure, maybe I just used him. I got away from Robbie, I got another drink to calm my nerves, but I don't have any desire to stick around him. That's not why I came here tonight. Paul's always been nice enough to me, but after the whole *Spin the Bottle* debacle at Denise's party...it just makes me uncomfortable to be with him. Especially when it's only the two of us. We aren't friends. We never have been. We have absolutely nothing in common. Just because I had an anger-induced momentary lapse in judgment that may have resulted in my tongue ending up in his mouth doesn't mean that Paul and I need to pretend this is anything that it isn't. I'll be kind to him in the way that he is kind to me, but it's not going further than that. I don't have any interest. But I also don't want to be rude.

Two minutes. I'll give him two minutes of casual conversation and then I'll say I need to get back to Alice. By then, I'm sure Robbie will have made his way into the party anyway and will be too distracted to even notice me before I convince Alice to leave.

"Cheers," I say brightly, forcing a smile on my face.

I start to pull my bottle away, but Paul's hand grabs my wrist, stopping me. "Here's to..." he says, trailing off with a grin on his face. Then, he puts his other hand on my shoulder, pulling me close enough so that he can whisper in my ear. "Here's to finding each other again. Here's to tonight. Let's make it a good one. What do you say, Cooper?"

A chill runs through me, and I know it's not just from the frigid breeze blowing through my hair right now. My heart begins to race, dropping into my stomach. And not in the good way. In an almost *painful* way. I can't exactly put my finger on it, but something in how Paul just said what he said makes me want to bolt for the door. The words themselves were innocent enough, but every ounce of his voice was laced with bad intentions. My reaction is so physical, that I have to shift my head away from him. And, when I do, my gaze collides perfectly with Robbie's across the pool.

There he is. Billy to his left, his ear turned to him as Billy animatedly tells him a story, and Kate Andrews to his right, his arm slung around her shoulders, and his eyes glued to my face.

Robbie shifts into slow motion as I completely freeze in place. Robbie's arm holding the beer bottle up to his mouth halts, slowly lowering back down as a deep indent forms between his brows. The lights reflecting off the pool flicker in his heated gaze, showing off the flecks of gold and caramel in the dark brown depths of his eyes. His jaw flexes as he gives the lightest shake of his head, one that I'm sure nobody but me notices because nobody is focused on him as intently as I am at this moment. Billy is still talking his ear off, completely unaware of how Robbie's attention is no longer on him. Completely unaware of everything he's saying with that silent shake of his head. I can hear his voice in my head rattling off so many different questions and accusations that they all start to blend together, creating a whirring sound that makes my ears feel like they're ringing. The one thing I can hear above all the chaos, however, is, *What the hell are you doing here?* The second is, *What the hell are you doing with* him?

And, I can't explain why, but something about those unspoken questions anger me. Because *who does he think he is?*

I have every right to be here that he does. What, did he think I was only capable of leaving my house if it was with him? I'm sure he'd be absolutely floored to learn that I was actually invited here tonight. That I was actually wanted, *without him.* And, *God forbid,* another boy wants to speak to me without it having anything to do with him. What a concept that must be for Robbie Summers to take in after two long months.

All of these irritating thoughts swirl through my head, and I try my best to just latch on to them, but I simply can't ignore the ache in my chest threatening to overpower them all.

The ache at seeing him here, perfectly back in his element, his arm around the type of girl that makes perfect sense for him, having the time of his life. I know–or at least I think I know– that there's nothing between Robbie and Kate. And, even if there was, it wouldn't be my business, but seeing the two of them so close is still just a painful reminder that he fits with someone like her in a way that he could never fit with me. There's no eyes on them because they simply work. They're *expected*. Nobody would even turn their head or raise a questioning brow at seeing Kate with Robbie because she's exactly the type of girl he should want. The type of girl that would last with him. They're not fire and ice. They're water and water. A combination that blends and flows easily. They're one of the same. Not one thing that snuffs out and destroys the other.

Sure, Robbie has a death glare in his eyes right now, but just moments before he saw me, he looked happy. He looked like he was having fun. He looked like his life had just picked up right where it left off. Like he hasn't woken up every single day for the last two months thinking of me and fallen asleep every single night seeing nothing but me behind his eyelids. Like he doesn't spend the days focusing on avoiding me in every way possible and the evenings just aching for me to be there. Like he hasn't spent any weekends just staring at his house phone on the wall, wondering if it might ring. No, he doesn't look like he's experienced any of that at all. And, as much as I know that should be a good thing, that I should *want* that for him, because it would make it that much easier for me to get over him...I hate it. I absolutely hate it with everything in me.

I blow a deep breath out of my nose, trying to calm down. And then I take a long sip of my wine cooler, my eyes still on Robbie because I'm not sure right now how to look away.

But then I feel fingers pressing into my hip, drawing me forward.

"How does that sound?"

My attention snaps back forward, back to Paul just in front of me. But I can't see his face, because it's practically buried in my neck.

"I– How does *what* sound?" I ask, trying to put some comfortable distance between us to no avail.

Paul pulls away just enough that I can see the curve of his smile in my peripheral vision. "C'mon, you can drop the act already."

I rear back, catching his eyes. "What are you talking about?" He reaches up, starting to run a hand through my hair, but I shake my head out of his grasp. "Paul? What act?"

He lets out a harsh laugh. "Your innocent Little Miss Valedictorian act. You don't need to keep it up anymore. Especially not around me."

My spine steels. "I'm not putting on any act."

"C'mon, darlin'..." Paul tuts, cocking his head to the side. "You don't have to pretend. You've already shown me what you can do. I know you showed Summers even more. Clearly he didn't appreciate you enough. Why don't you show me what he's been missing?"

He leans in suddenly, his lips brushing mine before I have time to shove my hand against his chest. "Paul, *stop*. What are you doing?" I try to shove him away further, but he's a step ahead of me, pulling me closer by both hips.

"What we should've started doing a long time ago," he huffs. "I mean, come on. You practically threw yourself at me at Denise's party. I haven't stopped thinking about it." He reaches up, cupping the side of my face with his hand and sinking his teeth into his lower lip. "Those little sounds you made while you were in my lap...*Mmm*."

My face heats and I push his hand away.

"Yeah, well, I hate to disappoint you, but I wasn't thinking about you when I made those sounds, Paul."

Paul stares at me for a long moment, his brows pulling together. And then, he laughs, advancing on me further. "Shit, Cooper, did you put up this much of a fight with Summers?"

"That's none of your business," I tell him, prying myself out of his grasp. "Thank you for the drink, Paul, but I'm not interested in anything else from you."

"Cooper–"

"I asked you *not* to call me that," I fume, my eyes shooting up to meet his.

Paul scoffs. "Well, you don't have to be such a bitch about it—"

"*What the hell is going on here?*"

Both our heads snap in the direction of the new voice, and I find a version of Robbie I've never seen before standing just behind Paul, his gaze burning into him. His hair is windblown and disheveled, his cheeks and the tips of his ears tinged with pink. He's panting as if he just completed a sprint, and his eyes are so dark I don't even think I can refer to them as chocolate anymore. He pushes up the sleeves of his gray Members Only jacket to his elbows, and I take Paul's momentary distraction of watching Robbie do so to fully remove myself from his grip.

"Nothing that concerns you, Summers," Paul snaps.

Robbie takes a step into Paul's personal space, not breaking his eye contact. "I didn't ask you. I asked her." He points in my direction, but doesn't look at me.

"Well, last I checked, she's not your concern anymore either," Paul says, chuckling darkly. Robbie's jaw flexes, but he doesn't back down. "You got your chance, and you blew it. So now, it's my turn."

"Your *turn*?" I question him, a humorless laugh bursting out of me. "I'm not a toy, Paul."

He turns back on me then. "Of course not. I'm sure you're way more fun to play with." He grabs my wrist, trying to tug me towards him, but I resist, leaning as far away from him as possible.

"I already told you, I'm not interested," I grit.

"Take your hands off of her right now," Robbie says, his voice low. When I look over at him, he's bunching the back of Paul's shirt up in his hand, pulling him backward.

Paul releases my wrist, and my arm falls back to my side with a thud.

"Smart choice," Robbie rasps, releasing Paul. "Now, come on, Cooper."

"I'm not going anywhere with you." I shake my head.

Robbie blows out an irritated breath. "Can you please, for once, just *not* be difficult?"

"Can you maybe look at me when you're speaking to me?" I shoot back at him.

Robbie stiffens, his eyes slowly raising to meet mine.

"Was that so hard?" I breathe.

His tongue pushes into his lower lip as his eyes dart between mine. "Yeah, it was."

I let out an incredulous chuckle.

"Now, will you come with me?" Robbie asks.

"No," I state, crossing my arms and spinning to walk the opposite direction, hoping to find Alice and leave, but instead, I run right into the wall of Paul's chest.

"Well, welcome back," Paul drawls, looping an arm around my back and caging me to him.

"Let go of me," I mutter, trying to wriggle out of his arms. I'm not fighting him for a full two seconds before I feel Robbie right behind me, wrapping an arm around my waist and shoving against Paul.

"You heard her, Paul. *Back the fuck off.*"

"Get off of me," I snap at Robbie over my shoulder.

"I'm trying to help you, Cooper," he scoffs.

"Yeah, well, I don't need your help."

My feet get twisted up as the three of us sway from side to side, and my wine cooler drops from my hands, smashing onto concrete.

"*Shit,*" I grit.

"*Sara?*" I hear the panicked voice of Alice from afar, and look up to see her running towards us.

"*Let me go!*" I practically shout at the same time Robbie says, "*Let her fucking go, Strothers!*"

I feel a deep laugh rattle Paul's chest right before he says, "Okay."

Then, all at once, he lets go of me.

The sudden release sends me stumbling backwards into Robbie, who lets out a grunting sound before he goes stumbling as well.

"Cooper–"

"Stop touching me–"

"What're you–"

"I can't–"

"Where are–"

"*Ahh!*"

I'm not sure which one of us is really at fault–which one of us trips first–but what I do know is that, right now, I'm in Robbie's arms. And we're falling, tumbling straight into the pool, breaking the surface of the freezing cold water, and then, everything going black.

forty-six

ROBBIE

I don't know how it happened.

One second, I'm ready to deck Paul across the face, and then the next, the wind is knocked out of me, I'm staggering backwards, Cooper and I are at each other's throats, my entire view becomes a mess of red hair and tangled limbs, and then we're falling.

Cooper's still in my arms when my back hits the surface of the pool water. The breath is pulled from my lungs, our bodies making a deafening smacking sound as we break the tension of the water, and then, all at once, we plummet like rocks.

It's early March and we live in the Bay Area, meaning this pool water would already be pretty chilly. But, with the cold front that came in tonight, it's *so* cold. *Painfully* cold. Freezing, honestly. It feels like time goes in slow motion as Cooper and I sink towards the bottom, our clothes weighing us down like heavy anchors.

The frigid temperature sends my body into something like shock, my muscles stiffening and not wanting to move, but my brain takes over, forcing my feet to kick off the ground of the pool. Somewhere on the way to the surface, Cooper slips from my grasp, and, when I finally come up for air, I find her coughing and sputtering, her soaking wet hair stuck to her forehead and hanging heavy around her face. I reflexively reach for her, pulling her to me as she continues to catch her breath. Even as she coughs, I can hear her teeth chattering from the cold, shivers wracking her body. Every time I nearly get a hold on her, she pulls back, beginning to sink again as she continues to choke. Finally, words manage to break through her strangled gasps.

"Stop it!" *Cough.* "Just leave me alone, would you?" *Cough.*

"*What?*" I question her, my head flying back.

"I know how to swim," she informs me, sputtering.

"Well, excuse me, Cooper," I scoff. "I just figured it's a little difficult to swim when you currently can't even seem to breathe."

At the same time, it appears Cooper and I both realize we don't need to tread water anymore, our feet finding the bottom of the pool. "I'd rather not breathe if it means I'm sharing the same air as you!" she shouts, shoving water in my direction.

"Wow." I bark out a laugh. "Real mature, Cooper."

She crosses her arms, speaking through her chattering teeth. "I wish you– I can't– Would you just–"

"What, Cooper? Spit it out."

"Just– *God!*" She shouts, exasperated. "*Shut. Up.*"

I take a step closer to her, laughing. "Is that the best you've got?"

Her gray eyes narrow at me.

"Well then, how about *you* shut up, Cooper?"

"Will you leave me alone if I do?" she fires back, quirking her brows.

"Probably not," I answer automatically.

"*Ugh!*" Cooper shoves at my chest, letting out a guttural cry.

When I don't budge after several attempts at knocking me over, she finally relents, crossing her arms once more.

"You done?" I ask her, my voice low.

Her eyes snap up to meet mine, but she doesn't say anything.

A few long seconds go by, both of our chests rising and falling, Cooper shuddering violently and her teeth clicking together, until the rest of the scene around us slowly breaches the bubble we've found ourselves in. The gasps and muttered whispers make their way into my ears, and I glance up to find what has to be damn near the entire party gathered around the pool with their wide eyes trained on Cooper and me.

"Come on, Cooper," I tell her out of the side of my mouth, not wanting to cause any further of a scene. "Let's get out of the pool."

"No."

I look down at her, taking in the shaking of her shoulders and the blue tinge of her lips I can see through her still half present red lipstick. She's clearly freezing. She looks absolutely miserable. *What is wrong with her?*

"Why not?" I ask.

"Be–because, I told you. I'm not going anywhere with you. So, *you* g–get out of the pool. I'll get out when I'm re–ready."

I run a hand through my wet hair, frustrated. "Are you kidding me right now?"

"D–does it look like I–I'm kidding?" she stammers.

"You certainly look like a joke, if that's what you mean."

The second the words are out of my mouth, I regret them.

Cooper's spine steels, her brows pulling together. She lets out a scoff, stepping back from me.

"Cooper," I shake my head, "I'm sorry. I didn't mean that–"

"Just g–get out," she mutters.

"*Sara?*"

Both of our heads turn to find Alice standing at the edge of the pool.

"What are you doing?" she questions Cooper, throwing her hands in the air. "Get out of there!" When Cooper doesn't respond, Alice looks at me. "Why is she still in there?"

"If you figure it out, let me know," I tell her.

"Sara, come on. Get out!" Alice shouts.

Cooper doesn't budge, just hugging her arms tighter around herself as she continues to pretend like she's not shaking like a leaf.

I blow out an irritated breath, tracing the length of her

shuddering body with my eyes. The red and black thin strapped dress she's wearing is soaking wet, molding to her body's every divot and curve. I swallow hard, forcing my eyes back to her face and quietly thanking God that this frigid water is slowing down the blood flow that's desperately trying to make its way to my groin at the image of her right now. The dress dry was enough to stop me in my damn tracks, but *this*, the way it's clinging to her now just simply isn't fair.

Who could stand a chance?

Alice calls Cooper's name again, but her infuriatingly stubborn best friend doesn't seem to be listening. I turn my head, meeting Alice's incredulous eyes, trying to pass a question to her through my gaze. The huff she lets out along with the hand she throws out in my direction gives me all the validation I need to make my next move.

I dart forward, bending over just enough to scoop Cooper up and throw her over my shoulder before she even has a chance to protest. It takes a couple of seconds before the realization seems to hit her, the low level hypothermia she's experiencing probably messing with her brain. I'm already reaching the first step of the pool before she starts smacking her fists against my back, grunting out curses and demands for me to put her down through her still chattering teeth.

When we hit the cold night air, Cooper starts to shiver even harder, her words not even making sense any longer. That only makes my feet move faster as I make a path through the crowd of people, not bothering to look at any of their faces. They're not my priority right now.

I push my way straight through the back door of Jesse's house, not caring one bit about the water trails and wet footprints I'm leaving in our wake. A few gasps sound and heads turn in our direction as I storm through the kitchen, making a beeline for the guest bathroom.

As soon as I turn the corner, I spot Grady Fisher, one of the freshmen basketball players, leaned up against the wall with his eyes trained on a brunette girl in front of him that's telling him a wildly uninteresting story that he's acting like he's eating up every second of.

"*Fisher*," I bark as I approach him.

Grady immediately snaps to attention at the sound of my voice, every bit of smoothness he was just able to feign melting off of him in an instant. He blinks hard at me, appearing extremely confused about why I would be addressing him.

Can't say I blame him.

"Uh...Robbie? What's up...man?" he asks, rubbing the back of his neck, his eyes flicking between me and the girl in front of him who is now fully focused on me.

I reach into my pocket, fishing out my car keys and tossing them at his chest. Caught off guard, he lets out a harsh breath as they knock the wind out of him, barely catching them before they hit the ground. "I'm parked around the corner. Go get my basketball bag out of my trunk and bring it to me," I tell him as I push open the door of the bathroom, maneuvering my way inside without letting any part of Cooper's writhing body hit the door frame.

Grady's mouth falls open, looking from my keys to me. "I–"

"Thanks, Fisher," I say, not giving him a chance to say anything else before I slam the bathroom door shut and lock it, leaving me and Cooper alone. I don't need to tell him what car I drive. Of course he already knows. He can figure everything else out.

"P–put me down ri–right this s–second or I will–"

Cooper doesn't get to finish her demand before I release my grip on her, letting her slide down the front of my chest. She hits the bathroom floor with unsteady feet, immediately trying to pull away from me but swaying and shivering too hard to get too far. I grip both of her elbows in my hands, holding her upright. She glares up at me, her nose flaring, but she doesn't try to pull away. Not yet.

"W–wow, I see we've upgraded from a cl–closet," she huffs, looking around the bathroom.

"Only the best for you, Cooper."

Her eyes snap back to my face, and she promptly steps back,

pulling her arms from my grasp and wrapping them around herself. *Well, that didn't take long.*

"Why are we in he–here? And wh–what the hell was that in the hall? Why did y–you send that k–kid to go f–fetch your bag like he was your se–servant?"

Now that we're inside and the air conditioning is cooling our already cold and wet clothes even further, Cooper is shuddering harder than ever.

"I have some extra clothes in my bag," I tell her.

"Okay," she quips, her brows pulling together. "A–and?"

"We need to get you out of this wet dress."

Cooper's spine snaps straight, her eyes widening to the size of gray saucers. "*Excuse me?*"

"You heard me. You're soaking wet."

"So are y–you!" she retorts. "And whose f–fault is that anyways?"

"*Yours,*" we both say at the same time, glaring at each other.

"Yeah, well, I have multiple changes of clothes in my bag. Hence me asking Fisher to bring it to me," I say.

Cooper laughs. "If you think I'm putting your c–clothes on–"

"I'm thinking you don't have much of a choice."

"I have m–my own c–clothes in Al–Alice's c–car!" she stammers, stomping her foot and fisting her hands at her side.

I take a step closer to Cooper, pointing at her chest. "You–" I start, but am cut off at the sound of the air conditioning starting up. Both of our heads raise, our eyes traveling up to the air vent directly above us as a gust of fresh cool air blows right onto us.

"*Je–Jesus Ch–Christ,*" Cooper curses, stepping back and crossing her arms, cowering in the corner of the bathroom.

I rake a hand through my hair, letting out a heavy breath as I watch her. She is shivering like she's a stray dog stuck out in a snowstorm. Her teeth click together and her fingers dig into her biceps as she tries to hug herself as tightly as possible, and her hair, now forming into light ringlets as it begins to dry, bounces around her face and shoulders as she shudders. I can't help but let my gaze trail further down, seeing how her dress is clinging to her for dear life, the peaks of her breasts formed into hard pebbles and straining against the thin fabric.

I shake my head, running a hand over my face, glancing between Cooper and the shower to my side. I know what she needs, and I don't give it another moment of thought before I walk over and pull the curtain to the side just enough to turn the shower on.

"Um, wh–what are you d–doing?" Cooper questions me.

"Get in," I tell her, nodding towards the shower.

Her mouth falls open, a confused laugh bursting out of her. "I'm sorry, wh–*what?*"

"Cooper, you're freezing. You can't even talk properly. Just get in the damn shower so you can warm up."

"B–but..." she stutters, gaze darting between me and the shower.

"What?" I demand, blowing out a frustrated breath.

"I'll get all w–wet!" she blurts, throwing her hands in the air for only a second before she's forced to cross her arms again.

I tilt my head at her, giving her a pointed look. "I think that ship has sailed, Cooper."

"But, m–my change of c–clothes–"

"I will go get your damn clothes if you're so insistent on being a stubborn pain in the ass and not wearing mine."

Cooper stands up straight, her teeth chewing at her trembling lower lip.

"Just get in the shower."

She shakes her head.

"Cooper."

"N–no," she insists, looking away from me.

"You're shivering harder by the second."

"I–I'm f–fine. I'll ju–just go g–get my change of c–clothes–"

That's it.

She can't even form a sentence. She looks as pale as a ghost. She needs to get in the damn shower and under the hot water.

I dart forward, grabbing her around the waist and picking her up.

"Wh–what the hell?! *P–put me d–down!*" Cooper shrieks, kicking her feet pathetically as she fights against me.

"If I put you down, will you get in the shower?" I ask.

"Yes! F–f–fine!"

I come to a stop just in front of the shower.

Really?

I hesitantly set Cooper on her feet, releasing my arm from around her waist.

And she bolts.

Or, at least, she tries.

She doesn't get far before I catch her, dragging her back to the shower.

"*Wh–what is your p–problem?!*" Cooper demands.

"*Me?* Cooper, what is *your* problem?" I shoot back as she continues to fight me.

"Currently, *you!*"

I lift Cooper up enough to get her feet over the lip of the tub, but she straightens her legs, pushing off of it. "I d–don't want to g–get in the sh–shower!"

Her skin is like ice against mine, goosebumps covering every exposed inch.

"You need to get warm!" I shout back at her, matching her volume. Luckily, the music playing from the party is so loud and certainly drowning out our voices from the other side of this door. We'd surely have raised a few eyebrows by now if not.

Cooper lets out a growl. "I don't n–need anything! Esp–especially from y–you!"

I manage to get her feet over the edge of the tub and plant them on the floor of the shower. She lets out a gasp as soon as the water hits her. I reach over, trying to turn the temperature even warmer, but she yanks back the curtain and tries to jump out as soon as I do.

"*Cooper!*"

"*Just le–leave me a–alone!*"

My body has a mind of its own, and before I even realize I'm doing it, I'm throwing my jacket off my shoulders and climbing into the shower, forcing Cooper back. She starts flailing her arms, but I reach up, grabbing her wrists in my hands.

"*Are you c–crazy?!* Wh–what are you d–doing?" Cooper growls.

I transfer her right wrist to hold it in my left hand with her left wrist long enough so I can whip the curtain closed behind me, sealing in the warmth. Within seconds of me doing so, I can see the color slowly returning to Cooper's face. She doesn't seem to care though, too focused on getting angrier at me by the second.

"*L–let me out!*" she screams, simultaneously shoving against my chest and shifting so she's out of the path of the shower stream.

"Why are you so goddamn stubborn?" I grit, forcing her back under the water.

"Why do you even c–care?" She snarls, spinning out of my grasp, escaping the water again.

I grit my teeth as I turn to face her, grabbing her and yanking her into my chest before she can even reach for the shower curtain.

"*Get off of me!*" she snaps. "Why does it m–matter to you anyways?"

Great question, I think to myself.

I don't even think I have an answer.

Liar.

It doesn't matter.

She matters.

Regardless of how much I wish she just wouldn't.

I spin both of us around, stepping forward so that the shower is running down Cooper's back, causing her to let out a hiss. "I'm trying to help you, Cooper."

"I don't need your h–help!" she grits, squirming in my arms.

"You are goddamn unbelievable," I mutter, forcing her back.

Heat rushes her face, her brows scrunching together in anger. "You are the most infuriating human I've ever met," she hisses through her teeth.

"*Ha!*" I throw my head back. "Try looking in a mirror sometime, Cooper."

She pushes against me, but I push harder, and her back hits the wall of the shower, the warm spray coming down hard over the two of us.

A humorless laugh comes out of Cooper. "God, I haven't appreciated the last two months enough," she shouts at me through the water.

My spine straightens. "What the hell is that supposed to mean?"

"I mean, don't get me wrong," she says, shaking her head. "It's been nice. But I think I forgot too quickly what it's like to not want to constantly wring someone's neck. To not feel like I'm going completely insane all the time."

My tongue pushes into my lower lip, catching the water droplets falling freely onto it. Shower steam clouds around us as I look down at Cooper, narrowing my eyes. "Yeah, you're right," I agree. "I forgot what it's like for my blood to not be boiling twenty-four hours a day. To not be fought tooth and fucking nail on every single thing I do and say."

"It's been freeing not to follow you around like a pet everywhere. To not have to spend lunch with you or pretend like holding your hand in the hallway is something I enjoy," Cooper says.

"It's been a weight off my back not having to haul you all around town every day. To not have to clean my car three times a week because there's so many goddamn red hairs in my seat and candy bar wrappers on the floor," I respond.

Cooper puffs her chest out, getting closer to me. "It's been *incredible* to hear only my own thoughts in my head at school, rather than your voice in my ear drawling out nonsensical bullshit and attempting to smooth talk me on a never ending loop," she growls.

I place my hand flat against the shower wall above her head. "It's been *delightful* going to parties and doing shit a normal teenager should want to do. To not have you there at my heels trying to drag me away from the fun and convince me to be someone that I'm not," I lie through my teeth.

A scoff escapes Cooper as she stares up at me through the curtain of water separating us for several long seconds. "I haven't missed you at all," she declares. Her lips twitch, and I don't miss it when she forces them to flatten again.

I swallow hard, feeling the crack in my voice before I even speak. "I haven't thought about you once," I mutter, blinking hard.

Cooper tilts her head back, fully meeting my gaze with her glassy one. "I hate you," she breathes, her eyes flicking between mine, lowering her voice even further as she adds, "*Robbie*."

And my name on her lips for the first time in months is all it takes.

My hand drops from the wall, my fingers snake into the hair at the nape of her neck, and I roughly yank her to me, crushing her mouth with mine.

A light gasp breaks through Cooper's lips, and I quickly swallow it down, parting my lips and breathing her in deep.

She reaches up, gripping my shoulders in her hands as if she's going to shove me away, but she doesn't. She's stiff and rigid for a few long seconds, her body seeming to be fighting her mind, but then, slowly, she relaxes into me. I can sense the moment that she finally lets go because she sighs against my mouth. I take the opportunity to sweep my tongue against hers, desperate for a taste of what I've been missing for far too long now.

A sound I thought I'd only hear in my dreams from here on out escapes Cooper, and it makes my heart thud against my chest at the same time it sends what feels like every ounce of my blood flowing south.

"*Robbie*," she murmurs against my mouth.

"*Cooper*."

She takes one more pull against my lips before she shifts back just enough so that I can make out her eyes.

"I–I..." she stutters, but it's not from being cold anymore. Her gaze shifts down to my lips, and I take it as a cue to kiss her again. She accepts it, then settles back on her heels, the top of her head at my chin.

Her mouth hangs open, and I know there's something she's wanting to say. I give her the time she needs to get it out, watching her gears in head turn.

"I...*I don't need you*," she finally whispers, barely audible. And I know she's saying it for herself far more than she's saying it for me. To remind herself what's true.

I blow out a breath, pulling her into my chest. I press my lips against the top of her head and then trail kisses down the side of her temple. "*I know, baby*," I mutter against her skin. "I know." When I reach the corner of her mouth, I find her lower lip quivering.

"But..." she breathes, shaking her head as she looks up at me. "I still want you." She reaches up hesitantly, running a finger over my bottom lip. "Why?" she asks.

"Honestly, I don't have a damn clue," I tell her honestly. "But it's good to know." Cooper tilts her head back, meeting my eyes hesitantly. "Because I'm pretty damn sure that I want you. But..." I trail off, letting out a breathy chuckle.

"What?" she asks.

"You may not need me, but I'm sure as I am of anything that I need you, Cooper."

She blinks at me, a single tear escaping from the corner of her glossy eye. I reach up immediately, catching it on the tip of my finger before it can run down her cheek. I'm not sure why I do it, because there's droplets of water freely streaming down her face from the shower above. The tear would've just added itself to the mix, making itself unknown as it joined the rest of the water.

But I'd know.

And I just don't want to know that I've allowed another tear to fall from Sara Cooper's eyes on my watch.

I move to flick the tear off of my finger, but Cooper's hand shoots up, wrapping around my wrist and stopping me. My gaze locks with hers, her lips part, and she manages to tell me a million things with a single word.

"Robbie."

I lean down, and she meets me halfway, barely brushing her lips against mine, just enough to make a growl slip from my throat.

"*Sara fucking Cooper.*"

We move in sync, Cooper jumping into my arms at the same moment I reach down to grip her smooth thighs. I hike her up so that her legs wrap around my waist, and then I press her against the shower wall. The shower head is directly above our heads now, but neither one of us cares, the water pounding down on us and running heavy streams through our hair as our mouths rejoin once more.

Cooper and I are ravenous for each other. It's like we're both addicts that chose this exact moment to say 'fuck it' and give in to our greatest weaknesses and deepest desires. I fold for her like a cheap suit. I can't keep my hands off of her. I need more of her. I feel like I might die without her if she took herself away from me right now. I'm not sure if that's healthy, but what I do know is, I'm not sure that I've ever felt more alive.

Cooper squirms against me, bucking her hips like she's searching for purchase. I'm trying to take it slow. I'm trying not to push her. I'm trying not to go too far with her too fast. But when she lets out a frustrated groan, fisting my soaking wet shirt to bring me closer to her so that she can sink her teeth into my lower lip, I lose all sense of self control and willpower.

I thrust against her, the hard ridge of me connecting with her warm center through the thick denim of my jeans. Of course, Cooper responds immediately, throwing her head back and gasping for air. I'm not sure what the use is. I don't think I've taken a breath in the last thirty seconds as I've watched the girl before me get set ablaze like the firecracker she is, her body reacting to *me*, to what *I'm* doing to her.

Yeah, forget air.

Who needs it when I have Sara Cooper in front of me?

She wraps her arms tighter around my neck, and I take it for what it is.

She wants more.

I grind up into her, harder this time, more forceful.

Because who am I to deny this girl?

Cooper whimpers, the ghost of my name falling from her lips.

There's shower steam all around us, but I can feel the warmth radiating from her where she wants me most, where I need her most. And, God, if she isn't the most exquisite thing I've ever seen, face flushed, hair wild and wet, and the prettiest little red dress ever made painted on her body by the shower stream acting like a spotlight on what must be the most incredible scene of my young life.

"Robbie, *please*–"

My face falls into the crook of Cooper's neck as I push against her. "God, I missed hearing you say my name."

My right hand unclenches around her thigh, running up the length of her side, brushing over the soaked lace and silky fabric of her dress. I pause when I reach the outer curve of her breast, then flick my thumb out, running it over one of the hardened peaks that's been teasing me for the last half hour. Cooper shudders, letting out a strangled moan as she rocks against me.

"*Oh, God*," she chokes.

"No, it's Robbie. We've been over this. But close enough I guess."

Cooper swats at me and I dodge her, chuckling against her neck. She stifles her own laugh, trying to cover it with a sigh. "Can't you think of something better to do with your mouth than talk right now?"

My fingers instantly flex, digging into her hip. I pull my head back just enough to find Cooper giving me a positively unholy grin, her teeth digging into her bottom red lip and her stormy eyes looking up at me through thick wet lashes.

"Now, Cooper," I say, shaking my head, my voice husky. "Don't go tempting me with a good time."

"Is it really temptation if I already know you'll give in?"

Fuck.

I lean forward, surprising Cooper and forcing her head to lay flat against the shower wall. I hear her breath catch in her throat as I get so close that my nose grazes hers. I look down at her, my tongue swiping over my lower lip. Her eyes trail the movement, the rise and fall of her chest growing more shallow with each bated breath that passes between us.

"Six."

"What?" Cooper questions me, her brows shooting up.

I tilt my head, eyeing her like the prey she's not so suddenly become to the animal inside of me.

"I can think of six better things to do with my mouth than talk right now."

Cooper's spine steels, and I watch her throat bob, which makes a smirk tilt my lips.

"Care for me to try any of them?" I ask.

If it was possible, Cooper's cheeks tint an even darker shade of red. She rolls her plump lips into her mouth, not removing her eyes from mine as she pulls me closer by the collar of my shirt, whispering, "*All of them.*"

"Guess we should get started then," I breathe.

I press up into her, holding her in place on the shower wall with just my hips and one hand supporting her under her left thigh as I bring my right hand up to her face. I lower my head until our lips are just a hair's width apart.

"*One,*" I whisper, then sink my mouth into hers.

I try to start gentle, low and slow, but only a few seconds pass before Cooper makes it obvious she's okay with me picking up the speed, her hands pawing at me and non-subtle moans bursting out of her.

God, I missed those moans.

Our tongues tangle, and I think I see stars as my dick painfully strains against my jeans. Everything in me would love to draw out this list all night if Cooper would let me, but my self control is lacking, and, now that I've gotten a taste of her, I have to have more.

I pull my mouth off of Cooper, and take a deep and shaky breath, her head falling to the side right where I want it.

My nose trails along the curve of her cheekbone, stopping right as I reach the outer shell of her ear. I graze my teeth along the edge of it, sending a shiver through her. She reflexively tries to pull away, but I hold her in place. "*Two*," I breathe, then bite down on her ear lobe. Cooper lets out a cry, arching her back and pressing her chest against my own.

"*Three*," I continue, knowing there's no stopping now.

I slowly lower my head resting my lips at the hollow of her throat just below her ear for a moment before I begin trailing hot wet kisses all over her neck.

Cooper cranes her neck, giving me better access as her fingers dig into the back of my shoulders, surely leaving half-moon marks from her fingernails.

God, I hope that's the case. I hope it scars. I hope there's permanent proof that I can have the same effect on Sara Beth Cooper that she has on me.

Between the shower water running hot down her neck and the wake of my mouth, the flush across Cooper's cheeks has worked its way promptly down her neck, leaving blossoms of red and a wet sheen coating her sensitive skin. Somehow it only makes her look more beautiful.

"*Robbie...*" she begs, writhing in my grasp.

"Giving up already, Cooper? We're only halfway there."

"No," she groans. "Just, please..."

"Please *what*, Cooper?"

"Don't stop touching me. Or I may have to kill you."

A sly smile crosses my face as I press a kiss at the crook of her neck before meeting her eyes. "Ready for number four?"

Cooper swallows, nodding.

I slide a hand all the way up the side of her right arm, pausing once I reach the spaghetti strap of her dress. I dip my finger underneath it, lifting it up slightly and running it back and forth across the pad of my pointer finger.

"Are you sure?" I ask, my voice low.

"Yes," Cooper says, nodding faster, looking up at me from under glossy eyelids.

I don't make her wait another second, dragging the strap down her shoulder. The drenched fabric of her dress slowly peels away from her skin an inch at a time. My mouth waters as the fabric dips lower, sweeping past the swell of her breast. I can't wait any longer, and it doesn't seem Cooper can either, her legs squeeze tighter around me in anticipation. I tug the strap down sharply, freeing her right breast. I only take the time to growl a quick "*Four*" before my head is dipping and my tongue swirls once over her pretty pink nipple before I wrap my lips around it, pulling it into my mouth with a gentle tug.

"*Ah*," Cooper whines. "Oh my– *Robbie*." Her fingers inch up the back of my neck, just barely grazing and pulling at the hair at the base of my skull.

I pull back, needing more, and she stiffens, pulling her hands away from me and holding them out to the side, staring at me with wide eyes. I ignore the fact that she just broke a rule by touching my hair, not too concerned with it at the moment, especially considering how far I've surpassed her no kissing rule. Instead, I take the opportunity to grab her extended left arm, pulling it down to the side so I can free it of that dress strap as well. I don't take my eyes off of her as I roll my lips into my mouth, wetting them before I dive in, claiming her left breast as well. I drag my tongue across her left nipple, and her body relaxes once more, pressing into me. I reach up, palming her right breast as I continue to play with her left.

God, they're perfect. Just more than a handful. They taste just as sweet as her mouth does. *I can only begin to imagine how she tastes in other places...*

I release my hold on Cooper, letting her feet hit the slick floor of the shower below us. Her breath stutters in shock, and she immediately pulls the top of her dress up, holding it to her chest to cover herself

"What're you–"

"I gotta tell you something," I say, cutting her off. "Or, really, admit something."

She narrows her eyes at me, her head tilting in suspicion. "Okay?"

I lean in, my lips at her ear. "I definitely don't hate you, Cooper."

I pull back, meeting her eyes again as she swallows hard.

I flash her a crooked grin, slowly sinking down to one knee. Her lips part, her brows raising. I run my hands up both of her thighs, over the red dress material I'd like to tear apart and frame to hang on my wall forever by the end of tonight. "Let me show you how much," I say, my voice husky as I glance up at her.

Cooper's chest rises and falls with shallow breaths as her back stays plastered to the shower wall. She sinks her teeth into her lower lip as she nods slowly. "Well, if you insist."

I let out a deep chuckle, my tongue pushing into the side of my cheek. *What a little shit.* "I do," I tell her, running my hand down the length of her left leg until my fingers wrap around her calf.

"I guess you better get started then," she breathes, her throat bobbing as she stares down at me.

"Better hold on tight, Cooper," I say, then grip her calf tightly, swiftly hiking it up and over my shoulder so that Cooper's standing on one shaky leg.

She lets out a gasp and I turn my head to kiss the side of her knee, working my lips up her inner thigh at a snail's pace, bunching up the silky fabric of her dress in my other hand. "I gotta know, Cooper..." I mutter against her soft skin. "Did you know I'd be here tonight? Were you trying to kill me with this dress?"

"N–no," she stammers, sounding honest as she shakes her head. "But I can't say it wouldn't have been a happy accident."

I nip at her thigh, making her jolt. "So you mean to tell me that I didn't even cross your mind as you slipped this silky little thing on?" I question her. "That you didn't picture my face when I saw you? That you didn't imagine what it would do to me? How I'd want nothing more once I saw you in it than to see you out of it? You didn't think about me pushing it up your pretty little thighs and spreading you wide to worship you like the fucking goddess you look like in this?"

Cooper doesn't respond right away, too busy panting and swaying on her one barely stable leg as I keep her steady with the other over my shoulder. I take the opportunity to reach down and adjust myself in my jeans, this squatting position doing nothing to help the rock hard situation happening in my pants. Cooper's eyes track my movement, her tongue darting out to wet her bottom lip as she does so, and I can't help the groan that escapes from my throat as I watch her do it.

I reach up again, fisting her dress in my hand and pushing it up higher until her panties are just barely exposed to me. "Mmm," I hum. "Maybe a goddess isn't the right word. I was thinking of an angel, but that doesn't quite fit either." I push my hand up, tracing my thumb over the outer edge of her panties, making her shiver and whine. "No," I tilt my head. "You're more like a little devil, aren't you, Cooper?" She shakes her head, biting her lip. "You were thinking all of those things, weren't you? You've probably been dreaming about them at night. Tell me, Cooper."

"Not...I– *Ugh*–" she stammers, her voice breaking off as I force her thighs wider just enough to run my thumb right down the center of her black panties.

"What was that?" I tease her.

Cooper lets out a strangled groan, throwing her head back as I press the heel of palm against her mound.

"*Hmm?*" I push. "What were you going to say?"

She sighs heavily. "I was going to say not everything is about you. But then I realized I'm too distracted to lie to you right now."

I drop my shoulders, my eyes narrowing on her. "Lie?"

"Do I really need to say it?" Cooper asks.

"Yes."

She rolls her lips into her mouth. "Everything is about you, Robbie. As much as I wish it wasn't, it just is. You're everywhere. You're in everything. I can't escape you."

I swallow hard, blinking. "Do you want to?" I ask her.

"I don't think I have the energy to try anymore."

A smirk pulls at the corner of my mouth. I gently pull her leg from my shoulder, setting her foot back on the ground before standing up. "Me neither, Cooper." I pull her face to mine, kissing her once deeply before pulling back, meeting her eyes. "So how about we stop trying?"

"Maybe ask me once we're out of the shower," she grins. "The steam might be going to our brains."

Is it crazy that I almost forgot we were even in the shower?

Maybe she has a point...

I laugh, giving her a shake of my head.

When she laughs in return, a smile lighting up her face all the way to her eyes, I immediately take back my last thought.

She has no point. It doesn't matter where we are. I know the way I feel about this girl.

I thread my fingers into her hair, pulling her in for one more kiss. "Fine," I tell her. "But, for now, back to business. I trace the bridge of her nose with mine. "No more distracting me, Cooper."

"I didn't do anything–" Cooper swallows her own words on a gasp as I slip my hand between her legs, cupping her center and running my hand up and down her slit over her drenched panties. Even though we're in the shower, I can distinguish the new wetness coating the cotton fabric from the old. Can feel the warmth pouring out of her.

"Sorry for getting you all wet," I murmur against her cheek, smiling to myself.

Cooper barely gets her scoff out before I'm gripping the waistband of her panties and bending down to drag them down her legs.

"I don't think we'll be needing these anymore," I tell her, looking up at her from under my lashes.

Her cheeks flush with warmth as she slowly steps out of her underwear, holding my shoulder for support. I tuck them into my back pocket once she's done, then immediately return her leg to where it was over my shoulder. "Now, where were we?" I ask her.

"Number five, I believe" Cooper breathes, squirming around and holding her dress down, acting shy.

"Right," I grin, dipping my head and running my nose along her inner thigh. "*Number five...*"

"Robbie, I..."

"*Relax, baby,*" I whisper, reassuring her like I know she needs me to.

"Robbie, what are you... *Ah... I... Robbie–*" Cooper stammers as she writhes uncontrollably in response to the heated kisses I'm trailing up her leg, slowly making my way to the place where I know she's aching for me, the place I've dreamed about ever since the last time I was blessed with the honor of seeing it...touching it. But, this time, *I want more.*

"Mmm..." I tut. "Cooper, I already told you how much I missed you saying my name." She looks down at me with heavy eyes, straining to keep holding her dress up with one hand while her other rakes through her wet hair. I grin up at her, my tongue tracing my bottom lip as I nudge her knee out further, spreading her legs for me. "Now, I think I'd like to hear you moan it."

Cooper doesn't have a moment to get her retort in before I'm pushing her dress up the last few inches, exposing her to me and ducking my head, giving her a flat hard swipe up my tongue over her glistening slit.

And that's all it takes for her to give me exactly what I want.

My name tears from Cooper's lips in the most sinful, spine-tingling, unforgettable way I could ever imagine.

Though I'd like to freeze this moment in time and drink in the image of her until my dying day, I don't let up. I don't even pause, lapping and swirling my tongue against Cooper's swollen bud like my life depends on it. I think it actually might. I look up at her, watching her watch me, and *God,* she's like a dream. Wet curls plastered to her forehead, eyes swirling with storm clouds, red cheeks and redder lips so desperate for my attention. But they'll have to wait. I thought her mouth tasted like candy, but *this...* This is what brings men to their knees. So here I am. And here I want to stay forever. I'm just not sure Cooper will last that long.

Her thighs are desperately fighting against me, clenching and quivering with every stroke of my tongue against her. I can see it in the pace of her breathing, the redness creeping up her chest, the way she's biting down on her lip to keep from coming apart. Cooper's almost there.

"I...I don't hate you either, Robbie," she tells me through breathy moans.

Well, I'll be damned.

I smile against her, removing my hand from her knee that's resting over my shoulder, hoping my head will be enough to keep her in place. I take my time, tracing circles up in her inner thigh, letting the anticipation build, and then I gently run two fingers against her soaking wet folds before slowly sinking them inside of her, curling them towards myself without ever removing my mouth from her pulsing bundle of nerves.

Cooper explodes, letting out a cry that competes with the wail of Ann Wilson from Heart, whose song is currently blaring from the other side of the door.

And, speaking of the door...

Three loud knocks rap against it before I hear the uneasy voice of Grady Fisher calling out. *"Uh...Robbie? You in there?"*

I pull my mouth away from Cooper just enough to respond, continuing to pump my fingers inside of her as I shout, *"Go away, Fisher!"*

A few seconds of silence go by before he calls out again. *"I...I have your bag."*

"Leave it!"

Cooper covers her face with her hands, shaking her head.

I let out an exasperated chuckle, diving in for one more lap of my tongue against her before I pull my fingers out, licking them clean before rising back to my feet. I'm just barely back at my full height before Cooper grabs me by my soaked shirt, pulling me in until our lips are touching.

"I want to feel you," she whispers, her mouth brushing mine with every word as she reaches for the button on my jeans.

My mouth falls open, my aching dick throbbing in my pants at her declaration. I place a gentle hand over Cooper's, stopping her movements. "Are you sure?" I ask her, meeting her eyes.

Her lips pull up at the corners and she nods firmly.

I blow out a steady breath as I slowly pull my hand from Cooper's, letting her finish opening the button. Once she does, I help her tug down my stiff wet jeans enough to show my embarrassingly hard erection pitching a four-person tent in my briefs. I watch Cooper closely, waiting for her reaction, waiting to see any hesitation or regret coming from her, but it never does. Instead, she wets her lips, her eyes darting up to meet mine once before she reaches out, wrapping a hand around me over my underwear.

I let out an involuntary hiss, my hand coming up to rest on the shower wall by Cooper's head. She only gives me one firm squeeze before I lose all control, grabbing two handfuls of her ass and hiking her up and pinning her against the shower wall once more. I press against her center, and, with my briefs as the only barrier between us, I see stars. *Goddamn* stars.

I think Cooper does too, judging by the way her head falls back and she cries out. She reaches down, tugging on the waistband of my underwear. "Can I..."

I smirk at her, tilting my head. "You want to meet Hank, Cooper?"

Her head falls into the crook of my neck as she laughs. "I hate you again," she says, but I know she doesn't mean it. Especially because her pointer finger is still pulling against the elastic of my briefs as she sighs. "I promise I'll be kind to him."

The smile slowly fades from my face. Cooper and I are so close yet so far from one another right now. I want more. I want it all. But I know that's not happening right now. Not here. Not in this shower. Not without a condom. Cooper deserves more than that. We've never officially discussed it, but I'm about ninety-nine percent sure that Cooper has never gone all the way with anyone. And, when she does, she deserves to be laid down right. I'll make sure that happens some day, but tonight, I'll give us as much as I can.

I nod at her, giving her permission. Cooper chews on her lower lip as she slowly works my underwear down. The moment she frees my dick, it flies straight up, bobbing against my stomach between us. Cooper and I are quiet and she takes it in, reaching hesitantly out after a few seconds to wrap her soft hand around me, making me groan.

"Cooper..." I grit out.

She looks up at me with bright eyes. "Yeah?" she asks softly.

"This...I mean, you've never..." I watch her throat bob. "This is your first time, right?"

"Yeah," she replies, not embarrassed or surprised by my question at all, and that makes me smile.

I run my hand through her hair, cupping her cheek. "Then we're gonna have to do it right. No more than this tonight, alright?"

She presses her lips together, and she nods evenly. "Alright," she says with a smile, stroking me.

Another hiss leaves my mouth. "Goddamn. You'll be the death of me, Sara Beth Cooper."

She pumps me several times in her hand, and I begin to work against her, the pressure at the base of my spine growing with every gentle pull of her hand. My fingers begin to dig into where I'm holding onto her. She's bringing me to the brink. I can feel it coming, and it's like I'm chasing it, but I'm also afraid to get there, not wanting this to be over so soon.

"Can I try something?" I choke out. Cooper's hand pauses, her brows pulling together. I lean in, pressing my lips to hers. "I want to feel you too," I say, running my thumb over her bottom lip.

She nods, smiling at me. "Okay. I trust you."

I trust you.

My heart nearly cracks in two at those three little words I never thought I'd hear from Sara Cooper again, but I force myself to focus on them later. I give a little hop, forcing Cooper higher up on the wall. I remove one hand from her backside, keeping her supported with the other as I position my length parallel to her center.

"What are you–"

Cooper doesn't finish her question, gasping as push forward, sliding through her folds but not entering her.

If I thought I saw stars before, I'm seeing the whole damn Milky Way galaxy right about now.

She's so warm and soft against me, wrapping partially around me. I can only imagine how it would feel to be inside of her. I can see Cooper already halfway to falling apart as I increase my speed and intensity. Between the warm shower water running between us, the humid steam sticking to our skins, and the slick moisture Cooper's creating all on her own, there is a perfect lack of friction as we slide against each other.

We're not one, but *almost*. There's something almost more intimate about this than going all the way. Something about the amount of willpower it takes to not take that final step, to not just change the angle slightly and let myself sink inside of her, to have the control to wait, to draw this out, to take my time with her. I've never experienced anything like it.

And then, all of the sudden, three knocks bang against the bathroom door again, this time much louder than when Grady knocked but a couple of minutes ago.

"*Sara? Are you in there?*"

Cooper's hand covers her mouth. "*Oh my God*," she mutters to herself, looking down at us and suddenly seeming to realize what's happening. "Ahh, yes, Alice! I am!" she calls out.

"*Sara, what the hell? Are you okay?*" Alice shouts.

"Yes! Totally fine!" Cooper calls back.

"Should I stop?" I mouth to Cooper.

Her mouth falls open, her brows pulling together like I just asked the most offensive question possible. "Don't you dare," she whispers back. So, I listen, continuing to work against her as she attempts to cover her whimpers.

"*Is...the shower on?*" Alice calls.

"Ah, yes! Yes it is. I'm–uh...showering. Because I fell in the pool. I, um, felt dirty. So, I'm showering," Cooper blabbers, slapping a palm to her forehead.

I drop my forehead to her shoulder, trying not to laugh out loud.

"*Um...okay,*" Alice replies. "*Well, I'll be in the living room. Let me know if you need anything.*"

"*Mmm*–Okay!" Cooper calls back, letting out a sigh of relief when a few seconds have gone by and we assume Alice has walked away.

"Feeling dirty, huh?" I ask her, waggling my eyebrows.

"Shut up," she says, promptly wrapping a hand around my dick and giving it a hard stroke.

"*Shit,*" I mutter, continuing to slide against her.

I figured Cooper was just punishing me for the dirty comment, but she doesn't stop pumping me, and I can feel my balls tightening by the millisecond with my thrusts against her center and the pulls of her hand.

"This isn't gonna last much longer if you keep doing that, Cooper," I grit.

"Then I guess we better give it all we got," she grins, increasing her speed and bucking her hips against me.

"*The death of me,*" I repeat, crushing my mouth with hers as I give her every bit of what I've got.

After a few more long heated seconds, like a beautiful symphony that could only be orchestrated by nature, the two of us come apart together, Cooper shaking against me and me wrapping a hand around myself to catch my release. There's not a chance in hell I was going to risk tainting that gorgeous dress in any form or fashion.

I let go of my hold on Cooper as I help her slide back down to the ground. Once she has her feet planted, I reach behind her, turning the shower off. The bathroom instantly becomes eerily quiet aside from our heavy breathing.

Cooper looks up at me, and I watch her face slowly twist up, her head tilting to the side.

I instantly feel a twist in my gut, wondering what's going through her head, wondering if she's regretting it all, if I went too far. "What is it?" I ask her.

She squints her eyes at me. "What about number six?"

A grin breaks out across my face. "As if I could forget," I chuckle, dropping back to my knees one last time. Cooper looks down at me with questioning in her gaze. "I hope you know that now that we've gotten to number five, there's not a chance in hell I'm letting go anywhere Cooper." Her mouth falls open. "Well, actually, you can go wherever you'd like. But I'll just follow you."

I start to inch her dress up her thighs again, and Cooper starts to reach for me. "Robbie, don't you think we should go–"

"Not what you think," I promise her, brushing my lips against her thigh as I give it the slightest push open. I trail a single finger over her skin, running it upwards until I'm just a few inches from the apex of her thighs. "Now, just in case, if over the next few days you might ever think that someone else's head could ever belong between your thighs, could ever do for you what only I can, I'll leave you this as a reminder."

"Robbie–"

"*Number six*," I announce, biting down on Cooper's inner thigh. She tenses up, letting out a moan laced with the perfect mixture of pleasure and the slightest ounce of pain. I suck her soft skin into my mouth, giving her an extra nip for good measure before tracing over the spot with my tongue, soothing it.

"Robbie, *what the hell?*" Cooper chuckles, running a hand down her face. She's trying to act annoyed, but I can see by the flush of her cheeks how much she really liked it.

Little devil, I think to myself.

I pull back, showing Cooper the light reddish-purple spot that's already forming on the inside of her thigh, a proud grin on my face.

"Did you seriously just give me a *hickey?*" she demands.

"Hey, you asked for all six," I tell her, pulling back the shower curtain.

She laughs, shaking her head as she steps out of the shower. "Remind me to never ask you for anything again."

"No chance, Cooper."

forty-seven

SARA

Robbie throws open the bathroom door and we're met with a wide-eyed Grady Fisher clutching Robbie's blue and yellow duffle bag and car keys to his chest.

"Oh," Robbie says, rubbing at the back of his neck. "Fisher, what are you still doing here? I told you to just leave the bag."

Like ten minutes ago, I add in my head, slightly mortified at what this freshman might have heard from the other side of the door.

"I...I was afraid someone might take your stuff... I–I didn't want to..." Grady stammers, trailing off as he tilts his head at us.

A weird feeling settles in my chest at how wrapped around his finger Robbie has so many people. How this boy just spent the last twenty minutes finding Robbie's car, rifling through his trunk in the dark for his bag, and standing in this hallway holding said bag in the midst of a party without question, just because Robbie asked him to. I'm not sure what I would even do with that kind of power. How I would even act simply knowing I have that power. But I guess that's just Robbie. Just his life. I'm not sure at the moment whether I feel envious of him or sorry for this freshman before me.

"How are you guys *more* wet than you were before?" Grady asks.

My blood drains from my face, my mouth falling open as I raise my hand to stifle my laughter. Robbie snatches the bag and keys from Grady, muttering a quick, "*Thanks, Fisher. Bye, Fisher*," before slamming the door in his face. Robbie rolls his eyes, shaking his head to himself.

Once my chuckles fade out, we're left staring at each other in the silent bathroom, and everything sort of just hits me. Like reality crashing down, whatever little bubble we were inside of in the shower popped wide open. Without our hands on each other, without the heat between us, there's nowhere to hide. No more walls. Nothing to shield us from each other.

And I have no idea what to do with that.

I don't regret what happened between us. Not at all, actually. Everything I told Robbie was true. I'm tired of trying to fight my feelings, tired of running away from him, tired of letting my fear consume me. We may come from different worlds, we may have lived different lives, but I'm not sure how much that matters anymore. Because all I know is that my world is brighter with Robbie in it, and my life is so much more exciting. He makes me feel alive. And I don't want that to stop.

But I also know that it isn't quite that simple. I can't just rewire my brain over the course of twenty unexpected, eye-opening, earth-shattering minutes. And trust isn't something that can just be given. It takes time. It has to be earned. But faith... Faith is something you choose. Something that has to be given for trust to ever be earned. I guess the only question is if I'm willing to find my faith. To dig it out of the box I shoved it in, locked, and buried deep inside my heart.

Robbie clears his throat, breaking me out of my spiral of thoughts. When I look at him, I see he's holding out a dry set of clothes to me, his open duffel bag on the ground between us and another fresh outfit in his other hand which I presume has to be for him to put on.

Robbie pushes the clothes closer to me, prompting me to take them from him, and I robotically do, words currently escaping me. I glance from the worn t-shirt and gym shorts combo in my hands to the jeans and golf shirt Robbie is holding, raising a brow at him.

"What?" Robbie questions me.

"Oh, nothing," I say. "Your outfit just looks a little more... presentable than mine."

"Well, what do they say?" Robbie asks, turning away from me to peel his wet shirt over his head and dry himself off with a towel he grabbed from the rack. I tilt my head at him, wondering why he'd feel the need to turn away when we just exposed far more than a little skin to each other mere minutes ago. "Beggars can't be choosers."

I scoff out a laugh. "I don't remember begging."

"Really?" Robbie asks, quirking a brow at me as he finishes slipping on his dry shirt, fixing the collar. "That's not how I remember it." He pushes off his wet jeans, running the towel over each of his legs before stepping into his fresh pair. "In fact..." he says as he turns back to face me. I force my eyes to stay on his face even though they are being drawn to his still undone jeans like the strongest magnet money can buy, pressing my lips together and praying my face doesn't look as warm as it suddenly feels. Robbie's face morphs into the slightest smirk as he approaches me. "You've actually been quite demanding ever since we stepped into this bathroom."

He suddenly leans in, coming so close that I'm sure he's about to kiss me, but then he stops his movement when his lips are only an inch from mine. My hands holding the change of clothes are suddenly pushed up into my chest by Robbie's hand gripping my wrist. My eyes, which I didn't even realize I had closed, snap open, meeting a new variation of Robbie's right in front of me.

Caramel milk chocolate?

"*Your turn*," he whispers against my lips before flashing me a grin and releasing me, spinning away like the gentleman I think he's trying to pretend that he is.

I blink at Robbie's backside several times, knowing fully well that he has a self-satisfied smile plastered across his face even though I'm staring at the back of his head. I shake my head, biting my tongue as I turn my attention to the clothes in my hands. I slowly unravel the blue gym shorts and heather gray t-shirt, my jaw coming unhinged when they are fully revealed to me.

"Oh, you've got to be kidding me," I say.

"What's that?" Robbie asks, appearing to play dumb.

I turn around the shirt and shorts, which I now realize are a set of his basketball practice clothes, so the fronts of them are facing him.

Robbie purses his lips, fighting a smile. "What's the problem?"

I give him a knowing look as I point to where *Robbie Summers* is written boldly in permanent marker across the name rectangle below the Bay View Bears logo on both the shirt and shorts. "You really expect me to put this on to walk out of this house?"

Robbie shrugs. "I mean, I could carry you out of the house if walking is too difficult. I know you had some trouble with swimming. And breathing."

My spine steels, my brows pulling together. "Hilarious, really."

"Thanks, Cooper. Now could you get dressed?"

"Oh, sure," I say, nodding with enthusiasm. "Did you want to pee on me first?"

Robbie nearly chokes. "*Excuse me?*"

"Because that's basically what you're doing by having me wear these out there," I tell him, pointing towards the door. "Marking me as your territory. Claiming me."

Robbie is quiet for a few moments, his eyes darting between mine before he takes a step closer to me, tilting his head. "Is there something so wrong with that?"

My lips part, but any words that may have had a chance to come out are quickly drowned out by knocks banging against the bathroom door.

"*Okay, Sara, I'm becoming concerned!*" Alice calls out. "*Are you still in there?*"

I take a shaky step back from Robbie, blowing a breath out before I answer her. "Yes, Alice, I'm in here. I'll be out in just a second."

"Is everything okay? Are you being held captive in there?" she asks, chuckling uncomfortably.

"Um...yes," I respond, not clarifying which question I'm answering. "Just a sec."

I walk past Robbie, grabbing a second towel off the rack before I start peeling my dress off my body and replacing it with the most ridiculous option for dry clothes I could imagine. I glance up at the mirror in front of me as I do so, expecting to catch Robbie at least attempting to steal a peek. But he doesn't, keeping his back to me and not uttering a word the entire time. I'm not quite sure what to think of that, his silence making the voices sounding off in my head suddenly deafening.

When I'm finished, I clear my throat once to catch Robbie's attention before I open the door for Alice, bracing myself for whatever her reaction might be. I'm honestly not sure after she let Robbie throw me over his shoulder and drag me out of the pool.

Actually, now that I'm thinking about it...

Should I be mad at her?

She definitely broke some form of girl code by letting that happen. She absolutely should have allowed me to freeze to death in the pool so I wouldn't be forced to swallow my pride, especially for Robbie.

God, it still feels like I'm doing something wrong when I let myself think his name after so long. It's so weird how natural it's coming to me now. It's even weirder how naturally I allowed myself to say it out loud once the floodgates burst.

God, I missed hearing you say my name

My face heats, my lower belly tightening at the reminder of all the things that just happened *after* I said his name.

Yeah...those things definitely didn't feel wrong. And absolutely were not weird.

Realization hits me that, in a way, I guess I have Alice to thank for those things.

Dammit.

I blow a strand of hair out of my face before resigning, reaching for the door knob.

When I pull open the door, Alice startles in front of me, her fist raised like she was just about to knock again. She lets out an exasperated breath, running her hand over her face before dropping it to her side.

"My God, Sara. There you are. Are you okay—"

Alice's voice abruptly cuts off at the same moment I feel a wave of heat against my back. Alice's gaze trails up and over my shoulder, and I don't have to turn my head to know that Robbie has joined me in the doorway. I take a deep breath, holding it in as Alice's eyes flick from Robbie to me, then down to the new clothes I'm wearing with his name all over them.

Back up to Robbie. Down slightly, I'm sure to the new outfit he's sporting. To the open shower curtain behind us. To the puddle covered linoleum floor. To our original clothes rumpled in heaps to the sides of the puddles. Back up to my face. Back to Robbie. Back to me.

"Oh," she utters.

A few awkwardly quiet seconds go by, and I see Alice slowly putting the puzzle pieces together in her mind. Then, gradually, a massive *smile* spreads across her face.

"What do we have here?" she asks.

"Nothing," I blurt, trying my best to seem casual.

"Nothing?" Alice repeats, her head tilting.

"Yep," I answer immediately, crossing my arms.

"Right." Her lips purse. "And *nothing* was going on in this bathroom for the last," she pauses, glancing down at her watch, "nearly half an hour?"

My mouth opens and closes several times as I give a halfway attempt at nodding.

"Robbie?" Alice asks, turning to him.

I stiffen, my eyes snapping wide open.

"Yes?" Robbie responds.

"Was nothing going on in this bathroom?" Alice repeats.

He won't say anything.

"Nothing happened in this bathroom."

I let out a subtle sigh of relief, smiling tightly at Alice.

"Huh," she huffs.

She still definitely looks suspicious, but I know we're in the clear now. Robbie backed me up, so she won't push it any further.

"But wait," Robbie suddenly says, and my spine instantly steels. "When you say 'in this bathroom', does that also include in the shower? Because lots of things happened in there."

I feel the blood drain from my face and I pivot on my heel to glare at him.

"Oh, *really?*" Alice asks brightly, clapping. She leans her head inside the doorframe, trying to get my attention. "*Lots* of things, you say?"

"Well, six–" Robbie begins.

"*Okay*, that's enough," I say, holding up my hands between the two of them, red staining my cheeks. I shoot Robbie a pointed look before I give him my back and step closer to Alice, huddling in front of her and lowering my voice to a barely audible whisper. "It's not what you think."

"I have no idea what you mean," she mouths back, fighting the grin on her face.

"It was just– It was nothing."

"Are you trying to convince me or yourself?"

"I..." I press my lips together. "I just did what you told me. It was just one of those bad decisions you said I should make. While I still have the chance."

Alice's mouth twists to the side, her eyes narrowing on me thoughtfully. "Yeah, I'm not so sure."

I open my mouth to argue, but Alice doesn't give me the chance

"Will Robbie be taking you home now?" she asks, much louder than necessary.

I pinch my brows, just getting another smile from her in response. "Wha...I...I don't..." I stammer.

"Yes."

Robbie's voice is firm from behind me. I swivel to look at him, and find his eyes trained on me, a serious look within them. One that tells me he's not taking no for an answer and to not even bother trying to fight him on it.

"Great," Alice says. "I guess you guys should get going then? Unless you were wanting to go back to the party, Sara?" She glances down at my shirt, her lips quirking. "You know, dressed in that—"

"No," I shake my head. "I'd like to go home."

I feel warm fingers slowly wrap around mine.

"Then let's go home."

I turn my head to find Robbie holding my hand, much closer than he just was, his head cocked as he looks down at me. When I tilt my head back to look up at him, a strand of hair falls in my eyes. Robbie quickly reaches out, pushing it behind my ear, creating a buzz under my skin where his fingers brush along the side of my face, eventually settling on my jaw. My lips part, eyes blinking as I watch his face soften, his lips pulling into a smirk.

"Well, you guys have fun with that," Alice says, bringing me back to reality, causing me to flinch away from Robbie's touch and turn to look at her. "Sara, you'll call me tomorrow?" As she says it, her eyes widen and head tilts in a way that tells me that I don't have a choice. That, whether I call her or not, we *will* be speaking tomorrow. Even if that means she has to show up at my front door and drag every last detail out of me.

"Sounds good," I tell her.

"Great," she replies, tapping the doorframe with her knuckle. "You kids be careful." She leaves us with one last grin and waggle of her eyebrows before she turns away, disappearing down the hallway.

My shoulders relax as soon as Alice is out of sight, but the moment I turn back to Robbie, they stiffen again. He's staring at me so intensely, and I have no idea how to read him. He's saying a million things within his gaze, but nothing to me aloud. His eyes are soft, but his jaw is hard set. He's wearing the faintest ghost of a smile, yet his brows are pinched together. His body is fully angled towards me, mirroring every shift of my feet, but his arms are crossed, like he's closed off somehow. Unsure, maybe. Hesitant.

"What?" I finally ask him, not able to attempt to psychoanalyze him for another minute without feeling like my brain is going to explode.

Robbie stares at me for a few moments, his eyes flicking between my own. I swallow down the rocks in my throat, waiting for him to speak. To make some grand declaration or maybe just run out of the door. But he doesn't. I just see his lips barely twitch before he uncrosses his arms, saying, "Nothing." I think about questioning him further, but he breaks my eye contact, ducking down to sweep his duffle bag off the floor. "Ready to go?" he asks once he's standing back up.

I lick my dry lips. "Yeah," I nod. "Sure." I walk past him to pick up my dress from where it's still rumpled in a pile on the ground. When I have it, I take the extra step I need to reach the sink, wringing as much water as I can out of it.

I'm reminded at this moment that this is, in fact, my mother's dress. And that makes me want to laugh as much as it makes me want to be sick. I wonder if she just wouldn't notice if it happened to go missing. I haven't seen her wear it since I was a kid, but I don't think I could chance having to control my reaction if I saw her in it again. A highlight reel of everything this dress just went through flashes through my head at warp speed, and my stomach does a flip flop.

Yeah, no. This dress will never see my mother's closet again.

I turn back towards Robbie and watch as he glances down at the now somewhat dry and wrinkled dress in my hands and can't help but wonder if he's thinking the same things I was just thinking. The way that his throat bobs and eyes darken just slightly tells me that he very well might be, and that sends a flutter low through my belly.

He eventually blinks a few times and clears his throat, seeming to snap out of wherever his mind was taking him, looking up to my face now.

"You sure you don't want to make a couple of laps around the party in that ensemble?" he asks, pointing to the clothes I'm wearing.

I let out a dry laugh. "I don't even want to show my face in this for the distance it takes to get out of the front door of the house."

Robbie blows out a breath, rolling his eyes. Then he tilts his head at me before looking down at his duffle bag, unzipping it and rifling through it. "Turn around."

"What?" I rear back. "Why?"

"I have a jacket you can wear," he says. "And it's still cold out anyways."

"Oh," I breathe, my shoulders falling. "That'd be great actually. Thank you."

I turn around, holding out my arms so he can slip his jacket on me, a warm feeling swirling through my chest at his consideration. I make out the sound of something being pulled from his bag before I feel the material sliding onto my arms and across my back. I straighten my arms out in front of me, pulling the jacket closer around myself and settling into its warmth. I start to turn around, but my eyes catch on the bright blue and yellow colors in the mirror in front of me, and that's when I realize.

I drop my head, letting out a chuckle before I spin around, looking over my shoulder in the mirror to read *Summers* clear as day across the back of the jacket. Because it's Robbie's letterman jacket. With his name and everything about him plastered all over it in embroidery and patches.

I look back at Robbie, finding one hand on his hip and the other halfway covering his upturned mouth. "I'm not sure how much of an improvement this is," I tell him.

He drops his hand from his mouth, revealing his full grin. "I don't think you've ever looked better."

I can't help but laugh, meeting his eyes as my chuckles fade out in a sigh. I raise my arms in the air, giving him a bow of sorts.

Robbie shakes his head, his tongue pushed into the side of his cheek. "Come on. Let's go."

———

The car ride to my house is almost entirely silent, but I wouldn't say that it's awkward. There's tension between us, but it's not heavy, not suffocating. It's more like a buzz of energy in the air, drawing the two of us together, but neither of us acting on it out of fear of giving in.

It's almost like when you run into static electricity, and you know if you touch the person or thing before you that you'll be shocked. You're often left in suspense, your finger floating in the air between yourself and the other object, afraid of the possible pain but also inexplicably drawn to it anyways. You know there's a chance you could regret giving it. It could simply hurt, leaving nothing but an aftershock and regret running through you. Or it could hurt just a little, but the satisfaction of giving in, of letting yourself feel it, far outweighs any hurt. In fact, it almost makes you feel stronger for having endured the pain. That shock is sometimes worth that blissful invincible feeling you get afterwards. The only issue is, you don't know unless you try. Unless you invite the pain in. You have no possibility of knowing how fulfilled and euphoric you can feel unless you allow yourself to get hurt. And I suppose that's the real test of it all. Whether or not to give in. Whether or not you're willing to risk the pain. Whether or not you're okay with never knowing what could be.

When Robbie pulls up to my house, my mom's car is already parked in the driveway. The lights in the house all seem to be off, so I'm sure she's already asleep. But that doesn't mean I'm about to prance through the front door with Robbie on my heels. Especially considering that I'm coming home much later than I normally ever would, the clothes that I'm wearing, the way half of my makeup is gone while the other half is smeared or running down my face, and the fact that we both have wet hair. With my mother's basic knowledge of me and Robbie's history and her awareness that I haven't been anywhere but home, school, or work in the two months since things between us ended, all of this would just lead to far too many questions that I don't have the brain capacity to answer right now.

I start to turn to him to tell him thank you and good night, but he's already opening his door and climbing out of the car.

"*Okay then*," I mutter to myself, doing the same.

By the time I close my door, Robbie's already rounded the car and is standing at the head of the walkway leading up to my house. He stops, looking over his shoulder with raised brows like he's waiting for me to hurry up.

I approach him hesitantly, my arms crossing. "Um...my mom's home," I mumble.

"Okay," Robbie says.

"Okay." I fidget, running a hand through my hair. "Well..." I flick my eyes in the direction of Robbie's car, expecting him to turn and go back to it.

"Does Sherri have rules against walking you to the door?"

I roll my lips into my mouth, fighting the urge to berate him for calling my mom by her first name again but also the automatic reflex to smile. "Not that I'm aware of," I tell him.

Robbie holds out an arm, telling me to lead the way, and I do. We quietly make our way up the walkway, the door feeling so much further away than it really is and time feeling like it slows with each step we take. Eventually, we reach the top step of my porch.

I turn towards Robbie to find his eyes already on me.

A few seconds go by of me averting his gaze and tapping my foot awkwardly before I finally blow out a breath, facing him. "Hey," I say dumbly.

"Hey, Cooper," he says back, his lips twitching into a smile for a moment before it fades, his brows pulling together. "Are you okay?" he asks, his voice gentle.

"Physically?" I ask.

"Sure," he nods.

"Yes, I'm okay."

Great, actually.

"And mentally?" he asks, taking a step closer. "Emotionally?"

"I..." I shake my head. "I'm not sure."

Robbie watches me for a few seconds, seeming to take me in. "What are you thinking?" he asks me.

"That's not a simple question."

"Actually, it may be the simplest question ever," he retorts. "Whatever's in your head right now, Cooper," he pauses, reaching up to brush his thumb across my temple, "just say it. Whatever it is. All of it."

I swallow hard, looking away from him. "I...I'm thinking..."

"So close. It's right there," Robbie pushes me, smirking.

"I'm thinking that... I'm freaking out a little. That...I don't really know *what* I'm thinking. I'm thinking that I don't really know if I trust you, but that everything in me wants to. I'm thinking about how no one has ever made me as angry as you have made me. Or sad. Or frustrated. Or enraged. But...I'm not sure if anyone has ever made me feel as happy either. As *alive*. And that...kinda scares the shit out of me. So, in a way...all those months ago...you were right. And I'm thinking about how I hate that you were right. I don't want to be scared...but I'm not sure how not to be. I'm also thinking that...if you meant what you said... If you want to stop trying to stay away from each other...which, I think you meant, but I–I don't know. I can't be sure. Things...things got heated...and I know we were in the moment... So, if you didn't mean it, that's fine. You can just tell me and we can move on with our lives. Get back to the status quo. But...if you *did* mean it. If you want to try to be around each other again, to be...whatever it is you want us to be...to be... together...in any way...I...I just...I think we need to take it slow."

I take a deep breath as I finish, looking up to find Robbie staring at me with wide, thoughtful eyes. Several seconds go by of me holding my breath and Robbie not saying anything.

Eventually, I'm forced to let out a weak chuckle, feeling like I might pass out if I don't get any new air into my lungs. Robbie still hasn't responded. He hasn't answered any of my questions. Or really addressed anything that I just word vomited out at him at his request. I shift on my feet, running my hands up and down my forearms uncomfortably, my eyes flicking between Robbie's unmoving face and my feet.

"What are *you* thinking?" I finally ask him.

"That I meant what I said." My gaze snaps up, and Robbie tilts his head at me, wetting his bottom lip with his tongue as he takes a step closer. "That you still scare me more than anything too, Cooper. And that I'd like to see you tomorrow."

My mouth falls open. A thousand thoughts run through my mind. Some that send heat rushing to my face, some that make my stomach sink, some that make my heart squeeze, and some that threaten to make my eyes water. I try to latch onto just one of those things to say, but I come up empty, the only thing I halfway manage to mutter being, "*Tomorrow?*"

"Yeah," Robbie says, a grin tilting his mouth. "Tomorrow."

I begin to chew on my bottom lip. "That's not taking things very slow."

Robbie breathes out a laugh, wrapping a hand around my elbow and pulling me closer to him, resting his other hand on my hip. He ducks his head, his face only a few inches from mine. "But it's a whole sleep away," he says, his voice low.

"Tomorrow's Sunday," I blurt.

"And?"

"Well...you know," I shrug.

He raises a brow at me, waiting for me to continue.

"It's the Lord's day."

Robbie snorts. "The *Lord's* day?" he repeats.

I cross my arms. "Yes?"

"When's the last time you went to church, Cooper?"

"Christmas," I say. Robbie's eyes narrow on me, making me avert my gaze. "...when I was seven," I add under my breath.

"Well then I'm in better graces than you."

I'm trying not to focus on the way Robbie's fingertips are circling against my hip and how they're sending a shiver straight down my spine with every movement. "Really?" I ask, attempting nonchalance. "When's the last time you went?"

"Sometime in junior high." Robbie reaches up, twirling a loose strand of my hair in his fingers. "But I practiced worship just about an hour ago. On my knees and everything."

My own knees nearly give out from under me. I lean back until my side comes into contact with the door frame, supporting myself against it. Robbie comes right along with me, sweeping that loose hair behind my ear. He looks down at me, his mouth quirking, just before he leans down and whispers in my ear.

"I suppose you deserve your day of rest. To confess for your sins and all."

Robbie pulls away, meeting my eyes again with a devilish grin. I swallow hard, squeezing my thighs together. "How considerate of you," I breathe.

Robbie reaches up, holding the side of my face as he brushes his thumb over the arch of my brow. Then he shifts down, sweeping it gently across the sensitive skin of my under eye, staring into my eyes like he's looking for something. "When can I see you, Cooper?"

"On Monday at school"

He leans back, giving me a sharp look.

"What?" I question him. "That's only the following day."

Robbie shakes his head. "That won't do."

"What do you mean?"

"I mean, when can I *actually* see you?" Robbie trails his pointer finger down the bridge of my nose. "Just us."

My teeth sink into my lower lip. "Saturday?"

"Friday."

I blow out a breath. "Fine. Friday."

Robbie's fingers move to my cheekbone, circling it. "And you'll sit with me at lunch this week?"

An unexpected laugh burst out of me. "*What?* Really?"

Robbie pauses the movement of his fingers, meeting my gaze and waiting for me to answer his question. I can hear his voice inside of my head quipping, *You heard me.*

"I..." I stammer. "I have to study for an algebra test this week..."

Robbie tilts his head at me, beginning his trail along my face again. "I can sit there at the same lunch table as you while you do that," he says.

"Well...if you really want to–"

"I wouldn't have asked if I didn't want to, Cooper."

I press my lips tightly together. "Fine. Lunch then."

"And you'll let me drive you to school?"

"You're pushing it, Summers."

Robbie's thumb presses into the center of my chin, a smile breaking across his face. "Aren't I always?"

I can't help but smile as well. Because, yes. *Yes, he is.*

I let out a sigh as Robbie's fingers brush the side of my jaw. "Yes to lunch. No to the ride."

No to confined spaces alone with you. At least for a few days. Until I can get my head on straight.

"Deal," Robbie utters, the tip of his thumb running along the outline of my bottom lip, his eyes tracking the motion intently.

"Robbie?" I breathe.

"Yeah, Cooper?"

"Why are you doing that?" I ask.

"*Hmm?*"

"Why are you...tracing me?"

Robbie hums, seeming to be lost in thought as he moves his thumb to follow the same path across my top lip. "I'm just trying to memorize you, Cooper."

"Why?" I ask him.

"Just in case I ever manage to lose you again." His finger goes back to the bridge of my nose. "I can't let myself forget anything. I'd already have a hard enough time sleeping without wracking my brain for how many of these nearly invisible freckles you have." His hand shifts up, fingers brushing the outer corner of my eye. "Or attempting to recall every shape and color of storm these babies hold within them." His finger trails painfully slow down my face, eventually reaching my bottom lip once more. "Or trying to remember the exact curve of your mouth, the naturally reddish tint it holds even before you put that red lipstick over it that makes me go damn near insane, the way your bottom lip is just a little bigger than your top, and how it feels dragging between my teeth."

I don't realize how close we've gotten until Robbie's forehead presses against mine. We stand there for a while, our breaths mingling, me staring up at Robbie, him staring down at my mouth. His fingers flex against my hip as he pulls me the slightest inch closer. "I'm taking it slow," he mutters.

"Right," I nod, breathless, my forehead stuck against Robbie's forcing him to nod as well. "Very slow."

Robbie's eyes are glued to mine for so long, I start to wonder if one of us is frozen. Then, suddenly, he leans down, ducking his head into the crook of my neck. And then he does the last thing I could have expected. He lets the hold of his fingers loosen on my hip, sliding his arms against my side and around my back until he fully wraps me in a hug.

My spine straightens, arching in surprise. My arms reflexively come up, wrapping around Robbie's neck. And then, I let out a sigh. One so heavy, that it feels like it releases two long months' worth of emotions, tension, and longing. I sink into his hold, my face pressing against his chest, my still semi-damp hair easily soaking into the front of his shirt. But he doesn't seem concerned about it.

I don't think either of us are concerned with much of anything right now.

We stand there for so long, just holding one another. It occurs to me that we've never done this. Never just hugged. Not once. And when Robbie subtly shifts his head just enough to smell my hair, this suddenly feels more intimate than anything else we've done.

My eyes flutter shut, soaking in every moment of it, willing this, willing *us*, to just last forever.

The words ring out clear in my head, almost as if I've said them out loud.

I missed you.

Robbie threads his fingers into my hair, nuzzling against me further.

"I missed you too, Cooper."

forty-eight

ROBBIE

My knuckle taps against the locked doors of Groovy Movie.

I lean my face against the glass door, placing my hand over my forehead and trying to peer inside. It's only a couple of seconds before I see a swish of red and a grin comes to my face. I pull away from the glass, stepping back so that Cooper can unlock the door.

She swings it open, looking me up and down as she leans against the doorway, still wearing her burnt orange Groovy Movie vest over the cream blouse and plaid skirt she wore to school today. Her arms fold and her ankles cross over one another, forcing my eyes to follow the dark pantyhose running up her long legs. My throat bobs, fantasies running wild in my mind and other parts of my body waking up in my brain's dream-like state.

"You're late," she says, snapping my gaze back to her face.

I lift the hand that is holding the heavy grocery bag up towards my face, reading my watch on my wrist. "Cooper, it's 9:01."

"And I agreed to 9:00," she retorts. I look up at her, finding her eyes narrowed on me but a smirk on her face. She pretends to yawn. "I'm not sure that I'm up for an outing anymore."

An outing.

That's what she keeps insisting on calling our first date.

It's what she referred to our date as every day this week when I'd remind her during lunch of our plans this Friday, just hoping to see her eyes turn on me and her cheeks flush pink. It's what she weakly threatened to cancel whenever I refused to tell her what we'd be doing, claiming she hates surprises. It's what I caught written in her open planner during Ms. Cage's class, which she promptly slammed close, blowing out a frustrated breath that reminded me far too much of other breathy sounds she has previously made for us to be sitting in history class together, me unable to pull her into my lap in my desk right there and make her make them again.

An outing.

Not a date.

Because calling it a date would mean she was making this easy for me. And there's no chance of that.

Because she's a stubborn little shit.

But, if I'm being honest, I can't even pretend that I mind.

I got to be around her this week. I got to look in her direction and not have to force my eyes away the moment she'd look back. I got to walk with her to Ms. Cage's class without either one of us deliberately speeding up or slowing down to avoid the other one. I got to watch her furrow her brow and chew on her bottom lip between sips of Jolt as she studied at lunch like her algebra notes contained the cure to cancer. I got to listen to my Journey *Frontiers* tape all the way through for the first time in months and think of her without it feeling like there was a hole in my chest. I got to play my first basketball game of the season last night knowing that her attention being on me wasn't *entirely* due to the photos she was taking.

When there was something I wanted to tell her, I was able to, because we were speaking again. When I wanted to scan the halls and find her, I could, because she wasn't hiding from me anymore. And when I felt like I may die if I didn't touch her, I was able to brush my fingers against her skin with only a half-hearted glare in response. And that was enough.

Things between us aren't perfect yet, but, for now, I'll take the things exactly as they are. As long as there's things to have at all. As long as Sara Cooper is slowly sliding her way back into my life– as long as it keeps feeling like the sun is finally rising for the first time in a long time– I'm content. I'm *happy.*

Cooper gives me another dramatic yawn, patting the palm of her hand against her mouth. "Perhaps we'll just have to save our outing for another day."

"Sounds great," I remark.

Cooper straightens in the doorway. "Um, really?"

"Sure, Cooper." I take a step closer to her. "I'd love to go on an outing with you another weekend."

"Well, okay then," she says, and, even though she's putting on her best show to hide it, I can see the slight shadow of disappointment flickering across her face.

She was looking forward to this.

A grin spreads across my face. "Great," I say, then push past her in the doorway.

Cooper spins around as I pass by her. "Um, what are you doing? I thought you just said we'd go out another weekend."

"Oh, yeah, we are," I confirm, setting the grocery bag down on the check-out counter. "But we're not going out tonight."

"What do you mean? And where are you going?" Cooper calls after me as I make my way to the far side of the store with a step stool I just pulled out from behind the counter.

I wait to answer her until I'm halfway up the steps of the stool, pulling down the old projector screen over the wall.

"Robbie, I– You can't just do that. We just use that screen for special events and during holidays and theme nights."

"Yes I can," I tell her, climbing down from the step stool and folding it closed before I head over to the action section of the store. I scan the shelves for just a couple of moments before I find what

I'm looking for, managing to snatch it up and hide it under my arm before Cooper reaches me.

"Excuse me?" Cooper whisper-shouts for some reason behind me as I round the corner of the shelf, moving to the front door to lock it.

"Do you trust me?" I ask.

"When my job is on the line? Not really."

I walk back to the check-out counter, returning the stool and beginning to dig into the grocery bag once again.

"You sure know your way around this store for someone that has literally never been in here," Cooper huffs.

"That's because I talked to Jack," I say, pulling a can of Jolt and a bottle of Pepsi from the bag.

Cooper's hands rest against the top of the counter, her brows raising. "I'm sorry, *Jack?*" she demands. "As in, *my boss?* Mr. Ritter?"

"Yep, that's him," I nod, taking out several options of candy and chocolate bars and an extra large bag of salt and vinegar chips. "Great guy."

"I'm so confused," she mutters. "Why did you talk to him?"

"So I could convince him to let me host our first date at his store, obviously."

Cooper's eyes go wide. "What? Are you serious?"

"Trying to be," I tell her.

"That's... I... You..." Cooper stammers, her bottom lip going into her mouth. "Are we...watching a movie?"

I give her a smirk, pulling out the VHS wedged against my side, and my heart nearly bursts at the look on her face when she realizes.

"We're watching *Top Gun*?"

I think she might cry, and I'm not sure what I'll do if she does. I vowed I'd never purposely make Cooper cry again. But I'm not sure it still counts if I know for a fact that they're happy tears.

Her glossy eyes trail from the movie in my hand down to the spread laid out on the counter. "You didn't have to do all this," she says, motioning towards it. "We have so many snacks here."

"But not your favorites."

I know for a fact, because I asked Jack what they keep in stock.

Cooper's lips pull up at the sides. "Thank you. This is... This is amazing."

I reach back into the large bag, pulling out the final item inside. I unroll the blanket, tucking it against my side as I walk around the counter.

"Nothing's even happened yet, Cooper," I say.

"And yet, somehow..." she pauses, pursing her lips as she meets my eyes, this still feels like everything." I reach up, pushing her hair out of her face and cupping her cheek. She shivers against my touch, pulling back like it's a reflex. Her brows pull together, and she gives me a weak smile as if to apologize. "Thank you," she says again, stepping closer to me.

"Of course, baby," I whisper, leaning forward.

Our noses graze, and we just look at each other for a few moments, both of us grinning like idiots and neither one of us knowing exactly what to do next.

Eventually, I decide to be the one to take charge of being smart, to take this slow. I raise my head, barely pressing my lips to her forehead before I pull back. I hold up *Top Gun* in front of Cooper, smiling down at her.

"Should we pop this sucker in?"

forty-nine

SARA

It's been about thirty minutes.

Thirty minutes since Robbie strolled into Groovy Movie like he owned the place, armed with all of my favorite things. Thirty minutes since he had me sit down on the softest blanket I've maybe ever felt on the floor in the middle of an aisle of movie stocked shelves while he turned down the lights and hit play on the VHS player. Thirty minutes since we started watching the movie that makes me feel more emotions than I thought I was capable of. The one that I've only ever opened up to Robbie about why it means so much to me.

Thirty minutes of him sipping his Pepsi and me sipping my Jolt, both of us seemingly too fidgety to go for any of the snacks just yet.

I keep feeling Robbie's eyes on the side of my face, but I keep my gaze forward on the projector screen, trying to hide the smile that pulls at my lips and the heat that grazes my cheeks every time I sense him watching me.

When a few minutes have passed without him looking my way, I decide to finally steal my own glance at him.

Robbie's leaned back, his elbows bent as his palms rest flat against the blanket to support him. He's discarded his jacket on the ground next to him, leaving him with only his dark t-shirt on top. I find myself ogling his tan forearms and the way the muscles and tendons strain within them as he holds himself up and wonder if it's weird that I find them attractive.

I decide that it's not.

Moving back to his face, I watch as the colors of the movie reflect in his focused eyes, showing every dimension within their depths. From this side angle, I can see his unfairly long sweeping eyelashes fluttering every time he blinks. I notice how his brow keeps furrowing and his lips keep twitching at the corners as he watches the current scene of Goose and Maverick attending their first day of training at TOPGUN, specifically the moment that Maverick realizes that the woman he was flirting with out the previous night is actually a civilian contractor for the Navy and one of his instructors.

I can't help but smile at Robbie's smile, because *of course* he would get a kick out of that.

As I continue to discreetly watch him watching the movie, I can't help but zone out some, my gaze shifting to the movie shelves behind him.

A few seconds go by before I see movement in my peripheral vision and find Robbie running a hand through his hair, his eyes trained on me.

"Whatcha doin', Cooper?" he whispers, as if we're actually in a movie theater.

That brings a small grin to my face. "I don't know," I tell him honestly. "Just...thinking, I guess."

"About what?"

I open my mouth and then press my lips together.

"Nope, don't do that," Robbie says, shaking his head.

"Do what?" I laugh.

"Sit there overthinking your response about what you were thinking. No more thinking about it. Just tell me what you were *just* thinking."

My brows knit at the amount of times Robbie just said the word *thinking*, but then I decide to just give him what he asked for.

"Well, I was just *thinking* about the amount of time throughout our relationship that you and I have spent between shelves. How many hours it must add up to."

Robbie's eyes search my face. Just as I'm about to regret being honest about what I was thinking, he smirks.

"Relationship, huh?"

I snort. "Calm down."

"You just said we're in a relationship, Cooper," he grins.

"I said we have a relationship, not that we're in one. That's two very different things."

"Seems like a pretty fine line between the two to me," he says.

"Then maybe you need to get your eyes checked. Know any places where you can do that?"

The response is out of my mouth before I can stop it, and I have to resist the urge to kick myself. It just came so naturally, slipping back into our old bantering ways.

Robbie's smile only flickers slightly. "None that would welcome me," he says quietly.

I open my mouth, not sure what I'm going to say but just knowing I need to say something. But Robbie clears his throat, cutting me off.

"You know, I think it's kind of cool."

"What?" I ask him.

"All our time between the shelves. Around books and movies."

I tilt my head at him.

"Since, you know, those are kind of your things," Robbie shrugs, dropping down on one elbow to tilt his body towards me. "And we've always been around them. We've been through a lot with no one but the shelves to see it. It's almost like...we've made a story between the stories. Or something."

My spine steels.

A story between the stories.

Robbie chuckles, reaching for a Red Vine from the package at his side. "Sorry. That may have been the cheesiest shit I've ever said. I take it back. Please, forget I said it."

"I don't want to," I breathe. Robbie glances up, meeting my eyes. I hold his gaze, rolling my lips into my mouth. "That may be my favorite thing you've ever said to me."

He takes a bite of his Red Vine, not forfeiting our staring game as he does. "You keep track of all the things I say to you?"

"Most of them."

"Do you write them down in your journal?"

I fight the urge to roll my eyes, a smile coming to my face. "Some of them."

"Really?" he asks, shifting up some so that he's at my eye level.

I shrug my shoulders. "I told you. I write down what inspires me. Anything that I think could become something more."

Robbie's tongue sweeps across his bottom lip as a few seconds of tense silence rest between us, only the sound of the movie playing in the background breaking it.

"Have you heard back about your scholarship yet?" he asks suddenly.

I shake my head. "Not yet. But I should know by mid-April."

"That doesn't really give you a lot of time to figure things out," Robbie says, picking up his Pepsi can.

"Well, there's really not much to figure out. Either I get the scholarship and go to NYU...or I stay here."

The Pepsi can stops in place against Robbie's lips, his eyes looking at me over the top of it.

"It's really just a matter of booking a flight and reserving a dorm room in New York. Or signing up for community college in San Francisco and mentally preparing for being a full-time movie rental store worker until I can make a new game plan."

Robbie lowers the can away from his face, something in his expression that I can't read as he picks at his soda's pop tab. When nearly a minute goes by without him saying anything, I pull my knees up to my chest, turning my attention back to the movie.

"Cooper?" Robbie says, his voice hoarse.

"Yeah?" I respond, chewing on my bottom lip.

I feel Robbie shift next to me, and when I look his way, I find him fully sat up and scooting closer into me. "When you're thinking about things that could become something more, do you ever think of us?"

There is so much to that question. So much more to clarify in what he means by *more*.

What is more? *For how long? Where would* more *even take place, depending on my currently very uncertain future and his future that he never even wants to talk about?*

There is so much I could say, so much I could ask him, so many possible caveats I could choose to point out. But instead, I let out a gentle sigh, choosing to answer the question for simply what it is.

"More than I care to admit," I say, echoing the same words I've heard his voice say in my mind over and over since holiday break.

Robbie reaches up, and I don't know why, but my body automatically stiffens against his touch. I'd like to think that it's my brain protecting my heart, but it's becoming frustrating. I'm trying to just be here. Trying to give myself a chance to be reckless and not think about the consequences of my actions for once. To just give in to what I want. But I know that's not going to be something that comes naturally to me.

Robbie lets his hand drop and he looks down, watching his fingers flexing at his side. He shakes his head, blowing out a shaky breath.

"You want to know what my favorite thing you've ever said to me was, Cooper?" he asks, looking up at me through the chestnut strands of hair that have perfectly fallen and swooped down across his line of sight.

I hug my knees tighter to my chest. "What?"

"It was just last week. You know, I don't have the writer brain or diary like you do–"

"Not a diary–"

"It was..." Robbie cuts me off, tilting his head up and smirking.

"It was when you told me...that everything is about me. That I'm everywhere and in everything."

I can feel the heat rush straight to my cheeks at the reminder of what I said to Robbie when I was in a more than compromised state last week. "You know," I let out an uncomfortable chuckle, playing with my hair so that it somewhat covers my surely very red cheeks, "I really figured we'd follow the Vegas rule with that." Robbie brows raise and I clarify. "What happens in the shower stays in the shower."

"Is that really what you want?" Robbie asks, his voice much more serious than I expected.

My grin slowly fades from my face. "Um...well...I..." I stammer.

"Cooper..."

I look up at him, meeting his piercing gaze. I can see the tight flex of his jaw and glance down to find his fingers still grasping at nothing for purchase. It's so automatic when I reach down and lace my fingers through his own.

The moment I do, Robbie stiffens, and then, he slowly raises our joined hands up to his face, shifting them from side to side as if examining them, trying to determine if they're real. He blows a long breath out through his nose, his eyes squeezing shut for a moment before opening them again and meeting mine.

"Cooper," he starts, his voice strained, "the reason that's my favorite thing you've ever said to me is because...it was exactly what I had been feeling for so long. It's like you yanked the painful ache from my chest and somehow put it into words. You said to me what I didn't know how to say to you at the time. But now..." He tilts his head, pursing his lips. "I think I'd like to give it another try."

I swallow against the tightness in my throat, giving him a nod. "Okay," I breathe.

Robbie takes a deep breath before beginning, shaking his head with a *'here goes nothing'* sort of flourish. "When this whole thing started between us, Cooper... I couldn't stand you. You drove me up a goddamn wall."

I bark out a laugh, completely caught off guard, but I let him continue.

"I've always felt on top of the world at Bay View. Nobody's ever questioned me, ever challenged me. But then, all of the sudden, I got detention. And here comes this little redheaded nightmare in Keds that's not even willing to pretend to put up with any of my shit."

I press my thumb hard against the soft spot between Robbie's thumb and pointer finger, making him jolt slightly.

"I think..." he carries on with a pointed look at me, "that before we crossed paths this year... I thought I was the only person around that was truly living. I thought I was taking in every ounce of life and savoring it where others were just letting it pass them by. I used to think kids our age that actually cared about school and were more focused on what was to come after high school rather than simply enjoying high school were idiots. It didn't make sense to me. What's the point in having dreams when you could be *living* the dream? Making the most out of each day as it comes? But I think... I think I may have had it all wrong. I think I was the zombie I liked to imagine everyone else but me was all along."

Robbie lets out a sigh, meeting my gaze that hasn't left his face since he started talking.

"You know, you were right before," he says, "all those months ago when you went off on me in your bedroom right before I convinced you to date me." He smirks, and I refrain from correcting him that it was *fake* dating. "When you told me that I was hiding behind an act. That it was easier than having to actually try. That keeping people at an arm's length prevented them from being disappointed in the real me."

"Robbie, I..."

"Please, Cooper, just let me finish. I'm kinda on a roll here."

I snap my mouth closed.

"But, it's funny," he continues. "The whole point of us dating... the whole...point of our arrangement, was to make you more like me. To make you someone I thought would be thought of as fun and considered cool enough by the whole school. As if...there was anything wrong with you in the first place."

"Robbie–"

"And *me*..." He shakes his head. "I was just trying to play the game. I just wanted to use you long enough so that I could pretend that I fit in with the crowd I thought I was practically the leader of before this school year. I felt it all beginning to slip away...that constructed image I thought I had so perfectly intact... The one that you saw right through." His throat bobs. "I just wanted to use you long enough to get that back. But then...it started to feel like there wasn't a *long enough*. Because...things changed, Cooper."

I squeeze his hand in the way I feel my heart squeeze.

Robbie's gaze drops to our hands, turning them over. "Things changed in that closet."

"Which one?" I ask.

"All of them," he says.

"They changed at the Back to School Dance. They also changed when I saw you get hurt. When I had to take you to my parents' office. When I caught you listening to my Journey tape in the library. When you gave that absolutely epic speech. When I had to watch you dance with Paul at the Homecoming dance...and then... well, you know."

I blink, averting my gaze as he trails off.

"They changed when you came to Thanksgiving," Robbie breathes, leaning closer to me. "When you stood up to my family for me in ways I never could." I feel the lightest touch of a finger against my chin, and find my head turning back in Robbie's direction. "They changed when I really got to kiss you for the first time." Butterflies instantly flutter against my ribcage, working their way down to my stomach. "They changed in the backseat of my car. And they especially changed...when I watched you walk away from me."

The backs of my eyes burn, but I don't allow myself to look away from Robbie, my breaths coming out shallow.

"Cooper...you said that I was in everything. But you...you *are* everything. At least to me."

It feels like a dam bursts in my chest, the floodgates of my heart busting wide open.

"You've absolutely ruined any type of weather for me," Robbie says, making me pull back just slightly, giving him a questioning look. "I instantly think of you when it's cold, wondering if you're inside or if you have a jacket to keep you warm if not. I feel you in the sun, the brightness in the morning reminding me of your smile when you laugh and the damn thing looking just like your hair when it's the perfect time of evening and it's starting to set, glowing bright reddish-orange." He ducks his head, his nose brushing against the top of my hair. "I smell you in the rain," he mutters against my temple before he pulls back enough to meet my gaze. "I see your eyes in every fucking storm, and I know for a fact I will for the rest of my life."

My teeth sink into my lower lip, my blood pumping in my ears. Robbie opens his mouth to continue, and it is beyond me how he still has more to say, how he doesn't know I'm already a puddle on the floor in front of him.

"I hear you in every love song I used to blast in my Camaro at top volume without ever paying attention to what the words were really saying. I taste you in anything sweet. But..." He reaches up gingerly, just barely brushing the back of his hand against my cheekbone. "I only ever touch you in my dreams anymore. And I don't want it to be like that. Please, Cooper, just...give me a chance. A real chance. Let me be serious about something for once. Let me be serious about you."

The last word is barely out of Robbie's mouth before I'm launching myself at him, my arms wrapping around his neck and my lips crushing against his.

It only takes a second for Robbie to catch up, his arms circling around his waist as he pulls me onto his lap.

The way this began, you'd think we'd have zero restraint, devouring each other and tearing our clothes off like our lives depend on it. But as soon as I'm settled into Robbie's hold, everything just slows down. We take our time, because suddenly it

544

feels like we have all the time in the world. Like this isn't something that's just going to be ripped out from under us at any moment. Like it's not just an illusion that's about to be shattered. No, this is different. Because, for the first time, we both know without a doubt that it's real. That it means something. That it's not just for show or the result of a heated moment. There's feelings attached to this. Meaning. Something that doesn't have an ulterior motive or pre-set expiration date.

This is just the two of us, being together. Giving each other everything we have to give and knowing this time that the other will give it in return.

Robbie slowly leans back, our lips never separating until he is flat on his back, my body parallel and flush to his. And then we both pull apart, our brows pinched together when we register at the same time the intro to *Take My Breath Away* by Berlin playing from the speakers, meaning the love scene between Maverick and Charlie is about to begin.

My hand covers my mouth as a giggle bursts out of me. Robbie's head falls back against the blanket, unable to stifle his laugh either.

"You really planned this evening down to a T, didn't you?" I ask.

Robbie brushes the hair out of my face, holding my cheek in his hand. "Cooper, I couldn't have planned for any of this if I tried."

My head tilts, a smile pulling at my lips. "Have you fallen for me, Lieutenant?"

Robbie's tongue presses against his bottom lip, his head shaking. "You've always seen right through me."

He lifts his head off the ground and I lower mine, our eyes searching each other's. When our lips are just a breath apart, Robbie surprises me, suddenly rolling us over so that he's now on top of me. I let out a small gasp as my back hits the blanket, but it's quickly swallowed by Robbie's mouth back on mine.

One of Robbie's hands stays holding my face while the other trails up my side, just slipping under the hem of my blouse. He trails circles against my skin, leaving goosebumps in his wake as he continues pressing bruising kisses against my mouth. My face feels warm, but pure liquid heat is pooling in my lower belly as the languid seconds go by. When Robbie's hand slides up further, his fingers gripping the side of my ribcage at the same moment his tongue tangles with mine, I find myself arching against him. Robbie responds immediately, letting out a groan against my mouth as he presses against me, making my legs automatically spread apart for him to settle between them.

I continue to kiss him back, but release my hold where my hands have been fisted in the front of his shirt, slowly pulling my arms back until they are fully extended, lying parallel to my head. Robbie finally takes notice, hesitantly pulling his face from mine as he looks down at me with a furrowed brow.

"Are you okay?" he breathes.

I nod, smiling. "Do it," I whisper.

"Do what?"

I tilt my head at him, watching the range of emotions flickering through his eyes as he looks down at me. "Touch me," I tell him. "Out of your dreams this time."

Robbie's eyelids grow heavy, his teeth grazing his bottom lip as he grips my blouse in his hands, inching it up just slightly before pausing, looking to my face once more for reassurance. When I give it to him, nodding, it only takes another second before the cream colored fabric is clouding my vision, being pushed over my head.

I hear the sound of my blouse landing gently in a pile on the ground near my head before my eyes flutter open and I find Robbie looming over me, his hand roughly rubbing over his jaw as he takes me in with nothing but a white lace bra on before him. I can't exactly decipher his expression, the look in his eyes something between a starving person seeing food for the first time in weeks and Ralphie when he opened the exact Red Ryder air rifle he'd been yearning for for months on Christmas morning in *A Christmas Story*. I'm not sure which of those looks brings a bigger smile to my face.

Robbie leans down, pressing a kiss to my collarbone. "Shit, Cooper. I'm not sure when you're gonna stop surprising me."

I place my hands on his hips, slipping them under his shirt and grazing my nails up his back, making Robbie shiver. He captures my lips in his, gentle but sure. "Your turn," I murmur against his mouth, fisting his shirt in my hands and giving it a gentle tug upwards. Robbie complies immediately, sitting up and pulling his shirt over the back of his head and off his body in one easy pull, revealing so much tan and toned skin that I just have to reach up and run my finger over.

I take my time, tracing across the line of his shoulder, through the thin smattering of hair covering his chest, down the plane of his abs, lean yet muscular. I take a moment to admire his arms, fully on display, toned from the thousands of hours of basketball he's played with them. Then my gaze is brought back upwards, to his perfectly mussed hair, those dark chocolate brown eyes, and those deep pink lips set into the most perfect, satisfied grin as he looks at me looking at me.

I blow out a deep breath, shaking my head. "You are..."

Robbie tilts his head. "What am I, Cooper?" he smirks.

"You're just really beautiful," I admit, meaning it wholeheartedly.

Robbie beams, leaning down to kiss me. "Well you're fucking gorgeous," he breathes. "And I'll never know how I went so many years without noticing."

"It's okay," I say, as he pulls his lips away from mine, peppering kisses across my cheek.

I let out a whimper as his teeth graze my earlobe. "I don't think I gave you much opportunity to notice me."

"Well, how about you give me the opportunity now to make it up to you anyways," Robbie mutters into my neck, working his way down.

I don't get the chance to answer before Robbie covers the left cup of my bra with his mouth, nipping and sucking, leaving the lacy fabric wet and straining against the pebbled point of my breast.

My head falls back against the blanket as I let out a strangled moan. Robbie moves to the other cup, not wasting any time with this one, pulling it down and exposing my bare flesh. He palms my other breast while he latches on to my nipple, giving it a hard suck followed by a lap of his tongue to soothe the pleasantly painful ache.

I'm squirming beneath him, putty in his hands as he continues to explore every inch of the upper half of my body, coming back to my face to kiss my lips intermittently. It catches me off guard every time he does it, making me smile. He's all over the place. Like he can't decide where to place his focus, but, at the same time, he's not in any rush, doing what feels right, paying attention to how my body responds, and it has my toes absolutely curling and my legs squeezing around him to pull him closer.

We're well past the love scene in *Top Gun* now, the sounds of fighter jets and radio communications filling the air around us, but it doesn't deter us any. If anything, it almost makes it more perfect. More *us*. Me and Robbie were never going to be your stereotypical romance novel couple. Everything between us has been a rollercoaster. Back and forth. Ups and down. Turbulence and explosions and high speed chases with moments sprinkled in that counteract it all. Moments that are quiet, peaceful, filled with longing, sprinkled with lust, heavy with purpose, and drowning in our reluctant but insistent want for each other.

"*Robbie*," I whine at the exact same moment he groans, "*Cooper*."

He braces himself up on his elbows to look down at me, eyes glossy and lips swollen, his chest rising and falling with uneven breaths.

"What is it, baby?" he whispers.

I swallow, reaching out and tugging him closer by the waistband of his jeans. "I want you."

Robbie looks down at where we're pressed together, only our pesky clothes separating us. His throat bobs as his eyes meet mine. "How much of me, Cooper?"

I don't hesitate, because I don't need to.

"All of you."

Robbie rakes a hand through his hair, shaking his head like he can't believe what he's hearing before he leans down, kissing me deeply. As our mouths mold together, exploring and tasting, Robbie slides a hand beneath my skirt, circling my hip and working to push the fabric further up my waist.

"Lift up for me, baby," he whispers against my lips, patting the side of my hip.

I do what he says, lifting my backside off the ground and letting him shimmy my skirt up until the top of it rests right at my midsection.

Robbie presses one last bruising kiss to my lips, and then a gentle one to my forehead before he works his way down my body. My chest heaves with anticipation. It feels like a century before he settles himself between my legs. Robbie fists the end of my skirt in his hand, slowly pushing it up, and then I watch as the arm supporting him nearly gives out.

"*Cooper*," he shudders, running a hand down his face.

"Yes?" I ask, playing coy.

"You could've warned me," Robbie practically chokes out, gently pushing my thigh further open.

I pull my lower lip into my mouth, fighting my grin. "Oh, did I not wear panties with my tights today? Sorry, I guess I forgot."

Without warning, Robbie drags the pad of his thumb over my pantyhose covered slit from bottom to top, the thin mesh-like fabric clinging to my damp center and firing off every nerve signal in my body.

I have to bite down on my knuckle to keep from crying out, my body feeling so raw and sensitive.

Robbie leans down, and I can feel his breath fanning over my inner thighs, making me shake. His eyes are glued to my core for several painfully long seconds before they flick up to me, something animalistic in them. He wets his lips before saying my name, his voice a low growl.

"Cooper?"

"Y–yes?"

Both of his hands slide languidly up my thighs, keeping them separated as my body reflexively fights to clamp them together. When he reaches the apex of my thighs, Robbie tilts his head, pinching the thin fabric of my pantyhose between two of his fingers and pulling up just slightly. "Are you particularly attached to these?"

My brows pinch. "My tights? Well, not exactly–"

The sound of ripping fabric shoots through the air as Robbie hooks his finger against the flimsy material, tearing the hem right down my center.

"*Robbie!*" I hiss out, my hips bucking as the cool air unexpectedly hit my exposed flesh.

"I gave you a chance to stop me," he says evenly, tearing the hole wider with each of his hands.

Something between a gasp and a giggle comes out of me as I kick my feet. "You didn't really give me much time to think."

"Sorry, baby," Robbie mutters, licking his lips. "Let me give you more time to decide if you'd like me to stop what I'm doing next."

"What are you–"

My voice gets stuck in my throat at the firm press of Robbie's flat tongue against me, swiping up the seam of my core at a pace so slow that he has me seeing stars. When he finally reaches the top, he fastens his mouth over my bundle of nerves, giving it a gentle suck and causing me to let out a deep moan.

"Was that enough time for you, baby?" Robbie drawls, swiping over the wetness covering his lips with two of his fingers.

"N–no," I shake my head. "I think I'm still deciding."

"Thank God," Robbie groans, sucking the same two fingers into his mouth, swirling his tongue around them before reaching down and sinking them into me.

I feel a kick in my lower belly, my hips jerking off the ground and rocking into Robbie's touch. "*Oh– Oh my...Robbie.*"

He takes his time, pumping his fingers in and out of me like he has all day. He sinks down resting his head against my thigh as he watches what he does to me, his gaze constantly flicking between my face and where he enters me, biting down on his lower lip like it's taking everything in him to restrain himself.

My hands are everywhere, gripping the blanket at my side, tugging at my skirt around my waist, and sweeping down to claw at Robbie's arms in any way I can. I keep almost going for his hair, the desire so strong and so reflexive to run my fingers through it and tug at the strands. But every time I start to reach for him, I pull back, going for anything else.

Robbie turns his head to the side, nipping at my sensitive skin while curling his fingers inside of me, and I think I'm going to lose it.

"*Robbie,*" I choke out.

"Yes, Cooper?" he mumbles casually, reaching his other hand up and pressing his thumb against my mound.

"*I–*" I gasp.

He ducks his head, replacing his thumb with his tongue, and I nearly scream.

"*Robbie–* Dammit. *Please!*" I cry.

Robbie shoots up, looming over me and pressing his lips to mine. One hand pushing my hair out of my face while the hand stays right where it's been. "Please what, baby?"

I let out a shaky sigh. "I need you."

Robbie stops moving, sitting up some to look at my face. "All of me?" he breathes.

I stare into his eyes, nodding firmly as I reach for the button on his jeans. "All of you. Please."

I just get his button undone when Robbie places his hand over mine, stopping me. "Cooper, hold on a second." He slowly removes his fingers from inside of me, and I instantly let out a weak sigh at the loss.

"Why?" I ask, squirming against the hold of his hand and new uncomfortable emptiness within me.

"*Baby,*" Robbie utters. "Please, look at me."

Something in his voice makes me listen, and I tilt my head back to look at him, all of the boldness I had mustered up quickly dissipating when I meet his concerned eyes.

"Are you sure?" Robbie asks gently.

I roll my lips into my mouth. "Yes."

Robbie's brows pinch, his face looking like he's deep in thought. Or maybe even pain.

"What's wrong?" I ask him.

My question seems to snap him out of whatever trance he's in, and he leans down to press a kiss to my forehead. "Nothing, baby. For once, absolutely nothing."

"Then what is it?"

"I just…" Robbie trails off. "You can't get this back. I just want to make sure it's what you really want. I want it to be perfect for you."

"Hey," I say, wrapping my hand around his cheek and making him look at me. "This is what I want. *You.*" Robbie blows out a breath, leaning into my touch. "And even if it's not perfect," I add, making his eyes widen, "I want it anyway."

Robbie smiles, grabbing my face in both of his hands and pressing his lips to mine gently. "Okay, Cooper. Then you got me."

He sits up slowly reaching into his back pocket and pulling out his wallet. He opens it up, pulling out a square foil packet and tossing it and his wallet just off to the side.

I see the shallow rise and fall of his chest and reach up, laying my hand flat against it and feeling the rapid thumping beneath.

"Your heart," I whisper. "It's racing."

Robbie covers my hand with his, wrapping his fingers around it. "Yeah, thanks a lot." I cock my head to the side. "You did that to me," he says.

I smile, reaching for his other hand and placing it over my heart. "You did that to me too."

A breath of silence stretches between us, our gazes locked and heart rates picking up by the second. And then, slowly, as if we've communicated to each other what we're about to do without words, our joined hands on Robbie's chest start trailing down, over his abs, through the thin patch of hair on his lower stomach, and past the place where his jeans are unbuttoned. Our fingers find his zipper, pulling it down a notch at a time until the pressure breaks, his hard length jutting out behind the confines of his briefs.

Robbie lets out a gentle sigh of relief at the release, gripping himself through his underwear. I follow his lead, tracing the length of him through the thin fabric before giving him a gentle squeeze. The groan that comes from Robbie has me reaching for the waistband of his open jeans, shoving them down over his hips. He helps me, rocking side to side, helping to force them down.

Once he has the denim pooled around his knees, he immediately turns his attention back on me, catching me off guard by leaning forward and capturing my lips with his before pressing hot wet kisses all down the side of my neck and across my chest until I'm worked up and panting again.

I reach down between us, dipping my fingers into the top of his briefs. "Can I..."

My question fades out as Robbie nods frantically into my chest.

I only manage to wrap my hand around the base of him and give him one firm pull before Robbie's snapping upwards, forcing his underwear down and freeing himself. He grips himself, shaking his head. "*Jesus*, Cooper, I..."

"What, Robbie?" I breathe.

He blows out a heated breath, gripping me by the back of the neck and pulling me up so that I'm eye to eye with him. "I'm gonna ask you one more time if you're sure. Because I feel like if I'm not inside of you in the next minute, I might die."

My throat bobs. "Well, we can't have you dying just as soon as I start to like you."

Robbie scoffs out a laugh, pressing his forehead to mine. I wrap my arms around his neck.

"I'm sure," I tell him.

Without breaking my eye contact, Robbie reaches out to the side, moving his hand around until he finds what he's looking for. He raises the foil packet up between us, tearing the edge of it open with his teeth. Now, he finally has to pull his eyes away from me as he looks down at what he's doing. I keep my eyes on his face, watching his brow furrow and his tongue poke out of the corner of his mouth in concentration as he pulls out the condom and rolls it onto himself.

He must have successfully figured it out, because now his eyes are back on my face and he's slowly laying us back down. I can feel both our hearts hammering against our pressed together chests, and it feels like it creates the perfect rhythm for whatever dance we're about to do. Robbie swallows hard, reaching one shaky hand between us, guiding his length to my entrance. He doesn't press into me right away, but simply against me, running his swollen tip through my slick folds. And just that alone sends a sensation through me that I've never felt before, a whine bursting out of me and my muscles tightening up.

"Baby, I need you to trust me," Robbie whispers. "Can you do that?"

"Yes," I answer instantly.

"I need you to relax."

Oh, how easy. No problem.

I try to force my body to go limp, but it's not working, my mind fighting against my muscles.

Robbie's thumb brushes my cheekbone as he places a kiss just below the hollow of my throat. "It's probably going to hurt a little at first, but you can take it."

My cheeks warm as I look up at Robbie under heavy eyelids, pride filling my chest at his words.

"Take a deep breath for me, baby," Robbie whispers.

I take the deepest breath I can manage, feeling Robbie just barely press forward as I do.

"Now, let it out. Let it all out, Cooper."

My lips part, the air blowing out of me, just as Robbie slides himself all the way inside me in one languid push.

My head falls back against the blanket. *"Oh my God."*

"Breathe, baby. Breathe," he whispers against my hair.

"I–I can't."

"You *can*," Robbie insists, turning my face so I have to meet his eyes. "You're okay. It's just me. You know you can take me, Cooper."

I bite down on my lip, nodding my head.

"I'm gonna move now, okay, baby?" Robbie says.

"Okay," I breathe.

And he does.

Slow, steady, and restrained, Robbie pulls out of me just a few inches before pushing back in, repeating the motion several times. At first, it stings. I'm not sure it feels right. I'm not sure that his confidence in me is warranted, because I really *don't* think I can take him.

But then, gradually, the pain starts to fade, replaced by something else entirely. And suddenly it feels more right than anything else in the world.

"Oh, *wow…*" I murmur.

"*That's my girl,*" Robbie drawls, his fingers gripping my hip.

His speed increases as I grow more comfortable, Robbie reading the way my body responds to him like a book. If Robbie liked my sounds before, he must be having a field day now as I feel completely out of control of my mouth, moans and whines and gasps slipping out with every thrust he makes inside of me.

Robbie looks down at me, his nose grazing mine as he watches me. At the same moment, his forearms hook around my thighs, dragging me closer and changing the angle just slightly, hitting an entirely new spot inside me that makes me feel euphoric. My hands shoot out, grabbing at any part of him that I can. I grasp at his shoulders and the back of his neck, but it doesn't feel like enough, and I hear myself let out a frustrated breath. Robbie's movements slow down as I do so, his lips pressing together and eyes squinting. And then, before I even realize what's happening, Robbie's reaching up and grabbing both of my hands and pushing them into his hair, using his fingers around my own to thread into his brunette locks. And it's not until he pulls his own hands away that my eyes go wide, realizing what he's done.

"Robbie, I–"

"It's okay," he nods, reassuring me.

"But–"

"I want you to, Cooper," he says, his eyes full of sincerity and his mouth pulled up into a small smile.

I roll my lips into my mouth, fighting at the tears threatening my eyes. "Okay," I nod, grabbing two handfuls of Robbie's hair as he sinks back into me all the way to the hilt. I give the strands of his hair a tug as I moan, pulling a groan from Robbie like I've never heard before.

"Cooper, I'm so close," he tells me.

"Ah– okay. That's okay," I stammer, feeling unable to come up with anymore words.

Robbie kisses me hard. "I'm only coming if you're coming with me," he says, pressing his forehead to mine and staring into my eyes as he drops his hand between us, pressing his fingers against me and circling that sensitive spot while he pumps into me faster than ever before. It only takes a few seconds before my vision blurs, every muscle in the lower half of my body tightening up before I come apart, fireworks shooting off behind my eyes and an explosion going off in my lower abdomen.

"*Robbie!*" I cry.

I just barely hear the whisper of "*Sara Beth*" against my lips before Robbie collapses on top of me.

I don't know how much time goes by as the two of us just lay there, Robbie's breath fanning against my neck and my fingers running gently through his hair.

"Are you okay?" Robbie eventually asks me, his voice quiet.

"Yes," I whisper. "I'm just..."

Robbie pushes up, bracing himself on his elbow. "What?" he questions me, his eyes filled with worry.

I let out a sigh. "I'm just wondering two things."

"Okay," Robbie says. "What are they?"

I reach up, tracing the outline of his lips. "Well, the first is, how do you ever expect me to be able to work a shift here again?"

The concern melts from Robbie's face as he lets out a chuckle. "I guess I didn't really think this through," he tells me. "I guess you'll just have to avoid this aisle."

"Oh, the romance and comedy aisle? Sure. It's not like anybody ever checks these movies out anyways," I deadpan, knowing they're easily our most popular rentals.

Robbie tuts. "Is it horrible if I'm not that sorry?"

"No," I laugh. "Because I'm not either."

"You're not?" he smirks.

I shake my head. "It's pretty epic to lose your virginity in a movie rental store if you ask me."

Robbie's tongue presses into his bottom lip. "Better add that to your stories."

I blink at him, a smile spreading across my face.

Stories.

Not diary.

"What was the other thing?" Robbie asks.

"*Hmm?*"

"The second thing you were wondering."

"Oh," I mutter, warmth spreading across my cheeks as I almost wish I could take back telling him there were two things.

"Cooper?"

"Uh...I was just gonna ask you...if it...if that..."

Robbie tilts his head. "What, baby?"

I blow a breath out of my nose, forcing myself to meet his eyes. "I was going to ask you if that's what it's usually like. If it was...good for you."

Robbie's lips press together, his eyes searching my face. I can hear my blood pumping inside my ears, and I start to think about telling him to forget it, but then Robbie speaks up. "It was absolutely incredible for me, Cooper."

"Oh," is all I can think to say before Robbie covers my lips with his, sweeping his tongue against the seam of my mouth and kissing me like he can't ever get enough of me.

"And, no," he whispers against my lips before pulling back to trail kisses across my jaw, "it's never like that."

ROBBIE

"Robbie, *please*," Cooper groans.

"Come on, Cooper," I whisper into the side of her neck. "Come with me. You know you want to."

"I can't."

I wrap my arms around her waist, pulling her back flush to me, moving my lips to the edge of her ear. "Do you have to be such a good girl all the time?"

"I think you've made sure that I'm not," she breathes, turning her head to press a kiss to my lips. "But, unfortunately, the yearbook isn't going to finish itself."

I let out a sigh as she pulls out of my grasp, turning back to the pile of pages laid out on the table before her.

I move to stand against the wall to the side, crossing my arms and leaning against it as I just watch her, a smirk pulling at my lips.

It's 4:30 p.m. on a Monday, and while every other student is long gone for the day, Cooper's still here at school, holed up in the yearbook room with no plans of leaving any time soon.

She's taking her duties as yearbook editor very seriously (*as if anything else would be expected*), reviewing each and every page she already meticulously planned and curated for the hundredth time now, making sure there's not a single error or way in which it could possibly be made better. You'd think she was organizing a precious historical museum exhibit or creating the most important issue of *Rolling Stone* or *Vogue* that the world has ever seen rather than a small town high school yearbook. But I suppose that's the thing about Cooper. Anything she works on is important. Anything she creates has to be the best in her eyes, or it's not even worth creating. It's not something I've ever related to, and it's certainly something I would have rolled my eyes at a few months back, but now, I can at least appreciate it. And I can certainly admire her while she does it.

I watch Cooper pick up two pages that look exactly the same to me, her brows pulling deeply together and her head swiveling back and forth between the two of them. Eventually, she seems to give up on them for now, blowing out a frustrated breath as she sets them off to the side, reaching for a box full of photos on the table to sort through. I discreetly sneak up behind her, looking over her shoulder and seeing that the pictures she's rifling through are ones she's taken at basketball games. I can't help but smile, thinking of our championship game just last week.

That was the first game where Cooper wore her *Bleacher Babe* t-shirt by choice, my last name and number proudly plastered across her back for the whole world to see as she stood on the sidelines taking photos. We may have lost the championship, and my final game as a student athlete, but I won that day. Because I got to take Cooper under the bleachers after the game and show her how much of a babe I really thought she was. Let's just say, curls of red hair fanning out over *Summers* and the number 24 is an image that won't be leaving my brain for a *very* long time.

It's been about three weeks since me and Cooper's Groovy Movie date, and three weeks since the two of us have stopped playing games. And, *God*, they may have been the best three weeks of my life so far.

We can't get enough of each other. I drive her to school every day and, by five minutes into first period, I'm already missing her.

We practically jump into each other's arms by the time we rejoin for Ms. Cage's class second period, then I barely scrape by through third period, bouncing my knee and staring at the clock until I get to see her again at lunch.

If I thought I had it bad for Cooper when we weren't together, I'm absolutely down for the count now. But I'm definitely not the only one. Even though she still likes to keep me on my toes from time to time and pretend like she isn't head over heels obsessed with me too, I know Cooper feels the same way.

She's been different the last few weeks, more carefree, less tense. The yearbook and school newspaper still mean the world to her, and I still catch her scribbling in her journal at least a few times a week, but, otherwise, she's really managed to let go. She's just been going with the flow, not constantly concerned with consequences and all the possible outcomes of every situation. And, even though it's not necessarily what I'm used to when it comes to Cooper, I have to say, I think it looks good on her.

I set my chin on Cooper's shoulder as she looks between two different pictures of me shooting a ball.

"Which one is your favorite?" she asks.

I take a moment to look between the two, then tap the left one with my finger.

"Me too," Cooper agrees, and I feel her smiling against my cheek. "You can see more of your face in this one."

"It's a pretty great face," I say.

"You know, I can't disagree." She looks between the pictures a couple of more times before setting down the one in her right hand on top of the page spread about the basketball team. My brows pull together in confusion, but then I see her fold the picture in her left hand in half, slipping it into her pocket.

"*Sara Cooper*," I gasp dramatically, spinning her around to face me. "That has to go against some sort of moral ethics code of yearbook editors everywhere."

"Oh well," she shrugs, looping her arms around my neck. "I

guess I'll just have to be selfish this one time. I would think you'd say rules are meant to be broken anyways."

I give her a grin, reaching down and lifting her up so that she's sitting on the table in front of me. "Do you think it would break any more rules if we hooked up on top of the yearbook proof pages?"

Cooper laughs, her head falling back. "Absolutely," she nods emphatically. "And even your face isn't worth going that far for."

"*Liar*," I whisper, nipping at her earlobe.

She shakes her head, giggling as she wiggles out of my hold, her feet landing flat on the ground. "I need to get back to work," she chuckles.

"No," I grumble, grabbing her face and kissing her. "Come get a burger with me."

"Robbie..." she shakes her head.

"Cooper."

"I really need to keep going," she insists, but kisses me back. "I was already supposed to have the final pages sent to print by last Friday."

"So, what's another day?"

Cooper blows a breath out of her nose. "And even after I finish this...I really need to study for my physics test this evening."

"And you will. After you eat dinner," I tell her, earning me a pointed look. "What, Cooper? You gotta eat."

She sighs, and when she looks up at me, I know I have her.

"Ten more minutes," she says. "And then we can go get dinner."

"*Five*," I correct her, pressing a kiss to her forehead before taking a step back.

"Fine," Cooper agrees, rolling her eyes with a smirk before spinning back around to the pages and photos.

She starts sorting through pages again when I move to her side, bracing my arms on the edge of the table and leaning my backside against it, letting her work for about thirty more seconds before I speak up again.

"While I have you agreeing to things..."

Cooper stiffens, blinking at the page in her hands for a few seconds before looking up at me. "Yes, Robbie?" she questions me.

I roll my lips into my mouth, fighting a grin. "I need you to go to Senior Prom with me."

I can see Cooper immediately gearing up to protest, but I don't give her the chance, rambling on.

"It's the week before graduation, so you have no excuses. The yearbooks will already have been handed out by then and there will be no more tests left to study for or schoolwork to stress over."

Cooper's lips part and then close again, making it seem like I stole the words right out of her mouth. She tilts her head at me "Haven't you been to enough dances?"

"With you? No." I reach out and grab her hand, pulling her closer. "Never."

She stares at me for several seconds, a smile tilting up the corners of her mouth. "Fine," she eventually agrees.

"*Yes*," I cheer, pumping my fist in the air before pulling her in to smack a wet kiss on her cheek.

Cooper chuckles, wiping at her cheek as she pulls back from me. "Geez, don't make me change my mind, Summers."

"Not an option," I tell her.

She breathes out a laugh. "Okay, fine. Now, let me just do one more thing–" She starts to turn back to the pages but I stand up, pulling her by the arm.

"Robbie, I–"

"Nope," I shake my head, reaching down and throwing her over my shoulder, making my way to the door. "You're coming with me."

"*Robbie!*" she squeals, chuckling. "I need to finish the yearbook!"

"There's always tomorrow," I say, patting her back as we make it into the empty hallway. "Let's go finish something else instead."

fifty-one

SARA

I try to take in the world around me in the mornings, tilting my head back to the feel the sun on my face and breathing in the cool spring breeze, but I can't, because he's invaded my every sense, the sun doing nothing to compare to the warmth I feel from him and the air around me having nothing on the blend of amber, spice, and wood that makes up his addicting, all-consuming scent.

I try to sit still in class, but all I can focus on is his touch forever lingering on my skin, his lips at my ear and his hands around my waist sending shivers running through me.

I try to look at what's in front of me, but, when I blink, all I see is him, those chocolate brown eyes and the most infuriating yet elating smirk forever in my sight.

I try to listen, but all I hear is—

"*Ms. Cooper?*"

"Yes?" I jolt, my vision coming back into focus as I zero in on my physics teacher, Mr. Norman, with his hands on his hips and a scowl on his face directed right at me.

"Ah, fourth time's the charm apparently today," he says, chuckling uncomfortably. "I was asking you if you could tell the class the answer to the final question on yesterday's homework assignment."

"Oh..." I mutter, pushing my hair behind my ear. "No, sir. I'm sorry. I can't."

Mr. Norman's graying brows shoot up. "Eh...excuse me?" he asks.

"I didn't get a chance to finish yesterday's homework yet," I tell him. "Sorry, Mr. Norman."

His eyes widen at me. "Well, okay, Ms. Cooper. That's... surprising. But I suppose we can't be rock stars every day. Just finish it and turn it in as soon as you can please."

"Yes, sir. I will," I nod.

"Does anyone else know the answer?" Mr. Norman asks.

Mary Ann Douglas promptly raises her hand from the back of the classroom and apparently gives him the answer he was looking for. I'm not sure what it is though, since I've found myself zoned out again.

I vaguely make out Mr. Norman asking Mary Ann to pass back last week's exams while the rest of the class does...*something*.

My mind just barely starts working through the possibilities of what Robbie and I could do this weekend when I hear a distinct hiss from my right.

"*Pssst!*"

I zero in on the clock on the wall in front of me. Just ten minutes until this class is over. Ten minutes until I get to go meet Robbie by the locker room entrance before he goes to off-season basketball practice and I go to algebra.

"*Pssst!*" the annoying sound echoes into my ear once again, this time joined with something bouncing off the side of my head.

"*What the hell?*" I mutter, snapping out of my trance and turning to find Alice staring at me from her desk, arm cocked to throw another wadded up sheet of notebook paper in my direction.

"What are you doing?" I question her.

"Seeing if you're okay," she says, her brows pinched like my questioning her made absolutely no sense.

"By throwing things at me?"

"Desperate times call for desperate measures," Alice says.

"What are you talking about?" I chuckle.

Alice narrows her eyes at me, lifting up her desk and scooting it over so that it's lined up directly with mine.

"Okay, ever heard of personal space?"

"Sara, what's the matter with you?"

"What?" I ask at the same moment Mary Ann drops off my exam on top of my desk.

Alice's eyes trail from my face over to the piece of paper in front of me, leaning in to look at it with me.

"Oh my gosh," she gasps lightly, covering her mouth. "Sara, I'm sorry. Are you okay?"

I look at her with knitted brows. "Um, yes? Why?"

"Your grade!" she exclaims.

"It's only a B," I tell her, picking up my binder from the floor and shoving the paper inside.

Alice barks out a laugh. "It's a B -. *Minus*."

"Thank you, Alice. I can actually read, believe it or not."

Her mouth falls open. "And you're okay with that?"

"Why wouldn't I be?"

"Because a B- is a cause for celebration in Alice Quinn's world," she says. "But in Sara Cooper's world, that's an act of war."

I stare back at her, blinking.

Alice leans forward, placing the back of her palm against my forehead. "Are you feeling okay?" she asks.

"*Yes*," I say, chuckling but getting somewhat irritated. "I don't get why you're freaking out so much."

"Because Sara..." Alice shakes her head. "I'm worried about you."

"Why?"

"Because you haven't been yourself lately."

My spine steels. "What does that even mean?"

"I don't know," Alice admits, her voice low. "You just seem...

distracted. Unfocused. Like you're just floating through life. It just seems like...." she trails off, blowing out a breath.

"What?" I push.

"It just seems like...ever since you got back Robbie...you're–"

"*Happy?*" I supply.

Alice's lips press together. "I mean... Yes. Of course you're happy. But–"

"But what, Alice?"

"I don't know!" she shrugs. "You're just not you."

"And what am *I?*" I ask. "Quiet? Sad? Lonely? Focused solely on school and work? Doing nothing fun? Just waiting around for you and only you to give me the time of day?"

"What?" Alice rears back. "Sara, no. That's not what I'm saying at all."

"Then what is it?" I demand. "Because, I swear, Alice, I'm starting to feel like I'll never make you happy."

"What is that supposed to mean?" she questions me.

I blow out a frustrated breath. "At the beginning of this year, you wanted things to be different, for me to be pushed outside of my comfort zone. Well, I did that. I ran for president. I got with Robbie. But, after the dust settled on that situation, once I was actually with Robbie, you were certainly lightning fast about running to me when you saw a chance for us to break up–"

"Sara, are you serious–"

"So, we break up," I continue. "But then, you start telling me I'm not *glowing* anymore. So you force me to go out, which results in me and Robbie getting back together and me being the happiest I've been in a long time. And now, you think I've changed? Now, you're still not happy with me?"

Alice shakes her head. "Sara–"

"So what is it, Alice? Because I don't understand what you want from me. I mean, is it just so unbelievably shocking to you that I'm actually with someone? That you're not the only one with a boyfriend now? That you're not the only person I have?"

"What's unbelievably shocking to me is how much of a bitch you're being right now," Alice growls.

I stiffen, my mouth falling open.

Alice ducks her head to speak to me. "Sara, I don't even know where this is coming from," she whisper-shouts. "I was so happy for you when you first got with Robbie. Hell, I encouraged it, maybe even instigated it. And I was more than supportive of you two getting back together. Robbie is not my issue. *You* are. Because *you're* my best friend. And you have been since we were in kindergarten. So don't try to act like I don't know you. And like I wouldn't obviously know when something in you has shifted. I'm just looking out for you because I know how hard you've worked to get to where you are."

I shake my head. "I missed one homework assignment and made one B- on a test. It's perfectly normal."

"Not for you," Alice says.

We stare off for a few moments before Alice leans closer, speaking again. "When's the last time you even wrote in your journal?"

I open my mouth to respond, but the school bell ringing cuts me off.

Alice pushes her desk back to its original spot, standing up and gathering her things. I robotically grab my things as well, and, once I get to my feet, I find her standing right in front of me.

"I love you, Sara," she says. "All I've ever wanted was to see you happy, to see you glow. But you can have a new flame without putting out the rest of your fires. They took a long time to build and a whole lot of energy for you to maintain. I'd just hate to see them smolder for nothing. Just...be careful."

And, with that, Alice walks out of the classroom, leaving me standing there slack-jawed and sick to my stomach.

It's not until Mr. Norman calls my name to let me know I'm the last person still in the classroom that I turn on my heel, making my way out and into the hallway. I feel like I'm in a fuzzy haze, operating on auto-pilot as my feet automatically drag me to the entrance of the boys' locker room.

"There she is!" a familiar voice calls.

I don't have time to even look up before Robbie is scooping me up into his arms, pressing my back against the hallway wall and kissing me hard. My eyes fall shut, everything from the last fifteen minutes slowly melting away as I feel Robbie's lips on mine. It's like I'm a toy that he's pressed the reset button on to return me to my factory settings. And when my arms wrap around his neck, it's like everything is back to normal, totally right in the world.

"Hey," Robbie says as he sets me back down on my feet.

"Hi there," I reply.

The grin on Robbie's face twitches, his brows pulling together. "You good?" he asks.

I press my lips together, nodding. "I am now."

"Great," he smirks, kissing me again. "I'm so glad you're here."

"I'm always here," I chuckle.

"Well, I'm especially glad today," Robbie says, grabbing my hand and dragging me a few feet down the hallway away from the locker room door. "Because I have a brilliant idea."

"And what's that?"

"We skip."

I tilt my head at him. "What?"

"I'm a senior. My basketball career is officially over. I'm washed up. I don't need to practice anymore. So let's skip seventh period." Robbie starts walking, pulling my hand behind him, but I don't move, making his feet come to a stop.

"What?" he asks.

"I have algebra seventh period."

"Yeah," Robbie says. "And you hate algebra. So that makes this an even more perfect plan."

My lips part. "What would we do?"

Robbie pushes my hair out of my face, cupping my cheek. "That's the thing, Cooper. We can do whatever we want. And," he adds, leaning down to whisper in my ear, "since it's Monday and you don't have work tonight, we can do whatever we want *all* night."

He pulls back, waggling his eyebrows at me, and I have to bite my lower lip to stifle a laugh. When I don't respond right away, Robbie's expression turns slightly more serious. "Or, you know, until midnight. Or ten. Whatever Sherri prefers

"Sherri doesn't really have many rules for me," I chuckle.

Because I've never given her a reason to.

"I knew I liked her," Robbie grins. "So, what do you say?"

I look up at him, my eyes searching his face.

There's a voice in the back of my mind telling me that this is a bad idea. Telling me that the reason I hate algebra is because it's my worst subject. That I'm already stressed for our final exam in a few weeks and missing a class would only set me behind further. That I haven't checked in on my grade point average in the last month or so and that I wouldn't want to let myself get too lazy with so little time left to go. It's suggesting to me that...*maybe Alice might have had somewhat of a point...*

But then, a stronger voice comes through. And it's real. It's Robbie, right in front of me, breathing against my ear, "*C'mon, Cooper.* It's just one class. One time."

And I can't help the way the smile that it brings to my face, pushing every other voice to the very back of my mind.

I pull back from Robbie, finding his gaze. "Fine, I'm in," I tell him. "But you better make it worth my while."

Robbie leans down, pressing a kiss to my lips before turning and pulling me along behind him, all the way out of the school and to his Camaro.

"I won't let you down, Cooper," he says as he starts the engine.

And he doesn't.

The afternoon honestly feels like a blur. One happy, blissful, euphoria-filled afternoon.

We get chocolate milkshakes. We stop and eat them in a park that I used to play at as a little kid. We talk about movies, about the ones that have made us laugh the most, the ones that have made us cry, and everything in between. I tell Robbie about the books that have been most popular at the school library recently, and about the ones I've been reading lately.

At some point, San Francisco is brought up and, when I say that I haven't been since I was a little kid, Robbie declares that we are driving there right this second. We make the forty-five minute drive, listening to *Frontiers* from top to bottom. And then, when we reach the city, we drive around for hours, stopping to park a few times for one reason or another, our final stop being a lookout point for the Golden Gate Bridge.

When we get there, Robbie switches out one Journey tape for another, starting up *Infinity*. And when *Lights* starts playing, which is evidently a love song to San Francisco, I feel my stomach knot and the backs of my eyes burn. Because, as I sit here on the hood of Robbie's Camaro with his arm around me, like the most perfect movie scene you could ever imagine, watching the lights go down in the city and the sun shining on the bay, I really do feel like I want to be here, in my city, and I wonder why exactly it is that I have been so intent on getting out of it.

We stay there, my head on Robbie's shoulder until the sun dips completely below the bay. And then even for a little while after. Eventually, the temperature drops due to the lack of sun and the breeze off the water below, and we decide to get back in the car. We make our way back towards Bay View, stopping for pizza along the way at a local mom and pop shop. And when we finally cross the city line of our small town around half past nine, the *Welcome to Bay View!* sign coming into view, I'm not at all ready for the night to end.

And luckily, Robbie doesn't seem to be ready either.

"You down for one more stop, Cooper?" he asks.

"What do you have in mind?"

He leans over, kissing my temple. "How about we let it be a surprise?"

Even though I usually hate surprises, I decide to just go with it. If the surprise of Robbie storming his way into my life worked out this well, I think it's best I allow them more often.

It's about ten minutes later when we're pulling up to a dark strip center in our main town square.

I used to come to this area all the time with my mom when I was younger, especially since Dolly's Diner where she works is right down the street, but it's been quite a while since the last time we each had a day off and time to spend together. From what I can tell, the square looks a little different than I remember, a few of the shops having switched out and others gone entirely. The fact that it's nearly black outside doesn't help me much in knowing for sure though. Since it's nearly ten on a Monday night, the place is a ghost town, all of the business closed and lights shut off. If we stayed here long enough, I half wonder if I'd see a tumbleweed roll by.

Robbie shuts the engine off once he's parked against the curb, and he opens his door, motioning for me to do the same.

I follow his lead, walking up to the front door of the business just to the side of his car. It's hard to read the writing on the door in the dark, but, when I glance up at the wooden hanging sign above us, I find the cut-out of a record hanging down.

"Where are we?" I ask. "A record store?"

Robbie leans in towards the front door, cupping his hands around his face and peering inside. "You know Billy Montgomery?" he asks, pulling back from the door once I assume he's confirmed the store is empty.

"Yeah, of course."

"Well," he says, standing up on his tiptoes, reaching up and running his hand across the top of the door frame. "This may be his older sister's shop."

"Oh?"

"And I may just know that she leaves a spare key out."

I raise my brows at him. "From previous experience?"

A grin flashes across Robbie's face as his arm stills. He drops back flat on his feet, flashing me a little gold key. "Perhaps," he says.

I shake my head as Robbie moves to unlock the door. "Is this a good idea?" I ask. "I mean, do you have permission to be in there?"

"Well, considering that Billy has permission to be in there, and considering that he has previously brought me and some of the guys here after hours..." Robbie stops speaking for a moment, waiting for the lock to click. "I'd say that basically means yes." A huge smile spreads across his face as he reaches for the door knob, turning it and pushing the door open. He motions his arm in a grand gesture, inviting me to walk inside.

"I'm not sure Billy's sister would agree with you. Or the police," I chuckle, walking past him in the doorway.

"But you'll go with it?" Robbie asks, closing the door behind him.

"Don't I always?"

Robbie uses the dim light of the single street lamp outside to find his way behind the check-out counter, flipping on a couple of light switches so that we're not in complete darkness anymore. When he does, the bright red and black mural reading *Monty's Records* is illuminated on the wall behind the counter. I stand back, admiring it as Robbie moves over to where the nicest record player setup I think I've ever seen in person is sitting just to the side of the painting, getting it started up.

"Pick a record, Cooper," Robbie says.

"Uh, me?"

He turns to look at me over his shoulder. "Is there another Cooper here I should know about?"

"No," I laugh. "I just never thought you'd pass over the responsibility of picking out music to me."

"Well, it's your lucky day."

"I'm not sure I've ever felt this much power," I say. "I'm not sure what to do with it."

Robbie shakes his head, hiding a grin. "Walk your pretty ass around this store and bring me something to play. Today, please."

"Fine, but only because you said I was pretty." I bat my eyelashes dramatically, ignoring his snort of laughter as I spin away, making my way into the aisles of records to choose from.

It only takes a minute or so of perusing the options until my gaze lands on one of the records I was hoping to find. I reach forward, plucking the black and white album from its place on the shelf and working my way back over to Robbie, proudly holding it out to him like a child showing one of their parents their latest art project from school.

Robbie's eyebrows raise when his eyes land on the record, looking from it up to me. "Tears For Fears?" he asks.

"Mhmm," I nod, crossing my arms and leaning against the table the record player is set up on.

Robbie lets out a whistle. "*Songs from the Big Chair*. Great choice, Cooper."

"I know, right?"

Robbie laughs, reaching up and wrapping his hand around my neck, joking for a second like he's going to strangle me before he instead pulls me in for a kiss.

After he releases me, he turns back to the album in his hands, removing the vinyl from the sleeve and placing it on the turntable. Once it starts spinning, he glances down at the back of the album cover before lifting the tonearm, setting it to play a specific song.

When *Everybody Wants to Rule the World* starts playing, a massive grin spreads across my face. I let out a sigh, tipping my head back as Robbie cranks up the volume.

"You like this song, Cooper?" Robbie asks.

"No," I shake my head, staring up at the ceiling. "I just think it may be the greatest one ever made."

"Well then," Robbie asks, tugging on my hand and making me look at him, "why the hell aren't we dancing to it?"

I let out a chuckle as I let him pull me towards him, spinning me around as he sings along to the intro lyrics. I join right in, swinging side to side with him and belting out the words at the top of my lungs, feeling so free with no one around to see us.

We start dancing our way through the aisles, signing to each other like we're two kids in a music video, acting like total goofballs and loving every second of it. I throw my hands in the air, snapping my fingers and swaying my hips while Robbie whips his head back and forth like he's a frontman on stage. By halfway through the song, I have a sheen of sweat coating my brow and Robbie's hairstyle is perfectly destroyed. He grabs my hand once more, spinning me into him, and I crash against his chest with laughter, my mouth finding his.

We stay that way for a few moments, our bodies still moving to the music but our lips locked, until a flash of light catches our attention and we're pulling back from one another.

We both look towards the front of the store, trying to find where the light may have come from. Robbie's eyes squint and then widen when he catches sight of headlights coming into view from down the road.

"*Shit*," he mutters.

"What?" I ask. "Do you think it's anyone we know?"

"Better to be safe than sorry," Robbie murmurs. "Stop the music, will you, baby?" He asks, squeezing my shoulders before letting me go and bolting towards the front door.

"Uh– I– Okay," I nod, stumbling over to where the record player sits. I shove the arm off of the spinning record with a loud scratch, internally cringing as Robbie visibly cringes, flicking the lock closed on the door.

"Sorry," I wince.

"I'll get over it," Robbie says as he jogs over to me. "Now, get down." He places his hand on my back and motions for me to crawl behind the counter.

"Should we turn off the lights first?" I ask.

Robbie shakes his head. "They would've already seen the lights. They're the only ones on in this whole strip center. Even though we only turned on a few, I'm sure this place looks like a beacon. We'll just draw more attention by turning them off now."

"Okay," I nod, thinking that makes sense. I glance over Robbie's shoulder, seeing the car approaching and realization hitting me. "Oh my God, Robbie, I think that's a cop car."

Robbie doesn't hesitate as he crouches down, bringing me with him. "It's fine. We're fine," he says, settling us behind the counter. "If they can't see us, they'll just assume Billy's sister accidentally left her lights on. The door's locked. They can't come in."

"Okay," I breathe, nodding. "Yeah, we're fine."

I hear the distinct sound of a car coming to a stop not too far away, followed by an engine being shut off. I swallow hard.

Totally fine.

A few seconds go by before Robbie starts inching towards the edge of the counter.

I grab his arm. *"What are you doing?"* I mouth, barely audible.

"Just checking. It's fine," Robbie whispers back, and I'm wondering at this point if he keeps saying it's fine because it's true or if it's for his own benefit.

He slowly leans over, just barely peeking around the corner before he snaps his head back. *"Goddammit,"* he grits.

"What is it?"

"Fucking Strothers," he mutters.

"Paul?" I question him, my brows pinching.

Robbie shakes his head. "No. His dad, who's an even bigger dick than he is."

"Oh my God," I whisper, covering my mouth with my hand.

"It's fine," Robbie murmurs. "Just give him a minute to feel like he's doing something. He'll eventually get bored and leave."

I try to sit still for a few moments, but the seconds feel like they're ticking by like hours. I keep glancing from the edge of the counter to Robbie's face. Then, slowly, as if we decided it telepathically, we both inch our way over, peering around the corner once more, my head below Robbie's.

I have to keep myself from letting out a gasp as I see an older, more burly version of Paul shining a flashlight into the store window. Luckily, he turns away only a second later, and my shoulders instantly drop in relief. Robbie reaches for my hand, squeezing it. I assume Officer Strothers is heading back to his car, but instead, he walks the opposite direction, making a beeline for where Robbie's Camaro is parked just in front of the store.

"That son of a..." Robbie grits, biting his knuckle.

Officer Strothers shines his flashlight into the front windshield of Robbie's car, then walks around it, bending down and looking in the driver's side window.

"Does he know that's your car?" I whisper.

"Everybody knows that's my car," Robbie responds, shaking his head. "And it definitely doesn't help that he's pulled me over in it a time or two."

"A time or two?" I ask, raising a brow.

"Or ten. What's the difference?" Robbie deadpans, keeping his eyes on the window.

"Robbie…"

"It's fine," he repeats. "The asshole sort of has it out for me, but he can't do anything with what he's found tonight. He didn't see us, and it's not illegal to park your car in our public town square."

I nod my head, chewing on my bottom lip as we watch Office Strothers make his third lap around Robbie's car. After his fourth trip around, and after one more glance inside the store, he seems to be frustrated, but content, making his way back to his police car.

Once he finally starts his engine and drives away until his taillights are no longer visible, Robbie and I let out matching sighs of relief.

"I'm sorry about that, Cooper," Robbie says. "It was stupid, coming here. I wasn't thinking."

When I don't respond right away, he reaches for my face, pushing my hair out of my eyes.

"Cooper, are you okay?"

I look between his eyes for several long seconds before a full blown laugh bursts out of me.

Robbie rears back, caught off guard. "What is it?" he questions me.

I shake my head, continuing to chuckle. "It's just…"

"What, Cooper?"

"That was kind of fun," I admit.

Robbie breathes out a laugh. "Are you serious?"

"Yeah, I think I am," I nod, placing a hand on my chest. "My heart is racing."

"Okay, adrenaline junkie," Robbie chuckles, his brows pulled together. "Who are you?"

"I don't know," I say. "But I think I like it."

ROBBIE

"Nope. Absolutely not."

"Oh, come on," I say.

"Robbie," Cooper sighs. "I'm not doing it."

"Why not?"

"Because it doesn't fit," she insists.

"If you don't think this fits, you're not the person I thought you were," I tell her.

Cooper spins away from the bulletin board, putting her hands on her hips. "And please explain how not adding *The Empire Strikes Back* to our plan for summer movie showings makes me someone different than who you thought I was?"

I lean against the check-out counter, cocking my head at her. "Because you're clearly not the exceptionally cultured film connoisseur I've had you pinned for all along."

Cooper scoffs out a laugh, running a hand down her face. "Robbie, it's not a summer movie."

"Explain to me how it's not."

"Explain to me how it *is*," she shoots back.

"It came out in the summertime."

She leans back, raising her brows. "So?"

"*So*," I throw my hands in the air, "it's a summer movie!"

Cooper shakes her head. "That really isn't how this works though. It's not about when the movie was released, it's about the feelings it gives off. You know, the vibes?"

"And what about interstellar rebellion doesn't give off summer vibes to you, Cooper?"

Her mouth falls open, then shuts again as she tries not to laugh. "Maybe if there were a few more beaches–"

Cooper doesn't get a chance to finish her weak argument as she's cut off by the bell on Groovy Movie's front door ringing as someone flings it open, barrelling inside.

We both spin around to find the source of the commotion, and, when we do, Cooper and I have very different reactions, her brows bunching together while a huge smile breaks across my face.

"Sherri," I grin, while Cooper questions, "*Mom?*"

Sherri Cooper comes stumbling towards the front counter like a bat out of hell, her hair disheveled and her waitressing uniform all out of sorts. "Hi, hon. Hi, Robbie."

I nod, the smile still on my face, which she quickly returns before turning back to her daughter.

Cooper's mom may have been hesitant when she first learned we were back together. Apparently, Cooper had given her a basic rundown of our history, which didn't paint me in the best possible light, but Sherri's always had a bit of a soft spot for me. And I'm thankful for that.

"Mom, what is it?" Cooper demands.

Her mom only pauses for a second once she reaches us to catch her breath, not saying a word before she slams some type of paper down on the counter.

"What..." Cooper begins, but trails off once she leans forward to look at what Sherri brought. It only takes a moment after I take a closer look as well for me to realize the paper she's brought is actually an envelope, and it only takes another second for me to immediately recognize the purple stamp from the sender.

NYU.

"I have to go to work," Sherri rasps. "I'm so late already, but this just came in the mail, and I won't be able to focus my entire shift if I don't know whether or not you've opened it. So please, open it."

Cooper's eyes flick from the envelope up to her mother's face, and then to mine.

I give her a nod. "Open it, Cooper."

She swallows hard, pushing her hair out of her face before she picks up the envelope with shaky hands, slowly tearing the edge open and pulling out the paper inside.

I feel Sherri and I gradually lean closer to both Cooper and each other as we watch her gray eyes scan over the words, not giving a single indication as to what any of them say. I halfway have the urge to reach out and grab Sherri's hand because I'm buzzing with so much anticipation and feel like I just need something to steady me.

I had no idea this was about to happen, but whatever Cooper reads on that piece of paper, whatever the outcome of her scholarship application is, it means big things. It determines so much for her and her future. What she'll do...where she'll be. There's a lot riding on this. And I'm not sure I've really allowed myself to think through all of the possible outcomes of this exact moment until now. And I just don't know what to feel.

I just need to know.

Whatever the answer is.

Based on the movement of Cooper's eyes, it seems like she's read through the entire paper once and has returned to the top to start over. After she reaches the bottom for the second time, the crease between her eyebrows deepening further, Sherri takes the plunge for both of us, grabbing my hand and squeezing hard.

"What does it say, hon?" she asks.

"I...I can't believe this..." Cooper mutters, shaking her head.

It feels like my heart sinks in my chest, dropping straight into my stomach.

"Did you not get the scholarship?" I ask.

She blinks at the paper a few times before raising her gaze to mine. Her eyes have a clear sheen in them, and that only makes the knot in my gut twist further.

"No," she breathes, shaking her head.

And now it's my turn to squeeze Sherri's hand. In fact, I'm pretty sure I squeeze it so hard that she'll have faint nail marks embedded in her skin, but she doesn't seem to notice or mind. Probably because she's feeling the same things as me.

Disbelief.

Disappointment.

Devastation.

I wasn't sure how I felt about knowing that Cooper would officially be heading to NYU in the fall, but now that it feels like that opportunity was ripped right out from under her– the opportunity I know she's worked incredibly hard for and sacrificed so much to achieve– I'm gutted. I'm furious *for* her. She deserves it more than anyone. She deserves the world. The world deserves *her*. To see what she's capable of.

"I got it."

My head snaps up.

"*What?*" Sherri and I both say at the same time, dropping each other's hands and moving around the corner of the counter to get closer to Cooper.

"I got it," she repeats.

She got it?

A smile slowly spreads across my face, every ounce of rage and dismay I just felt melting off of me.

But then I look at Cooper's face, and I can't help but feel confused. Because, if she really got the scholarship...

Why doesn't she look thrilled?

"And..." Cooper starts, but doesn't continue, tilting her head at the paper.

Sherri lets out something between a squeal and a yelp from beside me, waving her hands in the air. "And *what?*"

She looks up at her mom, her throat bobbing. "And...um..." she glances back at the paper, squinting her eyes as if she's not quite believing what she's reading, "they were so impressed with my application that they've also extended me an offer to come to New York early for an advanced creative writing summer program. Fully funded by the university, boarding included."

A beat of silence passes between us before Sherri asks the exact question standing out in my mind, "How early?"

Cooper sets the paper down on the counter. "The program starts two weeks after graduation."

A few moments go by as we all take in this information, Cooper seeming, oddly enough, to be having a harder time with it than any of us. But then, Sherri breaks the ice first, a cheer bursting out of her as she starts jumping up and down, clapping her hands together. She flits her way around me, scooping up her daughter in her arms and hugging her tight to her chest. And when she pulls back to kiss Cooper's cheek, tears are clear in her eyes.

"I'm so proud of you, hon," she says, beaming. "We'll talk more about this tonight when I get home, or first thing tomorrow morning if you're already asleep when I get there. I wish I could stay here celebrating with you for the rest of the night, but I have to go to work now."

Sherri steps back, giving a little shake of her hips. "Mama's gonna go get lots of tips tonight so that we can buy you a fresh new wardrobe for New York City," she tells Cooper, giving her a wink.

"Mom, really, you don't have to worry about that—"

"It's no worry at all. You deserve every bit of it, hon. It's the least I can do to reward you for all your hard work." Cooper opens her mouth to protest, but Sherri cuts her off with a raise of her hand. "Now, not another word on it or I'll never leave. I love you. I'll see you at home."

And with that, Sherri blows each of us a kiss and speed walks her way out of the front door. After the door swings closed, and Cooper and I are left alone, things grow quiet, only the sound of *E.T.* playing on the TV mounted in the corner of the store breaking the silence.

I'm resting my hands against the top of the counter, my eyes on

Cooper, while she's still clutching the scholarship decision letter to her chest, her eyes wide and vacant as she stares off at the door her mom just walked out of.

Several seconds go by, and I let them. I assume Cooper must be in shock. It would make sense that she needs a minute to process. I imagine it's a pretty crazy feeling seeing all your dreams come together right before your eyes.

But, of course, that's not something I would know anything about.

I wanted to let her be the one to speak first, but I can't take it any longer.

"Wow," I breathe. "Cooper, I..." Her eyes flick up to meet mine, the rest of her body unmoving. I run a hand through my hair, shaking my head before I reach for her, placing a hand on each of her shoulders. "I am so fucking proud of you."

Cooper's throat bobs, I'm sure from what has to be welling emotions, happiness about to spill over, but something in her eyes has me waiting cautiously for her to say something.

"It's..." she begins, her voice getting lost.

"It's incredible," I supply, kissing her forehead. "Amazing."

"So...soon."

I pull back, tilting my head at her.

"The program," she says.

I swallow, ignoring the strain in my chest, forcing myself to stand tall. "Yeah," I nod. "I guess it is. But you gotta do what you gotta do."

Cooper's teeth sink into her lower lip as her wide eyes lower to the paper in her hands once more.

"If I did it...that means I'd be in New York in less than six weeks. Just a little over a month from today, really."

"Yeah," I nod, my voice tight. "I guess that's pretty crazy to think about when you look at it that way."

A few moments go by without Cooper saying anything as she just continues to stare down at the letter, re-reading it for what must be the hundredth time.

"You must be so excited," I say, not phrasing it as a question, but hoping it'll get some sort of response out of her. I give her shoulders a slight shake, making her look at me. "I mean, Cooper, this is huge."

"Yeah," she says, "it is. Definitely." She smiles tightly.

"I know how long you've thought about this. Does it not feel real yet?" I ask. "I'm sure you don't even know how to feel."

"That's for sure," she nods, her eyes trailing back down.

"What's going through your head?"

"A lot," she whispers.

"Well, give me one thing."

Cooper blows a breath out of her nose. "It's just..."

"What?" I ask her.

She meets my gaze, her lips twisting to the side. "It would just be nice to have summer, you know? One last summer before having to start it all. Just...a few more months..."

Together.

She doesn't say it, but I know it's what she's thinking, what she's telling me with her eyes. And I have no idea how to respond to it. Because I couldn't agree with her more. Summer with Cooper would be incredible. I'd give anything for a few more months with her. Hell, I'd give more than anything for just any more time I can get with her, period. But I know I can't say that. I don't even want to say that. Because it won't make this any easier. And I'm not going to be the one to discourage her from doing what's best for her, what she's worked towards for so long. It's not an option. In fact, I'm honestly shocked Cooper's even acting like it is. That she's seeming reluctant over it at all. This is all she's ever wanted.

"I know, Cooper," I tell her. I reach for her face, holding it in my hands and tipping it up so she has to look at me. I brush my thumbs across her cheeks, looking into the swirling grays of her eyes. "But you have to take it."

Cooper's eyes flick between mine, a muscle in her jaw flexing. She reaches up, pulling one of my hands away from her face, giving my palm a quick kiss before she drops it, stepping back and out of my hold.

I'm still standing in place as she turns around, folding the letter and shoving it into the back pocket of her jeans before she bends down and picks up a box of VHS tapes from the floor behind the counter.

"Would you mind helping me reshelve these?" she asks.

I tilt my head at her, wondering if I'm overthinking, but then Cooper looks up at me and smiles.

"What? Getting déjà vu?" she asks.

I snort, a smirk coming to my face. "Definitely not. You never asked me that nicely in the library."

Cooper lets out a chuckle, ducking back down behind the counter. "Well, what can I say? Some things change." When she stands back up, she has another box in her hands.

"They sure do."

We look at each other for a moment, something passing over Cooper's face that I can't read before she clears her throat, moving around the counter and heading towards the shelves with her box in hand.

"Get started, Summers. If you're gonna distract me at my place of work, you're gonna have to help me make up the time."

"Happy to help," I say, grabbing my box and following after her. "As long as none of these movies belong in the romance or comedy aisle. Not sure how much help I'll be to you if we end up there."

fifty-three

SARA

"Baby, it's going to be perfect."

I bounce on my feet, trying to stand on my tip toes to sneak a glance.

"What if they got messed up?" I ask.

"How would they have gotten messed up?" Robbie asks.

"I don't know," I mumble, chewing on my bottom lip.

We move up a spot in line. Only three people left in front of us.

"You looked over every page like a thousand times, Cooper. You proofread every word, you reviewed every photo. You went through it with a fine-toothed comb."

"But...I... *Ugh*," I groan, running an exasperated hand through my hair.

Robbie's arms wrap around my waist from behind, pulling me into his chest so he can kiss the top of my head. "It's going to be the best high school yearbook the world has ever seen."

Fortunately, I don't have any time to argue with him or stress over it further, because we're next in line.

I step up, coming face to face with Mr. Hughes and Eugene standing behind the table. "Name?" Mr. Hughes asks as his eyes are still on the clipboard in front of him. But when he looks up just a second later, a huge grin spreads across his face. "Ah, *Sara*."

"Hi, Mr. Hughes," I smile, wringing my hands together.

Eugene comes up behind Mr. Hughes, handing him two yearbooks with sticky notes on them saying my and Robbie's names.

"Thanks, Eugene," I say, giving him a nod that he returns.

Mr. Hughes shakes his head, the grin still on his face. "You should be very proud, Sara. They came out absolutely beautiful." He leans closer, dropping his voice to a whisper. "Don't tell any Bay View yearbook club alumni you might run into in town, but this is by far the best yearbook we've had in all the years I've been in charge here."

Warmth spreads across my face along with my smile. "Really?" I breathe.

Mr. Hughes nods. "All the photos you took, the write-ups, the layout, the design, the way you pulled it all together." He taps his knuckle on top of the yearbooks in his hand. "The time and love you put into it is beyond evident. You told quite the story."

My cheeks hurt from how big I'm grinning. I feel Robbie squeeze my shoulders from behind and pride instantly swirls in my chest. "Wow, thank you, sir. I'm so happy you're happy with it."

"I always knew you could do it," Mr. Hughes says, giving me a wink. "I can't believe graduation is less than two weeks away. I can't lie, I'm going to miss having you in my class, but I'm just so excited to see what you do in the future." He tilts the yearbooks up towards his face, giving them one more look over. "I expect great things from you, Sara."

"Oh..." I mutter, my throat suddenly tight. "Well, thank you, Mr. Hughes. For pushing me. For believing in me."

And in this moment, I truly mean that. I feel really proud of what I created and even more proud that someone I admire so much was impressed with it. I think about how far I've come this year. About how I never would have even had the opportunity of having creative control over the yearbook if Mr. Hughes hadn't pushed me to run for student body president. I think about the risk I took in doing it, and the many risks I added along the way in hopes of achieving my goal, and how they all worked out in the end.

But what I don't want to think about, at least not right this second, is my future Mr. Hughes is so excited about. For just a little while longer, I'd like to just live in this moment. I'd like to let myself be the high schooler I pushed so hard against being for the last four years. I don't want to think about what's to come. I don't want to think about the plane ticket to New York City that I haven't bought yet. I don't want to think about where this all ends and where something new begins. But, I think I may have realized, I'm not quite ready or willing to give up what I have here. Not just yet.

"Thank you," I tell Mr. Hughes, "for...you know, everything."

"Of course. It was my pleasure," Mr. Hughes nods. "And, I just have to say, I didn't quite see your vision when you initially wanted to go with this as the cover, but I think it came out perfectly. It's as Bay View Class of '88 as it gets."

"Thanks," I smile. "Of course, I agree. And I'm really happy with it as well."

I can sense Robbie craning his neck behind me as Mr. Hughes hands me our two yearbooks, and, once they're in my hands, his spine steels.

"Cooper..."

"Thanks, Mr. Hughes. Thanks, Eugene." I give them both a wave as I scurry away from the table, Robbie hot on my heels.

"Cooper, what the hell did you do?" he asks.

I stop in place, spinning on my heel to face him, a devilish grin on my face. I take the sticky note off of the front of Robbie's yearbook, handing it to him.

His mouth falls open as he stares down at the cover, shaking his head in disbelief.

It just has the usual title words like it does every year at the top. *Bay View High School 1987-1988 Yearbook.* But the particular photo beneath the words is what's really worth noticing.

The picture on the front shows the front parking lot of the

school on a busy morning, the sun on the horizon, just the perfect amount of clouds in the sky, and tons of students walking around in blurry fashion. The top right area of the image shows a clear view of our white, blue, and yellow Bay View High School sign with *Home of the Bears* displayed beneath it along with our mascot.

And then, front and center, is Robbie.

His shiny red Camaro takes on most of the spotlight in the picture, but, of course, everyone's eyes are going to be drawn to the boy standing next to the Camaro. The face of Bay View High if there ever was one.

Robbie stands to the side of his open car door, sunglasses on, outfit effortlessly cool, hair perfectly imperfect, sliding his headphones onto his head.

It's my favorite photo I took all year. One I impulsively took a couple of months back when the two of us weren't even speaking.

I was getting off of the bus and walking into school. I had my camera slung around my neck because it was Valentine's Day and I was planning to take photos around the school. I had made it a habit at that point of never turning my head towards the parking lot when I walked in, to just actively avoid any place I thought Robbie might be. But, for whatever reason, I went against my own rules that day.

And there he was, looking like the perfect image of high school in California in the 80s. And I just knew, I had to capture it.

"Do you like it?" I ask him.

Robbie takes the yearbook from me, shaking his head. He stares down at it for so long that I lean closer, looking down at the picture to make sure there wasn't anything I missed, something that may have made him unhappy with me using it, but I don't find anything.

"Um...Rob–"

I don't get his full name out of my mouth before he's scooping me up in his arms, kissing me hard. I wrap my arms around his neck, smiling into his mouth and chuckling as he pulls back.

"So you *do* like it?" I grin.

"I think I love you."

My body goes limp in Robbie's arms, my eyes widening.

The words just came out of his mouth as easy and gentle as a breath. I blink several times, replaying him saying them in my head so many times that the words don't even seem like words anymore, and I start to question if he even really said them.

"Did you just casually tell me you love me in the middle of the school hallway?" I ask.

Robbie's eyes flick between mine, a smirk pulling at his lips. "Shit, I guess I did."

I swallow against the lump in my throat. "So I guess it's okay if I just nonchalantly say that I love you too?"

"Only if you mean it."

I nod, slowly and then near frantically. "I do."

Robbie's smile widens, his tongue pressing against his bottom lip. "Sweet."

I try to keep my lips pressed together, but fail, bursting out in chuckles. My head falls against Robbie's chest that's also shaking with laughter as he sets me back on my feet. He leans down, brushing a kiss against my temple.

"I love the yearbook cover, Cooper. Really, it means the world to me." I pull back from his chest, smiling up at him. He brushes my hair away from my face, running his thumb over my bottom lip. "You didn't have to do that, you know."

"Don't worry, it wasn't for you," I say, making Robbie tilt his head. "And I *did* have to do it. Like Mr. Hughes said, that photo perfectly represents our school at this moment in time. And that was my job when making the yearbook. To tell our class's story. There's no Bay View High story without Robbie Summers."

Robbie sighs. "I've said it before and I'll say it again. You never stop surprising me, Sara Cooper."

I give Robbie a smile, holding out my yearbook to him. "Will you sign my yearbook?"

"Only if you sign mine."

Robbie and I exchange books, settling our backs against the wall behind us to sign each other's inside pages. We lean away from one another, poking our tongues out and making idle threats towards the other person, neither of us wanting the other to see what we're writing. By the time we each finish our messages and signatures, several basketball boys approach us, all of them asking Robbie if he'll sign their yearbook.

While Robbie's busy with that, a handful of people approach me for signatures as well. I can't help but smile as I sign their yearbooks, thinking about how, as depressing as it might sound, I never would have expected half of these people to care to remember me at the beginning of the year. In fact, the only person I ever really thought about caring if I signed their yearbook was…

"Hey."

My posture stiffens at the gentle voice behind me. I turn around slowly, finding Alice behind me, holding her yearbook open against her chest.

"Oh, hey," I say back, my voice equally quiet and hesitant.

Alice and I have barely said more than a few words to each other in the last few weeks. Ever since…whatever it was that happened between us. I'm not mad at her, but I don't know why I still feel a sharp pain in my chest when I look at her. She glances behind me, craning her neck to look for something, and I just know that something is Robbie. I can't tell if she's looking for him because she wishes he were here or if she's hoping he's far away. Either way, she smiles tightly at me now, taking a step closer.

"The yearbook looks beautiful, Sara," she says, sounding entirely sincere.

"Thank you," I tell her. I try to think of something else to say. Anything I can add. We're both quiet for a few seconds, and then both suddenly try to speak at once.

"Do you think you could–"

"Would you maybe wanna–"

We both close our mouths awkwardly.

Alice lets out an uncomfortable chuckle. "Sorry, I was just going to ask if you wanted to sign my yearbook."

"Oh, yeah. Me too. Sure," I blurt, holding my yearbook out to her.

She gives me a small smile as she takes it, handing me hers in return. I let out a breath as I flip the book open to the blank inside page. I sit there twirling my pen for a moment, trying to think of something to write. After a few seconds, I decide to sign my name further down first, hoping the perfect message will magically come to me once I've done that. It doesn't, but it doesn't matter.

Because, right after I finish signing my name, the intercom above us crackles to life, Principal Whileyman's voice coming through. "*Attention, could Ms. Sara Cooper please make her way to my office as soon as possible? That's Sara Cooper. Thank you.*"

"Uh, I got to go, I guess," I murmur, handing Alice her yearbook back. "Can I finish it later?"

"Oh, yeah. Of course," she says, clearing her throat then motioning her head up towards the intercom. "Do you know what that's about?"

"No, I'm not sure," I tell her. "But I guess I'll go find out."

She nods, handing my yearbook back to me. "Best of luck."

I push my hair behind my ear, taking it from her hands. "Thanks."

When I turn around, I find Robbie a little ways down the hall in a huddle of athletes. He looks at me from over top of the crowd, tilting his head and holding his arms in the air, clearly asking about the announcement.

I shrug, mouthing to him that I'm not sure what it's about, then motion my head towards the direction of the front office, letting him know I'll be right back.

Once I make it inside, the secretary behind the desk says hello and tells me to go right in. I thank her, making my way down the short hallway towards the principal's office.

When I approach, the door is open, and I can see Principal Whileyman sitting at his desk. I approach hesitantly, knocking my fist against the wall just to the side of his door.

He instantly looks up, catching sight of me and waving me in, directing me towards the empty chair in front of him. "There you are, Ms. Cooper. Come on in." I start to make my way inside when he adds, "Thank you for joining us."

"Us?" I start to ask, but stop, stiffening when I see the other chair that wasn't visible from outside occupied. "Jesse?"

"Hi, Sara," Jesse nods, smiling tightly.

My brows pull together as I settle into my own chair.

"So, you're probably wondering why you both are here," Principal Whileyman says, and I resist the urge to blurt out that he's right.

"So, with graduation coming up next weekend and final grades being submitted for senior students, I just wanted to touch base on your valedictorian and salutatorian honors. We've got some things to discuss."

Oh.

I instantly relax into the chair, realizing he must want to talk to Jesse and me about our graduation speeches. It also occurs to me that I had completely forgotten about the fact that I would be required to give a speech at graduation, which means I haven't given a single thought to what I plan to say. Part of me wonders if anyone would notice if I just tweaked and repeated my student body president speech.

"Do I get equal time as salutatorian to give my speech?" Jesse speaks up.

"Oh," Mr. Whileyman says, seeming caught off guard by the question, "well, no. We have ten minutes allotted for the valedictorian and five minutes for the salutatorian."

"Wanna switch?" I ask Jesse, half serious. Surprisingly, he actually laughs, which makes me laugh in return.

"So...actually, about that..."

My and Jesse's heads both swivel back forward to where Mr. Whileyman sits.

"About what?" I ask him.

Principal Whileyman folds his hands on the desk, clearing his throat. "So, there's really no best way to say this."

I slowly sink back into my chair, bracing myself for what he's about to tell us.

"With the final grades being entered this week...it appears there were some shifts in the last grading period."

I swallow against the tightness in my throat, having a feeling I know exactly what those *shifts* are that he's referring to.

"This really wasn't expected, so I'm sorry to spring this on you both, but..."

Just say it.

"It came down to decimals."

"What did?" Jesse asks.

Say it.

"You both have worked very hard and should be extremely proud. I know you both have been accepted to universities and made future plans, so it's really just semantics at this point."

"Just say it."

Both sets of eyes in the room find me. Principal Whileyman blows out a breath. "Sara, Jesse has overtaken your grade point average. He'll be our valedictorian. You'll be our salutatorian."

I blink back at him, the air in my lungs feeling like it's been sucked out. "Okay," I breathe.

Jesse shifts forward in his seat next to me, the new information seeming to have just sunk in for him. "Wait, what? *Really?*"

I've already zoned out, their voices becoming muffled around me.

"Yes, Mr. Lamonte. Congratulations."

"I... Thank you, sir," Jesse says, shaking his head. "But, I just don't understand how. When we checked ranks after the holiday break...I just didn't think there was any chance."

I notice Principal Whileyman's head shift in my direction, but I don't meet his eyes. "Like I said, it was only by a fraction after some fluctuations in this final grading period."

Fluctuations.

As in, me, for once in all of high school, taking a month or so to somewhat slack off. To not have school be my sole focus. To allow myself to let loose and not fixate on each and every class assignment being finished ahead of time and without a single error. To trade a few of the hours I would normally spend poring over books and cramming for exams for, heaven forbid, spending some time with my boyfriend.

And, just like that, four years of work, four years of late nights and weekends spent inside, four years of sacrificing fun and exploration for stability and accomplishment, gone.

I grind my teeth together, forcing a smile on my face.

"Was there something else, Principal Whileyman?" I ask. "Or can I be dismissed?"

"That's all, Ms. Cooper. Thank you for coming in. And congratulations."

I don't feel anything as I robotically stand from the chair and make my way out of the office. It's not until I am stepping back into the hallway that I think I really let what I just learned sink in, and when it does....

I burst out laughing.

Because, really, it's kind of hilarious when you think about it.

What was even the point?

I cover my face with my hand, the chuckles not stopping.

A voice in the back of my head tries to chime in, telling me that Mr. Whileyman was right when he said it didn't really mean much at this point. Telling me that my good grades and (former) valedictorian status got me admitted to NYU. That even if Jesse just managed to pass me up at the last second, it doesn't discount all of my hard work and success. That I can't possibly say it was all for nothing.

But I ignore that voice. Because, right now, it sure feels that way. Right now, when I know I've truly enjoyed the last month of my high school experience more than I ever enjoyed any of the rest of it, it's difficult to not kick myself for my actions. For staying in the comfort of my little bubble, studying and scribbling about in my journal for so long when I could have been putting myself out there. When I could've been living a balanced life like every other high school student. When I could have been having fun.

Like Robbie.

"What's so funny?"

I tilt my head up, finding Robbie standing to my side. It's so automatic when I reach up, wrapping my arms around his neck and pulling his face down to mine. I kiss him for a long time. I'm not sure really how long, but Robbie is the one that eventually stops it, pulling back from me.

"What was that for?" he asks, lips and eyes glossy.

I shrug. "Just wanted to."

Robbie grins, letting out a scoff. "And you think I'm just an object for you to use whenever you please?"

I grip each side of his open jacket, pulling him closer to me. "Are you opposed to that?" I ask, tilting my head up towards him.

Robbie's tongue pushes into the side of his cheek, the mask he's put on flickering.

I raise my brows, pushing him to answer.

He rolls his lips into his mouth, shaking his head. "No, ma'am. I can't say that I am," he smirks. "Do with me what you will, baby."

"Great," I grin, standing on my tiptoes and leaning in close enough to brush his lips with mine. "Let's start now."

I drop back down on my heels, grabbing Robbie's hand and pulling him after me.

"Where are we going?" he asks.

"Your car."

"What? Really?" Robbie asks, his feet skidding to a stop.

I spin back around to face him. "Yeah," I say. "So you can drive us to get milkshakes." The shocked look on Robbie's face relaxes somewhat, but then I add, "But after the milkshakes, who knows?" I give him a wink, moving to drag him along again towards the front door of the school.

Robbie blows out a harsh breath, chuckling for a few seconds, but then I feel him slow again. "Wait, hold on for a second, Cooper."

"What?" I question him.

"Lunch is up in ten minutes."

"So?"

Robbie cocks his head. "So...we aren't going to have enough time to get milkshakes and get back before class starts."

"So, we don't go to class. The last half of my day is boring anyways."

His brows pull together. "You wanna skip the rest of the school day?"

"Don't you?" I ask him.

"I mean... Sure, I guess."

"Then it's settled," I smile, grabbing Robbie's hand again. I start walking once more, but only make it a couple of steps before Robbie speaks up again.

"Cooper?"

"Yeah?" I ask, not looking back at him.

"What was that about?"

"*Hmm?*"

"What did Principal Whileyman have to talk to you about?" Robbie asks.

"Oh," I say. "I'm not valedictorian anymore."

I'm instantly yanked back by the force of Robbie coming to a complete stop.

"*What?*"

"What?" I ask, my voice even.

"What do you mean you're not valedictorian anymore?" Robbie questions me.

"Jesse passed me," I shrug. "I'm graduating as salutatorian now."

Robbie simply blinks at me, not responding.

I stare back at him expectantly, but, once a few more seconds go by without him saying anything, I tilt my head at him. "You know, I always get chocolate milkshakes, but I think I could go for a strawberry one today. Doesn't that sound good?"

Silence.

"It definitely does," I say. "I'm gonna mix it up. Take a walk on the wide side." I shimmy my shoulders, winking at Robbie before turning around to continue heading to his car.

Robbie's hands quickly find my shoulders, spinning me back around to face him. "Okay, Cooper, whoa. I'm gonna need you to slow down and put it in reverse."

"What do you mean?" I ask.

Robbie shakes his head, an incredulous look on his face. "How are you just okay with this?"

I steel my spine. "Why shouldn't I be?" I ask him. "I can't change it. Not now. What's the point in getting upset?"

Robbie steps closer. "You've worked so hard for this though. I mean...how did this even happen? Did your grades drop?"

"It doesn't matter."

"*Of course* it matters," Robbie insists.

I rear back. "I'm sorry, what do your grades look like right now, Robbie?"

He barks out a laugh. "That's irrelevant. Because I don't care about my grades. I never have. But you do."

I press my lips together. "I'm still salutatorian. I'm still second in our class. It's not that big of a deal."

"I don't understand. In what world is this not a big deal to you, Cooper?"

"In this one, apparently," I insist. "Robbie, I just...don't care. Not anymore. It's done. And I'd really be happy if we could just not talk about it anymore."

"*Happy*..." Robbie repeats, shaking his head.

"Yes?" I question him.

"School makes you happy, Cooper. Working hard and pouring everything you have into an exam or project for the end result to be worth it. Taking pride in what you do, in who you are. Being a perfectionist and not being willing to accept less than the absolute best. *Being* the best... *That* makes you happy."

I blow out a deep breath, crossing my arms. "You make me happy."

Robbie's lips part, his head tilting just as the school bell rings, dismissing everyone from lunch.

"It's now or never," I say, taking the last few steps it takes to reach the door, pushing it open. "Are you coming with me or am I walking?"

Robbie looks at me for a few seconds, then reaches up, rubbing the back of his neck. He glances around us, seeing all of the people walking to class, and I know he wants to be one of them just about as much as I do right now. "Yeah, okay," he nods. "Fine. Let's go."

I clap my hands, standing aside for him to walk through the doorway. As we make our way down the steps, I reach for Robbie's hand. He lets me take it, lifting both of our hands up and pulling me to his side to wrap his arm around me.

We walk silently to his car, Robbie pressing a kiss to the top of my head just before we get there. I look up at him, catching his eyes.

"Still love me?" I ask, smiling.

His eyes are soft as he looks down at me, running a hand over the top of my hair. "Always, Cooper."

fifty-four

ROBBIE

Cooper's fingers thread into my hair, pulling hard enough to force my head back. I take the opportunity to catch my breath, then look down at her, grinning.

I can't believe how long I kept her from touching my hair. It may just be my favorite thing now. She's managed to wipe away any bad association I've ever had with it. There's no chance I'm thinking of my dad or older brother when Cooper's running her hands through my hair. Especially when she looks like how she does now.

Laid across my back seat, cheeks and lips stained red, with a dress the same shade of silver as her eyes, with the exact same glittery sheen present within them right now, bunched up around her waist, just for me.

I lean down, pressing a kiss just below her jaw, feeling her pulse spike beneath my lips as she arches into me.

"You know, you were the one that insisted we go to Prom," Cooper breathes.

"*Mhmm...*" I hum against her neck.

"So, it's funny how slim you're insisting on making the chances that we ever make it inside."

"Oh, trust me, I'll have no issues getting inside."

"But–"

Cooper starts to speak, but is quickly cut off by the press of my palm between her legs.

"*Robbie*," she groans, chuckling as she throws her head back.

"And were we definitely firm on the attachment to this particular pair of tights?"

"*Yes!*" she confirms, shoving her dress down and trying to wiggle away from me. I let her, quickly moving to sit up and pulling her onto my lap instead. She blows out a breath, settling into me. "I mean it, Robbie. This is the only pair of pantyhose I brought, and you've already caused a run in them."

"I like how you thought to bring clear nail polish in case you got a run in your tights but didn't think to simply bring another pair of tights," I tell her.

Cooper chuckles. "I probably should have known better, but I didn't. So, if you plan to go inside for the dance, hands off the tights until it's over."

I wrap my hands around her back, pulling her closer. "And what happens when it's over?"

"I guess we'll have to go to find out."

"Do you not think being in the parking lot for the last twenty minutes means that we technically went?" I ask.

Cooper leans back, grabbing her clutch purse from where it sits in the front seat. She pulls out her compact mirror and red lipstick, reapplying it. "No, Robbie, I don't. But I also think you're sounding a whole lot like somebody else that I know." She presses her lips together, checking them in the mirror, then scrunches her nose. "Or someone that I used to know, I guess."

"What's that supposed to mean?"

She closes her purse, shrugging her shoulders and smoothing her hair. "Oh, I don't know," she says.

I tilt my head at her. "You're still you, Cooper."

"I know," she nods, her voice low. "I just..."

I reach up a hand, cupping her cheek and making her look at me. "What?"

She puts her hand over mine, a smile light up her face. "I just think...you made me better. You know?"

My throat bobs, the corner of my mouth twitching.

No, I'm not sure that I do know, Cooper.

I pat the side of her thigh, giving her a gentle squeeze. "Ready to go in?" I ask.

"Let's get this over with," she winks, pressing a quick kiss to my lips before crawling off of me.

———

Even though I heard it over the announcements at least fifty times and read it plastered over dozens of posters in the last month, I forgot that the theme of this year's Prom is *Fire and Ice*. But when Cooper and I walk into the gym together, it's immediately obvious as the whole place is lit up in bright red and cool blue lights, cut-outs of snowflakes and flames strung up and hanging down from the ceiling. It seems we've even sprung for a small ice sculpture of a bear, one sitting on a table smack in the middle of the snack area, surrounded by tons of candlesticks just far enough away to keep it from melting.

As we make our way further into the room, I feel the need to loosen my tie, for some reason feeling a little overwhelmed by it all. The decorations are cool, but they're reminding me too much of how I feel on this inside right now. A little bit too much of what I'm feeling between me and Cooper.

I glance over at her, seeing how goddamn beautiful she looks underneath the blue lights, the glow of the candles lighting up her skin like she's some kind of an angel. Just looking at her sends warmth flowing through my chest. It's so hard to describe what I feel for her, what she's like to me. Love almost seems too simple, too mundane. What's between us is more than that. It's passion, it's heat.

It's *fire*.

All-consuming, addicting, impossible to look away from. The longer I spend with her, the greater it grows, the more she spreads through me, destroying everything I thought I knew and wanted and replacing it with her. I used to wonder what would happen to me if I fully let Cooper in, if she'd burn me if I allowed it. But, now, I don't fear that at all. I know what Cooper feels for me. I know she'd never do anything to hurt me. God, I'm more sure of that than I am of anything. So sure, in fact, that I've even wondered lately if she might hurt herself to avoid hurting me.

And that's where the ice comes in.

This sharp, cold, piercing feeling in the back of my mind that I've been doing everything in my power to ignore for the last few weeks. The one that sends a chill through me every time I look at a calendar and remember just how close we are to graduation. How close we are to her leaving.

Or, at least, when she's supposed to be leaving. We haven't talked about it. Cooper *won't* talk about it.

At first, I was fine with that, because I figured she was feeling the same way as me. That she wanted to put it off, that she wanted to just enjoy our time together before things had to get real, before decisions had to be made. But now, we're less than a week from graduation, just over two weeks away from the time she's supposed to be in New York, and she hasn't even mentioned it. Hasn't even told me if she's accepted the offer or if she's booked a flight. In some ways, I've been okay with it, with avoiding the conversation of our futures, because that would mean I could avoid talking about the fact that I haven't done a damn thing to prepare for mine.

I never applied for college. I don't have a job lined up. I don't have plans or aspirations of going anywhere other than Bay View. I'm just...*here*. Just existing. I was sure that something would come to me over the course of my senior year, that some inspiration would strike or that I would discover some grand passion that I knew I'd need to follow after high school. But, instead, I just stayed the same.

And then I found Cooper.

And, *God*, has she made me the happiest guy on the planet. She's taught me so many things, fulfilled me in so many ways, made me feel like I was someone worth doing something, but...I just still don't know what that *something* is. Cooper's seemed to always have her *something*, always known it, like she was made for it. Because she is. But me...I just don't know. And it's finally setting in just how quickly my window to not know is closing.

All I know is that I want Cooper. And I want her to be happy. She says that I make her happy. But how much of someone's happy can you really be responsible for? How much *should* you be responsible for? As someone that's basically never been responsible for anything, I have to be honest when I say it scares the shit out of me. The reliance on me that I've felt from her lately. The shifting of her priorities. The dreams of hers that used to be the only thing in her sight now taking a backseat to me. It makes me nervous. Frankly, it chills me to the bone.

And I don't want that. I don't want the ice. I'm here for the fire. I just want the fire forever. I guess the only question is whether my and Cooper's fire is destined to burn on forever or simply burn out like so many before.

"You love this song, don't you?" Cooper asks, making me realize that I've been staring at the ice sculpture and candle display for a good minute now.

"What?" I say automatically, snapping out of my trance.

Cooper chuckles. "This song," she repeats, pointing towards the dance floor. "You've sung along to it a few times in the car. And I've heard you listening to it on your Walkman. Blue Öyster Cult, right?"

I glance towards the dance floor, letting my ears focus in on the music the live band is playing, a laugh immediately bursting out of me when I identify the song.

"*Burnin' for You*," I confirm. "Very clever."

"Wanna dance?" Cooper asks, wiggling her eyebrows.

I tilt my head as I look down at her. She's bouncing on her feet, a smile bright across her face, her gorgeous red hair billowing out around her face, catching light in a way that puts every fire decoration in this gym to shame. "How could I ever say no to you?" I ask her.

"I guess you don't," she says, grinning as she pulls me onto the dance floor.

Cooper and I dance until we're out of breath and our hair is clinging to our foreheads, not able to escape the dance floor as the band plays one fantastic fire or ice themed song one after the other. *Burnin' for You* went straight into *Cold As Ice* by Foreigner, then was followed by Asia's *Heat of the Moment*. By the time we finish slow dancing to *The Flame* by Cheap Trick, we're both practically crawling to the punch table for a drink.

Cooper scoops us each a cup of the red colored punch full to the very top, us both downing it in seconds. It's not until we're each halfway through our second glasses and slowing down that I become aware of my surroundings, spotting Alice and Daniel just to the side of the snack table. Alice happens to turn her head in my direction at the same moment, and I raise a hand, waving her our way.

Her back straightens, a tight smile crossing her face as she waves back at me. I watch her eyes flick to Cooper at my side, who's still downing her punch. When Alice still doesn't move after a few more moments, I give her another wave of my hand towards us. This time, she turns to Daniel on the other side of her, his eyes on the stage. She leans in and whispers something in his ear, pointing in our direction. After that, I expect him to come over with her, but he doesn't, staying rooted to the spot as Alice makes her way over on her own.

"Hey Alice," I say to her, smiling.

I feel Cooper stiffen at my side, and I turn to see her slowly lowering her punch cup from her face, her posture rigid. My brows pull together as I look at her, but then my gaze is pulled away by Alice's voice.

"Hi, Robbie."

"Hey," I say again. "Long time, no see." And it's not until the words are out of my mouth that I realize I really mean them, and that it occurs to me that I haven't seen Alice in weeks. Now that I think of it, I haven't even heard Cooper mention Alice in weeks, which is about a thousand times less than she'd usually mention her in the same amount of time.

"Hi, Sara," Alice says, her voice sounding even less bright than it did when she greeted me.

"Hey, Al," Cooper says quietly, picking at the paper edge of her punch cup.

Alice crosses her arms in front of her. "Your dress is pretty," she tells Cooper, which makes her fidget with the skirt of the dress in question.

"Oh, thanks," she murmurs. "So is yours."

I look between the two girls, wondering what the hell I must have missed. Because their conversation right now sounds more like an awkward one between two girl cousins at a family reunion that secretly hate each other but are being forced to interact rather than a casual encounter between two best friends.

Silence stretches between the three of us for several seconds before Alice clears her throat, motioning behind her with her thumb. "Well, I better get back to Daniel. But it was good to see you. Both of you."

"Yeah, sure," Cooper nods, running a hand through her hair. "It was good to see you too."

Alice offers one last small smile before she turns and heads back to where she came from. The moment she is out of earshot, I turn back to Cooper. When I find her, she is fully turned towards the snack table, not acting like anything out of the ordinary just occurred.

"I can't decide what sounds more appetizing. A cocktail weiner or a meatball?"

"Cooper, what was that?" I ask.

She snorts. "A chance for you to make multiple weiner jokes. But now, it's just a missed opportunity, I guess," she says, popping a cocktail weiner into her mouth before taking another sip of her punch, strolling away from the table.

I follow after her, placing a hand on her shoulder to stop her.

"No, Cooper, I meant, what was that with Alice?"

"What do you mean?" she asks, playing with the puffy sleeve of her dress.

I cock my head at her, giving her a knowing look. "What's going on between you two? Something is obviously wrong."

"Nothing's wrong," Cooper insists. She lets out a sigh, looking down into her cup and tracing the outer edge of it with her finger. "We're just...not exactly getting along the best right now."

"*You and Alice?*" I question her, making sure I'm understanding correctly.

Cooper waves a hand at me. "It's fine, really."

She starts to walk away but I move around her, blocking her path. "Cooper, she's your best friend. It's not fine."

She opens her mouth and then closes it, glancing away.

I reach for her hand. "Baby, what happened between you two?"

"It's stupid," she mutters.

"It's not," I assure her, squeezing her hand. "Just tell me."

She blows out a breath, meeting my eyes. "She...thinks I've changed."

My shoulders fall, my heart instantly sinking in my chest.

"Since when?" I ask her calmly.

Cooper rolls her eyes. "Since you and I got together. You know, officially. She thinks I've lost focus, that my priorities have changed. She..." she trails off, shaking her head and letting out a laugh.

"What?" I breathe.

She turns back to me, rolling her lips into her mouth. "She said something ridiculous about me putting out all my fires for one new flame. She thinks I'm throwing away my life for you or something. I mean, that's crazy, isn't it?"

"Yeah," I nod, trying to swallow against the lump in my throat. "That would be crazy."

My throat tightens further, and I know it's to keep down the rest of the words threatening to spill out of my mouth. The ones telling her that I've had the same exact fears. The ones that tell her I'm not sure Alice is entirely off.

I should say them.

If I cared about her, I'd say them.

That's what love's all about, right? Putting someone else and their needs before your own? Being honest with them even if it hurts both of you in the process?

I should talk to her.

But I can't right now.

Because the thought of losing her has a knife twisting into my gut.

Cooper clears her throat, seemingly trying to break the silence we've found ourselves in. "Yeah, well, anyways," she chuckles uncomfortably. "I'm gonna need something a lot stronger than punch if we're going to keep talking about this."

I blow a deep, measured breath out of my nose.

"I..." I reach out, holding Cooper's face in my hand. She tilts her head into my touch, meeting my eyes with a small smile. "I need to go to the restroom real quick," I mutter. "Meet you right back here?"

"Sure," she says. "I'm not going anywhere."

I nod slowly, forcing a quick smile on my face. I start to pull away, but then, though I'm not sure what compels me to do it, I pull Cooper close, pressing a firm kiss to her lips. It's not the type of kiss you give someone that you know you'll be seeing again in five minutes. Neither is the one I press to her forehead for good measure before dropping my hand and practically bolting for the gym doors.

I burst out of the blue metal doors, loosening my tie around my neck as I speed walk towards the restroom. I'm not sure why I'm going there. I don't need to use it. I just knew that I needed to get out of that gym. Just for a few minutes. With the fire and ice coming at me from every angle, I started to feel like I was experiencing the effects of a fever, my skin warm and coated in a sheen of perspiration but my insides wracking with shivers and aching like there's ice in my joints.

When I reach the bathroom, I make a beeline for the sink, turning on the faucet and splashing water over my face within seconds of entering the room.

I'm running my hands down my face, pressing the heels of my palms against my eyes when I hear the sounds of flushes happening in succession behind me. I drop my hands to either side of the sink, glancing up into the mirror to find Jesse leaving the row of urinals and heading for the sinks.

Then Paul comes into view, following him.

I drop my head, blowing out a breath as I turn the sink back on, washing my hands to make myself look busy.

I can see the shift in Jesse's body as he approaches the sink next to me and realizes I'm here. "Hey, Rob," he says.

I look up. "Hey, man."

Paul moves to the sink next to Jesse, turning it on and beginning to wash his hands, not acknowledging me.

Jesse doesn't say anything else, just giving me a nod before he tosses the paper towel he was drying his hands with into the trash can and leaves the bathroom.

I continue washing my hands, waiting for Paul to leave. It takes me three pumps of soap though before I realize the water at his sink isn't running anymore and that he's just leaning against it, lingering.

I finally look at him, giving him what he obviously wants. "What?" I question him.

He tilts his head at me, his dirty blonde brows furrowing. "Rough night?" he asks.

"No," I say evenly, moving around him to grab a paper towel.

Paul's body turns, following my movement. "Really?" he asks, concern in his tone that I can only recognize as fake because I've known him for over a decade. "It just seemed like you might be going through something."

"Well, I'm not," I say, my voice clipped.

I wad up my paper towel into a far tighter ball than necessary, throwing it into the trash can with an equal amount of aggression as Paul watches me, his facial expression passive. His eyes search my face for a moment before he stands up straight, uncrossing his arms.

"Oh, well, okay then," he shrugs, walking around me to head for the door.

I shake my head, wondering what the hell any of that was about, before spinning around to leave as well. Only, I find Paul in the doorway, blocking my way.

"But, if you *were* having a bad night..." he muses.

"But I'm not," I grit, running an exasperated hand through my hair.

"Right," he agrees. "It's just that, if you were, I was gonna offer you some of this," he says.

My brows pinch together, irritation coursing through me as Paul pulls back one side of his sports coat. I think for two seconds about how much of a damper it would put on the night if I were to just sock him in the face, but then I see what he's pulling out of his jacket pocket, and I stiffen.

He holds up a hefty metal flask, shaking it.

I can hear the dull sound of the contents sloshing around inside of it, taking note that it must be nearly full. Just the thought of the liquid inside has my muscles relaxing, making my mouth water for it.

But then Paul's pulling it away, moving to slip the flask back in his pocket and turning to leave. "But if you don't need it—"

"Hold on," I blurt.

He turns back to me, his brows raised and a smirk on his face.

I chew on my bottom lip, my eyes narrowing on him. "What is it they say?" I ask.

Paul cocks his head.

"A shot a day keeps the doctor away?"

Paul breathes out a chuckle. "Sure, man," he agrees. "Let's go with that."

He pulls the flask from his jacket pocket once again, uncapping it and handing it to me.

I hesitate for only a moment before I take it from him, tipping it back and immediately relishing in the soothing burn of tequila down my throat. I let out a hum of satisfaction, feeling some of the weight that I've felt sitting on my chest for the last couple of weeks slowly being lifted away. I run my tongue across my lower lip, making sure I take in every last drop of the shot before holding the flask back out to Paul.

He shakes his head, pushing it back towards my chest. "Keep it," he says.

I rear back, my brows knitting in confusion.

"I've got another one stashed in my locker," Paul tells me. "And, besides, it looks like you need it more than me."

My mouth falls open, my head shaking. "I don't—"

"It's all good, man," he cuts me off, patting me on the shoulder and giving me a tight grin. "Have a good night." And then he walks out the door, leaving me in the bathroom alone with only the flask in my hand.

I swallow, glancing down at it. I move to slip it into my jacket pocket, then pause, deciding one more swig couldn't kill me.

When I walk back into the gym, I find Cooper right where I left her on the side of the dance floor. There's a smile on her face as she stands there with her arms crossed, gently swaying side to side as she observes the band and the people on the dance floor.

She must sense me watching her, because her head shifts in my direction, her grin instantly spreading to its full size as she skips over to me, looping her arms around my neck.

"Hey," she says, pulling me in for a kiss before I have time to respond.

I chuckle. "Did you miss me already?"

"Maybe," she admits. "Definitely." She crinkles her nose, glancing down at my mouth. "Have you...been drinking?"

My spine steels. "Uh...I..."

Cooper's arms unravel from my neck, her hands slowly sliding down my chest. Her eyes stay on my face as I stammer until her hand comes into contact with the square shape weighing down my suit pocket. Her brows raise in surprise, and, when I don't offer any explanation, she takes it upon herself to pull back my jacket, peering inside the side pocket.

"You didn't..." she says.

I shake my head. "I–"

"*Robbie.*"

My mouth snaps shut as I stare back at her, waiting for her to question me, or blow up on me, or maybe even call me a careless idiot.

But, instead, her face breaks out into a massive smile.

"I can't believe you," she chuckles.

"What do you mean?" I ask, confused by her reaction mixed with her words.

She catches me off guard, pressing her lips to mine. "I told you I needed something stronger than punch," she murmurs against my mouth with a grin.

fifty-five

SARA

"Come on! Keep up, Summers!" I shout in a hushed voice, giving Robbie's arm a firm pull as I drag him behind me.

Robbie's dress shoes skid against the floor as he nearly stumbles, making a loud squeaking sound. "*Shit!*" he mutters, making me burst out in giggles just as we round the corner.

I stop in place as soon as we are a few feet down the hallway and I feel comfortably concealed from view. Robbie nearly runs into my back, but quickly recovers. "*Jesus, Cooper,*" he huffs, straightening his jacket out. "Forget being a *Bleacher Babe*. I should've been convincing you all this time to get out on the court."

"No thanks," I say. "I'll leave the playing with balls to you."

Robbie leans against the locker to his side, raising a brow. "Do I even need to point out the obvious with what you just said?"

I run a hand down my face, shaking my head. "God, no. Definitely not–"

"Because if I remember correctly, last weekend you seemed to love–"

"Robbie, *please*, stop," I chuckle, covering his mouth with my hand, which he promptly licks.

I pull my hand back, moving to wipe it off on Robbie's pants, but he grabs my wrist, pinning it to the locker while he reaches down and digs his fingers into the side of my waist, tickling me.

I burst out in giggles, trying to catch my breath. "Would you stop? The whole point of coming over here was to not draw attention."

Robbie just barely lets up, giving me the chance to pull away. "Would you give me the flask already?" I chuckle, smoothing my dress out.

Robbie's laughter fades out, and he puts an arm up on the locker to steady himself. As he looks down on me, the smile on his face slowly fades.

I tilt my head at him, glancing towards his jacket pocket. "Um, today, please?" I ask playfully.

His lips press together, his head swiveling from left to right to make sure no one's around before he slowly reaches down and slips the flask from his pocket, uncapping it. I stretch my hand out for him to give it to me, and he starts to, but then pauses.

"C'mon, just a little further," I push.

Robbie rakes a hand through his hair, his gaze flicking up to mine. "Are you sure?" he asks. "I mean, that you want to?"

"It's just a drink, Robbie," I say, breathing out a laugh. "I mean, since when are you so responsible?"

Robbie's eyes squint, his mouth twitching. "Since never, I guess."

"Exactly," I grin, plucking the flash from his hands. "Thank you very much," I say, tipping it back for a shot.

I pinch my nose closed, forcing myself to swallow it down in one gulp. I hand the flask back to Robbie, trying to keep it together, but the burning in my throat wins, and I sputter out a cough. I stick out my tongue, wiggling my arms and legs to let the after effects pass. And then, I'm golden.

"You good?" Robbie asks, eyeing me.

"Never felt more alive."

Robbie's brows pinch, not even a smirk crossing his face.

I reach down, grabbing his hand and pressing a kiss to his palm. "What's that look for?" I ask him.

Robbie shakes his head, which seems to snap him out of whatever trance he was in, his face melting back into his usual easy, relaxed expression. "Nothing," he says, lifting up our joined hands to place his own kiss on my palm this time. He raises the flask up with his other hand, starting to flip the cap back onto it, but then hesitates, tilting it in his hands as he looks down at it. Then, suddenly, he raises it to his lips for one more long pull, before capping it and slipping it back in his pocket.

"Are you ready to go back in?" he asks me, pushing my hair away from my face and giving me a quick kiss.

I roll my lips into my mouth, hiding my grin. "Almost."

I reach down, slipping one heel off my foot, then use Robbie's shoulder for balance as I slip the other one off as well, leaving them on the floor next to Robbie as I turn to walk down the hallway in the opposite direction of the gym.

"Um, Cooper?" Robbie calls after me. "What are you doing?"

"Wait for it!"

It takes a few more seconds before I reach the end of the hallway, spinning on my heel to face Robbie. "Okay," I say, holding my arms out to the side.

Robbie tilts his head. "What am I supposed to be looking at?"

I stifle a laugh before taking a deep breath. And then I take off, jogging as fast as I can without slipping in my tights. I run straight for Robbie, and he jumps out of the way in surprise, thinking I'm about to run into him. But I don't, instead veering off to the side, throwing my hands in the air and sliding to a stop, my feet kicking out behind me.

Once I catch my footing, a huge smile comes to my face, and I bend my knees, giving Robbie a little curtsy.

He blinks at me, glances over his shoulder, then looks back at me. "What the hell was that?"

I let out a scoff. "Classic American film work!"

Robbie tilts his head, not responding.

"Iconic cinematography?" I try.

Still nothing.

I blow out a breath, making the hair in my face flip up.

"*The Breakfast Club*," I say.

Robbie's brows raise, a smile pulling at his lips. "*The Breakfast Club*," he repeats.

"Yeah," I nod. "You know, the scene where they're running through the hallways. Trying not to be caught by Vice Principal Vernon."

Robbie's tongue pushes into his lower lip. "You're cute, Cooper."

"Oh, just forget it," I say, rolling my eyes as I bend down to pick up my heels. When I stand back up, Robbie's there, wrapping his arms around me. "You're cute," he says again. "And so was your little scene reenactment. Very cool, actually."

He kisses my forehead, and I try to hide my smile as I look up at him.

"You know, lots of people think that scene is cool," I say.

"*Mmm*," Robbie hums, his lips grazing my neck. "Do they now?"

"They do," I confirm as his lips press against my throat, making my voice go up an octave. "And mark my words, your kids will too."

Robbie stiffens, pulling his head back up to look at me. "My kids?" he asks.

I shrug, the singular shot of liquor I took making me feel just a tad bit bolder. "Yours. Ours. Whatever."

Robbie's mouth falls open, his eyes searching my face. I give him a grin, standing up on my tiptoes and pressing a kiss to the tip of his nose before dropping my heels and dashing off towards the end of the hallway again.

"One more time for good measure," I call to Robbie over my shoulder.

I spin around as soon as I reach the end, dashing back just the way I came, making my skid to a stop even more dramatic this time, a chuckle bursting out of me as Robbie has to stick an arm out to help steady me.

I sigh as I catch my breath, bending down to slip my heels back on.

"And now we can go back to the dance."

———

Robbie and I won Prom King and Queen.

And, even though I already lived through the shock of winning Homecoming Queen, this time around didn't feel any less surreal. I felt on top of the world hearing my name called after Robbie's, hearing the entire gym burst into applause and walking on shaky legs up to the stage to get my crown. It's a feeling I never want to let go of. A feeling I don't think I'll ever have to as long as I have Robbie. He just has this way of making me feel infinite. And it just makes me love him more by the minute.

As Robbie and I are descending the stage, he stops us, leaning it to whisper in my ear that he'll be right back, that he'll meet me on the dance floor for our dance in just a second. I give him a hesitant nod, agreeing. As he jogs his way back up the steps and over to the frontman of the band, I catch sight of Alice standing just to my side.

"Oh, hey," I say, reaching up and fidgeting with my crown.

I feel like I've greeted her exclusively with an *oh* for the last several weeks, and I hate it. But I also can't help it. Things are weird between us. Strained. Ever since her weird come-to-Jesus moment with me, I've felt like I don't know how to talk to her anymore. Probably because I refuse to admit anything she said was right and because she refuses to take any of it back.

Alice smiles tightly at me. Another thing I've grown to resent, because Alice's smiles are *never* tight. "Another one to add to the collection, I guess," she says, motioning up towards my crown.

I attempt a laugh. "I guess. Kinda weird, isn't it?"

She shrugs. "Not really."

I swallow, glancing back to where Robbie is finishing up saying whatever he needed to say to the singer.

"Are you happy?" Alice asks.

"What?" I ask, turning back towards her.

"Are you happy?" she repeats, taking a step towards me. "Tonight? With him?"

"I am," I answer instantly.

I watch Alice's eyes trail over my shoulder, and when I follow her gaze, I find my spine straightening.

Robbie has made a stop on his way back from his conversation. Standing behind a little half curtain on the side of the stage, he's totally concealed from anyone looking at the stage from head-on, but from where we are watching from the side of the stage, we have the perfect view of him throwing back his flask, taking another long drink.

My head tilts as I watch him, concern prickling in the back of my mind. I clear my throat, forcing the feeling away as I turn back to Alice. When I meet her eyes, her face is surprisingly not showing any judgment. In fact, I'd say it's showing the opposite. She almost looks resigned. Impassive.

"I really am," I insist. "I'm always happy when I'm with him."

Alice's lips roll together as she nods. "Well, I guess that's all that matters." She steps closer, running her hand down my arm. "Have a good night, Sara."

I blink as I watch Alice walk away. I think I would have traced her entire path to find Daniel, but Robbie's voice in my ear and hand on my waist distract me.

"We're up, Cooper. Ready?" he asks.

"As I'll ever be," I nod, leaning into him as he takes my hand.

Robbie leads us to the spotlight waiting for us in the middle of the dance floor.

"Let's give it up for your 1988 Prom King and Queen!" the lead singer of the band calls out from the mic, earning a round of cheers from the crowd. "Now, for the lovely couple's dance, we have a very special request from the King himself. Haven't played this one in awhile, so if everybody could please show it some love."

I look at Robbie, my brows raised in confusion as he lifts my hands, wrapping my arms around his neck. I don't get to question him further, because the moment his hands land on my waist and the band starts playing, I instantly recognize the song.

Sara Smile by Hall & Oates.

And, boy, do I smile.

I tilt my head up at Robbie as we start to sway together. "You know, this song isn't very on theme with the Prom."

"Sure it is," Robbie insists.

"How?" I question him.

Robbie catches me off guard, spinning me around and dipping me back. He holds us there for a second, his glossy chocolate eyes boring into mine as a smirk pulls at his lips. "If fire was a person, it'd be you, Sara Cooper. No questions asked."

I can't even help the smile that breaks across my face right at Hall & Oates's cue.

"And maybe..." Robbie adds, as he stands us back upright, "I just happen to be very charming. And the singer of the band was very receptive to that."

"Now that sounds about right," I say.

Robbie presses his lips to my forehead as we continue to dance. I can faintly smell the tequila on his breath as it fans over the top of my head, and I can tell his movements are looser and less sure as we sway about the dance floor. But I don't mind, because this is him. He's having a good time. Because he's always having a good time. And he makes me have a good time. And I love him.

"I love you," I whisper, my face against Robbie's chest.

I feel his hands tighten on my waist as he lets out a shaky breath. "I love you too, Cooper," he mutters into my hair.

I smile, glancing up at him. "Is it you and me forever, Summers?" I ask, playing off of the lyrics in the song.

Robbie's face drops for a moment, like I caught him by surprise. His parted lips turn up at the corner a few times before he breathes out a soft laugh, grabbing me by the face and kissing me.

———

Thirty minutes later, the dance officially comes to an end and the chaperones are corralling us out of the gym like cows.

Robbie lets me know he needs to run to the restroom before we go home and tells me I can wait for him by his car before kissing the top of my head and dipping inside the bathroom.

I start to walk towards the door, but, with the traffic of every student trying to leave at once, I opt to just wait for Robbie outside the bathroom.

By the time he reappears a couple of minutes later, the hallway is almost entirely cleared out. I see Robbie's back first as he pushes out of the door, but then, when he spins around, I see him pulling the flask away from his face.

I cock my head to the side, waiting for him to notice me standing there, and, when he does, his spine steels.

"Cooper," he says.

"Having a little nightcap without me?" I ask, chuckling.

"Um..." Robbie trails off, glancing down at the flask and moving to put it back in his pocket.

"*Nuh uh*," I say, darting forward and grabbing it from his hand. Robbie is slow to react, and I'm able to uncap the flask and throw back a small sip before he takes it back from me. I register just before it leaves my hand how light it feels.

"Let's go home," Robbie says, throwing his arm around me and walking us towards the door.

We make our way out to Robbie's Camaro in the parking lot, Robbie releasing me just as we approach it. He gives me a funny look when he realizes that I've followed him over to the driver's side, cocking his head at me.

"What are you doing?" he asks.

"I'm driving," I say, holding out my hands for the keys.

"What?" he questions. "Why?"

"Because, I've had one and a half shots of tequila, one of those being over two hours ago, and you've had basically whatever else makes up that flask."

Robbie's brows pinch. "Cooper, I'm golden—"

"And I'm not discussing this," I insist. "Keys."

I hold out my hand, and Robbie looks down to it, letting out a sigh. "Fine, Cooper. You can drive my car if you want," he says. "In fact, I actually think it's pretty hot, so joke's on you."

"Whatever makes you feel better," I smirk, rolling my eyes.

Robbie pulls his car keys from his pocket, dropping them into my hand and then reaching up and patting the side of my cheek. "Glad to see you haven't totally given up on being the responsible one after all."

Robbie turns away, walking over to climb in the passenger side of the car.

And I'm left standing in place, blinking in the dark school parking lot with an open mouth and the keys still sitting in my outstretched hand.

I'm not sure how many seconds go by, but it's enough for Robbie to open his door again. "You coming, Cooper?" he asks.

I snap out of it, nodding even though I know he can't see me. "Uh– *Yeah*. Yeah, coming."

I get settled in the driver's seat, adjusting the seat and mirror as necessary– much to Robbie's dismay– before starting the car and pulling out of the parking lot.

We're silent for a couple of minutes as I drive, Robbie staring out of his window and my eyes on the road.

I try to let it go. I try to think about anything else. About how fun the dance was. About our Prom King and Queen crowns sitting in the back seat right now. But I just can't stop replaying the statement in my head.

The song on the radio fades out, beginning the next one, and Robbie instantly sits up in his seat.

"Oh, *yeah*" he says. "That's what I'm talking about, huh, Cooper?" He leans over, cranking up *Faithfully* loud enough to make the speakers rattle.

I press my lips together, flexing my fingers on the steering wheel, but I can't stop myself.

I lean over, turning the radio down enough so that I can hear my own voice.

"Robbie, what did you mean by that?"

Robbie doesn't seem phased by my question, his head bobbing along as he mouths the lyrics to the song. "By what?" he asks, his voice casual.

"By me not totally giving up on being responsible after all," I say.

I keep my eyes forward on the road, but when he doesn't respond, I have to glance over at him.

Robbie's posture is rigid, his gaze out the window and his hands in his lap. Several seconds go by of him not moving or saying anything before I say, "Robbie?"

Nothing.

"Hello? *Robbie?*"

"What, Cooper?" he mutters.

"Um...are you just not going to answer me?" I question him.

"What do you want me to say?" he asks, his voice even.

"I want you to tell me what you meant."

He finally moves, his head slowly turning in my direction in my peripheral vision. "What do you think I meant by it, Cooper?"

"Well, if I knew I wouldn't be asking," I say, blowing out an exasperated breath.

Robbie remains silent for several moments.

"This is a really fun way to have a conversation," I deadpan.

"When are you going to New York?"

My head snaps in Robbie's direction. "What?"

"I asked when you're going to New York," Robbie says.

I glance between him and the road, my mouth opening and closing.

Robbie's body fully turns in my direction. "What day do you leave? What time is your flight? Where are you staying when you get there?"

I bark out a laugh. "Okay, what is with the interrogation?"

"*Interrogation?*" Robbie repeats. "Cooper, these should be the easiest questions in the world for you to answer."

I shake my head. "I..."

"What all do you know about the summer writing course? What classes are you planning to take once the fall semester starts? What are you most excited to write about first?"

"Robbie, what are you doing?" I ask.

"*Answer the damn questions, Cooper,*" Robbie fumes, leaning closer to me.

"I–I can't!" I sputter.

"And *why not*, Cooper? Why the hell can't you answer questions about how you're about to be living your dream a few weeks from today? Why can't you gush to me over how damn excited you are to get out of this town and go to New York City where you belong, where you've worked all of high school to get to?"

The backs of my eyes burn, my chest aching. "Robbie, please, stop," I beg, shaking my head.

"Because you're planning to throw it all away, aren't you?"

I shake my head. "*Please...*"

"*Aren't you?*"

My lips part as I attempt to answer him, but a silent sob just comes out instead.

"Cooper–" Robbie begins, but cuts off, both of us stiffening in our seats as red and blue lights fill the car, reflecting in the rear view mirror.

"Oh... Oh my God," I say, my hands shaking as I glance down at the speedometer. "I was distracted," I breathe, slowing the car down and settling on the shoulder of the road. "I think I was speeding. Probably swerving some."

Robbie looks over his shoulder and out the back window, cursing as realization passes over his face. "Wouldn't have mattered if you weren't," he says. "We'd still be getting pulled over."

I feel my heart hammering in my chest as I glance up at the rear view mirror, spotting a silhouette stepping out of the cop car, closing the door. I let out a shaky breath, watching as the silhouette starts to make its way towards us.

I've never been pulled over before. I don't know what to do, how to act. I'm not exactly one for breaking the rules. I swallow hard, feeling like I might be sick. But then I feel a hand on my bicep.

"Cooper, switch with me."

"*What?*" I demand as Robbie is clicking the button to release my seat belt.

Robbie blows a breath out of his nose, gritting his teeth. "Switch seats with me. *Right now.*"

"What? No. I can't. I was driving. I was the one pulled over."

"In *my* car. By the jackass who's had it out for me since the moment I got my driver's license. You're not taking the fall for it."

"Robbie—"

"Cooper, you have to move. It's now or never."

"But I—"

I don't get a chance to finish my argument, because Robbie is grabbing me, slipping one arm under my thighs and the other behind my back, and hauling me over his lap.

"Robbie, *no!*" I cry, kicking my feet and trying to fight him. But it's no use.

He plops me down on the other side of him, flinging his body into the driver's seat and clicking his seat belt on just before the cop approaches the car window.

"Robbie—" I whisper-shout, two tears streaming down my face.

"*Stop,*" he mouths at me silently, his jaw set.

I wipe my tears away, swallowing my sob just as the cop knocks on Robbie's window, prompting Robbie to roll it down.

Officer Strothers's face comes into view a few seconds later, looking as smug and menacing as the last time I saw him.

"Evening, kids," he says, a Cheshire cat smile on his face that makes a shiver run through me.

"Evening, Officer," Robbie replies, his voice tight.

"Where are you kids coming from tonight?"

Robbie scoffs, mumbling under his breath.

"What's that, son?"

"I said, you know we're coming from Prom," Robbie grits, making me stiffen at his harsh tone. "Along with every other kid in town, including your son."

Officer Strothers's tongue presses into his bottom lip. "You know what? You're right," he says. "I know tonight was Prom. Which means I know what every kid has been getting up to, including my son."

Robbie blows out a measured breath, looking up at the officer. "Sir, I'd like to get my girlfriend home. So, if you could either tell me why you pulled me over or let me go–"

"Have anything to drink tonight, son?"

I feel my heart stutter in my chest. I swallow hard, slowly glancing over to look at Robbie, who, even though he's certainly had plenty to drink, doesn't react at all to the officer's questioning.

"No, sir," he says.

"Is that so?"

"Should I repeat myself?" Robbie asks, and, if we weren't currently in the presence of a police officer, I would kick him for being a smart ass to a police officer. I rest my elbow against the side of my door, biting down on my nails to distract myself, keeping my eyes on the floor.

Officer Strothers breathes out a chuckle. "You know, it's just that you were going pretty fast and swerving around quite a bit for someone that hasn't been drinking."

I feel my pulse pounding in my ears, and I resort to counting in my head to drown out the noise, convincing myself that this is going to be over any second.

"I'm sorry about that, Officer," Robbie says. "You see, we were just pretty wired coming home from Prom. I had some music playing. Probably a little too loud, if I'm honest. We were just singing along and having a good time. It may have caused a little distraction in my driving on this open empty road."

My eyes widen, surprise coursing through me at Robbie's ability to stay calm and come up with such a coherent believable answer when he's half past drunk while I'm currently sitting here, essentially sober and am on the verge of being sick.

I steal a glance at Officer Strothers, trying to determine if he's buying any of this. His brow is furrowed, his eyes narrowed as he lifts the flashlight he's carrying up to Robbie's face. It's so bright that I have to look away, but Robbie barely flinches, just squinting into the light.

"Hmm..." the officer muses. "Eyes are pretty glossy and bloodshot to be sober."

"Strothers, if you wanted to stare longingly into my eyes, you could've just asked."

I cover my mouth, blocking the unexpected laugh trying to burst out of me and also keeping myself from berating Robbie for his actions.

Officer Strothers drops his flashlight, taking a step back from the car, and a sigh of relief instantly flows out of me.

"Step out of the vehicle, please."

My head snaps in Robbie's direction, every ounce of blood draining from my face.

"Is that really necessary–"

"*Now*," Officer Strothers barks, silencing Robbie.

Robbie blows a breath out of his nose, squeezing his eyes shut once before reaching for the door handle.

My hand shoots out, grabbing his arm. "*I– I– Please– Don't–*"

"It's fine, Cooper," Robbie insists, cutting off my stammering. He covers my hand with his, giving me a gentle nod. "It's gonna be fine."

My hand slips out of his as he pushes his car door open, climbing out.

I don't even think before I act, throwing my car door open as well.

"Cooper, don't–"

"Young lady, I'm going to need you to stay where you are," Officer Strothers says, holding up his hand towards me from the other side of the car.

My mouth falls open, but no actual words come out, every one of them getting stuck in my throat as my eyes stay glued to Robbie.

"What's it gonna be, Officer?" Robbie asks, his voice steady.

Officer Strothers moves to stand directly in front of Robbie, crossing his arms.

"Say the alphabet, backwards, starting with Q."

"*Excuse me?*" Robbie says at the same time I think, *What?*

"Alphabet. Backwards. Q. Tell me the rest."

"Who the hell can do that?" Robbie demands.

"It's a standard sobriety test requirement, son," Office Strothers states, cocking his head. "Are you refusing to participate?"

Robbie lets out a deep sigh, and I can tell he's fuming on the inside. "Fine," he says. "Okay, Q. Then, P. *Uh...*" he trails off, his brows knitting together. "O? Then, um, M—"

"*Wrong.*" Officer Strothers declares.

"Oh, c'mon man—"

"This line," the officer says, pointing downwards and cutting off Robbie's protests. "Walk on it."

My nails dig into my palm as I watch Robbie straddle the line on the side of the road. I don't know how confident I am in Robbie's gracefulness, much less with the current state he's in.

"One foot in front of the other," Office Strothers instructs Robbie once he's in place. "Go."

I hold my breath as Robbie takes one step, and then another.

He's golden.

But then the third step comes, and he has to hold his arms out for balance.

He recovers, taking a fourth and fifth step.

And then on the sixth step, he completely wobbles, losing his balance and stepping completely off the line, muttering "*Shit.*"

He tries to pick up where he left off, but he never fully recovers, shaking and stumbling through the next few steps. It's less than convincing, and it sends my stomach sinking straight to my toes.

"I've seen enough," Office Strothers says.

Robbie swallows, straightening out his jacket, and, even from here, as best as he's trying to hide it, I can see he's shaken. And it has a lump settling in my throat so tight that it's painful.

"So, can we go?" Robbie asks.

Office Strothers is quiet for a moment. "Hold out your arms to the side, son."

I'm confused by the instruction, and clearly so is Robbie by the look on his face, but he does as he's told. As soon as Robbie's arms are up at his side, the officer moves to stand behind him, and, when he reaches out, patting at Robbie's sides with both of his hands, I feel my knees start to give out. I stand there, helpless, only able to watch Robbie's face as he realizes what's happening. What's about to happen.

Office Strothers continues to move down, patting Robbie in search until he reaches his lower waist, his hand coming straight over top of the rectangular shape in Robbie's jacket pocket. I feel the breath slowly leave my lungs as he pulls back Robbie's jacket, reaching inside the pocket and pulling out the flask.

"And what's this?" he asks Robbie, not even attempting to conceal the look of triumph on his face.

Robbie clears his throat, glancing over at me before looking back to the officer in front of him. "Gatorade," he says, shrugging. "You know, gotta keep the electrolytes up."

Office Strothers uncaps the flask, taking a sniff of it. "Doesn't smell like there's many electrolytes in here to me, kid."

"You'd be surprised," Robbie mutters.

"Hmm," the officer hums, recapping the flask. "Right, well, I think we're gonna have to examine this a little more closely. Down at the station."

I can't stop them. Tears stream down my face. I start to move towards him, but Robbie shoots me a look that stops me in my tracks.

"Is that really necessary?" Robbie asks, his cool demeanor finally wavering.

"Afraid so," Office Strothers says. "Turn around, son."

Robbie's jaw flexes as he gives him his back. Office Strothers doesn't take any time, pulling both of his arms together and snapping handcuffs onto Robbie.

"And, now, if you don't mind. I'm just gonna need to take a look inside your car," Officer Strothers says, patting Robbie's shoulder. "Just to make sure we got all the *Gatorade*."

Finally able to speak, I stand my ground. "You can't just do that," I cry.

"Actually, Miss, I can," the officer says, giving me a patronizing look as he opens Robbie's driver's side door. He sits down in Robbie's seat, and the sight alone sends me into a blinding rage, making me step back from the car. It feels like he's invading Robbie's space. *Our* space.

"But you–"

"Cooper, it's fine," Robbie insists. "Just let him have his fun." Officer Strothers seems to be ignoring us, looking under Robbie's seats with his flashlight and digging around in the back floorboards. "There's nothing in there to find anyways."

I drop my face into my hands, shaking my head, trying to retrace the steps of our night to understand how we could have possibly gotten here. I hear the click of a glove box opening as I run a hand down my face, surely smearing my already half wrecked makeup.

"Huh. Nothing to find, you say?" Officer Strothers asks.

"That's what I said," Robbie confirms, all niceties gone from his voice.

"Well, kid, then what's this?"

It feels like all the blood in my veins freezes as I pull my hands from my face, slowly bending down to look inside of Robbie's car. To where Office Strothers is leaned over into the passenger seat, one hand in Robbie's open glove box, and the other raised, holding up the same joint he's had in there for months.

"*Oh my God*," I breathe, barely audible.

This isn't happening.

Office Strothers whistles, stepping back out of the car. "Yep, we are definitely gonna have to take a trip to the station."

I can't breathe.

He grabs Robbie's arm, starting to drag him in the direction of his police cruiser. "I guess it turns out your visit there may be a little longer than we originally thought."

I'm trying to step forward.

Why aren't my legs working?

I grip the top of the car, trying to catch my breath.

"I hate to say it, but I told you so, Summers. When I have them pinned, I'm always right. I always get 'em."

They reach the car, and Officer Strothers opens the back door, stepping to the side to help Robbie into the back seat.

Robbie looks up, trying to catch my eye.

But I can't see him.

My vision's blurry.

I can't breathe.

Everything's blurry.

My legs aren't working.

And then it all goes black.

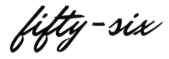

ROBBIE

I let my eyes fall shut, blowing a deep breath out of my nose as I hold out my hands.

I hear the faint click of a lock, followed by a voice I'd frankly be happy to never hear another day for the rest of my life.

"Ten minutes, kid," Officer Strothers says, removing my handcuffs.

Too bad I'm going to be hearing it every day for the foreseeable future instead.

I don't respond, watching as he unlocks the door in front of me and just wishing I could make time slow down.

I don't want to do this.

I have to do this.

"Clock is ticking," Officer Strothers tuts.

I grit my teeth, glaring up at him before yanking the door open.

The room is much lighter than the dingy hallway I just came from, making my eyes need a minute to adjust. I opt for keeping them on the floor as I slowly walk forward, clenching my fists at my side. I know it probably makes me a coward, but I just need a little more time. I need a few more seconds to prepare myself. I

631

need a moment to let it really sink in that when I look at her for the first time today, it's going to be the last first time for a very long time.

I make it to the booth I was directed to. The first one, and one of only three total, because this is a small town where basically no one manages to get arrested.

Yet, somehow, I did.

I guess you can't say I was never the best at something difficult.

I pull back the chair, slowly sinking down into it and settling my elbows on the counter in front of me. I let out a heavy sigh, reaching up for the telephone on the wall and bringing it to my ear.

With nothing left to procrastinate with, I finally look up.

And the sight before me nearly kills me on the spot.

Cooper sits on the other side of the glass, looking like she's been through hell and back.

She has the telephone on her side of the glass in one hand while her other hand is pressed against the glass, reaching out to me in the only way she can right now. Her eyes are red-rimmed and the dullest shade of gray I've yet to see, the dark circles beneath them only sucking the life out of them further. The usual red glow to her cheeks and lips is gone. Even her hair seems to be lacking its usual fiery hue, hanging limp and lifeless around her face. And then, worst of all, the top left corner of her forehead is covered with a giant bandage, the edges frayed and dark spots of blood still shadowed beneath it from where she hit her head when she fell. From when she passed out right in front of me and I couldn't do a damn thing to help her because my hands were in cuffs and I was being shoved into a cop car.

Just seeing it now, I'm brought right back to that moment, replaying it over and over in my head. I keep watching her get so overwhelmed with stress and sick with worry that it makes her blackout, her knees giving out from under her and her going head-first into the asphalt.

And then, I'm forced to revisit every moment before that, wracking my brain for what could have possibly led her there.

Trying to understand in what world this could ever be something that's a part of Sara Cooper's story. And I know what my answer is.

I know it all began with me.

"Hey," I hear her voice come through the phone line, soft and raspy, bringing me back to reality.

"Hey, Cooper," I say, trying to force a smile on my face.

Her throat bobs. "How are you doing?" she asks.

"Well, surprisingly, I think orange might be my color, so I'm feeling pretty good about that."

Cooper doesn't laugh, her lips pressing tightly together. "Robbie…"

I let out a sigh, running a hand down my face.

"I heard…" Cooper mutters. "About your parents."

I look down at the countertop, letting out a humorless laugh. "What about them?" I ask her. "That when I used my one phone call on them last night, my dad laughed and hung up on me? Or was it about when the station called my house this morning and my mom answered the phone saying they didn't have a son named Robert?"

"Both," she whispers, her voice cracking in a way that makes me want to bust through this glass and wrap her in my arms. But I can't.

"You know…you could have called me."

I force myself to look at her.

"What were you supposed to do?" I ask her.

I watch her lips quiver and her hand raise to swipe a tear away from her eye. "Robbie…I talked to Officer Keller up front. She said… that if your parents don't bail you out…that you'll be here at least sixty days. That you could even be transferred to a different jail if your hearing doesn't go well."

I blink at her, my tongue pushing into my cheek as I nod. "Mhmm. She told me that too."

"So then it's obvious, isn't it?" Cooper asks.

"What is?"

She scoots her chair closer, hugging the phone to her face. "Robbie…let me help you–"

"No," I say immediately, cutting her off.

"But–"

I shake my head. "It's not happening."

"*Robbie*–"

"Cooper, I said *no*," I grit.

Her brows pinch. "Let me bail you out."

"I'm not going to let you do that," I insist, angry tears prickling at the corners of my eyes. "You're not spending a dime on me, Cooper."

"Robbie, I have lots of savings. You're not understanding–"

"No, Cooper. *You're* not understanding apparently. So much so that I'm concerned."

"What do you mean?" she whines.

"Cooper," I say, blowing out a frustrated breath and meeting her eyes, "all of those savings were saved for *you*. To go to NYU."

"I–"

I don't let her interrupt me, barrelling on. "They're for your housing and living expenses. For your food. For your entertainment. For everything that you need to live the next four years to your fullest while you are in school. While you're in your screenwriting program. While you're creating art. While you're doing what you've been dreaming of all this time."

Cooper swallows hard, her eyes spilling over with tears. "But I don't need... I don't have to–"

"Yes, you do, Cooper. And you will."

She shakes her head, complete desperation written all over her face. "I can reapply next year. If you won't let me bail you out, at least let me wait for you. NYU will still be there. I can figure it out."

I lean forward, pressing my hand against the glass separating us. "Cooper..." I whisper, "it's everything you've worked for. It means everything to you."

"No," she says, choking out a sob. "Robbie, *you* mean everything to me."

I straighten in my seat as Cooper cries, and when my hand falls away from the glass, she looks up at me, a confused expression on her face. I grind my teeth together, my jaw flexing as I look off to the side.

"Robbie?"

I shake my head, my pulse pounding too hard in my ears for me to think straight.

"Talk to me, Goose," she pleads.

My head snaps in her direction. "Cooper, come on. Just stop it," I demand, standing up from my chair and raking a hand roughly through my hair.

Cooper stands up too, a shocked look on her face as she tucks the phone to her ear. "Stop what?"

"Being ridiculous," I tell her.

She opens her mouth, then closes it, her brows pinching. "*Excuse me?*"

"I mean, come on, what did you really think was gonna happen here?" I question her, throwing my hand out to the side. "That you and I would get together in the last couple months of high school and that we'd just stay together forever? That's it? *Happily ever after?*"

She doesn't say anything, but the look in her eyes and slump of her shoulders tells me that maybe that was exactly what she was thinking.

I tilt my head at her, shaking it. "C'mon, Cooper," I beg. "I *know* your imagination is bigger than that. I know your dreams are at least."

She rears back. "Why are you being like this? Why are you trying to act like what we've had isn't real?"

"Baby, *trust me*, it's been real. It's about as real between us as it gets. But..." I trail off, biting down on my shaky bottom lip, determined to keep it together. "That doesn't mean it's meant to last."

Cooper flinches, grabbing her chest as if she's just been shot, her eyes narrowing on me. "Are you just trying to hurt me?"

"Cooper, I'm trying to *save* you. From me."

She catches me off guard, barking out a laugh. "Well, I wish you would've thought of that a little sooner. Because it's too late, Robbie. I'm too far gone. You're already my–"

"Don't you *dare* say I'm your everything again."

"*Why not?*"

"Because that's exactly the problem!" I fume. "Don't you understand? I can't be your everything because *everything* is waiting for you out there!" I shove my finger towards the door leading outside. The one that's on her side of the glass. The one that I can't get to. "Cooper, I'm only gonna hold you back."

I watch her shake her head at me, but I can tell she's slipping, mentally and physically. She's sinking down, settling on top of the counter, her eyes searching my face.

I mirror her, sitting down on the counter as well, swallowing hard as I lock in on those sad storms through the window. "Look," I breathe, "I'm going to be in here for sixty days. Minimum. So, for eight weeks, I'll be here. But, as for you..." I raise my hand, tracing her features with my finger through the glass, trying to memorize them all over again, making sure I got them absolutely perfect the first time. "You're gonna walk that stage in a few days, and you're gonna graduate with our class–"

"Robbie..."

"And you're going to give a salutatorian speech twice as epic as your student body president speech. You're going to bring a smile to every student's face and a tear to every parent's eye. *Especially* Sherri's. You're going to take pictures with Alice, and you two are going to make up. You're going to forget whatever happened between the two of you and move on. Because you're best friends. Because you need each other. Because you're *good* for each other. And because she loves you just as much as you love her, despite how much of a stubborn pain in the ass you may be about it."

Cooper breathes out a laugh, shaking her head as she wipes away a tear.

"And then," I continue, "two weeks after that, you're going to go to New York–"

"But, I–"

"You're going to go to New York City," I say firmly. "And you aren't gonna think about me for a damn second, Cooper. Do you hear me?"

She chokes on a sob, looking down.

"Cooper, do you hear me?"

"I hear you," she mutters, "but I'm not listening."

She looks back up at me, her eyes full of so much emotion that it almost makes me want to take it all back. To beg her to stay. To make her wait for me. But I won't do that. I'd never do that.

"Robbie, I can't."

"You can and you will," I tell her, and she immediately looks away. "Cooper, please look at me."

She blinks hard, forcing herself to face me once more.

"Cooper, I know you think I'm everything to you, but you've got it so wrong. Because, actually, *you* are everything to *me*. You are the greatest thing that's ever happened to me. In the short time I've been with you, you've done more for me than I've ever done for myself. You're the dream I never even knew to have. The first thing I've truly ever cared about. The only thing I've ever worked for. You are the thing about myself that has made me the proudest. You're the landmark of my existence. But *me?*" I shake my head, letting out a scoff. "I'm *nothing* in the greater picture of what's gonna be *your* life. I'm barely a blip on the map. I'm a stepping stone to so much more. I'm a memory you look back on in a couple of decades and laugh about."

"I wish you'd stop talking that way about yourself. Really, it's killing me." Cooper looks at me, her voice raw and her eyes finally dry of tears. "Do you remember when you told me that?"

"Of course I remember, Cooper. I'll always remember," I tell her, meaning every word of it. "But the difference now is, what *I'm* saying is true."

She's quiet for a moment, her eyes considering me.

"I peaked in high school," I say. "But it's barely even your starting point. So, I'm going to stay here, and you're going to move on. You're gonna go on without me. You're gonna start your life.

You're going to realize your dreams. And you're going to do something so rad that the whole world will know your name."

Cooper rolls her lips into her mouth, a single tear slipping from her eye. I watch her as she reaches up, swiping it away, and I can't help the ghost of a smile that traces my lips. Because something about that tear is different. It's not a tear of sadness, or desperation, or frustration. It's a tear of grief. Of acceptance. It's the type of tear you cry over a change that's hard, but necessary. The type of tear you cry when you're scared out of your mind, but you know you're doing the right thing, and that you need to do it anyway. It's a tear that I can live with. A tear I'm okay with making her cry, because it means that I haven't ruined her for good. It means she's heard me. That she's going to let me let her go.

"And what about you?" Cooper asks, blowing out a breath. "What are you going to do after sixty days? After you get out of here?"

I glance around the room, taking it all in before I meet her eyes again. "I guess that's for me to figure out. It's probably long past due, if I'm being honest." Cooper tilts her head at me. "I haven't made any plans for my life," I say, "so it's probably good that I'll have nothing but time for the next couple of months to think about what exactly it is I might want my life to be."

Cooper traces circles on the glass, her gaze distant and full of thought. After a few moments, she lets out a gentle sigh, her finger pausing its movement. "I hope you figure it out," she whispers.

I adjust the phone against my ear, flattening my hand against the window over where Cooper's fingers still rest. She takes notice, her fingers slowly spreading out, her hand flattening perfectly parallel to mine through the glass. "I hope so too," I breathe.

Cooper's eyes flick up to meet mine, and I swear the hurt in them looks like lightning crackling throughout the storm clouds. But, through it all, I can see the truth. That I've gotten through to her. And that's all that matters.

"Goodbye, Robbie," she says.

I pull back, standing up so I can get one more good look at her, smirking involuntarily as I do it, tears welling in the corners of my eyes. "Bye, Sara Beth Cooper."

She hangs up her phone. And so do I.

Then we let our hands slide down the glass, dropping them back to our sides.

We stare at each other for a few more seconds, brown meeting gray, chocolate meeting storms, a smile meeting a frown, the past meeting the future, the end meeting the beginning.

And then she turns and walks away.

And, thankfully, she doesn't even look back once.

1996
Los Angeles, California

epilogue

SARA

"Any plans this weekend?" the taxi driver asks me.

I peel my eyes away from my window, turning my head to catch his gaze in the rear view mirror. "Oh, nothing much," I say. "Just have a work event to attend."

The old man lets out a whistle, raising his gray eyebrows at me as he joins the line of cars to drop me off. "You're far too young to be working on the weekends, young lady. You better make some time to enjoy yourself."

"I'll try my best," I tell him, a smile coming to my face. "What about you? What are you up to this weekend?"

"A whole lot of nothing. I can't wait," he says.

I chuckle as we approach the front of the line.

"Actually, I just remembered. My wife and I are going to the movies tomorrow night."

"Oh? Well, that should be fun," I say.

"I'm not sure how I could've forgotten." The driver shakes his head. "Seeing this movie is all my wife has talked about for weeks. She read the book it's based on last year and it hasn't left her night stand since. I've never seen her laugh and cry so much in the same few days." He purses his lips, his brows scrunching as he parks the car against the curb. "I wish I could remember what it was called."

I roll my lips into my mouth. "It sounds like quite the story."

"*Story!* That's it," he declares, waving a finger in the air. "Something like that."

We both open our doors, stepping out of the taxi and heading around to the trunk. The driver hands me my suitcase and I thank him, telling him to enjoy his weekend and his movie with his wife before I turn away and head through the doors of LAX.

I slide my headphones up from around my neck and onto my ears as I make my way through the airport terminal. I'm extra early for my flight, as always, but I check the status board just in case. When I confirm that I have about an hour before my flight takes off, I decide to check out some of the shops and grab a snack to kill some time.

I head for my favorite one-stop-shop convenience store in the terminal, purposely entering through the side entrance so I can avoid the book section, at least at first. A coy smile plays on my face as I try not to turn my head in the direction of that wall, instead making a beeline for the drink coolers. I grab a Coke and, as I'm in the process of picking up a bag of salt and vinegar chips, the Cranberries CD I'm listening to comes to an end.

I reach into the tote bag on my shoulder for my Discman, popping the CD out. I start to dig around in my bag for another album to listen to when I remember that I left my CD case sitting on my desk. I blow out a breath, deciding I'll just restart my Cranberries one, but then a small CD section catches my eye across the store.

With time to burn, I decide to walk over to it, seeing if they have anything in stock that I may want to listen to. My eyes scan over the several rows of CDs, not seeing much that I'm interested in or don't already have at home. Just as I'm about to turn away, a flash of blue catches my eye, making my heart stutter in my chest. I blink at the CD, my mouth twitching into a grin. Before I even know what I'm doing, it's in my hands and I'm headed for the register.

I set it on the counter, reaching in my tote bag for my wallet.

"Journey *Frontiers*, huh? That's a good one," the woman behind the counter says, making me look up at her. She appears to just be a few years older than me, bright highlights in her hair and soft brown lipstick on her lips.

"Yeah," I agree. "Yeah, it is."

"Really takes me back to high school," she sighs, entering the CD into the register.

"I know exactly what you mean," I agree, pressing my lips together as I hand her a twenty dollar bill.

She takes it from me, turning away to make change, and I find my eyes trailing to the side. My head pulls back as I register the large display right to the side of the check-out counter all full of the same book. I reflexively reach out, picking one up and holding it in my hands as I look over the cover. A smile tilts my lips as I flip the book over, reading the synopsis.

"Have you read that one?" the cashier asks me.

I glance up at her. "Uh, no," I shake my head. "I haven't."

"*Oh my God*," she says, shoving the register closed and leaning forward as she hands me back my change. "You absolutely have to."

My smile grows. "Yeah?"

"*Yes*," the woman insists. "It's incredible."

"You really think so?" I ask.

"Honey, I *know* so," the cashier states. "I'm not even much of a reader, but...that book made me feel something. More than I've felt in a long time. It really did a number on me." My teeth sink into my bottom lip as my hand tightens on the book. "It's actually about to come out as a movie. Like, this week, I'm pretty sure."

"No kidding?"

"For real," she nods. "I'm so excited to go see it. I'm honestly surprised you haven't heard of it. I feel like everyone's talking about it right now."

"Guess I'm just a little out of the loop," I say.

"Well, my recommendation: get in the loop," the cashier says, tapping the top of the book with her finger. "If I ever met that author out in the wild, I'd probably have to give her a hug. And then bill her for my therapy."

I let out a chuckle, turning the book over in my hands.

And effectively covering the author headshot on the back.

"That Sara Cooper really is something."

I look up at the woman, my smile reaching my eyes as I stare at her.

She smiles back, then flicks her gaze downward, clearing her throat.

"So, are you gonna buy it?" she asks.

"What?"

"Uh...the book?"

"*Oh,*" I blurt out. "Eh...Sure...Yes. Please," I stammer, handing my change right back to the cashier with a tight grin.

When I walk out of the store, I take a pause at a bench by the doorway, unwrapping *Frontiers* and slipping it inside my Discman, resecuring my headphones on my head. A warm wave of nostalgia washes over me and a prickly sensation prods at my heartstrings as soon as *Separate Ways* begins to play. I take a deep breath as I pick up my book from where I set it down on the bench, flipping it over to re-read the synopsis I already know every word to as I make my way towards my gate, my feet knowing this airport like the back of my hand at this point.

After a minute or so of walking, a flash of light reflects into my eyes, making me glance up. And then it all happens so fast.

I only have a second to register a man wearing aviators in front of me and to think, *Who the hell wears sunglasses inside?*, before my shoulder slams directly into his, pulling a grunt out of him and sending my book flying out of my hands.

"*Oh my gosh,*" I gasp, my headphones falling off the back of my head. I secure them with one hand as I use the other to somewhat steady myself against the man, my eyes staying on his chest as I'm too flustered to look at his face yet. From where I'm standing, I can see he's wearing jeans and...

My head tilts.

A flight jacket?

I swallow.

Aviators? A flight jacket?

I shake my head.

Did I seriously just assault a pilot?

"*Sheesh*," the man groans as he stands up straight.

"I'm sorry," I repeat. "I– I wasn't paying attention." I start to bend down to pick up my book, but decide to just leave it. I have hundreds at home. Instead, I grab the handle of my suitcase, moving past the man.

"Watch where you're walking, would you?" he grunts.

"Sorry," I mutter over my shoulder as I continue speed-walking towards my gate.

"Hey, I think you forgot something," he calls after me.

"I don't need it. It's not even mine," I insist, not looking at him.

"Running right into me *and* letting a good book go to waste? *Wow*, Cooper."

I'm a good ten feet away from him now. *Why won't he just let me leave?* "I'm sorry," I repeat as a last-ditch effort. "I'm so sor–"

My feet jerk to a stop.

I blink hard, trying to replay what I just heard, my spine ramrod straight.

Cooper?

I turn slowly on my heel, my pulse pounding in my ears. After what feels like ten long, breathless minutes, I'm finally facing him.

The pilot is standing there, a duffle bag slung over his right shoulder, with the type of smirk on his face that I thought only existed in my dreams anymore. My mouth falls open as I my eyes trace over his shiny chestnut brown hair, cropped short on the sides with just a little extra length on top, perfectly mussed. He reaches up, pulling off his aviators, and it's like time slows down. It's like a movie. Like my life's a movie. My feet stumble a couple of hesitant steps forward. And then, the sunglasses are totally gone.

And I find double milk chocolate eyes staring back at me.

"*Robbie?*" I breathe.

His tongue pushes into his lower lip, a grin spreading across his face. "Hey, Cooper."

I shake my head. I don't know for how long. But clearly not long enough, because I'm still not capable of forming words.

"Your hair's grown," Robbie says, tilting his head.

Apparently words have escaped even the smoothest of wordsmiths at this moment.

"It's been eight years," I reply.

He nods. "It has."

"You cut yours," I say, motioning towards his hair.

"I had to."

"Why?"

"I joined the Navy."

My eyes widen, my mouth falling open. "*You did?*" I ask, my voice cracking.

Robbie rolls his lips into his mouth, nodding. "For the last six years, that's where I've been. I didn't really have much to go home to after my sixty days were up." He meets my eyes, and I have to swallow against the lump that instantly forms in my throat. "And since my grades were in no place to go to college and my parents weren't exactly willing to support me otherwise...the idea just sort of came to me."

"*You*..." I choke, the backs of my eyes suddenly burning as I can't contain my smile. "You figured it out."

"I did," he nods, a grin of pride filling his face. "And you, Cooper," he says, taking a step in my direction and extending his hand towards me, "you did something too."

I look down, seeing him holding my book out to me, the image on the cover displaying rows of shelves filled with books, movies, and cassette tapes.

"*A Story Between the Stories*," Robbie smiles, shaking his head. "I haven't been able to go in a store without finding this book on the shelves, and I've been seeing ads for your movie everywhere. I'll be damned. You really did it."

Tears blur the edges of my vision, and I have to look away to wipe my eyes, a breathy chuckle escaping me. I feel so overwhelmed with emotions, not even knowing where to begin this conversation. I've laid awake for so many nights wondering if this exact conversation would ever happen, and, now that it's here, I'm not sure how to know if it's real.

"I... I can't believe you're here," I say. "Actually, what *are* you doing here?"

"Well," Robbie says, rubbing the back of his neck. "I actually just finished my contract with the Navy a few weeks ago. I've been in LA visiting for the last two weeks, but now...I'm not totally sure."

He's been in LA for two whole weeks?

"I have a flight back to San Francisco in about an hour," he says, "but..."

"What?" I question him.

"I'm just not sure if there's much back there for me," Robbie answers, giving me a tight smile. "So I was thinking of going to the ticket counter and seeing what other flights are heading out in the next few hours instead. I think I may just go somewhere new. At least for the next few months. I'm planning to start college in the fall."

"College?"

"Yeah," Robbie nods. "We get to attend for free with our military benefits. I think...I'd like to go for coaching. I wanna coach high school basketball."

I can't stop the smile that breaks out across my face. "I think you'd be amazing at that."

"I hope so," he smirks, shrugging. "But anyways, what are you doing here, Cooper? In LA?"

"Well," I chuckle, pushing my hair behind my ear. "I kinda live here now. I have for the last four years. Ever since I graduated from NYU."

A smirk tilts Robbie's lips. "NYU?"

"Yeah," I nod, "NYU."

He takes a step closer, his voice quiet when he asks, "Was it everything you dreamed of?"

"It was," I confirm, chewing on my lower lip. "Everything and more. But I'm more movies and beaches than plays and cold winters. So I came back to California to start working."

"You got the best of both worlds then?" Robbie asks. "You did everything I said?"

I smile tightly, giving him a shrug.

He takes another step. "You got it all?" he asks.

"It sure feels that way," I say softly.

His eyes search my face, milk chocolate shifting to caramel. "Good," he whispers.

I stare back at him, feeling like I could stay frozen to the spot forever. But then, a voice comes over the terminal intercom.

"*Attention, we are now beginning the boarding process for American Airlines Flight 7891 to New York City. Passengers, please proceed to Gate C24.*"

I clear my throat, taking a step back from Robbie and pointing over my shoulder. "That's gonna be me."

He tilts his head. "Back to New York?"

"Just for the weekend," I say. "It's actually...for my movie premiere. It's tomorrow."

Robbie's brows raise. "It is, isn't it?" He blows out a whistle, running a hand through his hair. "Well, shit, Cooper. That's...that's amazing. Congratulations."

"Thank you," I smile.

We look at each other for a few seconds, neither of us moving or saying anything.

Eventually, Robbie takes one for the team, breaking the silence. "Well," he shakes his head, dropping his duffle bag to his side. "It was really great to see you."

"You too," I nod, my throat feeling like it's closing up.

Robbie gives me one last smile, raising his hand towards me before turning to walk away.

"*Wait,*" I blurt.

He looks back, raising a brow as I close the distance between us, the words flying out of my mouth.

"Why don't you come with me?"

Robbie turns back to face me. "To your gate?"

"To New York."

"To New York?" he repeats.

"Yeah," I nod.

We stand there for a moment, our shoulders stiff and our eyes darting between each other's, before both of us suddenly break, laughter spilling out of us.

"You are something else, Sara Cooper."

"Sorry," I mumble, running a hand down my face. "That was crazy. Just a very crazy, spontaneous thought. Just forget it. It was, uh, good to see you as well." I start to spin away, but something catches my wrist.

I look back, finding Robbie with not an ounce of humor left on his face.

"Doesn't sound so crazy to me," he says.

My throat bobs. "Really?"

"Yeah," Robbie nods. "Actually, it sounds pretty rad."

I chuckle, shaking my head, and a huge smile comes to Robbie's face. "Nobody says rad anymore, Robbie."

"Only the cool kids," he grins.

I look down at the floor, continuing to laugh until I sigh. It registers then that Robbie's hand is still wrapped around my wrist.

I raise my arm, pulling back just enough so that his hand is now wrapped around mine. I look down at our intertwined fingers, blowing out a breath.

"I have to be honest with you," I tell him, glancing up to meet his eyes. "I didn't really do everything you said."

"Have you ever?" Robbie asks.

I shake my head, returning his smile. "I've thought about you," I say. "A lot."

Robbie tilts his head, reaching up and brushing his thumb across my cheek as he looks into my eyes. "It doesn't storm nearly enough in California. But I've thought about you a lot too, Cooper. And I'm proud to admit it."

acknowledgments

For as long as I can remember, all I've ever wanted to do is make people feel something. To write stories. To make something that matters to somebody. To create a world that allows someone out there some form of escapism, or brings them back to exactly where they need to be. In short, I've always wanted to do something rad. And, as much as I like to pretend like I can do it all on my own, rad things simply can't happen without a few rad people to help you along the way. And they certainly don't matter as much without those people to share it with.

To my parents, Shaunna and Randy (or Cora and Randall, as I call them. *Don't ask.*) Thank you for being my biggest cheerleaders and supporting me in each and every ambitious fixation, creative whim, and life decision. Thank you for keeping the decade of the 80s alive throughout my life and for being there to answer every late night text and phone call quizzing you about it for the nine months it took me to write this book. It couldn't have happened without you. And it certainly wouldn't have felt so special.

To my sister, Jess. For always being there for a good laugh and a brutally honest opinion. For loving music more than anyone I know, and sharing so many special moments with me within it. And for watching *Dirty Dancing*, *Top Gun*, and *Rock of Ages* with me a million times over the course of our lives. Let's watch them a million more.

To Leigh Ann, *my* Alice. Thank you for being the person I can always count on to know me better than I know myself. For loving and supporting me just the same at my absolute worst as you do at my absolute best. For finding a way to feel right by my side even if you're a million miles away. For manifesting greatness and happiness with me since high school. We've come *so* far. Let's take it all the way.

To Hailey. Thank you for being just as absurdly spontaneous, restless, and dying to experience the world as me. For always being a voice of reason and a friend to turn to. And, most seriously, for being the catalyst that turned my life around. For encouraging me to move to Dallas and allowing me to fall in love with this city. Who would've thought we'd end up here? Certainly not either of us. Anyways, Go Stars!

To Morgan. I'm so thankful that Penelope Douglas and my YouTube channel brought us together, and that you randomly decided to send me a voice note one day. If only I knew at that time that we'd be sending each other voice notes daily from there on out and that you'd become my writing partner in crime. Thank you for every bit of your help on this book and all the books that are to come. I can't wait for the day that we can say we really did it.

To Taylor Jenkins Reid and John Green for making me experience emotions I didn't know I was capable of, for making me feel a little less alone in my thoughts of this world, and for being my biggest inspirations when it comes to writing. If I can one day write something that makes a single person feel what a single one of your books has made me feel, I'll know I've made it.

To the Duffer brothers for creating the character of Steve Harrington and to Joe Keery for bringing him to life in a way that spoke to me so deeply that I had to write a whole damn book inspired by him.

To the 80s, the era I never lived through but has always felt like home. To nostalgia, carefree love, and the feeling like anything is possible. To the movies that made me want to be the main character and to the music that's made me feel the most alive. To Steve Perry and Journey for bringing my family together and never failing to bring a smile to my face. I'm listening to *Faithfully* as I write these acknowledgements, and I wouldn't want it any other way. Thank you. I'll never let you go.

And, last but certainly not least, to *you*. Words don't mean anything unless there's someone willing to read them, and I couldn't be more thankful that you took the time to read my book. Whether you found it and me through my Nikki's Book Nook social media channels or you just stumbled upon us, I appreciate and love you all the same. With all my heart, thank you.

about the author

Nikki Witt is a writer of slow burn, all-consuming romance books. She is a graduate of Texas A&M University and currently resides in Dallas, Texas.

When Nikki isn't writing or reading, you can find her snuggling with her two cat children, Draco and Kiwi, watching Dallas Stars hockey, listening to Taylor Swift or Harry Styles, or traveling to whatever destination is offering a flight deal that week.

For more information, visit authornikkiwitt.com.

youtube.com/nikkisbooknook

tiktok.com/@nikkis.book.nook

instagram.com/nikkis.book.nook

Printed in Great Britain
by Amazon